Collected Fiction: 1888–1895

ARTHUR MACHEN

Collected Fiction

Volume 1: 1888–1895

Edited by S. T. Joshi

Hippocampus Press

New York

Published by Hippocampus Press
P.O. Box 641, New York, NY 10156.
www.hippocampuspress.com

Cover illustration © 2019 by Matthew Jaffe, MatthewRJaffe.com.
Frontispiece photograph by E. O. Hoppé, provided by Mark Valentine.
Cover design by Daniel V. Sauer, DanSauerDesign.com
Hippocampus Press logo designed by Anastasia Damianakos.

First edition
1 3 5 7 9 8 6 4 2

ISBN 978-1-61498-285-2 three-volume set
ISBN 978-1-61498-248-7 volume 1
ISBN 978-1-61498-251-7 ebook

Contents

Introduction

This is the first complete edition of the fiction of Anglo-Welsh writer Arthur Machen (1863–1947) ever published. It includes the totality of his short fiction, novelettes, novels, and prose poems. While there is some debate as to what actually constitutes a short story in Machen's work—especially given his bountiful array of journalism, some of which borders on fiction—the works in this volume are unquestionably narratives that feature one or more elements of fictional composition. A substantial majority of these works are tales of horror and the supernatural—a genre in which Machen has made a lasting and ever-expanding impression.

Machen's two principal autobiographies (*Far Off Things*, 1922; *Things Near and Far*, 1923) and other writings often supply dates of the composition of his novels and tales, and this edition is therefore arranged chronologically by date of composition insofar as it can be accurately established. He declares that *The Chronicle of Clemendy* (1888)—a series of tales imitative of such mediaeval or Renaissance works as the *Decameron* or the *Canterbury Tales*—was written in 1885–86, a few years after he had left his native Wales to come to London in 1883. It was around this time that Machen, in order to make an income, produced a translation of the *Heptameron* of Marguerite de Navarre (1886) and did other miscellaneous work for publishers and booksellers.

In 1887 Machen's father died, and the inheritance that he subsequently received was sufficient for his financial needs for the next fourteen years—augmented by his immense translation of the *Memoirs of Jacques Casanova* (1894) and of Béroalde de Verville's *Le Moyen de Parvenir* (1890). In 1890 the first section of "The Great God Pan" appeared in a magazine; the composition of that novella extended into the next year. It was at this time that he produced a number of tales or sketches for various magazines, notably *St. James's Gazette* and the

Whirlwind. In the 1923 introduction to *The Hill of Dreams* (included in the Appendix to Volume 2 of this edition) Machen describes these works as "'smart' tales contributed to an extinct, or almost extinct, family of journals; the 'society' papers." They are purportedly humorous or whimsical, often with covert sexual implications. "The Inmost Light" was composed in 1892; it and "The Great God Pan" were published as *The Great God Pan and The Inmost Light* (1894), creating a sensation because of the manifest undercurrent of aberrant sexuality in "The Great God Pan."

The Three Impostors (1895) is a curiosity. Machen explicitly declares (in the aforementioned introduction to *The Hill of Dreams*) that "in the spring and summer of '94 I was busy with *The Three Impostors*," completing it early the next year. But one segment of this episodic novel, "Novel of the Iron Maid," had appeared in *St. James's Gazette* as early as the issue for 13 November 1890; the suggestion is that this tale was only incorporated into the fabric of *The Three Impostors* at some point during its composition in 1894–95. The novel therefore appears here after the tales of 1888–92.

"The Red Hand" and "The Shining Pyramid" were both written in 1895, and were both first published in that year.

This is not the place for an extended critical assessment of Machen's work, early or late; I have in any case done so elsewhere.[1] Here we can refer to one of the defining characteristics of Machen's weird work—his employment of the "little people," purported to be a race of primitive quasi-human creatures dwelling on the underside of civilisation, whose occasional encounters with human beings creates havoc and destruction. In this volume, the segment "Novel of the Black Seal" in *The Three Impostors* and "The Shining Pyramid" express this conception most concentratedly. That Machen gave serious thought to this idea is indicated by his review-article "Folklore and Legends of the North" (1898), printed in the Appendix. Further light is shed on the idea, and on Machen's early writing in general, in the 1923 introduction to *The Three Impostors* and on a late piece, "On Re-reading *The Three Im-*

---

1. See my chapter "Arthur Machen: The Mystery of the Universe" in *The Weird Tale* (1990), and my introduction to *The White People and Other Weird Stories* (Penguin Classics, 2011).

postors and the Wonder Story," apparently written in the 1940s when August Derleth was contemplating reprinting *The Three Impostors* for his fledgling small press, Arkham House.

This is the first edition of Machen's fiction to present corrected texts based on consultation of manuscripts and early publications. Handwritten or typed manuscripts of Machen's fiction or other work—aside from letters—are very few, and extensive use has been made of the final two chapters of *The Secret Glory* (found in Volume 2 of this edition), which were not published when the novel appeared in 1922 and which are in the holdings of the Beinecke Rare Book and Manuscript Library of Yale University. The essay "On Re-reading *The Three Impostors* and the Wonder Story" exists in a typed manuscript at the Wisconsin Historical Society (Madison, WI).

These and other documents indicate that Machen utilised British spellings for the most part, with some exceptions (e.g., "judgment" instead of "judgement"; "connection" instead of "connexion"). He also uses "shew" (for "show" [as a verb]) quite consistently in his manuscripts, and this spelling has been used throughout the three volumes of this set. Those manuscripts also reveal that Machen preferred to place punctuation outside of quotation marks except in dialogue, or when a complete sentence is quoted, or a few other instances.

In the absence of actual manuscripts of the specific works of fiction contained in this volume, care has been taken to choose those texts by Machen that most clearly reflect his stylistic, textual, and grammatical preferences. For example, there is clear evidence that Machen revised the text of *The Chronicle of Clemendy* for the 1923 reprint, so that text has been used here. Conversely, I have determined that the first edition of *The Three Impostors* is closer to Machen's wishes than the (very slightly) revised text of 1923. For "The Great God Pan," "The Inmost Light," and "The Red Hand" the text from *The House of Souls* (1906) has been used; for "The Shining Pyramid" the text from *The Shining Pyramid* (1925) has been used. Most of the brief sketches of 1890–91 were not reprinted beyond their initial magazine appearances, so those appearances perforce have served as the basis of the texts. "A Double Return" and "The Lost Club" did appear in *The Cosy Room and Other Stories* (1936), so those texts have been used. "A Wonderful

Woman" appeared in two Machen collections in the 1920s, but neither of these were supervised or authorised by Machen, so use has been made of the original appearance.

I have prepared a bibliography of Machen's fiction, listing publications of his novels and story collections during his lifetime (also including *Tales of Horror and the Supernatural* [1948], in which he probably had some input prior to his death in 1947), as well as appearances of the individual stories. This bibliography can be found at the end of the volume.

I am enormously indebted to David E. Schultz and Jordan Smith for their assistance in securing the texts of some of the rarer items in this volume.

—S. T. JOSHI

A Chapter from the Book Called The Ingenious Gentleman Don Quijote de la Mancha Which by Some Mischance Has Not Till Now Been Printed

The grand and diverting Scrutiny made by the Priest and the Barber in the Library in York Street.

It is mighty well," said the priest, "but now we are in York Street, let us see this library of which you have told us so much." "With all my heart," answered the barber, and calling the housekeeper, he bade her light the way to the room containing so many curious books. They went up more flights of stairs than I can number, in short the sky was not far off, when the housekeeper stopped before a door and presently unlocked it. This she did, not without terror, knowing that many of the books treated of Magic, Necromancy, Spells, and Incantations, but the priest told her not to be afraid, since he was a Bachelor in Arts, and had his exorcisms on the tip of his tongue. He said this in jest, for he knew that books seldom hurt men in any other way than by sending them to sleep, and without more ado they all went in, and setting down the candle, began to look around them. And the first book that Master Nicholas the barber put into the priest's hands was a piece written with the pen, being the two last books of "Ptolemy's Quadripartite or Tetrabiblion". "This," said the Licentiate, "seems a thing of mystery, for I suppose that the 'Quadripartite' was the first work on Astrology, of any account, written in the learned tongues; and from it have arisen an infinite swarm of commentaries, paraphrases, volumes of cloudy annotations, and the like. And from its weight and authority it has been done into all our modern languages." "That is true," said the barber, "and this volume was first translated into the Latin by Melancthon, and from his Latin into English. But I see here another version of it, the four books translated by one James Wilson; and yet another, with notes, by James Ashmead. But tell me, Master Licentiate, what is this book I have, the title of which I cannot read, for I do not know Chinese?" "Nor is it necessary that you should," answered the priest, "but for all that, this writing is not Chinese, nor yet Arabic, but good Greek, and spells: *Christologia.* This is a curious book, and should be curiously kept, for it is by that learned and exact Divine, Doctor Butler, Bishop of Durham, who wrote the 'Analogy'. It is said that he began to write this piece to confute Astrologers, and ended by becoming one himself. But what are those books bound in boards on that shelf at the back?" Taking the candle, the barber began to examine the books in question and to read out their titles. "Here," said he, "are the Select Works of one Porpery, or Borphery—." "Porphyry, you would say," struck in the Licentiate, "I know him well, though I do not understand him, since he is an obscure writer. And in this volume, I perceive, is contained the 'Care of the Nymphs', wherein he makes old Homer as fantastic as himself; but yet his allegorical notions are beautifully set forth, and well contrived. But the translation, I see, was done by Thomas Taylor, the famous Platonist, who is reported to have sacrificed a bull to Jove in the back parlour of his lodging." "And here," said the barber, as he groped in his dusty and dark corner, "are more translations by this same Taylor, who indeed seems to have been a very notable botcher of ancient doublets. This is the 'Fragments of the Ancient Pythagoreans', this, 'Plato's Dialogues', and here we have 'The Lost Writings of Proclus', surnamed the Successor. Pray, Master Licentiate, where do these Successors live, for I know no family of that name?" "You mistake, you mistake, Master Nicholas," said the priest, not without smiling, "this Proclus was the successor of Plato, and (so he said) the last link of the Hermaic Chain. But let us have done with him, for I see on the shelf 'The Triumphal Chariot of Antimony', by Basilius Valentinus, with 'Anima Magica Abscondita', and 'Lumen de Lumine', by Thomas Vaughan, called in Alchemy, Eugenius Philalethes. And just beyond is the 'Victorious Philosophical Stone', and, by St. Chrysostom, 'The Comte de Gabalis'. All these, Master Nicholas, are exceeding choice reading, and books not to be found every day. But while I dip into these, do you put that great folio to the question, for though it be a big book, it may chance to be a good one also." And while the barber struggled with the folio aforesaid, drawing it from under quartos, octavos, and duodecimos innumerable, the priest lifting his eyes happened to catch sight of a volume which made him put back "Lumen de Lumine" into darkness. "A jewel! A jewel! Master Nicholas," cried he, in so high a tone, that the barber left his task and came running, and said, "by what chance could a jewel or anything of worth come in a room where there are only books?" "I would not say," answered the Licentiate, "that I have here the shining and unconquerable diamond, or any store of right orient pearls, or mystical opals; but for all that, I have a book full joyous. It is, in fine, the treatise of Henry Cornelius Agrippa, or, Herr Trippa, as Rabelais styles him, on 'The Vanity and Uncertainty of all the Sciences and Arts'. Truly this is *liber jucundissimus,* and full of curious learning also. But bring hither that great folio and open it on the table." And when the book was brought into the light, it was found to be "Zoega de origine et usu Obeliscorum", and the priest began to examine it with great curiosity, for it had many plates of obelisks, choicely printed. However, he is not recorded to have said anything about this book, or concerning obelisks; and in this it would have been well if others had followed his example of silence, for few can speak of obelisks and to the point at the same time.

But while the Licentiate was investigating the obelisks Master Nicholas was by no means idle, and presently called out, "Here, master priest, I have found a whole nest of curious books, and all engrossed by hand, and painted and adorned with figures, but as easy to read as print." "Declare to me the titles of some of them," answered the priest, "and we shall see if they be of any account." Forthwith the barber began: "'Collectanea Chimica: a Collection of Rare and Curious Treatises on Hermetic Science', 'Mr. Yardley's Process for Making Gold', 'Book of the Offices and Orders of Spirits', 'Key of Solomon the King'," and would have gone on had not the priest stopped him, that he might himself look into these volumes. But as he turned the leaves over, admiring the seals, pentacles, magic writings, circles, figures of the Cabala, and the like wonders of Theurgy, there slipped out a sheet of paper closely written on in a fine character. "What is that?" said the barber, as the priest picked it up and began to read it; but he got no answer for some while. At last the priest said: "This, Master Nicholas, is a Relation of an Interview with a Spirit, shewing how a man conjured a demon to appear and how they spoke together. But put it back in the volume of Divine Magic whence it came, since my blood begins to run cold. And see, what is that worthy folio yonder?" "This," said the barber, "is 'The Herball', by Gerarde; and, as I am a Catholic Christian, here are images of all manner of sweet and whole-some herbs set in lively portraiture on every page. To speak the truth, this is just as if I walked in my own garden; why, I could almost pluck this sprig of borage and put it in a cup of wine (would that I had such, for this learned dust makes my throat mighty dry). And Lord! here is bugloss, of which a neighbour of mine makes so comfortable a syrup, and thyme, and vervain, and balm." It is probable that Master Nicholas would in this fashion have run over the whole Generall Historie of Plants, "from the cedar tree that is in Lebanon even unto the hyssop that springeth out of the wall", but the priest cut him short with, "Master Nicholas, Master Nicholas, we are come here to see books, not to hear nor to deliver lectures and discourses, unless, indeed, I have occasion to speak a word in season, to do which is a privilege that pertains to bachelors and doctors. Do you, therefore, instead of prat-ing, proclaim, like a King-at-Armes, the style and title of the several books." Forthwith the barber began: "Oriatrike, or Physick Refined, being a new Rise and Progress of Philosophy and Medicine for the Destruction of Diseases and the Prolongation of Life." "Stay," said the Licentiate, "since this seems no common book, pray declare who wrote it." "One Val Helmont, it appears," answered the barber. "Say not one Val Helmont, for there is but one, and a most ingenious, subtle doctor. In his Oriatrike and his Ternary of Paradoxes you will find strange, unheard-of curiosities; as the Birth of Tartar in Wine and the Deliramenta Catarrhi, which means the Ravings of the Rheum. But read on." "The Discovery of Witchcraft, wherein is displayed Lewde Unchristian Practices of Witchmongers." "That, Master Nicholas, is Scot's Discovery, and a kind of barn where conjurations, horoscopes, witches' Sabbaths, necromancies, and the like are stacked roof high." "That were an ill barn to sleep in on an Eve of May. But I have here a book that pleases me, for it is the Prognostications of Nostradamus, and that, I am sure, must be a very comfortable book." "It is so," answered the priest; "but do not read it, neighbour, for fear you should also begin to prognosticate, and so turn from an honest barber into a false prophet. Instead read me the title of that small volume you are handling." "The Open Entrance to the Shut Palace of the King." "I know the book, and have read it in the Latin, but can scarce say the entrance is altogether an open one. Rather it is a wonderful maze, adorned with mystical figures that shadow forth the Great Work. But what is that chest of books that you have opened?" "It seems to me," said Master Nicholas, "that this chest is full of Magnetisms, Somnambulisms, and Phrenologies." "I think you are right," said the priest, as he picked out one or two of the volumes, "and in the chest they shall for the present time remain, except this Swedenborg and Mesmer, which seem noteworthy." "But I wonder by what strange chance this old book called 'Sciographia, or the Art of Shadows', has got among these modern tracts on magnetisms, mesmerisms, and somnambulisms." (This came from the barber, who should have been an Inquisitor.) "It were hard indeed to say," answered the priest, "what shadows have to do with such grave and weighty books; but I see this is a work on making dials, printed in the seventeenth century, which may be called the age of dials, as this present time is the age of clocks. But what have we here? by Virgil's tomb none less than Delrio on Magic, and in vellum too. These, Master Nicholas, are, I verily believe, the most curious and wonderful six books in the world, fitted out with all manner of strange stories and quaint, stupend relations. For, believe me, the good father Delrio was not like one of our modern scribblers, who pick here and pick there, mingling scraps of all sorts like a cook making a stew, but rather one of those learned persons called by the author of Pantagruel quintessencers, or extractors of fifth essence, who do everything judiciously and admirably. Take him from my hands and lay him back softly in his stall, for fear he should fascinate me, and with his incantations root my eyes to his page." But as the barber did this, whether he was over careful, or whether it was so fated, a whole battalion of books slipped out, and, without crying "Santiago," came charging on his skull, like men in mail. "Why this," said the barber, as he rubbed his pate, "is just as if the church tower or some such mass of masonry had fallen on one." "You say truly," answered the priest, picking up the volumes that had well-nigh overwhelmed the barber, "for here are whole hosts of masonic books concerning the Royal Arch Degree, the Flower Shushan, the Divine name, and the like secret matters of the Craft. But cheer up, it was not fated that you should die so, as you may see, if you will, in this Complete Book of Knowledge, shewing the Effects of the Planets, also Pythagoras's Wheel of Fortune, Palmistry, and the Interpretation of Dreams. But here I see all the wonderful works of Jacob Behmen, that Prince and Prodigy of all Theosophers. Here we behold, like Daphnis in Virgil, both the clouds and the stars, the Aurora, the Tables of Divine Revelation, and the Discourse of Souls, all irradiated in a wonderful and awful light. But read on, what have you there?" "'Anima Astrologiæ; or a Guide for Astrologers', by Mr. William Lilly, printed in 1676." "I know the book well," answered the Licentiate; "in it are the one hundred and forty-six Considerations of Guido Bonatus, and the Choicest Aphorisms of the Seven Segments of Jerom Cardan of Milan; but this edition of 1676 I have not seen before, since it is of the rarest." "And here, Master Licentiate, is another book by this same Lilly—namely, his Christian Astrology, modestly treated of in Three Books; and at hand I see a whole pile of thick and glossy books called Ephemeris, a word I do not remember to have heard before." "It is merely Greek for an Almanack," the priest answered, "and the plural is Ephemerides, though indeed it is not necessary for you, who are a barber, to know so much." "But pray, sir, among so many curious books, treating of wonderful arts, is there no pleasant and easy work shewing a man how to live his hundred years or so with less trouble than many take now to live to fifty or sixty?" "We have seen something of this sort already, but I have here a choicer way," answered the priest, "namely, 'Hermippus Redivivus', and a merry, witty, treatise it is. But I am grievously afraid your wife would mislike the method, and would have you reinforce your radical heat and moisture after some other fashion." Now, as may be imagined, all this precise scrutiny had not been done in a moment; and as the barber began to say: "I think, Master Licentiate, we might do worse than cast our eyes over the books in those top-shelves yonder," the housekeeper adjured them from below to come down presently, unless they both had a mind to pass the rest of the night in cock-loft land. And so, with many regrets that they could not linger any more in this dusty and fantastic realm, the Licentiate and the barber went out and left the books in darkness.

The Chronicle of Clemendy

or, The History of the IX. Joyous Journeys. *In which are contained the amorous inventions and facetious tales of* Master GERVASE PERROT, *Gent., now for the first time done into English, by* ARTHUR MACHEN, *translator of the Hepatameron of Margaret of Navarre.*

CONTENTS

EPISTLE DEDICATORY

To the Right Honourable, Illustrious and Puissant Prince,
HUMPHREY, DUKE OF GLOUCESTER,
Knight of the Most Noble Order of the Garter, &c. &c.

It were but lost labour on my part (most illustrious) should I presume to give the especial reasons or prerogative instances whereby I am moved to offer unto Your Grace these poor ingatherings of a scholar's toil. For your universal favour and benevolent encouragement towards men of letters is a thing widely known; and if amongst scholars, that are vulgarly supposed to form a Commonwealth, it be lawful to set up lordship, this I make no doubt shall by the consent of all be assigned unto you. Of late years, I confess, Patronage hath been a thing little used and but meanly conceited of; but indeed I know not how it would have gone with myself and many others of like employ, had it not been for Your Grace's hospitality. How many a poor author hath had at home but a scurvy bin and piggin, a bare floor and barer trencher, a cup void not only of canary, but even of small ale. How many a scholar, I say, hath passed away the best years of his life, the flower of his age, in some mean cock-loft, with scarce enough air, (let alone meat and drink) for his sustenance; the which lack of air being by itself well recognised for a sufficient cause of melancholy. And when we consider the other misfortunes which are rather to be esteemed essential than accidental to such a life: the slow decay of hope, the loneliness of days and weeks and years, the scorn of others, and (often) the contempt of one's very self, it will readily be received that whosoever doth aught to mitigate the hardships of this estate is most worthy of praise, thankofferings, and lowly service. The which hath been Your Grace's office, I mean to entertain a sort of men mighty little esteemed in the Commonwealth, being held by the most of the people at an equal price with mere strollers or common vagabonds; differing only in this, that we scholars so far from roaming about do rather use not to venture out of doors, for fear and shame lest our ragged small-clothes and greasy doublets should draw on us open scorn and derision. But I suspect that in this particular I shall scarcely gain much credit, scholarship and shame being generally accounted as incompatibles, and as little likely to coexist in one person as heat and cold, at the same time, in one and the same substance. And indeed it were well for us if this should be so: and let him that leaveth the shelter of his chimney corner (though it be in a kitchen) and adventureth up to town to make his fortune by letters, take heed that he have about his heart that harness of strong oak and triple brass that Horace writes of. I say nothing of them that are driven by ill hap to try their luck (as the phrase goes), they have no choice, and may be are as well off as they expected. But I would have him who abandons of his own free will a good home, kindred, acquaintance, and the like to make account of these things. That for plenty, he shall have want, for love, scorn and contempt, for familiarity, loneliness and desolation. For pure air he shall gain a Stygian fume, a black mist, a sooty smoke: for those delicious meadows, heathery mountains, rustling woods, and all such prospects of delight, a Cretan Labyrinth, a stony wilderness, a dædal wandering along whose turnings and returnings do go such companies and pomps as the old Tuscan Poet beheld in his vision. *Vexilla regis prodeunt inferni,* said he of them, in a parody of Vincentius his hymn; and I doubt not that the line would stand as good in application to certain of our trained bands as to those of Hell itself. Truly then do we poor folk owe what service we are able to pay Your Grace, who, spite of mean dress and poverty (justly accounted by Mr. Hobbes for shame and dishonour) is pleased to entertain us at that board, where so great a multitude of our brotherhood has feasted before. For your illustrious line hath now for many generations made it a peculiar glory to supply the needs of lettered men; and as we sit at meat it seems (methinks) as if those mighty men of old did sit beside us and taste with us once more the mingled cup we drink. The ingenious author of Don Quixote de la Mancha must, I suppose, have often dined with the Duke of his age, Mr. Peter Corneille and Mr. Otway, Senhor Camoens, Rare Old Ben, Signori Tasso and Ariosto, not seldom: while young Mr. Chatterton the poet did not only dine, but break his fast, take his morning draught, and sup with Your Grace's great-grandfather, till at last he died of a mere repletion. In fine, throughout all ages the House of Gloucester hath stood our friend; and not one whit do you (most honourable) degenerate from the Dukes of the former time. Nay, I believe that there are as many bucks killed and butts of claret and canary tapped, as many benches round the board now as ever there were; for our race doth in these days discover no very manifest signs of diminution: I can assert at all events that did we (like Holy Church) draw our graces and inspiration as by a chain and a continual succession, there would be no fear warranted lest the line should become extinct.

This poor offering then I am bold to present for Your Grace's acceptance; and if there shall be found in it aught of sweet savour or pleasant discoursing, lay it not up to my poor wit (or at least in but a small degree) but to Your Grace's entertainment and familiarity. And let it please you, my Lord, to be assured of this: that the butler may always set a cup and trencher on the board for me, since (unlike to some others) I shall never scorn Your Grace's hospitality:

> But do now, and ever shall remain
>> Your Grace's most obliged,
>> humble Servant,
>> ARTHUR MACHEN, Silurist.

Here begins the veracious Chronicle of Clemendy, the which was compiled and written by Gervase Perrot of Clemendy, Gentleman, Lord of the Manour of Pwllcwrw (Beerpool) and Tankard Marshall of the Assize of Ale. And in this volume are contained all those witty and facetious discourses, jests and histories done in the parlour of Clemendy, on the Forest Road, and in the town of Uske, when the Silurists journeyed thither on the Portreeve's festival. And first is set down the Discourse of Ale, the same standing first in the Latin book.

JOURNEY THE FIRST.

MASTER PERROT'S DISCOURSE OF ALE

Of the invention of beer divers tales are told; for some say that the Egyptians first concocted this super-excellent and glorious juice; some place that primitive brewery among the Germans, lauding their King Gambrinus, and some stiffly maintain that those Asiatic peoples that fought with Xenophon did use to get drunk on ale, and nothing else. But I believe these be idle tales, legendary fables, and false conceits, for our old bards in their Triads name cwrw (and that is ale) as one of the three special blessings of the Land of Summer. Hence I believe that the Silurians, while they dwelt in that land, by some happy chance brewed beer, and, as they journeyed westward, imparted the secret of its concoction to the races through whose midst they passed; and finally, having brought their ships to anchor off the coast of Gwent, made a stay at last to all their wandering, and set up their vats beside the waters of the Uske. And this Manour of Pwllcwrw, in which I dwell, I suspect to have been from the very first a moist yet ever thirsty soil; for the word meaneth Beer Pool, or in the Latin tongue, as it is styled in the ancient Court Rolls, Stagnum de Cervisiâ. And unto this day, if you shall ask a man in the manour who is casting barley-seed upon the ground, "Friend, what sow you?" he will answer, without more ado, "Hot beer." Whereby you will perceive how subtle a people we are, and how keenly we search into eschatology, looking rather to final ends and effects than to what is but passing and transitory. And, if you come to practice and leave theories, I suppose there is not a man amongst us that loveth not a cup of old and corny ale, who will not joyfully dip his beard into the foam, turn up the can, and pour the torrent down. Wherefore amongst us the Mystery of Ale Drapers is held in great honour and repute, from the highest unto the lowest, from the little taverns on lonely roads, atop of hills, and in forgotten valleys to the great masters of the Tankard that fill the can in our fenced cities and towns of frequentation. Of these last we have some egregious specimens, fellows with round paunches and long heads, who have seen so many generations of travellers, and such diversity of morals, trickeries, methods, humours, counterfeits, revelries, noses, doublets, lecheries, japes, breeches, arguments, and appetites that their wits have grown very sharp, so that they perfectly comprehend the difference between a cassock and a smock, understand when it is wise to ask questions, and when to lay finger unto nose, when to call the crier, and when mumchance is the only word. Sometimes these gentry lose all sense of hearing and seeing to boot, and inquisitive strangers who wish to find out things, and have a well-founded conceit that the master of the Ivy-Bush sees what is done under the ivy, are greatly astonished at a deep, impenetrable ignorance, and go away as they deserve, no wiser than they came. But at other times Red Lion and Boar's Head see through the blankets and hear through the keyhole most wondrously well; they have, I believe, a special kind of tankard in the which they look when they desire to learn the A B C of an affair, and likewise a fashion of ear-trumpet that carries the click (it is some such sound, at all events) of a kiss from the cock-loft to the cellar. These Master Tankards are, in fact, mighty pleasant fellows, who bear witness to the error of giving the name "fuddlecap" to them that have much traffic with ale; and this is, it seems certain, a very great mistake, which all good Christians ought to avoid. A man who comes home late, goes to bed by a lanthorn which he has forgotten to light, and blows it out heedfully before he gets between the sheets, doubtless seems a little foolish; but, if you should interrogate him, he would be able to give good reasons and arguments of justification, shewing that he was a judicious and agreeable Silurian, and that you were a jolterhead. Well, then! leave Silurians alone when they come home late and do strange things, for you must know they have been gazing, for I wis not how many hours, into a certain dark brown, foaming, silvery fountain, wherein they have seen all manner of strange sights, visions, hieroglyphics, steganographics, pyramids, triangles, spells, perpetual motions, hot fiery conjunctions, drolleries, and mosaics; they are therefore illuminated with a transcendent science which often makes them laugh very heartily to themselves, whenas they think how ignorant and silly others are. And, from seeing in that admirable fountain and abysmal well how this earthly sphere does certainly whirl around the sun in an everlasting gyre (indeed Pythagoras taught as much, but nobody would listen to him), Silurians are obnoxious to a circularity of motion after these meditations, the which the old hieroglyphical writers symbolise by the likeness of a man driving turkeys along a road.

Praised be the home of the Greyhound in Abergavenny, and the habitation of the Salmons in Uske; thither we all hasten after we have crossed the bridge, for we see the shield from afar, azure, three salmons nayant in pale argent; 'tis a very goodly coat. But all the company within must be blazoned hauriant and not naiant, for they sit drinking and drinking evermore, forgetful that the Portreeve passeth along the road, they hear not the noise of his trumpets nor the beating of his drums. No thought give they to the high service in St. Mary's quire, nor to dalliance with fair ladies in the castle that overlooks the town; but the tankards, and cans, and cups foam up, and foam again, and in the Salmons they sit still drinking, and drinking evermore. And thou, most swift Greyhound, that swingest in the city dreaming below great hills, where the Gavenny and the Uske do meet and interflow, for thee, I say, they have set up a rare kennel, a kennel with a courtyard and low passages, where is stored baronial ale, ale such as was pleasant to De Braose what time he had lordship here, and dwelt in a mighty fortress. Hither journey weary men who have crossed mountains and are sore afoot; along the road they come at evensong and count the miles unto thy gate, till the noise of chiming bells grows near, and they enter in and sit them down, and with a long breath do drain oblivion of all their toils. Hither come the cold and melancholic people and go away duly spiced, and warmed and gingered; hither also do the merry folk hold their synods; and Silurianise till the flame leapeth out through the chimney-top, and the tiles clatter together with their singing and their mirth. Gather ye, O gather ye, and pull the greyhound's tail, all dumpish and doting men. I cite, summon, and admonish you to be and appear before the High Court of Cervisage holden within the afore-named tavern at six of the clock in the afternoon on the Calends of May, that ye may there and then purge ye of your contempt towards this honourable Silurian Assize. Fill your purses, and be ready to do suit and service and pay your quit rents to the High Tosspot our lord paramount, and to his magistrates the Lords Maltworm of Wales, humbly craving pardon for past sadness, dolour, wry mouths, cramped foreheads, knitted brows, griefs, illhaps, and all the like iniquities. For 'tis a very merciful Court, and will ever pardon them that desire to amend. I have known one come before the Most High and Mighty Lord Tosspot confessing that he had fared well in no single undertaking of this life, that all the glad hopes and expectations of his youth had come to nought, that his days were passed in misery and woe, and that he wished for nothing better than to die; yet he submitted himself to his liege lord, and craved mercy. But my lord looked pitifully upon this wretched sinner, and charged Levrier d'Argent, his herald, to set him in the ingle-nook, and there to deliver to him the sentence of the Court; and that was brought in a great tankard of old ale, so strong that it burned upon the fire like oil, so concocted that it smelt as a garden of spices of Arabia. Then the session went on, and the Sub-chanter raised the song—

Potus blandus! Potus fortis
Regibus, cleris et scortis
Et in hortis atque portis
O dulcis cervisia:

after the order appointed in the Consuetudinary of the Court. Then
was read a piece from "The Red Book of Rabanus Jocosus," and the
whole assembly from the High Tosspot to the Clericus Spigotti recounted tales so quaint and admirable that the guilty, pardoned man
was like to have been bursten with laughter, notably at the tale of a certain clerk, called *The History of the Silver Tankard with the Golden Spout, and
how rain water flowed forth from it.* Which I would gladly set down here
had I not sworn by Gwen-Wen and the Round Table not to publish
nor blaze abroad the acts done in Cervisage at the Greyhound; but this
tale is engrossed on the Court Rolls, with many other choice relations
that the Court has heard told and laughed at, you may be sure, as they
have deserved. This ancient society of Cwrw Dda was founded, it
seems certain, in the time of King Arthur, and sat for many years in
that quarter of Caerleon which has ever since been renowned for its
malt-houses; but about the time that the Normans came over great alterations and reformations were made, and, on account of the decayed
magnificence and dimished frequentation of Caerleon, the Court was
removed to Abergavenny and the day of session fixed for the Calends
of May, being the day on which the great May Mart is held at the
aforesaid town. And shortly after this, summons was directed to
Gruffydd Perrot, assigning to him the office of Tankard Marshal, unto
him and his heirs for ever—"quia ille et antecessores sui semper ha-
buerunt domum Columbariam in manerio de Stagno Cervisiæ"—for
that he and his forefathers have alway held Clemendy in the Manour of
Beerpool. And then I think this High Court was constituted as it is
now, and records kept by the Clerk of the Acts in Cervisage; yet all
customs and precedents of weight were curiously maintained and are
observed unto this day as they were in the reign of King Arthur. For
all our doctors and antiquaries who have searched the Chronicles and
turned up the soil of the Caerleon meadows are agreed that the High
Tosspot, and his proctors, lieutenants, summoners, clerks and surrogates, with all their acts, arrests, prescriptions, methods and consuetu-
dinaries, their *merum et mixtum cervisium,* their writ of *Cyathum hausit*

extremum and all other their benefices, exemptions and immunities, have their source and beginning from that wonderful Round Table, which is as potent now as when King Arthur and his Knights first made it famous. From this origin proceeds the Benefice of Free Sokage and the famous charter of *Terra Sabulosa* or Sandy Soil. And this latter name is given to no desert place nor stony land but rather to the fairest and most delicious manours, and the merriest cities of Gwent, and confers inestimable privileges. But, before it be granted and sent forth under the seal of the High Tosspot, the Clericus Spigotti visits the place and strictly interrogates all men, gentle and simple, whether they be verily addicted to strong ale and waggish ways; and, if he find so much as one politique or rancorous meddler therein, without more ado he tears his mandate in twain and rides hot foot away. But if the Spigot Clerk find the folk to be true Silurians, mellow men; the girls comely and jesticulous; the country provided with sunny nooks for winter and shadowed summer byways; and, above all, the ale mighty and sound to the core; he brings a good report to the Court and speaks favourably of that land. And if it be a town the Spigot Clerk must find a fair open street or square for wags to walk in; and walled gardens and trees and orchards, without which the largest town is no better than a rat-hole and fitter for brutes than Christian men. Then is the charter engrossed, and signed and sealed by the High Tosspot, and carried with pomp and worship to the place with trumpets, and vyalls and banners and the rarest show imaginable. The which place is thenceforth called Sandy Soil, because the thirst of it is insatiable, and craving moisture without end. Observe, then, what lordship Ale hath over us Silurians, and especially over the folk of Pwllcwrw; for 'twas by virtue of holding land in this gracious manour that my ancestor was cited to the Court and had an honourable office given him at the Reformation, which he and those who have come from his body have fulfilled through rain and sun ever since, both at High Sessions in Abergavenny, and at Petty Sessions in Uske. We Perrots indeed have gone wet foot and dry foot to these solemnities, not let by turmoil or distress, and when Levrier d'Argent calls *Canthari Mareschallus,* our *adsum* never fails, nor the function of our Marshalsea, nor have we broken faith with the Round Table. And know that by this Sassion Cwrw Dda ale is ennobled and glorified for us, exalted from a tinker's drain to a sempiternal spring of deep signification and high method, whence comes Silurianism and all that joyous knowledge which will not let us be dumpish, disconsolate, nor over-sorrowful have we never so much reason for sadness and dolour. Of these sweet thoughts the Saxons know nothing at all, and hold our mirth for folly and dotage, and, merely seeing that many of us are poor and meanly clad, deride and despise Silurians more than all other men, declaring that we are fools, dolts, jolterheads, idlers, whoremongers, drunkards, and so forth, and at the best pity us with a kind of scorn as a moon-struck silly folk, harmless for want of sense. But we, though we hear these people so declaring in their pride that our Round Table is noth-ing more than a Roman shambles or slaughter-house, merely shrug up our shoulders, smile under our beards, and utter some quaint saying as to the foolishness of men talking about a place to which they have never been, or at least do not understand in the smallest degree. But by the Oar and the Stillions! by the Spigot and the Pitch! these stupid per-sons are not worthy of a seat in the Greyhound nor the Salmons nei-ther; nor should they be allowed so much as to cross the boundaries of the Land of the Moon, lest they make us as dull and dismal as they themselves always are and always have been. But, if you wish to learn a little Silurian wisdom, go any day to Uske, and spend a few hours and a little money at the Salmons, taking the seat between the fire and the window which looks out on a fair open place, where there is always some pleasantry or racy galliardise on foot. Then you shall go to the Boar's Head, and there they will give you all you want, whatever it may be or how much so ever of it you require at their hands. 'Tis the first degree in Cervisage, and so you must go on, till the fame of your deeds and conversation come to the ears of the High Court, who will in due course issue the writ, *Bene, Bene, Bene Bibere,* and cite you to their Petty Sessions. It may be that I have said too much of the customs of Cer-visage, and am growing somewhat wearisome; but, by the Bottomless Vat! I have looked so long into the Tankard that it is still dancing, shimmering, brawling, foaming, ebbing, flowing, before my eyes; and as for my ears there is ever a humming, a surging on the Brim, a deep thorough Bassus sounding in them, with treble, tenor, and counter-tenor, duly falling in and making up the concert in more descants, symphonies, antiphons, fugues, madrigals, rounds, canons, and catches, than it is convenient for one man to listen to. And the chime of silver cans is still changing, ringing, and tingling against the tympanum, the meatus, and Eustachius his tubes, running back and fore from the outer ear to the inner, so that I can hear nothing else. In fine, all my five senses (some naughty fellow has added a sixth, fye on him!) rational and vegetal soul, sensus communis, memory, understanding, will, and phantasy, are quite absorbed in this one object; and, if you talk to me of letters, I can but think of the Library of Burgavenny, where are so many great embossed books clothed in skins, and bound in chains; such chests of parchments and rolls, where is kept the Silver Oar borne before the High Tosspot, where are desks, lecterns, and stalls for learned Silurists, where in the midst hangs a silver lamp, fed with pure and quintessential ale, and such a store of wonderful and joyous histories, and phantastic inventions that a London bookseller would go raving mad to think thereon. Am I not, then, a complete and special Tankard Marshall, and a true Silurian? One of that company who cannot laugh too much or turn the tap too often; and in truth, whether it be good or bad, that is all our philosophy. As for the rest; reforming, regenerating, couzening, amending, perfecting, leading-by-the-nose, and beatifying our fellow-men, we leave to the wise folks, those I mean that have a finger in every pie, and whose pockets never lack plums; maybe we should be tempted to follow their example did we not see these same righteous busybodies, and sanctified intermeddlers sometimes giving one another odd, sour looks, and drawing their foreheads into all manner of comical shapes, which they call gravity and expect us to consider mighty solemn. But we Silurians had rather laugh and lie still, leaving other matters to God and the King, who (it is lawful to say) can be trusted to do what is best. What ho! My Lord High Tosspot cometh with his Silver Oar and Great Seals, and all his merry company. There go the vyalls and the horns to the tune of *O my Madam in the Can.* Lo! you; in crossing the brook the Clericus Spigotti hath been spilt; there'll be a tang of beer about the water till it flows into the Uske hard by Caerleon. Fill up a foaming measure, and make all ready for the joyous session of the Cwrw Dda.

THE PORTREEVE'S GAUDY-DAY

1.—THE PREPARATION.

In the midst of the journey of my mortal life, I sent one day letters to three friends of mine, asking them to come to me at Clemendy, and make merry with me for a little while; ere the honeysuckle and the roses had fallen to earth once more. For it must be understood that I had been taking a dip into the Devil's Bath; and being recovered was willing to celebrate my happy case in some fitting and joyful manner. I know not whether any of you who may read the Silurian Mythologies have ever had a plunge into this same Balneum Diaboli; but if not let me tell you 'tis a mighty hot fountain; and yet has lumps of ice floating in it that freeze the heart while the head's on fire. In fine 'tis a bath to be remembered all the days of a man's life, a bath held in especial abhorrence by Silurists, because, whenas they are in it, they laugh little, drink less, and will scarce say "thank you" if a pretty lass beckon with her finger, and pout her lips into shapes never so enticing. And, as it is well known in what esteem Love, Ale, and Laughter are held by the good folk of Gwent, you may conceive how sorely sick they must be to have no relish for these delights, and even to rail against them and to blaspheme; uttering all manner of waspish censures against broad grins, brown bowls, and cherry lips. It is in these sad times when Beelzebub takes us by the neck, dips us under, and asks, "How do you like that?" that we say sour and ill-natured things against everybody, pry into matters which should be covered with leaves like the baskets in Ceres' Pomp, and find fault with everything. Others write books while they are soused in the Bath; works full of unpleasant doctrines and sad moralities to the intent that our Mortal Life is a pitiful Tragic Show, full of tears, and sighing, and sorrow; instead of the true, veracious, and Silurian position, namely that it is the drollest, merriest, wildest, most fantastical comedy; a comedy better than any that the witty clerk Aristophanes invented for the men of Athens, and rigged out with the rarest jokes, trickeries, brawls, intrigues, miz-mazes, counterfeits, gods-from-the-machine, choruses, waggeries, oil-flasks, wineskins, masks, and music. This is what it really is, tho' when one is in the Devil's Bath it seems quite different; but then it is silly to touch the quill at such a season, and can only waste time, ink, and paper.

And since I had come once more to my right reason, and the blue sky opened no more for me a pall of blackness, as I have said, I bade my friends come and sleep for a few nights under my roof, that we all of us might get some gladness whilst we were able. And on the appointed day I waited for them, sitting in an elbow chair set in the shade of the lawn, and had on a little table beside me a flagon of wine, a cup, and the famous books called *The Red Book of Rabanus,* and *The Joyous Inventions of the Monk Galliardus.* With these good fellows I passed the afternoon, lying well back in my stall with my legs stretched out, reading with grave delight the pleasant adventures of the Seigneur of Ville-aux-Echelles and Madam Amalaswonda, and the wonderful history of the Rose-Chapter held in the Abbey of Arsanno on the Vigil of St. Ypocras. And amongst other strange relations I read as follows from the *Periphrasis* of the Spanish friar, Antonio of Calvados; the which plainly declares the delight taken in our land by the nations oversea:

STRANGE STORY OF A RED JAR

If you ever chance to spend a few weeks in the County of Monmouth, and are one of those clever people who know where to look for what is good, you will not fail to roam over the hills and across the valleys till you come to a little town called Uske. This town lies beside the fair river of the same name, and is sheltered on every side by wooded hills and sweet, greeny slopes; and to the east you can see the enchanted forest of Wentwood, where there are deep dells, shady alleys, rocks with water everlastingly dripping from them, and the finest black cherries that anybody could wish to taste. But, if you once cross the bridge and get into Uske, you will have plenty to look at without thinking of Wentwood, that is, if you are fond of quaint houses, wild old-fashioned gardens, and odd nooks and corners of every sort. And, better than all, there are old tales and legends still lingering about the sunny streets, and sleeping on the settles next to the fire; but it is getting rather difficult to wake them up now, because you see they are very old. They are, in fact, the last vestiges of the good old monks, who had a Priory in Uske, and this tale I am going to tell is considered by experienced judges to be as pleasant a story as any of them, because it has such a fine moral, without which a story is no more use than a wasp without his sting.

You must know, then, that there was once a monk at the Priory, named Brother Drogo, who was regarded by everybody as a splendid specimen of a monk; and not without reason, for he stood six feet high, and had a waist like a wine-tub. He had roving twinkling black eyes, a firm mouth, and a voice like the roar of the pedal-pipes of the organ, and it must be confessed that in his quire habit he looked a well-proportioned man, and a pillar of the Church. As for his intellect, all the brethren allowed him to be an admirable logician, an orthodox divine, and the best judge of sauces, seasonings, hot relishes, sweet-meats, and preserved dainties of the whole convent, and this was say-ing a great deal. It was Brother Drogo's science and deep knowledge of the nature of things, and of how to mingle hot and sweet together, that made the pious brethren long for Lent and fast-days, and desire to mortify their throats with curious dishes, of which none but himself and the cook ever understood the composition. But yet this was not Brother Drogo's greatest art; for he was the Cellarer of the Priory, and took care of the casks in the cellar, and of that pleasant vineyard on a southern slope, where the sun was nearly always to be found; and if he were great in the kitchen and the larder, he was far greater in the affairs of the fragrant world below. But here his one fault got the better of him, and sometimes played him queer tricks; for, to tell the truth, Brother Drogo used now and then to get very drunk. When in this state he usually saw visions, which made some esteem him a very holy man (since it is only such that are blessed in this fashion); but others said that his visions were of the wrong sort and should be kept out of the monastic Chronicle. However this may be, the last vision that he ever saw was such a wonderful one that it lasted him the rest of his life, since he never touched anything but water afterwards; and this was the manner of it.

It was a very hot drowsy sort of day in the beginning of Septem-ber; a day when the sickles were busy in the corn-fields round Uske, a day of blue dim mists over the woods and hills and the river, a day of mellowed golden sunlight good for the vines and apples and pears and plums, and all the autumn fruits that were ripening in those tangled gardens of Gwent. In the castle above the town the lords and ladies were lying in the shade upon the grass and listening to the ballads and love-songs of the minstrel Master Jehan de Laune of Paris town; and the girls let the squires and pages tickle them and snatch sly kisses as much as ever they liked; because it was too hot to scream and they knew it was right to bear and forbear. In the Priory the monks were (most of them) asleep and dreaming holy dreams that made them smile as they slept; but Brother Drogo was wide awake and walking up and down the cloister. Why was this? Well, it was because he was terribly thirsty, and felt as if a Lollard were being roasted somewhere at the back of his throat, and the reason that he did not drink was that he had doubts whether he should ever stop if he once began. This was in fact a knotty case of conscience and it puzzled the good man and made him feel thirstier than ever; the which was natural since theology is known to be a dry and thirsty science. It is bad enough when two or three divines are muddling a question between them, but this unfortunate monk had to be Præses, Opponent, and Respondent all at once; and he found that it was necessary for him to take a little wine to clear his brain, for being a conscientious man he wished to settle this point before doing anything else. He therefore picked his way past a dozen or so of monks, all smiling very hard, and went along a dark passage, and began to go down the steps to the cellar. Now the steps were many and by reason of their great age, uneven; so it was slow work getting to the bottom, and the Cellarer had to stop short very often and tap his skull, for the cool air from below seemed to make his blood hotter than before. And when he stopped he held up his lamp and looked at the walls, which had been decorated in rather a curious manner by an ancient monk who had been dead a good many hundred years. This artist's fancy had led him to suppose that views of Purgatory and warmer places would be a nice ornament to the cellar stair; but whether he intended all these flames, fagots, and streams of fire as a sort of whet for the wine, or whether he meant to say "that's what'll come to you if you get drunk" is more than I can tell. But these pictures made Brother Drogo feel warmer and warmer, though he couldn't help looking at them; and in one place where a fine powerful demon was sousing a big monk in a cauldron of fire and poking him with a three-pronged fork to see if he were done, the Cellarer was forced to discern a huge resemblance between the monk's features and his own. However he trod the last step in due time, and stood in the vaulted cellar, the which had aisles, transepts, side chapels, and ambulatories in abundance, but there were casks everywhere of all shapes and sizes, and a few curious-looking jars with Greek letters cut on them. In this shadowy world of wine Brother Drogo stood awhile and gazed about in an abstracted kind of way, rolling his tongue in his mouth and telling his tale on his fingers as he thought of Burgundy, Beaulne, Champagne, and all the vintages of the fair land of France, of Valdepenas and Amontillado, of the juice of the Rhine mountains, and of the famous wines of Italy, which are drawn from the very mouth of the fire below. But the Cellarer's thirst was such a stupendous one that he could not see his way to allaying it on any of these; so he just drew himself a pint of his own red wine of Uske, and sat down on a stone form to consider things. When he had finished his draught he began to walk about among the casks and to peer into odd shelves and crannies in out of the way recesses and blind corners of the cellar, muttering to himself all the time "Burgundy, Beaulne, Champagne, Valdepenas, Amontillado, Montepulciano" as if he were bidding the beads of St. Bacchus. By chance he came to a nook in the darkest part of the cellar, in the which nothing was kept, nor had been for many a long day; and holding up his lamp and peering about the dim and shadowy wall he saw faintly a great red jar, of the most ancient and uncouth form imaginable, graved all over with ivy leaves, vine tendrils, pine cones and a pomp of nymphs and fauns dancing all around it. But there was no mark, nor label to say what this jar held; so Brother Drogo found it was his duty as Cellarer to look a little more closely into the matter. Indeed he had his doubts as to whether this jar was a good Christian, so he got on a stone step and began to use his tools on the jar's mouth, which was covered tightly with black pitch. And as he cut this pitch away faint odours of delicious fragrance began to steal out tickling Brother Drogo's weakest places. "The Prior will thank me for this day's work" thought he; and thus he cut the last piece away and the soul of the jar poured its whole fragrance out upon him like a breeze from the Islands in the High Levant, and went past into the cellar, and up the stair into the cloister where the monks were asleep, and out into the town so that the townsfolk said to one another "'Tis a balmy day, indeed marvellously balmy." As for the girls in the castle their gallants squeezed them a little more closely, and they smiled and seemed to think everything was being properly performed and going on nicely;

but then it was a sweet gale that blew upon them.

But Brother Drogo said to himself "one cup—one little cup—of this wonderful wine will quite quench my thirst; better than a hogshead of any other wine; indeed if I were now half-seas-over, it would be my duty to taste it; am I not Cellarer? How shall I bring the matter before the Prior without having tasted?" You see Brother Drogo had not read Aristotle for nothing, so he gently inclined the jar to his cup, and let a dark purple stream run slowly like oil into it, till it was quite full. And when he tasted he had drained the cup, and when he had drained the cup he knew that he, the Cellarer of the Convent of St. Mary, was a sinful man that had gloried all his days in a nice discrimination of various juices, when in point of fact, he had that moment tasted wine for the first time in his life. But instead of running up the stairs and telling the Prior, Brother Drogo drank and drank again, cup after cup, till he got chimes in his ears, fire in his veins, and a miz-maze in his brain. This veracious history does not say how many cups Brother Drogo lifted out of the red jar; but it was certainly a great many for he was a man of large capabilities. However, as he was drawing down the jar to fill once more that little cup, he seemed suddenly to fall asleep, and to have down cushions laid under his head, but this strange circumstance happened so suddenly that he had no time to take notes; and it is not possible to give so full a description of the affair as I should have wished. But the really strange part of the tale is that when he had slept till he could sleep no more, and woke up again, he was no longer in the cellar of the Convent at Uske; how this happened neither he nor I nor anybody else have ever made out, but it is certainly a fact that Brother Drogo rubbed his eyes and found himself lying on green grass. And when he had rubbed his eyes a second time, had stood up and looked about him, he saw that he was standing on the highest point of a mountain girt around with woods of dark pine-trees, and dwarf oak thickets, and brakes of tangled undergrowth. Below very far was a city of a strange fashion, and beyond the city mountains rising one above the other; and behind him was the sea of a very deep blue. Before the Cellarer had finished wondering where he was and how he got there, his ears caught a noise of jangling and clashing of brass on brass, with shrill flute notes, beating of drums, and loud cries and hails now from one quarter and now from another, gathering together and drawing towards him. I do not see what Brother Drogo could do but open his mouth; it is certain that he did so, for he could not recollect what passage it was that led out of the cellar to the top of this mountain. But while he was thinking the matter over, the drums, tambourines, cymbals, single flutes, double flutes, and loud calling grew loud enough to deafen one; and all at once he was surrounded on all sides by a company of girls whose clothes seemed to be at the wash, for there was not enough of linen (or of anything else) to make a kerchief on the whole company. And when they began to dance round the poor man, calling to him in a tongue he did not understand, he began to be afraid he had got into bad company, not suited for a monk of St. Bennet's rule. But he could not help allowing that these girls had very nice figures and seemed to be able to make a great noise. "If I were a layman," thought he, "it would be different, but these amusements are not quite proper for ecclesiastical persons." Round, around they whirled in dancing and the din of cymbals clashed louder yet; but then the figures of the naked girls became shadows and their music was hushed to a dull murmur. The next thing Brother Drogo heard was the words of the Prior of his Convent, saying "He will yet live, and drink another cup." "Of water only" answered the poor Cellarer, who began to think he was always to be moving, from cellar to mountain and from mountain to his bed. In fact, he had been found, after much seeking, lying on his back in the cellar, with a nasty cut on his head, a great wine jar lying in shards beside him, and a pool of dark red wine on the floor giving forth a fragrance that made the monks sniff eagerly. Some persons have said that Brother Drogo must have slipped backwards, knocking his skull against the edge of a stone ascent, and pulling the wine jar after him. These persons make out that he dreamt whatever he saw, but I am disposed to think them rather too clever for this dull world of ours. But as I said at the beginning of the tale the Cellarer kept to water for the rest of his life, and leaving the cellar to another hand became the chief gardener of the Priory, and grew such worts, and flowers, and fruits as were not to be seen elsewhere in all Gwent. Indeed he invented that great green plum, as big as an egg, that melts in the mouth as sweet as honey, and is rightly called "Soif de Dru," or "Drogo's Thirst."

And the moral of this history is—Leave old jars on the shelf. It seems to me a good one.

*   *   *

And when the shadows began to climb up from the brook Gwith-ian and the valley of Deep Dendraeth, and to give coolness to the western hills; far away I heard a horn winding, and knew the notes for the call of Nick Leonard, of Uske. But presently two other bugles joined in the music and told me that Tom Bamfylde of Abergavenny, and Phil Ambrose of Penyrhayle were also journeying to Clemendy. After the horns came the noise of horses' feet; so I went forth to meet my guests and saw them soon coming at a sober pace, one after anoth-er along the depths of the road. So to greeting and to supper and wine-reward for the journey done; which with certain pipes of tobacco and a canon sung made us fit for no unwelcome rest. But on the morrow we agreed to be merry, remembering that we were officers of the Cwrw Dda, having Free Sokage and dwelling *in Terra Sabulosa.*

THE SPIGOT CLERK'S FIRST TALE

On the morrow when we had breakfasted, we got out our pipes and began to smoke tobacco as we all of us did use, and soon the parlour was decked out with those blue clouds that savour so sweetly of a morning, and each was filled with a grave contentment with the world, and especially with the Land of the Moon (that is Gwent) as being the most productive in pleasant things of all countries whatsoever. And after some time I thought fit to say "What contentment shall we use this morning that we may pass the time cheerfully and not grow weary and wish the sun a-bed? For my part I am content to sit still and smoke, but I know that in Uske and Abergavenny this employment is not held sufficient." Whereon Dick Leonard said "Let us play at bowls, 'tis a hearty game and a choice diversion, and not laborious like Tennis which sweats a body half away." "The devil loveth the bias, and useth bowls of liquid fire; if you believe me not, read the Itinerario Infernale of the Licentiate Sanctius, who saw the fiends playing with the heads of Kings and Cardinals." Thus Tom Bamfylde spoke contra, and to him assented Master Ambrose, who protested that he cared not a tittle whether the devil used bowls, but was hot enough already and deter-mined to sit still. "But," quoth he, "let us rather tell tales in turn, so

that three may smoke while one recounts, and 'tis odd if we four Silurians are not able to furnish each other with entertainment till the
clock strike dinner-time. Placetne vobis, domini?" "We might do
worse," said Master Leonard, "and your entertainment may serve our
occasions; but it is but just that as Spigot Clerk will have stories told,
Spigot Clerk should make a beginning of telling stories, wherefore hold
ye your peace, most gentle Knights, and hearken to the fat products of
Ambrosius his brain." "Not so," cried Phil, "but rather we will recount
by lot, and leave the judgment to our sweet lady Chance who still deals
kindly with us." "Your lady Chance is no Christian, she hath not been
sanctified," said the Rubrican, "but is a mere Pagan, and a slut to boot:
yet we will use her for this turn, since it is a trivial. But what manner of
lot shall we employ?" "Why this," I answered: "Let him whose pipe
first goeth out tell the first tale, and have likewise the power to name
his successor, and so on, till we have all devised some history. And the
deviser shall for his turn sit in the chair by the window, the which was
made after the conceit of one of our house that was a great bard, and it
is alleged that this seat maketh him who sitteth thereon to be fertile
and mightily productive." "How precious a chair is this," quoth Dick
Leonard, "and in what esteem would I hold such an one if such were
in my possession. Truly I believe there are a few households in Gwent
that would find a chair of these properties convenient, for it would explain matters that are now a mystery. By the Round Table a very special chair, and worthy of the Manour of Pwllcwrw. But hush! for we
must all smoke slow, if we wish not for the prerogative in devising."
So all applied them to the task of burning tobacco by slow degrees, but
Phil Ambrose in his caution let the fire in his pipe die out altogether,
and though he might puff and blow, he blew nothing but ashes from
the bowl, and so in spite of all he had to begin our pastime. But first I
duly took him by the hand and set him in his stall, with as much ridiculous solemnity and observance as I could master, and said to Tom
Bamfylde "Do you, O learned Rubrican, use the words of the herald
when an Act in Cervisage is to be discharged." Then the tenor in a
plain song, after the manner of distinct reading—*With closed lips and gap-
ing ears, I pray you, I charge you, good Lords of Gwent hearken to what is to come,
then be joyous and laugh gaily. Seal up the door.*

HOW THE FOLK OF ABERGAVENNY WERE PESTERED BY AN ACCURSÉD KNIGHT

All good Silurists love the sweet town of Abergavenny, wherefore I need crave no pardon in telling a tale of it. But you know there stands outside the east gate a very fine church that was formerly the quire of the good old monks, settled there by the great Lord Marcher Hamelin de Baladun, not by Drogo de Baladun nor Bryan de Insula, as some have said; though indeed this question is of little importance to my history. And you know what curious and special works are to be seen in this quire, what storied and annealed windows, with monuments of charge and show most choicely wrought, and blazoned with right noble bearings. There the great lords lie well, as it becomes lords to lie, decked out in their harness, their head and feet resting on strange monstrous creatures and with calm faces and uplifted hands, wrought full rarely in the goodly stone and alabaster. Beside these are their dear wives and sweethearts vested in wimple, couvre-chef, and cote-hardie, with their little pets cut beside them. One of these sweet ladies hath a squirrel in her hand and they say that while she ran after the merry little beast she fell down from the castle wall and quite lost her breath. Is it not pitiful to think of this and of all these ladies and their knights, who of old time loved and laughed right heartily and were warm and glowing from head to foot, and are now so cold and quiet? But it was certainly a sorrowful thing to die for a little fellow with bright eyes and a curly tail; 'twas bad enough when a lady died for her big pet, who could put his arms all round the cote-hardie, and fondle it, and say pretty things, and kiss those full red lips, that are now so white and chilly. But yet 'tis of none of these dear dead maidens that I am going to talk, nor of their brave Knights that payed quit rent to them in kisses, and did with their embraces full knightly suit and service. Though one wrestled with a bull till the brute's horns broke off, and another charged twice through the stricken field of Banbury, pole-axe in hand, though one fought two days and nights with a few small ships against a host of French and Spanish galleys (hard by to Rochelle, this did Jehan de Hastings, third of that name), yet I know you care not much about them, or their noble and ancient coats, and I wis that you would not weep at the fate of the last Seigneur who died when he was but seven-

teen being pierced through the body in a tourney. I will therefore devise you a tale of another marvel of the minster, which (to speak the
plain truth) made a great noise in its day, was a notable nuisance to the
lords and ladies aforesaid, pestered the good monks till their stalls were
too hot to hold them, and played the very deuce with the honest
townsfolk of Burgavenny, who then, as now, lived a quiet life and
asked for nothing but to be left alone. And what was this marvel? How
could anything about a church be so wicked as to worry people and
make them say naughty words in the old French Tongue, in the Dog-
Latin Tongue, and in the language of Paradise itself, for everybody
knows that Adam was a Welshman, that from his body come all the
Ap-Adams, one of the largest and noblest families in the world, who
have made themselves loved, feared, reverenced, and honoured both
in the lands on this side the sea and in the lands beyond seas. There are
some currish fellows now (and I suppose there always have been
such), who say there never was, never is, and never will be an Ap-
Adam good for anything alive or dead but fattening the soil, that this
earth would be passably pleasant if there were no Ap-Adams on it, that
the young Ap-Adams who are round and soft and wear cote-hardies
cause more burning plagues and hot damnifications than the old ones
with bristly beards, breeches, and grisly oaths. But these are ill-natured
folks who have been crossed in love, so you mustn't mind what they
say; and besides in this very church outside the east gate of Burgavenny lies the glorious tomb of Sir William ap-Thomas from whose body
cometh the worshipful and illustrious house of Herbert, and he was
the grandson of Jenkin ap-Adam, nor can the heralds trace this house
back any further. But after all this genealogical and moral discourse
you are still in the dark as to what it was that made all Abergavenny
into a stewpan with a hot, glowing fire under it, and in it a heap of
Drogos, Humphreys, Mauds, Matildas, Efans, Owens, Jorwerths, and
Gwrgans with Prior Hadrian de Mortuo Mari and his monks, all snort-
ing, blowing, thinning down, murmuring and crying *Splendeur Diou, Di-
aoul, in ignem aeternam et favillam cum Diabolo et angelis suis*—for the good
old monks were the only people then who really understood theological arrangements, so they naturally expressed their thoughts with better
grace and at more length. Well I will out with it; it was a mere clock, a
thing of cogs and wheels and bells to tick off hours and minutes and

seconds, to strike eating time and drinking time and kissing time, by which conceptions, horoscopes, and all the products of mind and body might be dated, in sun and shade, in the which point clocks are better than Dials, for these latter are not very useful on cloudy days, and moreover on each and every Diál are the words *We Must,* and people do not like to be always drinking the joyous sunshine and sweet nectar of the air from a death's head, unless they are fantastic and tired of the blue sky, the green earth and the Ap-Adams upon the earth. Now this clock aforesaid lived in a tower built on to the monastic church solely for its use and benefit to the intent that it might be plainly seen and clearly heard, and tell the Burgavennians when to breakfast, dine, and sup, when to yawn and awake, when to yawn and go to sleep, when to squeeze the ladies hard and to kiss their nice red lips till they were out of breath (these kisses leave blisters) and when to listen to the juice going guggle, guggle, guggle into the cups. Besides this it marked off Mass and Matins, separated Sext and called to Compline, and as I have said dwelt in a high campanile, that looked over the town walls and peeped into all the bye-ways, dark alleys, walled gardens, pleasaunces and closes of Abergavenny, indeed it is supposed that the clock was the witness of many a little matter known only to two besides. Now the tintinnabulous functions thereof were performed by a very fine piece of mechanique, I would say by the statue of an armed knight standing in a habitacle with a double row of bells hung beside him on which he smote the hours and the quarters with his axe, and also at the Canonical Hours struck out a verse of the hymn appointed to be sung, the which duties he discharged to admiration, and was accounted an honest fellow, notwithstanding all the ugly dragons, basilisks, and serpents that were cut in the stone all about him. To be short he was called by the common people Sir Jenkin Thomas, and was known by report all over Gwent, aye, and had had bequests and charges and rents erected for him by pious people, who thought Sir Jenkin looked after them and kept Abergavenny quiet and in good order. There was a charge of three shillings and four pence per annum on the meadow called Tirgwain-y-groes, of one shilling and ninepence on the seigneur's mill, of sixpence three farthings on the land called Penycoed; while my lady Loys had given him a pair of gold spurs and a certain Sir Reginald de Braose had devised ten golden pounds to the knight: all these benefactions being for the renewing of the gilt on Sir Jenkin's armour, the repainting of his face, and also the repairing and beautifying of the tower whereon he dwelt. And as all rent-charges due to the Priory were collected by the Prior, we may be pretty certain that Sir Jenkin was not defrauded of his due. But you will ask how came this clock in Abergavenny? Well it was one of the fruits of the leisure of the good old monks, who even in their idlest hours were not entirely idle, but rather were for ever inventing, fertilising, concocting, devising, fabricating, producing and making productive. Ah! we owe a great deal to these holy men who saw into the essence of things and knew more than we do about juices and the *perpetuum mobile*. Accordingly one of them at Burgavenny Priory as he sat in the sunny garden looking at the wonderful hill called the Blorenge, and meditating upon what mechanical device he should next put his hands and mind to, suddenly bethought him that they had no clock worthy of their quire, and presently determined that he would make a clock that should be the pride of the Convent, the town, and the Lordship. And when this canon (his name was Dom. Maria de Wick) told the Prior of what he intended to do the Prior said O *Admirabile,* and nothing doubted that they would have a very special clock as Dom. Maria was known to have made an instrument in which was a wheel eternally moving and yet not finishing one revolution in seven thousand years. And in much less time than that Dom. Maria had made all his wheels, and cogs and chains and had fitted them with weights, having likewise fashioned the face, splendidly coloured in red and blue and gold, and all manner of astrological tables written on it, so that this clock got the name, among the curious, of *Medulla Quadripartiti*—the marrow of the Quadripartitum which as you know is the Institutes of Astrology. In the meantime the Prior had paid a visit to the Baron in his castle, and had talked very kindly to the brave honest knight, explaining to him that one of the canons was making a very fine clock for the Priory Church, and that it was necessary that this clock should be provided with a tower. Just then pretty Eva or Maud or Isabella came in, and the Prior's affair was done in no time, and the campanile as good as built, for the Prior was a very holy man and a great favourite with the ladies, his penitents. To be short the tower was built at the Baron's charges, and the clock set up in it, and then and not till then did Dom. Maria lead forth Sir Jenkin, whom he had concealed in his laboratory, for he had worked on this figure with great ingenuity, and thought even better of it than of his wheel, which to be sure did nothing but go round somewhat leisurely. And when the Prior, the Sub-prior, the canons, and the monks saw this admirable statue, so artificially perfected with helmet, coif, hauberk, condiéres, baldrick, and chausses, and marked how the face was enamelled to the life, they knew not exactly what to say; some cried *"miles ad vivum,"* and others *"admirabile,"* only the sub-prior muttered something to himself about *"sollers hominem ponere"* and *"plane perfectum est,"* but then he knew rather too much and afterwards came to grief. Then Dom. Maria expounded his great work to them, and shewed that he could easily link it to his clock and make it strike the hours and even play tunes with a moderate amount of contrivance; and of this the Prior altogether approved—"'Twill sanctify the town" said he. Thus the habitacle was fashioned high up on the tower, and the dragons, lizards, and other monsters choicely cut out by a Freemason who had come to the great Fair on May Day, and had been chosen by Dom. Maria to execute the work. Finally on St. Petronilla's Day Sir Jenkin Thomas was hoisted to his place and with his axe (the oblation of the Mystery of Cordwainers) knocked off *Jam lucis orto sidere* on the peal of bells (the oblation of the Mystery of Ale-Drapers) and shortly after struck six o'clock as coolly as a husband kisses his wife. I need say nothing of the rites and ceremonies observed, but you may be sure the Prior wore his gold cope with the orphrey of roses and lilies and the peacock hood, that wax tapers, incense, holy water, and holy men were as thick about that tower as flies round a cow's head on Midsummer Day. And besides the monks the castle and the town and all the country side had come to see this sanctification: there was the Baron with his little son, and the Lords Marcher of Estrighoil and Uske, wearing splendid surcoats bejewelled and glowing with lions, ravens, boars' heads, and flower-deluces; there was the Baron's Lieutenant Sir Raoul Lezayre (but he was looking all the while at the ladies instead of Sir Jenkin), to say nothing of Esquires, Captains, and men-at-arms. As for the ladies they were there also finely tricked out in silk, and velvet, and sly smiles; and to mention things unlike together, the Chancery of Burgavenny was present in black gown and square cap, together with the Rolls and the Requests wagging their heads and looking solemn; and lastly all the

commonalty of the town and country from the Mayor to the wild
shepherds from the mountains. Thus was Dom. Maria's work hal-
lowed in the presence of a great multitude, yet it was noted that after
the consecration, after Sir Jenkin, his battle-axe and bells had been
sprinkled with the holy water, the Freemason who had cut the stone-
work, craved leave to go up and set his mark thereon, saying that he
had by some mischance forgotten to do this before. Which leave was
given him, and it is alleged that when he had come down again, and
had vanished back into the crowd he was heard to laugh indecently
and full scornfully, and the Burgavennians assert that this Freemason
was no more nor less than one of Hell's Commissioners, who by that
mark he set upon the stone undid all that the holy water and benedic-
tions had effected, and in fine, was the author of all the mischief that
came to pass. They say also that the Baron hearing how the fellow had
laughed, was willing to have spoken with him in his castle (or may be
under it) and bade a man-at-arms attach his person; but to no effect,
since there was no Freemason to be seen, either then or afterwards in
all the coasts of Gwent.

But nobody thought very much about him at the time, for they
had plenty of other things to take up their thoughts, namely feasting
and drinking; for never was there such a festival at Abergavenny as
that of St. Petronilla de Clochasterio, as this lady (virgo non m'ra) was
called by the monks ever after. For first of all there was a very sufficient table at the Priory, where the great Lords and Ladies, their Esquires, Pages, and Fools (so they named Men of Letters in those days)
were so stuffed with peacocks, pheasants, swans, partridges, capons,
salmon, carp, trout, boars' heads, larded beef, and venison of all sorts
and sizes, to say nothing of the rivers of sauces monastically concocted
of spices (such as the cursed monk &c. &c.), of cunning condiments,
of sweet confections with one notable device in marchpane, imaging
the new tower, that they must but for the wine assuredly have choked.
But the wine saved them for it was ecclesiastical and entirely canonical
both as to quantity and quality; so that between the monastic spices
and the purple juices this was a day remembered by lords and ladies in
more ways than one. Nor did the townsfolk or the countryfolk starve,
and if you put for peacocks, ducks, and for swans, geese, for boar's
head, pork, for venison, mutton, and for wine strong ale, they made as

hearty a banquet in the meadow as their betters did in the refectory, and were no more fit to hear Evensong than the monks were to sing it; and indeed you could scarcely make out the Psalms for the clatter of the *misereres,* as one monk after another fell forwards and lost his balance. And that night at the castle it is said that the three Lords Marcher began to discuss theological questions, the which proves that they must have been half-seas-over. Why? Because when these great seigneurs were sober they never talked of such things, knowing that matters ecclesiastical are beyond a curly pate which must pass under the razor to tackle these dogmatical affairs. Nevertheless, on St. Petronilla de Clochasterio her feast they not only discussed Divinity and the Symbols of Holy Church, but even wrangled thereon, contradicting one another bitterly and stubbornly; and pelting each other with infamous accusations and malevolent censures all as if they had been Præses, Opponent and Respondent in the Schools at Oxon. At last my lord Bryan de Monte-Fixo of Estrighoil, and my lord Lawrence de Salso Marisco of Uske, fell together on my lord of Burgavenny, insinuating with indecent perspicuity that his ancestor Walter de Baladun had brought home counterfeit reliques from the Holy Land; whereupon there was a silence, for this was a dreadful thing to say, and my lord of Burgavenny's moustachios grew as stiff and upright as the tails of two dogs before they begin to fly at each other's throats. But in this silence voices came up from the lower table where the squires were sitting, and lo and behold these gentry were doing exactly the same thing as their lords, namely wrangling and disputing on the tenets of our Holy Church. The which was evidently pernicious and unbearable, so the three Barons vehemently commanded their esquires to hold their peace and go on drinking like honest gentlemen, and moreover they enforced this pious precept by example, till they were as drunk as it is possible for Lord Marcher to be; and finally were carried to bed by six of their Clerks in Chancery. And this is the very manner in which the Burgavennians celebrated the festival of St. Petronilla de Clochasterio. And for the space of a hundred years Sir Jenkin Thomas (but the monks called him Bramantip) struck the hours and played his hymns to the admiration of all men, and, as I have said, won great fame in Gwent for a doughty knight; and had monies and rents and charges devised to him, so that seventy years after Dom. Maria was buried (he became sub-prior of the Convent) Sir Jenkin glittered all over with gold and silver, and was as fresh and ruddy of countenance as on the day he was set in his place. And in course of time a new officer was created in the Convent, who was called Clochasteriarius and had a cell in the tower, his duty being to keep in order the curious mechanique of the clock, also to astrologise or star-gaze: but one or two of them that held this office are reported to have abused it, that is in place of prying into matters sidereal they pryed into matters Burgavennian, and what was worse talked of what they had seen, by which bad conduct much scandal arose. And certainly they that devised those curious optical glasses by the which we can see what kind of a place Venus is, never intended us to use them for spying into orchards or walled gardens to the great annoyance of respectable people. And one of these holy star-gazers, Brother Roger by name, when reproved by the Prior for this same misplaced curiosity, replied that a strong conceit had possessed him to the effect that Venus was as a matter of fact the earth and the earth Venus, and so he thought it his business to see what was being done on that planet: but the Prior would not listen to these refine-ments, and gave the post of Clochasteriarius to the oldest monk in the Convent, who merely sang with an open book before him for form's sake, since his sight had failed him in his eighty-ninth year.

But when Sir Jenkin (or Bramantip if you like it better) had rung out *Now that the star of day doth rise* about thirty-six thousand, five hun-dred times, the cursed mark of the Freemason began to take effect, though why the devil had waited all these years is more than I can say, unless it be true that Satan loves to do everything in a cross-grained roundabout kind of way, unlike everybody else. And the first folk that Bramantip worried were the monks, and the first monk to be used spitefully was his own special monk or keeper, the monk who loved him and oiled him, brushed him down, burnished his gold, saw that his bells were nicely hung, and now and again dabbed his face with paint so that Saxons and strangers from outlandish countries beyond seas might not say when they came to the great May Fair: "The Knight of Burgavenny groweth old and wrinklesome, he botched his hymn most woefully, his armour is dull and tarnished, and his arm stiff with age. In fine Sir Jenkin plainly dotes, and is altogether decayed." Yet it was upon the good monk who loved him and cared for him that the old rascal played a scurvy unhandsome trick in the manner following, as it was told by the monk aforesaid, called in religion Brother John. Who deponed before the Prior, the Sub-prior and the Canons that whilst he sat in his cell ravished in celestial speculations, he suddenly heard a great blow struck on his door as it had been a battle-axe smiting violently upon it, and immediately the door flew open, so that, turning round in great dismay, he beheld the statue, called of the monks Bramantip and of the townsfolk Sir Jenkin Thomas, standing in the doorway, with a wrathful and indignant countenance and his axe uplifted as if to smite him Brother John aforesaid, dead as he sat. Thereupon overcome by grievous terror and affright he made the sign of the cross and swooned away, and remained without knowing anything until he was revived by the Sub-prior, who found him lying at full length upon the floor. The which relation was confirmed by the Sub-prior so far as he was able to speak of his own knowledge; but he said also that going up into the tower to talk with Brother John, he met a woman (as he conceived) who seemed to be in great distress and misery, and fled past him on the stair, hiding her face with her robe. But whether this woman were only a vision, or an evil spirit, or whether she had aught to do with this affair, he, the Sub-prior aforesaid, was not able to determine. And on being interrogated by the Prior Dom. Hadrian de Mortuo Mari, whether any audible species were emitted by her footfalls, he answered Yes, but it was found on consideration that demons were not seldom audible; and, further interrogated, he confessed that she appeared to him to be a young woman, and if he might judge by certain curves and spherical indications a right comely wench, but refused to take any oath as touching this strange appearance in question. Thereupon the Prior bade all leave him, save only Brother John, whom he is said to have interrogated sharply and persistently both in Chapter and in camera; but nothing more was known of this matter, some saying one thing and some another; and this was Sir Jenkin's first act of malice, the rumour of which went not beyond the Convent walls.

And his second foul practice was done in this wise. You must know that the then Lord of Abergavenny had a daughter, Isabella by name, who at this time was in her sixteenth year, of a most beautiful and exquisite feature, a woman in all but age, and (so says the old Chronicle) evidently made for Love. And in the castle was a young gentleman who bore on a very noble coat, the baton sinister, the same having been from his youth in the service of the Baron, who had trained him in arms and in all that it becomes a gentleman to learn. Who being now seventeen years of age was, it is conceived, pricked and stung * * * * by the adorable and ravishing beauty of the Lady Isabella, in such wise that he was quite unable to contain himself, and finding the lady aforesaid to look not unkindly on him, became against all honour and religion her lover *par amours*. And so it fell out on a hot afternoon in May, they two being together in a retired arbour hard by the castle, were terribly and fearfully surprised by the Knight of the Tower, standing after an enraged and malevolent sort over against them, having his axe uplifted in the air. So the lover and his mistress became as dead for fear, thinking the Knight was come to kill them both their souls and their bodies, for their outrecuidance and impudency; and were found as they lay by the Baron, the young gentleman having his arms about the body of the Lady Isabella aforesaid. But what came of this adventure I will not tell you, for it were a sorrowful and piteous story: but this was the second mischief done of Sir Jenkin; and this could not be concealed but the rumour of it was rather blazed all over the town and Lordship.

And the third appearance of this villainous and malicious Knight was in the town of Abergavenny, and came about as follows. There lived hard by the Parish Church a fellow called Hên* Phil yr† Salutation; being a taverner and host of the Salutation Inn, the which was much resorted to by the townsfolk of the baser sort, who met there to exercise their wit on matters beyond them and to drink small ale and sour cider. This Philip was known to be a fellow of craft and marvellous skill in money-grubbing, being moreover suspected by many of unduly and unlawfully concocting his ale with water and strong drugs, so that his customers were sooner fuddled and made utterly foolish than at any tavern in the town. And how Sir Jenkin dealt with him was not clearly understood, but most said that while Phil was in his cellar, foully practising alchemy on his ale, he heard a clanging step come down the stairs, the door (which he had barred and bolted) was smit-

*Old.
†Of the.

ten open with a single blow, and by the light of his lanthorn he saw Sir Jenkin making toward him as if to cleave him asunder. Whereupon he fainted away, and fell with his head against the edge of a cask, and was struck silly for the remnant of his days, and these were few. But the Monk John de Ferula who lived at that time in Abergavenny, and left behind him a curious book of Annals, insinuates that besides practising baratry with his ale, Phil did also meddle with his wife's maid, and that she was in the cellar with him when Sir Jenkin burst open the door.

And from that time there was no more peace at all in Abergavenny, nor for gentle nor simple, clergy nor lay folk, but all in turn were continually pestered by this fearsome and horrible statue, who seemed to know all that was being done from the lardarium of the convent to the bower of the castle, and interfered as readily as can be imagined with the privity of the whole town, sparing none but molesting all. Hence all the pleasantry of the place decayed, the young squires and frolicsome ladies, the jolly old monks and the hearty men-at-arms, with all the fat inn-keepers, buxom widows, merry jokers and witty wags were tormented out of their lives by this fellow with his nasty battle-axe, who made no scruple of turning up at a confidential colloquy when he ought to have been standing in his tabernacle on the tower and hammering away at his bells; for it was no use to make little arrangements to transact business at Evensong nor Compline nor Matins neither, since Sir Jenkin always made a third at these small parties. But what puzzled the good people so terribly was that the hours were rung out just the same, as also the hymns without a note missing; and this indeed the Burgavennians could scarcely be expected to take quietly, and as a matter of fact not a few men who had hitherto borne a large paunch with great credit, grew thin and pale through endeavouring to untie this knot. Once the good folk tried making a ring round the tower to watch for Sir Jenkin's descent; but then one cannot stand with one's head in the air all day and all night, and to do so for a couple of hours makes a body's neck ache terribly. And then it began to rain and hail and snow all at once, so everybody went home, and the Knight was at his old work again before the day was done. Nor could any walls, doors, locks, bolts or bars, keep him out, however high or strong they were; and the Baron gained nothing by lowering the portcullis, raising the drawbridge, setting a double watch on the barbican, barti-

sans, and battlements; for Sir Jenkin knocked at his door and interrupted him and altogether muddled things in the castle. It is said there
were two special cauldrons of boiling lead kept simmering day and
night for a week above the main entrance and two cauldrons of boiling
oil maintained for the same period above the postern, but though the
machicolations were beautifully made and the baron's men handy fellows with the ladle they saw no one, and yet the Knight got into the
interior parts of the fortress somehow or other. And since the Baron
of Burgavenny, Lord Marcher of Wales, was not able to defend his
strong place against Sir Jenkin, the small gentry, and petty merchants
knew they might as well give up trying: as for the monks they had giv-
en in long ago and had taken to horse-hair, knotted scourges, dreadful
penances, all-night vigils, fasting on bread and water, and general morality, the which was a state of things unknown at the Priory since the
days of the pious founder. But everybody confessed that it was not
pleasant to live at Abergavenny as it formerly had been, and agreed
that if Sir Jenkin were not done away with the castle, convent and city
would all go to the devil together. And then began consultations and
whisperings and conferences to take place and messengers were running all day from the castle to the convent, and from the convent to
the town; and at last half a score of humble petitions were delivered to
the Prior, the first beautifully engrossed by the best clerk in the Chancery of Burgavenny, and sealed with a great lump of wax as big as a
French pear, with boars' heads and lions, and flower-de-luces on it,
and the last rather blotted and scurvily written with no seal at all, from
the poorest people in the place (for though a man be poor he doesn't
like his little pleasures to be interfered with). But all these petitions
were very humble and reverent, and all craved the same boon, namely
that the false Knight, Sir Jenkin Thomas de Clochasterio, should be
seized and haled before the Ecclesiastical Court, for that he harboured
within him a certain foul, damnable, pestilent, and infernal spirit or
demon, the name of the demon aforesaid being unknown, and this to
the great loss and hurt of the petitioners, who prayed that without
needless delay or adjournment the Knight aforesaid should be brought
to account for his horrid crimes and notorious iniquities. Which petitions were received by the Prior in full chapter after High Mass had
been sung on the Festival of St. Benedict, the said Prior being pleased

to use great courtesy toward the petitioners, promising to consider their desires, and finally sending them away with his benediction. And after this you may conceive what a stir and work there was amongst the ecclesiastics, what letters passed between the Prior and the Bishop of Llandaff, the Abbot of Tintern, the Abbot of Caerleon, the Abbot of Grace-Dieu, and the Priors of Uske, and Estrighoil and Llanthony; what questions were put to the Canonists and grave Doctors of the Church; for Dom. Hadrian de Mortuo Mari had sworn a great oath to do the business thoroughly and to leave no stone unturned. At last when St. Petronilla de Clochasterio her feast day came round every thing had been settled, matters were in trim, and if Sir Jenkin had had an ounce of brains under his helmet he would have got down from his habitacle on the tower for good and all, and gone in search of Dom. Maria or the Freemason or the Devil or whomsoever was his responsible author. But then you see he had nothing inside his head or his belly either but brass wheels and cogs, and it seems that though these contrivances were sufficient to plague a lot of harmless quiet people, they were not clever enough to let Sir Jenkin know that he was in a nasty scrape and stood a decent chance of being burned. But on St. Petronilla's vigil, the convent and the castle and the city were as full as they could hold of Churchmen, Canonists, Casuists, Surrogates, Lawyers, Chancellors, Summoners, Apparitors, and Clerks, together with a great army of hangers-on and camp followers, who all ate and drank and walked and talked from one end of the town to the other; but kept themselves very quiet for all that, since they were terribly afraid that the Knight knew their business and would burst upon them and make holes in their skulls with that axe of his to let out the Canon Law and Divinity and Clergy and so render any processes invalid. Certainly Sir Jenkin must have been somewhat thick-headed, for he could not help seeing a great big stake driven into the ground by the west door of the Priory Church as one might say right under his nose, and likewise fellows coming in from the country bringing huge loads of dry sticks on their backs, and on mules, and in wagons, and any man-of-letters could have told him that these preparations looked very bad indeed. But on the morrow when the Abbot of Tintern had sung Pontifical High Mass, the Abbot of Caerleon being deacon and the Abbot of Grace-Dieu Sub-deacon, the Court was formed in the Chapter House, and the sub-prior of Abergavenny read a great many letters from the Churchmen who hold the chief authority in these merry affairs, by which the Court was fully constituted and invested with plenary power to deal with this detestable and monstrous case. Then Sir Jenkin Thomas was summoned to appear in the Chapter House by a grim-looking personage in a yellow skin and square cap, and this preconisation was so formal and lengthy an affair that before square-cap had called the luckless Knight's name for the ninth time, the workmen had hauled him down, and dragged him to the door, whereat his body was presently attached by the Sergeant, and he was seated in a chair straight in front of my lord Abbot of Tintern who was the chief judge. Then came the pleadings, which I would like to rehearse to you for they are pleasant reading and admirably expressed, but I have them not, and my memory will not suffice for the recollection of all the sworn statements, deeds, depositions, warrants, petitions, bills of accusation, incriminating documents, evidences by word of mouth; together with precedents, recitations, Decretals, Extravagants, Authorities, Scriptures, Rescripts, and extracts put in by the gentry in square caps: all being set down in that delicious Latin dialect that seems made for cases of this kind. But I believe that no less than a hundred witnesses were cited before my Lord Abbot and examined in his presence, and the clerks (there was a long row of them) wrote hard all the time and enjoyed it, for it was not often they had a chance of covering their yellow skins (of parchment I mean) with such curious histories, or of moistening their yellow lips to such good purpose as they still wrote on and on. And at Evensong time the great silver lamp that hung in the middle of the Chapter House was lighted and sconces also all round the walls, and the trial still proceeded, while outside the Priory was a great multitude of people of all conditions and from all the coasts of Gwent waiting to hear sentence given. And all the while Sir Jenkin never moved, and would not answer a single question; but perhaps he knew it would be no good, and so held his tongue to save trouble. But if he held his tongue other people did not, for they felt that such a chance as this was too good to be lost, since it might never occur again and all sorts of interruptions to the real business took place, some of which were quite indecent. I believe that close upon Midnight a young Canonist put in an objection to the effect that a device of metal work, not having any soul nor principle of life, was incapable of being judged by the Ecclesiastical Law; whereupon there was first of all a terrible wrangle about the nature of the soul which gave the young Canonist his opportunity to read out Aristotle, Averroes, St. Denys the Areopagite, Erigena, St. Thomas d'Aquinas, Duns Scotus, Peter Lombard, &c., &c., till he had to be stopped by force, for he never would have stopped of his own accord. But my Lord Abbot made short work with this objection, proving syllogistically and illatively that nothing in the whole world was outside the Laws Ecclesiastical which go over everything like a blanket, and keep the earth warm. Indeed this remark of the young Canonist's was a very foolish one, and shewed that he was fresh to his work. Finally, some time on the next morning, the judges held a short conference apart, and then they proceeded to the judgment which was delivered on these four Articles of the Bill of Accusation; namely:—

I°.　That the accursed Knight Sir Jenkin Thomas of the Tower was able to do what no man could do; much less a figure of metal, insomuch as he was proved to have often climbed over high walls, and burst open strong doors barred with iron.

II°.　That the accursed Knight aforesaid always caused them that beheld him to swoon away.

III°.　That the accursed Knight aforesaid had often intermeddled in the private affairs of religious men.

IV°.　That the accursed Knight aforesaid was able to be in two places at the same time; the which was a pernicious, hurtful and heretical practice, of itself very worthy of the stake.

Now these four counts stood in the Bill as IX, XXXI, L, and LXXXIX respectively; there being in all a hundred charges against Sir Jenkin, but some of these were rather frivolous, so my Lord Abbot of Tintern, my Lord Abbot of Caerleon, my Lord Abbot of Grace-Dieu, and the Priors of Burgavenny, Uske, and Estrighoil directed the Clerk to strike out ninety-six counts, and then proceeded to give judgment upon the remaining four; and this reformation of the Articles was allowed by the lawyers to be just and according to precedent. Then my Lord Abbot of Tintern stood up and everyone saw what a splendid man he was, tall and white-haired, with a glitter in the corner of his eyes. And he adjudged Sir Jenkin to be guilty of all these four charges, by the plain evidence of many persons freely given before the Court and by many depositions of people of every sort and condition, but notably by the deposition of the Baron of Burgavenny Lord Marcher of Wales, who had put himself and his clerk to much pains that the several circumstances might be made manifest to the Court, as they had fallen out. On the second count my lord Abbot spoke to the effect that this was evident art magic and diabolic contrivance, for the persons who had swooned, swooned not from fear of death (though perchance they themselves might think so) but rather from a trembling and awful dread stirred up in the breast of man when brought near to a demon. On the third count my Lord Abbot said that these acts of intermeddling with religious persons and holy men of the Order of St. Benedict were further marks of Satan's handiwork, since none but a devil or one possessed of a devil would pester and annoy men sanctified and set apart for the service of God. And on the fourth account my Lord Abbot said that to be in two places at the same time was a noisome, hideous, and unutterable offence (scelus tetrum, horribile, et infandum) well worthy, as the accuser had said, of fire and fagot. And Sir Jenkin being pronounced guilty of all these crimes was asked by the Clerk if he could shew cause why sentence of combustion should not be pronounced against him, but gave no answer and sat quite still. Then the Abbot arose again and signed himself with the sign of our Holy Faith and condemned the Knight of the tower to be burned with fire, and presently, and in a place provided for that end hard by the quire of the Convent. Then Sir Jenkin was dragged out, and the people shouted with such a shout that for a week after they could not so much as whisper, so glad were they to see this bad Knight doomed to die, and he was chained to the stake, and an incredible pile of wood lighted all around him and below him, and in this sort he was burned with fire and the lump of metal that was found cast into a hole in the earth and covered up out of sight. And it is related that the monks of Llanthony heard the great shouting of the people when Sir Jenkin was brought forth, and looked toward Abergavenny and lo! the sky grew red as blood with the flame of the fire; and they certainly thought that the Welsh had stormed the Castle, were burning the town and slaugh-

tering the people. And after this Abergavenny returned to its old ways
of pleasantness and began to laugh again, and drink and make love
without fear of Sir Jenkin or his horrid battle-axe, and indeed began to
laugh at him in his turn, though nobody who had seen him at close-
quarters did this. And the tower being stripped of its roof fell by degrees into decay, and in the course of a hundred years there was not
one stone of it to be seen on its original position, but a great many
stones of it might be seen in Abergavenny and the country round
about, where they were doing duty in walls and houses, and indeed
they were very special achiler stones, too good to pave the roads with.
As to the Freemason's carven work of dragons and other beasts
whereon he had set his damnable mark, by the earnest counsel of the
Prior of Estrighoil it was smitten into powder and cast into the air; for
this Prior had been in France and Spain and knew all the crafty tricks
of the Prince of Darkness, who must be entirely brought low, or he
will jump up again as frisky as ever he was before. And here I would
end my tale were it not that the monk John de Ferula in his exact annals hath set down a report concerning these curious circumstances
which I must tell you of, for I will imitate that good monk and leave
nothing out. And this report was to the effect that the Prior, the Baron
and the townsfolk, had one and all been most thoroughly and deli-
ciously duped and deceived in this matter; for the whole affair was a
piece of trickery contrived by a company of merry wags of the place,
the sole end and aim of whose lives was to serve up bamboozlements,
trumperies, balderdashes, impostures and beguilements to their fellow
men, and their greatest delight to watch them digesting these gallimaw-
fries and moreover concocting sauces of their own to make the dish
yet more pleasant. And John de Ferula declares that these jokers of
Burgavenny were bound together into a Mystery or Corporate Body,
with pass-words and secret signs, and that some of them were young
esquires in the Baron's household, that some were monks, and some
the sons of the gentry in the town, so that they were verily and indeed
able to be in a good many places at one and the same time, and had a
perfect intelligence of all the pleasant treaties, Cyprian covenants, and
amorous pacifications that were afoot. Thus with a suit of armour and
a mask their designs were accomplished with great ease, and to ward
off suspicion one of the company would now and again pretend the

Knight had visited him; and some were for prolonging the trickery after Sir Jenkin had been burned, but 'twas judged wise to stop there for
fear lest some one should pluck up a heart and tackle the demon with
the carnal arm. And John de Ferula (some called him plain John Rodd)
says that this waggish invention was engendered in the brain of one Sir
Peter de Fontibus who was also of the Society called the Cwrw Dda
(qui erat quoque Sodus Societatis Bonæ Cervisiæ q. v. Cwrw Dda). But
the exact annalist says openly that all this was mere rumour, not talked
of or noised about till long after Sir Jenkin was burnt, and believed by
very few and not at all by himself for, says he, I know that the Devil is
very strong in Burgavenny, and to his malice there are no bounds. And
the only circumstance that at all confirms this story is that Sir Peter de
Fontibus aforesaid, who was a gentleman of consideration in the town,
and was present at the famous trial of Sir Jenkin, was heard all the
while to gurgle and make a clicking noise to himself, when the more
curious circumstances were recited, but he was known to be tormented
by defluctions of rheum to the teeth which caused him great anguish,
and as at that time to grow purple in the face and twist his body to and
fro. But I believe that it is true that this gentleman was of our Sokage:
what say you Master Bamfylde, is it not so?

"Sir Peter de Fontibus," answered the Rubrican, "was without
doubt of our Sokage, and in point of fact was called in Cervisage Ratabus the Powt, being the same that instituted the Charter of 'Thirsty
Soil', as Dick Leonard will tell you. But if he did verily contrive the
joyous trumpery, the which you have so choicely narrated to us, he left
no record thereof, at the least none that I have seen; nor is it in the
Red Book of Rabanus. But whom do you will should come after you in
devising; for it is your part to choose a tale-teller?" "The next deviser,"
quoth I, "shall be Master Cook, for it wants but twenty minutes to
noon, and there would be no time to tell another tale. But if this affair
of the clock were indeed a piece of cozenage, as I believe it was, it is
surely as choice a deceit as ever sprang from the fertile soil of old Siluria." Then Dick Leonard said: "What takes me most is the Court, with
all the Abbots, Priors, and Decretalists, the row of parchment scrapers,
and the officers of the ecclesiastical law, sitting all through the night
under the silver lamp, digesting this fantastic lump of trickery and
sending it down with the strong wine of their own imaginations."

"Now let's dine," said I, "and though you will not have a feast like the banquet of the monks that Spigot Clerk hath so wittily delineated for us; yet my cook is a good disguiser of raw stuff, and a man of some invention, and for your drink I have a very sufficient Rhenish wine, in the which we will give a health to the waggish memory of Ratabus, who was called the Powt."

THE LORD MALTWORM'S FIRST TALE

When we had sufficiently nourished our internal juices by dining I let my three worshipful jokers know that there was a spacious shadow ready for them on the lawn, where I had caused chairs to be set as easy as I had, for a man who has made a good dinner needs gentle treatment and a little luxury of comfort, so that he may meditate on nothing, and stroke himself down without let or hindrance. Some people cannot sit still and do nothing even after dinner, they must still be fretting and fuming, still reforming, still setting matters right. O miserable race of men; tell me how comes it that there is any wrong or crookedness upon the earth, for since your great Originall began to mend our fortunes, you, his apes, have never ceased to botch, to rip, to tear, to drive in nails and pull them out, to loosen the tight and to tighten the loose, and all the while to go solemnly to work, to use long words and to drink cold water. But we four Silurians were not of this Reforming and Beatifying company, and were able to sit very still in the shade, watching the sunlight play upon the trees, and the filmy clouds floating across the sky, and listening to the ripple of the brook as it sped over the stones toward Caerleon. Phil Ambrose the Spigot Clerk, who had in the morning told the rare tale of Sir Jenkin, was especially resigned and calm, and leant back in his elbow chair, smoking a mighty long clay pipe, seeming to my eyes a very mellow personage and a dignified also, if you take away his shape, for he was a little barrel of a man. And after he had sat thus somewhile he began to be inquisitive and to ask questions about old sayings and proverbs and those quaint words used by our forefathers, which we now hold for condemned or at least suspect. But I believe that if we persevere in this sort much longer a man will be ashamed to speak of his belly or his guts, and be shewn the door if he name these members in a polite assembly. However that may be, nothing passed between us worthy of note, for it is not good for a man to put out his mind in the afternoon, the which has been provided for us to dream in, and talk lightly, and idly to pursue small love-affairs; for I deny not that this petty exertion is to be allowed after four o'clock; indeed if properly discharged it may give a man a gust for his supper. But I forbid all kissing, since this amusement makes one warm, and is hard to leave off, besides.

But after we had supped and the bottle began to go round, the Rubrican, Tom Bamfylde, began one of those dissertations he was addicted to relating to the old privileges and customs of the Court of Cervisage; I think he was trying to clear up our understandings on one of the knotty points in our *Rituale*, namely the circumstance of a Death's Head being placed before the High Tosspot and delineated on one of the quarters of his seal; the which hath perplexed many of us, for in our teaching we utterly abhor all doleful, hypochondriac imaginations. And the Rubrican, being somewhat drunk, was fumbling desperately at this entanglement, quoting the old Annals of the Court, and moralising our Legends and Songs till he seemed to himself to have found out a high method and signification in this terrible symbol; "'tis the very pith and most dogmatical article of our knowledge," said he. "For you must consider that the whole world and all our life is a most rare and quintessential jest or merry piece, so subtile indeed is the peal of joyous laughter that sounds through it that the gross ears perceive it not and imagine that the noises they hear are a continual sobbing, a bitter ceaseless wailing, a crying and lamentable moan for mercy, and sighs and weeping without end. But these noises we Silurists know well to be mere fictions, like the sounds heard by deaf people of drums and bells; and are all of us agreed that to see the best play one need only live. So the world being shewn to be an exceeding merry world, and man being of it the microcosm (as it is well termed by the Brethren of the R. C.), it would follow that the image of a man might stand for the effigies and symbol of the Silurian Knowledge and joyous philosophy. But the great sages who founded the Session Cwrw Dda, and in their Round Table have mystically taught us whence all things come and whither all things go, have refined upon this conceit, and truly considering that a man standing for the world, his head may best represent man (for the head is in fact that admirable aumbry holding inventions, wit, methods, conceits, fantasies; a storehouse of delights) have chosen a Deathshead as an image of the Cwrw Dda, and I believe it to be both suitable (as I have shewn) and subtle. For many by this symbol are puzzled, and scratch their heads, and wander into wrong tracks; and all this for our enjoyment; and in short I would have you believe that by it is meant 'The Merriment of the Whole World'". This farrago was received in silence, Dick Leonard only saying mildly, "Master Perrot's wine is very strong; but I believe there is some truth in what the Rubrican says, for though drunk he is a learned man and accustomed to peer into the essence of things. And now I think of it a conceit has come into my brain touching the morrow, the which I believe will please you all; let us, I say, go to Uske." "Why should we especially go to-morrow?" "Because 'tis to-morrow that the burgesses proceed to the solemn election of a worshipful Portreeve, whom they choose with many admirable rites and significant ceremonies; and all the town is full of gentry, rogues, Egyptians, wits, saltimbancos, zanies; clerks and birds of our feather." "We will certainly go then," said I, "if Phil Ambrose and Tom Bamfylde be well-disposed unto this journey." "We are so," quoth the Spigot Clerk, "for we are not accustomed to miss these solemnities, insomuch as they furnish us with gay adventures, choice comedies, and a fine stock of tales and pleasant sayings for the winter nights. For a man should be ever heedful of that hutch or cupboard of his, the brain; to keep the shelves well-stocked with good fare, duly spiced and seasoned, thus he is ever able to draw out a dainty dish and to set it before his friend." "Let us go, let us go," assented Tom Bamfylde, "I warrant we shall return the wiser, and carry back with us more than we brought." "Of that I am not altogether certain," said Nick Leonard, "sometimes it happens so, and sometimes contrariwise, but it is of no great consequence. And now, my merry jokers, what says the wise Hebdomadarius of the Eighth Week" (he was speaking of the "Joyous Inventions" of the monk Galliard) *"Be not dull at sunset when the rain falls and the night comes on, but search for sweet memories through the byways of your brains, be droll and witty, and the devil take him that keeps a sour countenance.'* Wherefore let some one tell a tale and strive to match the relation we heard in the forenoon." "You have spoken," said Phil Ambrose, "and you shall devise for us, for it is my part to choose a successor." "So be it then," quoth Nick Leonard, "but first let me sit in the Bardic Chair, that my cervical substance may be fertilised, and bring forth ripe fruit. And do you, Master Rubrican, intone us the Herald's Proclamation, or some chant fit for our occasion, if your plain song be not altogether drowned in Rhenish wine." Then the Rubrican sang as follows: *If any speak while these things are being set forth, may he quaff water for the remainder of his days; but when all is done, laugh and drink unto the nail.*

HOW A MAN OF CAERLEON FOUND A GREAT TREASURE

My tale shall be of Caerleon-on-Uske; and since the Spigot Clerk devised his history of Abergavenny wherein our Court now holds session, it will not be amiss if I speak somewhat of Caerleon, whereat the tosspots of Gwent were first banded together by our glorious King Arthur, of right worthy memory. But I will not tell you any stories of roofs shining like gold, or of the tower that overtopped Christchurch Hill and looked on to the Severn Sea, or of chargeable palaces, standing splendidly in the little town, since all these things are underground like the Barons of Burgavenny and have become somewhat wearisome. But what I have to tell happened about two hundred years agone, when Caerleon was little different from what it is now, or from what it will be two hundred years hence, if the curtain do not fall on our merry Comedy, ere that time be accomplished. Now you have it well set in your heads that as there are two Sicilies, so there are two Caerleons, one on this side the bridge, and one on the other; and there being two Caerleons I must tell you that he, concerning whom this history is related, dwelt in Caerleon-over-Bridge, and in a little hut by the river's bank, not far from the bridge itself. As for his name it was Griffith, and he was called Griffith the Delver, and sometimes Twrch Ddær which is in the letter Earth-Hog and in the spirit Mole; hence we see how poetical and florid is the language of the Welsh. This Griffith was in fact one of those that are eternally digging, who dig early and late and leave no rest for our old Mother Earth, who must surely be more patient than most ladies, since they heartily dislike being scratched. It is true that a girl does not object to be tickled, if you do it nicely, and choose the right places; but there can be no resemblance between a lover's finger-tips "desipientes in loco" and the rough blows of spade, mattock, and pick-axe striking here, there, and everywhere, turning everything upside down. And of all diggers and delvers Griffith was the most sempiternal, for he dug deep, turned the clods well over, and never left off. And yet he was not a common spade-man, and never thought of planting anything in the bares he made, and indeed his operations were in no way agricultural; since in place of putting seeds into the ground, his aim was to draw something out of it. He was in fine a treasure monger, having been bitten with this madness when a boy, and when he was a good many years better than three-score, was not yet cured. His malady was caused by his overhearing two monks talking together of the enormous treasure that the old Romans and the British Kings had concealed; and as these two ecclesiastics were very great liars and engaged at that time in compiling a Chronicle, you may be sure that they heaped up gold, silver, and jewels to an incredible and monstrous degree. One was describing with minute exactitude the twelve chests of pure silver, each of two feet in length, two feet in breadth, and two feet in depth, each sealed with King Arthur's seal, the Red Dragon, and buried in the midst of St. Julian's wood, under a great stone. "And the first," said the holy man, "hath in it twelve diamonds, each several diamond being cut in twelve facets and each standing for a Knight of the Round Table. And the twelfth of the price of a single stone would suffice to build a Cathedral Church, more chargeable than any church in Christendom, and plentifully to endow it with lands for the Dean, Canons, Vicars, Prebends, songmen, and quiristers, so that it should be better served than the quire of Canterbury." "And the second," broke in the other monk, "hath in it twelve Rubies, each ruby the size of a man's head, and each standing for a saint of Britain." "And the third," quoth the first monk, "hath in it twelve opals, shining with every colour in the universe, most glorious to see, and each personates a beautiful lady of King Arthur's Court." In this fashion they ran through the twelve chests as if it had been a grocer and his man, ticking off casks of sugar; and never a smile on the faces of them. Next they made a bill of ingots of gold, to the number of one hundred and twenty five, sunken in the Uske, in a straight line from Merthollye Chapel, each ingot being stamped with the name of a Roman Emperor, but they could not quite agree together as to which of the Emperors had owned this great treasure. So they proceeded to emerald vases filled to the brim and over-running with gold pieces, to cups and chalices of pure gold and of a monstrous size, with pattens, flagons, brooches, chains (one was of a thousand links, and did use to be hung across the lists of turney), crosses, mitres, rings, candelabra, till the lad's head fairly went round to hear of all this wealth, and much of it within a few yards of him. For the two Cistercians left nothing conjectural, but laid down precisely where each hoard was to be sought for, and seemed likely to continue the list to infinity. But just as one of them was speaking of the great bell twelve feet high, and fashioned of pure gold that hung in the Castle Mound, the bells of his Abbey rung out and called them both away to Evensong. But Master Griffith stood still where he was, being quite unable to move, since it never came into his head that the two monks were mere historians, who were getting their hands in for the writing-room. But hearing them note every particular so exactly and precisely, even to the depth in feet and inches below the surface, he conceived them to be speaking the truth, as some people have done since his time, and with less excuse, for Griffith was thought to have always been a little simple. And from the time when he heard these ecclesiastical narrations the poor lad became unable to sleep well at night, for the light of the jewells shone before his eyes and filled the nasty dirty room with a splendid and wonderful glow, blood-red, and golden, and sapphire, and twelve blinding rays from the twelve diamonds shot through all the other hues, and dimmed his eyes with glory. Then the walls changed to gold and silver, the door was a slice of a single emerald, and his head got muddled, and he began to fancy all sorts of things still more extraordinary. As for eating and drinking it became tedious to him, for a wooden platter and piggin were not nearly so fine as the pattens and chalices he had heard tell of, and so he did not trouble himself to devour their contents, the which was somewhat foolish, it must be confessed. And when he was sauntering about in the meadows he did nothing but twist his neck and try to stare the sun out of countenance; for he had heard one monk telling the other of a marvellous dish, "whereof the compass was one twelfth of the compass of the Round Table, of a metal that was neither gold nor silver, but more excellent than either, and having in its centre the Name Iao, written in the character of the magicians. Which dish was made by no artificer nor mortal worker in metal, but proceeded from a supernatural marriage or conjunction of the sun and moon, and was

drawn down to earth by Merlin, and now lies five feet three inches below the midst of the Round Table." Of this extraordinary nonsense
much was lost on Griffith, but he nevertheless made it his business to
keep a sharp look out on the heavenly bodies, in order to catch them
at their amorous play, the nature of which he understood very imper-
fectly and was desirous of learning. But this amusement brought him
nothing better than a wry neck, and he was forced to conclude that
love-affairs up above were transacted much as they are down here, that
is in strict privacy. And he was no sooner able to get a spade than he
began to dig and make holes wherever he thought there was treasure;
for though Griffith's wits were not perhaps of the brightest, yet he
perfectly remembered every circumstance he had heard, and indeed the
whole story seemed written in fiery letters on the air. So he sought
now in one place and now in another for all these fine things, and
folks soon became aware of his folly, the which was deemed very entertaining, and a piece of a blessing in dull times when there was very
little to laugh at. But when the two historians heard of the Delver, they
understood the matter thoroughly, and were vexed at it, for they were
pious men, desirous of amusing people and not of driving them mad.
So they went together to Griffith and endeavoured to open his understanding and to shew him the true state of the case; but to no avail, for
he, an unlettered man, had no notion of History, and thought the two
monks were trying to make a fool of him that they might keep all the
treasure for themselves. Perceiving the poor man's madness the historians did the best they were able, and interceded with the Abbot so
that the Delver was fed at the Almonry every day for the rest of his
life, the which was, as I said at the beginning of my tale, spent in turning earth upside down, wandering through St. Julian's wood, prodding
walls, poking under the roots of trees, and the like investigations. Before long the Caerleon people had got used to Griffith, and no longer
took the trouble to laugh at him; indeed a gentleman who had a large
garden tried to profit by his little infirmity, and caused it to be con-
veyed to the Mole that this garden aforesaid certainly contained gold
and silver in abundance to be had for the digging. By which device he
hoped to have his soil turned over very cheaply, but the fish, as the
saying goes, would not bite; Griffith having certain fixed notions of his
own capable of no amendment or alteration. So for forty years and

more he persisted in this folly, for the twelve rays of the twelve diamonds still blinded him, and the great golden bell within the Castle
Mound rung all through the night in a deep mellow voice, and to him
the painted images in the windows of the Quire were rubies and sapphires beyond all price. And in these fantastic imaginations he would
doubtless have died peacefully enough, had it not been for the coming
of a stranger to Caerleon, a merry young gentleman, who was fond of
folly and always encouraged it to the best of his ability, who seeing
Griffith mooning about the place and driving his spade into the earth,
enquired as to the reason of these proceedings, and was observed
when his understanding had been enlightened, to grow suddenly grave
and thoughtful, as he was accustomed when a joke came into his head.
And henceforth the wag watched the Delver at his work, and noted
how he often came back to one place, namely the bottom of the
Round Table; for the great dish neither gold nor silver but better than
either, had taken Griffith's fancy, perhaps because it was a little out of
the common. But if I had been in his place I believe I should have let
this dish lie, since the goldsmiths would be very likely to say unkind
things about it, as stupid people always do of matters beyond their
comprehension. But the young gentleman seeing how Griffith was everlastingly at the bottom of the hollow took his measures, and then sat
down to see what would come of them. And of a dark, windy night,
with sudden gusts of rain blowing up from Severn Sea; as Griffith the
Delver sat in his horrible little den by the riverside his thoughts ran as
usual on the buried treasure of Caerleon; and the notion, species and
imagination of the wonderful dish pricked him more violently than it
had ever done, so that he was forced to take his spade, light his lantern, and sally forth without delay. And as he went over the bridge, the
wind gave a howl, and the rain dashed in his face, and he felt the whole
scaffold shake and quiver beneath him, as if it desired to sail down the
river into the open sea. In fine it was precisely the sort of night to have
put out an ordinary lantern in what is sometimes called a brace of
shakes, but Griffith's lantern had been made by himself on scientific
principles and would have hung from the mast of a ship off Cape
Thundertops, without so much as a wink or half a twinkle. It was a
glorious lantern, a credit to the town, and had been out in all weathers
and at all times of the day and night in search of ideas, conceits, fic-

tions, and all the flowery inventions of the monastic chroniclers. With this treasure of a lantern and the sempiternal light which the diamonds flashed into the Delver's brain, he made his way in a few minutes to the Round Table and was soon digging away as if he were twenty and going to work for the first time, instead of being as he was sixty and more, and a very old hand at this foolish business. And when he had dug to the depth of about three feet his spade struck somewhat that was neither earth nor stone and made a clanging noise, the which was the sweetest sound the Delver had heard since the monks talked together of the twelve chests of pure silver. So he propped the lantern on a lump of earth and stooped down, and felt warily with his hands in the place the noise came from; and before long drew out a quaintly shapen vase, of a greenish colour and mighty heavy in the hands. Just then the lantern overbalanced and fell into the hole, but of course that did not make it go out or burn its own sides, like lanterns do nowadays; so Griffith set it back in its place more securely, and sat down and dipped his hand into the green vase. It was very nearly full to the brim with coins; they slipped between his fingers and slid along his palm, and went chink, chink, chink either against other, and against the vase, and then the golden bell inside the mound began to toll and the glorious ruby and sapphire lights glowed out and filled all the Round Table with their flames. And Griffith saw the Twelve Knights sitting each in his place guarding the mystic rose, and each Knight had on his forehead a diamond cut in twelve facets, from which the rays shot forth with incredible brightness: and above all the Knights the great King Arthur, into whose eyes it was impossible to look, for they were of a very terrible beauty. Then these things faded and a mist closed about the Delver, who sat in the place he had made for himself, clutching the vase with one hand, the lantern with another, and having the spade between his legs. And this mist was pearly white, but yet it was also of manifold colours, that went and came and glowed and faded and seemed full of lovely faces and figures that might have attracted the poor man if he had not been getting rather astonished at these strange sights. In a desperate sort of way he drove his hand again into the vase and felt the coins, and all these glamours immediately vanished; but the lantern still burnt on, and Griffith thought that he would like to have a look at his treasure trove. And to have this pleasure he accordingly turned the vase upside down and a great stream of coins poured out; at the sight of which Griffith's heart stood still and he swooned quite away. For you see they were only copper coins of modern date which the wag had buried a few days before; but the Delver was terribly disappointed that they were not gold. You and I and everybody else would be glad enough to find a crown's worth in pence and halfpence; one can buy a good deal with five shillings, but the Delver had hoped for rather more than he got, and his animal spirits and humours for the next ten minutes had a bad time of it. And I daresay you would guess that when he regained his senses there were very few left to him, you would say, in short, that though he was crazy before, now he was a raving madman. But the real facts were quite opposite; for instead of losing his wits altogether he got back those he had lost forty years before, and sat down and began to ponder matters reasonably, and consider what was best to be done. And now all sorts of notions came into his head, and notions to some purpose, for among the rest in some wonderful way the Delver found out who had put this trick upon him, and determined to cry quits before another nightfall. So without delay he emptied the coppers into a bag he had about him, threw the vase back into the hole and heaped the earth over it, and then with his bag, lantern, and spade he set off at a sharp walk for the house of him who had devised this piece of trickery. And having reached his doorway, Griffith fell once more to his old trade, I mean of digging, and long before the light dawned he had constructed a spacious and luxurious pit, fairly deep, with a puddle at the bottom of it, and also a few sharp jagged stones by way of relish. And why or wherefore old Twrch Ddær took all this trouble, is more than I can tell you; but it certainly seemed rather likely that any one going in or coming out of the house, without due warning, would fall into this pit aforesaid, and so indeed it happened. For the gay young joker came home with a companion early in the morning, their heads being in a very muddled state and their notions in great confusion, and their throats spouting out scraps of drinking songs. *Cor imbutum nectare volat ad superna*, hiccoughs one; *Nasonem post calices faci le praeibo* stutters the other; and then they began to quote all the most wanton pieces of Ovidius Naso they could remember, which were not very many, seeing they were too drunk. However they made shift to help one another through that naughty and amorous canticle *'Twas very hot, when at noon-day;* and then they began to discuss the beauties of certain ladies of their acquaintance, so you may judge what sort of a night they had been spending in the house where the lights never went out, for the porter was too deaf to hear the curfew, and the ladies and their friends were dancing, laughing, singing, and fiddling in such wise that they heard no noises save those of their own making. And being in this state of mind you will not wonder that in the dim twilight of dawn the two companions saw nothing of the Delver's preparations for their comfort, but went merrily on, and in the natural course of things fell one on top of the other into the pit, where they sustained a good many bruises against the sharp stones, and (it is said) quite dried up the pool of water at the bottom, being young gentlemen of a mighty warm complexion. Here they lay very quietly, not puzzling their heads about anything, but taking it easily and keeping still, until a servant opened the door an hour or two later, and saw his master and his friend wait-ing to be let in after the fashion I have described. In the meantime Griffith the Mole had gone into exile somewhere on the other side of Wentwood Chase, since he suspected that this item might be set down to his account, and the bill presented in a manner not at all to his taste. However a few weeks after the wag left Caerleon, not liking the Welsh way of joking, and it is said that he died shortly afterwards of a bad sore throat, a complaint which was very common in those glorious old days, in fine he lost his head, and that is a loss fatal to all of us unless we happen to be saints and then, you know, one can pick up one's head and go up the hill. As for Griffith the Delver he returned to his hovel in Caerleon-over-Bridge, and though he missed at first the flam-ing light of the jewells and the tolling of the golden bell, yet he settled down and passed the remnant of his days in great comfort. But he did no more digging for he had found a much better employment than scratching and tormenting Mother Earth. What was that? Why to do nothing, of which he soon learnt the art, for he was a good Silurian at bottom and most likely never would have done anything all his life, if he had not been so unfortunate as to hear how History is written. So he sat in the sun in summer and by the fire in winter, and the good old monks took care of him and gave him plenty to eat and drink while he was alive, and a handsome funeral with plenty of tapers after that he had finished with this world; the which event happened when he was aged ninety-five and getting rather tired. For this is what we must all come to, even if we pass our days in the beautiful sunlight and by the warm hearth, doing nothing; since even of this a man gets tired in time. And then he looks out for a nice quiet corner in the churchyard and curls himself round and goes to sleep, and doesn't answer when they come to call him in the morning. Then it's no good to hammer at the door and bellow "Hi! get up, it's half-past twelve. Are you going to sleep all day?" since the old Silurian doesn't hear anything and lies very still. But of this story there are two morals: and the first is Don't believe everything the historians tell you; and the second Keep sober till the joke be over: and I think these are good morals, especially the last.

Thus Nick Leonard brought his tale of Caerleon to a close; and we all praised him for it, though we had found it in parts a little tedious; but yet on the whole it is a pleasant, moral story. The Rubrican however said: "I find fault with this tale and also the tale of Sir Jenkin, and my fault is that in the both of them the wrong circumstance hath been chosen, and the less made the greater. For consider, Phil, what a sweet mournful tale of love you could have devised of the Noble Bastard and the Lady Isabella; and you Nick I believe could have told us some adventure of the waggish gentleman far more pleasant than the folly of the old Mole, who was, I am convinced, an ass." "It always seems thus," answered Phil Ambrose, "to those who hear the stories; but if you will take thought you will see plainly that piteous love *par amours* is a tale that has been told many times; aye, verily since the world was in her orchard days and apples meant more than they do now, this story has been still weaving; and so soon as ever the scissors cut one smock in twain another is on the loom." But Nick Leonard said: "Since Tom doth take on him the part of Cato, he shall tell the next story and sit in the Bard's seat; and there let him shew his right to draw the thumbnail under our fine phrases and moralities, or else for ever hold his peace." "It is decreed," said I, "squat thee down Master Rubrican; and the Spigot Clerk shall preconise silence after our laudable custom and use." Then Phil Ambrose poured out a glass of wine, sent it down fairly, and sang in a severe and ancient mode—*O let not any voice be heard, my lords of Gwent: for by these things the sweet method of laughter is shewn to you, and how the ale surges upon the Brim of the whole world.*

WHAT FELL OUT IN THE ANCIENT KEEP OF CALDICOT

Of my lord Humphrey de Bohun, tenth and last of that name, many pleasant adventures are related, for he had livery of Caldicot Castle when he was but a young man, and so was disposed to hold a merry court therein. In this he succeeded admirably; but not so well in his designs of afterwards turning over a new leaf and being gravely sober, since he died young, as if to shew there was quite enough gravity already if not too much. But during the ten or twelve years of his reign that fine Castle of Caldicot was full of jokes and entertainments; indeed some have supposed that this plenitude of jest caused the walls to bulge out and afterwards to crack; but I believe the great hole by the eastern tower was made in the muddled times of the Roses when Earl Humphrey had been under earth for many years. You know he married my lady Joan of Arundel, with whom he had been brought up, so that husband and wife understood each other's little ways, and managed to live together very comfortably at Caldicot, where there was plenty of room for everybody. And one of my lord's whims was to gather about him a company of those quaint fellows sometimes called "men of genius"; for what reason I know not, but so goes the phrase. But I certainly think the genii in attendance on these gentlemen are by no means to be envied, since the work is hard, the laud little, and the wages less; and if "like master like man" hold good these poor devils must have but a scurvy life of it. Nevertheless some people profess great love for these queer customers, and the High Constable was one of them, and he would have stowed inside the castle a small army of poets, romancers, stargazers, scholars, cunning mechanics, and dabblers in Hermetical affairs, and all at the same time; and they say that he got his money's worth out of them for they often made him laugh till he cried. Others think he might have been more thrifty in his amusements and declare that he would have done well to content himself with his household fool who made folly his profession whereas the rest were mere virtuosi or amateurs of foolishness. Yet by this assemblage of oddities my lord enjoyed a great variety and diversity of doublets, faces, and methods of madness; and he delighted in nothing so much as to watch his jokers at dinner, or in their other employments the which were manifold. It is reported that in an apartment of the south-western tower, somewhat near the sky but provided with a fair hanging gallery, Master Jehan Doucereutz perfected his rare piece called *Le Roman de la Mouche,* admired by all virtuous people for its fine colloquies, dialogues, allegories, fables, and moralities, though some critics call it a tedious and lengthy poem. But in these dissolute times a piece of more than twelve thousand lines tires out our patience, and really good poets of severe morality like Maistre Jehan can gain no hearing. Formerly no maiden of gentle blood would have dared to skip a line of *Le Roman de la Mouche,* and many right virtuous and illustrious ladies have confessed that they owe all their good qualities to it and their tapestry work; but all this is changed. Hard by the postern gate was lodged Master Geoffrey Tudor, and here he wrote the fifth Book of *Sir Percival of Trematon,* a romance stuffed fuller of enchantments, battles, dragons, giants, magicians, peerless ladies, mirrors of chivalry and coat-armour than any other work of the species; and it is stated that the exquisite delineation of the Castle of Joyous Garde in the fifth book is the exact portraiture of Caldicot as it was in the reign of the last De Bohun. Atop of the south-eastern tower was the apartment of Master Ignoramus de Prato, one of those gentry who interfere with the privacy of the Lunatics, Mercurials, Jovials, and (worst of all) Venerians, who know rather more about the future than about the present, and who will tell you whether you will dance from a ladder or say your prayers kneeling—at the block: and what's more they'll shew you the reasons of it, and how it must be so from a malign aspect of Saturn, and in such wise and in so many hard words that for very decency's sake you'll not presume to die in your bed. Master Ignoramus his little tract (500 pp. folio) on Decumbitures was first printed at Venice in the year of grace 1495, and with it is his Dedication to "The Most Noble Prince, Humphrey, Earl of Hereford Lord Marcher of Wales and Lord High Constable of the Realm of England." Underneath this astrological personage, sometime dwelt Messer Antonio dei Coglonieri, a Venetian and a great clerk, who knew Greek and many things besides; but both his temper and his complexion were too hot to be pleasant, and everybody from my lord to the serving-maids agreed that there was no satisfying him, and that the sooner he were gone the better it would be. In the western tower of the grand gate-house was the apartment of Master Nicholas Bubbewyth, a man far gone in mechanical knowledge, who was able to twist a large river round his little finger, and to make it go up or down, to right or left, in a straight line, a spiral, or in maze-wise just as he pleased without any reference to the natural predilections of the water. It was Master Bubbewyth who perfected that pleasant contrivance by the which all the meadows about the castle could be put under water in five minutes; and also a device, not less pleasant, for shooting boiling lead through the air; but he was a man of wit and merry fancy who knew what a joke was, and understood the violent, mixt, and natural motion of projectiles. Last and best of all this company came Dom Benedict Rotherham who had been in Arabia and Syria and amongst the Moors both of Spain and Africa, and in these places had practised the art of multiplication, and was affirmed to be an adept in the operation of Hermes. And besides those high mysteries that relate to the making of gold, and the preparation of the life-giving essence, he was learned in the physick of the Arabians, and understood the concoction of potions and powders of wonderful efficacy, whether to kill or cure, and it was whispered that he knew enough of magick to set down Caldicot Castle in the realms of the Great Cham between the hours of matins and prime. In fine the High Constable regarded Dom Rotherham as his rarest diamond, and had given him at his own desire an apartment in the great keep. Which keep was the oldest part of the castle, and stood at the north-western angle of the wall, on a lofty mound, having been built in the gloriously muddled days of King Stephen, when it was well if one had a good thickness of wall between the vital parts of one's body and the austerities of the climate. For in those days it rained spears, hailed battle-axes, and snowed iron-headed shafts, and in Gwent there was often a Welsh frost besides: and all these weathers were noisome for man and calculated to bring on bad complaints. Therefore Humphrey de Bohun, third of that name, who married Margaret, daughter to Earl Milo of Hereford, made the walls of his mistress' tower ten feet thick, and took great care that the masons set the stones truly to the square, and filled up the chinks and crannies with mortar, lest perchance there should be a draught. You will wonder that this lusty lord was so particular not to have a blast of cold air blowing at the back of his neck, but I assure you there was nothing that our old nobles hated more than a draught. Why was that? Well, you see a draught was more hurtful then than now-a-days; for in our times it breeds a rheum and sets our noses running, but in the days of Humphrey III. it was very apt (if the hole were large enough) to breed men-at-arms and set blood running; the which sanguinary defluction is worse than any rheum, and cannot be treated with hot water and a handkerchief. Below the ground story, some ten feet beneath the earth, and full twenty feet from the slope of the mound, was a sweet capacious dungeon, a dungeon where a man could lie snug and still, without bothering his head about politics or theology or any knotty points, since nobody could disturb him in this retreat. For some reason or other Dom Benedict when he first came to Caldicot, and saw all the splendour of the palace (for in the later days it was no less), the fair rooms on the walls and in the towers, whence one could step out on the alures or galleries and take the air easily and pleasantly, came to a stand at the old donjon and would have my lord assign him an apartment there, saying that it was very fit for his purposes. The High Constable was astonished at this request, and shewed him how much fairer and better rooms there were in Caldicot, and wondered greatly when the adept still desired a place in the keep. But here it was that Dom Benedict went to work and lit his fires, filling the whole tower with dreadful stenches, that seemed to make their way even through those mighty walls and float out on to the court and to the noses of the lords and ladies as they sat in the hall or in the bowers. Father Raymond the chaplain swore by the Gospels that he looked one night out of window and saw the whole keep aglow with fire, and every joining of the stones marked out in a blinding line of light; others professed that they had heard dreadful noises issuing from it, as it were of a storm of thunder; a few had seen a flaming cloud float across the sky and hover over the tower; but the High Constable was glad to hear these reports, since they shewed he had got a man who understood his business and had some little interest with the fiends and elemental spirits. But though the adept was assuredly a clever fellow, who had gone deeper into the nature of things than most of us, he could not justly be called a pretty man, nor a well-favoured, nor a handsome; since his face was too yellow, and had too many wrinkles in it to be altogether a nice countenance. Moreover his eyes were uncertain and variable, some said they were coal-black, some that they were blue, and some that they were sea-green; but all agreed they were more like two small fire-balls than anything else, since a look out of them shot through you, disturbed your faculties, and confused your understanding, like a swinging fisticuff, fairly delivered above the nose. And the body of Dom Benedict was mighty lean, and clothed in a black cassock, and appeared to be thoroughly dried up by the hot suns of Africa and Syria and the fetid smoke of his furnaces; in such wise that all the ladies and women of the castle had a very poor conceit of him, as being more of a bellows than a man. But in this they were mistaken as ladies sometimes are, even in matters that concern them nearest, for the adept was very strong and had worked up all sorts of things in those crucibles of his besides The Green Lion and The Son blessed of the Fire. Sometimes he would come out of his laboratory and walk in the galleries whence he could see the country far and wide, and look down into the bailey and watched the Knights pass to and fro and the men at arms, but he spoke only when he could not help speaking, and few save the High Constable troubled him with their conversation. In fact Dom Benedict stunk abominably of chemical materials, and it was best to keep at a distance from him, since he made one feel faint and sickly and dried up the throat: but my lord when he would talk with him always had a boy with a flagon of wine by his side; and as he drank all the time he was in the tower it is no great wonder that he often felt confused about the operation of Hermes when he came out, and found going down the ladder a mighty ticklish affair. There could be no doubt that the alchemist was a very different personage to all the other ingenious gentlemen entertained in the castle, for Maistre Jehan Doucereutz, though a moral and didactical versifier, more profitable for young maidens than any other tutor, was a great favourite with everybody and fitted his conversation to all needs, for as he moralises in his poem the wise man is like a key that will turn back any bolt, and open every door. To my lord he told tales, some say better and pithier relations than any in the *Roman de la Mouche;* to my lady and her cousins he read what he had written the night before, with the knights and esquires he was mirthful, and all the maidens loved him, and he them: though none could wag his head in time with Father Raymond's better than this witty and excellent man. And it was the same with the rest, for they all tried to make the time pass pleasantly, as it should in a castle; and if men did not try to be companionable, what would the poor girls do; for they cannot play their little games all by themselves, or if they try they soon begin to yawn and get dull; and this shews that we men are intended to be always with them, to help them laugh and cry, eat and drink, dance and sing, keep still and make a noise. Why even Master Nick Bubbewyth, who was a plain outspoken kind of man, did his best and made the ladies little mechanical toys, most ingeniously and artificially invented and cut out; and as for Master Geoffrey Tudor when he began to tell a chivalrous adventure full of dwarfs, spired towers, magick swords, and enchanted forests, the whole hall grew as still as death; and when he had done all the maids wanted to kiss him, to which I am sure he would have had no objection. But this alchemical personage was entirely disagreeable both to mind and body, and even my lord, though he was proud to have a man at Caldicot that could make gold and knew all about the fiends, yet confessed that Dom Benedict was an unwholesome fellow and smelt very strong. But still the adept abode in the keep and pursued his investigations; and it is said that he made by art a great store of gold, with which the High Constable enriched the castle with rare metal work from Flanders and finished the Tennis Court so that it was finer than the King's Jeu de Paume in France.

Now among the women of my lady Joan there was a girl named Loyse, who came from Bretagne, and was a great favourite with the Countess, perchance with the Earl also, for she was good to look upon, and well shaped all over. But however this may be it is certain that she gave none of her favours to anybody else, nay, not so much as a kiss, and yet had lips that seemed devised for nothing besides, and as sweet a little body as any Christian woman could desire. But she seemed, somehow or other to be still waiting for something or somebody, and would stand for hours on the alures, gazing across the plain, or watching the gilt vanes swing from north to south. Loyse was in short a grave quiet girl, and on that account loved by the Countess, who found her other maidens rather too fond of amusing themselves with the pages and young gentlemen who were learning their business at Caldicot; but as she said it was all her husband's fault, since he was never better pleased than when he caught a page with his arms round a maiden's neck, kissing her like anything, and putting all manner of foolish notions into the poor girl's head. This always made the High Constable laugh tremendously, and he would say to the pair "That's right my children, be sure to enjoy yourselves, and don't mind me." So it is not to be wondered at that these pastimes became very popular at Caldicot, and the esquires, pages, captains, and lieutenants were always tickling, squeezing, enticing, and kissing some girl or another, but never Loyse for she did not appear to care about enjoying herself like the rest of them. Yet they all loved her for she was a kind, pitiful girl, and so beautiful withal that a good deed done by her seemed somehow of a much better quality than the good deeds of the governess Mistress Eleanora Malkin, who was not exactly well favoured, nor quite as young as she had been. How this was I can't tell you, but it is just the same in our days, and I expect never will be different. Moreover each and every of the young gallants hoped to overcome her scruples before next July, and treated themselves with imaginations of the first kiss on those maiden lips, for the sprouting chivalry of Caldicot was point de vice and thought no small beer of itself in war, or love or tennis; the which were the principal amusements of those days. And the three pastimes are alike in many ways: in each victory is very sweet and defeat as bitter, for each one must be strong and a thorough man, and in each great practice and long experience is required if you want to divide your enemy scientifically into two equal parts, to take your lady's heart quite out of her body, or to best "better than half-a-yard." And every gentleman at Caldicot wished to do these things, and worked hard from morning to night and from night to morning, at one or the other, and the ladies helped them as well as they were able, since one could not be unkind to people who were so persevering. I suppose that even the smallest page, little Raoul de Monthermer, who was only ten (it was pleasant to hear him talking of his mistress and the lady of his thoughts) would be dead by this time in the natural course of nature; but many of the High Constable's establishment died young from a too rigorous pursuit of their favourite amusements, for they forgot that one should be temperate in all things and seemed to think themselves as strong as that Seigneur d'Ercules who was a Lord Marcher of Greece and did things that are too hard for us now. And this courageous chivalry was madly in love with Loyse, partly because she really had a nice figure (*droit corsage* the French call it) and partly because she would have nothing to do with it, and when it began to say pretty things and to stretch out a wanton hand, she would move further off

and begin to talk about something else. And once there was a Court of
Love held at Caldicot, to the which came Ladies, Knights, poets, and
pursuivants d'amour from all Christendom, and the Assize was held in
a tent set up in a meadow, most gorgeous to behold, all shining and
glittering and glowing with gold cloth, and noble blazons, and banners
of the Knights. Hereat arose so sweet a noise of sonnets and canzones,
of amorous rhapsodies and songs burning with love, of gitterns and of
lutes; that if you stand under the old ruinous Castle walls in June
whiles the sun is setting, you may chance to hear some few faint notes
of that delicious musique, and catch a glimpse of the fluttering banners, though it was all done many an hundred year ago. And to this
Court came many petitions from the Castle, and pleaded the Rebellion
against our Liege Lord Love of Mistress Loyse, shewing that she had
never paid to him who is paramount lord of all women and men, her
suit and service. And the *Arrest d'Amour* was duly proclaimed bidding
this rebel make amends to her sovereign, and choose some gentleman
to be her true lover, as you may read in the *Paictes et Gestes joyeuses de la
Cour Dorée,* a book which is now in the King's Library at Paris. But still
Loyse continued obstinate and kissed nobody but her mistress and the
other girls, liked to have a room to herself, and went about dreamily,
heeding not at all the frolicsome, merry, wanton life that everybody
beside herself was leading; I should say beside herself and the Hermetic Philosopher Dom Benedict Rotherham; but sweet Loyse did not
remind one in the least of the adept, since, as I have above noted, his
skin was too yellow and his eyes too burning to be pleasant to look at.
Not to speak of his figure which was of quite a different shape from
the maiden's.

But one day after Evensong, when the whole house was sitting
down to supper, it appeared that Loyse was nowhere to be seen, for
many soon missed her, though she gave *droit d'amour* to none. And first
they went to her chamber, but she was not there; nor indeed in any
other part of the castle, though no coign nor carrel was left unsearched
from my lady's bower to the guard-room by the grand gateway. At the
latter place the men-at-arms answered that they had seen nothing of
her, sorrowfully enough, since it was like asking a poor shepherd if he
had a pipe of malmsey in his cabin: and the watch were quite assured
that Mistress Loyse had not left the castle; in fine, she seemed utterly

to have vanished like a puff of smoke on a windy day. I need not say that the keep was searched from top to bottom, from the wooden gallery on the roof, to the dungeon below the mound: but as one might expect there were no maidens of any kind to be seen within the walls thereof. There was however a most fetid and noisome stench proceeding from some *prima materia* that was gaily purging itself of its gross qualities over a brisk fire, and in truth everybody judged these qualities to be as gross as could be reasonably desired. Dom Benedict indeed was hanging his nose over the crucible as if he rather liked these vapours which made the throats of the searchers feel like a ploughed field after a long drought with a hot sun shining on it; but then he was a man of peculiar tastes and not a little eccentric. He did not seem thoroughly to comprehend what all this curious rout was doing in his laboratory and when the High Constable endeavoured to enlighten his understanding he merely said "Mistress Loyse, Mistress Loyse" as if he were thinking of something else; and as it was very evident that she was not there they all left him and tumbled down the ladder, and ran to the buttery directly to take the taste of the *prima materia* out of their throats. But every other place was searched again and again, even to the lockers in the walls and the chests in the Record Room of the Chancery of Caldicot, but there was no Loyse anywhere, neither amidst the towels nor the rolls. And this was indeed a wonderful affair which puzzled all the lay-people tremendously, but Father Raymond is alleged to have had his eyes open at a very early stage of this business and to have smelt sulphur in it from the first. He certainly sent letters to Oxon, which brought a learned clerk to Caldicot, a man of great skill in matters wherein the devil was thought to have his finger, who understood all the intricacies of affairs like this; yet even he was for a long time quite at fault. But if anybody could have seen through the walls of the keep and looked into Dom Benedict's laboratory, they would have beheld a very strange sight, as appears from the confession of the adept, made by him on the fifth day of the question, and written down by Giles Sandys one of the clerks to the Chapter of St. Peters at Llandaff. The which document sets forth that the accused person Benedictus de Rotherham, a native of the county Palatine of Durham, and aged fifty-five years, three months, and ten days at the time in which this confession was made; had formerly been a monk of the Benedic-

tine House of Religion at Durham, but was beset even from his boy-
hood by an itching desire for knowledge, and more especially for
knowledge which is occult, and not lawfully to be acquired by Christians. And Benedictus de Rotherham, the accused person aforesaid,
having found out, by reading a certain book in the monastic Library,
that the highest and most magistral secrets of the occult philosophy are
not to be discovered in the Realm of England, nor in any other Christian land, but must be sought amongst the followers of the Accursed
Prophet Mahommed (whom God confound), broke his monastic vows
and fled the cloister, having stolen a jewell from the shrine of St.
Cuthbert, worth better than a hundred pounds. By means of which the
accused person aforesaid journeyed to the Levant and lived for many
years amongst the Infidels, having renounced his Saviour, and becoming in all respects an outcast from our Holy Faith, so that he might attain to the knowledge of Alchemy and Diabolical Magick, and have
intercourse with demons and the fiends of hell. And being as he professes a man of a natural and acute wit, he came in course of years to
know greater secrets than the Magicians, his tutors; and has confessed
to deeds which it were not fit to set down on any parchment, being
that they would set the parchment crackling and the ink hissing and are
altogether abominable and accursed, and moreover not necessary to
the process now directed against this man under the Ecclesiastical Law
by and with the authority of Roger Lord Bishop of the See of Llandaff.
But the accused person, Benedictus de Rotherham aforesaid, has also
made full confession as regarding the crime for which he has now been
arraigned; namely that he did by magic arts seduce the person of one
Loyse de la Haye, who has afterwards died without making any confession or receiving absolution for her sins; her body having been exhausted and her reason destroyed by the usage she endured. But
before the hand of death cut short her life she raved continually of a
lover, whom she called by the pagan and outlandish name of Yussef,
and still murmured words taken from Love's Promptorium, the which
was never known to be in her hands. And the accused person Benedictus de Rotherham aforesaid having been subjected to torments unen-
durable, that the truth might appear the more clearly, has confessed
that when he had inhabited the Castle of Caldicot for the space of
three months he became possessed with a stronger lust to enjoy the

body of Loyse de la Haye, than had ever affected him towards other women, though he had dwelt for many years among the Infidels who are known to be preposterously and beyond all measure addicted to venery. And this desire so inflamed him that he had almost died of it, and often he swooned away and became senseless from hot, intolerable imaginations in the which the beautiful body of Loyse de la Haye was continually presented to him in such wise that all his inward parts appeared to burn with the unquenchable flames of Hell. And being well assured that he was not able to get possession of her by natural means, by which maidens are used to be won, he determined to enjoy her by the power of his art, not doubting its sufficiency for this or any other purpose. And as the girl Loyse aforesaid passed below his lodging he appeared to her at the head of the stair, having transformed himself into the appearance of a young man of very great beauty, vested in rich stuffs of the Moorish fashion. Then as she came to the foot of the ladder, curious to know who this might be so handsome of feature and in such gorgeous attire, he called her to mount up and cast a spell over her so that she must needs obey whether she would or no. And when the maiden had climbed the stair he went on before her, and immediately bestowed her in a secret place contrived in the thickness of the wall, whereon, by his art, he was advertised so soon as he beheld the tower on his first coming to Caldicot; and this he did knowing that she would presently be missed, and a search made everywhere. But after the High Constable and his people were gone from the keep, he led forth Loyse and drew her to him, caressing and fondling her and slaking on her lips the intolerable thirst by which he was consumed, and so working with his enchantments that before night fell she was more eager for love than even he, and gave him back all his embraces and fiery kisses in a manner which shewed that she was by nature hot-blooded, and had long restrained herself. And the accused person Benedictus de Rotherham aforesaid states that they spent the night in the dungeon of the keep which by art magick was changed into a delicious bower, draped about with hangings and tapestry work, furnished with couches and stools of velvet and samite, and lighted by a jewell hung from the vault by one hundred chains of fine gold, and shedding a light as it were of a harvest moon of fourteen nights. And in the midst of this chamber, so artificially prepared was spread a banquet of delicates and the most potent wine that was ever pressed from the days of Noe until now; for a few drops of it would turn the most holy of the saints into the most infuriate of sinners. And while they feasted and toyed with one another the magick harmonies seemed to swell into their ears, and thrilled every nerve and vein in their bodies with a sharp and exquisite pleasure. * * * * * In this wise they lived together in the tower of Caldicot Castle, the accused person, Benedictus de Rotherham aforesaid, sometimes leaving his mistress and shewing himself to the High Constable and his people, so that no suspicion might be stirred up against him. And when he returned to the dungeon that had been transformed into the temple of Venus, he ever found Loyse hungering for him, and remembering nothing of the Countess or her former virtuous life. But at last, by the great skill and prudence of the clerk from Oxon, their wickedness was discovered and the whole matter brought to light, as has been declared in the evidence delivered before the Ecclesiastical Court, and written down by me, Giles Sandys, appointed as scrivener to the Court on this behalf. And here the accused person, Benedictus de Rotherham aforesaid became silent, and would say nothing more; whereupon he was questioned as before, but swooned away, and was pronounced by the physician, employed by the Ecclesiastical Court on this behalf, to be in danger of death; and was accordingly led back to his cell.

How like you the flavour of the old Records of St. Peter's, my merry masters? Do they not make your throats as dry and husky as mine is growing with all this talk? But I thought I would give you a taste of an old fashioned dish, though the sauces and condiments have somewhat of a fiery smack to which we are unaccustomed: and you must acknowledge that Giles the Scrivener knew how to make a confession and write it down ecclesiastically and minutely. But if you want to know what became of the accused person Benedictus de Rotherham aforesaid, I can tell you this much that he died soon after he made confession of his detestable enormities, and indeed he had made the world too hot to hold him, for he was burnt to death. It is said that no sooner was he chained to the stake than the fagots burst into flame without any torch being set to them, which circumstance seems to prove that this alchemist was rather a bad fellow, who deserved everything he got. There is always one thing however which is pleasing in these affairs, namely that work was found for the parchment-scrapers, canonists, and ecclesiastical quill-drivers, who lead for the most part dull lives enough, and are glad to have a little variety. This mishap was also a warning to the girls at Caldicot, not to be too virtuous and severe, not to bind the devil with iron chains; since this makes Satan angry and inclined to do mischief when he gets loose, which he is sure to do sooner or later. Mind you, I do not know that they particularly needed this cautel, but at all events it made them be careful what they were about. But the Countess was sorry for Loyse.

Ending with these words his tale of Nether-went, our Rubrican upheaved himself from the wondrous chair, and stood up, looking round as who should say "you can find no fault in my relation, I believe." But we sat in a row with our heads on one side, each man holding his pipe to his lips, and puffing pensively, for we could not exactly discover what we thought of this story. At last Tom sat down again and filled his glass and his pipe and began to drink and smoke himself; for he was not going to wait to receive judgement like a felon before the justice. Then Nick Leonard commenced to say "'Tis not altogether a bad tale, but neither is it a good one, at least to my taste; there's too great a heat about those old ecclesiastical arraigns for July, and the fable seems to me somewhat of a hellish one." To this the Rubrican answered "Do you assert that my story, which I have told, is not a moral story?" "Nay, Nay," I cried out, "he says nothing of the kind, for 'tis assuredly a very moral story, but there's a whiff of sulphur about it for all that, and you know, Master Rubrican, that the old records are apt to be strongly flavoured." "How is it," put in Phil Ambrose, "that the ink in which such things are written doth never lose its sheen, and that the gold and gules, azure and purple are still as fresh as though the pen were hardly dried." "The reason of this is," quoth the Rubrican, "that the scribes were the old monks, who did everything thoroughly; who, when they have once set foot in a country, can never be blotted out of it, nor die away into forgetfulness. Doubtless they were mortal men, even as we are, and had their little failings, but they were very strong men and knew how to make red ink and build monastic edifices. And now Abergavenny Fair is the only place where this ink can be bought, and the scriptorium of the Cwrw Dda the only place wherein it is used: and who knows how long the Sokage hold together in these days whenas all good ancient customs are dying out or being uprooted by main force?" "Take comfort," said Nick, "for there will always be Silurians as long as the world doth last; though I believe they will sometimes be very few and scattered about the land, and forced to work hard for hard masters, and be roughly treated in many ways. But still they will remain until King Arthur come once more, with his Twelve Knights and all his wonderful array, riding through the woods and across the hills to the musick of his magick horn. Then shall old Dubric sing mass in the metropolitical city, and then shall begin the great Silurian year. But lo! the night goes on and we waste the time by talking of what shall be, when we, at all events, shall have been borne with singing along the valley and up the slope of the long hill to our quiet home beneath the grass, where are no storms, nor rains, and the roaring October winds shall sound merely through the boughs above us, nor break at all our rest. Search, search my masters through the fantastick alleys of your mind, and set some merry tale on foot; recall again the joyous days of old, and let the owls hoot as mournfully as they please." "I give my place unto mine host, the good Tankard Marshall," said Tom, "I will sing mumchance through my nose, lest any babbler break the story short." Then came the chant: *Hear and speak not a word, for merriment is a-making and a strong concoction of choicer wit; and the blacksmith forgeth on his ringing anvil drolls.*

THE QUEST OF THE DIAL AND THE VANE

Humphrey de Bohun, the High Constable, of whom we have heard somewhat before, once upon a time kept Eastertide with great pomp and ceremony, assembling in his hall as many ladies and knights as he could gather together and doing his best to entertain them merrily. Dim and dark personages, whom you and I know very well (for the genus doth remain immortal) shortly say that my lord and all his guests did eat, drink, laugh, dance, sing, and make love to a most scandalous extent; they say to be sure that each and every of the company at Caldicot enjoyed a great deal too much of all these pleasures. But we know well enough what this means, we understand, I believe, what kind of a world these sour fellows would make if they had the chance. First they would paint the blue sky black and the green trees white, all flowers should be dark brown, all meats loathsome, all sounds hideous, and all girls ugly. 'Tis a good thing, is it not, that these godly men are not yet quite strong enough for this; truly they do as much as they are able by making themselves as loathsome and hideous as is possible; but our precious world still laughs, whirls round, and keeps up the dance with the circling stars. And at Caldicot everybody from the Earl to the scullions did his best to keep pace with this mad and joyous melody and now at Eastertide when so great a company of fair and beauteous ladies and noble warriors were gathered together, some said the good old days had returned again and that they might look before long for King Arthur himself with all his host to return again. And Maistre Jehan Doucereutz the moral rhymer made a piece, richly rhymed, which he called "The Argument of the Dial and the Vane, or Constancy and Variety in Love." This he taught to two young ladies called Alicia and Avisa, and shewed them how to stand and hold their figures, while they repeated it; and one evening when the serving men had borne in the tapers and lighted the lamps, this fine poem was recited before all, with so ravishing a grace and gestures so lovely that the High Constable's guests gazed silently at the young maids' lips, without uttering a word. But when it was finished a great dispute arose as to the arguments and conclusions between the Dial and the Vane, for in his wisdom Maistre Jehan had left the matter doubtful, and none could determine which of the two he thought was best. Every lady and most of the young knights swore by the pheasant and the peacock that Variety in amours was treason to love; that no virtuous lady would listen to a gentleman that was variable, and that Constancy was one of love's sweetest graces. "What though our ladies slight us, and speak scornfully of us," said Sir Nicholas Kemeys, a young and high-flown gallant, "what though they frown upon us, and turn away when we look at them. Let us honour them yet more reverently and with a perfect worship bow down at their feet, holding but the sight of their beauty too great a reward for our poor service and adoration." Every lady in the hall lauded these words and some let their eyes rove slyly towards him, and thus the champion of Constancy was treated with Variety; as if to shew us the way to get praise and pudding by one stroke. But the High Constable and the more experienced knights laughed at these fine Platonic sentiments and said there was nothing like Variety in everything

and especially in love and my lord shewed paradoxically and philo-
sophically that before a gentleman can be constant he must first be
variable; since constancy is bottomed on good judging and good judging on wide experience and many trials. "One must love," said he, "at
least a dozen maids, every one of a different pattern and each one in a
different manner, before one can be fixed at last; so the mariner shall
sail over various floods and many waters ere he drop anchor in the still
waters of his haven." So between ladies and knights the field was
stricken, and now one and now another champion came forth to onset
armed with pompous phrases and muddled arguments; but my lady
Joan would say nothing alleging that she had always known my lord to
be a reprobate; but she spoke with laughter, and was answered by him
with certain gestures which made her laugh still more. Meanwhile the
lettered men had listened and held their tongues, Maistre Jehan being
mightily delighted at the good success of his piece and the entertainment it had made for all the noble folk; and presently he and Master
Geoffrey Tudor the romancer were observed to put their heads together, as if they were concocting some good and joyous invention.
And while somebody was saying, "We see the preëxcellence of the one
over the other by the lively symbols wherein Maistre Jehan has set
forth his parable; for the vane is ever gay and merry, still on the viretot,
and always tells us something; whereas the dial has no story in the
shadow, and is but a useless piece of brass while the vanes are clatter-
ing and swinging joyously"; Master Tudor stood up and prayed for the
High Constable's ear, the which was readily granted him and all kept
silence. "I would make an oration to you, my lord," said he, "for that
my brother, Maistre Jehan Doucereutz and I, have, unless I am mistak-
en, concocted for your pleasure and the pleasure of fair ladies and the
noble chivalry of Christendom, so choice an adventure and rare an
emprise that I believe no deeds that are written in the Book of the
Round Table nor in any writings of errantry shall be found worthy to
be compared with it. And in fine our plan is this: namely, let each array
in this gentle battle choose a champion, the most worthy and knightly
that may be, and let them ride forth, the one in quest of Constancy and
the other of Variety; and let the one bear the badge of a dial and the
other the badge of a vane; so when their quest be done they shall return again to Caldicot and give us the history of whatsoever they have

done or seen. I pray you my lord consider this, and advise with yourself and your knights whether it be not a rare design." But forthwith the High Constable smote the table with glee and swore by the Ships of the Air, by the Ways through the Mountains, by the Castles under the Sea, and by many other things, that this quest should be made, and he charged each side to choose a knight, and set Brother Benignus the German Monk to work on the two badges, the which were fashioned by the cunning artificer aforesaid in gold, curiously and choicely. And presently two champions were chosen; for Constancy was Sir Nicholas Kemeys by the suffrages of all the ladies, and for Variety Sir Dru de Braose, a knight full hardy and experienced in many affairs. Then vast cups passed round to the health of these noble champions; and the High Constable named Maistre Jehan and Master Geoffrey clerks of this high emprise to keep records and to write histories of all the fair deeds that should be done in the quest, so that it might never be forgotten but be written in the Rolls of the Court of Caldicot. But when the talk began to be of sleeping my lord commended to Sir Nicholas and to Sir Dru the ministrations of his fool Thomas, whom he affirmed to be a very comfortable person and able to give them weighty counsels as to the conduct of their adventure. And to Sir Nicholas Thomas said, amongst other foolish things "Above all beware of rope-ladders" the which words he pronounced with such a knowing smile that the Champion of the Dial suspected there was something besides folly in them. But the fool's counsel to Sir Dru was "Have nothing to do with any one driving nine black hogs, for they will lead you to the devil." And after wishing both knights plenty of folly wantonness, trickery, queer sights, broken sounds, and odd odours on their quest, the very precious and jocular Thomas withdrew himself chuckling hugely; and so all slept hard without rolling. But on the morrow, when they had dined, the two knights began to arm, the two girls Alicia and Avisa helping them and binding on their badges to the delight of all the company. And when they had bidden farewell to the High Constable the knights mounted their horses and rode forth from the grand gateway, the trumpets sounding for them, and all the walks along the battlements and the high galleries being thronged with ladies, and with knights who waved scarves and shouted good luck as their warriors pricked across the meadows. And the Champion of the Dial and the

Champion of the Vane were last seen riding together by the limits of a great wood of beeches; when one turned to the right and the other to the left and so rode out of sight.

Thus the knights errant started on their quest; to ride far and wide by land and sea in search of Constancy and Variety, and often they were spoken of at Caldicot of evenings, all longing for their return and to hear the tale of their adventures. Once after they had departed six months and more a man came with a wild story to the intent that he had seen both of them together at Abergavenny but, though he affirmed he knew well the faces of Sir Nicholas and Sir Dru, he was considered to lie; since they were certainly very far away, and most like, in the lands beyond the seas. But the two Clerks, who had been appointed by their lord scriveners and prothonotaries in this behalf, had each a mighty quill cut broadly, and two fair skins of vellum, the one of which bore atop the limning of a dial and the words "The History of the Quest of Constancy"; and the other the limning of a vane and the words "The History of the Quest of Variety." So summer and harvest-time and Michaelmas did pass by and Christmas came bringing high revel; but the knights came not. And the snow lay deep in Wentwood as January came in; in February the rain fell down, all through the month, and March brought winds, merchandise of Moscovy; while the High Constable and his house waited for the return of the two champions. But when Eastertide was come and the hall triumphed with banqueting and mirth as it had done a year ago; the watchman above the gate called out that he saw a knight riding toward the Castle at about a mile's distance and my lord when he heard of it said "'Tis one of them returned with his story," and so all the company went up to the high alures along the southern wall and watched the knight as he rode along. What chattering and dispute arose as to which of the two it were, or whether it were either of them, I need not tell you; but presently Mistress Alicia cried out "'Tis our true knight Sir Nicholas, I know his bearing and the paces of his horse," and she was indeed in the right. Then the High Constable bade his trumpeters sound a welcome on their clarions to this mirror of chivalry, and the guard were set all in order clothed in mail, and the portcullis men and the drawbridge men stood by their chains lest the gallant knight after many perils and hazards should end by falling into a pit. So as the trumpets

pealed forth their close the bridge fell down, and bowing low to his
lord above the gate Sir Nicholas was received once more within the
bailey of Caldicot. First, as was right, the maids disarmed him and bore
basins of fair water, and unguents and odours, and clothed him in a
surcoat fit for the King's Majesty and tenderly handled him; for they
saw Sir Nicholas was pale and thin and judged him to have gone
through divers sore dangers in their behalf. Then (as if he had been a
boar's head or peacock) he was brought into the hall in a pomp, to wit
by the steward, the castellan, and the sergeant-marshal, with a music of
pipes and vyalls and sweet singing, and the fool Thomas walked behind for his reward; and so was set at the Earl's right-hand, and feasted
with the most delicate and opiparous fare and the most curious wines
imaginable; for the High Constable noted that Sir Nicholas seemed all
the while like a man in his twy-senses, between the call and the awakening. Scarce a word moreover came from his lips, but he knit his
brows, tapped his skull, and was heard once or twice to mutter "Surely
I am myself and this is the hall of Caldicot in Netherwent, and my lord
Humphrey sits beside me." They that heard these conjectures concluded therefrom that the poor gentleman's head was dazed and somewhat
muddled, but we must not say hard things of them on this account,
because, you know, they lived a long while ago and were ignorant of
true science. But in our days if a man desire to make a noise in the
world, and to be accounted a philosopher whose thoughts are deep
down below the form and nature of things, he has only to write his
Meditations or Considerations declaring in quaint and quidditative
terms how uncertain it is whether "I" is "I." And all this is quite right,
but to each age pertain its own perfections. But my lord, the ladies and
the knights waited anxiously for Sir Nicholas his lips to open to better
purpose; and had good hopes of hearing a fine history when the
Knight of the Dial had drunk his wits back again. At last my lady Joan
could wait no longer, but cried "Sir Nicholas, Sir Nicholas begin your
tale, or else it will be cock-crow before you are half-way through." "It
shall be so," answered he, "I will tell all and would have begun before
were not my adventures so wonderful as to be almost beyond belief;
but now since you bid me, I will omit nothing." Then the company
about the board was hushed to silence, and the fool closed one eye,
while the chins of Maistre Jehan and Master Geoffrey sought their

hands, since it was their function to chronicle what was to come. Then Sir Nicholas Kemeys, the Knight of the Dial, began his relation of

THE QUEST OF CONSTANCY

speaking for some tway turnings of the horologe in a voice of grave sweetness that drew all eyes intent upon him. In this history he told them how he had lost his way in a vast forest, where he was beset by the folk of Faerie, who played him a thousand tricks and bewildered his sight and mind and all his rational faculties with their enchantments, shewing him the sweet unearthly bodies of ladies lying asleep beneath the trees, and sending dwarfs to waylay him and draw him aside from his track. Nevertheless through all these magic meshes he won through, and at last reached a flat land on the summit of a mountain, where he found the people celebrating the Festival of Wine Skins, with songs and music and interludes and many pleasant diversions, but there was nothing like Constancy to be met with among them in love or in anything else. Thence Sir Nicholas went down to the valley beyond, and saw in the midst thereof a great city on a hill, having a spire rising from it of incredible height that seemed to sway to and fro from star to star. And the hill whereon the city stood was so steep that no horse nor mule might mount it, and the only way for a man to ascend was by way of four stout and well-set ladders, made of ropes, one on each side of the city. "So," said the Knight, "I was forced to leave my horse below while I mounted upwards, till I had laid my foot on two thousand steps, and stood before the northern gate; and blew my horn before the drawbridge that I might have entrance. The which without question or delay was granted me, and I came through a broad and sunny street, planted with trees and established with high-built houses, to the market place before the great spire, and here the people bought and sold, and played at tables and flew enormous kites shaped in the similitude of dragons and birds of ravine, and monstrous creatures: and on a high seat sat the king of that city clothed in blood-red vestments, holding a golden rod; and there was his court before him. To the king himself I shewed my quest, and told him all my desire; and when I had finished he answered: 'You could have chosen no better place, Sir Knight, than my fair town of Ladders; for we have here an example of splendid constancy, and this you shall see presently.' Then he called ten men-at-arms, and whispered apart to their captain, who beckoned me to follow him. This did I, and we went out of the square down a narrow alley, till we came to a door-way and this being opened shewed a winding stair rising from it. But I would not go up as the captain asked me, for I had had enough of mounting; whereupon he and his soldiers fell on me all at once and grasped my head and throat and body and arms and legs so that I could not stir; then one bound my hands and 'climb' they said and I had no choice for the spears of that city have sharp points. And when I had gone round and round up that stair, so that my limbs sunk from under me, and my senses were confounded, I became like one who walks in his sleep and could count the steps no more; but before this I had surmounted five thousand of them. At last we came to a door in the wall, and here they unbound my hands and unlocked the door and bade me go in and gaze as long as I would above or below it mattered not which, for either way there was constancy and plenty of it 'Since most gallant knight errant and mirror of chivalry, if you look over your shoulder you will have a close view of a special vane of beaten brass, the which follows the wind whither-soever it leadeth it, and this it does in all weathers, by day or night. But if you yourself are not over constant, and like change, you have but to look down on our square, when you will see us all constant in con-stantly taking our pleasure; only go not too near the ledge of your hab-itacle, since a mile through the air is a long fall.'" Here Sir Nicholas groaned deeply and went on to explain that he found himself in a little cell or habitacle made some ten feet under the capstone of that spire he had seen from afar, and, as he judges, full a mile from solid earth. And all the company groaned and cried 'las!' and called on the dear saints, hearing of such a fearful adventure; and some of the girls fan-cied they were falling from that tremendous height, but in fact they were deceived since most of them were borne up by an arm in need ere they had gone back three inches. "And there indeed for many days and nights also (so said Sir Nicholas) have I seen the mighty vane of shining brass in the image of a most foul and malicious dragon, swing-ing to and fro above my head and screaming as it went, like a woman in her agony; but my greatest terror was the swaying of the spire the which seemed to be in sempiternal motion and rocked continually as a tree upon the mountains. As for looking beneath I durst not do it, for I feared that I should instantly fall down and doubted whether they would pick me up alive after such a tumble. And my food no man brought to me; but just after sunrise and sunset, I would hear a noise like wings beating the air; and opposite to my habitacle there would flutter a great kite, having fastened to it a flask of wine, a little meat, and a loaf of bread, all of which were good enough, the wine indeed being of Catholic and Christian quiddity. And with a hook on a spear shaft I would draw the kite to me and take my victual and then let go again; so I lived in this place for better than nine months." Herewith the Knight of the Vane came to a full stop, and only by slow degrees was the history of his escape drawn from him by the Countess and the fair ladies. And the Chronicle indited by the skilful hand of Maistre Jehan Doucereutz proceeds to relate how Sir Nicholas grew desperate on the lofty spire and how one evening when the great kite drew near to him, it being made like a bird of prey with mighty flapping wings, he took not his provision from it nor let it go, as he was used, but leapt upon it floating in the air and cut the cord that held it with his dagger. "Then with a great shout of the people ringing up into mine ears, in place of falling to the earth, I floated away, being carried far above their heads by a fair breeze, and soon was beyond that hateful ladder city. And now for six days and nights I was borne amidst the clouds over deep woods and mountain tops, and lakes, pinnacled castles, and walled cities, and they that looked up and saw me were in terror, thinking, as I suppose, some fearful monster was about to waste their land. Now the wind lifted me high towards the heavens, where I looked upon the stars and saw clouds rolling beneath me, like the billows of the sea; and now I swam the air but a little distance above the earth, and have thus passed over dreaming towns, and armies in array, and have gazed on the wandering miz-maze of the world. Sometimes have I flown swiftly before a tempest, and heard the wind rush by as an onset of battle; and have passed unstricken amid the flame of rapid lightnings and the roaring of the thunder; and anon the air hath been still and peaceful and (I think) filled with the chiming of many bells from the churches and snatches of organ musick; or else my brain was sick and imagined to itself these harmonies. But on the morning of the seventh day, as I hung over a great forest, stretching far and wide to the limit of my vision, I felt that the bird was slowly sinking downwards, and was glad, for I was sorely in need of food and of drink. To be short it descended on to an oak, and I making haste to set my feet amid the boughs, let it go for an instant; and thus it is that I can shew you no proof of my story; for the kite was seized by a sudden breeze and rose aloft into the air till it was but a speck against the blue, and afterwards I have not seen it. And lo! beneath the tree was my horse that I had left behind when I climbed up into Ladder Town; and how this happened is beyond my wit, neither can I get to the bottom of it at all. Then rode I away, and for three months have I journeyed through wild lands, foreign peoples, many perils, and much misery; but the vane on the spire of the accursed city is the only constant creature that I have beheld in this my quest."

No sooner had Sir Nicholas brought this stupendous history to a close than the blast of a horn, blown long and loud, assailed the ears of the High Constable and his company, who marvelled so at this circumstance that they forgot to marvel at the story. "Go, Thomas," said my lord to the fool, "go quickly and see who it is that is without so late; since a fool is best to open to one that comes on a fool's errand." "Truly I think I am the right man for this occasion," answered the precious Thomas, who kept one eye still closed, so that they said "He is, in fact, a great fool," and that is how the phrase originated. Remember this when you speak of your friends behind their backs, and forget not to feel thankful to the witty lords and ladies who have furnished you with this expression of true friendship. But Thomas went forth, while the horn still rang through the towers, along the alures, and into the hall; and ere long returned leading with him no less a personage than Sir Dru de Braose, who looked hearty and well, and had not so warm a welcome from the ladies as Sir Nicholas; both because he was on the wrong side in the quarrel, and because he seemed in full possession of his mental faculties. But then he had fewer of these to take care of than the Knight of the Dial, and so kept what he had in better order. But the Earl took care of him and saw that the jovial knight was duly stuffed with good things, and his throat well swilled with wine; and all expected to hear from him a history of pleasant and amorous adventures and some rather juicy tales, and the ladies prepared to blush, as it is proper for ladies to do on such an occasion. Some of the prettiest of them were blushing already, but these were mere private and peculiar blushes, not connected with the public business or necessities. But it appeared when Sir Dru began the story of the

QUEST OF VARIETY

that he had had almost as rough a time of it as Sir Nicholas himself; but to be sure he spoke at much shorter length and appeared now and then to stop short and knit his brow as if he had forgotten what had next befallen him. And thus he began: "After that I had parted from my companion I rode onward over the level many miles till I came to a stream with high banks of yellow mud, and no bridge was to be seen, whereby I might have passed over. But presently I beheld a large boat moored to a post on the bank, and into this boat I and my horse descended. But as I would have steered it over to the other side the wind rose suddenly and caught the sails and the force of the water took the boat and drove it violently down the brook till we came into the open sea. And here again, as I strove to guide my vessel the rudder broke in pieces, and the might of wind and wave growing in violence urged us onward, and the air grew dark with the storm, so that I gave myself up for lost, and thought each moment to be overwhelmed amidst the high billows. And for three days and three nights the tempest continued; and all the while we lay in thick darkness as if it had been a continual night, so that at last I fell asleep from hunger and weariness and slept, as I believe, for many hours. For when I woke no clouds were on the sky and no longer in mid ocean, the boat slowly sailed along the shore of a deep bay in still water; but out at sea I saw all the waves ridged with white foam because of the storm that was overpast. And seeing the water was shallow, I made shift with my lance to guide the boat aground and mounted my horse once more and set forth through a narrow valley that I might discover to what manner of country I had come." Here Sir Dru paused and laid his finger for a minute to his skull; and then began to speak of his inland journey; of green lawns, brooks of sweet water, delicious fruits, sweet singing of birds, and many other pleasant circumstances such as sailors conceive in a calenture; but which are neither new nor over pertinent to the story. "And before I had ridden for an hour," said he, "I overtook an old hideous woman who drove before her nine black hogs, very monstrous and fierce to behold, having tusks like to wild boars' tusks, and the grunting of them was like the noise of a fierce lion. The old woman I addressed and asked her if there were no lord in the country that shewed hospitality to wandering knights and refreshed them after they had undergone great peril and distress. 'Truly,' she made answer, 'most hardy and gallant knight, you have but to follow me, and I will take you to a very great lord, who loves nothing better than to entertain strangers and weary men, notably if they be mighty warriors of gentle birth as you are. And to his castle I am now driving these nine hogs that have of late had pannage in the woods hard by the sea.' Thus the old woman with the swine led me through a fair open country till we came to a high wall of stone around a castle, having towers and alures and a strong gate house, even as this castle of Caldicot. At this gate house the old woman bade me wait while she drove her hogs round by the postern, and in a little while the drawbridge fell down, and the lord of the castle came forth to meet me, a grave and comely man with blue eyes and a long white beard. And he took me by the hand and led me in, calling me brother and bidding me command him and all his men to do whatsoever I would. 'Many a year gone by,' said he, 'a gallant knight like you came here in search of adventures, and so fertile a land did he find it that he never returned to his country, but died here; and he too was of Gwent.' With these words we came to the banqueting house, lofty and magnificent, and in a gallery was a quire that sang and played every manner of instrument while the company were at meat. Then mine host made me sit beside him at the high table, whereat sat also his nine daughters, such girls as it does a man's eyes good to gaze upon, for one of them would turn an abbey upside down. And at the board below was as brave a sort of ladies and of knights as I ever desire to see, all gallant and gay, and dressed in splendid robes of velvet and silk and golden stuff, enriched with jewells beyond all price. Let me say nothing of the feast or of the wine that graced it, for neither surely did come from any earthly cook or perishable vineyard, but were rather drawn down from Olympus Hill on the Marches of Greece; being altogether most delicious and wondrously tasty on the tongue. And before I had rinsed my mouth with many cups of those celestial juices, my eyes began to wander over the nine maidens, and soon met with an answer from the eyes of one them, joined to sly smiles and downcast looks that, to speak the truth, made me desirous of knowing more of her. Ladies, I crave your pardon, but I tell you this girl's lips were mighty red. But when we had finished feasting, and I had informed my host how I had wandered away from Gwent in the quest of Variety, curtains fell over the windows and the hall was suddenly darkened; but only for a moment; and I heard a sound of most strange palpitating music that swelled and died away and rose again; then were the doors thrown open, and two tall men entered carrying great tapers of wax aloft; and after them the minstrels, and then fifty more men bearing tapers, and these stood around the hall. So the music that had entered went up to the high table and played there; they that were in the gallery answering them, and the ladies and the knights began to tread a dance, weaving and unweaving perplex'd figures continually. But seeing the girl I had marked out still sitting I drew near to her, and endeavoured as courteously as I could to entertain her with such polished phrases and gentle discourse as my wit supplied. And to speak the truth she was not backward, her eyes consumed my soul and her voice thrilled through me as we talked and we told one another old flaming tales of passionate lovers, how that fire of love had burnt to the ground many noble houses, and had brought to desolation lordships, and dominions and mighty kingdoms, as it was with Queen Guinevere and Sir Lancelot du Lac. And in some way or other, as we were rehearsing these fair conclusions, I found her hand in mine, but I profess I know not how it got there; yet 'twas not at all unpleasant, and I had an inclination to prolong our discourse. But as we were debating some knotty point in gallantry my girl said to me 'Surely, fair sir, we could solve these intricate questions better in quietness by ourselves; come then, follow me and I will lead you to a fit school, but we will have no præses, for there is no need for one.' And I made no scruple at all to follow Madam Enantha (this was her name) out of the noise of music, and dancing and laughter; and she went before me through a side door, along a passage, and up a stairway till we stood together on the alures. Then what with the moonlight that shone through the open casements, the faint sound of the lutes and vyalls, and the strangeness of the adventure my head became confused for some while; but when I awoke I found Enantha's arms about my neck and her lips set fast on mine, indeed she was a nice girl and seemed mighty affectionate. Then we paced along the alures till we came to a tower, and whilst we delighted ourselves there with warm caresses, a voice that turned my heart to ice sounded (as it appeared) from close beside us. 'Now farewell (it said) most courteous and loving knight, descend without steps and at dawning look on the dial, and find there in the ever shifting shadow the true exemplar of variety.' But before mine host, (for I know it was none other) had finished this strange speech the floor beneath me began to sink and I passed from the arms of my mistress down through the tower into darkness till I was at the bottom of this secret shaft, far below the earth. Here I might beat the walls and cry out and none hindered me; and all through the night I raved like one written in the Books of the Moon even till the dawning came and one long ray came into that foul and loathsome pit lighting upon a dial set in the midst. And this place was so contrived with squint holes fashioned through the walls, that all the day the sunshine fell upon the dial and marked the hour, and by its brightness made my prison-house yet more noisome and abhorred. What food I had was flung down to me from above, but I saw no face and heard no spoken words throughout all the time I was thus clapped up, namely for nine months, more or less. And there doubtless I had died wretchedly, save that one day in my frenzy I cast mine arms about the pillar on which the dial stood and pulled with all my might striving to uproot it. And after many a grievous tug, in the strength of my madness, what I endeavoured I at last effected, and the pillar yielded and fell to one side, bringing with it the floor around in a circle of a cubit's diameter. And the beam of sunlight shining on this place shewed me a steep flight of steps, and beyond an odd glistening of some other brightness. My way it seems is lower still, said I to myself, and as quickly as I could I ran down the stairs and found myself in a passage lined with smooth mirrors of steel, and illuminated by small lamps hanging from the roof at equal distances apart. From these lamps came pleasant odours, as they burnt, but I stayed not to examine anything, rather coursing along for my life, for I feared there had been a watch set on me in my dungeon, though I knew not of it. And when I had run three or four miles, and was nearly breathless, the lamps ceased, and I was in darkness, and the track grew rough and stony; and the walls when I felt them were of hewn rock. Then the way widened, and my feet trod over sand, till I saw once more the light of heaven, that I had not beheld except on that cursed dial for many a weary week. To be short I came out by a cave on the sea shore, and had not far to go before I found my boat lying just as I had left it above the wash of the tide. I need not say how swift I was to embark and sail away with a blessed wind from those shores, nor how by land and sea I have returned to Gwent once more, since I have devised for you all the matter pertinent to this my quest of variety."

Herewith Sir Dru's tongue ceased from wagging and Master Geoffrey's pen from flickering; and none knew what to say, for it seemed as if the Argument of the Dial and the Vane had not been concluded by the knightly quests; but rather mixed, muddled, confounded, obscured, dedalised, and entangled to an intolerable extent. Then by the High Constable's solemn decree this great question was adjourned, prorogued, and continued to next Easter; and they all went to bed hoping that the morrow would be a warm and shiny day. But both the histories were curiously engrossed by the lettered men and laid up amongst the records of the Castle for the admiration of the after-ages. But it was discovered a short while afterwards that in neither of them was there one jot or tittle of the truth, since they both proceeded from the fertile brain of Sir Nicholas Kemeys, who had taken the hints of that great fool Thomas in the management of his fables. And in fact the two knights errant had been enjoying themselves all the time at Abergavenny, revelling, feasting, and making love to their hearts' content; drinking the strongest men under the table and hiding in aumbries and in dark corners till the town was too hot to hold them. And when my lord Humphrey had the real truth of this affair carried to him, so well-pleased was he with the ingenious and finely conceited lying of Sir Nicholas and Sir Dru that he gave to each of them a fat manor in his lordship of Netherwent, and would have them always in presence at Caldicot till he died.

Thus I brought my relation to a close; and it was then found to be time for sleeping, so that no man laid his thumb nail on what I had said, unless he did it in his dreams.

BY THE WAY

On the next morning while the darkness still palpitated in the sky, and the lucent day-star shone over the dreaming woods and rivulets; a tread of heavy boots clamoured about the passages and stairs, and at our doors was a knocking and a voice crying "Domini ocula aperiatis," or words resembling these, for I could never teach Efan to latinise honestly though I had laboured a whole month to put some learning into him. But I was pleased to hear Tom Bamfylde responding in a set Latin speech beginning "Justum: nam ibimus per vias nemorosas et vireta locorum amœna"—It is meet: for we are to go by wooded ways and pleasant greeny places—"by streams of water and running brooks," he went on, "by the castle on the hill and the church by the road, even unto that delicious city the very jewell of sweet old Gwent." For Latin came from his tongue full smoothly, and hearing that tongue spoken half asleep he answered in it, much to the confusion and dismay of Efan who hated the language he was compelled now and again to speak; and as he would say "The words do rankle in my belly like sour ale, for they be not good words nor wholesome; but loathsome and hideous." And hearing this flight of Latin whistling about his ears, he made haste, and cursed himself in Welsh, and having sworn profanely, withdrew himself as quickly as he could. Then was great haste made on our part also and before long we were dressed in point; for I took out a fine habit I had of crimson velvet, well laced and purfled: and my three guests had, as I have said, vestments of murry and tawny plush, so that we were, all four of us, right gallant and brave and fit for Uske on the Portreeve's holyday. So one after another stamped down the stairs, and felt his way in the dim twilight along the passages and stumbled into the parlour; here was a fire burning, the shutters closed, and six tapers lighted, for us to see our breakfast, on which we fell solemnly and earnestly to work and passed around a tankard of the Brown Nut. And outside we heard the cocks singing lauds, with festal antiphons and ruling of the quire; for by Clemendy they had a house under a Chanticleer and sub-chanticleer and lived together as virtuously as could be expected. And when we had done with cup and platter we sallied forth and got into the saddle, just as the sun rose above Kemeys and Wentwood and flung his light right over the great round hills that are in the west. Then the horns began to play before the porch at Clemendy; a rousing melody they made with tarantaras and magistral flourishes; full pompously and gorgeously we rode out at the gate, doffed our feathers to the church and turned up the road to Uske. But for all our clamour I heard a full rich voice swelling up from the village—*"What bird is this, I pray thee tell me, That carolleth so loud at dawning, O dear mother"* and in the fine trills and graces of the old Welsh song, I recognised very well the sweet throat of a sweetheart of mine called Mevamwy, who thus (dear merry maiden) sent us on our merry way. Then along the deep and narrow road, one riding after another between high banks of flowers and green leaves, till we began to pass through the midst of the forest, and here the buglers ceased, for with blowing their throats were dry, and with puffing their cheeks weary; and the way being wider we were able to go more together and to talk at our ease. "Here halt," said Nick Leonard the Lord Maltworm, "and cease horn, and strike flint on steel, for I am minded to smoke a strong whiffling pipe of tobacco." "So we, for one cannot relish the morning air without tobacco smoke, this forest roadway is so sweetly sheltered and embowered on either side that the blue clouds we blow, shall float and die into the larger blue, gently and by slow degrees." Thus the Rubrican answered for us all, and the smoke's wreaths rose upwards as he had said, and truly I shall never forget, so long as I live, the delicious savour of that pipe of Trinidado, taken in midforest and mingled with the morning, and gladness, sunlight, and green leaves and many roadside flowers. So we rode slowly along, and after a little while Tom Bamfylde (ah what a fair monument has poor Tom in Abergavenny minster) said "Let the fat Spigot Clerk smoke out his pipe and shew forth one of the best tales he has in his hutch; and when we have to ride singly again, he shall be second, and bawl out the phrases of his story, as if he were a herald on coronacion day." "Well well," replied Phil Ambrose, "it is my turn, and I will do my best to add one more pleasant circumstance to the Uske Roadway and the Forest of Gyronne." "Of Flower de Luce and the Lyonne Rampant you should rather say," quoth I. "I speak of the field," said he, "I speak of the field; for there are no lions in the forest nor flower-de-luces; but the subtilest foxes and vixens in all Gwent, and an undergrowth of daffodils and afterwards of red campion and the purple Iacinth, the flower that cries woe. And before Michaelmas it is truly gyronny of gules and or. But talk not to me now, but let me smoke my pipe to the last ash, and then you shall have my tale." And before long the pipe came to an end, and Phil looked around him: "Blow horns," said he, "sound me one long and glorious strain as for the knights' onsetting, make me purple musick, my companions; before I devise my story of old Gwent." Then the bugles rang out full and clearly, till all the valley and the wood seemed satiate with sound; and as the last dying note dropped back from the hilltops upon us the Spigot Clerk began his tale.

How a Knight of Uske Kept Guard over a Tree

It appears to me, gentlemen, that since we are going this day to Uske with the deliberate intent and fixed resolve of taking our pleasure there, it would be well for me to devise a tale concerning that town aforesaid, and so I will bring a text for you out of its byways and make an ancient moral story. You shall understand then that a good many years ago (how many I will not say, lest the Rubrican catch me tripping in my antiquities) there was a young gentleman living in Uske, called the Sieur Payne Martell, whose coat was so splendid and princely a one that he could never have it blazoned on his vestments in full, because the bill would have been too long for anything, or for his purse at all events. When I say never I speak not by the book, for I mean to say in his young days with which my tale is concerned; but when he was about fifty years old he went as brave as any one; and for this you may look in the tournament-rolls of Windsor and in the *Inquisitio Post Mortem* held some years afterwards. This young knight then lived at Uske in a very pleasant and retired manner, subsisting on the contents of a small chest he had; the said chest containing a beggarly number of gold pieces; how gained I will not dare to say: because I really don't know. For all I can pronounce they might have been the few remaining feathers of a fine bird that had flown away; an estate to wit, maybe they came from the high toby; in which case we should call them extract of moonlight and fifth essence of the dark lantern. But since it is of no great consequence how money be gotten, it would be waste of time to discuss these hypotheticals; for the fact that I want to get into your heads is that these yellowboys kept disappearing till at last there were very few left. Not that there was any mystery in the matter, any more than there is in the necessity our mortal nature has for meat and drink; but there was a good deal of mystery in Sir Payne's mind as to how he should refill his chest again. This question he endeavoured to solve in lonely walks about the woods and hillsides, and along the banks of the fair water of the Uske, lying full length in the long grass under the shade of a hedgerow and looking hard into the river. I believe he expected a river-maiden to take a fancy to him and bring up her treasure from the chambers below the Uske; for he was not a bad looking gentleman and your nymphs and all their sort are notoriously addicted to imprudent wedlock with mortal men. But Sir Payne was never startled out of his dreamy gazing by the sudden radiance of dripping golden hair and he began to be afraid that the tales of these damp ardent girls were not quite true. This thought made him feel sadder than before, since he was a knight loving of wonders, full of faith, as poor as a rat, and fond of fine girls: but he did not despair and still chiefly frequented the Uske, sometimes amusing himself by throwing sticks into the stream and watching them float away. And when the angelus sounded in the valley (though he sometimes waited till the sunset) he would get on his legs with a sigh and trudge home, and then lie down in his cockloft and fall asleep, muttering to himself "I don't much care if I never wake again in this horrible earth"—though, to be sure, he did not quite mean it. But you see the poor gentleman was in want of everything that makes life pleasant; and there are times when all of us, with cause and without, read King Solomon's Sermons with a sad relish. But Sir Payne would have done well to remember that this good King wrote a Song (and a Song of Songs) as well as a Sermon; and if one has a smack or two of the whip, why by the splendour of Love's firmament! there's a smack of a kiss and the unction (what sweeter, what more comfortable) distilled from a pair of darling lips, also. In our degenerate days, doubtless, it would be thought unwise of a man to spend his days by the riverside, waiting for a water-maid to woo him; but Sir Payne was no pagan and had great faith; and from my history you will understand that he was in the right and could have chosen no better way to mend his fortune. It was one day in June, between Midsummer and Petertide, a highday of Beelzebub (if he in truth have lordship over the flies), a day of swarming bees, of ripening cherries, of chiming foxglove, of still air moved now and again by faint breezes, but most of all a day of roses. Roses did hang everywhere, by hedgerow and byway and brake and river, white and red, in bud and blossoming, filling the fields with a faint scent that could scarce be perceived but might not be denied. And on this day Sir Payne was lying according to his use by the Uske, keeping well in the hedge's shadow, and just above him with boughs falling to his hand was a great bush of pink roses, and here and there was a blossom almost as red as blood, but most were paler. But their odour came not to his nostrils since beside the rose bush grew an elder tree, the bloom of which is strongly fragrant, and it made the air heavy all around. And while he thus lay, pondering and dreaming and listening to the perpetual ripple of the river (for on the opposite side it was shallow) the bell of the Priory began to ring for Nonesong very sweetly, and looking up he noticed the roses, and a quaint thought came into his head. How these fancies are engendered I know not; but it is certain that if one seek for them they are not to be found, but they come and go at their pleasure and are altogether licentious. And this thought of Sir Payne's was to fashion a wreath of roses and to cast it on the current of the Uske; and thus to make an oblation to those maidens of high race of Færie, to whom belongeth every winding of the river, every ripple and little tributary brooklet, all broad spaces and reaches of still and glassy water, from the wells in the mountains unto Severn Sea. And so he twined his fret of blossoms, setting four of the reddest at four points of the circle, and cast it well out into the stream. At first he was afraid, for the wreath floated to the other side and seemed in danger of being caught by a great bramble that hung from the bank; but it did but touch a thorn and swam out again into midstream, and passed round the bend of the river. And to speak the truth Payne had not long to wait for an answer to his flower offering; for in less time than a good church clock takes to strike noon, he heard the even plash of oars, mingling with vyall notes and the sound of singing, coming towards him from the way of Caerleon. The knight made no doubt at all that he was about to be borne away to Avilion like King Arthur by three fair ladies of Færie; but herein he went a little too far, for that Island is kept for great lords and princes, else it would be overcrowded. But presently (the music and the noise of oars growing louder and more plainly measured) Payne saw a painted barge swing round into his view, rowed by six rowers who now held their oars aloft; and an old white-bearded knight in glittering vesture held artfully the helm. Below him sat three or four ladies with as many knights and beyond them was the musick, who now ceased a little while, to rest. But as they came nearer Sir Payne saw to his wonder and rejoicing that his rose-garland crowned one of the ladies and instantly he plucked another of the redder blossoms and held it in his hand. Now as the barge grew point by point along the river the musick fell to again and began with long drawn harmony of vyalls and a deep tenor throat that divine ballad *Soubz cest Amour mon coeur est endormy*. And as they passed by, Sir Payne gazed a moment into the eyes of the girl sitting nearest to the helmsman, who wore his rosy fret, and he saw that she was very beautiful. And she, who was keen of wit and sight, noted the red rose in the poor knight's fingers, and smiled on him: ah! such a smile, that made the earth seem lovelier; and the passionate melody thrilled to his heart—*mon coeur est endormy* he sang to himself softly and the barge had passed. And soon by another winding of the river it was hidden from his sight and the musick came faintly on the summer air, and Sir Payne was alone once more. But can we call him alone when on the swirl of the water he saw that gilded, painted barge perpetually advancing, heard the stroke of the oars, and the first long sweep of the bow upon the vyalls. And there in the marvellous mirror of the Uske he likewise saw the maiden sitting beneath his rose garland, a maiden clad in white velvet, wearing a collar of jewells, and having wings of golden gauze floating from her head, like the wings of a gorgeous butterfly! All this was a rare and curious sight for the eyes of a gallant gentleman to feast upon, and Payne saw everything very clearly, for you must remember he had been fasting for some time like any hermit, and was therefore in the right state to see visions. He found them indeed so entirely to his taste that neither evensong, nor curfew, nor compline stirred him; and it was in the meadow by the riverside that he took his sleep that night and woke up the next morning rather hungry and quite ready for breakfast and whatsoever should happen to come after it. As to the former contentment he was fortunate in having the acquaintance of the Lardarius of the Priory at Uske, one brother Pacificus, a monk to the backbone. The which is so much as to say, a man with strong sinews, a deep bass voice and a sound heart. This honest monk Sir Payne sought out in his larder, a small room, but a fragrant, and full of good things such as sauces, condiments, old cheese, tasty preserved meats and sausages, with odd-looking little flasks stowed away here and there in nooks and crannies. Herein the hungry knight found the Larderer who had just taken off his quire habit, for primesong was scarcely over, and Sir Payne hinted that if anybody thought of taking breakfast he should not be averse to fall in with the notion. "Surely, fair son," answered the monk; "I am about to take some little refreshment myself and here there is always a cup and platter for you: and for a beginning try these cherries from our orchard, just gathered, one of these white manchets, a few strawberries and a flask of cool red wine that has spent an hour or two in the well." With these simple dainties they began and then Brother Pacificus drew out the substantial part and the truly monastic fare. This was a sausage about as long as a man's arm, rather crooked, but splendidly attired in a vestment of gold leaf, as though it had been an uncial J in a Missal. In short it was one of those "Uske Puddings" for which the Priory had been famed time out of mind, of which the Prior made an Easter offering every year to the Bishop of Llandaff, and on which many high ecclesiastical persons had been regaled on Gaudy-Days. While Brother Pacificus was stripping this peppery unctuous customer of his skin, Sir Payne's blue eyes twinkled finely, for he knew the taste of these gay fellows and was aware that it was always necessary to drink a lot of good wine afterwards; and when a man had done this he was in the humour to pull Satan's tail and follow up the attention with a hearty kick. And when the two comrades were in the midst of their disjune the knight began to ask the monk (who knew everybody) about the barge he had seen the day before. "An old knight, Father, steered it; a well-looking man with a white beard and a gyppon all glistening with gold; and below him sat a fair young lady, golden haired and intolerably beautiful, in a tunic of white velours: and other ladies and knights were there, and minstrels also." "You saw, I think, Sir Rowland Bluet; for he often goes thus on the water, and his daughter Alianor is truly a comely maiden; but what was his coat, since you doubtless noted it?" "He bore three golden chevrons on a sanguine field crusoly of the first, and the maiden's cote hardie was pounced all over with the golden crosses." "That to be sure is Sir Rowland's coat; a good knight, a very worshipful gentleman, but somewhat stern and not by any man to be trifled with. But you may see his house not far from the Castle, with a high wall all around it and a great chestnut tree growing in the court. As for Mistress Alianor, she is the child of his old age, very dear to him, and intended for some great lord; and to be sure together with her beauty she will bring her husband a comfortable dowry and many a fat meadow in the vale of Uske." This comfortable news was the best sauce in the larder for Sir Payne, and he got very genial over his tenth cup, since he made no account of Sir Rowland Bluet's severity or of his dispositions of his daughter, justly reckoning such matters of small importance. And by the time the bell began to ring for terce Sir Payne thought a little rest and meditation in some shady place would be good for him; as his head was very clear, and he felt that if he could have quiet he would soon be able to make excellent arrangements. The people of Porth-y-carne street who saw him walking towards the bridge said he was drunk, but for once, they made a mistake I believe: since it is wrong to call a man drunk or fuddled who is arguing and smiling to himself so brightly and merrily that the very children laugh to see him. In this agreeable state Sir Payne met at least five pretty girls, and he kissed every one in a calm but decided manner. The which shews his wits were in good order, for one cannot mark one's approbation of a nice feature in a nicer way. Will anybody deny this? I believe not. And after resolutely and admirably discharging these duties the knight got away to his old nook by the river and there dreamt a thousand pleasant dreams, wove innumerable fancies, bathed his head in sunshine and the water of the Uske, and perceived that the brightest butterflies all carry on their backs a little naked boy, and that every flower whereon they rest hath a little maid of færy in it. He saw also long pomps of folk in green array pass below the tall grasses, with minstrels blowing great honeysuckle trumpets and heralds in golden tabards; and down in the river the stars were shining. I suppose it was in these stars that he saw it figured that Mistress Alianor Bluet would walk on the river bank after Evensong with no more retinue than her page and a girl; but however that may be he discovered this fact and duly betook himself to thitherward, wearing on his sleeve a red rose and looking for all his poor vestments a gentleman of true blood and loyal lineage. It is in this high regard that a man of quality is easily discerned and distinguished from a rich scurf whose only arms are the royal ones on his gold crowns. There by the woods and waterside Sir Payne met the lady of his thoughts slowly and gently pacing, and whispering to the girl beside her; who was only a little way behind her mistress in beauty. From afar off the pair spied one another, and like the afterglow of sunset flushed Alianor's cheeks, so that she was considered to blush, and she caught her fellow tightly by the arm, murmuring "He whom you see approaching it was that sent me the garland yesterday. Shall we not turn and pass away through the woods." "Courage! mistress," answered the girl; "he seems to me a proper gentleman enough and a hardy; and you know:

> *Jamais d'amoureux couard*
> *Oyez bien dire.*

However let us see how he carries himself at close quarters, and then you can turn back if it be your pleasure." This advice suited Alianor very well, so they paced still slowly on, till they met Sir Payne Martell, who took care to let his rose be seen, and directed one look of humble supplication towards the lovely Alianor. And when they had gone a little way he turned and followed them, the which was soon perceived by the waiting-maid who beckoned to him with her eyes and lips to have a good heart and not to be afraid. Thus encouraged Sir Payne followed in their footsteps hoping to see Alianor turn her face a little toward him, but she was indeed too bashful, and her maid had much ado to bring her up to the mark. At last when they came to a very quiet bend, thickly wooded on both sides (but one or two spaces of sunset flame appeared between the leaves) the page left his lady's train and coming to the knight said "my lady Alianor Bluet bids you come before her presently." This did Sir Payne, you may be sure, and found the two maidens seated on the grass, the servant glancing roguishly at him, and Alianor half smiling half frowning, but altogether almost too lovely even for Gwent and the purlieus of Uske. "What makes you follow me thus?" said she as the knight bent before her, for she wished to begin the service in a high tone, trusting they might come to the *secreta* afterwards, contrary to the use of ecclesiastics. "I guard your ways, sweet mistress," answered he, "for that I am a knight of the Rose and bound by my vows and solemn promises to wait on the chiefest of all roses, in whom alone is conjoined the perfect red and white." "By St. Dorothy, sir knight, I have never heard tell of such an order, pray teach me who is the sovereign of it." "He is called by some the Lord of Love, for he is a mighty and puissant prince." "Are there many knights then enrolled in this order?" "Many, for one cannot be a perfect knight without a lot in this brotherhood, in which high courage and the worship of loveliness are taught us, and all the service of incomparable beauty." ("He uses mighty fine words" said the serving maid, "he talks like a grammarian, and hath a noble nose.") "And how fares your brotherhood in poverty," went on Alianor, "for perhaps some of you have not very large estates and are not able to make a brave show, nor to sit beside the ladies you adore, nor to lead them out to dance." "'Tis then our sovereign lord doth succour us and opens to us the wicket into his close, and there we either live most blissfully or gladly die seised of Love's demesne." Thus Alianor and her knight played at question and answer, like two girls on a lawn tossing the ball either to other and coming nearer at every throw. Meanwhile the maid and page were playing amidst the trees and laughing, for the boy wished to kiss the girl, she said he was too young for kissing, told him to wait a year or two and then he might do what he liked with her lips. But he could not wait and chased her round and round the oaks till her foot slipped and she fell right into his arms and lay still there thinking a pretty boy of thirteen better than nothing. And as these pastimes went on the ball turned and returned between Alianor and Payne till at last they got so close together that the poor knight ventured to slide his fingers into the lady's hand, and not long after to draw her to him, supposing that as she said not a word she found his ways not quite distasteful. But by the time Payne was beginning to discover what it was to have won the love of the prettiest girl along the Uske, the serving-maid and page came up with reverent faces to let the lovers know that it was almost dark and full time to separate; and indeed it is likely that neither of them would have found out these facts without some prompting. However they made an appointment to meet again in certain woods that lie on the hills to northward of the town and said goodnight fondly to one another. Maybe you remember the first time that your sweetheart said goodnight to you in sweetheart-wise, for there are circumstances therein that make the blood run swiftly and raise golden fancies in the mind. And if you have not forgotten you will understand how Payne wandered home to his garret, marvelling how happy a world it is and how beautiful all things surely are. In fact the streets of Uske grew very spacious, and loftily the houses rose upward in the gloom, especially the mansion of Sir Rowland Bluet that had a high wall all around, above which one could see the great chestnut tree. Sir Payne slept that night a happy sleep, a sleep furnished with fragments of sweet musick, snatches of quaint song, curious scents and pinnacled castles, a sleep rigged out with the most rarest dreams and illuminated with red stars. The which must be set down I suppose to the gentleman's being in love, a complaint that bears the responsibility of a good many transactions and is as needful to a tale as a nose is to a face. Depend upon it a face without a nose is no true face, it is incomplete, and the like may be said of a story that lacks love. But this matter at Uske was indeed a fine love affair, secret, ardent and well-planned from the beginning; daily calling for fresh stratagems and new meeting-places and all those counterfeits that lovers take delight in, though to be sure they are made more for show than use. Yet I suppose this couple might have learnt the alphabet together for a long time without being found out, if Payne had been content to bear his mistress company in her country walks and sunset meditations in the woods by the river. But being a young fellow of adventure, fond of dangerous places and warm corners he must needs propose a midnight interview, notwithstanding that he knew well enough Sir Rowland's sharp ways and his dislike of uninvited guests. Alianor received this plan with a shake of the head at first, but before long became convinced that it would be rather pleasant, and at last agreed to Payne's desire. This was dead against the counsel of her maid who affirmed that such meetings often led to bad blood, cuts, slashes, and strong language, nay, she said, brave gallant gentlemen had sometimes left the world on such occasions without having leisure to see after their affairs. However nobody paid any attention to this wise girl, who was fond of pleasure but very wary, having noticed that people who enjoy themselves too much often die young. In short Alianor agreed to keep wide awake on the Wednesday night following, the which arrangement left Payne two clear days to knock his notions into shape and to perfect whatever contrivances he had in his brain. The Tuesday he spent chiefly at the Priory, eating and drinking of the best and hearing conclusions from the most experienced monks concerning the excellent and kindred arts of getting into and getting out of difficult and perilous places. On these points Payne heard some curious discourses and Breviates, but the advice that pleased him best was that delivered by a very ancient monk who had seen many Priors enthroned and had helped to sing the *Dirige* and the *De Profundis* over most of them. "My son," said Brother Audœnus, "take the nearest path, follow your nose, go on steadily, and if necessary fall asleep till the coast be clear. For thus you will imitate the pious example *Sanctorum vij Dormientium*—of the Seven Sleepers, whose holyday we keep to-morrow: and they, you know, slept hard and went on sleeping as only saints can sleep, till the right time came to them for rubbing their eyes. And don't forget that though you may seem to be sliding down hill very fast, yet it's probable you may strike upon a side passage that will lead you to the top." "Brethren, pray fill this holy man a full cup, for I think we have in his words the kernel of the matter." This was done and Brother Audœnus raised his chalice in the air and drank to the pious memory of the Seven Sleepers, and Sir Payne went home to ponder over the counsels of the ancient monk, and to discover how they might be fitted to his necessities. But just as he was going out Brother Pacificus the Larderer slipt something into his hand, muttering "take this, it will be sure to come in useful" and this something proved to be one of the monastic sausages, royally arrayed in cloth of gold. On the night following close upon Midnight Sir Payne began his enterprise by scaling the court-wall of Sir Rowland Bluet's mansion, the which he accomplished not without difficulty, but at last came to the top and set forth straightway on his journey to his lady's lattice, the road being along the boughs of the chestnut tree that spread from the wall to the house. You may be sure he trod softly and made no more noise than he was able, often stopping and peering about to discover whether he was on the right road, for the branches went in all directions and Payne had no great desire for an interview with Sir Rowland, who might wish to know what he wanted with him. However by slow degrees he reached a bough overhanging Alianor's window and began to sing under his breath *Soubz cest Amour* as was agreed upon; when the lattice was swiftly opened and his sweetheart's face looked out and her hand beckoned to him to come. This he did quickly enough, swinging himself down as aptly as if he were a mariner; and the lovers began to busily engage themselves in making up for the time they had lost, fondly gazing into each other's eyes and again and again drawing close together to drink that sweet essence that some set far above the rarest wine. But in the midst of this pleasant pastime, whiles their blood ran hot and swiftly, and their cheeks were close together, their arms twined round one another's necks, they heard suddenly deep oaths, clashing steel, and trampling feet, all these noises manifestly rolling toward Alianor's chamber and growing every moment louder and more vehement. I do not doubt that those of my hearers who are sharp-witted have guessed that Sir Rowland had discovered he had more guests under his roof than he was aware, and while Payne and Alianor are cooling down a little and making the best of their short time for reflection I will tell you how the old knight had gained his knowledge. You must understand then that there dwelt in the house an animal called a scholar, by name Master Lawrence, the same being some kind of kinsman to Sir Rowland, and having free lodging with him whenever he chose to lie at Uske. Most part of this fellow's time was spent in dodging between Oxford and Paris, Padua and Salamanca, in which places he peddled philosophy always finding people ready to deal in his wares, for he cast a confused light on places that had hitherto been plain enough, and wrapped up what was obscure in the dark mists of his brain. This Master Lawrence was also known to have a new system of his own invention, the which was very quidditative and had statements in it that made simple people stare and press their hands to their heads: and thereat he was now labouring in his apartment not very far from Alianor's. You see if he had been a true scholar the noise of some one feeling his way along the branches of the chestnut would not have moved him in the least; but as it was he put out his lamp and set himself to watch for what should come next. We know of course that Sir Payne came next, and no sooner had he set his feet on the floor of his sweetheart's room than Master Lawrence posted off to the old knight's bedside and then and there let him know that his daughter had a friend staying with her, just arrived from anywhere you like by way of the tree. I confess the news was rather startling, but I don't think it was right for an old man to swear so violently, and to abuse his servants because they were asleep and not awake at midnight was clearly unreasonable. However they were all

armed to the teeth in fifty *Aves,* and began their march to the lady's
bower, and Sir Rowland led the cursing which was not pleasant to listen to. When this noise and the noise of steel first came to Payne's ears
he wished to stand beside Alianor and make a fight of it, though a
short sword was the only arm he had, but she would by no means suffer him, bidding him begone as he came through the window. But just
as he put his foot on the ledge a shout arose from the court, and there
he saw plainly enough four stout fellows with torches and drawn
swords, who had that instant come forth from within; and the red
glare from the street told him that he was expected there also. Circumstances of this kind try a man's wits, and Payne stood still a moment
doubtful what to do, but a rush against the door and a cry from Alianor pricked him on; so drawing the golden sausage from his sleeve
and whirling it round and round in the air he leapt into the midst of
the leaves with a fearful din ringing in his ears, and a howl from one of
the men below on whose nose a piece of dead wood had dropped unexpectedly, much to his terror and annoyance. However they all
thought they had caught their bird as certainly as if they had him in the
cage; Sir Rowland and the scholar waiting in the room to guard the
window and the rest going down into the court and the street, where
they stood in a ring with their swords in readiness and their faces all
turned upwards like a sort of astrologers on a quodlibet day. One or
two hardy souls were for mounting up there and then and taking captive or putting to the sword, but they who had seen Payne come forth
would have none of that "He hath, look you," said they, "a great brand
that he whirls around like lightning, and would kill every soul of us,
one by one, if we went up in the dark." So it was agreed to wait till
dawn and then to bring ladders and plant them all round and carry the
place by storm; to which Sir Rowland consented, for he perceived that
his men would not do otherwise. To Alianor he said little, keeping all
his wrath for her gallant, and from what he did say he got little satisfaction, since she flatly denied that any one had been with her. Thus was
watch and ward kept around the chestnut tree all through that night,
till the day dawned and people in Uske began to run together, to stand
in rows, to roar with laughter, to chuckle and to grin at the sight of
half a dozen men armed to the teeth with drawn swords and ghastly
torches, standing under a wall holding their heads on one side, and not

speaking a word. But it was sorry fun to them on guard for they ached all over, and their necks had become fixed awry, and not one relished the prospect of encountering the sausage which they had made into a sword; even in broad daylight.

But when the sun was well above the woods, strong cordial waters were served out to each, and Sir Rowland made an oration to them from the window promising fine things to the man who should make capture of the miscreant. Then by way of beginning fairly they shot three flights of arrows into the tree waiting after each volley for a groan or a heavy fall, but there was not a sound, and poor Alianor, whose soul was in her ears, began to take courage and to hope that her lover had contrived somehow to steal away. Then ladders were brought and fixed all round the stem of the tree, and whilst the chosen men began to climb the rest kept double watch determined to be taken aback by no sudden leaps. But the crowd (which grew every minute) when they saw the men's heads appear above the wall, as they mounted upwards, grew silent, for this seemed an entertainment too good for common mirth, and by a great deal better than a hanging. I think indeed that the explorers went up the steps very much as if they were about to be hanged; however this perilous climb was accomplished in safety and they began to tread the boughs warily and tenderly as if they trod eggs, expecting at each step the onset of the enemy. But the fates did not will that any should die by that fearful sword, and they wandered unharmed from one side to the other, from the top to the bottom, and found not him they sought nor any trace of him at all. So they called for more to help them, and one or two young rascals of the town, mere jackanapes at climbing, swarmed up to the swaying summit and lay out on the farthest boughs, these squinting crosswise and those downward, whilst the solid serving men poked and beat and squatted and leaned over in the more central and secure places. But after an hour of this curious forestcraft it evidently appeared that he whom the searchers searched for was not there; and then I must confess the crowd began to jeer and hoot and make horns; since to keep guard all night over nothing and then to seek for it at dawning seemed to them an act of folly. But Sir Rowland was fit to burst with rage, and stamped about reviling his daughter and cursing his men, who (he swore) had slept standing, and at last turned on Master Lawrence, telling him that he had conceived the whole affair in his cloudy besotted brain, and this was all the reward Lawrence got for his pains. But when the story reached the Priory the monks made a shrewd guess as to who had got into this scrape and doubted not that he had crawled out of it by following the advice of Brother Audœnus—and by the aid of the gilt pudding, said the Larderer unto himself. But as a matter of fact Payne had taken a long leap through the gloom of midnight, across the flame of torches into the depths of the tree; and while he steadied himself a moment his hand pressed hard on a bough above his head, just in the place where there was an odd lump in the bark. Then strange to say the solid wood gave way from beneath his feet and he began to go down and down; down a-down, steadily and swiftly to silence and pitch darkness, till he verily believed that he should soon discover whether Sir John Maundeville were right or wrong concerning the antipodes. Not that he cared two pins about the matter, but he thought since he had come so far it would be as well to look into it. However the earth brought at last his deep courses to a stay, and Payne was free to choose his own path and go wherever he liked, by which I mean to say, wherever he could. And now I am going to be exact and mighty positive about what happened down below; since I do not wish you to swallow a pack of fantastick lying legends, but only the exact truth. But the old Canon who told me this story thought fit to do quite otherwise (I suppose he took me for a fool); and gravely enough, without a crease in his cassock, shewed how Sir Payne struck upon a passage that led to the underground Abbey of Thermopota, and lay there for eight nights, while the monks celebrated the high feast of St. Ypocras, and held their great Rose-Chapter. But I take it there is no truth in this; rather, when Sir Payne found there was no more falling to be done, he proceeded to strike a light to a wax taper, and with this to speculate and survey into what kind of a place he had come. But before proceeding about this business in earnest he had a hearty laugh over the people up above, who were on the look out for his descent, and firmly resolved to follow religiously the advice of old Audœnus, who clearly understood these matters. Looking around he then perceived that he was in a small vaulted chamber with an opening in the stones through which he came, and the walls were strangely painted with mystical devices in red and gold and on them were carven symbols and hieroglyphical emblems, like those they say adorn the wonderful Cloud Castle of Rohalgo. But of more account than these curiosities he held the oaken door thickly pounced with great iron nails, and feeling the handle he found that it moved easily and so was the way laid open before him. Therewith went Payne from the vaulted room below the roots of the tree, and saw that he had come to a level passage, in height about six feet and four in breadth, and in length as it might be, for one taper will not light an alley. With his nose for leader he began to pace along this dark alure, comforting himself with the thought that it certainly led somewhither, and praising himself for his foresight in bringing a candle with him, but 'twas not before he had gone a hundred paces that he found out what fine things this candle was able to shew him. Then casting a side glance to his right he saw a painting on the wall, as fresh and gay as if it had just received the last touch, and furnished with some curious conceits. On a marble bench, overshadowed with mulberry trees, he saw an ugly old man with goggle eyes sitting, and beside him were masks of all shapes and forms, each one wrinkled into a stupendous grin; and with his hands the old fellow was kneading and twisting the mouth of one of these masks, while at his elbow lay one whose nose he had adorned with warts and knobs most hideous to behold. And beneath this picture was written in Latin *The Invention of Laughter.* A little beyond stood painted a Court of ancient, black gowned men sitting at a table; with their clerks beneath them writing on great rolls of parchment; and before this court were a naked youth and a maiden, hand in hand, who seemed to plead for mercy. This was called *The Court Baron of Love.* I pass over other pictures that Sir Payne did see, called *Joyous Disport, The Triumph of Folly,* and *The Battle of the Rocks;* and stop at the likeness of a great white goose, standing by a stream and bending her neck round to her tail, for under this was a long legend, beginning *Form and Matter.* Next was a maiden of bewitching comeliness, lying amidst flowers beside a wandering brooklet, with flashes of sunlight lighting on her beautiful færy body, but vainly matching itself against the glory of her black eyes, and the roguish smile on her full red lips. Her name was set down in large characters, and she was no less than *The Muse of Gwent.* Here was a chemist's elaboratory, wherein a man of savage and starved countenance and tattered vestments stirred a great furnace, for he was *Extracting Fifth Es-*

sence; and to cut short the last picture Payne saw was entitled *The Manour Perpetual*—a sheltered, wooded valley; a place of lawns, and quiet waters and tall blossoming hedges, beneath which lay men who seemed to rest at last. But these devices I have named are not the tenth part of them that he beheld on the walls of the dim passage; so that when he had gazed upon them all and the way began to mount again, he was weary and was fain to dout his light and lie down to sleep. How long he slept I know not, but when he awoke he lit again his taper, and joyfully remembering the sausage fell upon it with a will, drinking a little out of a cordial flask he had about him. This refreshment gave Payne courage for the upward journey; though to be sure he had to drain his flask before his mounting was done, for it seemed to be without end. Now he turned to right and now to left; now went round and round as in a tower, till at last to his joy he heard a voice close to him, and what is more, a voice somewhat familiar and dear; for it was Alianor's. Then with his candle he viewed the wall to search for an escape, and presently came to a wood panel with a boss of wood in the midst of it. And he listened again and heard that it was Alianor and her maid who talked; and then once more softly came from his lips the song *Soubz cest amour mon coeur est endormy.* In a moment his sweetheart ran forward, and as she came to the wall Sir Payne pressed the boss and half the panel sank down, and once more her arms did twine about his neck. One cannot speak of meetings of this kind, for it is not possible to describe what they are like, and to be short, if you wish to know, you must have them, and then you will understand quite perfectly. And since I hear the bells of Uske begin to chime I will tell you in brief that Payne lay hid in Alianor's chamber till the coast was clear, and then slipt away with her and her maid and became a servant of the Baron of Burgavenny, for whom he struck many a weighty stroke in the wars of the Marches. But since the panel was in place again when Sir Rowland came in and found the room empty, this affair was never rightly understood at Uske, though most who passed along Porthycarne Street looked wise when they saw the great chestnut. And the moral of this story is that we may reach our goal by a crooked path through an opening in an unexpected place.

The Portreeve's Solemnity

From St. Madoc's Church to Uske is a short mile in distance and the road doth follow the river, passing under a high cliff mantled with trees; the same being a sweet road and a pleasant ennobled by the prospect of the embowered town, distant greeny hills, and the neighbourhood of the clearly flowing water. No sooner had we left the narrow byway from Landevennoc than we were in the midst of a great throng of people, tramping a-foot, riding on horses, nags, and mules, and pressing forward, as we, unto the great solemnity. Here was a fine patchwork quilt, the which did one's eyes good to look at, for in one place was a piece of satin and gold lace, in another dusky subfusc tatters: there was a parson in his priest's cloak and cassock, there an esquire glittering with gold galoon, there an Egyptian with his bien morte, there a handsome, laughing maiden walking beside her lover. Close beside us were three comely wenches, berubanded like a Maypole, and with them joked three gentlemen of Newport who tried to perplex them and make them blush: and on the other side was an ecclesiastic tall and broad, riding on a proper nag, and especially cassocked and buckled up with silver. Behind him rode his serving man with his mails, and behind the serving man a rout of Gypsies, tinkers, sweetmeat sellers, and gay ladies, discoursing together after their use and making a great uproar. In front were some half-dozen mariners from Caerleon; two poor clerks in torn cassocks, expatiating rhetorically in the Latin tongue on this admirable admixture; a lawyer with a keen eye and a stooping back; and a body of minstrels, dressed in motley and fantastick guise, and carrying in their hands horns, vyalls, and lutes. All clamoured together, some sang, some strove to dance short steps; and all pressed onward; while the sun baked us so that we should have dried up had it not been for the sight of the river and a cool breeze blowing from the eastward slope of Wentwood Chase. I turned me round to a fellow walking at my horse's tail, who bore a heavy pack, and asked him what he did at Uske, and he told me that he would sell there certain sweet cakes of his making, and that he stood for the better part of the day by the Minster gate. Then, burdened with his load of delicates, he fell behind, and another took his place, with a wallet of ballads, one of which he roared out in a rattling bass as a sample of his wares, and sang all the way. At last we came to the bridge and passed into Uske; and as we crossed the river, the bells which for a little while had kept silence, began to chime anew, and up the street called Maryport we made our way slowly amidst a still greater and more various copie of people, and from the castle battlements above us they began to shoot off guns. And as we rode up the street Phil Ambrose put his finger to his nose, and vanished away, down a narrow passage to the left hand, the which so far as I could see, appeared to lead into a garden.

Then, when we came into the square, and saw the Moot House in front of us, there rose a shout from the great congregation of people; the doors were thrown open and the pomp began to come down the stairs. First walked two tabarders wearing surcoats of blue silk, and blowing a blast of musick on their trumpets; next, the eleven yeomen of the guard carrying pikes, thirdly the two Master Sergeants in black cassocks and square caps, then the three macemen, who bore black wands tipped with gold, and wore heavy mantles of blue cloth, with red tassels hanging from the shoulders. To these succeeded the two Chamberlains, the Recorder or Prothonotary, and the Town Clerk, with the Water Bailiffs, all decently vested and carrying the symbols of their several functions; and for a finish walked, to the right hand, the Constable of the Castle, and to the left hand the Portreeve, both being clothed most gorgeously and magnificently in satin and velvet and furs; and behind them came the bailiffs, who are the Portreeve's assessors. And at the foot of the stairs of the Moot House, the trumpeters sounded a halt and the Prothonotary began to read clearly and audibly the *Inspeximus* of King Edward IV. whereby all powers, benefits and privileges formerly enjoyed by ancient charters are confirmed and established to the Portreeve, Bailiffs, and Burgesses of this borough of Uske. And by it the burgesses of Uske are declared free and exempt of all murage, pontage, pickage, tronage, kayage, lastage, passage, portage and terrage throughout the kingdoms of Great Britain and Ireland, and Gascony, and Aquitaine and all other lands within the Realm of England, both on this side the sea and beyond seas. From the street to the left the town musique advanced to meet them, and so soon as the procession was at the foot of the steps, their melody began, and the minstrels went forth before the tabarders down the street unto the river till they reached the Water Gate. Hither we followed them, through the press, amid a din and clamour indescribable; and when we gained the water side, we found the whole pomp standing in a half-circle by the gate with a trumpeter at either end and the Portreeve in the middle; and the musick was hushed. "Now watch the river," said Nick Leonard, "for it is time for the officer of our Sokage to appear from above the bridge, since he by a fiction is supposed to row in a boat all the way from Abergavenny, but to speak exactly, steps into a coracle a few yards beyond the bridge." So I looked up the river and presently a small wicker boat, used in these waters shot under the bridge, and in it was Phil Ambrose the Spigot Clerk of the Cwrw Dda, for this was his office if he were present. And guiding his craft skilfully across the rapids, he brought it to a stand over against the water-gate, and took out a great roll of parchment, which he held in his hand. To whom the Portreeve, "Whence come you, and on what errand?" Then the clerk began "I come from the town of Burgavenny, from the Most High and Mighty Tosspot Ratabus, third of that name, from the worshipful Lords Maltworm of Wales, and from all the whole Court of Cervisage; and herewith I give you my authority and letters of credence." Then he hands his roll up to a yeoman of the guard who gives it to the Portreeve that he may read it. This done the Portreeve asked, "What is it you would have of me?" "I would ask you these things—In Primis: will you drive away from your borough of Uske all erroneous, blasphemous, heretical and strange doctrines, such as and especially that it is good for man to drink water rather than ale?" And the Portreeve answers: "I will do so, for a year and a day, while I hold mine office." Spigot Clerk, "Will you promote laughter, and joyous conversation, discourage gravity and pensiveness, and temper justice with jokes?" The Portreeve answers as before. Spigot Clerk, "Will you, to the utmost of your power, be an abettor and fautor of the Most High and Mighty Tosspot, the Lords Maltworm and the whole Sokage of the Cwrw Dda so far as the High Tosspot aforesaid is concerned with you and your town?" And the Portreeve again answering that he will do what is required of him, the Spigot Clerk takes off his cap, stands up in the boat and cries out in a loud voice, "Then a good greeting to John, twentieth of that name, the right worshipful Portreeve of Uske. A fair voyage to him and a dry throat and wine enow for ten; may the plague consume his enemies, and the sun keep him warm. All this by and with the authority of Ratabus, High Tosspot of the Cwrw Dda. Fare ye well." Then the Clerk ran his boat ashore some way farther down and did reverence to the Portreeve and came amongst us again, and the musick swelled forth gladly and joyously and the bells crashed all together. But now to answer them the bells of St. Madoc's Church down the river began to chime, and a whole host of coracles were drawn near the water-gate, for the Portreeve and all his company have been used from time immemorial to sail down the river to St. Madoc's Church and there to hear a solemn service. And for the magistrate and the Constable of the Castle, and the Bailiffs a very large wicker boat is provided and another for the musique who play their water piece; but all the rest go each man in a coracle apart; and they must steer warily, for the river is shallow by Uske, and there is only a narrow passage that a boat can use. But my comrades and I would not go upon the river, but watched the college getting one by one into the boats, and saw them sailing down in a long line, so far as we could make out without any mishap. It is said that once upon a time a Portreeve, magnificently inclined, endeavoured to have his coracle drawn by swans; but the birds would not go by rule and landed the magistrate in the water, if it is lawful to say so. It is, indeed, without swans, a most rare and delicious solemnity, smacking strongly of the days of old, that were so fertile in rituals, observances, processions, ceremonies, pomps, and pageantries: and should be curiously observed and held in honour, for these vestiges of antiquity are becoming scarce. But let this be enough to say concerning it; and let us begone to the glorious Salmons, who have opened their mouths very wide. Here we asked the Host to put us in a room by ourselves, for the common rooms were replete and roaring with laughter from many throats; but he said that he would set us in a chamber where there was good company and not too much of it; and this pleased us better than privity would have done. So we go down a long passage and mount three steps and find ourselves in a low room looking on the garden of the Inn, and in it are the ecclesiastic we saw on the way and a young gentleman gallantly dressed, who was speaking when we came in, and was manifestly a stranger from the lands over sea. And from his talk it appeared that he was giving the clergyman some notions of the Ecclesiastical Polity of France and of the various oddities and queer theological habits certain of the sacred personages had in that realm, and at his account our Welsh churchman was evidently much pleased; for the cassocks like to hear how their brethren abroad are faring. With this odd brace we made haste to be acquainted, and gave and received titles, localities, coat-armour, ancestry, estates, styles, dignities, and all such epithetic ware, for without this truck we could not be true commensals nor give opinions on any matter. And firstly the churchman; who told us that he was named David Phillips of Fleur-de-Lys in the shire of Cardigan, that he was a Cursal Canon in the Cathedral Church of St. David, the worship of which stall he mightily extolled, "for," said he, "in our Chapter the King's Majesty is but Cursal the First, and 'tis an august office to be Sacristan." Somewhat he spoke of great princes, his ancestors, somewhat of cheeky, crusoly, martlets, ermines, and gringolly, somewhat of the castle of Fleur-de-Lys, and ancient vessels of silver: but most of this is impertinent and I pass to the young gallant. Who told us that he came from the Realm of France, that he was of the house of La Roche Nemours (de Rupe Nemorosa) in Brittany, and was travelling in Gwent for his curiosity, which made him go whither his fellows went not. But as we understood his English poorly and he our French no better we agreed to speak Latin together, the which we all pronounced monastically and not after the picked, newfangled fashion. And since it appeared that we were all somewhat addicted to the exhaustion of claret before other wines, I called the Host and instructed him how to provide for us. "Bring hither," quoth I, "the most convenient and decent drinking-cup you have, and pour me into it as much claret as it will carry, and serve us some kind of drawer-on." Forthwith he brought us a silver chalice brimming with about a quart of scented wine, and set down some bottles in a corner if we were thirstier than we thought, for there is no possibility of exact calculation, and to chase a landlord to and fro for more when one journey sufficeth, misbecomes a gentleman. With this he bore a service of broiled fowl, hissing hot from the flames, and in truth it tasted in the mouth like burning coals. But the wine was well cooled in the bubbling fountain of the Salmons, and was very fragrant delicious claret, and light and easily carried in the belly and the head; so we were comfortable enough by dinner time. But when our meal was duly discharged, we called our host again, and craved him to set us a table and chairs under a shady mulberry in his garden, and this he easily granted us; so we were greatly at our ease, and sat listening to the roaring and shouting and singing of the multitude, whom no sun could keep quiet. But when the day began to cool and our wits to grow clear, we all asked the Seigneur of La Roche Nemours to devise some relation for us, since he came from beyond seas and could tell us of what we knew not. "Nay," answered he, "but the pleasantest adventure I have in my head was produced by your own soil of Gwent, and was recounted to me by a young clerk of Chepstow, with whom I journeyed this very day." "Let us hear it, by all means," quoth the Canon Cursal, "for I know this soil to be a rich and racy one teeming with good things both for mind and body. Wait but a moment while I move my chair, for the sun is gaining on me; and then do you devise." So sitting in the shade, hearing now and again above the noise and clamour closes and intonations of strange solemn music, that seemed to come from a ruined realm of faery, we hearkened to the stranger's tale of our own dear land.

THE QUAINT HISTORY OF A LORD OF GWENT, AND HOW HIS WIFE DESIRED TO SMELL A ROSE

Roger de Sco. Mauro was seised of his castle of Penhow when he was about twenty-five years of age, and was thought a fortunate young knight, since the estates of the St. Maurs were just now beginning to be in a very fat and prosperous condition, and to draw some blood out of the country. This was partly owing to a little agreement of three parts between Gilbert Marshall Seigneur of Estrighoil, Sir William de Sco. Mauro, and Morgan Howell, Seigneur of Caerleon; and the event of this agreement was that this Morgan Howell, aforesaid, was gently eased and relieved of his Manor of Woundy in Gwent Level; the which for the future did appertain to the noble house of St. Maur, who do not appear to have left their wits behind in Normandy. And with the manor went many a pleasant fish-pool, and mills and quit-rents and estovers, and a good slice by way of house-bote and hay-bote out of Wentwood Chase, as the old records of the Jury will tell you. With this, and a few small easements in addition, the walls of Penhow grew warm and comfortable, and when the place came to Roger, and the Steward had given him an account of his possessions, he determined to lose no time but to enjoy himself with all speed. So he called together a goodly flock of his boon companions who were many, and now increased every day, and bade them to Penhow that they might try his cellars, test the merits of the manorial preserves, and receive joy-bote and jest-bote from their entertainment. This summons, it will be supposed, met with few nays, and before long the manor-house overflowed with gay surcoats, who ate, drank, hunted, tilted, made love, and played ball with laudable hardiness; indeed between one thing and another, they gave themselves but little time for sleeping. Among these laborious persons were Sir Bogo de Knovill, Sir Dru de Dynam, Sir Philip de Bendeville, Sir William Denford de Crick, and many another stalwart lusty man, who was rather more important a few hundred years ago than now, the which must be my excuse for not giving you a roll of them all like the old blind clerk of Scio, or the glorious Virgilius; since they doubtless took time over their catalogues and trimmed and garnished them with choice adornments so that they are not tedious but smack smoothly in the mouth. But you may conceive if you can the trampling of the horses of this company as they rode up to Penhow, the glittering of the steel, the blaze of coat armour, and the fine clatter of old French, scraps of love-songs of Provence, or merry ballads from Paris town, and every now and then a rather strong expression by way of comma. I leave the gentlemen and pass to the ladies, who come last, like the canons in a procession; for one should always keep the best for last, and these ladies were assuredly creatures of rarity and art, diamonds of clear water. I know not precisely where they all came from, but they were finely dressed and well proportioned and seemed always cheerful and ready for a joke, in fact there is little doubt that Roger's feminine guests were exceedingly nice girls, though some severe persons have chid him for keeping bad company. I do not exactly understand what this phrase means, for no company is bad for a wise man; and I think the people who talk in this way cannot have heard tell of Socrates, the king of wisdom, who no sooner was advised of the advent of Madam Theodota, a notorious strumpet, to the dearly-beloved city of Cecrops than he cried out "by the dog" and (as if he had been bitten by a mad one) posted off to this pretty piece in a tremendous hurry. And you remember how he found a painter pleasantly employed in setting her on canvas, and how these two, the beautiful witty strumpet and the old goggle-eyed flat-nosed quintessencer, talked together, for you have without doubt read the *Pellakis ethaumasa.* And the moral of this is that Socrates knew what he was about, for he was a very great extractor of fifth essence, and that all of us, who are as logs compared to him, must touch our caps and not venture to contradict a word he said. And how anybody could call the Fair Ladies of Penhow, as this gay sisterhood was termed during their reign, bad company, is beyond my conceit; for I do assure you they had the most joyous dancing eyes,—blue, brown, grey, and black,—the sweetest little lips, soft sanguine cushions whereon the bare Lord of Love held Assize sempiternal, ever issuing blithe decrees, enunciating arrests, forging endless golden chains with sharp hooks to fasten hearts together, and engaging in his daintiest workmanship of kisses, to the which wares he imparts a perpetual variety, an unfailing sweetness, joys continual and ecstasies that are never wearisome. Shall we not therefore honour and reverence the place which gives us all these nice things; and is it right to talk of "bad company" in connection with such delicious dainties? But Loyse, Isobelle, and Erminie and Rosamonde served up all this fare in perfection, and pleased the gentlemen exceedingly, for they were not like some ignorant awkward girls that we have nowadays to whom a man is obliged to teach everything, owing to the horrible deficiencies in their education. But these damsels kept the knights amused, roused them up, and prevented them from being dull, if it rained; contrived all manner of jokes, sang love-ballads, played on the lute, and were all over the house, and on fine days, all round it; sitting in quiet nooks and putting their lovers through their paces. All this was fine sport for Sir Roger and his guests; but it must be confessed that it came rather expensive, since Penhow got such a name, that as soon as one knight had gone out at the gatehouse with his suite of steel-clad, bottle-nosed, and ever-draughty followers, two more came in, very hot and thirsty and ready for anything that was to be had. The ladies too could not live on air and love, poor dears, and their sweet little bodies and smooth dainty skins had to be filled with sweetmeats and choice wines; and besides these they had several small necessities, without which ladies cannot get on, but which cost a good deal of money when one has to pay the shot for a dozen or more. Whence it came about that after a few months of this fine fun it became expedient that Sir Roger de Sco. Mauro should try to draw his purse strings in very tight, and send all his merry guests about their business if he did not want them to run away with his woods and meadows, his commons, estovers, house-botes and heybotes, mills, fishpools, and everything that he had. But yet he was very loathe to do this, and had long conversation with Master Robert Pykott his steward, Father Hadrian his chaplain, and Dom. Hierome Jessaye, a man of law, who was full of expedients, and had assisted at synods like these many times before. And so it came pass that Sir Roger was forced often to leave all the mirth, laughter, and mellow sounding of the lutes, vyalls, and hand-organs, the fantastic quips of gallantry and the beautiful theories of the wondrous clerk of the Academy, the tales of chivalry and love, and the swift ball play against the high wall at the angle where it joins the tower; to meet the three sages who were all of them a little musty, and whose talk was dull. Inside a room of the tower they sat, with chests and hanapers and coffers all around them, and before the steward and the man-of-law were great vessels of ink, and long vicious-looking goosequills that made ugly marks against everything and wrote down unpleasant items. And the business was to inspect, peer into, tote up, balance, and certi-fy, charters, copyhold-rolls, receipts, grants, manor-lists; and to set these against sundry bills of debts that filled a capacious chest and seemed likely to lift the lid off their receptacle, to say nothing of lifting the lead off Penhow, the cattle off the meadows, and the fish out of the pool, if some order were not taken with them. Against these hideous bills the manor-rolls shewed very poorly, though they were famously written and engrossed on great skins of parchment, and as Master Hi-erome Jessaye declared, had been executed by an Italian clerk as beauti-fully and artificially as any he had ever seen. But as the man-of-law was pleased also to remark fair flourishes fill not full flagons, nor gold frets an abounding chest, and sometimes 'tis better to have a single live sheep than a dozen sheepskins; and the next time Master Hierome came to Penhow after making these facetious observations, he brought a little horn of red ink with him with which he wrote down terrible things that seemed to promise abundance of dry bread and as much cold water as it liked you for Penhow; and Roger began to recollect that there was no well in the castle and all the water had to be fetched in a bouget from the fountain down below, for hitherto he had looked upon his cellar and his ale-tubs as the only fountains with which he was concerned. Meanwhile Master Pykott was hard at work with a lot of little sticks notched all over with lines and figures, but the tallies had no more comfort in them than the rolls since the bills of debt were too strong for anything. In the midst of all this ink, parchment, and law-latin, Roger grew very sad, for he was not a good clerk, and did not like to see how fast Master Hierome's enormous quill leapt and flick-ered over the parchment, as if it were a bird of ravine; and it seemed to him that a man who wrote so quickly could not be good for any re-spectable family, in the which conjecture he may not have been far from the truth. And though the chaplain tried to ease his heart with comfortable and pious allusions to a fiery furnace, he got to feel quite down in the mouth, especially when a long bright ray of sunlight shot through the lattice and lighted on the municipal and forensic nose of Master Hierome Jessaye, shewing a few flaws and patches of faulty colour on this grand member, for one cannot expect to be good all round, and the carnations of the man-at-law were, it must be con-fessed, miserably botched. Then Sir Roger would fall to making com-parisons (impertinent as I conceive) between this nose and other noses he knew something about, especially the nose of dark eyed Maud, with whom he was said to be on very friendly terms. And by some Cervical Capitulary or Notional Law, the nature of which you will find fully ex-plained in Aristotle, Alexander Aphrodisiensis, Plotinus and other learned clerks, nose led him to eyes, eyes to cheeks, cheeks to lips, and so on, and so on; till he was deep in the consideration of privileges, quit-rents, and tolls entirely different from those noted in his muni-ments. How this came about I cannot exactly tell you, nor am I entirely certain as to whether all the doctors I have mentioned agree in their definitions and explanations; I thought the matter out some years ago but I confess that at present my head is slightly muddled on the sub-ject. But I have reason to think that this Law of the Brain is made ex-pressly on the behalf of hapless lovers, so that whether they see a squirrel eating nuts on a bough, a girl carrying clothes from the wash, or a man with a brown doublet, it is all one to them and in about a mi-nute and a half they are muttering to themselves "O my darling, my love, my dear, dear sweetheart, let me kiss thee, let me fondle thee, let me embrace thee but once again," or some nonsense of this description. And then they begin to recollect and run over everything, and their hearts seem to melt away and their throats get husky. So merely a sunbeam on a lawyer's nose sent Sir Roger off to a land of pretty fancies, and while he was thus a-maze, the sound of a rich mellow voice mounted up and came in like the ray of sunlight through the lattice, and with it tender lute-notes that tickled the heart, and bred love in excess. And this is what Sir Roger heard above the scraping and squeaking of Master Hierome's quill, in the muniment room of the tower of Penhow.

> *All through the nightertale I longed for thee,*
> *In loneliness, and hearkened for the door*
> *To open, or a footstep on the floor.*
>
> *O lief sweetheart, I pray thee pity me,*
> *I hunger for thy kisses evermore;*
> *All through the nightertale I longed for thee.*
>
> *Joyesse is turned to wo, and misery*
> *Is my solace, certes, my heart is sore.*
> *Yet these poor lips a smile at morning bore,*
> *Though all the nightertale I longed for thee.*

And then a slowly dying close on the lute, that seemed to tremble and thrill with love like the "yes" that comes at last, and to beat against the lattice like a bird against the bars of its cage. And seeing that Madam Maud was the chorister, you will not wonder that Sir Roger's head got between his hands, since this pretty girl was expensive in her habits and had cost him a lot of money, and he was so unfortunate as to be dreadfully fond of her; indeed her reproachful song was far from being deserved by her lover. But he knew that she was too great a luxury for a poor man, and it troubled him exceedingly to think with what inferior wares he would be forced to put up for the future. But his meditations were cut short by Master Hierome giving his final judgment that all these frolics must come to an end without delay, and that Sir Roger de Sco. Mauro would have to be content for a good many years to come with a rather retired and secluded manner of living. And the steward and the chaplain were obliged to confirm this decree, because

they saw there was nothing else to be done; so the man-of-law took a
new pen and began to make his arrangements for the payment of that
monstrous pile of debts, and Roger had to look on. And in a week's
time all the pleasant company had gone from Penhow to search for the
four winds, and Sir Roger was left to himself and had plenty of time to
consider affairs in general, and his lack of everything that was pleasant
and desirable, in particular; and it was at this cheerful season that a
white hair or two began to hang about his ears, and his smooth young
forehead began to shew faint lines here and there. And finding his
lonely life quite intolerable after the gay racket of the past, he determined to get out his best suit of armour, grind a keener edge to his
sword, sharpen his lance-head to as fine a point as a lady's little finger-
tip, and see if he could not pick up a living by breaking heads and
bounteous bloodletting. The which was, it must be agreed, a resolution
worthy of a brave man, the descendant of an ancient house, and
moreover a very salutary one, for anybody who understands mankind,
knows that the blood of most people is far too hot and superabundant,
hence he who makes it his business in one way or another to cool our
passions and make us more reasonable and less violent, is evidently a
great benefactor and philanthropist. But misfortune was already beginning to improve Sir Roger, and it made him come to this laudable determination of leaving his castle in Gwent Level, and going over sea to
ameliorate the condition of mankind and his own purse at the same
time. And before he had been seised of Penhow for a year and a day
he was on shipboard, having with him as esquire a young fellow from
his Manor of Woundy, whom he had noticed to be sharp witted and
handy in many ways, and not addicted to asking questions when his
lord told him to do anything. This esquire's name was Gilbert Tapp,
and though young, he was grim and stern-set of feature, and slow to
take in a joke; for this was the nature he had received from his father
and mother, who were by no means pleasant people. Thus the Knight
and Esquire made their way by land and sea to Germany, and some say
they remained there for more than twenty years in the service of divers
great nobles, now fighting for one and now for another, since so long
as the pay was good and there was plenty of employment neither Sir
Roger nor Gilbert cared a rap for whom they warrayed. Some say that
they went to the peninsula of Italy as well, and assisted to conclude the

various disagreements between the cities, duchies, principalities and kingdoms by vigorous applications of the Gwentian sword, spear, and battle axe; and that they were at the stricken field of La Grandella and in many other affairs of the same kind in connection with those troublesome two Sicilies. It is likewise recorded by one or two annalists that Sir Roger served Baldwin, second of that name, Emperor of Constantinople, and had to get out of the way very quickly on the night of July the twenty-fifth, when Alexius Strategopulos climbed over the wall and cleared out the Latins. But all agree that the Knight of Penhow carried the golden wings over battlements and breaches, through blood and fire and steel-hedges, most knightly and gloriously; and Gilbert Tapp followed close at his heels so that when Sir Roger poked a man in the ribs with his spear, the Esquire hit him hard over the head with his sword, and relieved him of any troubles that he might be destined to have in this mortal life. In this fashion they made themselves useful to their employers and got together a good many gold pieces, but the work was very hard and grew in time to be wearisome. For there are only a certain number of ways in which a man may be killed, and when you have gone through all these and begun again at the beginning, and are still drudging at the same mill, you begin to long for something fresh and cannot run your enemy through the breast or cleave him to the spine with any true art or relish for the business. Besides this constant warfare is like old Time and leaves certain indelible memorials in the way of scars, seams, holes, hacks, unhealed wounds, and tender places, for people will not be killed if they can help it and when hard pressed are apt to cut out their epitaphs on a hostile surface of flesh. And by the time Sir Roger had acquired a broad blue seam from his forehead to his jawbone, another across his left cheek, had lost one ear, and had gained a nasty wound in the side (Gilbert being rather worse off, for he was more obstinate) he began to consider that he had about enough of these memorial inscriptions written on him and that it would be a good thing to leave fighting to younger men for the future and rest his bones again in Gwent. And he felt that he might do this very comfortably, for besides a good round sum in money, he had some five or six chests full of brooches, rings, chains, and bracelets fashioned of the precious metals and for the most part of gold, together with a few emeralds, sapphires, rubies, diamonds and such like gauds, which he had picked up in the course of his busy life, for he was fond of curiosities of this kind and would say jokingly that no collector had such opportunities as a free-lance. I believe indeed that Sir Roger had enjoyed his little pleasures as well as worked hard during this stormy period of war and battle; and it seems credible that he had forgotten Madam Maud a good many years ago having in his time seen a great variety of ladies, grave and gay, hot and cold, moist and dry, black, brown, and tawny-yellow. Altogether he felt that it was high time to take things more quietly and to hang up the red banner with the golden wings in the hall at Penhow. And when he got home and began to examine into his accounts he found that all the old debts were paid, excepted only an item due to Master Hierome Jessaye, who had kept the manors warm, or as some said, had been kept warm by them. And since from an accurate observation and adding up it appeared that the man-of-law had already made a tolerable swarf-penny out of his stewardship, Sir Roger refused in a very decided kind of voice to pay him another farthing; and as his moustachios began to bristle like a hog's back and the scars of him to turn a fiery purple, Master Hierome was generous and forgave him his debt. This is what it is to deal with an upright honest lawyer; but some of them rob and pill their clients without mercy. And from that time Sir Roger led a very happy and respectable life at Penhow, amusing himself with keeping the people round about in order, looking after his privileges, and building a bit to the castle here and there, and maintaining open house and a hospitable table for all comers, but especially folk from over sea, for he liked to talk over old times and to hear how things were going on in the castles he had burnt, the towns he had stormed, and the families whose numbers he had reduced. To Gilbert Tapp he had given the captainship over the garrison, for it was necessary to be on the safe side and not to tempt one's neighbours to ransack one's money chest; a very sinful habit but a common one in those days and accompanied by such annotations as throat-cutting and general destruction and deviltry, so that the gloss was worse than the text. On this account a strong body of men-at-arms was maintained at Penhow, and the old battered and scored esquire took good care that they were well up to the mark and perfect in their exercises. In this sort Sir Roger lived till he was getting on in life and had seen the sun set on his grand climacteric; but as he was riding one day through the village it chanced that he met an old woman trotting along as fast as her legs would carry her. "Whither go you so fast, mother?" said Sir Roger. "If it please you to the wife of John-ap-Griffith," answered she. "And what would you do with her?" asked the Knight, for he felt curious, he knew not why. "Why I would be with her in her labour and ease her of her first child," answered the old woman, and this reply set Sir Roger a-thinking, though as I have said he was no great clerk. But it seemed very plain to him that if he waited much longer before begetting a lawful heir of his body the business was likely to fall through and the castle and manors would pass to his cousin, whose conversation he did not much relish. Wherefore he determined to set this matter in train as soon as might be, and to cast his eyes round the castles of Gwent for a pretty modest maiden to be his wife and to bear him (if God willed) a son, who should succeed him. On this behalf he consulted Gilbert, but not to any great purpose, forasmuch as the esquire was not addicted to the company of ladies, and even in his youth had had as little to do with them as he was able, and "I suppose we can't very well do without them" was the best word he had ever said of women-folk. But Sir Roger looked about him and took stock of all the noble marriageable maidens in Gwent, and found out as far as he could their virtues and defects, for he was determined that his wife should be somewhere near perfection (that is so near as a woman can be expected to attain) and it would have grieved him to have thrown himself and all his experience away on a girl that was at all flighty or misdemeanant in her habits. And as he had still that old weakness of his for black eyes and a well moulded breast; he had a good deal of trouble, for beauty and sense are not often met with in the same skin. But at last, when he was beginning to grow desperate, he saw one day at the Castle of Estrighoil a pair of eyes that pierced to his heart quite in the old delicious way, and on enquiry he found that the young lady to whom they belonged was called Eva de St. Pol and was of French parentage but had been an orphan for many years. And hearing from all hands sunset accounts of her, her beauty and her virtues, and being himself altogether in love with her innocent beseeching face, exquisite curves, and gracious ways, he in due form craved her hand of the Lord of Estrighoil who was her guardian and had authority over her. And as Sir Roger was known to have lined his coat pretty warmly with gold besants and was besides a very gentle and perfect knight who had maintained the honour of the Marches full valorously in the lands beyond sea, my lord and lady of Estrighoil considered him a good match for Eva who was poor and had hardly a carucate of land that she could call her own. As for the maid she made no difficulty over the business (not that it would have gone for much if she had) since she was sharp enough to find out that the old knight was deeply dyed with love for her, and hence Madam Eva foresaw that she would get her own way with him and rule joyously at Penhow. Of course she had one or two scruples over her betrothal, and could not help thinking rather sadly of the pretty speeches a young gentleman named Rupert de Launay had whispered in her ear; nay of certain occasions when he had misjudged his distance and put his mouth rather lower down; but perhaps Rupert knew something about the inwards of the ear and wished to communicate his intelligence by way of those pipes at the back of the gullet. But all these little talks had taken place the summer before, after evensong, in the alleys of the Rose Garden, and Rupert was far away, in strange countries; so it was no good speculating about him or his nice manners. Therefore in due course of time Eva de St. Pol was wed to Roger de St. Maur by my lord of Llandaff, who was observed to glance at the bridegroom rather doubtfully while he sang certain prayers, as if he thought he was wasting his breath. Nevertheless the old and the young were securely tied together and Eva pledged her troth to Sir Roger to be bonour and buxom in bed and at board, and there was feasting and high holiday in the hall of Estrighoil. So the knight took home his wife, who soon began to make the castle more lively than it had ever been since Madam Maud ruled the roast, for a girl of seventeen years will chase dulness out of most places with trills of laughter and song, bright eyes, gay gowns, and all those pleasant varieties, modes, and manners which do entrance us ever. And with the young wife comes a joyous procession of keen pages and artful chambermaids, who are versed in all sorts of tricks and waggeries, and run up and down the stairs and galleries, hide in the big aumbries, and are always inventing some fresh mystery, though the fable is always much the same. Well-nigh the first thing that Eva did was to ransack her husband's jewell caskets, trying on all the necklaces and brooches, and fitting her little white fingers with the finest rings she could discover, while her good man looked on, and at last pulled her on his knee and stroked her beautiful brown hair and kissed her, for he loved her better every day. And nine months after the wedding Eva gave her lord a sturdy son, who would doubtless have been like his father if he had happened to be seventy years old instead of an hour, and to have a bristling white moustache and shaggy eyebrows. It will be supposed that Sir Roger loved his wife none the worse after all his hopes were thus fulfilled, nevertheless his love was henceforth Platonicall; for he was not so strong as when he came to his estates, and had knocked about a good deal in his time. But though he was quite satisfied with one heir, Eva thought very differently on the matter, as was to be expected of a girl of eighteen, and kept exhorting her husband to the intent that it was advisable to provide Penhow with another branch, in case the first were by some misadventure to fail. And finding her admonitions, soft speeches, kisses, caresses and blandishments had no effect, only making Sir Roger look sheepish and ashamed of himself, she rang this peal in his ears all day and night, and endeavoured by every method to bring him to a sense of his duties towards her. But it was to no purpose, since the old knight could kiss her and stroke her and fondle her but nothing more, though he made himself rather ill by drinking the vile concoctions flavoured and spiced by a doctor of medicine, who had won a high repute by his treatment of these cases. It is to be feared however (by the leave of the Fratres Fraternitatis R. C.) that no beverages, though they be sopho-spagirically concocted, can make a young man out of an old one; certainly they did Sir Roger more harm than good and made him say ill-natured things of the physician and smash his vials. Hence poor Eva became very melancholy for want of love, and hushed her joyous singing and laughter, and spoke seldom and in a plaintive voice to the distress of her husband, who was happy in all else and especially in his son who grew every day to be a finer specimen of the stout old stock of St. Maur. And the pages looked at Eva slyly, as if they knew what ailed her, and with her women she often wept over her fate, as they worked at the tapestry; but it seemed as if there was no help for it, since Sir Roger was not likely to grow more vigorous as he got older. It is not to be wondered at then that Eva became fantastic in her habits, and thought strange sick thoughts within herself; on Monday she would be racing all over the house and making everybody stare at her frolics, and on Tuesday she sat in the same place from Prime to Evensong, spoke not a word, and ate nothing. On Wednesday she would hardly leave the Lady Chapel of the church, but on Thursday her romping mood returned again; so that in one way or another she did her best to torment her husband and her companions out of their lives, for no one ever knew what would happen next. But one day it fell out that as Sir Roger and his lady sat at meat, a stranger came into the hall, for the knight still continued to welcome travellers and to listen to their tales and adventures. This man was clothed in a habit of brown and yellow with long hanging sleeves and there was a gold bracelet of curious workmanship on the wrist of his right arm; his face was quaint and his eyes most keen and piercing. And while he spoke all kept silence and held the morsel they were to eat in their fingers, waiting for his words; because he told them of wonders in a deep sweet voice that seemed to come from far away; and none had ever heard stories like these told of the man in brown and yellow. For all his talk was of the High Levant, and the Isles of India, and the great marvels and miracles that are done in those parts, and the curious arts that are understood there, such as negromancy, geomancy, pyromancy and the like, and how there are islands and cities in the which dwell no living man, but multitudes of spirits and ghostly people, who now and again come among men and take mortal women to wife. And while he recounted these strange histories his face never changed a whit, but his voice rose and fell and thrilled like the organs when they are played skilfully, and it sank deep into the hearts of all who were at the board. But Eva was more enchanted than the rest by the odd deviser, and would have him come to her bower after dinner, that she might still listen to him, for his voice stirred up old memories in her heart and made her think of the alleys of Estrighoil Castle and likewise of Rupert de Launay, though for the life of her she could not discover why it was so. And being seated on a stool, the stranger began his incantations anew, and talked more and more wildly and fantastically, till Eva and her women thought the walls were turning round and the floor heaving, and took hold of each other's hands and squeezed them hard as though they had been a bevy of lovers. And this is how the brown and yellow man brought his histories to a close. "Now," said he, "'tis almost time for me to be gone, since I must sup tonight with the Lord of the Castle of Rohalgo; but one more relation I will devise for you. Know that in the realm of the Great Chan there is an exceeding vast desert, to cross the which you shall journey five years, if you have good camels and skilled guides who lead you by the shortest way. But 'tis more like that you take ten years, and few care to travel through this wilderness, preferring to journey along the border of it, by a track where there is victual and provender for them and their beasts. And some say that there are no wells nor fountains, nor trees, nor any green thing nor living creatures throughout the whole length and breadth of this desert; but this is not the truth, for I talked with a wise man of Cathay who used geomancy, and he shewed me the nature of the place, and gave me such reasons that I perceived he was not lying nor deceiving me. Know then that toward the midst of the wilderness there is a great circle of sand that never is still, but heaves up and down in waves and breakers like the waves of Ocean, and this compass of sandy sea is about ten miles in breadth, so that none can pass through it save by a miracle and art magick. For so quick is it that it sucks in and draws down whatever is cast into it and in a moment of time, since it is full of whirlpools. But if any man could reach the other side, he would see a country as fair and fruitful as any in the world, with meadows, woods, running brooks, orchards all most green and pleasant to the sight. And on the hills are castles, fairer and stronger than any in Christendom, with towers and pinnacles that cannot be conceived, insomuch as the images adorning them are ten times the height of a man, and from the ground seem to be puppets; and the sound of the bells chiming in the high belfries is heard of still evenings in Ermony and India from a distance of many thousand leagues. And they who live in that country are men descended from the giants that in old time dwelt upon the earth, and they have many arts and mysteries of which we can understand nothing, and to strive after this secret knowledge is great sin in common men. But one marvel they have that they sometimes impart to us; for they know of our affairs and have intelligence of things which are done by us in privity, and sometimes will grant boons to them that are deserving of the same. Understand then that there grows in this land a manner of tree, with a blossom somewhat like a rose, for it is red in colour, but in each flower there are twelve leaves, and it is fairer to see than any rose, because the hue of it is not fixed nor always the same, but seems like fire all glowing and palpitating, so that it is a very glorious sight. And whosoever smells the scent of one of these flowers forgets all the bitter memories and sorrows of his past life, grieveth no more for present woe, nor is able to be touched by any ill fortune that may come; since from the eyes of him that smelleth the thick veil falleth away, and he beholdeth the wondrous beauty of the things which verily are; and his ears are opened and the everlasting musick soundeth in them, so that in a moment of time his old life becomes like a dream a man dreamt when he was a boy, and remembers faintly all his days. And the sweet imaginations which come now and again into the minds of all of us, dimly and staying but an instant, by the scent of the rose blossom gloriously like unto it, and abide for evermore; and in the brain of him that has smelt this bloom of færy an old rhyme still runs—

> *We have a quiet place wherein to dwell.*
> *A quiet place wherein to hear the swell*
> *Break with a deep dull roar upon the land*
> *And rattle of the pebbles on the strand*
> *And rain come pattering on the closed door*
> *But we shall rest for evermore.*

And, as he finished the rhyme, the stranger rose upon his feet and looked Eva de St. Maur through and through for a moment, then he did reverence and went forth, and they never saw his face again; though some pretended to see the brown and yellow robe moving swiftly along the passages of the Castle of hot summer nights, for many a year after; but these clever personages are suspected to have had the sun still in their eyes or to have seen double. But when the stranger had left the bower Eva and her ladies all sat quite still and close together, for their hearts were beating swiftly and their breasts heaving violently, and their breath came quick and short; while the blood ran a furious course through their veins even as the knights make their onset of battle. And it is well known that all these symptoms are bad ones, prognostic of mischief, especially if ladies are thus affected, since they are a little apt to let their imagination get the better of them, and to kick poor old Master Logick in his tattered gown and rusty cassock out of doors. And who comes in when Genus and Species go out? Why the most puissant prince and paramount Lord Phantasy, all gallantly bedecked in gold and green, bringing with him a host of mad whimsies, who are his great officers of state; and his Lord Marshall is none but Love. And to be plain these giddy girls made wild work that night, and for some nights after, and stored up trouble for themselves which made them wish they had never heard the stranger's voice, for they all agreed that it was this, rather than the matter of his stories, which turned their heads and made them forgetful when they ought to have remembered. But in Eva's brain the relation of the Rose took root, and grew day by day, till she forgot or seemed to forget her old trouble in this new one, for now her one desire was to smell the wondrous blossoms, and she longed for the scent continually and was always saying to herself "Oh, if I could but smell the flower!" Sir Roger, who as I have shewn had seen a good deal of the world in his time, had heard many strange stories, and talked with many strange people, endeavoured to laugh this notion out of his wife's head; for as he told her he had lived long enough to find out that all soils produced an abundant crop of lies, but especially the soil of the Levant, where fictions attained to a monstrous height and luxuriance. As for the man in brown and yellow he cursed him and denounced him for the most malicious and damnable liar that this world had ever generated, and swore by *Corpus Domini,* St. Michael the Archangel, the candid host of martyrs, and all the whole company of saints that if he ever came within the lordship again, he should go hot-foot to his father, the devil, and tell his tales to the fiends of hell. This was, it must be confessed, rather violent language, but Sir Roger was in fact a little angry with the man for turning Penhow upside down, making the girls giddier than they were before, and crazing Eva by his nonsensical tales which nobody in his wits credited, though the knight confessed that they were amusing enough to listen to. And if the traveller had returned it is probable that Gilbert Tapp would have treated him roughly and played him some scurvy tricks; but he knew better, and those who saw his vestment were never able to catch him up for he walked too fast. Meanwhile Eva still pined after the rose, thinking of it during the day, and dreaming hot dreams of it at night, and still, sleeping or waking her words were "Oh, if I could but smell the flower."

But who do you think was seen at Penhow one fine morning in

May, when the shade began to be more pleasant than the sun, and the young beech-leaves shone like silver? Why none but the old lover Rupert de Launay, who had returned from over sea no richer than when he left Estrighoil, for he had not Sir Roger's wit, but was stuffed with all sorts of rubbish about glory and gentle deeds, and a fair fame; so you may be sure he found that most people took him at his word, and let him fight for these fine entities and abstractions without troubling such a mirror of chivalry with more salt than would keep his lance in rest and his arm strong. By some means he tickled Sir Roger in the right spot and obtained free quarters and a hearty welcome at Penhow, where he took the pages under his care and taught them the science of arms, and all manner of knightly courtesies, philosophies, and refinements, such as they would never have learned from Gilbert, who looked very grim when he heard the things that began to be spoken of at dinner and in the evening, for these niceties did not enter into his system of chivalry, which dealt less with theory than practice. As for Sir Roger he leant back in his high elbow-chair and laughed at all the high-flown nonsense and romantic methods with which Rupert seasoned his discourse; and as he laughed he asked himself "where should I have been now, if I had warrayed for the love of glory?" and then he shook his head and looked wise and winked at Gilbert Tapp. But Eva paid little or no heed to Rupert or his talk, and tho' she would speak to him kindly enough it was plain that she had quite forgotten the sweet susurrations of the garden of Estrighoil, or if she remembered them it was with no particular desire to renew an ancient amity. And Rupert on his side was either with the sprouting chivalry, or hunting in Wentwood Chase, or talking to the old knight, to whom he did great reverence, as to a right worshipful and valiant warrior (and indeed Sir Roger had been all this in his day) and listened to his tales of fights, sieges, and stormings of strong places. And in appearance Rupert de Launay was as proper and personable a man as the chivalry of Christendom could shew, standing six feet high, and well proportioned in his limbs, and being somewhat thin of face, though very handsome with a clear olive skin and deep blue eyes. And when he wore the surcoat given to him by the Emperor, which had his bearings exquisitely worked thereon—or, three ravens sable party per pale a palise gules and or—he looked a very fine specimen of a knight and seemed to have stepped out of the great book of romances from which he was used to read aloud on wet days and at candle-time. Hence you will not wonder that the girls grew soft hearted over this fine gentleman, for they love strength, valour, and gallant manhood and also high-flown romantic fantasy; so that when these qualities cohere in the same substance they are by nature strongly drawn and attracted to it. But Rupert de Launay seems not to have troubled himself greatly to encourage their fancies; for he was flying at more noble game, and studying the ground before he sat down and besieged the place in form. And it appears that he took the trouble to make himself throughly acquainted with the Chronicles of Penhow, so far as they related to my lady Eva, thus the keen pages told him all about her melancholy because she might not have another child, and also of the visit of the man in brown and yellow, and of her longing to smell the wonderful twelve-petaled rose that grew in the great wilderness. And when Rupert had found out these facts, and pondered them over in his mind, it is likely that he put them together and found links where nobody else had seen any, for he is acknowledged to have been very artful in the conduct of this affair, and to have shewn great strategy and opiniastrety therein. For you must understand that all the while he was oversea he had cherished and cockered up his love for Eva St. Pol, keeping her portraiture before him when the trumpets sounded, and the steel began to ring; never telling his nearest friend a word about her, but burning his lamp of love in secrecy till the flame of it made the heart of him white hot and scorched his brain. And when at last he returned to Gwent and found his mistress the wife of old Sir Roger, he would doubtless have done well to look out for another sweetheart, but he rather added oil to the flame and determined to win her by one means or another. And after he had been about three months at Penhow, he found himself walking in the garden in the cool of evening, knowing, it may be, that Eva often came there after evensong alone, to gaze at the sun sinking slowly into the deep glades of Wentwood, and to fancy it the likeness of the rose of Cathay, as the red lights began to burn and glow. And in due time, after Rupert had cast many a glance at the opening in the box hedges, his lady came, clothed in a dress of creamy white, the which fitted the curves of her body to admiration, and did not make the lover any cooler or less ardent. And it may be noted that these two seemed intended for one another, for both had skins of clear olive, and a feature beautifully cut out; and in Eva's eyes there was a great yearning and desire for she knew not exactly what, and also in Rupert's though he understood quite plainly what he wanted. And when she saw Rupert, she seemed to wonder a little, for the garden was no haunt of his; but merely gave him good evening as he bent before her, and then they stood a long time side by side watching the sunset. And when the lord of day had descended some while into his western habitations, a curving line of dappled cloud that rose like a serpent from above old Kemeys tower, and mounted afar into the vault of heaven, began to change from pale yellow to deep gold, from gold to red, and at last became most bloody and fiery gules, which signifieth the love of our neighbour. And for a moment Rupert gave a side glance at Eva's face and saw tears in those beautiful yearning eyes, then he broke silence saying "And yet that streaming sanguine cloud is pale beside the ardour of the petals of the Rose." Instantly his lady turned to him, full eagerly and impatiently, and said "What do you know of the Rose, who can gain a blossom for me, is it indeed so precious and beautiful?" "No man can tell its excellence," answered he, "its glory goes beyond all mortal wit, and they who talk of pleasure, not having smelt its fragrance, do but babble out of square, and speak of that they know not." And she "Ah, who will gain it for me, since my husband says that it is a lie and a deceit." And he answered "I, Rupert de Launay, have crossed the whirl of sand and the terrible billows of the quaking wilderness; and for you and you alone, I gathered a blossom from the fairest tree of all, that grows in the pleasaunce of the Cloud Castle of Rohalgo. Hark do you not hear the chiming of a hundred bells as from a far distance; for this is a sign from the Lords of the Land?" And indeed Eva heard bells enow deeply ringing, but 'twas within her brain they rung, for she was filled with rapturous joy. And she said "Give me the flower O thou true loyal knight, that I may satisfy my longing." But Rupert answered "That will I, but O my darling, my delight, my treasure, let me kiss thy lips and take thee to my arms, let me slake the thirst with which I am consumed; for am I not thy lief sweetheart who has never ceased to long for thee." And without waiting for an answer he cast his arms about her neck and drew all her body and her face close to him, and kissed her lips as though he would never have done. And

Eva said not a word but let him squeeze her and kiss her to his heart's content since she thought it a small price to pay for the thing he had promised her; and beside she was a woman who, in fact, had no husband so that this love dalliance was by no means disagreeable. And before very long she answered his lips with hers, after the manner prescribed in the Use of Paffo, and practised by all lovers, and threw one white arm around Rupert's neck, so that altogether there was not much room left between them. And while they still kissed and clung to one another; there came a man stealthily and secretly behind the high hedge of the garden, moving like a cat before it springs, and bending down and listening for the sound of his own breath. This was none other than the old esquire Gilbert Tapp, who had seen Rupert go into the garden, and had watched him there from the tower; hence he had perceived how the knight talked with Eva; but when it came to kissing, he felt that he had his sword and ran down the tower stair, for it seemed to Gilbert that this fine couple were getting on rather friendly terms. Then he went softly and quickly beside the hedge, intending to creep behind Rupert and to kill him as he stood, the which he could have done very easily and not have hurt Eva, being an exceeding cunning and dexterous swordsman. And it seems probable that he would have accomplished his desire; but just as Rupert began to grow more ardent and his hands to wander indiscreetly; Gilbert entangled his foot in a bough that stretched across the path, and fell headlong to the ground with a hideous clatter of steel and a dreadful storm of oaths, for this mischance vexed him. At this Eva cried out "O leave me, begone, there's no time to spare, in five minutes the guard will be out, and we surrounded, make haste, speed you, make haste, for your life." And Rupert answered speaking swiftly as well he might: "Farewell; but when you hear them singing *It is ordained by Love's decree*, look for me." So saying he leapt away, and vanished into the woods, while Gilbert swore hard, since when he got to his feet, he was dizzy and staggered from side to side, as if he were half seas over. Meanwhile Eva ran by another way to her bower, and sat down in no little fear as to what her husband might do or say when he came to hear Gilbert's story. The which, you may be sure, was recounted presently, with due emphasis and perspicuity, to the great astonishment of Sir Roger, who had never thought to be troubled with an adventure of this kind; and passed his hand across his forehead as if he expected to find certain protuberances already sprouting out therefrom. Gilbert was for sending out a party to raise hutesium et clamorem, to scour the woods, ransack the barns, poke spears into the mows of hay, and explore the ditches: "'tis ten to one," said. he, "we should catch the young devil curled up in some cranny, and thus take away the risk of any mistakes in the future." But Sir Roger answered "No, no, he's far away by this, you may be sure, and I expect will put Severn Sea betwixt him and Penhow before morning; and I suppose we shall hear his tales of chivalry no more. Let him go then, for after all there was no great harm done, and you know Gilbert, young blood is warm." Then Sir Roger dismissed his captain, and sent for Eva, to whom he discoursed at some length on her folly and misdemeanour, promised her faithfully to cut Rupert de Launay into little pieces if he could catch him, and sent her away, to all appearance penitent, but in fact exultant, since Eva was now very artful. How was this? Why, because she was in love and had all the chambers of her mind illuminated by a clear dazzling light that shewed her everything more plainly than the tapers shew the waxen images on a king's hearse; and as she went she laughed to herself and sang *It is ordained by Love's Decree* but very softly. But you must observe that she flattered herself all the while that it was the Rose she longed for and not her lover's lips; though she confessed that Rupert's system of kissing was vastly superior to any methods her husband practised. So from this sweet yet dreadful night Eva walked about the castle delicately, living in a beautiful dream world full of rosy clouds and fancies, and languorous delights which made her blush when she was alone. But you may be sure that as she walked, stood, sat, or lay down, in hall or bower, in her garden or on her bed, she kept her ears wide open for the signal, knowing not from what quarter it should come. And her husband on his part forbade her to go beyond the walls of the castle, and set a watch upon her, whilst Gilbert and his men at arms were continually vigilant, and let not so much as an old woman pass the gate unquestioned. And Eva smiled to see their care, for she knew that Rupert loved her, and that no portcullis can keep out love, who always manages to slip through the holes and to pass the guard on his blind side, for the little god is very crafty. And one evening about six o'clock as Eva paced beside the box hedges in her clinging dress, looking very beautiful in the mellow light of evening, a boy's voice suddenly began to sing *It is ordained by Love's Decree* and looking upward she saw one of the pages walking on the gallery of the tower, and trilling out his melody carelessly and gaily enough as if he knew of nothing better to do. Quickly she turned away and leant against a plum tree, for the fierce blood surged up over her breasts and neck and face, and she trembled exceedingly, not knowing what might happen next, or whether Rupert might not be within a stone's throw of her. But looking all around she saw no one, and the page's song had come to an end, and he was leaning against the beams of the gallery with his chin on his hands. And soon after the twilight came on, and Eva walked unsteadily to her bedchamber and made her women undress her and then leave her, save one girl whom she trusted and who slept in the same room on a smaller bed. But Sir Roger slept not with her and had not done so for many years. This wench Eva cautioned, so soon as they were alone, and bade her sleep her soundest and on no account to see or hear anything till dawn, speaking half in jest and half in earnest; and the girl laughed merrily and promised to be as deaf and blind as the bed-posts, for she scented a mystery, and relished having some sort of a part to play therein, though it were a mute one. And Eva lay with her eyes wide open, listening for every sound, and thinking every moment that the door was moving; but it was midnight before her wish was fulfilled. And I believe she had at last fallen asleep, and was aroused in the sweetest manner that can possibly be conceived, namely by the warmth of a pair of eager lips pressing on her own, and the first words she heard were pleasant words enough though trite being "my darling." And here I think we had better leave Eva and her gallant who had to make the best excuses he was able for not bringing the Rose with him, the which I doubt not, he did to admiration. But I deem it worth while to tell you how he contrived to get inside Penhow, guarded as it was by men trained in war, for the manner of it was very curious and artful. You must know then that Rupert, in those days when he was elaborating his plans and marking out a course of amorous adventure, had foreseen that he was more likely than not to be surprised in the midst of his first onset, and like a wise general had heedfully provided for this event. For so gallant and brave a knight was he that the risk and hazard spurred him on and strengthened his resolve; and well he knew how swiftly his sword leapt from the scabbard, and how surely it cut through steel and flesh and bone, for he had made this blade to drink the life-blood of mighty warriors. Therefore he was all the more re-solved to bring the affair to a conclusion, and took order wisely so as to be prepared for the event. For he practised with a page whom he favoured above his fellows, and instructed him that if he, Rupert, went suddenly from Penhow, this page was to coin an excuse and the third morning after come to the tallest oak tree by Kemeys Tower, and there wait for him. Also Rupert had won over by fair words and gold pieces the two men in the castle who commonly fetched water from the well below, and they had promised him to do his pleasure in the fashion he shewed to them. And when Rupert was forced suddenly to flee away, right as Sir Roger said, he passed over Severn Sea; but returned in time to meet his factor by Kemeys, and then and there taught him how he was to sing the song in Eva's hearing, and likewise charged him to warn the two watermen, that they should delay their office as late as they were able, and drive all folk away from the well. Thus these fel-lows waited till it was quite dark, and then drew the great barrel-on-wheels down to the fountain, giving many a glance to right and left, for they knew that if this complot were discovered, there would be a noose and a ladder for each of them. And no sooner did they come to the well than Rupert de Launay stepped out of the darkness; off went the head of the barrel, and in he crept, and so was drawn up the hill and through the gateway of Penhow and remained curled up where the water should have been, till he thought all safe and made his way across the courtyard and up the stair, and so woke his sweetheart with a kiss. But the next day it was discovered that there was no sign of moisture in the cask, it was as droughty as a field in summer; every-body was interrogated as to this strange circumstance, but none knew anything of the matter; and the watermen swore that the machine was heavy enough to draw up the night before; and this indeed was noth-ing but the truth. And Rupert lay concealed all through that day in Eva's chamber; nor did the time pass wearily, for his mistress came to him ever and anon, and stayed with him as long as she dared, since she thought no more of any rose but love, the which she now tasted for the first time, and could not satiate herself therewith. But you may suppose that the girl who slept with Eva was posted conveniently and kept a sharp look out for the enemy, lest the sweethearts should be interrupted in their sport by the whistling of a sword blade, and have no time to put their affairs in order, or to look about them. To be short the dear day of love came to a close all too soon, as such days mostly do, and when it was dark again the wench rapped at the door of the chamber and said "They are ready." I doubt not gentlemen you have heard and read a good deal about the farewells that take place on these occasions, and maybe have had experience in the matter (saving always your Canonical reverence) so I will cut my tale as short as the lover's final kiss was long, and briefly tell you that by good luck, (as I believe) more than anything else, the gallant got again into the barrel and was trundled out of Penhow Castle and down the hill. I conceive however that he laid as firm a hold upon his sword as he was able when Gilbert stopped them by the gate, and adjured the men to make no more mistakes as to the water, if they desired to escape the lash: and as he spoke gave the cask a sounding blow with his truncheon by way of emphasis. But that was all; so Rupert leapt out in safety, bountifully rewarded the carriers, and sped away, no one knows whither, for his hiding place at this period has never been revealed. And so soon as Sir Roger's mind was set at ease about his wife, he hindered her not from walking abroad with her women, as she had formerly been used; and one day not long after whenas Eva and the girl in whom she trusted were pacing through a wood near Penhow, a splendid knight and his yeoman came riding after them and reined in their horses. Then the knight drew up Eva bidding her fear not and cling close to him, and the yeoman made a place for the wench, so with a joyous blast on the horn, they rode away beneath the trees, the boughs closed behind them and they were seen no more in Gwent. But that very morning Gilbert Tapp had cursed a page for trilling out from the gallery *The swallows fly the greenwood shade, To flit across the sea, And there the joyous sun hath made A merry home for me: Far from the forest glade.* Hence it came to pass that Sir Roger de Sco. Mauro was left alone with the grim old squire; and passed his time chiefly in looking at the rings and jewells Eva had liked best and in wondering what she could have found so desirable in Rupert de Launay. But he died soon after, expressing to the last a poor opinion of wedlock, and exhorting his son to feel his way very carefully when he came to have truck with womenfolk. As for Eva and her paramour they are stated to have fled to France, and to have lived a merry life there, meeting with no particular misfortunes, but getting off scot-free in this world at any rate. And there is certainly in Picardy a right noble and illustrious house of that name, who dwell in a fine castle, and trace their line to one of Charlemagne's Paladins; but whether this family had its root in the unlawful love of Eva and Rupert does not certainly appear. But there is trouble when seventy is matched with seventeen.

Thus the Seigneur of Roche-Nemours brought his tale to an end, and as he finished the strange musick that had sounded brokenly all the while, came clearly on the cool breeze of evening to our ears, and died away to a wistful sighing close. And we all praised the story, but the Cursal Canon could not bear that Eva and her leman should escape their temporal punishment. And he urged my lord to mend this, if he recounted it again, and to drown the pair of lovers within sight of France, especially if any illiterate persons were within earshot. "For" (said he) "though the dull and gross idiots are slow enough to extract morality from what they hear, they snuff out lechery, give tongue, and follow after it as briskly as a good hound scents the fox. And the very same folk are the worst backbiters and most malicious, and if they heard your name would turn up their eyes and whine out 'Alas! Alas! he tells very wanton tales. I fear he lives but lewdly.'" "Truly, father, I believe you speak the truth," answered my lord, "and for the future I will follow your counsels and make these poor sinners die most miserably and wretchedly; or better still, Eva shall live and turn into a shrew, and so make Rupert's days a burthen unto him." And now the sky began to darken, and the mists to rise from the river, so we called our host and paid our shot, and went forth into the town, that was by this time beginning to resound with genuine mirth and to exhibit pleasant personages far gone in Silurianism. But the Cursal Canon gave us his blessing and bade us farewell, for he was purposed to ride as far as Abergavenny and to lie there for the night. And at his departure we were sorry, for he was a devout, fat man, and we had hoped to hear from his lips some fine story of the old Decretal Days, or other pleasant case drawn from the Records of St. David's Chapter. Nevertheless we passed an hour or two pleasantly, wandering to and fro among the Silurians, and watching their amusements, and above all we delighted to hear odd scraps of talk as folk went by us, and strove to make sense out of such phrases as "came softly and scraped the key-hole," "she knows you not yet, and asked me the other day who you were," "it was for the third time and her mother." But I strove all the while to find out the musick I had heard from the garden, being desirous of hearing them play some piece from beginning to end, but there was no vestige of them to be seen. I believe Phil Ambrose would have willingly stayed in the streets all the night, for such festivals as this were his chiefest joy, and he walked with his head on one side smiling quaintly to himself. But since the Rubrican, Tom Bamfylde, by dint of running like a coney into every burrow with a sign or a bush above it, was becoming very drunk and somewhat tedious, we were resolved to make a start, and waited for him at the door of an inn, but still he came not forth. At last I went after him and going dubiously along a passage that seemed to be without end, found my companion seated in the easiest chair, smoking, drinking, and talking all at once; and in front of him on the settle was a row of olden gray-beards of Uske, who seemed to be listening attentively to his facetious discourses. Forthwith I made my way through a thick cloud of smoke and made Tom follow me out; the which he was very loathe to do, since he was a man apt to hang over his cups. Yet before ten struck we were on horseback, and had sped over the bridge; and went together till the turning to Landevennoc, and here my Lord of Roche-Nemours left us, for his way was to Caerleon. Then we fell into single file, and Phil Ambrose set a catch going, and so with singing we passed through the solemn scented night, and strove to make the journey fro as pleasant as it had been to.

THE JOURNEY HOMEWARD

Thus we had accomplished about a half-part of our returning, when we came to a place where a steep hill rises from the road, and a path goeth up therefrom, passing through a thicket on the bank, and leading into a deep and gloomy wood. And in the midst of this brake is a tall beech-tree, and around it a space of smooth, short grass, the which is cool and green even in the thirstiest droughts of August. And as we drew near to this place we saw the flame of a fire burning therein, and suddenly came a strain of sweetly measured musick, like a nightingale singing, and we could hear voices speaking a foreign tongue. Then the flute (for such it was) hushed, and a violin began a low descant, but swelled and thrilled, and rose (it seemed) in lamentation; but changed anon to a solemn tune like church musick, with long sustained notes and ancient closes. Then a lute began its amorous song, and a tenor voice chimed in with it and sang so sweetly a love-song of Italy that each of us thought of his mistress and wished her at hand. But when this was finished they all began to talk again in their vowelled speech, and then we determined to send an ambassador to this company that, if they willed, we might hear something more of their art. So I got off my nag and began to climb the bank, making my way in and out among the hazel-bushes, the wild raspberries, the maples, and the brambles, now ducking my head to escape a stiff bough, and now picking my way amidst the thorns, guiding my steps by the glare of the fire, and the sound of voices. At last I pushed aside two meeting bushes of may-thorn and stood within the circle. In the midst was the great beech, and its boughs stretched widely out on all sides, and rustled in the wind; below it a fire of dry sticks was piled up, crackling and blazing bravely and casting an uncertain and fantastic light on the musicians who sat around it. To whom I doffed my beaver and told them that I with some other honest gentlemen had heard their choice melodies as we passed on our way, and by their leave would gladly join their session under the beech-tree, and pay handsomely to hear them at greater length. And when I had done, a man who seemed to be the eldest of them answered me in indifferent English, bidding me and my companions welcome, very courteously and floridly, "for," said he, "all lovers of good musick are our brothers." So I called out to Nick Leonard and he and the other two came slowly up, as best they could, cursing now and then as a bough rapped in their eyes or a bramble tripped them up. And when they had found their way, we all sat down together, and the elder man began to inform us as to the condition of his band, and their manner of living. "We are," he began, "a company of musicians from Italy; this young fellow who is sitting on the root of the tree and eating sweet-cakes is called Giacomo Corelli of Aspignano; he plays the viol d'amore and is something of a poet. Next to him you see there squats a little fat fellow (by your leave Nanni); his name is Giovanni Mosca, Siena gave him birth, and the flute is his instrument.

Next you have the sweet lutist, who softens maidens' hearts and makes lovers sigh, he is of Babbiena, and is called Piero Latini. Fourthly Coppo Cacci of Pisa, whose art on the violin you heard but lately; and lastly myself, who love the bass-viol better than any other instrument, and am styled Andrea Galliano of Perugia. As to our business it is to wander upon the earth, and make musick for men, who are good enough to let us live in return, and indeed your men are as a rule harmless creatures enough, though sometimes a little brutish." "And how did you fare today?" asked Phil Ambrose, "for I suppose you have been at Uske." "Right well," answered Andrea, "for the people made much of our musick all the morning and thumped down their pieces as heartily as one could wish; and indeed your folk are by no means devoid of harmony; for as we played I noted often how now one, now another of the crowd would edge close to us, hum the tune over once or twice to himself, then throw his head back, and sing to our playing in a full tenor voice, though somewhat slowly. And they tell me that the words are improvised, even after our own Italian manner, and that your Welshmen commonly practise this art, and glory in it: and it seemed to me that the Welsh tongue is very fit for singing and rolls from the throat richly and gloriously. But lord! how the people delighted themselves when the singing and the musick came together, and showered money on us, and would have us drink ale and still drink more, and themselves swilled down more of ale and cyder than I could have conceived. But the best part of our day was in the afternoon, when as we were going up the street a serving-man came and fetched us into a house, and led us through a long passage into a court, and from the court by a green alure, and thence into a fair garden, where were several ladies and gentlemen, of right noble houses as I suppose. These were sitting under a yew tree and had a table spread with a very white and comely piece of damask before them, and on it were flasks of wine, and cups of Venetian glass, and plates of sweetmeats. Then they bade us play for them our most excellent and curious musick; and I was in some doubt as to what I should choose, so I asked Giacomo and he bade me notice that these personages were all noble lovers, and must be fed with strange mystical melodies, and quaint dances, joyous exaltant love-songs, and wailing, forlorn lamentations, following fast upon one another. So we made them as fantastic fare as we were able, and it pleased us to note how hands stole together, and shy glances were interchanged; one put his arm upon the table and so shielded bent down and kissed his sweetheart's forehead, and none could laugh for all were stung alike. Then at sunset a gentleman, whose garden it seemed to be, rose up and praised us mightily for our musique, 'and all of us,' said he, 'praise you, but the ladies (and here he took off his hat) most of all, and if you and your company were ever with us our mistresses would never have to call us to account for hearts tender and soft no more.' Then he himself served us with wine and sweetmeats and we drank a health to those beautiful ladies, whose comeliness is more perfect than that of Tuscan maidens, for our girls are burnt up by the sun. And when the servant led us away he gave me a purseful of gold, and so we shall think often of that garden of Uske and pray for the good success of the noble lovers in love and in all other their concernments." "And whither are you now bound?" said I. "We are never bound," answered the young man, Giacomo Corelli, "but wander hither and thither as the fancy takes us, setting smooth times against rough, and warm sunshine against the bitter wind and sky of lead. For our chief delight is to have no fixed times or places but to go where we list, and to be ready for any adventure that may befall us, since if our affairs are unprosperous and our hearts sad, we have our musick and our songs of Tuscany; and he that has art, whether of sweet colour, or sweetly measured words, or sweet closes of melody, should deem himself blessed and be very thankful to God, though his cup be dry, his platter empty and his journey through life grievous." "You speak with reason, I think," said the little fellow called Mosca, "but yet meat and wine are good creatures and make the skin smooth and comfortable; wherefore let us sup, and afterwards these gentlemen shall hear how we fulfil all our bragging of our art." Nor did they delay but opened their wallets and drew out little dainties and sundry flasks and made us share with them: and piled more sticks on the fire from a heap at hand, and then was heard a crackling and hissing from the greener bark, joined to a gurgling noise as one flask after another was tossed into the air. "Certainly," said Tom, the Rubrican, "if this be a sample of your victual, I think you fare well, and I believe I shall take down my father's old vial and join your company." "Ah! sir," answered Piero Latini (a man with thin jaws that worked fast) "'tis not often that we sup so decently. But you must know that having our purses full this evening we determined to give our bellies good cheer, and looked about us to find a confectioner. And after some dispute we fixed on a little shop near the bridge, with a window hanging over the road; and bade the girl who waited bring us the choicest delicates she had. But this wench was one of your modest maidens with a black and roving eye, who see more of what goes on in the street than in the shop, so she called her father, who was certainly a very capable man and a complete cook. And he soon filled our wallets with savoury pies, brawn, tongues, sausages, sweet-cakes, confects, tarts, and puddings, and as he brought them out from one bin or another described each piece very exquisitely, telling us its properties and good parts, and finished up by asking a scandalous sum the which we brought down to half with a little trouble. Now this piece I am eating is a fair sample of his craft, it is, he told us, a compost of capon's flesh, and veal, and pigeons, and ham, brayed together in a mortar and flavoured with herbs and spices and curious condiments, and indeed it is good provision and gives a relish to the wine." "And what fine sausages are these," said Phil Ambrose, holding one up and then gnawing at it, with an evident gust: but I was busy with some sort of a pie, I know not of what essence, but certainly the cook that made it must have had a great intellect and a painful, elaborate artfulness. In fine we supped as handsomely as it is possible to sup, and when all the meats were entombed, the Italians began to stand in order and to finger their instruments, talking to themselves in Tuscan: but we drew out our tobacco pipes and lit them with chips of burning wood, which are the rarest pipe lights in the world. Then beyond the flickering flame and the fragrant curling smoke of Trinidado a low sweet musick came, for the Signor Mosca was moving his lips along his flute, and the nightingales in the wood ceased to listen to him; and Coppo Cacci, and Corelli, and Andrea followed after with violin, viol d'amore, and bass-viol; and thus I heard the symphony of which some faint snatches came to my ears while I listened to the Seigneur de Roche-Nemours his story. For they told me afterwards that this was what they played in the garden to the lovers. Truly it was a wonderful musick and full of strange fancies for which I tried to find a meaning but could not; since it seems probable that such harmonies are drawn from the Outside Realm, and are in themselves but semi-

tones and broken voices from the concert sempiternal and transcendent. And it appeared that Giacomo Corelli, whom Andrea had called a
poet, himself had devised this symphony (as he told us) in times when
he was hungry and thirsty and a-cold; and when I looked at him he appeared to me like one who listens for sounds not heard of other men.
And when the last deep thunder came from the bass-viol, and the final
dying close wandered away into the darkness of the wood, the circle
closed again about the fire, and we fell to talking of indifferent matters.
And all the musicians had curious tales to tell concerning their instruments, their strange virtues and properties, how they are answerable to
one another, and occasionally make them that handle the bow their
servants, and play them all manner of tricks. Messer Corelli was good
enough to give me the complete anatomy of the vyall, according to the
most approved theories, and from what he said it appears that vyalls
certainly have souls, indeed he shewed me the exact position thereof as
Master René of the Rolls has pinned down the reasonable soul of man
to the pineal gland. Then Messer Cacci made a very ingenious relation
of two companions and two violins, and shewed how when one was
played, the other of itself echoed the musick, though many hundred
miles were between them; and how the companions answered, either
to other, in like manner, and dying at the same instant of time, their
vyalls likewise in that hour fell to pieces with a loud twang. "And this,"
said he, "was made evidently to appear, and is commonly believed all
over Italy": "Is commonly believed to be a lie you would say," quoth
Mosca, "for he who credits these violin histories must have soft
brains." But all the others cried out upon him with one voice, and
promised that so soon as they set foot again in Tuscany the Holy Office should take order with him and eradicate his unbelief: "Certainly,
Nanni," said Andrea, "the fagots that shall make a roast of thee have
begun to sprout, for thou wilt assuredly come to be burnt." And seeing
that the little man did not relish these jokes over much, Nick Leonard
asked the musicians if they knew of any curious or fantastic case, besides their craft-tales, "for these," said the Lord Maltworm, "seem to
breed dispute, a thing detested by us of Gwent, who are accustomed to
take everything quietly and as it comes. And if as you say, Signor Mosca's notions have really a taste of the faggot about them, doubtless the
Holy Office will attend to him in due time; and you need not therefore

to grow solicitous concerning the poor gentleman." "'Tis well spoken Nick," said Tom Bamfylde, "come my masters, surely in your wanderings you have picked up some curious and well-seasoned tales; and though I have both devised histories and listened to them, yet I have never seen a time or place or company fitter for the production of these commodities. And as to Signor Mosca, why, you may set your minds at ease as to that false damnable and pernicious position of his viz. that in vyalls there is merely natural wood and sheep's-gut, and no rational soul nor sympathy. For I assure you that the Venerable Philip Jenkins Archdeacon of Monmouth would give odds to the Inquisitors of the Holy Office, so capable a divine is he, and so vigilant to uproot erroneous doctrines and heresy. And moreover he's a kinsman of mine, and I'll make interest with him, and have Signor Mosca presented in the next Consistory Court at Caerleon, and I promise you it shall go very hard with him." After this pledge they could dispute no more, but began to advise together as to who had the best and strangest relation in his head, and it was agreed that Piero Latini of Babbiena was seised of a mighty quaint history, the which had been mellowed and ripened by age, so that there was no sourness or crudity left in it. And Andrea declared that Piero was able to talk nonsense with a graver face than any one of them, and so was fittest to entertain us. Forthwith he struck one or two deep notes from his bass-viol, and Piero began his story.

HOW THE DUKE OF SAN GIULIANO MADE BUILD A HIGH WALL

Upon the northern slope of the Mountain di San Giuliano a good many stones have been piled together and erected into walls and towers, the which taken together make up a considerable castle, and seem to have been well arranged, for they shew no sign of old age or decay, though they have stood there for five hundred years and more. This fine building is the nest of the Dukes of San Giuliano, who trace their line very far back, and are mixed up with the old Patricians and pagan knights, till at last you find yourself in a thick brake on a Sabine hill, the which brake is the resort of a nymph or some such special wanton, and here civil people stop short, for it is well known these nymphs did not relish being peeped at, and were used to be respectfully spoken of.

And inquisitive intermeddling personages who wished to know more than other people they taught manners and afflicted them grievously, turning them into stags, softening their brains, and altogether making examples of them, so that others might clearly understand that nymphs are best left alone. Wherefore we will not enquire further into the far-back affairs of this noble house; but merely say that they chose the mountain for their abode so long ago as the time of the Emperor Charlemagne, and were continually strengthening their castle, building thick walls and running up high towers, until it became as safe a place as any in Tuscany, and very fit for the habitation of great princes who require retreats of this description wherein they can contemplate at their ease the silly passions of the common people and the violence of party spirit. Some of the Tuscan nobles have chosen to leave the brave old strongholds of their forefathers, and have come down to the cities in the vales, but the lords of San Giuliano knew better than this, and though they were always glad to see the townsfolk climb puffing and panting up the mountain side, and never failed to welcome them heart-ily if rudely, with spear-heads and arrow-shafts, they still clung to their battlements and gilt pinnacles above the broad mountain woods. They had noticed, you see, that nobles who dwelt in towns became towns-folk, and got involved in town disputes, and sometimes came off sec-ond best and had to sit below some stupid fat huckster who called himself Podesta, Gonfaloniere, or Consul, and tried to persuade him-self and other people that they were on the whole a finer and more spirited sort of men than the old pagan Romans. This rubbish always made the Dukes of San Giuliano sick, and irritable in temper besides; and as I have said they took good care to stay up on the mountain and made it very hot climbing for anybody who wished to hang his cap on the vanes of the castle or to discover the thickness of the walls by the process of pulling them down. Duke Mark (who had to wife Yolande of Perpignan) was especially averse to the townsfolk, and when they gave him any trouble, always burnt a village, without stopping to en-quire whether it were the right one; and thus his neighbours grew to understand him and his odd ways, and agreed to let him go his own road. Fourth in descent from Duke Mark was Duke Guido, and he it is of whom I am about to devise, for searching in the byways of my brain I can find no better tale than this, which is still relished of cool evenings in the taverns of Tuscany, though the case fell out three hundred years ago, or maybe more. Now this Duke Guido di San Giuliano is confessed to have been a very witty and ingenious personage, and to have had a good knowledge of Grammar, Law, Logic and Philosophy, and some say he smattered in Theology to boot; but I believe he was too wise a man to do so, since he must have known that our Holy Religion is under the charge of the Holy Father and the Cardinals who do not require any help in their duties. And they are quite right to keep these affairs tight under their fists; for what should I say to a plough-boy who would teach me how to tune my lute, and for laymen to dispute over weighty matters of clergy is not a jot the wiser. But in all other learning I am convinced that the duke was far gone; and he had learnt the Greek tongue from one Argyropulo, a scholar from Byzantium, who was then in Italy, being an envoy from the Patriarch to the Pope. Also he shewed great favour to those who did things in the vulgar speech, to painters and to skilful carvers, so that Monte di San Giuliano became our Italian Parnassus, and the castle the watch-tower of the Arts and Humanities. My lord had for wife a beautiful and illustrious lady, called Constance degli Interminelli, the same being of a right noble house, of an angelic comeliness, and endowed with a cheerful imagination which got fun out of everything and even out of her husband, who, in spite of his learning and good parts, was somewhat gloomy and austere. And though this couple were well matched in years, yet they had no children, and people said that my lord spent his nights chiefly in mending and annotating Greek and Latin texts, and labouring to find out whether *et ita* or *itaque* was most to Tully's liking, and holding up old deeds and charters to the lamp to see if they were written over some golden work of the ancients. But the duchess never remonstrated with him or spoke angrily about his bad taste in preferring his parchments to his wife, for he was a young man, and she thought he would sow these learned oats of his and come to his senses before very long. And then, Constance would whisper to herself, my lord will notice my golden hair and blue eyes, and forget all about these heathens and their cold philosophy. She once tried meddling with his lamp, in such wise that it went out in a slow and sickly manner, just as the duke had taken out his manuscript of Homer, and was sitting down to make a night of it; but my lord flew into such a furious rage (being a choleric man when provoked) that this expedient was never again attempted. But after six years or more of this manner of living Constance perceived that her husband's case (and her own) was becoming desperate, and that some sharp remedy must be applied if things were to be mended, for the duke grew worse every day and began to stoop and peer and fumble about the castle all as if he had been a poor bachelor at the University, instead of being a very mighty prince, whose bearings the English Heralds would blazon in precious stones and jewells if not with the stars of heaven. This scholarly behaviour was certainly not worthy of one whose ancestors, the mighty nobles of the old time, had always been found where hard knocks were to be got, where the trumpets smote through the air, where the hammering of steel on steel was like the noise of a thousand smithies. And still less did it become my lord of San Giuliano thus to neglect his wife, seeing that the ancient princes of his line made no less of Venus than of her leman Monsignor Mars, and had loved so heartily that they furnished many a pleasant tale to the craftsmen of Paris who dressed their adventures up and tricked them out in fine language. Altogether you will agree with me that Constance had good ground for complaint, and with those blue eyes and golden locks of hers had a just title to the duke's love and affection, especially since her only rivals were a lot of nasty mouldy parchments, which had much better have been left to perish decently in the black holes of the monasteries. And being purposed to cure her lord of his Ciceronianism by some means or another she consulted her ladies one summer evening, while they were walking together in the shady alleys that were all around the castle, as to how she should best make the duke to amend his ways and live more like a good Christian gentleman for the future. And they all said that to consider this matter it was necessary that they should be seated and at their ease, for it was a knotty question and the very mention of it made them warm. So they walked on until they came to a large and special seat, placed under a great oak, and most exquisitely cut out in marble, and adorned with admirable devices that had generated in the brain and were shapen by the chisel of a young gentleman of Florence employed by the duke in the beautifying of his castle. Then my lady took her place in the centre of this fine form, and the rest who were (most of them) dark beauties, sat down with much rustling of silk and satin on either side of her; the girls who could not find places lying down on the grass in all sorts of pretty postures, and thus this brave Parliament proceeded to debate. And as is usual with assemblies of this kind there was a great diversity of opinions, theories, speculations, and methods: some would have Constance smile more on her lord, beguile him with allurements, and gently draw him into the mesh of love; some were for frowns, black looks, and words of reproach; some for floods of tears, long drawn sighs, and a pitiful beseeching countenance. Francesca of Mantua, who was one of the Bedchamber women, counselled Constance never to leave the duke by night or day, but to be ever beside him; and Laura degli Cavalcanti bade her go still abroad, and when she was at home, to keep her chamber "for so" said she, "my lord will feel the lack of you." But a girl named Agnes, who lay upon the ground, and had a face full of maliciousness and wit plainly told her mistress that there was only one cure for the duke's sickness; "and this," she said, "is for you to choose some young gallant from among the gentlemen of your court, and openly to shew your kindness for him by pleasant words and by acceptance of his service; the which I warrant me will open my lord's eyes, and shew him along what manner of road he is posting. This is a medicine I have known operate most marvellously, and unless I am much mistaken it will teach your husband that there is more wit in women than in Cicero, or any man at all, dead or alive." At this hardy speech Constance looked down and was thought to blush but ever so little, and the ladies agreed that though Agnes was young there was some tincture of sense in what she said, and that if my lady furnished her husband with a pair of horns he would have no right to be angry, since he had of his own acts and deeds (or rather want of them) forfeited all his claims and privileges. But an old dame with white hair, who had seen a good deal of life, and knew that such remedies as these now and then turn out worse than the sickness itself and bring on bad complaints, advised Constance not to be hasty in the matter, but to send for some learned physician, and consult with him, and open up all her grief "since," (quoth the old dame) "the doctors understand these affairs better than any one, and are often able to give comfort, when there seems to be no hope." And with this their session broke up, and the marble fauns at either end of the bench were left alone, to look slyly at one another as if they knew that there was mischief a-brewing. Perhaps unkind people would say that when a company of ladies plot schemes together, the results are not likely to be very salutary to any one concerned; but this is an opinion to which I do not consent, since it proceeds from a bad source, namely from the brains of ugly men whose lips are so large that no girl will kiss them; hence it is evident that whatever comes from those lips aforesaid should be looked upon with suspicion and in most cases rejected. However that may be, it chanced next morning that the duchess was seised with a violent pain in the head, just as she came out from hearing Mass, and was borne fainting to her chamber and put to bed by her women, who at first did not perceive the trickery, for, to be short, it was nothing else. But the duke verily believed his wife to be in grievous case and, since he loved her well enough in his quiet way, sat down and wrote letters and sealed them with a curious seal he had, it being the likeness of a man in armour, with two snakes for feet, and his face turned away, driving four horses in a chariot: and on one side of him was a star, and on the other a half moon; this seal being artfully cut out in green jasper. The letters, thus sealed, were given into the hands of messengers, who rode swiftly, and in due course brought back with them to San Giuliano no less a person than the renowned physician Signor Albericus of Padua, whose consultations are still made much of and esteemed not only by doctors but by curious persons and lettered men, who find therein many strange diseases and witty cures, set down in grave and choice phrases, and enlivened by some flashes of mirth. This learned person having heard what the duke could tell him, was taken to Constance's chamber, and there left alone with her, because as he merrily said he was used to this kind of thing and might be trusted. And indeed he was a good distance on the wrong side of sixty, fat and rotund in person, and altogether not a man to make a jealous husband put his hand to his forehead, though the wife were never so beautiful. And so soon as the door was shut and the duke out of earshot, Constance eagerly began to pour her woes out before the good doctor, whose brain she bewildered with an infinity of feminine lamentations and prayers for aid. And when Albericus had heard the whole story and put the fragments all together, he perceived that he had got mixed up in rather a ticklish business, the which might possibly give him trouble and disturb his peace and quietness. And since he loved an easy life above everything, he determined to be wary in the matter and keep a good look out for pitfalls; so when Constance began delicately to throw out hints about philters and full-flavoured medicaments of the same kind, he cut her short by saying that his system of medicine did not allow of such remedies, which he affirmed to be of an uncertain and hazardous nature, the manner of whose operations it was impossible to predict. However he promised to speak earnestly to her husband, and to admonish him that his wife required different treatment at his hands, or else would fade away like a flower shut out from the sun. The which promise Albericus faithfully fulfilled, and bade my lord look more into Constance's beautiful eyes and less into his manuscripts; "since," said he, "change of all things is sweet, and you, my lord duke, have surely had enough of yellow and black, and would do well to inspect and examine a little more closely that admirable red and white; in the which process you will discover more poetry, philosophy, science, and measured eloquence than there is in all the books of the ancients." I think this was excellent advice, and well worthy the author of the Consultations; but as it fell out the doctor made a slip which quite spoilt everything. For he thought to humour the duke by speaking to him in Latin, and strove to do so elegantly, and indeed he rounded off his periods very floridly and pompously, and avoided ending a sentence with a word of one syllable as is done in the Missal and Breviary. But unfortunately he used a word found only in very early writers and very late ones, which twanged so hideously in my lord's ears that he paid Signor Albericus his fee and sent him away without more ado, and read Cicero all night, like a man that has tasted an addled egg and must swill out his mouth with pure water and choice wine, to purify it. Hence Constance fared not a whit the better for the physician's counsel, for the duke made no account of a man who used such solecisms, and troubled himself the less when he heard that my lady went abroad again; and indeed she found staying in bed dull work enough. And it seems likely that Constance began to weigh in her mind what that mischievous Agnes had advised, for she was observed to look curiously on the gentlemen of her court, now gazing at one and now at another, as if she wished to know which was most fit to be used as an emplaster. I mean a plaster of the fiery burning sort, concocted out of the most furious virtuous mustard, to be laid on Duke

Guido's heart, and to draw out the love that doubtless was there. And it must be confessed that one could not wish to see a more gallant company of young gentlemen than that which sat down at the ducal table, for they were gathered from all the most noble and illustrious families of Italy, and thought it honour to call themselves the servants of so mighty a prince as my lord of San Giuliano. In fact Constance must have been very hard to please if she could not have fancied one or other of them; since they ranged in age from fourteen up to forty, and were nearly all gentlemen of pleasant manners and few scruples, who would have done a great deal at the command of their master, and in point of fact adored their mistress and grew rapturous over her rare beauty, as is the manner of Italian nobles, who are wanting in moderation. So you may guess that if Constance had bent her little finger in the direction of one of these gallants, she might have had him body and soul, for life and death; but it seems that for some reason or another she passed over all this gay silken company, and left them to content themselves with such divinities of lesser rank as they could propitiate and make look kindly on them. And after these fine gentlemen there were artists whom the duke entertained, namely artists in marble, and metal-work, and colour, some of them being young and proper men, and besides their craft-skill, of sharp wit and good address. There was for example Messer Belacqua the painter, who was limning Domesday above the altar of the chapel in fresco, and marshalling on the high space of wall all ancient prophets and patriarchs, apostles, elders, martyrs, and the virgins feeding amidst lilies, all in solemn order and degree by their companies, and the strong and most awful angels were flying forth from the throne under their captain St. Michael to set this last assize. But the glory of the colours it is impossible to describe, for they were of the sunlight and the blue sky of heaven, and the red clouds of the Northern Light. And the painter Belacqua was a sweet courteous gentleman, a lover of fair ladies, and would have been well content to serve the duchess in any fashion, but certainly would have most blithely assisted her in the way of making the duke jealous. Yet she passed him and his fellows by and made an odd choice, which proves her to have had a good heart, as some think, and as others declare, a mighty weak head. For she must needs pick out a little scholar and poet, Luigi Cortanto by name, who was not

held in much esteem by anybody, being of a low family, as poor as a
rat, and of a small insignificant figure. Besides these defects he was a
quiet and shy sort of a man, who was happiest when people would
leave him alone either with his lamp, his papers and his ink, or in some
cool alley or arbour where he could pace up and down with his eyes on
the ground, or sit dreaming and imagining those choice conceits which
have earned an eternal glory for him. And the duke had summoned
him to San Giuliano and entertained him there, because of some verses in the Greek language made by this Luigi aforesaid, the which were
so artfully conceited and ingeniously made out that they were published among all the lettered men of Italy, and so mightily enchanted
my lord that he must needs have the author at his castle. But in fact
Messer Cortanto did not himself esteem highly this kind of work, for
his whole delight was in a Book of Pastoralls in the speech of Tuscany;
the which he was fashioning: with sweet and mellifluous eloquence after the model of Virgil the great master. And this piece it is which has
kept his name alive and is to this day a fragrant memorial of him, but
then all these pastoral songs were known only to himself, and were
hidden in a chest in his cell at San Giuliano. Who then was surprised
but Messer Luigi when his mistress began to make sweet eyes at him,
and to let glances fall in his way that no man might mistake; since he
thought his cassock was shabby enough to keep off all darts of Love,
and had been used to look at Constance from a great distance, below
all the fine gentlemen and young nobles of the court. And certainly it
did not seem likely that this beautiful lady would take the trouble to
climb up the many stairs that led to the poet's chamber, and lighten his
dark room with the golden glory of her hair, and the rays from those
deep blue eyes of hers: when there was such brave lodging to be had
on the ground floor amid silk and velvet and all manner of rich furniture. But one can never get at the Rhyme and Reason of Love, whose
decrees are not to be questioned nor reformed, one must only bow the
head and say 'So be it' without enquiring into the why and wherefore.
And perhaps Constance saw something in Luigi's features not visible
to other people at that time; I mean, all those sweet amorous conclusions and gracious meditations which you may find in the twelve
books of "Il Pastor Intronato," which, as I have said, were fashioned
with such curious and painful art that they have never been surpassed

nor equalled by any of our Tuscan poets. But let the reasons be what
they may, it became very plain to Luigi that those swift glances were
meant for none but himself, and before long he shyly ventured to return them, and was not less than rapturous when one day the duchess
drew him apart before all her ladies and courtiers, and walked with him
in the garden, though, indeed, he could find but little wit wherewith to
answer all the pleasant speeches and delicate little compliments of his
noble mistress. But that malicious maiden Agnes laughed, for she saw
that her counsel was being taken after all; and then laughed again saying to herself "Truly these great ladies make an odd choice." As for the
poet, his ideas and rational faculties were in a very confused state, and
obscured, pleasantly enough, by golden and rosy-coloured clouds
which floated in his brain; but before the actual sun had set that night,
the sun of love rose for poor Luigi and began to shine upon him and
to scorch his heart with a heat that was of the noonday. And whereas
the duchess had merely intended to make her husband's conscience
prick him, she had made this fierce flame of love lighten the poor
scholar, kindling in his breast all manner of desires and cravings which
poverty had hitherto effectually subdued, and illuminating his cell with
the blaze of that ardent lamp which shews everything so plainly. But
her husband made no account of Constance's kindness to Messer Luigi, nor is it clearly ascertained that he so much as saw it, though it became every day more evident to the ladies and nobles of the Court,
who began to think there must be rather more in the poet than they
had suspected. And so long as this strangely matched couple merely
sauntered about the walks of the garden before the eyes of all, I don't
think much harm was done, though Luigi's compliments were getting
rather high-flown and fetched from a tremendous distance, and Constance looked more and more softly upon him, perceiving that his
mind was lovelier than his body, though even in this latter she tried to
see some excellence and worship. But when it came to the mistress
and her servant dropping far behind the rest in their walks along the
alleys, I believe the duke would have done well to take some order
with them, and to become jealous as was expected of him. But he had
peered so long at his manuscripts that he had become rather short-
sighted in other affairs; so that Constance and Luigi by slow degrees
became lovers in real earnest on both sides, instead of on one only, as

it had been at the beginning. I know not precisely how, when, or where this was declared between them, or if it were ever so declared, since the fair dialects of passion in those days led noble lovers onward by fine phrases and Platonical sentiments, so that all abrupt and sudden falls from friendship into love were avoided, and from *Ville des pensées* to *Chasteau de par amours* was a brave road through a delicious country, abounding in sunlit meadows, shady groves and rippling brooks, thrilling with the song of nightingales. Imagine then, I pray you, my beautiful Constance (who assuredly must have carried in her bosom a wonderful spell against Sirius, for that malefic star could not hurt her nor scorch her red and white), and the little dark man with hungry eyes in his dingy scholar's vestment walking hand in hand (ah! how fiercely pressed together) down the long road; and halting now and again for a little while in the arbours by the way. But mark, now the poor poet leads and beckons Constance to hasten onward, and she cannot disobey him, and had he bade her kiss him before the whole court I verily believe she would not have refused, since he was her Lord Paramount and held that enchanting body with all its loveliness bound fast in his service. In short they reached the valley together and mounted up unto the wonderful Chasteau de Par Amours, where, certes, there is choice entertainment and soft lodging; musick too from horns, harps, and vyalls to pierce the heart; and deambulatories in rose-gardens and along incredible galleries hanging from the summits of pinnacled tower and of stony wall. But alas! one must pay one's shot for all this, the musick turns at last to sickness and fear, there's nightshade amidst the rose hedges, and sharp rocks below those high hanging ways. What shall I say of the overshadowed parliaments in the woods, their countersigns and secret signals to one another, and of the times when Constance, full of shame yet fuller of love, went stealthily in the dead of night along the dark passages by the savage warriors of the arras, and up the long weary winding stair to Luigi's chamber? Once Duke Guido met her and asked her what she did at such an hour, but the keen wit of a woman in love easily found an excuse to satisfy her husband, so the revelling at the Castle went on gaily. You see all her notions of winning her husband's love had quite fallen into forgetfulness, and she thought only of enjoying Luigi's, wondering dimly, now and then, as she lay in his arms, at her old innocent life, but never desiring that it might come back. For when it has come to this pass, and the drawbridge of the castle has been drawn up, a woman who is sharp-witted knows that there is no returning: the card is on the board and may not be taken again. How this strange affair would have ended, if it had been left alone, is more than I can tell, but I suspect Luigi would have tired of his mistress, and have gone back quite easily and contentedly to his garret in Florence, there to put the last finish to his pastoral pieces and then to set them forth. For now he wrote verses no more, being his brain was burnt up and adust with hot passion, which could not find voice in the calmly measured and perfect sweetness of duly chosen words. But it fell out that a gentleman of the Court, near akin by blood to the Marquis of Mantua, who had formerly pressed Constance hard to no avail, and was now the lover of Agnes, by the intelligence this girl gave him, and his own wit, had come to understand how things were going between his mistress and Messer Luigi, and spied upon them constantly. In this gallant there was only one fault, and that a fixed habit of keeping old insults and bad turns in a warm, dry corner of his heart, whence every night and morning he brought forth these commodities, looked at them, and returned them again, till the time came to give them back to their rightful possessors. And since he had taken Constance's refusal of his love very grievously and had long cherished a sincere desire of crying quits with her, he began to see daylight, and to say, like the rest of the courtiers, that the poor scholar was after all an admirable sort of man; for through him he saw a door leading to the sweet desert of vengeance. And by dint of hiding in the trees by the most retired alleys, lurking behind arbours, and in the recesses of the castle stairs he was soon able to make out a very pretty process of arraignment, for he became a party to the plot, which before was only known to Luigi and Constance, and the marble satyrs, and the mighty warriors waving on the arras. Thus he felt himself in good company, and was observed by his friends to be in high spirits, for generally he had the repute of being somewhat gloomy and of sullen conversation. Indeed this gentleman enjoyed himself greatly in these days, and needed no fire of cold nights, for he warmed his heart with the view of a rare revenge, worthy of his ancestry and noble bearings, and well befitting an illustrious house. But he waited for some time that there might be no mistake or bungling in the matter, since he knew that a trifling miscalculation might cost him his head and leave Constance and her sweetheart to make merry at his expense above ground, while he would be taking his ease in Phlegethon below. And to make everything complete he entered into close acquaintance with Luigi, and by dint of flattery and his knowledge soon heard the whole tale from the scholar's own mouth, and applauded him mightily, only bidding him consider how various and unstable were all earthly concernments, especially those which appertained to the Lordship of Love. At last all was in train and the noble gentleman of Mantua had arranged in his mind the time, place and manner of his repaying to Constance this his just debt. You must understand then, that in the gardens of the castle of San Giuliano there was a great and admirable labyrinth or Siege of Troy, contrived of laurels, cypresses, and box trees, with windings in and out, turnings, returnings, dædal wanderings and perplexed passages, almost beyond conceit or imagination. And in the courses of the maze were arbours here and there with seats for them to rest a while, who took the pains to tread these windings; and many of the trees were cut out into the fantastick similitude of towers and castle walls, strange monstrous beasts, and symbols of secret meaning. And at the entrance was a stone pillar, about four feet in height, and on the top was this legend:

Hic quem Creticus edit Dædalus est Laberinthus,
De quo nullus vadere quivit qui fuit intus,
Ni Theseus gratis Ariadne stamine jutus.

And in the midst of the labyrinth was a very fair and pleasant bower of box, with the likenesses of peacocks, foxes, pheasants, and doves de- vised in the topiary manner, and a seat of marble very exquisitely carved. Now this place was often resorted to by Constance and the scholar, who were never weary of tracking out its windings in compa- ny, and had found out a secret concerning it; namely that one of the hedges was in fact double and had within itself a passage, which might only be entered by pressing down a certain bough at a certain place; and when they had gone in they perceived that none who passed by could spy them out since the green walls on either side were thick and impenetrable. And you may guess that they often came hither, for it seemed a very secure place; but so did the noble gentleman of Mantua who had enough craft to see rather than be seen, and marked the trick of the bough to a nicety, while the lovers thought there was not a soul within the whole labyrinth. But in the cool of a memorable day this gentleman contrived so that Duke Guido should walk with him in the garden, and as they paced up and down he shewed his master what kind of a wife Constance was, speaking softly with picked words, and using no sort of violence or indignation. At first the duke would believe none of it and began to frown in a fashion that made the courtier grow sick and pass his hand to the back of his neck, for he seemed to feel the rope squeezing and the first prick of the axe at the same time. But nevertheless he gave the duke such proofs and insisted so on what he had said that my lord began to grow uneasy in his turn, and at last said "Are you able to shew me them together in such wise that I cannot fail to be convinced?" And the gentleman answered "Come with me." So he took this poor husband toward the Siege of Troy and led him in, and then along the wandering endless passages, between the high green hedges, now to the right and now to the left, and stopped at last before a smooth wall of box and pointed with his finger as if to say that the lovers were within it. But the duke himself knew not of this cranny, and would have spoken, but the gentleman held up his hand again and drew his sword. Then he slowly and warily put down his hand among the leaves and caught the bough with a grasp like a smith's vice: and in an instant had torn it away so that the duke saw Constance his wife and Luigi Cortanto the scholar with their lips hard set together, and their arms around one another's necks. And the gentleman thought that his master would have leapt in and made short work of them both, and had turned away, for he rather liked the scholar and had no particular wish to see him die violently, only he listened for Constance her death scream. But the duke did not so much as draw his sword; merely looking once into his wife's eyes, and then going back, he took hold of the gentleman's arm and led him forth. But when they had again come to the entrance my lord of San Giuliano put his finger on top of the pillar and pointed to the line *De quo nullus vadere qui fuit intus,* and said no more but only bade the courtier go to the castle and fetch an hundred men-at-arms to that place. This done, the soldiers were set all round the labyrinth, and their charge was to keep close watch, and if any one strove to come out, by no means to kill but

merely to push them back again within the maze. And the duke likewise sent messengers to the officers over all the towns within his lordship, to what intent you shall presently understand. Thus the hanging
gallery of the Chasteau de Par Amours had fallen beneath Constance
and her lover, and they were now tasting the points of the rocks beneath. But how they fared together, whether they reproached or con-
soled one another is not known, only before long one of the soldiers
heard a rustling in the leaves opposite to him, and Luigi's head came
out. And seeing the men-at-arms made no sign of hurting him the
poor poet gave a whistle and a swift pattering of feet came along the
passage inside the labyrinth. Then Luigi began slowly to ease himself
out, and still the soldier did nothing, but when he was clear of the
hedge and had turned to help Constance, the man seized him by his
neck and pushed him back again by force, so that all his struggling
could not keep him on the right side of his prison, and while he was
doing this the pikeman heard some one's breath caught sharply, and a
noise like sobbing. And once or twice Luigi tried to escape that night
and put his head out as before, and saw standing by each soldier a
serving man holding a great torch, and neither said anything, but let
him painfully work his way out as before, and then thrust him back.
And just as the sun set at the close of the next day the messengers the
duke had sent began to return, and with them came companies of
men, whom my lord himself received, and shewed them where they
might get stones, rough and smooth, for these fellows were masons.
Straightway they went to their work, and as more came, they too fell to
their tools, and at midnight many score of men were a-labouring by
torchlight, and a place had been made ready for the foundations of a
wall right around the maze. Nor was there any delay, but the stones
were set one above other, and compacted with mortar, and still the
men-at-arms stood in their order, but Luigi only came out once more.
And it chanced that as he did so the duke stood opposite to him by the
wall which was beginning to rise above the earth, and the poet looked
into the eyes of his lord and went back of his own will into the windings of his prison. But the duke remembered the old saw "God keep
you from the eye of a lettered man," and knew that the masons might
set about his own tomb also. Nevertheless he made no sign, and night
and day the work went on; and the guard was changed, and none in

the castle dared to ask a question, or so much as to see the wall before their eyes, for by this time everybody was aware that Duke Guido was a chip of the old block, whose answers would be a gibbet and a rope. But the gentleman who had played the spy, and given the duke his information, had grown gloomy and sour again, for he was obliged to confess to himself that this vengeance of his master's was more curiously and choicely invented than anything he had conceited of; and this thought mortified him and made him wish he had not interfered in the matter, since he could not bear to be in anywise surpassed. To be short, before a week had passed the labyrinth was shut in by a great wall forty feet in height, without doorway or entrance, only in the place over against the pillar there was cut the line from it *Nemo vadere quivit qui fuit intus* in fair and deep letters on a smooth ashlar. Then the masons received six times the price of their labour and were sent back again to their several towns, and the guard was kept no longer, since there was not likely to be any one inside who was able to climb that lofty wall. And about three months after this fine monument of love was concluded, Duke Guido caught the pestilence and died miserably, for Luigi had looked upon him, and woe is ever in store for them upon whom hath fallen the eye of a lettered man. But the noble gentleman of Mantua went up to the poet's chamber, and in a mournful meditative way, began to burst open his chests and to ransack his wallets, for indeed he was sorry for the poor scholar, against whom he had no grudge. "Alas! alas!" murmured he to himself, "all the evil that we men suffer in this vale of misery must be put down to the wickedness and devilish entanglements of the women. And now this Constance hath made three honest gentlemen to suffer for her sins, and hath killed two outright. Truly it were well for us poor silly men, if there were no women in the world." Sadly and pensively musing in this wise the noble gentleman ran through all Luigi's papers; for he loved good letters and understood well how to distinguish choice writing from mean. And when he came to "Il Pastor Intronato," and saw what a rarest work of art was in his hands, he well-nigh wept, saying: "Alack! alack! a very admirable poet, a gentle witty clerk; dear soul, and he's come to this pitiful end, and all through woman's wanton, wicked ways." And thus it was by this gentleman's hands that this delicious piece of Luigi's was set forth, and remains, as I have said, a fragrant and everlasting memorial of him, together with the great stone wall around the miz-maze of San Giuliano. The which stands there to this day, and none has ever climbed it, nor entered the labyrinth; and so it is not known at all how the lovers lie, or whether they met their doom together or apart. But I must tell you that when Duke Guido's brother who came after him had been seised of the Lordship of San Giuliano for a year or so, the malicious rout of certain cities sub-adjacent began again their old villanous seditions, clamouring that the bodies of the lovers should be buried with rites of Holy Church, and the monstrous wall thrown to the ground; and thence fell once more to their rubbish about the Romans, talking of the Tarquins, Gracchi, tyrants, tribunes and the devil knows what infernal nonsense besides. And in their blustering speeches they confounded dates so scandalously, and got Roman History into such a woeful muddle that Duke Antony (who like his brother was something of a scholar and precisian) became annoyed, and was obliged to take a leaf out of Duke Mark's book, and to remind his subjects, by means of fire, sword, and halter, that all their pagan Pompeys and Brutuses had been put under the sod a long time ago. And as to the wall I have seen it with mine eyes, and it is indeed a very special wall.

No sooner had Piero brought his story to an end than Messer Mosca drew out from his wallet a bottle, round bellied and thin necked, and gave it to me bidding me to drink and pass it round. And when we had emptied it of its fragrant, oily juice Giacomo Corelli began to chide Piero for his lack of art in telling the tale, "since," said he, "you should have enlarged upon the shadowy terrors of Constance's midnight journeys to her lover, and have made the warriors of the arras play her all manner of tricks, as is customary in Romances. Likewise you fell short in the building of the wall, and did not hold your torches on high and make them flame and smoke and cast strange lights around, nor did you cause the harness of the men-at-arms to glitter, nor the moon to shine with a calm golden effulgence on that fantastic scene." "I have told the tale as I received it," answered Piero, "and all these graces that you speak of can very easily be conceived by the hearers, without the trouble of recounting them, since such ornaments are, as you say, common to all romances." "And now, sirs," broke in Coppo Cacci, the cunning player of the violin, "it is time for you to pay your shot, and this you shall do by devising us some history of your own country, and in no other way whatsoever." "Nay," said Nick Leonard, "we will content you in both ways, for I am in the humour to tell a merry case, and I think I have one in my head which will be found not altogether unpleasant, though it is but an old song." And Andrea answered, "We listen and await your musick, for I expect it will be no less."

THE AFFAIR DONE AT THE HOUSE WITH THE LATTICE

In the time of Jehan de Hastings, third of that name, Baron of Burgavenny, and Earl of Pembroke, there came a young knight to the town of Abergavenny, having the style of Sir Philip Meyrick of Caerwent, and being on the whole rather a pleasant young gentleman. That is to say he was of a moderate height, had yellow hair and blue eyes, and a cheerful grin, of the which commodity he was very liberal. You will know what I mean when I tell you that some ladies called him an impudent fellow, whilst others had nothing to say when Sir Philip's name was mentioned, but blushed and smiled a little to themselves, as people do when they have pleasant recollections. This knight was lodged, I believe, at the Priory, where he had an uncle, an old Canon of some eighty odd years, who had begun life by enjoying it, and still persisted in this course, only he had changed his methods; for a spark of twenty and a Canonicus of eighty go to work in different ways. On this good old ecclesiastic Sir Philip is supposed to have fastened, and at the Priory he lived some while snug and at his ease, though the Cellarius hinted once or twice to the Prior that all the casks in the cellar had sprung a leak of late, and that if things went on in this style much longer, they would infallibly run dry. But the Prior rebuked him for his want of faith and shewed him plainly how the saints love monks and casks and take care of them, and even when hard put to it, have been known to work great miracles in their behalf. I suppose however you would be glad to hear some few particulars about Sir Philip, and how he came to test the barrels of Burgavenny and the faith of the monks. And if you have ever walked through Abergavenny with your heads on one side you will doubtless be inquisitive about that fine house a little way out of the town, that seems to have just stopped short of being a castle, and has an extensive and complicated coat of arms cut over the porch.

But I am going to tell you all about these matters, and you shall understand how this mansion was built, and what it had to do with Sir Philip Meyrick. Who, as I have said, was styled of Caerwent, and indeed he came from the neighbourhood of that town of an old Welsh family, whose pedigree kept getting longer and longer, and their rent roll shorter and shorter as the Saxons followed the Romans, the Danes the Saxons, and the Normans the Danes. Every century in fact added quarters to their shield, and subtracted carucates from their possessions, until uncivil people began to whisper that the Meyricks of Caerwent were decaying and would ere long be all uprooted from the soil or rooted under it; it did not matter which. But you may judge what a sound old family this was by the time it took them to fall to pieces, your modern houses give a crack and thunder in a moment to the earth in a cloud of dust and mortar, and dirt of all sorts, but this old ancient race who had once ruled all Gwent, and had furnished the Calendar with three or four saints, merely dropped a stone here and there, and then went on quietly for another hundred years. However when Sir Philip took possession he found the house, the garden, a field or two, and little else; and the rain came through the roof and soaked him through when he was in bed. These circumstances would have discouraged many young gentlemen, but being a Meyrick he had the hole mended and sat down to do a little thinking, for he perceived that the family was in a languid state and needed to be revived. Sir Philip had, to be sure, that cheerful confidence in himself, which helps a man on in the world, and fills his cup for him, and it need not be said that he considered himself equal to the task of restoring his house and collecting together a few acres of that dust whence we come and which bears corn and oak trees as well as men—some say a good field of corn is worth more than a fool; but I suspect this opinion is heretical and unreasonable besides. Why? Because rain sometimes falls and spoils the ingathering of the wheat; whereas no rain beats down, nor does the mildew destroy the plentiful and everlasting crop of folly, which is ripe all the year round and groweth more luxuriant every day. But I return to Sir Philip, who when he had laudably determined in one way or another to magnify once more the name of Meyrick, began to go farther and to consider in what way he should do this. And finding himself master of no arts but those of warfare and horsemanship, he deter-

mined to try what chivalry would do for him and made the journey
oversea to France, the which realm one of our glorious kings was at
that time engaged in tormenting. This expedition Sir Philip performed
in company with a band of pretty fellows of Gwent, of whom some
had made the country too warm for them, some found the times dull
at home, some like himself were desirous of mending divers rags and
tatters in their estates. And I believe that this Silurian band did not disgrace their ancestors, and came to be much respected by the French as
a sturdy set of men who made large gaps and cut to the bone. This was
well enough, but yet Sir Philip did not find his pockets get any fuller,
and heard no talk of a grant of land or lordship, or office about the
Court, or government of an island, or any of those contentments
which are good for an old decayed family. Hence he made his way
home again, perceiving that chivalry was going to the devil, and that
this war was a very unrighteous war that did nobody any good. For he
was not so silly as to think that killing Peers of France, burning their
towns and castles and pilling the people was in itself a comely undertaking; though he might have excused it if it had brought him one or
two of those little easements that I have mentioned. After this disappointment he was for a few weeks perplexed as to what he should turn
his hands to, and at last concluded to roam for a while about the country, keeping his eyes open and his brain clear, since no one knows after
what fashion good luck shall come to us. It really is a very simple thing
this finding of the golden cup at the foot of the rainbow, that cup I
mean which delights our eyes, moistens our throats, and casts its own
original radiance on the remnant of our lives. But somehow or other,
most men bungle sadly over the search, and grumble horribly if they
are not successful directly they have started on their journey. They forget, you see, that before there can be a golden cup there must be a
rainbow, and a rainbow generally follows rain and storm and driving
clouds. Some few there are who profess to care nothing for this quest
and spend their days in the courtyard, looking down into the dim old
well, and dazzling their eyes with the stars they see therein. They think
themselves wise, and in point of fact they are quaint fellows, which
perhaps comes to the same thing. But Sir Philip knew better than they,
and had no intention of leading this dreamy sort of life, for his great
ambition (or so he said) was to have at last a good monument over

him in alabaster, carved artfully, with all his quarters painted on the stone and in the window above. To enjoy this benefit, and to lie like a Christian when he was dead, it was necessary to lie like one when he was alive; that is, of course, in a warm bed under a leaden roof, with a full belly. And he was too wise a man (though he was a young one) to vex his heart over his poor estate and ill success at the wars; for he understood the benefit of misfortune and early buffets, the which give a vast relish to the warm hearth and good wine of after years. Hence he proceeded cheerfully to his geographical studies, strolling discursively from town to town, from castle to castle, and from convent to convent; never hurrying himself in the least, and always finding out the pleasantest paths and the most sheltered nooks. In this pilgrimage he acquired an immense amount of knowledge, and found out all the fine things our land is fertile in, tasting the full-flavoured gilded sausages of Uske Priory, the products of the vineyards of Lantonia Abbey in Gloucester, the hams of Caerleon, and the larded meats and sweet cakes of Monmouth. And since he always made himself agreeable, sang a pretty French song, and kissed the black-eyed Silurian maidens with liberality and in a pleasing manner, Sir Philip was welcomed by all and enjoyed himself exceedingly, as he deserved to do. But he never forgot business in his amusements, still keeping his eyes open, and sharpening his wits every day against other folks' brains, as he sat in the snuggest seat of the common-room, or hall, or tavern, ever ready to catch the morsel which should satisfy him for the remainder of his days. After about a year of this life, wherein he learnt more than Oxford, Paris, Padua, and Salamanca could have taught him, he hit upon the notion of visiting his uncle, the old Canon Ambrosius, of Abergavenny; for he was a pious young man, and had heard tell that the cook of the Priory had a curious art of preserving ducks in hot sauces, and that his condiments were on the whole more ecclesiastical than any in the Marches. So between the desire of enjoying the conversation of this admirable cook, and of dutifully serving his uncle, who came of a jovial stock, namely the Ap Adams of Hafod, Sir Philip used more speed in his journey to the Grand Seignory of Burgavenny than he was accustomed, and had to sit very still for many days after he had got there. As for the old Canonicus he welcomed his nephew, made much of him, and saw that he had plenty to eat and drink, and was lodged

well; and listened to the Silurian wisdom he had acquired in his wanderings, for the good man relished the sapience of the tankard and the
sparkling black eyes, having himself compiled some Breviates of this
pleasant philosophy in his younger days. To be short Sir Philip found
himself in desirable quarters, and sometimes of a morning after he had
been mortifying his flesh with the warm sauces of Master Cook and
the cool juices of Master Cellarer, he would grow melancholy and
think of turning monk himself, so that he might keep his throat in a
continual state of mortification. But these pensive thoughts went off
with his morning draught, after which he commonly went his rounds
about Abergavenny to his own delight and that of the townsfolk, who
loved a pretty man in a gay surcoat who could tell a merry tale. His
chief guide and Cicero was a certain lawyer of the place, called John of
Gloucester, the same being an officer of the Chancery of Burgavenny,
and by no means bearing the gown in vain. He certainly did not look
over sharp, being pudding-faced (if it be lawful to say so) and of a
squat figure, but nevertheless his upper stories were well furnished,
and he shewed Sir Philip all the entertainments that were being performed in the town, and told him below what windows it was amusing
to wait after dusk. By the advertisements he received of this witty lawyer Sir Philip threaded many a maze and soon knew the histories and
adventures of the townsfolk very perfectly; but found nothing of solid
advantage therein, until he had been in Abergavenny better than six
months. And one evening as he was passing along a bye street with his
companion, he saw a large well-compacted house, as fair as, or fairer
than any in the town; but on the face of it there appeared but one lattice window, and this high up above the door. "Who dwells there?"
said he to Master John. "Why nobody exactly knows," answered the
lawyer, "for the inhabitants of this house are what is called quiet people who mind their own business so well that they give other folk no
opportunity of helping them. But I believe that one Maurice Torlesse
doth actually dwell here, with two servants, an old man and an old
woman, very hideous to behold, and also his daughter whose name I
know not, though I have seen her." "Where did you catch a sight of
her?" asked Philip, pricking up his ears, for he loved mysteries. "At
that very lattice I have once seen the lady, as I passed below, and by
corpus Domini I thought I should have swooned away." "Was she then

so foul to look upon?" "Sir Philip, Sir Philip, she was as fair as a lady of færy, and had oh! (here the little man sighed deeply to himself) such eyes. 'Las! they pierced utterly to my heart, and taught me that all the beauties I had seen before were mere clumsy wenches. And I have seen her also going to the Mass and vesper-music at the Monastic Church, but shrouded and hidden by a thick veil and attended by the old hideous woman, who seems to be her governess." "Her father then keeps her very close?" "Right as he keeps his treasure, whereof I believe he hath good store; and I may tell you what a porter once told me; namely that going to the house on a certain day he was let in with his load and found the walls most chargeably adorned with hangings, and golden vessells on the cupboard finer than my lord has in the castle. But, as you may guess, he was in the street again before very long, and though he troubled himself to invent many ingenious tales as to what he had seen and heard, they are too improbable to be worth recounting." "And has this beautiful young lady no lovers?" "Not one, saving myself, who can never forget her." "Why in that case (with your leave) I can do no less than be her sweetheart," said Sir Philip. "I love beautiful eyes, and golden vessells, and comely hangings, and have always used to look closely into such ware; and I believe this damsel will suit me well enough—that is if she be well proportioned." "I should judge that her taille is a rarer and more lautitious taille than that of Madam Phryne; but, by cock! if you win this lady you must be a very discreet knight, and a cunning, and a daring to boot; since Master Torlesse will have no gallants, keeps his doors bolted, and shoots bolts at any he sees lurking about." "Well well, I must advise and consider, and concoct plans and strategies, and call me a fool if I do not give you some parchments to engross before the year is done." With this they parted and Philip passed the night in trying to get some sense out of this queer sort of household, applying all his experience and rules of art to it, but nevertheless the morning found him muddled, for though he had heard of many pretty girls with three or four lovers, and understood the complications arising therefrom, a pretty girl with no lovers at all was an entirely new leaf in his book. He perceived therefore that he must gather more facts and look into the affair himself; and so made it his business to walk slowly between the church and the house of Master Torlesse, about Evensong time, in hopes to meet the lady who had done such damage to the heart of John of Gloucester. And this he did for a week and saw nothing; but one stormy rainy evening as he was loitering along a narrow passage, he perceived two persons coming swiftly and shyly towards him, who when they saw him seemed at first minded to turn back, but in the end pressed on, more hastily than before. And as they passed Sir Philip doffed his cap, and bowed low, equally to both, since he was not quite a fool, and knew that it is rather more important in the beginning of a love affair to have the good will of the governess than the mistress. But they seemed to make no account of his civility and courteous observance; and he could only mark that the young lady was indeed of a fine shape, richly dressed and specially scented, but so closely veiled that he could not lighten his heart with a glint of those marvellous eyes of hers. And as they fared along this passage, the trees that hung over the wall of it, wept and rained upon them, as the gusts of wind came up; and Sir Philip stood gazing dizzily, for though he had seen little, yet the strange influence of a perfect grace and beauty had fallen on his soul, so that his brain was mazed and wildered. But after a little while he followed the lady of his thoughts to the church, and found the monks at Evensong, and looking around saw the two figures kneeling together in a pew. Forthwith he set himself in a convenient place behind a pillar and watched them attentively, hoping the young lady might raise her veil, but she remained with head bent and enshrouded all through Evensong, and the service sung, went forth as if she saw no one save her old governess, who should certainly have been veiled herself, for her countenance was of a mystical and stupendous ugliness. In this wise Sir Philip saw his lady once or twice and still bowed low before her, and worshipped her presence, and likewise the presence of the hag, who, he thought, looked at him not unpleasantly; but he spoke not a word, for he considered that it was not yet time for speaking. And in the next place he began to linger in the neighbourhood of their house, casting many wistful glances up at the lattice, and expecting every moment to have a dose of boiling water, or maybe an iron bolt through his body, since Master Torlesse appeared from all accounts to be a man who did not like to have his mansion or his daughter stared at. But a really gallant gentleman cares nothing for the anger of parents or guardians, trusting in his own manly feature, the courage of his heart, and above all in the très-noble and puissant God of Love, who still prevents and succours true, loyal, and steadfast lovers, his liege subjects, delighting in their service and helping them to make a mock and a song of those silly persons who guard beauty, and think themselves strong enough to keep Love out of a lady's heart. It is this same Diou Damur that is Chancellor of the Schools of Lovers, and teaches therein by his professors (who have many names) a joyous Trivium and Quadrivium, giving some to drink of the red wine of Desire, feeding others with the sweet apples of Cozenage and Trompery, and making all more sharp and cunning than the subtlest doctors, or masters in philosophy. And those that serve him well he will never desert. Hence one night, about the time of the Compline-song, as Sir Philip paced to and fro beneath the high house of Master Maurice Torlesse, in the dusky radiance of a moon seven days old, he suddenly saw a light gleam through the lattice of his longing; then a hand pushed the cancels open, and lo! his lady looked forth upon him. "Come near," said she, in a voice sweet and plaintive as a virelai, that drew Sir Philip more strongly and graciously than the west wind draweth the ships of holy pilgrims to the port of their desire. And coming close under the wall he looked upwards to her face leaning out of the window, and gazed into her most beautiful brown eyes, which would have made St. Benedict himself tear up his Rule, and would have burnt up all stern Capitularies and Edicts in their liquid fire. But now they were pitiful and moist with tears, and as she spoke to her true knight her voice ever and again broke short. "Are you not young," said she, "or have you lost the desire to live, that you come to this house so often and so hardily. Certainly you cannot know what fashion of man my father is; but know now that the next time you hie hither will be the last, since he to-day oiled his cross-bow and bade Richard dig a grave, as he said, for a proper man." "And if you will look forth and smile upon me dying, I would it were now to-morrow and your father's bolt was sped. But understand O maiden most beauteous and adorable, that my heart and life and soul are yours altogether; I am your mere creature and desire but to gaze upon that super-excellent loveliness and worship it; and if you should scorn my service I shall indeed die more miserably than by any bolt or sword." Perhaps you may divine that while these pretty speeches so gallantly phrased and amorously conceited were being delivered, the two were gazing either on other, and Sir Philip's eyes spoke more fairly and delivered more honest arguments than his lips; for you see he was too many feet below his mistress to make any effectual use of this latter organ; by the which a girl is more thoroughly convinced *ex opere operato,* in five minutes without a word being uttered than if her lover spoke like Demosthenes, Æschines, Cicero and Chrysostom all at once. However the young knight did what he could with his fine blue eyes, and between them and his hardy and knightly orations, full of amorous doctrines and high courage, the maid began to feel a fluttering at her heart, and a strange delicious sensation that made her wish Sir Philip had a ladder. But as she heard her governess's footstep tottering along the passage, she merely answered "Sir Knight I do not quite conceive your meaning; but if you are not weary of the sun come not in my path to-morrow, since I am purposed to shrive me at the monastic church, and if my father hear that you were to be seen on the way, he will assuredly cause you to die." And with that she clapped the window to, and Sir Philip was fain to begone, for he had noted the shy smile that played about her lips as she finished speaking, and understood her intent to perfection. Hence he betook himself to Master Cellarer at the priory, and astonished that good monk with his capacity for drinking, till the man crossed himself violently, thinking this guest was a kind of incarnate Wine-God, who had come over the hills to Abergavenny, as Bacchus came to Thebes, and would do damage to somebody ere he left it. Indeed Brother Toricellus expected every moment to see vine leaves wreathing round Philip's temples, and to hear cymbals clanging: but as a matter of fact the knight was only anxious to have his brain in good order, so that he might reason clearly, and see his way through this strange dædal of Love. At last he left the cellarer to his devotions, very solemnly and earnestly charging him to be moderate in his cups, and walked steadily to his lodging with about a gallon of French wine in his inwards and a fertile crop of ideas and conceptions in his brain. And the next morning he sought out his uncle, the old Canon, and explained the whole matter to him, dropping some hints as to a new roodscreen for the quire when the marriage was concluded. The which hit Father Ambrosius in the soft place, for he was zealous for the good of the community: but yet when he heard the name of Torlesse he looked grave and explained to his nephew that this man was indeed a crusty customer, who was suspected of heresy by the church, but lived in peace by making large oblations to the parson and the prior. "Leave that all to me," answered the young knight, "but tell me who shall shrive Mistress Torlesse to-day?" "Father Andrew," answered the Canon. "And is he not a man somewhat resembling myself in figure?" "Yea, but stoops exceedingly and shambles in his walk." "That is well, and with your favour and his, I will take his place and inspect the conscience of the fair penitent, and prescribe a penance for her, better than any in Father Andrew's brain." To be short Sir Philip got on the blind side of Father Andrew and obtained the loan of his habit, and at the appointed time for hearing confessions, shambled with his eyes bent on the ground into what is now called the Herbert Chapel, and there awaited his mistress, with the cowl drawn over his head, and his hands on his knees, in the shriving pew. Thither also came the girl, pale and trembling between joy and fear, for her heart had been beating terribly all the way, and at every step she looked for her lover; and, to be sure, she had dreamt of nothing else all through the night, in her little chamber of the lattice. And having left her governess kneeling in the church, she came slowly and totteringly to the chapel, stopping now and then for a moment to lay her hand upon the tombs of the old lords, for she had scarce strength to walk. And as the false monk heard those footsteps, his heart also leapt, but joyfully, and when she was within a few paces of him he started up, and then those poor trembling limbs of hers were, you may be sure, rarely sustained, and the red maiden lips felt what delight there is in a kiss. Some there are who say that all this rapture is a mere fantasy, the concept of a mind extravagant and delirious, but I believe, for my part that it is as real as any other earthly thing. At all events young people will always take a certain pleasure in the business, and certainly this penitent and confessor did so kiss, fondle, hug, and caress, murmuring such fervent endearments and pretty phrases, that poor Eva de Braose must have heard them from her monument hard by, and moved her right hand a little nearer to her stony heart. In fine Mistress Torlesse made a very famous shrift, confessing in the first place that her name was Edith, and in the second that she accepted Sir Philip's service, and would take him for her true loyal lover. But she bade him by no means come before her window any more, since her father had a keen eye and a cool aim, "and," said she, "I would rather never see your face again, my darling, than have you die for the love of me and my poor loveliness." Then Sir Philip (after that he had answered in a proper manner to this nice speech) began to enquire as to the old governess, and found that she was somewhat favourably inclined towards him, though she feared her master more than God, the saints and the devil, but yet a little gold might work wonders with her. "Then give her this," said he, drawing forth a purse with a matter of twenty pieces in it, "and promise her five times as much on our wedding day." And after making certain arrangements and appointments, the time came for them to part, the which they did, not without some trouble, for at these farewells each desires to give the last caress, and to kiss but once more, and all this takes time. However Edith went away at last, and the Pseudo-Andrew shuffled back to the convent, and gave the priest back his vestments, assuring him that things were in a very prosperous state. And from that time Sir Philip knelt beside his Edith on most days whereon she came to Mass and Evensong, with the connivance of the ancient hideous governess, to whom he persisted in paying most lowly reverence, continually dropping little purses into her hand, the which he obtained from the Canon Ambrosius. And once or twice instead of going to the monastic quire his lady met him just outside the town, and they pleased themselves by walking beside the Gavenny hand in hand. And the more Sir Philip heard of Master Maurice Torlesse the less he liked him, for everything that could be told of him was bad, save only that he was undoubtedly very rich, and kept in his house chests full of good things; besants, rose-nobles, flagons, and chalices of gold, to wit. But it fell out one day (it was in autumn, as the story was told to me) when the lovers were parting fondly after their vesper-musick was duly and sweetly sung, Edith bade her lover by no means look for her on the morrow, "since," said she, "there will be a dreadful and violent storm of thunder and lightning and furious rain, that will slay many men, and beasts, and tear up the oaks on the mountain side, and pour the brooks and the river all across the land." At this prophecy Sir Philip was in no little astonishment, for the air was dry and not too clear, no cloud was in the sky, and the western heaven was filled with the clear red glow of the sunset. And with many questions he tried to make Edith tell him what her intent was, or how she knew of tempests before they fell, when there was no sign or apparent likelihood of the same; but she would not resolve him, replying with put-offs and kisses, and twining her arms fast round his neck, so that he had to be content with these doubtful though pleasant explanations. And as he went home he saw an old husband working in the fields, whom he asked plainly if he thought a storm was approaching, receiving for answer that there could be no better prospect of fine weather; though the man, who was a wary old Silurist, ended his reply by saying "so we should think, however," but this he always did, knowing by long experience that there is no certitude or sure opinion in mortal affairs. But he always excepted one thing, and still stiffly maintained that strong ale was a good drink and a desirable. In this as we know, he was right, as he was in his all but universal cautel judicious and philosophical, notably in this matter of the weather, for on the morrow there burst a terrible and destroying storm over the town, bearing rain in torrents, and winds that hurled down wall and tower, flung heavy stones into the air, and tore up tall trees and whirled them as though they had been hazel saplings. And all the sky crashed with thunder, and the lightning seemed as if it shot up into the black accursed air from the rocks of the Grat Skirrid and the mighty dome of the Blorenge, and the peak of the Sugar Loaf; and the waters of the Uske and the Gavenny boiled and seethed and streamed out all upon the land. Then did the great bells of the Priory chime out, and the bells of St. John's, and of the Churches of St. Michael and St. Tillio, and the two St. Davids, even till all the quires of the mountains were ringing down the storm and matching the voices of the bells with the roaring of the thunder. In this wise they of course got the storm under at last, for no tempest can withstand the chime of bells, if they be rung aright; but everybody wished the wind and lightning had given in a little sooner before half-a-dozen men, a score of beasts, and as many sheep and horses had been struck dead; to say nothing of houses in flames or else quite ruinated. But it was noted that of late years there had been several of these cursed storms at Abergavenny, and some tried to prove that the weather like everything else was getting into a bad predicament and wanted the Holy Father after it. As for Sir Philip, he was in a perturbed state of mind, not wishing to have a prophetess to wife, believing that such personages were well enough in the old time, but now inconvenient, and likely to bring a man into trouble with the Archdeacon and the ecclesiastical courts. Wherefore he pressed his sweetheart strongly to tell him how she came to know anything about futurity, and perceived that his words annoyed her and drew tears into her eyes, and made her lips tremble. So with comforting the poor girl, stroking her soft hair, and kissing away the tears he forgot all about his perplexities, till he was alone again. And then they bothered him worse than before, because he saw she was afraid to resolve him, the which made Sir Philip suspect that this was a bad business. After such sort a good many interviews were held between them, always with the same beginning and end; and Philip was so strongly bound with love's tendrils that he could not break away; but he got rather thin about the face, and a hogshead of Bordeaux wine lost all but the scent and fragrance of what it had once held. In these days Brother Toricellus the Cellarer would not patiently listen to any one who affirmed Sir Philip Meyrick of Caerwent to be made of the same stuff as common men. "The times are coming," he would say, "when the Prior, the Sub-Prior, the Canons, and you and I, unworthy brethren and chiefest of sinners, shall drink water; *de torrente in via bibemus,* for there soon will be no wine left in the casks"; and all the monks grew pale and crossed themselves, for they began to think Sir Philip was a Silenus sent to chastise them for their shortcomings and misdemeanours. But Brother Toricellus, a man without faith, had led them astray, and made them shoot wide of the mark. But about a month after the storm, as Sir Philip and Edith were talking in their accustomed manner, he pressing her to clear up his doubts, and she sadly and silently hanging down her head, her love for him prevailed, and she said at last, "Well then if it must be so, come to the back of our house to-morrow evening, at four o'clock, and wait by the door of the garden wall till I open to you. But if you die, your death will be of your own seeking, and my soul shall soon follow yours, for I am not able to live apart from you, my true knight. But if you will enter this perilous tourney, put on a surcoat of green, a green cap, and be prepared to lie closely and privily." With that she burst into tears and clung to her lover, weeping as if her heart was rent in twain. But Sir Philip was overjoyed at her words, and went to his comrade the lawyer, and told him that the Romance was getting into its last books. "And John," said he, "prepare choice skins, and cut your quills very aptly, for I will have my marriage deeds executed by you and by none else." At this the lawyer puckered up his mouth, and put his hand to his head, for musing, he conceived that rolls pertaining to other matters might have to be engrossed before the contracts of marriage were made out. But he willingly obtained for Sir Philip a green surcoat and cap of soft cloth; "She will make you hide amongst leaves," said he. "So I suppose" answered the knight, "and look you, I'll have my sword not very far from me, and if there be a burial, 'twill not be of a Meyrick of Caerwent." So, like a knight of færy, he went all in green, to the appointed place, by a door in a high wall; and sat down on the grass, with his hand on his sword, looking somewhat grimly on it, for Master Torlesse had put him to great inconvenience and trouble, and he would have relished no task better than that of piercing this sour old devil to the heart. It was on occasions of this kind that Sir Philip's jaws shut tight down, and his brows and moustache went up, and between ourselves I should have preferred to let him alone, if I had seen him in such a mood, for to speak the truth when he was in the humour, and his teeth were clenched, he would have fought all the hosts of hell. *Requiem aeternam,* he was a true son of Gwent and a very perfect knight. But when the dials marked four of the afternoon, Sir Philip heard a gentle rustle at his back, and looking up he saw the door slowly open, and his lady standing with a pale face, beckoning to him. Then did Sir Philip enter, and found himself in a thick grove of trees, growing close to one another, and after that with one long and solemn kiss they had kissed each other's lips, she set him in his place, where he could lie down and look through the leaves, and forthwith left him, telling him not to stir nor make a sound, on peril of his life. And for the next hour or two the knight had full leisure allotted him, wherein to meditate on this strange case, and what he was to see that should explain his sweetheart's foreknowledge of the storm. As for the garden he found it ordinary enough, in nothing different from other closes, unless for one or two flowers of exceeding sweet fragrance and rare beauty, the which he had never seen before. But when he had turned over everything in his mind a good many times, and was feeling puzzled, weary, and very thirsty, he saw a tall old man, grey-bearded and hawk-nosed, come into the midst of the pleasaunce from the house, the same being in fact Master Torlesse, and his habit was a dark brown cloak with long hanging sleeves of tawny yellow, a black undervest, and a yellow cap on his head, shaped like a cap of maintenance, having on the front of it a jewell in silver, being the image of an eagle holding a serpent in its beak. And in his right hand was a long black wand, and from his baldrick hung a sword, and what Sir Philip saw afterwards you will find recorded in the chests of the Court *In Banco Domini* of the old Lordship and Grand Seigneury of Burgavenny. The which parchments are marked on the outside *"In the affair of the pardon of Phillippus Meyrick de Caerwent, Miles Auratus, for the murder of Mauritius called Torlesse, a man of unknown lineage and estate."* And as I myself, by the favour of the Clerk, have seen these strange documents, have indeed fingered them and held them under my nose for many hours together till I seemed to hear an ancient law-man reciting and droning the dim old story in my ears, I will make an abbreviature and digest of it for you using as far as I can the phrase of the original. The which beginneth somewhat as follows. In the year of our Saviour MCCCLXXII, the forty-fifth year of our Sovereign Lord King Edward third of that name since the Conquest, the fourth of our Lord Jehan third of that name, Baron of Burgavenny, Earl of Pembroke, Lieutenant of Acquitaine, and Lord Marcher of Wales; on St. Denys his day at eleven o'clock in the forenoon there came before us, Guillaume de Oskington, being the judge appointed under the seal of our Lord Jehan aforesaid, to rightly and duly discharge, do and execute justice in his Lordship of Burgavenny, Clement la Touche Prior of the Convent of St. Mary the Virgin, in the town of Abergavenny, the same appearing in the stead of the Canon Ambrosius, who professes that he is from age and infirmity unable himself to appear and plead his petition. And Prior Clement the above-named ecclesiastic, being honourably received by us, and we having allowed him to plead in the place of the Canon Ambrosius, he has humbly sued that a pardon shall be made out, granted, and published to the person named Philip Meyrick, a knight, who, having been delivered into the hands of our Master Sergeant, is now in the prison of the Court, and there awaits his trial on the ground that he did violently and maliciously take away the life of a certain Maurice Torlesse, an inhabitant of this town, unduly, unlawfully, feloniously and against the peace of our Lord Jehan, third of that name. And we having consented to receive this petition and to hear testimony and witness upon it, so that, if it may be, it shall be supported, buttressed, and firmly established out of the mouths of several persons, who have professed themselves willing to give evidence before us, Guillaume de Oskington, on this behalf; we have caused our clerk to write down the matter of their depositions, so that the truth of this affair may be the more clearly known and understanded. And in the first place has come before us John of Gloucester, a lawyer of the Chancery of this Lordship, who has read to the Court the relation of this affair taken down by him in cursive characters from the lips of Sir Philip Meyrick, to the which document Sir Philip Meyrick has affixed his seal in token that it is the truth. And in this deed is shewn how the petitioner having become enamoured of Mistress Edith Torlesse . . . . (Here I shall leave out a page, for we have heard all this before) . . . . and that after he had lain hidden in the grove, as he conceives for the space of two hours, he saw the late Maurice Torlesse come into the garden and stand in the midst thereof, holding in his hand a long wand, the which is now in the keeping of the court. And he affirms that up to this time it was as fine and as dry a day, as he had ever seen, and that there were no clouds to be made out from one side of heaven to the other. But he states that Maurice Torlesse, standing in the midst of the close, first struck the earth with his wand, then throwing up both his hands, with the palms turned out and open. Forthwith the ground began to tremble and shake, and to heave up and down, sending out evil vapours, which curled in wreaths and floated in the air. Then Maurice Torlesse struck the earth a second time, pronouncing with a loud voice the name Sabiao; and the earth shook more violently, and in the one place piled itself into the similitude of mountains, and in another fell as it were into valleys; and springs of water burst forth and flowed between the hills like to brooks and rivers. Then was the bare earth covered with grass and trees and cornfields, and whilst the wizard continually uttered invocations (which the petitioner does not recollect, for he professes not to be a clerk, and affirms moreover that with this wild monstrous work his brain was muddled) slowly was built up in a valley below a bare round hill, twice the height of an ant-hill, the walls of a town, and the houses of it, and without one gate was a castle, and without the other gate a quire. Then mansions and churches and farmsteads and cabins appeared on the face of the country around, and cattle and horses and sheep were made, and last of all men and women walking through the town, or labouring in the fields. Then did Sir Philip Meyrick perceive that he saw before him in little, the likeness of the town of Abergavenny; and the hills were the Blorenge, and Skirrid, and Sugar Loaf, and the streams the Honthy and Gavenny and Uske. But as he beheld this wonder the wreaths of accursed smoke, which came forth from the earth, began to mix with one another, and to gather together, and spread out above the earth, like clouds, and to drift across the mountains, as Maurice Torlesse continually waved his wand above them. Then did they change to a black colour, and seemed like ink, and the wizard smote the earth, where it resembled the cleft of the Great Skirrid, and flame gushed out from the end of the wand and ran all along the clouds as it had been lightning, and a noise of thunder began to sound, and the clouds poured forth a storm of rain upon the earth. But whilst all this was being done in little by art magic and devilish contrivance, the same was performed in great, and in truth a very terrible storm of rain and thunder had fallen on Abergavenny, and the church bells were set ringing, at the sound whereof the wizard laughed aloud, and smote his clouds asunder so that he might look down upon the town and see here a burnt mansion, here a heap of ruins, and here a man scorched and blackened with the forking fire, or struggling for his life in the flood. But as he gazed thus, it is supposed that he must have glanced at his own garden, and so have seen Sir Philip Meyrick hiding amidst the trees; for without more ado, he drew his sword, and rushed furiously towards him, leaving the storm to take care of itself. And the petitioner deposeth that seeing this dreadful wizard coming thus with sword in hand, he was in some dismay, not for fear of his adversary's arm, but for terror of his art; and also because he was an old gray beard, whom to kill would bring no honour nor worship. Yet, seeing no choice in the matter, and not wishing to die by hands so vile and abominable, he called upon the Heavenly Host and especially upon his patron St. Philip the Apostle, and drawing his sword, went forth against Maurice Torlesse, and had need of all his capacity, or else he affirms he would have been pierced through at the first onset. But never has he had so bitter a fight, in any battle oversea against knights of renown and fame, mighty warriors clad cap-a-pé in steel harness, as against this old man, for the sword of him seemed to dart from all quarters at once, and ever sought to home within his heart. And in this fight Sir Philip Meyrick received ten grievous wounds, some of which did put his life in danger, but at last, he suddenly stepped back, and with all the hatred of his soul whirling his sword aloft cleft the wizard from top to toe, so that he died not long after. And at the death of him all his fantastic device of mountains and streams and the walled town seemed to melt away, and the clouds also as they appeared, in thin wreaths; and at that time the veritable storm of heaven ceased to rage. And this he professes is the whole truth of the matter, no more and no less, wherefore he craves of his liege Lord Jehan, third of that name, misericorde and pardon, for that the late Maurice Torlesse was a right foul and pestilent wizard, to send whom to his eternal torment of hell-fire was well done and thankworthy. And here endeth the relation and prayer of Sir Philip Meyrick, Knight of Caerwent; the which deed we have read and inspected, and declare that it is duly signed, sealed, witnessed, and attested.

Next have come before us, Guillaume de Oskington, Masters Robin Pyatt and Samuel Owen, surgeons, who state that they have had experience in sword cuts, spear thrusts, hacks, stabs, and the like wounds, having been in the wars oversea against the French and Spaniards. And they declare themselves to be competent persons, sufficiently learned in the ancient physical authors, and have produced for our satisfaction divers parchments, the which we have read and find them sufficient witness and surety for the aptness of these persons. Who declare that they have made examination of the body of Sir Philip Meyrick, and have found upon it ten wounds, being about the head, midriff, arms and breast, and they declare that five of these wounds are grievous and should have been mortal, had not the blood of the wounded man been pure and uncorrupted, and his strength very great. And they have also examined the body of the late Maurice Torlesse, and find that it was cleft into two equal parts by a most admirable and artificial stroke, the which no bone or sinew could resist. And they have found no other wound upon the dead man, from his head to his feet. But craving the indulgence and consideration of the Court, they have prayed us to look favourably upon the accused knight, saying that a man who cuts so clean is too good for the axe or halter, since there are no traces of bungling or awkwardness about his handiwork.

Next has come before us Mistress Edith Torlesse, the sweetheart of Sir Philip Meyrick, who has shewn us how this affair came about, confirming in all respects the words of the knight. And having lifted her veil, at our desire, she has answered all such questions as we have thought fit to put her, in a modest and maidenly manner; only with great difficulty confessing her father to have been a man in all respects malicious and cruel, but could say nothing as to his parentage, nor from whence he came at the first, for she knew nought on these matters. And having been interrogated by us, as to how she knew when her father was about to do these works of the devil, she has replied that from his laughter and glee she ever knew when he had this operation in his mind. And being further questioned by us, for what cause was it that her father would not give her in marriage, or allow her to meddle with love affairs, the which, *obiter dicendo,* we Guillaume de Oskington affirmed to be the natural, fit, and laudable employment for so rare a beauty and perfect grace of maidenhood; she has answered to us, not without blushes, that it was for fear lest her lover might come to be informed of her father's practices, and so bring him to ruin. And hereupon we have ended our interrogation, and have had this maiden honourably escorted back to her own house.

And lastly has come before us Dom. Anthony Flambard, a Canon of the Cathedral Church of St. Paul, in the City of London; an ecclesiastic well acquainted with the Canon Law, and a very sound and capable divine. Who, having read all the depositions relating to this affair of the murder of Maurice called Torlesse, and having talked at length with Sir Philip Meyrick and Mistress Edith Torlesse, has come to a thorough understanding of the matter; and has declared to us the whole nature and essence of the incantations whereby storms and tempests are drawn down to earth. And all his opinions and doctrines he has confirmed and maintained out of Holy Writ, the holy Fathers and Doctors of the Church, and out of the works of learned men of the Universities of Salamanca and Padua; so that in all of what he has said there are no mistakes at all. And he declares that this operation and invocation of tempests is done by means of devils and fiends of hell, and that it is a foul sin and shame in any Christian man to do such works. Wherefore he is of opinion (speaking with all submission toward my Lord Jehan de Hastings, third of that name, and this honourable

Court) that Maurice Torlesse was fitly punished by the hands of Sir Philip Meyrick. Though he declares that he would this accursed wizard could have been taken alive and delivered into the hands of Holy Church, that a fit punishment might have been meted out to him, who was not worthy of so knightly a death.

And we, Guillaume de Oskington, having received authority from my Lord Jehan, third of that name, Baron of Burgavenny, Earl of Pembroke, Lieutenant of Acquitaine, and Lord Marcher of Wales, in this behalf, for that our Lord aforesaid is now beyond seas in the service of our Lord the King; and having power in this affair either to give doom of death or life whichever shall seem good to us; having duly gone through all the evidence that could be brought before us, and having examined Sir Philip Meyrick of Caerwent, both publickly and privily, have determined to grant the petition of Clement La Touche, Prior of the Convent of St. Mary, the same being proctor for the Canon Ambrosius, as is aforesaid. And we have therefore caused a pardon to be made out in the form accustomed and sealed with the Great Seal of my Lord Jehan; and have decreed that Sir Philip Meyrick shall be forthwith enlarged from his captivity and be no more in the custody of our Master Sergeant; and that no fines nor amercements of any kind be taken from him, on this behalf, neither now, nor hereafter.

So the old record ends, and under the name of the good judge is the great waxen seal of the Barons of Burgavenny; which in those days was strong enough to open dungeons and shut them, to kill or to save. Hence it was that Sir Philip and Edith were brought together before the altar of the conventual church of St. Mary's, and became the bravest couple in all Gwent. And the first thing that Sir Philip did, after he had received Maurice Torlesse his estate by right of his wife, was to bear a thousand pieces of gold to the Prior, that the roodscreen and loft, with a fair rood and images of St. Mary and St. John, might be forthwith executed, the which was done so sumptuously and honestly that there was not another to compare with it in all the Marches of Wales. And every year Sir Philip made an oblation of a hogshead of French wine to the monastery, and he made build also the chapel of St. Philip, having an altar of alabaster, and a shrine adorned with jewells, and stories annealed in the window o'er the altar: and this he did because the saint had succoured him in his great necessity. And here he and his wife were buried, when they had lived for long years together happily and their last day was done, and a glorious tomb was made over them carved with images, and coat armour, very specially and decently cut out. But all this chapel has since been ruined and prophaned by wicked men, on whose heads may God's curse alight, both here and hereafter. But the Prior Clement la Touche said to the Cellarer "Next time, Brother Toricellus, have a little more faith." In such wise was renewed again the house of Meyrick, and so firmly established that it hath never been more prosperous than now. But you see how foolishly the old wizard conducted his affairs, and what an ass he was to think he could subdue the God of Love, and shut his doors upon lovers. It was this folly of his that brought death and dishonour to him at last; for I daresay that if he had behaved like a sensible man, and treated Sir Philip courteously and honourably, his son-in-law would have looked over his little eccentricities and let him die in peace. But I suppose he would have made him live a good way off, because a father-in-law who deals in storms and is in the habit of pumping thunder, is by no means a desirable neighbour. However I dare say everything happened for the best, and certainly Sir Philip and his sweetheart got on very well without this unpleasant old personage, who not content with being a wizard, must needs be also a fool. But let all of us ever serve our Liege Lord Love, and worship him with a perfect worship; swearing still by the Ladies and the Peacock.

So did Nick Leonard bring his tale of the Lady of the Lattice to an end; and we clapped our hands, for we had relished it mightily all through, and thought it might compare with the story of Abergavenny told by Master Ambrose. The musicians praised it also to excess, for they had not heard anything quite like this before; though I should suspect that some fine strokes were lost upon them. And while we were discussing and pointing out to these good fellows the beauties and Silurian wisdom of the relation, we began to wonder at the marvellous art and grammar of the old wizard, who was able to perform such a magistery. All of us agreed that there is no such work done in our days, and Mosca said, "If you, sir, had not so clearly and evidently shewn the matter to us, I should have thought this a thing impossible to men." "Why, signor," answered Nick, "you must know that it is not altogether of faith to believe the story, though I myself credit it entirely; as I do everything set forth and approved by the good judge Guillaume; and he it is plain believed every word of Sir Philip's deposition, or else had not granted him his pardon. But I must in honesty tell you that there is another account of the affair done at the House with the Lattice; the source of which is the mouths of evil-speakers, who are always ready to spit upon dead men's graves and to defile honourable families. These fellows tell us that Sir Philip was a profligate and idle rascal, my sweet Edith a harebrained foolish wench, and Maurice Torlesse an honest grave gentleman, who with much ado tried to keep his daughter a virtuous woman. And they declare that Sir Philip murdered the poor man in cold blood, and with his sweetheart concocted all the strange story of the incantation, because the elder would not give this rakish wastrel his daughter. But who would credit such an idle story? None I believe but a foolish, malicious personage, whose heart was galled with the dignity and worship of a right illustrious, honourable and ancient house. However 'tis of no more use to get warm and use strong language concerning this matter than any other; for trust me, gentlemen, all things are solved by sitting still, and not by walking about with cheeks puffed out with big words. Come Tom, spit out a tale, but by the Dogstar and the full moon in glory, let's have no more of your devilish alchemists or any theological tales or records." The good Rubrican was hurt by this address, for he had a great notion of his story of Caldicot, the which he considered a moral and profitable relation; however he suffered the insult to pass and stroked his stomach softly for a few seconds, then put his finger to his nose, and thus began.

THE TRIUMPH OF LOVE

One fine morning in July, just as the shadows were equal all round the world (or at all events in Gwent, and that is sufficient for our purposes) and the clocks of our holy faith were confessing in a variety of manners that it was noonday; the Fair Folk of Wentwood Chase were amusing themselves by the spectacle of a young knight, wandering about under the greenwood in a perplexed and vagrant fashion, as if he did not exactly know whitherwards to go or what to do with himself. What the Fair Folk thought of him, I can't tell you, because I am unhappily unlearned in the Language of Færy, and have read none of their Chronicles, Memorabilia, Annals, or Commentaries; but I have reason to think they approved of him because he chanced to wear a green surcoat and was a proper man besides. On this green vestment were blazed three golden stags in pale; and to speak the truth they paced through herbage of a faded and autumnal sort, which bore the russet vestiges of many a storm of wine, and had undoubtedly done good service in its day. From my mention of the knight's coat you will have guessed, of course, that he was one of the d'Espalions of Gascony, and this is indeed the fact; and he of whom I tell you bore the name of Sir Symon d'Espalion and thus was the son of a right illustrious house forced to wander through the forests of a foreign land. Is not this shocking? But there was no help for it, since he had been so unfortunate as to get mixed up in disputes with the High Sheriff of Gascony, who grew violent and desired to hang Sir Symon by the neck; but the knight thought it would be foolhardy to try this experiment, and left France suddenly. Never enter into arguments with these Sheriffs, because they are testy fellows, and have friends who are rather fond of trying how long one can live without any breath. However Symon was young and somewhat untried in the wickedness of the world, so it is not admirable that he made a few mistakes at the beginning—some men do nothing else from beginning to end, and are it is plain themselves mere incarnate fallacies. It needs not to enquire concerning the matter of the discussion between the Sheriff and the Knight; but I am pretty certain that in this case as in all others love was at the bottom of the mischief. Possibly it was love of black eyes, red lips, and a neat figure, or maybe of curiosities such as coins, jewells, bracelets and gauds of that description, or perchance merely a love of a complete vengeance—it's of no importance. But I incline to think it was the last item that sent Sir Symon abroad, from certain hints and dark sayings in the Chronicle; and certainly Vengeance was the mistress of many in that age; whereby she is proven to be a notorious slut and wanton as well as an ill-tempered harridan. But however that may be, here was the knight a good many miles away from his native castle, with very few nobles in his pocket, and not too much victual or drink in his stomach, wandering on this fine July morrow through the wet glades of Wentwood Chase. For it had rained without ceasing a whole week, and even now the great white clouds were slowly rolling away to westward like tall ships in full sail, and leaving behind them a deep blue firmament and a hot sun, which made everything smoke and steam. You will suppose perhaps that the warmth and light and pleasant air caused the exile to cheer up and sing snatches of ballads and rondels; but I assure you it was not so. For what good is an azure heaven to a man when his heart is shrouded in sable and thick darkness; or do you think a joyous dancing air that sets the boughs a-tremble and the fairy-bells a-chiming can rejoice him whose soul is driven across a wilderness of sorrow without hope? Nay these things do but increase our grief (unless we be thoroughly indoctrinated and inebriated with the subtlest and mellowest knowledge of Siluria) and only made Sir Symon regret with sharper anguish the misfortunes that had reft him from the bluer sky of his own country. But as it happened he was one of those persons who are well taken care of, and somehow or other, set upon their legs. People fortunate in the same way declare the cause to be a keen wit and a skill in untying tangles; others who are poor all their days and leave no money for wax tapers or masses, say it's all luck and impudence. I don't pretend to decide which of the two opinions be the verity; and I really don't think it matters a pin's head, for our business is to take whatever comes without noise either of rejoicing or lamentation, since neither will last for very long. As for the wandering knight he chanced upon a road leading through the forest to a castle built there by the Lord Marcher of Estrighoil, both for the defence of his lordship and for his pleasure when he would leave his halls above Wye water, and go-a-hunting in Wentwood. This castle was at first only one great round tower, but afterwards it had been made larger and furnished with an eight-sided tower and a hall, and surrounded by a pool of water; and it was on a high place looking over the greeny billows of the forest and many a hill and valley and long level of the beloved Gwentian land. As for the name I am in some difficulty for some called it Taroggy, some Strogul, and others Struggle, which has made learned men mix things up and confound this forest fort with the great castle of Estrighoil above the Wye and the Severn and Chepstow town. But I believe Struggle will suit us best, for it means something, and this is more than can be said of Taroggy, unless one happens to understand the niceties, contractions, mutations and amplifications of the tongue of the Terrestrial Paradise. And it so fell out that Sir Symon d'Espalion found himself about half-a-mile from this place, and as he stood musing and doubting whether to toil up or shamble down, the faint notes of a horn wound afar off were borne unto his ears; and looking to the quarter whence this music came, he saw in the valley below a goodly company on horseback, knights in glittering steel, with bannerets; and as he rightly judged ladies also, and men following a-foot; all coming leisurely in brave array toward him, and sounding the horn by turns. And again Sir Symon was in doubt, namely as to whether he should run into the deep hollows of the wood and hide himself; or rather run to meet this gallant band; and his difficulty he solved by sitting down on the roots of a beech-tree as being a less troublesome method than either of the other two. This was certainly a moderate and contemplative conclusion and was perhaps the best he could have made; and to be short it served his occasions. For two knights rode on in front of the main body, whose business it was to keep a sharp look out for cutthroats, high and low tobies, banded robbers and other bad characters who are to be met with in large woods; I must crave pardon for calling these artists bad, but in fact they are not salutary for travellers. And the two knights spying out Sir Symon rode up to him cautiously, for there might possibly be more in him than met the eye, and more of him behind the trees; however no cross-bolts rapped their armour, and they halted opposite to the knight and began to ask him questions, in order to find out whether he were a rogue or an honest man; or, to be more precise, Silurian, and philosophical, whether there were more of roguery or of honesty in him. But when he answered them courteously in fine phrases of Paris town, that he was of the d'Espalions, pointing to the blazon of his surcoat; they perceived at once that he was a good Christian and a virtuous gentleman; and if a due and melodious accent, a pleasant smile, and a good coat are not sufficient evidences of virtue and a good heart underneath, I profess I know not what are. In fine Sir Symon prayed the knights to take him before their lord, who they let him know was no less than Ivo Fitz-Baderon, Earl of Estrighoil, and Lord of Netherwent on the Marches of Wales. And when he drew near to and met this nobleman as he rode at the head of his band, Symon perceived that this was indeed a great lord and worshipful, for, in the words of the old poem, there was:

A ramping lyon on his breast;
Five golden lilies gay
About it were, and for his crest
He bore a raven aye.

And beside him rode his daughter Bertha, of whom I will speak more hereafter, and behind him ladies, knights, esquires, pages, men-at-arms, and serving men and, to be short, it was a right brave array glittering with gold and silken stuff and stronger steel and dark eyes of maidens strongest of all. And when Sir Symon came before the Lord Ivo Fitz-Baderon, he bowed low and craved leave to address him: which being granted he thus began. "You see before you, my lord, a poor, banished, and luckless knight, whom envy and severity have driven away from his country and who is now forced to lie like a robber in woods and mountains and secret places, and to live like a wild-beast rather than a gentleman; and all this to his great hurt, sorrow, and ennuy. Wherefore I humbly crave your help and aid, and for ever I will be your liege man and warray against all your enemies." And the Earl, a noble of a large heart and some sense, seeing that Sir Symon was a well made man whose arm might come useful, replied by bidding one of the men at arms give the knight his horse, and then made him ride at his side, while he asked him a few questions and made sure that he wore his own coat and that his genealogy was a tolerably long one. As to the reasons which brought Sir Symon across the water the Earl left them alone, knowing that knights of the best kind sometimes have to leave their homes rapidly and pick up a living roughly in odd places. Soon they reached the utmost height of the hill and came before the gate of Struggle where was the Ranger of Wentwood and his men bowing low; for you must understand that Earl Ivo intended to lie here some weeks and to kill a good many fat bucks or whatever he could find even if it chanced to be a marten or a fox. And since I have said that there had been great rains for some time before, I will tell you that things had been terribly dull at Estrighoil; there had been yawning from dawn to dusk and melancholy listening to the plash of the rain and the rattle of the vanes as they swung round from south to west and from west to south. Some people, I know, think Dullness a young deity born late and in our own days, and conceive that the lords of the old time had so many battles, sieges, storms, rebellions, jousts and tournaments to attend to that they never were idle; but this is not the truth. Some of them amused themselves in dull times by looking after the morals of their subjects and hanging folks by the neck, but this made them unpopular because the common people have no patience with anybody who tells them they are doing wrong and tries to raise them heaven-ward. Earl Ivo certainly, an easy-going, merry, old lord who knew he was made of clay himself, was not the sort of man to take advantage of others' flaws and cracks, and never strangled any one unless he was obliged to, even in rainy weather. But his temper, it must be confessed, used to get terribly short, and his odd profane expressions in which he mixed up all sorts of things, made the gargoyles laugh; but then they had plenty to do and spouted water all day and all night. And Bertha his daughter and her ladies were in not much better case; being bored and ready to say yes to anything, or to anybody that would invent some new entertainment for them. The which is a very dangerous state for maidens to be in; and if I were master of a house of them, I would myself draw my mouth into queer shapes, squint, and play the fool to make them laugh: but I hope I shall never have very many to look after. Some of the knights and pages did their best to amuse the poor girls by making love to them; but somehow they were not in the humour for it, and only yawned at the very finest speeches and most passionate orations. The fool also had done his best and was more successful for a while, since he was no ordinary jester or concocter of stale jokes; but a man of subtle and curious wit who played with a merry sadness on the black keys of this our Mortal Life, and drew therefrom quaint harmony that made one cry and laugh at the same time. But the lords and ladies grew weary of him also and called him hard names, since they were all in that cheerful humour which tires and grows sick of everything, and conceives the worst torment of Hell to be an everlasting Dullness. On the whole therefore, it was rather fortunate, when the drip, drip, drip of the rain ceased and the sun shone down through the high windows of the hall, casting many a glorious tincture of blazonry on the floor and on the arras. Without much consideration or brow-knitting Earl Ivo determined to hold a hunting month at Struggle, and told Bertha to gather her gear together, which she did very willingly, loving the greenwood and the woodland air. Perhaps you would like to know what Bertha was like, and if this be so

I will endeavour to satisfy you; though in my own opinion all young maids are just alike—that is, to them that like them. However this was the fashion of her, and this is the kind of girl that makes a Silurian's lips pucker up into an O, his right arm bend into a curve, his heart beat fast, and his mouth water. Understand then that her hair (to begin where one should begin) was like an old bronze medal that has been dipped a moment into *aqua fortis,* and shews here like red gold, there well-nigh black, and here, there and everywhere all manner of glints and shadows between the two extremes. Of forehead there was not much, for forehead we ask not, and shall not cry "gra'merci" if you exhibit to us one never so lofty and well-compacted; but what eyebrows and lashes, and below what eyes—black, or say rather, like two deep wells at noonday, with stars shining in them, and in these wells many were drowned, and all swore there's none such pleasant death as drowning. Her nose was a special nose, neither too long nor too short, too flat nor too high, too thin nor too thick, but had just that little turn at the end which virtuosi in noses declare to be desirable. For these gentlemen aver that this dainty button says as much as "I'm a woman and not an angel," and is a sure sign of those charming imperfections which make the ladies perfect. As for Bertha's mouth it was (to be honest with you) the only member of her that could be taxed or censured. Why? For that it was incomplete and not perfect nor sufficient in itself, being so choicely and rarely contrived with concave and convex parts that it was evidently devised to fit into another piece of like workmanship, if nature had turned out any at all comparable with it. Of her chin I must maintain that it was a chin dear, delicate, and intolerably precious, with dimples playing at Barley Break across it, as sunshine quivers across the rippling water of a pebbly brook, when it has to pass through many leaves, and lights now here, now there, according as the breeze stirs the boughs high or low, to right or left. And what a figure had this noble maiden! One must not go closely into these matters, but know that Bertha was of a most exquisite taille, which matched her face in every respect, and would have made Madam Phryne feel spiteful. But now I have said all these nice things about this nice girl, I am compelled in common honesty to tell you that those fine eyes of hers were roving eyes which glanced here, there and everywhere, and when joined to her smile, were known to have made

Canons and Archdeacons stutter and lose their places. And while Earl Ivo, and Bertha, knights, esquires, pages, and Sir Symon d'Espalion were nourishing themselves and irrigating their throats in the hall at Struggle, my lady looked once or twice so sweetly and shyly on the stranger that he forgot all his troubles in a moment, and understood that he was in for a pretty sharp attack of love. He resigned himself to the disease quietly, knowing that love is on the whole an amusing affair enough, full of various experiences and novelties, and sometimes not without solid profit, if it be judiciously conducted. As for Bertha she had dropped her lashes once too often; since Sir Symon was a blade of keener metal than any she had dealt with, and she found him before long to be a doctor in that science of which all profess to know a piece; and they that talk least of it often know most. However Sir Symon had other things to think of that evening, for Earl Ivo proposed to take him into his service, to give him a new surcoat twice a year and as much meat and drink as a gentleman ought to have—*e a sustenir le devant dit Symon taunt come il vivera en manager e en beovere avenauntement come a gental homme a peut*—as it stands in the indenture drawn up by Master David, the Earl's scrivener. I do not think it necessary to tell you all the particulars of this document; because you might grow rather weary, and besides, (to speak the truth) the learned disagree as to the quantity of oats that Sir Symon's horses were to eat in a day, and I should be sorry to put any false notions into your heads on this important point. But you may depend upon it that the knight agreed pretty quickly to this offer, as he would have done in any case, but now all the more since he had farsed the indenture in his own mind with another item, namely "e en amur," for a gentleman requires something more besides meat and drink and two robes yearly. This agreement dated, witnessed, signed and sealed, Sir Symon made himself very agreeable to everybody by telling the newest tales that were being relished in Gascony; regular candle-time relations, the which raised such deep roars of laughter that the oak-trees of Wentwood heard the sound and have been laughing among themselves ever since, though silly people call it sighing. As if a stout old oak, sound to the heart, and devoid of care, ever did anything so foolish as to sigh! But these numskulls think the whole world is in the dumps as they themselves are. And from that day began the pleasantest time Sir Symon had in his life; for the sun, that puissant Lord Marcher, swept the clouds right away into Severn Sea and ruled in a Lordship of perpetual azure. Then was it pleasant to ride beneath the branches beside Bertha and her ladies, and to study the sweet varieties of maidenhood, the which is indeed an enchanting thing—when it happens to be in a good temper. But we may be sure Sir Symon had changed his dress and smartened himself up, for he knew that ladies have almost as much liking for a surcoat rightly embroidered and cut to the fashion as for the Theological Virtues, and much more than for the first two Evangelical Counsels, though they think that the third, Obedience, is becoming in a husband. But while Sir Symon made good cheer for all the girls, he kept his choicest fare for Bertha, and little by little wove his incantations round her till her girlish soul was quite hushed and submissive under the sweetest and strangest of all spells on earth. There are many methods and systems in this curious magic, and I suppose everybody puts some little originality into his love-making; but one thing is very certain, namely that love is a thing which does not grow stale: a doctrine which is clearly proved by the persistence and obstinacy of the human race in this pursuit. I suppose it is more than five thousand years since the first kiss came off; concerning which you may read in the books written by the Rosy Cross Fraternity, and therein you will find the *Ubi* and *Quando,* and *Relatio* of it. But it is wonderful to think how much kissing has been going on ever since, and not a sign, so far, of its going out of fashion. And after Bertha and her knight had ridden a good many times side by side and he had said a number of pretty things which she had answered with glances that slid out of her eyes like summer lightning from an ebon sky; it fell out that they rode one day before all the rest, and roamed even farther, till the sound of voices and laughing was broken and died into silence. And now the only sounds were a gentle rustling as the boughs above swayed to and fro in the southern wind, and that continual murmur of summer time, which tells us of the labour of the bees. And the voices of Bertha and Sir Symon were hushed also, but they rode very close together and seemed to lean toward one another; so that Gwyn-ap-Neath the King of Færy who happened to be going the same way, held his little sides for laughing and poked his little Prothonotary hard in the ribs, to make him understand there was a joke. You will wonder perhaps that the knight did not set about his business in earnest, finding himself thus alone with his dear lady; but the reason is that love is fearful; though at the same time it is most hardy; the which is a dogma to be believed without any questions, cavils, or argumentations. But before long, finding they were far away from their fellows he leant toward Bertha and kissed her on the cheek, without asking leave or license, whence we may perceive that the field was ready for the crop, the fagots for the torch, the bread for the oven, and, in effect, Bertha's cheek for her lover's lips. For indeed she made no remonstrance whatever, only a crimson dawn of Very Love flushed from her breast to her forehead; and since she had been anxiously expecting some such pleasant occurrence for the last mile, it would have been foolish to scream when it came about. But it is really impossible to talk to one's sweetheart, as she should be talked to, on horseback (unless you are both on the same horse) wherefore Sir Symon presently jumped down, and laying his arm delicately round Bertha's waist, had her most exquisite arms twined about his neck and so brought her to the ground. Then did he spread her a soft throne of ferns on the roots of a tree, and kneeling at her feet, began to intone the Hours of Paphos in a mellow and passionate voice, for they had said the *secreta* some time before. Perhaps you do not understand me and have never heard of these offices, and indeed they are no longer sung in the flaming old-fashioned manner; for the times are degenerate. Well this is how Sir Symon began—"Darling, when the sun ariseth he shines in through my window and finds me awake and pale for thinking of thee; and when he sinketh below the western hills he leaves me still enlightened with the rarer glories of thine eyes." "'Las, dear love," answered Bertha, "far away below us are the level moors; but we are in a greeny dell of Wentwood Chase; so was my life before thou camest compared to what it now is. O my sweetheart how shall I love thee aright?" "Love me and the kisses of my mouth even as the meadows love the dew in August, as the stones love the ripple of the brook, as the cornfields love the harvest moon ruddily ascending or shaped in sickle wise." "Thou art my mighty glorious sun and I thine earth yearning for the rays of thy love." "Thou art mine evening star, shining in the glow of sunset; my rose-garden and my paradise wherein I take my pleasure." The King of Færy heard all this and a great deal more; but he found a little of it go a long way and moved on with his train to hold a speech-court under a great oak, whither all the Fair Folk of Wentwood assembled. And after Bertha and Sir Symon d'Espalion had brought their service to an end, had kissed and colled and looked into one another's eyes, had spoken and remained silent; they began to consider that it would be as well to mount and make their way to Struggle without delay, since folks are apt to be suspicious and say nasty things of a knight and a lady who get lost in the woods together. The general lack of charity indeed, was and is, a most sorrowful thing; one has only to be seen going by the same road once or twice in a week and they say directly "What wench is he after?" "Who lives on the other side of the hill?" And if a young gentleman is seen alone with a lady there are seldom wanting malicious personages who declare they are lovers. I hope you will always avoid these courses and if you see me at any time rather close to a girl with black eyes; say presently "They are discussing philosophical questions," in the which statement you cannot fail to be right and accurate. But the two lovers of Wentwood, in mortal fear of busybodies and unkind observations rode swiftly, or as swiftly as the undergrowth would let them, to Struggle and found the knights and hunting men in the court slicing up a few bucks and drinking as much as gentlemen ought to drink. Here Sir Symon handed Bertha down with such a complete and icy courtesy that several knowing winks were nipped short, and mouths were opened instead of eyes being shut; for they were simple men and unversed in stratagems and deceits. And all the evening Sir Symon clung to the skirts of a nice girl with yellow hair and long fingers, whom he entertained with ballads, canzonets, little stories, and odd questions, and, I am afraid, rather turned her head; for his manners, it must be confessed, were extremely pleasing. And using some caution and looking out for brambles in his path Sir Symon contrived to live as joyously as any knight could desire for the next week or two; for how pleasant are the beginnings of love and the various wandering byways which all lead to the same place. Byways, do I say? Rather ladders, graduals to the Mount Marvellous and the Castle beyond Conceit, mounting through deep blossoming orchards, flowery closes, and boskages of solemn scent; and the way now illuminate and radiant, now dim and mystical; but all most lovely, sweet, unearthly, quite passing all compare. Here we cannot climb alone, to the solitary the gate is barred, and the bridge drawn up across

the deep blackness of the moat of melancholy; but hither maiden
hands do guide us, red lips entice, and a girl's eyes are lamps before us.
From what I have said before of my Bertha, you know that she was
one whom the stars had shapen marvellously, and choicely well, and
Sir Symon found that she led him by sweeter paths to bliss than any
that his dreaming soul had trodden; or any that he had fashioned formerly in the bygone ballad of his life. Let us no more say that they rode
through Wentwood, or looked on Severn Sea and the waving cornfields
of Gwent; but rather wandering they went among the mazes of a Forest
of Phansy; rested beneath trees of might unimaginable; and saw below
them golden clouds, shining water, and glittering vanes, high turrets, and
pinnacles now lifted merely above a silver misty sea, and now rising
from tower and gateway and stony wall. And oh! the pomps and glorious shows they beheld (when their hands were clasped) in the courts of
the castle; for thither *all ancient noble lovers did resort* as the old poet tells us.
For he says—

> *They that have truly kept the ordinance*
> *The King has made, which is our Lord Royall,*
> *With perfect love and leal observance;*
> *When that the doom of death do on them fall*
> *Then do they win their bliss and maintenance*
> *And joyous pleasure in a wondrous hall.*
> *It is so fair, I guess it passeth thought,*
> *And by no rhyming may at all be sought.*

Hither then did Bertha and Symon look from the greeny lattices that
the hazel and the rose and honeysuckle twisted; since they had vowed,
either to other, a perfect and enduring love, and so had fellowship with
the true lovers of the old time, who for their King's sake had endured
pain and sorrow, shame, death and dishonour rather than transgress
their faith and law. But one day as these two sweethearts were busily
engaged in their favourite occupations; that is to say the business and
quidditative investigation of searching for the soul of a kiss; pursuing
that queer, subtle, and undoubtedly delicious entity through all its
transformations; a sudden thought came into Bertha's depositary of
notions, and this thought made her knit her brows. "Do you think my
Father would like to see us thus?" asked she, stroking Sir Symon's
curly hair in a meditative kind of way. "Hardly I suppose," answered

the knight, "seeing that I am an exiled man, living only from his board: but it isn't of much consequence, is it?" "Only that my Father is Ivo Fitz-Baderon, Lord of Estrighoil, and master here of all men's lives and liberties." "Well he could only hang me." "I dont think I should altogether like to see you hanged; besides if that happened you would not be able to marry me, and you would like me to be your wife, wouldn't you?" "Yes I should certainly like to marry you now you re-mind me, and as you say, the ecclesiastical law forbids wedlock with ghostly men. But do you think my Lord suspects anything?" "He never suspects, but he sometimes hangs when he thinks he is in danger of being suspicious, for he says this is a very sinful state of mind." "Then shall we ride away together?" "To whitherward?" "Why I don't know exactly, but I suppose there are other lords on the Marches, who would willingly buy the sword of a gallant gentleman and shelter him against his enemies." "Ay, there is my lord Humphrey de Bohun of Caldicot, to whose son I am promised; and the Baron of Burgavenny my father's brother-in-arms, and the Lord of Uske our cousin: think you that these would have warm sheets ready for us." "Well, yes; but perhaps too warm; and now I think I should like to kiss you." Then they began their game of sweetlips over again, for this was their anti-phon which began and ended every thing they did. But for all that, a short time after as Sir Symon was riding with a knight of the company, named Sir Rouf de la Grave; a good natured young fellow with no guile at all in him, the Frenchman began suddenly "What do you con-jecture would happen if I were to marry Bertha?" Sir Rouf jerked the reins, rubbed his eyes, and looked into Sir Symon's face, to discover if he were in earnest, but saw about as much expression there as there is in the face of a man who asks his sweetheart how her mother does to-day. He concluded therefore that the Frenchman, being a joker, was playing on him and endeavouring to make his chin fall—that is to say to make a fool of him: and answered with as empty a face as Sir Sy-mon's: "I suppose you would dance." "How?" "With high steps, Sir Symon, most gracefully and wondrously." "This is too deep for me; let me have your meaning plainer." "Why then you would swing." "Swing what?" "A mere trifle, no more than your body; and that to be sure would be a lighter burden than it is now, for it would be relieved of its soul before very long." "It is not possible you mean I should be hanged?" said the French knight, laughing all the while to himself at Sir Rouf's poor wit and thick head. "I do not know about being hanged, since that is not a polite expression, nor one used by people of good breeding; but I am quite certain that you would feel it necessary to mount a ladder, tie a scarf rather tightly round your neck; and then begin to foot the mazles of the air, as I have said." "Ah, what would I give to have been nurtured in this land where air and wit are of equal sharpness; but to speak the truth the hot sun of Gascony spoilt my brains when I was quite a little boy." With that Sir Symon talked no more of marrying or hanging, but began to speak of the fights and battles he had seen; and Sir Rouf looking at his broad shoulders and thick arms thought to himself "He may not have much to boast of in the way of brains but he would be an awkward customer to meet in a stricken field or joust or tournament." But some years afterwards, Sir Rouf having pondered these matters over in his leisure moments (for he could not eat or fight or drink or make love and think at the same time) all at once smote his head and said so that his wife could not hear him "he was certainly making an ass of me." But Sir Symon, after duly considering this affair, was forced to believe that if he married his dear Bertha, he would come to grief in some way or another, if not by rope then by axe, and to his mind there was not a pin to choose between either, and both were an abomination to him. Altogether he did not like the look of things and almost wished he had been hanged in France, which was his native country; and a true patriot like Sir Symon always chooses to give employment to his countrymen rather than strangers. But this wish seems to me not very sensible, since if he were hanged for carrying off the sweet body and unspeakable charms of Bertha, he would have so to speak, his money's worth; nay I profess it were well worth to be the husband of such a girl for a week and then to swing away. And, in effect, he determined to make her his wife, come what might, and they began to plot together how best to bring their love to its consummation. Then Bertha remembered that below Wentwood not far from the Uske river is a little church called Kemeys; by the which the road from Caerleon to Uske passeth—a small church it is in truth and lowly, being named Inferior to distinguish it from that other Kemeys beyond called Commander. But here Bertha said the parson was an old priest who had once looked after souls at Estrighoil

Castle, and had loved her beyond all (as was indeed natural) and she believed that he would knot them together ecclesiastically in the sacrament of matrimony. But it was as well, (they thought), to be sure of this beforehand; because if the parson took it into his head to curse instead of to bless it would be rather awkward. Wherefore Bertha wrote a letter (the which she could do very well) superscribing it *"For the hands of Dom. Andrew de Fago, parson of Kemeys: these:"* and this she gave to Sir Symon who rode down through the wood and came out on the road to Uske not far from Kemeys Church. He had not, as you will suppose, much trouble to find the parson; though the good man had taken to call himself Beeche since he had changed the Wye for the Uske, thinking perhaps that his parishioners had quite enough Latin on Sundays and holidays. But Sir Symon soon made out the parsonage and found Master Andrew dogmatising and theologically disporting himself in company with a volume of the "Questions," and a flagon of wine; for he was not ignorant of any philosophy. Hospitably he received the stranger and gave him his best chair, and bore another flagon of wine for refreshment and post-viaticum; and then received his daughter Bertha's letter; which made him stare and disturbed his brain. For he thought within himself "If I don't marry them they will certainly agree to dispense with any service at all; and thus they and I through them shall be guilty of mortal sin; to say nothing of robbing the Church of her dues. But if I do marry them there'll be trouble for me and the Archdeacon of Monmouth will doubtless be moved to interfere and take order in the matter to my no small discomfort and annoy." This, you see, was what is called a dilemma, a dilemma that pushed hard and had sharp horns; but since Father Andrew loved Bertha exceedingly and cared more for her health and pleasure than his own; he concluded *affirmative*, after subjecting Sir Symon to a short examination to make sure that he had no pestilent notions in him, and believed entirely all the doctrines of our Holy Faith. Here indeed he was on safe ground; since the knight hated hereticks as the devil, and it was safer to call him a recreant and a coward than to speak a word in his hearing against the Church or the doctrines thereof. But at the same time the parson warned him that he was putting his body into the dungeon and may be his neck into the noose; though since Father Andrew de Fago had been young himself once upon a time he did not expect his words to have much effect. In fine, he agreed to join this fine couple together in three days' time, and he let Sir Symon know that there was a ship that should weigh anchor from Caerleon that very morning and its voyage was to Venice in Italy. And as it seemed certain that it would be a good thing for the knight and his lady to get beyond call of Estrighoil Castle and Earl Ivo Fitz-Baderon it was determined that they should sail in the *Torchbearer* and hasten to southward ere the stormy weather and troublous time began. And the good old parson promised to agree with the master of the ship (to whom he was akin) so that all should be in readiness for them; and sent Sir Symon away up the hill with his blessing. So was this affair brought to a conclusion, for a man and a woman, the one dressed like a poor clerk and the other as a merchant's daughter, stole away from Struggle and vanished into the mist of the morning, and not a soul of the Earl's company could perceive to whitherward they had gone, when the hue and cry should have been raised after them. But old parson Andrew de Fago joined them in wed-lock, and after houselled them at the altar of the little church between the wood and the water; hence good Silurians hold Kemeys Church in special reverence and pray there for the souls of the fortunate lovers, who found, either in other, what each desired. And after they were married they sped away to Caerleon and got on board the *Torchbearer;* and so sailed down the Uske into Severn Sea, following the triumph of the sun. Here dimness closes around them and their happy love, as the ship vanisheth into the flushing clouds of sunset; but we think we can see Bertha and her lover standing upon the deck, hand in hand gazing into the west, and heeding not the rush of water nor the noise of the wind that speeds them. But soon the glory fades and they turn and find no weariness in looking into one another's eyes, for there truly are the torches burning of light celestial and unspeakable, since they were kindled at the altar of Love the Sovereign and Lord Royall.

Thus did close our Rubrican's story; and the fire was burning low, and I heard the wind upon the hill wailing sadly, as it is wont when it calls to the clouds and draweth them from the western sea. So we bade farewell to the Tuscans, and made them for all their denials a little purse for their hour of adversity. Then to their music we rode away once more, and thus did close the Portreeve's Gaudy-Day.

(*Here ends the* CHRONICLE OF CLEMENDY or HISTORY OF THE NINE JOYOUS JOURNEYS.)

EPILOGUE

Here, it appears, the first tome of the Silurian Mythologies comes to an end, and you are at liberty to take off your spectacles (if you have any) and to make use of the expressions made and provided for such occasions. But if you and I have here to grin and say "good-day," I have to part also with my sweet companion, who has come all the way to Cock-Loft Land to help me and to whisper strange stories in my ear; I mean no less an one than the merry Muse of Gwent. There she is standing by the door, my lovely mistress of quaint fancies and odd memories, laughing that magic laugh that makes my landlady look grave when she sees me, since she is of London town and does not understand Silurianism, nor how Muses with flashing eyes and cherry lips come to moping scholars at midnight to comfort them. But some people always put a bad construction on everything they see and hear, and in fact they are very troublesome folks.

But now the joyous maiden must return to her hedgerows, and rivulets, and meadow realm of flowers; since in all likelihood my days and nights will shortly be wholly devoted and given over to weighty matters of state and the service of my lord of Gloucester. For a few days ago His Grace did take me aside into his cabinet, and looking kindly upon me (though some call him a stern and awful noble) said: "Why Master Leolinus you look but sickly, poor gentleman, poor gentleman, I protest you're but a shadow, do not your Abbreviatures bring you in a goodly revenue?" "Not so, Your Grace," answered I, "to the present time I have abbreviated all in vain, and were it not for the hospitality of your table, I know not how I should win through." "How goes it then with your Silurian Histories, with which I am mightily in love by your talk of them, and would by no means have them remain unfinished." "With them, may it please Your Grace, it fares exceedingly well, and this very morning I have made an end of writing the First Journey, containing many agreeable histories and choice discourses." "I believe indeed it will be a rare book, fit to read to the monks of Tintern while they dine. But yet I will have you lay it aside a little, since I have a good piece of preferment for you, an office (or I mistake you) altogether to your taste. What say you, Master Scholar, to the lordship of an Island and no less an Island than Farre Joyaunce in the Western Seas? How stand you thitherwards? Will you take ship presently?" At hearing this, I was, as you may guess, half bewildered with sudden joy, that is apt to bring tears into the eyes of them that have toiled in many a weary struggle with adversity: I could but kneel and kiss His Grace's hand, and say, "My lord." "Enough, enough," said this kind nobleman, "I have long desired this place for you; when you first broke bread with me, I said to my chaplain, 'That man hath in him all the essentials of a Governour, for he eats clean and drinks very dry. Farre Joyaunce shall certainly have him, so soon as my cozen Gwared dies.' And this day the ship came into the river from Sure Haven, bringing letters from the Bishop to the intent that Gwared fell asleep a month ago, and that the people of the Island anxiously await a new Governour. So if you will, the office is your own, the ship *Salutation* will trip anchor on St. Denys his day, and can bear Leolinus, first of that name since the Conquest, to his Island of Farre Joyaunce."

So it has come to pass that in a few days I shall be bound for Sure Haven in that pleasant island of the west, and shall be forced to put aside my writings that I may advise concerning the duties of my lordship, its law, civil and ecclesiastical, its privileges, tolls, heriots, estovers, and all customary dues. And that I may sooner comprehend them I have much talk with the Paumier du Seigneur, who came in the ship *Salutation,* and is a high officer in Farre Joyaunce, where the chief disport is tennis-play, and a skilful player more worshipful and honoured than almost any one. Surely this shall be a Blessed Isle; but ere we drop anchor we shall be, I fear, sorely buffeted by storm and tempest, and shall scarcely sight the castle towers before the clerks are singing the O Sapientia. Nevertheless I am in good hopes of keeping Christmas in my castle aforesaid, and will endeavour to shew my subjects what it is to have a Governour that has dwelt in Cock-Loft Land. And then once more to my book that I may make it an acceptable and a worthy offering to my lord, slowly and artfully brewing my strong ale, storing up in fair bins and vessels my curious sausages, my mangoes hot and sweet, spices, delicate liquors, and choice confections, until at last I have such mauresque fare to offer as shall be very pleasant to the taste, and shall make men come and come again, and incite and spur them to the Silurian Wisdom. So my book shall be shewn in the after time, when I am gone to the Abiding Home—"This is the Chronicle of Clemendy, and a curious piece. Master Leolinus, the Silurist, who was sometime Lord of Farre Joyaunce, wrote it; a painful man and mightily addicted to good letters, good ale, and good tobacco."

But here is my Paumier, with his parchments, to advise with me concerning a grant of Water Baylage to the Abbey of St. Michael, and also concerning the ceremonies observed in the island at Christmastide. He tells me that the voyage will surely be a rough and tempestuous one, but with the captain of the *Salutation* there need be no fear. And so farewell, till the anchor be dropt in the Sure Haven of Farre Joyaunce.

The Spagyric Quest
of Beroaldus Cosmopolita

When the worthy quintessencer and most respectable traveller in the subterranean Heaven, Master Beroalde, of fragrant and delectable memory, had reduced into elemental powder and sopho-spagyrick dust all his worldly goods and found himself so sophisticated, metallurgised, suffused, salivated, and petrobolised that he had not a crown in his pouch, he cried out without caring who heard him, *Accursed be my furnace,* and proceeded to drive his servant away, which was wrong, for he was a canon, and as such should not have endeavoured to be better than his neighbours, who were all canons, and who all kept serving-maids. Hence we may conclude that he was extremely annoyed and desperately despairing, which indeed was the case, for he had passed the following articles through the furnace without any result:—

> *Item.*—Twelve meadows by the river.
>
> *Item.*—A house, by the same.
>
> *Item.*—Three orchards.
>
> *Item.*—A vineyard.
>
> *Item.*—A medlar tree, bearing one hundred sacks of medlars every year.
>
> *Item.*—Three cows, whose tails had been docked as a sign of mortification, to shew that they were theological animals.
>
> *Item.*—A house with a garden in the best street of Tours (where can one find in these days such a house and such a garden as this was?).
>
> *Item.*—Three thousand crowns; and there remained not a farthing or an apple, or a wine-flask, or a blade of grass, or a medlar.—*Amen.*

The devil take those who endeavour to lead us the wrong way and make us meddle with metals, or medals; persons whose throats are dry with smoke so that they cannot taste good wine! Let us leave such men and their devices and search for the delectable quintessence of the true Alchemy and the first matter of the world, which cannot thus be obtained, since it is mystagorical and resides in the mountains of the Moon. Be silent! This is the true path, and it was opened to the Canon Beroaldus that very night in which he cursed his furnace; and for seven days he was not to be found in his stall, nor anywhere else. At this much popular indignation was aroused, for his disappearance was connected, with his sending away his poor girl, who had served him well and theologically, and had done her best. But people said that the produce of his own country was not good enough for Beroaldus, and he was gone to Paris to see what he could find. There were some in the chapter who said he had thereby offended ecclesiastically, and should be admonished to be content with what came to his hand, like the countryman of whom it is said that on whatever, or whomsoever, he put his hand, he did it with all his might. Some of the canons, however, thought differently, and a dispute arose *concerning warming-pans*. (I make no apology for using theological terms, for the story is a theological one.)

Stay! Let us argue no more, but search for the cause of things, which is to be found in certain circular vessels well known to œnologists, and the brethren of the Holy Jar. This treatise teaches the true way of the Spagyrick Quest, and is the most opuscular of all opus-culums, *opus-coleorum,* as an old canon used to call but he lived in the old scholastic days, when ecclesiastics could dispute in mode and figure.

Beroaldus then having foresworn his furnace, became in a state to receive grace *ex congruo;* which is a theological mystery not to be disputed, though some persons have not been able to understand how he could receive anything *ex congruo* after sending away his maid. Peace! do not tamper with the faith, or your fate will be like that of the student who undertook to see a girl named Faith home from the fair, and was afterwards burnt alive for heresy: he had tampered with Faith. Let this be a lesson to you.

The canon sat alone in his room, which smelt like the Bottomless Pit smells on melting-day when there is a heavy consignment of fat

heretics, smug water-drinkers, and blasphemers of joyous diversions to
be boiled down. His furnace was empty; the room was dark, and the
books sat still on the shelves, looking about as lively as an Œcumenical
Council, a row of empty bottles, or the Three Barbels on the sign.
Thus dark and drear sat Beroalde in his room, when, as he gazed before him, expecting I do not know what, there rose light at the window, which grew brighter and brighter, fumes of sweet-scented
vapour, smelling like the incense at the Introit, gathered below and
above and all around the light so glorious, and in the midst and inmost
brightness Beroalde saw written these high and famous sentences,
which are the essence, groundwork, foundation *ante sæcula,* interior
meaning, full commentary, perspicuous gloss, hypothetical symbol,
cabalistic import, and gnostic mystigorification of all tomes of true science and registers of ancient wisdom. It is certain that on the Tomb of
the Scarab, on the Gate of the Abyss of Demiourgos, on the tables of
the Sephiroth, near to the Ayin-Soph, in the lightened places of the
Subterranean Heaven, and in the Authentic Formula of the first matter
of the world, this magistral breviate is inscribed. For it means—Hush!
let us have it first, and the meaning will become apparent. On the outer circle was written:—ALGAR+ALGASTNA+++AMRTET+. On
the inner circle was written:—TE+DAGIRAM ✠ ADAM ✠. And on
the inmost circle was written the four letters R T N T. There! you who
have been working at the bellows and calling on Baal, you who have
ridden post through wet and dry, up hill and down dale in Valentine's
Triumphal Chariot, and have never reached the Mons Magorum Invis-
ibilis, you who have taken Our Sulphur, Our Salt, Our Earth, and Our
Mercury, you who live on Cabalistic Sauces and drink the juices of the
Green Dragon, you know now how to philosophise to some purpose,
and by philosophise I mean, the obtaining of the Philosophal Stone;
the source of which is contained in the letters of the above juicy inscription or conscription, as the Penitentiarius, who was noted for beginning everything with *con,* would have called it. You ask why I call
the above inscription or conscription juicy? I bid you who ask go and
search in that rich treasure-house of conceptions, interludes, furnaces,
fountains, sauces, records, mirrors, high tomes of weighty meaning,
and lamps for sages to lanternise withal, where our Great Master dis-
penses wisdom in eternal paraphrases, while the great golden clouds

cease their flight to listen to him. There are stored in golden vessels those juices which alone avail to the completion of the Spagyrick Quest, which are called in good lingo the Sum of the Stars. Wait! let us come to our purpose. The Canon got up from his chair and gazed at the appearance like dogs gaze at the full moon, and then he saw a hand pointing to a wheel of fire at one side of the circle, and then another hand beside it, and strange to say he saw two arms which appeared to pertain to the two hands. "Good," said he to himself, "now we are getting at it; they will bring you strong wine if you drink all day." When he had gazed till the words of light were deeply printed in the hollows of his skull, all of a sudden the whole blaze vanished out of sight, and instead of it there was the sun shining in at the window, though it was an hour after sunset. Beroalde, the Spagyrist, stared long enough at this marvel, as he thought somebody must have been saying mass backwards over him; but his wonder was much increased when he heard a mellow voice saying "Shall we set out now?" He looked at the place where the voice came from, and there he saw a short thick-set man, yellow-skinned and black-haired, with a mouth as large as a cow's, and eyes of fire. He wore a square cap and scholar's gown, and stood just under the window where the vision had appeared. "Who are you, and where should we go?" said the Canon, in whose body butter was flowing. "I am sent," said the short man, "to lead you to the place where what is below is that which is above, where the earth is separated from the fire, where the brood of the crow change their feathers and are made like unto doves, where is performed the engendering of the sun from the Philosophal Egg. For know that of your own wit you can never attain to this work, but in a manner you are found worthy. Follow me." Forthwith he touched the window and the glass melted away, and Beroalde followed him, and saw that from the window was built a very great flight of steps of white marble, that descended and went down, and was prolonged, extended, pursued, multiplied, and reduplicated, till it became black and invisible, and (as it was revealed) it consists only of seven steps added to one another in a certain mystic manner. And the guide said again, "Follow me, but look not to the right or to the left where is the Abyss, but only beyond and above." And Beroalde, looking beyond, saw only the stairs, and above he saw how the heaven was divided, and half of it was night with the moon and stars, and half of it was light with the sun shining. "This is the mystery of the heaven above the earth called celestial, we seek the mystery of the heaven below the earth called subterranean," said the guide; and forthwith he began to descend the stairs, Beroalde following closely behind him. Verily, it seemed as if they would never reach the deepest depth, as the king once observed on a notorious occasion, which cost some persons who had pushed the matter on their share of the royal favour. Well, but all things come to an end at last; wedding-nights, the generating of fools and of quintessencers, the dreams of dreamers, organ-sounds and singers' voices; the pinnacles of the Cloud Castle of Rohalgo and the old Canon's Easter sermon, and the journey across the Waste, do they not all cease? Truly they do, and, in one way or another, sleep. Amen. So then it came to pass that Beroalde and his guide came at last to the lowest stair, and the man in the scholar's gown told the Canon to look round, and there he saw far off as far could be the top of the stair leading into his house, and the city of Tours with clouds all around it. This was a marvel, but the guide led him on through a narrow passage, which was quite dark, but short enough, and then he knocked at a door five times, and it was opened. And as it was being opened the guide whispered to Beroalde, "Enter into the Four-square Garden, where all things are lawful, and here you shall learn what you desire." "Here comes the Spagyrist," cried out the porter, whom Beroalde knew very well, for he kept the *Three Puddings* in Tours; "come in, come in, most worthy sir, there are puddings enough here, and chitterlings, and sauces, and enough mustard for the Great Master himself, and a puncheonful of grape-guts. What the devil! Ora pro nobis in omnia sæcula sæculorum, amen, alleluia, alleluia; there are girls, too, Deo Gratias, the fields are ready for the harvest, ut bos locutus est in populo barbaro, O Domine feliposophidexterandorum." Beroalde made no answer to this intelligible discourse, for he was looking before him, and turning to his guide said to him, "Tell me, most admirable leader, what these things mean." "Call me Liripipiastor," answered he; "and come forward, and I will shew everything to you, as you have indeed much to learn, and many doctrines wherewith to be indoctrinated. But tell me, before we go farther, can you answer me this: *In quo sit bonum vinum continendum?*" "In boteliis, et flaccis, et barillis, et tonnis," answered Beroalde, who was a learned metaphysician and jurist, and had taken a great part in the trial before the Cathedral Penitentiary of the woman accused of offending with a wine-skin. This great case, be it added, was tried before the Penitentiary Raoul de Fermeboise, lasted for two years, and resulted in the condemnation of the accused, whereby great tumults were excited among the Tourainian women, who considered the sentence as an unjust abbreviature of their liberties. The Canon therefore answered firmly, and looked the scholar in the face, but Master Liripipiastor said, "'Tis answered carnally and according to the wisdom of the flesh, which, as the Apostle teacheth, is accursed, such answers will not pass here. Come with me and hear how the matter stands." And Beroalde followed him, but what was it that he saw the meaning of which he craved to know? He saw the four-square garden. What is that? It is a garden of pleasure, of high discourse, of wisdom, of sages, of good wine, of philosophising, lanternising, symbolising, spagyrising, the garden of the old concoction and the new juice, of songs and melodies, where there are hundreds piping and hundreds playing on viols; it is a garden to look for maidens in. Did I say to find them? No; then do not interrupt me. It is a garden of games and pastimes and joyous diversions, where they play and extract fifth essence, and toss balls, and drink all day; in fine, it is a garden whence all good books proceed. What books are good? Why those which teach us in a thousand ways to laugh, and therefore contain all wisdom; books of concubines, multiplication, entrances into secret places, books full of merry demons who dance and twine about every page. It is a garden full of sun and shade, of groves and lawns, and hedgerows and rivulets, and pools, and wells; of marble seats and carven stalls, of rich stuffs, of halls, sculptures, towers, bells, chimes, cupboards; a garden where they make green sauce all night. All these circumstances and pursuits made the Canon Beroalde wish to know about things, and the scholar Liripipiastor drew him through the throng who were amusing themselves to a well where the Great Master sat on a marble seat, and was discoursing to a few apart. And what a man was he, of what a noble presence, with long white beard and a cassock flowing royally about him like a king's robe. He made Beroalde look down, since the Canon had never met such a gaze before, and he asked, "Who is this, Liripipiastor? Is he dogmatised sufficiently to come here?" "He is the alchemist Beroalde, whom I led

down the stairs to-night as he desires to attain the spagyrick quest."
"Ha! ha! he comes from Tours, I swear, his father sold onions in the
Rue Chaude; well, son, do you know in what good wine should be
contained, or, in other words, what is the temple of good wine?" "He
lacks right knowledge on that point," said Liripipiastor, "for he says it
is contained in boteliis, et flaccis, et barillis, et tonnis; wherefore I have
brought him to you to be instructed." "Listen, then, Beroalde, and you
Liripipiastor, Grobiscornus, Ratifuntulus, and Patuloformus, and you
other wenches. What, there are no wenches; well, bottles then, and let
us see whether they are not *ejusdem substantiæ. Sic probatur!* What would
be the use of bottles without openings? The wine would have to be
drunk *inclusivè;* that is to say, it would be included in the bottles and secluded from you, therefore it would not be drunk at all; or, better still,
it would be drunk and not drunk, *ut probatum est,* which is a contradiction, *ergo non esse Deum.* What do you say to this, philosophasters and
lanternisers? But let us return to our potage, or rather our *potus.* Bottles
must have openings, *ut probatum est,* and so must girls, for if they had
not openings they could not eat; therefore bottles and wenches are of
the same substance, *ut probatum est.* Listen to that, you doggrelisers of
good logic, and learn what it is to conclude in *primâ figurâ, modo Bacchi.*
As I was saying, listen, you other bottles, and learn what is the temple
of good wine. What is wine? It is the true *primum mobile* which turns the
spheres. You will see that proved in Raymond Lully and Bernard of
Trevisan, and Arnold de Villa Nova and Aristotle *De Gluc,* chapter
three. Wine therefore contains the universe, and makes the planets
dance and engender stars; and how can anything contain that which
contains all things? Listen: this is a great mystery, not to be revealed to
the vulgar, but only to the true tosspots of true poculations, who live
vivified and permeated with right doctrine. Matter is contained in
space, but the soul contains space, the clouds, the sun and the stars,
the oceans, and the heavens. *Ergo,* the soul contains *bonum vinum,* and
by soul I mean the belly; therefore the sage's belly is the temple of
good wine, *ut probatum est.* And the corollary of this fundamental dogma is that the soul must be purged and prepared, cleansed, sanctified,
mystagorified, and enlightened by the mystagorical preparation, which
is mustard. Now you have heard the reason of these things; and we
will now sanctify our souls, I mean drink good wine, or rather make

that which is above descend to that which is below, or perform the transmutation of juice into laughter, or what you please." "Master," said Liripipiastor, "I heard a bottle chink from the well." "Hush, it is an oracle, a globular omen, a regurgitation, an influence from the spheres. Stoop down, Rotifuntulus, and listen to the voice from the well of science." The young man, Rotifuntulus, who looked to Beroalde an angel of beauty, stooped down and put his ear to the bubbling well, and listened, but not a sound did Beroalde hear except the noise of the water. But the listener presently got up and said, "The holy and omniscient oracle has been delivered in my ear of the word *Algarum*, and from inspection of the well I foresee that a transmutation is at hand." "Son," said the Master to the alchemist, "this is a word for you, and you are now about to learn the First Matter of the work. (Give me some more wine, for I am dry. Ah, ha! that smacks well, *nota bene*.) Know that the interpretation of the mystical and regenerating symbol and allegorised paraphrase *Algarum* (a word well known to the magicians, who make children with it; ask again how it is done) is as follows: IN THE FRUIT OF THE TREE OF THE SECOND JUICE, which indeed is evident, as in the word there are seven letters, and in the interpretation there are five times seven letters, which render these paraphrases so mystagorical that mixed with water they turn it into wine. Let him listen to me if any sophister or spagyrist desire to know how to turn water into wine by the addition of paraphrases, since the method is contained in these discourses. But I have spoken enough: go, son, and seek for that which is in the fruit of the tree of the second juice." "Who will shew me how this is to be performed?" said the Canon. "Go, go, get into the midst of the garden and ask for the tree and it will be shewn to you and everything else. *Pax vobiscum amen, venite compotemus.*" At this Beroalde was compelled to depart, and, as it is related, he turned now to the right and now to the left and became entangled in a *Labyrinth* (for he was now without a guide) which would have put Dædalus to shame; it turned and returned a thousand times upon itself, and was so dark and vast a place that the Canon grew near to despair. But at last he came to a place where lamps were set, each lamp hanging by a golden chain, as it seemed, from empty space, and the light they gave him shewed what was painted on the wall. And there was delineated in the most admirable colours and the most glorious gold the whole Operation of the Sons of Wisdom, or the Heavenly Marriage; proceeding from the First Concoction, the Birth of the Eagle, the Engendring of the Crow, the Balneum Solis, the Great Procession, the Torchbearers, the Storm at Night, the White Woman in the Purple Field, and the Son blessed of the Fire, so that Beroalde was utterly amazed, but yet without understanding, since he knew not the First Matter of the Work, nor how the White Woman could have copulation with the Red Man. So he wandered around and around in this Labyrinth, passing from Light to Dark and from Dark to Light, seeing now and again Pictures at the lasciviousness of which he was astonished, for he did not understand the spirit but only the letter. At last, weary and sick of all, he cried out, "O Domine Deus, if I could have a seat in the sun and a flask of wine I should be content, for this labyrinth is toil without knowledge." No sooner had he said this than he beheld a little door in the wall, and over it was written SOLUS INTROITUS IN V.S.D.M., and Beroalde lifted up the latch and passed through, and from black his garments had turned to white, and his hand feeling in the air closed upon a wine flask. Now, indeed, he had attained through the Labyrinth to the place called the Magician's Heavenly Chaos, where the subterranean sun shines eternally, bringing the magic fruit to perfection. It was surrounded with a wall of trees, thick, high, and dark; it was a green meadow of the softest grass, with banks whereon to lie in the sunlight. In the midst Beroalde beheld the so famous Seven Fountains which are set about the Tree of the Second Juice, and are as follows, according to the description of the best authors.

The first is the fountain of the Spiritual Sol; it is a golden bowl, having carven on it the thousand names, the Process, the Multiplication, the Colour, the Immensity, the Depth, the Sound, the Voice, in short what is whispered at the Door. You understand what I mean; silence! This bowl is immeasurable, no one can say how broad it is; it in fact, a golden sea, welling up with an eternal spring; in the depths of its waters are all things reflected, the water magical, a fluid in which to bathe most of the volumes that have been written.

The Second is the fountain of the Spiritual Luna, and contains the liquid from which beautiful girls with enticing shapes are produced by quintessential process. In shape it is a spire of light, continually ascending, pointed like a spear, and having its base in the floods and waters. With a drop of this liquid of Luna philosopher once anointed his flagon, and ever after it was full of wine.

The Third the fountain of the Spiritual Venus, in shape a sphere, abounding and glowing with ruddy light. In the liquid of this sphere the Great Master beheld his Voyages and discovered the Way to Attain, for it contains all philosophies: in it may be seen the flights of all the Stars and the most precious secret of the Generation of Fools; a mystic matter; in it is delivered the sense of the words Κογξ ὀμπαξ.

The Fourth is the fountain of the Spiritual Mercurius, the *Argent Vive*, full of a thick viscid and spermatic fluid which runs a race round a Bowl of Earth, and from it doves rise up continually and fly away into the heaven. I read in an ancient book that this liquor is the seed of the world and makes everything fertile; it was symbolised in those mysteries of Priapus, the Father of the Chitterlings, now counted obscene.

The Fifth, Sixth, and Seventh, are not, as might be thought, Fountains of Saturn, Jupiter, and Mars, but are Mirrors in which each man sees what he desires; in them are cities, maidens, dances, clouds, stars, spires, phrases, allegories, treatises, breviates, tomes, songs and chanting, hieroglyphics, visions, and tennis-balls. Look in them for facetious sayings, you whose brains run dry; look for sunlight in the dark days, when a fine rain falls continually, these mirrors are magistral and enigmatical, fit only for sages.

While Beroalde was busily engaged in sucking in all these mysteries, without lifting an eye to what stood in the midst, he heard a voice saying, "First drink, and then demand what you will," and Beroalde saw an old man standing beside him, in a robe of ash-grey. "What shall I drink?" asked the Canon. "Drink the volume of delectation in your hand; it is the true wine, the comfortable potation, the orthodox commentary; it is full of reasons of everything, it warms the skull, and fills its dark places with the sun." So Beroalde drank and became full of boldness, and said with great courage, "I come here in search of Algarum; otherwise what is contained in the fruit of the tree of the Second Juice." "Where do you come from?" "The World." "What is the World?" "Listen; for I am drunk and full of reasons. Once there was a true world, a holy, spiritual city; but long ago, before the secrets of hot sauces were discovered, the Arch Concocter of Bad Productions dreamt an ill dream which we now call the world." "Well answered. How came you?" "By the Seven Stairs, and through the Four-square Garden, to the presence of the Master and to the Oracular Well. Hence I came through the Labyrinth, fortified with the word of Algarum, a paraphrase which turns water into wine." "Then behold, son of regeneration, the Tree of the Second Juice, and the fruit thereof." And Beroalde lifted up his face, and beheld in the midst of the fountains the mightiest tree he had ever seen, so lofty that the clouds swam across its top, and in breadth a day's journey, covered with dark green leaves from which is prepared the Green Sauce of the Philosophers, and with the golden fruit, somewhat like an apple, which the world desires in vain. And amidst the branches were cities, and castles, and golden spires, inhabited by the Homunculi; and Beroalde was bidden to climb this tree if he would gain the fruit. He therefore took of the Spiritual Mercurius and the Spiritual Sol from the fountains, and anointing himself, was carried on high into the tree, where he underwent the seven transmutations. He became a volume, a cloud, a star, a pinnacle, a faun, a song, a dream; he ate the fruit and drank the mixed draught, and was wedded to the Queen Soteris in the mystical marriage. And when he returned to the ground, he carried with him a book containing one leaf, and in it written: "IN THE SIXTH HOUR OF THE NIGHT SEARCH NOTHING BUT THYSELF, AND THOU SHALT FIND THE FIRST MATTER OF THE STONE, AND IN NO OTHER PLACE IN THE WHOLE WIDE WORLD SHALT THOU FIND IT."

The Great God Pan

I

THE EXPERIMENT

I am glad you came, Clarke; very glad indeed. I was not sure you could spare the time."

"I was able to make arrangements for a few days; things are not very lively just now. But have you no misgivings, Raymond? Is it absolutely safe?"

The two men were slowly pacing the terrace in front of Dr. Raymond's house. The sun still hung above the western mountain-line, but it shone with a dull red glow that cast no shadows, and all the air was quiet; a sweet breath came from the great wood on the hillside above, and with it, at intervals, the soft murmuring call of the wild doves. Below, in the long lovely valley, the river wound in and out between the lonely hills, and, as the sun hovered and vanished into the west, a faint mist, pure white, began to rise from the banks. Dr. Raymond turned sharply to his friend.

"Safe? Of course it is. In itself the operation is a perfectly simple one; any surgeon could do it."

"And there is no danger at any other stage?"

"None; absolutely no physical danger whatever, I give you my word. You were always timid, Clarke, always; but you know my history. I have devoted myself to transcendental medicine for the last twenty years. I have heard myself called quack and charlatan and impostor, but all the while I knew I was on the right path. Five years ago I reached the goal, and since then every day has been a preparation for what we shall do to-night."

"I should like to believe it is all true." Clarke knit his brows, and looked doubtfully at Dr. Raymond. "Are you perfectly sure, Raymond, that your theory is not a phantasmagoria—a splendid vision, certainly, but a mere vision after all?"

Dr. Raymond stopped in his walk and turned sharply. He was a middle-aged man, gaunt and thin, of a pale yellow complexion, but as he answered Clarke and faced him, there was a flush on his cheek.

"Look about you, Clarke. You see the mountain, and hill following after hill, as wave on wave, you see the woods and orchards, the fields of ripe corn, and the meadows reaching to the reed-beds by the river. You see me standing here beside you, and hear my voice; but I tell you that all these things—yes, from that star that has just shone out in the sky to the solid ground beneath our feet—I say that all these are but dreams and shadows: the shadows that hide the real world from our eyes. There *is* a real world, but it is beyond this glamour and this vision, beyond these 'chases in Arras, dreams in a career', beyond them all as beyond a veil. I do not know whether any human being has ever lifted that veil; but I do know, Clarke, that you and I shall see it lifted this very night from before another's eyes. You may think all this strange nonsense; it may be strange, but it is true, and the ancients knew what lifting the veil means. They called it seeing the god Pan."

Clarke shivered; the white mist gathering over the river was chilly.

"It is wonderful indeed," he said. "We are standing on the brink of a strange world, Raymond, if what you say is true. I suppose the knife is absolutely necessary?"

"Yes; a slight lesion in the grey matter, that is all; a trifling rearrangement of certain cells, a microscopical alteration that would escape the attention of ninety-nine brain specialists out of a hundred. I don't want to bother you with 'shop', Clarke; I might give you a mass of technical detail which would sound very imposing, and would leave you as enlightened as you are now. But I suppose you have read, casually, in out-of-the-way corners of your paper, that immense strides have been made recently in the physiology of the brain. I saw a paragraph the other day about Digby's theory, and Browne Faber's discoveries. Theories and discoveries! Where they are standing now, I stood fifteen years ago, and I need not tell you that I have not been standing still for the last fifteen years. It will be enough if I say that five years ago I made the discovery to which I alluded when I said that then I reached the goal. After years of labour, after years of toiling and groping in the dark, after days and nights of disappointment and sometimes of despair, in which I used now and then to tremble and grow cold with the thought that perhaps there were others seeking for what I sought, at last, after so long, a pang of sudden joy thrilled my soul, and I knew the long journey was at an end. By what seemed then and still seems a chance, the suggestion of a moment's idle thought followed up upon familiar lines and paths that I had tracked a hundred times already, the great truth burst upon me, and I saw, mapped out in lines of light, a whole world, a sphere unknown; continents and islands, and great oceans in which no ship has sailed (to my belief) since a Man first lifted up his eyes and beheld the sun, and the stars of heaven, and the quiet earth beneath. You will think all this high-flown language, Clarke, but it is hard to be literal. And yet; I do not know whether what I am hinting at cannot be set forth in plain and homely terms. For instance, this world of ours is pretty well girdled now with the telegraph wires and cables; thought, with something less than the speed of thought, flashes from sunrise to sunset, from north to south, across the floods and the desert places. Suppose that an electrician of to-day were suddenly to perceive that he and his friends have merely been playing with pebbles and mistaking them for the foundations of the world; suppose that such a man saw uttermost space lie open before the current, and words of men flash forth to the sun and beyond the sun into the systems beyond, and the voices of articulate-speaking men echo in the waste void that bounds our thought. As analogies go, that is a pretty good analogy of what I have done; you can understand now a little of what I felt as I stood here one evening; it was a summer evening, and the valley looked much as it does now; I stood here, and saw before me the unutterable, the unthinkable gulf that yawns profound between two worlds, the world of matter and the world of spirit; I saw the great empty deep stretch dim before me, and in that instant a bridge of light leapt from the earth to the unknown shore, and the abyss was spanned. You may look in Browne Faber's book, if you like, and you will find that to the present day men of science are unable to account for the presence, or to specify the functions of a certain group of nerve-cells in the brain. That group is, as it were, land to let, a mere waste place for fanciful theories. I am not in the position of Browne Faber and the specialists, I am perfectly instructed as to the possible functions of those nerve-centres in the scheme of things. With a touch I can bring them into play, with a touch, I say, I can set free the current, with a touch I can complete the communication between this world of sense and—we shall be able to finish the sentence later on. Yes, the knife is necessary; but think what that knife will effect. It will level utterly the solid wall of sense, and probably for the first time since man was made, a spirit will gaze on a spirit-world. Clarke, Mary will see the god Pan!"

"But you remember what you wrote to me? I thought it would be requisite that she—"

He whispered the rest into the doctor's ear.

"Not at all, not at all. That is nonsense, I assure you. Indeed, it is better as it is; I am quite certain of that."

"Consider the matter well, Raymond. It's a great responsibility. Something might go wrong; you would be a miserable man for the rest of your days."

"No, I think not, even if the worst happened. As you know, I rescued Mary from the gutter, and from almost certain starvation, when she was a child; I think her life is mine to use as I see fit. Come, it is getting late; we had better go in."

Dr. Raymond led the way into the house, through the hall, and down a long dark passage. He took a key from his pocket and opened a heavy door, and motioned Clarke into his laboratory. It had once been a billiard-room, and was lighted by a glass dome in the centre of the ceiling, whence there still shone a sad grey light on the figure of the doctor as he lit a lamp with a heavy shade and placed it on a table in the middle of the room.

Clarke looked about him. Scarcely a foot of wall remained bare; there were shelves all around laden with bottles and phials of all shapes and colours, and at one end stood a little Chippendale book-case. Raymond pointed to this.

"You see that parchment Oswald Crollius? He was one of the first to shew me the way, though I don't think he ever found it himself. That is a strange saying of his: 'In every grain of wheat there lies hidden the soul of a star.'"

There was not much of furniture in the laboratory. The table in the centre, a stone slab with a drain in one corner, the two armchairs on which Raymond and Clarke were sitting; that was all, except an odd-looking chair at the furthest end of the room. Clarke looked at it, and raised his eyebrows.

"Yes, that is the chair," said Raymond. "We may as well place it in position." He got up and wheeled the chair to the light, and began raising and lowering it, letting down the seat, setting the back at various angles, and adjusting the foot-rest. It looked comfortable enough, and Clarke passed his hand over the soft green velvet, as the doctor manipulated the levers.

"Now, Clarke, make yourself quite comfortable. I have a couple of hours' work before me; I was obliged to leave certain matters to the last."

Raymond went to the stone slab, and Clarke watched him drearily as he bent over a row of phials and lit the flame under the crucible. The doctor had a small hand-lamp, shaded as the larger one, on a ledge above his apparatus, and Clarke, who sat in the shadows, looked down the great dreary room, wondering at the bizarre effects of brilliant light and undefined darkness contrasting with one another. Soon he became conscious of an odd odour, at first the merest suggestion of odour, in the room; and as it grew more decided he felt surprised that he was not reminded of the chemist's shop or the surgery. Clarke found himself idly endeavouring to analyse the sensation, and, half conscious, he began to think of a day, fifteen years ago, that he had spent in roaming through the woods and meadows near his old home. It was a burning day at the beginning of August, the heat had dimmed the outlines of all things and all distances with a faint mist, and people who observed the thermometer spoke of an abnormal register, of a temperature that was almost tropical. Strangely that wonderful hot day of the 'fifties rose up in Clarke's imagination; the sense of dazzling all-pervading sunlight seemed to blot out the shadows and the lights of the laboratory, and he felt again the heated air beating in gusts about his face, saw the shimmer rising from the turf, and heard the myriad murmur of the summer.

"I hope the smell doesn't annoy you, Clarke; there's nothing unwholesome about it. It may make you a bit sleepy, that's all."

Clarke heard the words quite distinctly, and knew that Raymond was speaking to him, but for the life of him he could not rouse himself from his lethargy. He could only think of the lonely walk he had taken fifteen years ago; it was his last look at the fields and woods he had known since he was a child, and now it all stood out in brilliant light, as a picture, before him. Above all there came to his nostrils the scent of summer, the smell of flowers mingled, and the odour of the woods, of cool shaded places, deep in the green depths, drawn forth by the sun's heat; and the scent of the good earth, lying as it were with arms stretched forth, and smiling lips, overpowered all. His fancies made him wander, as he had wandered long ago, from the fields into the wood, tracking a little path between the shining undergrowth of beech-trees; and the trickle of water dropping from the limestone rock sounded as a clear melody in the dream. Thoughts began to go astray and to mingle with other recollections; the beech alley was trans-formed to a path beneath ilex-trees, and here and there a vine climbed from bough to bough, and sent up waving tendrils and drooped with purple grapes, and the sparse grey-green leaves of a wild olive-tree stood out against the dark shadows of the ilex. Clarke, in the deep folds of dream, was conscious that the path from his father's house had led him into an undiscovered country, and he was wondering at the strangeness of it all, when suddenly, in place of the hum and mur-mur of the summer, an infinite silence seemed to fall on all things, and the wood was hushed, and for a moment of time he stood face to face there with a presence, that was neither man nor beast, neither the liv-ing nor the dead, but all things mingled, the form of all things but de-void of all form. And in that moment, the sacrament of body and soul was dissolved, and a voice seemed to cry "Let us go hence," and then the darkness of darkness beyond the stars, the darkness of everlasting.

When Clarke woke up with a start he saw Raymond pouring a few drops of some oily fluid into a green phial, which he stoppered tightly.

"You have been dozing," he said; "the journey must have tired you out. It is done now. I am going to fetch Mary; I shall be back in ten minutes."

Clarke lay back in his chair and wondered. It seemed as if he had but passed from one dream into another. He half expected to see the walls of the laboratory melt and disappear, and to awake in London, shuddering at his own sleeping fancies. But at last the door opened, and the doctor returned and behind him came a girl of about seventeen, dressed all in white. She was so beautiful that Clarke did not wonder at what the doctor had written to him. She was blushing now over face and neck and arms, but Raymond seemed unmoved.

"Mary," he said, "the time has come. You are quite free. Are you willing to trust yourself to me entirely?"

"Yes, dear."

"You hear that, Clarke? You are my witness. Here is the chair, Mary. It is quite easy. Just sit in it and lean back. Are you ready?"

"Yes, dear, quite ready. Give me a kiss before you begin."

The doctor stooped and kissed her mouth, kindly enough. "Now shut your eyes," he said. The girl closed her eyelids, as if she were tired, and longed for sleep, and Raymond held the green phial to her nostrils. Her face grew white, whiter than her dress; she struggled faintly, and then with the feeling of submission strong within her, crossed her arms upon her breast as a little child about to say her prayers. The bright light of the lamp beat full upon her, and Clarke watched changes fleeting over that face as the changes of the hills when the summer clouds float across the sun. And then she lay all white and still, and the doctor turned up one of her eyelids. She was quite unconscious. Raymond pressed hard on one of the levers and the chair instantly sank back. Clarke saw him cutting away a circle, like a tonsure, from her hair, and the lamp was moved nearer. Raymond took a small glittering instrument from a little case, and Clarke turned away shuddering. When he looked again the doctor was binding up the wound he had made.

"She will awake in five minutes." Raymond was still perfectly cool. "There is nothing more to be done; we can only wait."

The minutes passed slowly; they could hear a slow, heavy ticking. There was an old clock in the passage. Clarke felt sick and faint; his knees shook beneath him, he could hardly stand.

Suddenly, as they watched, they heard a long-drawn sigh, and suddenly did the colour that had vanished return to the girl's cheeks, and suddenly her eyes opened. Clarke quailed before them. They shone with an awful light, looking far away, and a great wonder fell upon her face, and her hands stretched out as if to touch what was invisible; but in an instant the wonder faded, and gave place to the most awful terror. The muscles of her face were hideously convulsed, she shook from head to foot; the soul seemed struggling and shuddering within the house of flesh. It was a horrible sight, and Clarke rushed forward, as she fell shrieking to the floor.

Three days later Raymond took Clarke to Mary's bedside. She was lying wide-awake, rolling her head from side to side, and grinning vacantly.

"Yes," said the doctor, still quite cool, "it is a great pity; she is a hopeless idiot. However, it could not be helped; and, after all, she has seen the Great God Pan."

II
MR. CLARKE'S MEMOIRS

Mr. Clarke, the gentleman chosen by Dr. Raymond to witness the strange experiment of the god Pan, was a person in whose character caution and curiosity were oddly mingled; in his sober moments he thought of the unusual and the eccentric with undisguised aversion, and yet, deep in his heart, there was a wide-eyed inquisitiveness with respect to all the more recondite and esoteric elements in the nature of men. The latter tendency had prevailed when he accepted Raymond's invitation, for though his considered judgment had always repudiated the doctor's theories as the wildest nonsense, yet he secretly hugged a belief in fantasy, and would have rejoiced to see that belief confirmed. The horrors that he witnessed in the dreary laboratory were to a certain extent salutary; he was conscious of being involved in an affair not altogether reputable, and for many years afterwards he clung bravely to the commonplace, and rejected all occasions of occult investigation. Indeed, on some homœopathic principle, he for some time attended the séances of distinguished mediums, hoping that the clumsy tricks of these gentlemen would make him altogether disgusted with mysticism of every kind, but the remedy, though caustic, was not efficacious. Clarke knew that he still pined for the unseen, and little by little, the old passion began to reassert itself, as the face of Mary, shuddering and convulsed with an unknowable terror, faded slowly from his memory. Occupied all day in pursuits both serious and lucrative, the temptation to relax in the evening was too great, especially in the winter months, when the fire cast a warm glow over his snug bachelor apartment, and a bottle of some choice claret stood ready by his elbow. His dinner digested, he would make a brief pretence of reading the evening paper, but the mere catalogue of news soon palled upon him, and Clarke would find himself casting glances of warm desire in the direction of an old Japanese bureau, which stood at a pleasant distance from the hearth. Like a boy before a jam-closet, for a few minutes he would hover indecisive, but lust always prevailed, and Clarke ended by drawing up his chair, lighting a candle, and sitting down before the bureau. Its pigeon-holes and drawers teemed with documents on the most morbid subjects, and in the well reposed a large manuscript volume, in which he had painfully entered the gems of his collection. Clarke had a fine contempt for published literature; the most ghostly story ceased to interest him if it happened to be printed; his sole pleasure was in the reading, compiling, arranging, and rearranging what he called his "Memoirs to prove the Existence of the Devil", and engaged in this pursuit the evening seemed to fly and the night appeared too short.

On one particular evening, an ugly December night, black with fog, and raw with frost, Clarke hurried over his dinner, and scarcely deigned to observe his customary ritual of taking up the paper and laying it down again. He paced two or three times up and down the room, and opened the bureau, stood still a moment, and sat down. He leant back, absorbed in one of those dreams to which he was subject, and at length drew out his book, and opened it at the last entry. There were three or four pages densely covered with Clarke's round, set penmanship, and at the beginning he had written in a somewhat larger hand:

> Singular Narrative told me by my Friend, Dr. Phillips. He assures me that all the Facts related therein are strictly and wholly True, but refuses to give either the Surnames of the Persons concerned, or the Place where these Extraordinary Events occurred.

Mr. Clarke began to read over the account for the tenth time, glancing now and then at the pencil notes he had made when it was told him by his friend. It was one of his humours to pride himself on a certain literary ability; he thought well of his style, and took pains in arranging the circumstances in dramatic order. He read the following story:—

The persons concerned in this statement are Helen V., who, if she is still alive, must now be a woman of twenty-three, Rachel M., since deceased, who was a year younger than the above, and Trevor W., an imbecile, aged eighteen. These persons were at the period of the story inhabitants of a village on the borders of Wales, a place of some importance in the time of the Roman occupation, but now a scattered hamlet, of not more than five hundred souls. It is situated on rising ground, about six miles from the sea, and is sheltered by a large and picturesque forest.

Some eleven years ago, Helen V. came to the village under rather peculiar circumstances. It is understood that she, being an orphan, was adopted in her infancy by a distant relative, who brought her up in his own house till she was twelve years old. Thinking, however, that it would be better for the child to have playmates of her own age, he advertised in several local papers for a good home in a comfortable farmhouse for a girl of twelve, and this advertisement was answered by Mr. R., a well-to-do farmer in the above-mentioned village. His references proving satisfactory, the gentleman sent his adopted daughter to Mr. R., with a letter, in which he stipulated that the girl should have a room to herself, and stated that her guardians need be at no trouble in the matter of education, as she was already sufficiently educated for the position in life which she would occupy. In fact, Mr. R. was given to understand that the girl was to be allowed to find her own occupations, and to spend her time almost as she liked. Mr. R. duly met her at the nearest station, a town some seven miles away from his house, and seems to have remarked nothing extraordinary about the child, except that she was reticent as to her former life and her adopted father. She was, however, of a very different type from the inhabitants of the village; her skin was a pale, clear olive, and her features were strongly marked, and of a somewhat foreign character. She appears to have settled down easily enough into farmhouse life, and became a favourite with the children, who sometimes went with her on her rambles in the forest, for this was her amusement. Mr. R. states that he has known her to go out by herself directly after their early breakfast, and not return till after dusk, and that, feeling uneasy at a young girl being out alone for so many hours, he communicated with her adopted father, who replied in a brief note that Helen must do as she chose. In the winter, when the forest paths are impassable, she spent most of her time in her bedroom, where she slept alone, according to the instructions of her relative. It was on one of these expeditions to the forest that the first of the singular incidents with which this girl is connected occurred, the date being about a year after her arrival at the village. The preceding winter had been remarkably severe, the snow drifting to a great depth, and the frost continuing for an unexampled period, and the summer following was as noteworthy for its extreme heat. On one of the very hottest days in this summer, Helen V. left the farmhouse for one of her long rambles in the forest, taking with her, as usual, some bread and meat for lunch. She was seen by some men in the fields making for the old Roman Road, a green causeway which traverses the highest part of the wood, and they were astonished to observe that the girl had taken off her hat, though the heat of the sun was already almost tropical. As it happened, a labourer, Joseph W. by name, was working in the forest near the Roman Road, and at twelve o'clock his little son, Trevor, brought the man his dinner of bread and cheese. After the meal, the boy, who was about seven years old at the time, left his father at work, and, as he said, went to look for flowers in the wood, and the man, who could hear him shouting with delight over his discoveries, felt no uneasiness. Suddenly, however, he was horrified at hearing the most dreadful screams, evidently the result of great terror, proceeding from the direction in which his son had gone, and he hastily threw down his tools and ran to see what had happened. Tracing his path by the sound, he met the little boy, who was running headlong, and was evidently terribly frightened, and on questioning him the man at last elicited that after picking a posy of flowers he felt tired, and lay down on the grass and fell asleep. He was suddenly awakened, as he stated, by a peculiar noise, a sort of singing he called it, and on peeping through the branches he saw Helen V. playing on the grass with a "strange naked man", whom he seemed unable to describe more fully. He said he felt dreadfully frightened, and ran away crying for his father. Joseph W. proceeded in the direction indicated by his son, and found Helen V. sitting on the grass in the middle of a glade or open space left by charcoal burners. He angrily charged her with frightening his little boy, but she entirely denied the accusation and laughed at the child's story of a "strange man", to which he himself did not attach much credence. Joseph W. came to the conclusion that the boy had woke up with a sudden fright, as children sometimes do, but Trevor persisted in his story, and continued in such evident distress that at last his father took him home, hoping that his mother would be able to soothe him. For many weeks, however, the boy gave his parents much anxiety; he became nervous and strange in his manner, refusing to leave the cottage by himself, and constantly alarming the household by waking in the night with cries of "The man in the wood! father! father!"

In course of time, however, the impression seemed to have worn off, and about three months later he accompanied his father to the house of a gentleman in the neighbourhood, for whom Joseph W. occasionally did work. The man was shewn into the study, and the little boy was left sitting in the hall, and a few minutes later, while the gentleman was giving W. his instructions, they were both horrified by a piercing shriek and the sound of a fall, and rushing out, they found the child lying senseless on the floor, his face contorted with terror. The doctor was immediately summoned, and after some examination he pronounced the child to be suffering from a kind of fit, apparently produced by a sudden shock. The boy was taken to one of the bedrooms, and after some time recovered consciousness, but only to pass into a condition described by the medical man as one of violent hysteria. The doctor administered a strong sedative, and in the course of two hours pronounced him fit to walk home, but in passing through the hall the paroxysms of fright returned and with additional violence. The father perceived that the child was pointing at some object, and heard the old cry, "The man in the wood," and looking in the direction indicated saw a stone head of grotesque appearance, which had been built into the wall above one of the doors. It seems that the owner of the house had recently made alterations in his premises, and on digging the foundations for some offices, the men had found a curious head, evidently of the Roman period, which had been placed in the hall in the manner described. The head is pronounced by the most experienced archæologists of the district to be that of a faun or satyr.*

---

*Dr. Phillips tells me that he has seen the head in question, and assures me that he has never received such a vivid presentment of intense evil.

From whatever cause arising, this second shock seemed too severe for the boy Trevor, and at the present date he suffers from a weakness of intellect, which gives but little promise of amending. The matter caused a good deal of sensation at the time, and the girl Helen was closely questioned by Mr. R., but to no purpose, she steadfastly denying that she had frightened or in any way molested Trevor.

The second event with which this girl's name is connected took place about six years ago, and is of a still more extraordinary character.

At the beginning of the summer of 1882 Helen contracted a friendship of a peculiarly intimate character with Rachel M., the daughter of a prosperous farmer in the neighbourhood. This girl, who was a year younger than Helen, was considered by most people to be the prettier of the two, though Helen's features had to a great extent softened as she became older. The two girls, who were together on every available opportunity, presented a singular contrast, the one with her clear olive skin and almost Italian appearance, and the other of the proverbial red and white of our rural districts. It must be stated that the payments made to Mr. R. for the maintenance of Helen were known in the village for their excessive liberality, and the impression was general that she would one day inherit a large sum of money from her relative. The parents of Rachel were therefore not averse from their daughter's friendship with the girl, and even encouraged the intimacy, though they now bitterly regret having done so. Helen still retained her extraordinary fondness for the forest, and on several occasions Rachel accompanied her, the two friends setting out early in the morning, and remaining in the wood till dusk. Once or twice after these excursions Mrs. M. thought her daughter's manner rather peculiar; she seemed languid and dreamy, and as it has been expressed, "different from herself", but these peculiarities seem to have been thought too trifling for remark. One evening, however, after Rachel had come home, her mother heard a noise which sounded like suppressed weeping in the girl's room, and on going in found her lying, half undressed, upon the bed, evidently in the greatest distress. As soon as she saw her mother, she exclaimed, "Ah, mother, mother, why did you let me go to the forest with Helen?" Mrs. M. was astonished at so strange a question, and proceeded to make enquiries. Rachel told her a wild story. She said—

Clarke closed the book with a snap, and turned his chair towards the fire. When his friend sat one evening in that very chair, and told his story, Clarke had interrupted him at a point a little subsequent to this, had cut short his words in a paroxysm of horror. "My God!" he exclaimed, "think, think what you are saying! It is too incredible, too monstrous; such things can never be in this quiet world, where men and women live and die, and struggle, and conquer, or maybe fail, and fall down under sorrow, and grieve and suffer strange fortunes for many a year; but not this, Phillips, not such things as this. There must be some explanation, some way out of the terror. Why, man, if such a case were possible, our earth would be a nightmare."

But Phillips had told his story to the end, concluding:

"Her flight remains a mystery to this day; she vanished in broad sunlight; they saw her walking in a meadow, and a few moments later she was not there."

Clarke tried to conceive the thing again, as he sat by the fire, and again his mind shuddered and shrank back, appalled before the sight of such awful, unspeakable elements enthroned as it were, and triumphant in human flesh. Before him stretched the long dim vista of the green causeway in the forest, as his friend had described it: he saw the swaying leaves and the quivering shadows on the grass, he saw the sunlight and the flowers, and far away, far in the long distance, the two figures moved towards him. One was Rachel, but the other?

Clarke had tried his best to disbelieve it all, but at the end of the account, as he had written it in his book, he had placed the inscription:

ET DIABOLUS INCARNATUS EST. ET HOMO FACTUS EST.

III
THE CITY OF RESURRECTIONS

"Herbert! Good God! Is it possible?"

"Yes, my name's Herbert. I think I know your face too, but I don't remember your name. My memory is very queer."

"Don't you recollect Villiers of Wadham?"

"So it is, so it is. I beg your pardon, Villiers, I didn't think I was begging of an old college friend. Good-night."

"My dear fellow, this haste is unnecessary. My rooms are close by, but we won't go there just yet. Suppose we walk up Shaftesbury Avenue a little way? But how in heaven's name have you come to this pass, Herbert?"

"It's a long story, Villiers, and a strange one too, but you can hear it if you like."

"Come on, then. Take my arm, you don't seem very strong."

The ill-assorted pair moved slowly up Rupert Street; the one in dirty, evil-looking rags, and the other attired in the regulation uniform of a man about town, trim, glossy, and eminently well-to-do. Villiers had emerged from his restaurant after an excellent dinner of many courses, assisted by an ingratiating little flask of Chianti, and, in that frame of mind which was with him almost chronic, had delayed a moment by the door, peering round in the dimly-lighted street in search of those mysterious incidents and persons with which the streets of London teem in every quarter and at every hour. Villiers prided himself as a practised explorer of such obscure mazes and by-ways of London life, and in this unprofitable pursuit he displayed an assiduity which was worthy of more serious employment. Thus he stood beside the lamp-post surveying the passers-by with undisguised curiosity, and with that gravity only known to the systematic diner, had just enunciated in his mind the formula: "London has been called the city of encounters; it is more than that, it is the city of Resurrections," when these reflections were suddenly interrupted by a piteous whine at his elbow, and a deplorable appeal for alms. He looked round in some irritation, and with a sudden shock found himself confronted with the embodied proof of his somewhat stilted fancies. There, close beside him, his face altered and disfigured by poverty and disgrace, his body barely covered by greasy ill-fitting rags, stood his old friend Charles Herbert, who had matriculated on the same day as himself, with whom he had been merry and wise for twelve revolving terms. Different oc-cupations and varying interests had interrupted the friendship, and it was six years since Villiers had seen Herbert; and now he looked upon this wreck of a man with grief and dismay, mingled with a certain in-quisitiveness as to what dreary chain of circumstance had dragged him down to such a doleful pass. Villiers felt together with compassion all the relish of the amateur in mysteries, and congratulated himself on his leisurely speculations outside the restaurant.

They walked on in silence for some time, and more than one passer-by stared in astonishment at the unaccustomed spectacle of a well-dressed man with an unmistakable beggar hanging on to his arm, and, observing this, Villiers led the way to an obscure street in Soho. Here he repeated his question.

"How on earth has it happened, Herbert? I always understood you would succeed to an excellent position in Dorsetshire. Did your father disinherit you? Surely not?"

"No, Villiers; I came into all the property at my poor father's death; he died a year after I left Oxford. He was a very good father to me, and I mourned his death sincerely enough. But you know what young men are; a few months later I came up to town and went a good deal into society. Of course I had excellent introductions, and I managed to enjoy myself very much in a harmless sort of way. I played a little, certainly, but never for heavy stakes, and the few bets I made on races brought me in money—only a few pounds, you know, but enough to pay for cigars and such petty pleasures. It was in my second season that the tide turned. Of course you have heard of my marriage?"

"No, I never heard anything about it."

"Yes, I married, Villiers. I met a girl, a girl of the most wonderful and most strange beauty, at the house of some people whom I knew. I cannot tell you her age; I never knew it, but, so far as I can guess, I should think she must have been about nineteen when I made her acquaintance. My friends had come to know her at Florence; she told them she was an orphan, the child of an English father and an Italian mother, and she charmed them as she charmed me. The first time I saw her was at an evening party. I was standing by the door talking to a friend, when suddenly above the hum and babble of conversation I heard a voice, which seemed to thrill to my heart. She was singing an Italian song. I was introduced to her that evening, and in three months I married Helen. Villiers, that woman, if I can call her woman, corrupted my soul. The night of the wedding I found myself sitting in her bedroom in the hotel, listening to her talk. She was sitting up in bed, and I listened to her as she spoke in her beautiful voice, spoke of things which even now I would not dare whisper in blackest night, though I stood in the midst of a wilderness. You, Villiers, you may think you know life, and London, and what goes on day and night in this dreadful city; for all I can say you may have heard the talk of the vilest, but I tell you, you can have no conception of what I know, no, not in your most fantastic, hideous dreams can you have imaged forth the faintest shadow of what I have heard—and seen. Yes, seen. I have seen the incredible, such horrors that even I myself sometimes stop in the middle of the street, and ask whether it is possible for a man to behold such things and live. In a year, Villiers, I was a ruined man, in body and soul—in body and soul."

"But your property, Herbert? You had land in Dorset."

"I sold it all; the fields and woods, the dear old house—everything."

"And the money?"

"She took it all from me."

"And then left you?"

"Yes; she disappeared one night. I don't know where she went, but I am sure if I saw her again it would kill me. The rest of my story is of no interest; sordid misery, that is all. You may think, Villiers, that I have exaggerated and talked for effect; but I have not told you half. I could tell you certain things which would convince you, but you would never know a happy day again. You would pass the rest of your life, as I pass mine, a haunted man, a man who has seen hell."

Villiers took the unfortunate man to his rooms, and gave him a meal. Herbert could eat little, and scarcely touched the glass of wine set before him. He sat moody and silent by the fire, and seemed relieved when Villiers sent him away with a small present of money.

"By the way, Herbert," said Villiers as they parted at the door, "what was your wife's name? You said Helen, I think? Helen what?"

"The name she passed under when I met her was Helen Vaughan, but what her real name was I can't say. I don't think she had a name. No, no, not in that sense. Only human beings have names, Villiers; I can't say any more. Good-bye; yes, I will not fail to call if I see any way in which you can help me. Good-night."

The man went out into the bitter night, and Villiers returned to his fireside. There was something about Herbert which shocked him inexpressibly; not his poor rags nor the marks which poverty had set upon his face, but rather an indefinite terror which hung about him like a mist. He had acknowledged that he himself was not devoid of blame; the woman, he had avowed, had corrupted him body and soul, and Villiers felt that this man, once his friend, had been an actor in scenes evil beyond the power of words. His story needed no confirmation: he himself was the embodied proof of it. Villiers mused curiously over the story he had heard, and wondered whether he had heard both the first and the last of it. "No," he thought, "certainly not the last, probably only the beginning. A case like this is like a nest of Chinese boxes; you open one after another and find a quainter workmanship in every box. Most likely poor Herbert is merely one of the outside boxes; there are stranger ones to follow."

Villiers could not take his mind away from Herbert and his story, which seemed to grow wilder as the night wore on. The fire began to burn low, and the chilly air of the morning crept into the room; Villiers got up with a glance over his shoulder, and shivering slightly, went to bed.

A few days later he saw in his club a gentleman of his acquaintance, named Austin, who was famous for his intimate knowledge of London life, both in its tenebrous and luminous phases. Villiers, still full of his encounter in Soho and its consequences, thought Austin might possibly be able to shed some light on Herbert's history, and so after some casual talk he suddenly put the question:

"Do you happen to know anything of a man named Herbert— Charles Herbert?"

Austin turned round sharply and stared at Villiers with some astonishment.

"Charles Herbert? Weren't you in town three years ago? No; then you have not heard of the Paul Street case? It caused a good deal of sensation at the time."

"What was the case?"

"Well, a gentleman, a man of very good position, was found dead, stark dead, in the area of a certain house in Paul Street, off Tottenham Court Road. Of course the police did not make the discovery; if you happen to be sitting up all night and have a light in your window, the constable will ring the bell, but if you happen to be lying dead in somebody's area, you will be left alone. In this instance as in many others the alarm was raised by some kind of vagabond; I don't mean a common tramp, or a public-house loafer, but a gentleman, whose business or pleasure, or both, made him a spectator of the London streets at five o'clock in the morning. This individual was, as he said, 'going home', it did not appear whence or whither, and had occasion to pass through Paul Street between four and five a.m. Something or other caught his eye at Number 20; he said, absurdly enough, that the house had the most unpleasant physiognomy he had ever observed, but, at any rate, he glanced down the area, and was a good deal astonished to see a man lying on the stones, his limbs all huddled together, and his face turned up. Our gentleman thought this face looked peculiarly ghastly, and so set off at a run in search of the nearest policeman. The constable was at first inclined to treat the matter lightly, suspecting common drunkenness; however, he came, and after looking at the man's face, changed his tone, quickly enough. The early bird, who had picked up this fine worm, was sent off for a doctor, and the policeman rang and knocked at the door till a slatternly servant girl came down looking more than half asleep. The constable pointed out the contents of the area to the maid, who screamed loudly enough to wake up the street, but she knew nothing of the man; had never seen him at the house, and so forth. Meanwhile the original discoverer had come back with a medical man, and the next thing was to get into the area. The gate was open, so the whole quartet stumped down the steps. The doctor hardly needed a moment's examination; he said the poor fellow had been dead for several hours, and it was then the case began to get interesting. The dead man had not been robbed, and in one of his pockets were papers identifying him as—well, as a man of good family and means, a favourite in society, and nobody's enemy, so far as could be known. I don't give his name, Villiers, because it has nothing to do with the story, and because it's no good raking up these affairs about the dead when there are relations living. The next curious point was that the medical men couldn't agree as to how he met his death. There were some slight bruises on his shoulders, but they were so slight that it looked as if he had been pushed roughly out of the kitchen door, and not thrown over the railings from the street, or even dragged down the steps. But there were positively no other marks of violence about him, certainly none that would account for his death; and when they came to the autopsy there wasn't a trace of poison of any kind. Of course the police wanted to know all about the people at Number 20, and here again, so I have heard from private sources, one or two other very curious points came out. It appears that the occupants of the house were a Mr. and Mrs. Charles Herbert; he was said to be a landed proprietor, though it struck most people that Paul Street was not exactly the place to look for county gentry. As for Mrs. Herbert, nobody seemed to know who or what she was, and, between ourselves, I fancy the divers after her history found themselves in rather strange waters. Of course they both denied knowing anything about the deceased, and in default of any evidence against them they were discharged. But some very odd things came out about them. Though it was between five and six in the morning when the dead man was removed, a large crowd had collected, and several of the neighbours ran to see what was going on. They were pretty free with their comments, by all accounts, and from these it appeared that Number 20 was in very bad odour in Paul Street. The detectives tried to trace down these rumours to some solid foundation of fact, but could not get hold of anything. People shook their heads and raised their eyebrows and thought the Herberts rather 'queer', 'would rather not be seen going into their house', and so on, but there was nothing tangible. The authorities were morally certain that the man met his death in some way or another in the house and was thrown out by the kitchen door, but they couldn't prove it, and the absence of any indications of violence or poisoning left them helpless. An odd case, wasn't it? But curiously enough, there's something more that I haven't told you. I happened to know one of the doctors who was consulted as to the cause of death, and some time after the inquest I met him, and asked him about it. 'Do you really mean to tell me,' I said, 'that you were baffled by the case, that you actually don't know what the man died of?' 'Pardon me,' he replied, 'I know perfectly well what caused death. Blank died of fright, of sheer, awful terror; I never saw features so hideously contorted in the entire course of my practice, and I have seen the faces of a whole host of dead.' The doctor was usually a cool customer enough, and a certain vehemence in his manner struck me, but I couldn't get anything more out of him. I suppose the Treasury didn't see their way to prosecuting the Herberts for frightening a man to death; at any rate, nothing was done, and the case dropped out of men's minds. Do you happen to know anything of Herbert?"

"Well," replied Villiers, "he was an old college friend of mine."

"You don't say so? Have you ever seen his wife?"

"No, I haven't. I have lost sight of Herbert for many years."

"It's queer, isn't it, parting with a man at the college gate or at Paddington, seeing nothing of him for years, and then finding him pop up his head in such an odd place. But I should like to have seen Mrs. Herbert; people said extraordinary things about her."

"What sort of things?"

"Well, I hardly know how to tell you. Every one who saw her at the police court said she was at once the most beautiful woman and the most repulsive they had ever set eyes on. I have spoken to a man who saw her, and I assure you he positively shuddered as he tried to describe the woman, but he couldn't tell why. She seems to have been a sort of enigma; and I expect if that one dead man could have told tales, he would have told some uncommonly queer ones. And there you are again in another puzzle; what could a respectable country gentleman like Mr. Blank (we'll call him that if you don't mind) want in such a very queer house as Number 20? It's altogether a very odd case, isn't it?"

"It is indeed, Austin; an extraordinary case. I didn't think, when I asked you about my old friend, I should strike on such strange metal. Well, I must be off; good-day."

Villiers went away, thinking of his own conceit of the Chinese boxes; here was quaint workmanship indeed.

IV

THE DISCOVERY IN PAUL STREET

A few months after Villiers' meeting with Herbert, Mr. Clarke was sitting, as usual, by his after-dinner hearth, resolutely guarding his fancies from wandering in the direction of the bureau. For more than a week he had succeeded in keeping away from the "Memoirs", and he cherished hopes of a complete self-reformation; but, in spite of his endeavours, he could not hush the wonder and the strange curiosity that that last case he had written down had excited within him. He had put the case, or rather the outline of it, conjecturally to a scientific friend, who shook his head, and thought Clarke getting queer, and on this particular evening Clarke was making an effort to rationalise the story, when a sudden knock at his door roused him from his meditations.

"Mr. Villiers to see you, sir."

"Dear me, Villiers, it is very kind of you to look me up; I have not seen you for many months; I should think nearly a year. Come in, come in. And how are you, Villiers? Want any advice about investments?"

"No, thanks; I fancy everything I have in that way is pretty safe. No, Clarke, I have really come to consult you about a rather curious matter that has been brought under my notice of late. I am afraid you will think it all rather absurd when I tell my tale. I sometimes think so myself, and that's just why I made up my mind to come to you, as I know you're a practical man."

Mr. Villiers was ignorant of the "Memoirs to prove the Existence of the Devil".

"Well, Villiers, I shall be happy to give you my advice, to the best of my ability. What is the nature of the case?"

"It's an extraordinary thing altogether. You know my ways; I always keep my eyes open in the streets, and in my time I have chanced upon some queer customers, and queer cases, too, but this, I think, beats all. I was coming out of a restaurant one nasty winter night about three months ago; I had had a capital dinner and a good bottle of Chianti, and I stood for a moment on the pavement, thinking what a mystery there is about London streets and the companies that pass along them. A bottle of red wine encourages these fancies, Clarke, and I dare say I should have thought a page of small type, but I was cut short by a beggar who had come behind me, and was making the usual appeals. Of course I looked round, and this beggar turned out to be what was left of an old friend of mine, a man named Herbert. I asked him how he had come to such a wretched pass, and he told me. We walked up and down one of those long dark Soho streets, and there I listened to his story. He said he had married a beautiful girl, some years younger than himself, and, as he put it, she had corrupted him body and soul. He wouldn't go into details; he said he dare not, that what he had seen and heard haunted him by night and day, and when I looked in his face I knew he was speaking the truth. There was something about the man that made me shiver. I don't know why, but it was there. I gave him a little money and sent him away, and I assure you that when he was gone I gasped for breath. His presence seemed to chill one's blood."

"Isn't all this just a little fanciful, Villiers? I suppose the poor fellow had made an imprudent marriage, and, in plain English, gone to the bad."

"Well, listen to this." Villiers told Clarke the story he had heard from Austin.

"You see," he concluded, "there can be but little doubt that this Mr. Blank, whoever he was, died of sheer terror; he saw something so awful, so terrible, that it cut short his life. And what he saw, he most certainly saw in that house, which, somehow or other, had got a bad name in the neighbourhood. I had the curiosity to go and look at the place for myself. It's a saddening kind of street; the houses are old enough to be mean and dreary, but not old enough to be quaint. As far as I could see most of them are let in lodgings, furnished and unfurnished, and almost every door has three bells to it. Here and there the ground floors have been made into shops of the commonest kind; it's a dismal street in every way. I found Number 20 was to let, and I went to the agent's and got the key. Of course I should have heard nothing of the Herberts in that quarter, but I asked the man, fair and square, how long they had left the house, and whether there had been other tenants in the meanwhile. He looked at me queerly for a minute, and told me the Herberts had left immediately after the unpleasantness, as he called it, and since then the house had been empty."

Mr. Villiers paused for a moment.

"I have always been rather fond of going over empty houses; there's a sort of fascination about the desolate empty rooms, with the nails sticking in the walls, and the dust thick upon the window-sills. But I didn't enjoy going over Number 20, Paul Street. I had hardly put my foot inside the passage before I noticed a queer, heavy feeling about the air of the house. Of course all empty houses are stuffy, and so forth, but this was something quite different; I can't describe it to you, but it seemed to stop the breath. I went into the front room and the back room, and the kitchens downstairs; they were all dirty and dusty enough, as you would expect, but there was something strange about them all. I couldn't define it to you, I only know I felt queer. It was one of the rooms on the first floor, though, that was the worst. It was a largish room, and once on a time the paper must have been cheerful enough, but when I saw it, paint, paper, and everything were most doleful. But the room was full of horror; I felt my teeth grinding as I put my hand on the door, and when I went in, I thought I should have fallen fainting to the floor. However, I pulled myself together, and stood against the end wall, wondering what on earth there could be about the room to make my limbs tremble, and my heart beat as if I were at the hour of death. In one corner there was a pile of newspapers littered about on the floor, and I began looking at them; they were papers of three or four years ago, some of them half torn, and some crumpled as if they had been used for packing. I turned the whole pile over, and amongst them I found a curious drawing; I will shew it you presently. But I couldn't stay in the room; I felt it was overpowering me. I was thankful to come out, safe and sound, into the open air. People stared at me as I walked along the street, and one man said I was drunk. I was staggering about from one side of the pavement to the other, and it was as much as I could do to take the key back to the agent and get home. I was in bed for a week, suffering from what my doctor called nervous shock and exhaustion. One of those days I was reading the evening paper, and happened to notice a paragraph headed: 'Starved to Death.' It was the usual style of thing; a model lodging-house in Marylebone, a door locked for several days, and a dead man in his chair when they broke in. 'The deceased,' said the paragraph, 'was known as Charles Herbert, and is believed to have been once a prosperous country gentleman. His name was familiar to the public three years ago in connection with the mysterious death in Paul Street, Tottenham Court Road, the deceased being the tenant of the house Number 20, in the area of which a gentleman of good position was found dead under circumstances not devoid of suspicion.' A tragic ending, wasn't it? But, after all, if what he told me were true, which I am sure it was, the man's life was all a tragedy, and a tragedy of a stranger sort than they put on the boards."

"And that is the story, is it?" said Clarke musingly.

"Yes, that is the story."

"Well, really, Villiers, I scarcely know what to say about it. There are, no doubt, circumstances in the case which seem peculiar, the finding of the dead man in the area of Herbert's house, for instance, and the extraordinary opinion of the physician as to the cause of death; but, after all, it is conceivable that the facts may be explained in a straightforward manner. As to your own sensations, when you went to see the house, I would suggest that they were due to a vivid imagination; you must have been brooding, in a semi-conscious way, over what you had heard. I don't exactly see what more can be said or done in the matter; you evidently think there is a mystery of some kind, but Herbert is dead; where then do you propose to look?"

"I propose to look for the woman; the woman whom he married. *She* is the mystery."

The two men sat silent by the fireside; Clarke secretly congratulating himself on having successfully kept up the character of advocate of the commonplace, and Villiers wrapt in his gloomy fancies.

"I think I will have a cigarette," he said at last, and put his hand in his pocket to feel for the cigarette-case.

"Ah!" he said, starting slightly, "I forgot I had something to shew you. You remember my saying that I had found a rather curious sketch amongst the pile of old newspapers at the house in Paul Street? Here it is."

Villiers drew out a small thin parcel from his pocket. It was covered with brown paper, and secured with string, and the knots were troublesome. In spite of himself Clarke felt inquisitive; he bent forward on his chair as Villiers painfully undid the string, and unfolded the outer covering. Inside was a second wrapping of tissue, and Villiers took it off and handed the small piece of paper to Clarke without a word.

There was dead silence in the room for five minutes or more; the two men sat so still that they could hear the ticking of the tall old-fashioned clock that stood outside in the hall, and in the mind of one of them the slow monotony of sound woke up a far, far memory. He was looking intently at the small pen-and-ink sketch of a woman's head; it had evidently been drawn with great care, and by a true artist, for the woman's soul looked out of the eyes, and the lips were parted with a strange smile. Clarke gazed still at the face; it brought to his memory one summer evening long ago; he saw again the long lovely valley, the river winding between the hills, the meadows and the corn-fields, the dull red sun, and the cold white mist rising from the water. He heard a voice speaking to him across the waves of many years, and saying, "Clarke, Mary will see the God Pan!" and then he was standing in the grim room beside the doctor, listening to the heavy ticking of the clock, waiting and watching, watching the figure lying on the green chair beneath the lamp-light. Mary rose up, and he looked into her eyes, and his heart grew cold within him.

"Who is this woman?" he said at last. His voice was dry and hoarse.

"That is the woman whom Herbert married."

Clarke looked again at the sketch; it was not Mary after all. There certainly was Mary's face, but there was something else, something he had not seen on Mary's features when the white-clad girl entered the laboratory with the doctor, nor at her terrible awakening, nor when she lay grinning on the bed. Whatever it was, the glance that came from those eyes, the smile on the full lips, or the expression of the whole face, Clarke shuddered before it in his inmost soul, and thought unconsciously of Dr. Phillips's words, "the most vivid presentment of evil I have ever seen". He turned the paper over mechanically in his hand and glanced at the back.

"Good God, Clarke, what is the matter? You are as white as death."

Villiers had started wildly from his chair, as Clarke fell back with a groan, and let the paper drop from his hands.

"I don't feel very well, Villiers, I am subject to these attacks. Pour me out a little wine; thanks, that will do. I shall feel better in a few minutes."

Villiers picked up the fallen sketch and turned it over as Clarke had done.

"You saw that?" he said. "That's how I identified it as being a portrait of Herbert's wife, or I should say his widow. How do you feel now?"

"Better, thanks, it was only a passing faintness. I don't think I quite catch your meaning. What did you say enabled you to identify the picture?"

"This word—'Helen'—written on the back. Didn't I tell you her name was Helen? Yes; Helen Vaughan."

Clarke groaned; there could be no shadow of doubt.

"Now don't you agree with me," said Villiers, "that in the story I have told you to-night, and in the part this woman plays in it, there are some very strange points?"

"Yes, Villiers," Clarke muttered, "it is a strange story indeed; a strange story indeed. You must give me time to think it over; I may be able to help you or I may not. Must you be going now? Well, good-night, Villiers, good-night. Come and see me in the course of a week."

V
THE LETTER OF ADVICE

"Do you know, Austin," said Villiers, as the two friends were pacing sedately along Piccadilly one pleasant morning in May, "do you know I am convinced that what you told me about Paul Street and the Herberts is a mere episode in an extraordinary history? I may as well confess to you that when I asked you about Herbert a few months ago I had just seen him."

"You had seen him? Where?"

"He begged of me in the street one night. He was in the most pitiable plight, but I recognised the man, and I got him to tell me his history, or at least the outline of it. In brief, it amounted to this—he had been ruined by his wife."

"In what manner?"

"He would not tell me; he would only say that she had destroyed him, body and soul. The man is dead now."

"And what has become of his wife?"

"Ah, that's what I should like to know, and I mean to find her sooner or later. I know a man named Clarke, a dry fellow, in fact a man of business, but shrewd enough. You understand my meaning; not shrewd in the mere business sense of the word, but a man who really knows something about men and life. Well, I laid the case before him, and he was evidently impressed. He said it needed consideration, and asked me to come again in the course of a week. A few days later I received this extraordinary letter."

Austin took the envelope, drew out the letter, and read it curiously. It ran as follows:—

"MY DEAR VILLIERS,—I have thought over the matter on which you consulted me the other night, and my advice to you is this. Throw the portrait into the fire, blot out the story from your mind. Never give it another thought, Villiers, or you will be sorry. You will think, no doubt, that I am in possession of some secret information, and to a certain extent that is the case. But I only know a little; I am like a traveller who has peered

COLLECTED FICTION: 1888–1895

over an abyss, and has drawn back in terror. What I know is strange enough and horrible enough, but beyond my knowledge there are depths and horrors more frightful still, more incredible than any tale told of winter nights about the fire. I have resolved, and nothing shall shake that resolve, to explore no whit farther, and if you value your happiness you will make the same determination.

"Come and see me by all means; but we will talk on more cheerful topics than this."

Austin folded the letter methodically and returned it to Villiers.

"It is certainly an extraordinary letter," he said; "what does he mean by the portrait?"

"Ah! I forgot to tell you I have been to Paul Street and have made a discovery."

Villiers told his story as he had told it to Clarke, and Austin listened in silence. He seemed puzzled.

"How very curious that you should experience such an unpleasant sensation in that room!" he said at length. "I hardly gather that it was a mere matter of the imagination; a feeling of repulsion, in short."

"No, it was more physical than mental. It was as if I were inhaling at every breath some deadly fume, which seemed to penetrate to every nerve and bone and sinew of my body. I felt racked from head to foot, my eyes began to grow dim; it was like the entrance of death."

"Yes, yes, very strange, certainly. You see, your friend confesses that there is some very black story connected with this woman. Did you notice any particular emotion in him when you were telling your tale?"

"Yes, I did. He became very faint, but he assured me that it was a mere passing attack to which he was subject."

"Did you believe him?"

"I did at the time, but I don't now. He heard what I had to say with a good deal of indifference, till I shewed him the portrait. It was then he was seized with the attack of which I spoke. He looked ghastly, I assure you."

"Then he must have seen the woman before. But there might be another explanation; it might have been the name, and not the face, which was familiar to him. What do you think?"

"I couldn't say. To the best of my belief it was after turning the portrait in his hands that he nearly dropped from his chair. The name, you know, was written on the back."

"Quite so. After all, it is impossible to come to any resolution in a case like this. I hate melodrama, and nothing strikes me as more commonplace and tedious than the ordinary ghost story of commerce; but really, Villiers, it looks as if there were something very queer at the bottom of all this."

The two men had, without noticing it, turned up Ashley Street, leading northward from Piccadilly. It was a long street, and rather a gloomy one, but here and there a brighter taste had illuminated the dark houses with flowers, and gay curtains, and a cheerful paint on the doors. Villiers glanced up as Austin stopped speaking, and looked at one of these houses; geraniums, red and white, drooped from every sill, and daffodil-coloured curtains were draped back from each window.

"It looks cheerful, doesn't it?" he said.

"Yes, and the inside is still more cheery. One of the pleasantest houses of the season, so I have heard. I haven't been there myself, but I've met several men who have, and they tell me it's uncommonly jovial."

"Whose house is it?"

"A Mrs. Beaumont's."

"And who is she?"

"I couldn't tell you. I have heard she comes from South America, but, after all, who she is is of little consequence. She is a very wealthy woman, there's no doubt of that, and some of the best people have taken her up. I hear she has some wonderful claret, really marvellous wine, which must have cost a fabulous sum. Lord Argentine was telling me about it; he was there last Sunday evening. He assures me he has never tasted such a wine, and Argentine, as you know, is an expert. By the way, that reminds me, she must be an oddish sort of woman, this Mrs. Beaumont. Argentine asked her how old the wine was, and what do you think she said? 'About a thousand years, I believe.' Lord Argentine thought she was chaffing him, you know, but when he laughed she said she was speaking quite seriously, and offered to shew him the jar. Of course, he couldn't say anything more after that; but it seems rather antiquated for a beverage, doesn't it? Why, here we are at my rooms. Come in, won't you?"

"Thanks, I think I will. I haven't seen the curiosity-shop for some time."

It was a room furnished richly, yet oddly, where every chair and bookcase and table, and every rug and jar and ornament seemed to be a thing apart, preserving its own individuality.

"Anything fresh lately?" said Villiers after a while.

"No, I think not; you saw those queer jugs, didn't you? I thought so. I don't think I have come across anything for the last few weeks."

Austin glanced round the room from cupboard to cupboard, from shelf to shelf, in search of some new oddity. His eyes fell at last on an old chest, pleasantly and quaintly carved, which stood in a dark corner of the room.

"Ah," he said, "I was forgetting, I have got something to shew you." Austin unlocked the chest, drew out a thick quarto volume, laid it on the table, and resumed the cigar he had put down.

"Did you know Arthur Meyrick the painter, Villiers?"

"A little; I met him two or three times at the house of a friend of mine. What has become of him? I haven't heard his name mentioned for some time."

"He's dead."

"You don't say so! Quite young, wasn't he?"

"Yes; only thirty when he died."

"What did he die of?"

"I don't know. He was an intimate friend of mine, and a thoroughly good fellow. He used to come here and talk to me for hours, and he was one of the best talkers I have met. He could even talk about painting, and that's more than can be said of most painters. About eighteen months ago he was feeling rather overworked, and partly at my suggestion he went off on a sort of roving expedition, with no very definite end or aim about it. I believe New York was to be his first port, but I never heard from him. Three months ago I got this book, with a very civil letter from an English doctor practising at Buenos Ayres, stating that he had attended the late Mr. Meyrick during his illness, and that the deceased had expressed an earnest wish that the enclosed packet should be sent to me after his death. That was all."

"And haven't you written for further particulars?"

"I have been thinking of doing so. You would advise me to write to the doctor?"

"Certainly. And what about the book?"

"It was sealed up when I got it. I don't think the doctor had seen it."

"It is something very rare? Meyrick was a collector, perhaps?"

"No, I think not, hardly a collector. Now, what do you think of those Ainu jugs?"

"They are peculiar, but I like them. But aren't you going to shew me poor Meyrick's legacy?"

"Yes, yes, to be sure. The fact is, it's rather a peculiar sort of thing, and I haven't shewn it to any one. I wouldn't say anything about it if I were you. There it is."

Villiers took the book and opened it at haphazard.

"It isn't a printed volume, then?" he said.

"No. It is a collection of drawings in black and white by my poor friend Meyrick."

Villiers turned to the first page, it was blank; the second bore a brief inscription, which he read:

> *Silet per diem universus, nec sine horrore secretus est; lucet nocturnis ignibus, chorus Ægipanum undique personatur: audiuntur et cantus tibiarum, et tinnitus cymbalorum per oram maritimam.*

On the third page was a design which made Villiers start and look up at Austin; he was gazing abstractedly out of the window. Villiers turned page after page, absorbed, in spite of himself, in the frightful Walpurgis Night of evil, strange monstrous evil, that the dead artist had set forth in hard black and white. The figures of Fauns and Satyrs and Ægipans danced before his eyes, the darkness of the thicket, the dance on the mountain-top, the scenes by lonely shores, in green vineyards, by rocks and desert places, passed before him: a world before which the human soul seemed to shrink back and shudder. Villiers whirled over the remaining pages; he had seen enough, but the picture on the last leaf caught his eye, as he almost closed the book.

"Austin!"

"Well, what is it?"

"Do you know who that is?"

It was a woman's face, alone on the white page.

"Know who it is? No, of course not."

"I do."

"Who is it?"

"It is Mrs. Herbert."

"Are you sure?"

"I am perfectly certain of it. Poor Meyrick! He is one more chapter in her history."

"But what do you think of the designs?"

"They are frightful. Lock the book up again, Austin. If I were you I would burn it; it must be a terrible companion even though it be in a chest."

"Yes, they are singular drawings. But I wonder what connection there could be between Meyrick and Mrs. Herbert, or what link between her and these designs?"

"Ah, who can say? It is possible that the matter may end here, and we shall never know, but in my own opinion this Helen Vaughan, or Mrs. Herbert, is only beginning. She will come back to London, Austin; depend upon it, she will come back and we shall hear more about her then. I don't think it will be very pleasant news."

VI
THE SUICIDES

Lord Argentine was a great favourite in London Society. At twenty he had been a poor man, decked with the surname of an illustrious family, but forced to earn a livelihood as best he could, and the most speculative of money-lenders would not have entrusted him with fifty pounds on the chance of his ever changing his name for a title, and his poverty for a great fortune. His father had been near enough to the fountain of good things to secure one of the family livings, but the son, even if he had taken orders, would scarcely have obtained so much as this, and moreover felt no vocation for the ecclesiastical estate. Thus he fronted the world with no better armour than the bachelor's gown and the wits of a younger son's grandson, with which equipment he contrived in some way to make a very tolerable fight of it. At twenty-five Mr. Charles Aubernoun saw himself still a man of struggles and of warfare with the world, but out of the seven who stood between him and the high places of his family three only remained. These three, however, were "good lives", but yet not proof against the Zulu assegais and typhoid fever, and so one morning Aubernoun woke up and found himself Lord Argentine, a man of thirty who had faced the difficulties of existence, and had conquered. The situation amused him immensely, and he resolved that riches should be as pleasant to him as poverty had always been. Argentine, after some little consideration, came to the conclusion that dining, regarded as a fine art, was perhaps the most amusing pursuit open to fallen humanity, and thus his dinners became famous in London, and an invitation to his table a thing covetously desired. After ten years of lordship and dinners Argentine still declined to be jaded, still persisted in enjoying life, and by a kind of infection had become recognised as the cause of joy in others, in short, as the best of company. His sudden and tragical death therefore caused a wide and deep sensation. People could scarce believe it, even though the newspaper was before their eyes, and the cry of "Mysterious Death of a Nobleman" came ringing up from the street. But there stood the brief paragraph: "Lord Argentine was found dead this morning by his valet under distressing circumstances. It is stated that there can be no doubt that his lordship committed suicide, though no motive can be assigned for the act. The deceased nobleman was widely known in society, and much liked for his genial manner and sumptuous hospitality. He is succeeded by," etc., etc.

By slow degrees the details came to light, but the case still remained a mystery. The chief witness at the inquest was the dead nobleman's valet, who said that the night before his death Lord Argentine had dined with a lady of good position, whose name was suppressed in the newspaper reports. At about eleven o'clock Lord Argentine had returned, and informed his man that he should not require his services till the next morning. A little later the valet had occasion to cross the hall and was somewhat astonished to see his master quietly letting himself out at the front door. He had taken off his evening clothes, and was dressed in a Norfolk coat and knickerbockers, and wore a low brown hat. The valet had no reason to suppose that Lord Argentine had seen him, and though his master rarely kept late hours, thought little of the occurrence till the next morning, when he knocked at the bedroom door at a quarter to nine as usual. He received no answer, and, after knocking two or three times, entered the room, and saw Lord Argentine's body leaning forward at an angle from the bottom of the bed. He found that his master had tied a cord securely to one of the short bed-posts, and, after making a running noose and slipping it round his neck, the unfortunate man must have resolutely fallen forward, to die by slow strangulation. He was dressed in the light suit in which the valet had seen him go out, and the doctor who was summoned pronounced that life had been extinct for more than four hours. All papers, letters, and so forth seemed in perfect order, and nothing was discovered which pointed in the most remote way to any scandal either great or small. Here the evidence ended; nothing more could be discovered. Several persons had been present at the dinner-party at which Lord Argentine had assisted, and to all these he seemed in his usual genial spirits. The valet, indeed, said he thought his master appeared a little excited when he came home, but he confessed that the alteration in his manner was very slight, hardly noticeable, indeed. It seemed hopeless to seek for any clue, and the suggestion that Lord Argentine had been suddenly attacked by acute suicidal mania was generally accepted.

It was otherwise, however, when within three weeks, three more gentlemen, one of them a nobleman, and the two others men of good position and ample means, perished miserably in almost precisely the same manner. Lord Swanleigh was found one morning in his dressing-room, hanging from a peg affixed to the wall, and Mr. Collier-Stuart and Mr. Herries had chosen to die as Lord Argentine. There was no explanation in either case; a few bald facts; a living man in the evening, and a dead body with a black swollen face in the morning. The police had been forced to confess themselves powerless to arrest or to explain the sordid murders of Whitechapel; but before the horrible suicides of Piccadilly and Mayfair they were dumbfounded, for not even the mere ferocity which did duty as an explanation of the crimes of the East End, could be of service in the West. Each of these men who had resolved to die a tortured shameful death was rich, prosperous, and to all appearance in love with the world, and not the acutest research could ferret out any shadow of a lurking motive in either case. There was a horror in the air, and men looked at one another's faces when they met, each wondering whether the other was to be the victim of the fifth nameless tragedy. Journalists sought in vain in their scrap-books for materials whereof to concoct reminiscent articles; and the morning paper was unfolded in many a house with a feeling of awe; no man knew when or where the blow would next light.

A short while after the last of these terrible events, Austin came to see Mr. Villiers. He was curious to know whether Villiers had succeeded in discovering any fresh traces of Mrs. Herbert, either through Clarke or by other sources, and he asked the question soon after he had sat down.

"No," said Villiers, "I wrote to Clarke, but he remains obdurate, and I have tried other channels, but without any result. I can't find out what became of Helen Vaughan after she left Paul Street, but I think she must have gone abroad. But to tell the truth, Austin, I haven't paid very much attention to the matter for the last few weeks; I knew poor Herries intimately, and his terrible death has been a great shock to me, a great shock."

"I can well believe it," answered Austin gravely; "you know Argentine was a friend of mine. If I remember rightly, we were speaking of him that day you came to my rooms."

"Yes; it was in connection with that house in Ashley Street, Mrs. Beaumont's house. You said something about Argentine's dining there."

"Quite so. Of course you know it was there Argentine dined the night before—before his death."

"No, I haven't heard that."

"Oh, yes; the name was kept out of the papers to spare Mrs. Beaumont. Argentine was a great favourite of hers, and it is said she was in a terrible state for some time after."

A curious look came over Villiers's face; he seemed undecided whether to speak or not. Austin began again.

"I never experienced such a feeling of horror as when I read the account of Argentine's death. I didn't understand it at the time, and I don't now. I knew him well, and it completely passes my understanding for what possible cause he—or any of the others for the matter of that—could have resolved in cold blood to die in such an awful manner. You know how men babble away each other's characters in London, you may be sure any buried scandal or hidden skeleton would have been brought to light in such a case as this; but nothing of the sort has taken place. As for the theory of mania, that is very well, of course, for the coroner's jury, but everybody knows that it's all nonsense. Suicidal mania is not small-pox."

Austin relapsed into gloomy silence. Villiers sat silent also, watching his friend. The expression of indecision still fleeted across his face; he seemed as if weighing his thoughts in the balance, and the considerations he was revolving left him still silent. Austin tried to shake off the remembrance of tragedies as hopeless and perplexed as the labyrinth of Dædalus, and began to talk in an indifferent voice of the more pleasant incidents and adventures of the season.

"That Mrs. Beaumont," he said, "of whom we were speaking, is a great success; she has taken London almost by storm. I met her the other night at Fulham's; she is really a remarkable woman."

"You have met Mrs. Beaumont?"

"Yes; she had quite a court around her. She would be called very handsome, I suppose, and yet there is something about her face which I didn't like. The features are exquisite, but the expression is strange. And all the time I was looking at her, and afterwards, when I was going home, I had a curious feeling that that very expression was in some way or other familiar to me."

"You must have seen her in the Row."

"No, I am sure I never set eyes on the woman before; it is that which makes it puzzling. And to the best of my belief I have never seen anybody like her; what I felt was a kind of dim far-off memory, vague but persistent. The only sensation I can compare it to, is that odd feeling one sometimes has in a dream, when fantastic cities and wondrous lands and phantom personages appear familiar and accustomed."

Villiers nodded and glanced aimlessly round the room, possibly in search of something on which to turn the conversation. His eyes fell on an old chest somewhat like that in which the artist's strange legacy lay hid beneath a Gothic scutcheon.

"Have you written to the doctor about poor Meyrick?" he asked.

"Yes; I wrote asking for full particulars as to his illness and death. I don't expect to have an answer for another three weeks or a month. I thought I might as well enquire whether Meyrick knew an Englishwoman named Herbert, and if so, whether the doctor could give me any information about her. But it's very possible that Meyrick fell in with her at New York, or Mexico, or San Francisco; I have no idea as to the extent or direction of his travels."

"Yes, and it's very possible that the woman may have more than one name."

"Exactly. I wish I had thought of asking you to lend me the portrait of her which you possess. I might have enclosed it in my letter to Dr. Matthews."

"So you might; that never occurred to me. We might send it now. Hark! what are those boys calling?"

While the two men had been talking together a confused noise of shouting had been gradually growing louder. The noise rose from the eastward and swelled down Piccadilly, drawing nearer and nearer, a very torrent of sound; surging up streets usually quiet, and making every window a frame for a face, curious or excited. The cries and voices came echoing up the silent street where Villiers lived, growing more distinct as they advanced, and, as Villiers spoke, an answer rang up from the pavement:

"The West End Horrors; Another Awful Suicide; Full Details!"

Austin rushed down the stairs and bought a paper and read out the paragraph to Villiers as the uproar in the street rose and fell. The window was open and the air seemed full of noise and terror.

"Another gentleman has fallen a victim to the terrible epidemic of suicide which for the last month has prevailed in the West End. Mr. Sidney Crashaw, of Stoke House, Fulham, and King's Pomeroy, Devon, was found, after a prolonged search, hanging from the branch of a tree in his garden at one o'clock to-day. The deceased gentleman dined last night at the Carlton Club and seemed in his usual health and spirits. He left the Club at about ten o'clock, and was seen walking leisurely up St. James's Street a little later. Subsequent to this his movements cannot be traced. On the discovery of the body medical aid was at once summoned, but life had evidently been long extinct. So far as is known, Mr. Crashaw had no trouble or anxiety of any kind. This painful suicide, it will be remembered, is the fifth of the kind in the last month. The authorities at Scotland Yard are unable to suggest any explanation of these terrible occurrences."

Austin put down the paper in mute horror.

"I shall leave London to-morrow," he said, "it is a city of nightmares. How awful this is, Villiers!"

Villiers was sitting by the window quietly looking out into the street. He had listened to the newspaper report attentively, and the hint of indecision was no longer on his face.

"Wait a moment, Austin," he replied, "I have made up my mind to mention a little matter that occurred last night. It is stated, I think, that Crashaw was last seen alive in St. James's Street shortly after ten?"

"Yes, I think so. I will look again. Yes, you are quite right."

"Quite so. Well, I am in a position to contradict that statement at all events. Crashaw was seen after that; considerably later indeed."

"How do you know?"

"Because I happened to see Crashaw myself at about two o'clock this morning."

"You saw Crashaw? You, Villiers?"

"Yes, I saw him quite distinctly; indeed, there were but a few feet between us."

"Where, in Heaven's name, did you see him?"

"Not far from here. I saw him in Ashley Street. He was just leaving a house."

"Did you notice what house it was?"

"Yes. It was Mrs. Beaumont's."

"Villiers! Think what you are saying; there must be some mistake. How could Crashaw be in Mrs. Beaumont's house at two o'clock in the morning? Surely, surely, you must have been dreaming, Villiers, you were always rather fanciful."

"No; I was wide awake enough. Even if I had been dreaming as you say, what I saw would have roused me effectually."

"What you saw? What did you see? Was there anything strange about Crashaw? But I can't believe it; it is impossible."

"Well, if you like I will tell you what I saw, or if you please, what I think I saw, and you can judge for yourself."

"Very good, Villiers."

The noise and clamour of the street had died away, though now and then the sound of shouting still came from the distance, and the dull, leaden silence seemed like the quiet after an earthquake or a storm. Villiers turned from the window and began speaking.

"I was at a house near Regent's Park last night, and when I came away the fancy took me to walk home instead of taking a hansom. It was a clear pleasant night enough, and after a few minutes I had the streets pretty much to myself. It's a curious thing, Austin, to be alone in London at night, the gas-lamps stretching away in perspective, and the dead silence, and then perhaps the rush and clatter of a hansom on the stones, and the fire starting up under the horse's hoofs. I walked along pretty briskly, for I was feeling a little tired of being out in the night, and as the clocks were striking two I turned down Ashley Street, which, you know, is on my way. It was quieter than ever there, and the lamps were fewer; altogether, it looked as dark and gloomy as a forest in winter. I had done about half the length of the street when I heard a door closed very softly, and naturally I looked up to see who was abroad like myself at such an hour. As it happens, there is a street lamp close to the house in question, and I saw a man standing on the step. He had just shut the door and his face was towards me, and I recognised Crashaw directly. I never knew him to speak to, but I had often seen him, and I am positive that I was not mistaken in my man. I looked into his face for a moment, and then—I will confess the truth—I set off at a good run, and kept it up till I was within my own door."

"Why?"

"Why? Because it made my blood run cold to see that man's face. I could never have supposed that such an infernal medley of passions could have glared out of any human eyes; I almost fainted as I looked. I knew I had looked into the eyes of a lost soul, Austin, the man's outward form remained, but all hell was within it. Furious lust, and hate that was like fire, and the loss of all hope and horror that seemed to shriek aloud to the night, though his teeth were shut; and the utter blackness of despair. I am sure he did not see me; he saw nothing that you or I can see, but he saw what I hope we never shall. I do not know when he died; I suppose in an hour, or perhaps two, but when I passed down Ashley Street and heard the closing door, that man no longer belonged to this world; it was a devil's face that I looked upon."

There was an interval of silence in the room when Villiers ceased speaking. The light was failing, and all the tumult of an hour ago was quite hushed. Austin had bent his head at the close of the story, and his hand covered his eyes.

"What can it mean?" he said at length.

"Who knows, Austin, who knows? It's a black business, but I think we had better keep it to ourselves, for the present at any rate. I will see if I cannot learn anything about that house through private channels of information, and if I do light upon anything I will let you know."

VII

THE ENCOUNTER IN SOHO

Three weeks later Austin received a note from Villiers, asking him to call either that afternoon or the next. He chose the nearer date, and found Villiers sitting as usual by the window, apparently lost in meditation on the drowsy traffic of the street. There was a bamboo table by his side, a fantastic thing, enriched with gilding and queer painted scenes, and on it lay a little pile of papers arranged and docketed as neatly as anything in Mr. Clarke's office.

"Well, Villiers, have you made any discoveries in the last three weeks?"

"I think so; I have here one or two memoranda which struck me as singular, and there is a statement to which I shall call your attention."

"And these documents relate to Mrs. Beaumont? It was really Crashaw whom you saw that night standing on the doorstep of the house in Ashley Street?"

"As to that matter my belief remains unchanged, but neither my enquiries nor their results have any special relation to Crashaw. But my investigations have had a strange issue. I have found out who Mrs. Beaumont is!"

"Who is she? In what way do you mean?"

"I mean that you and I know her better under another name."

"What name is that?"

"Herbert."

"Herbert!" Austin repeated the word, dazed with astonishment.

"Yes, Mrs. Herbert of Paul Street, Helen Vaughan of earlier adventures unknown to me. You had reason to recognise the expression of her face; when you go home look at the face in Meyrick's book of horrors, and you will know the sources of your recollection."

"And you have proof of this?"

"Yes, the best of proof; I have seen Mrs. Beaumont, or shall we say Mrs. Herbert?"

"Where did you see her?"

"Hardly in a place where you would expect to see a lady who lives in Ashley Street, Piccadilly. I saw her entering a house in one of the meanest and most disreputable streets in Soho. In fact, I had made an appointment, though not with her, and she was precise both to time and place."

"All this seems very wonderful, but I cannot call it incredible. You must remember, Villiers, that I have seen this woman, in the ordinary adventure of London society, talking and laughing, and sipping her coffee in a commonplace drawing-room with commonplace people. But you know what you are saying."

"I do; I have not allowed myself to be led by surmises or fancies. It was with no thought of finding Helen Vaughan that I searched for Mrs. Beaumont in the dark waters of the life of London, but such has been the issue."

"You must have been in strange places, Villiers."

"Yes, I have been in very strange places. It would have been useless, you know, to go to Ashley Street, and ask Mrs. Beaumont to give me a short sketch of her previous history. No; assuming, as I had to assume, that her record was not of the cleanest, it would be pretty certain that at some previous time she must have moved in circles not quite so refined as her present ones. If you see mud on the top of a stream, you may be sure that it was once at the bottom. I went to the bottom. I have always been fond of diving into Queer Street for my amusement, and I found my knowledge of that locality and its inhabitants very useful. It is, perhaps, needless to say that my friends had never heard the name of Beaumont, and as I had never seen the lady, and was quite unable to describe her, I had to set to work in an indirect way. The people there know me; I have been able to do some of them a service now and again, so they made no difficulty about giving their information; they were aware I had no communication direct or indirect with Scotland Yard. I had to cast out a good many lines, though, before I got what I wanted, and when I landed the fish I did not for a moment suppose it was my fish. But I listened to what I was told out of a constitutional liking for useless information, and I found myself in possession of a very curious story, though, as I imagined, not the story I was looking for. It was to this effect. Some five or six years ago, a woman named Raymond suddenly made her appearance in the neighbourhood to which I am referring. She was described to me as being quite young, probably not more than seventeen or eighteen, very handsome, and looking as if she came from the country. I should be wrong in saying that she found her level in going to this particular quarter, or associating with these people, for from what I was told, I should think the worst den in London far too good for her. The person from whom I got my information, as you may suppose, no great Puritan, shuddered and grew sick in telling me of the nameless infamies which were laid to her charge. After living there for a year, or perhaps a little more, she disappeared as suddenly as she came, and they saw nothing of her till about the time of the Paul Street case. At first she came to her old haunts only occasionally, then more frequently, and finally took up her abode there as before, and remained for six or eight months. It's of no use my going into details as to the life that woman led; if you want particulars you can look at Meyrick's legacy. Those designs were not drawn from his imagination. She again disappeared, and the people of the place saw nothing of her till a few months ago. My informant told me that she had taken some rooms in a house which he pointed out, and these rooms she was in the habit of visiting two or three times a week and always at ten in the morning. I was led to expect that one of these visits would be paid on a certain day about a week ago, and I accordingly managed to be on the look-out in company with my cicerone at a quarter to ten, and the hour and the lady came with equal punctuality. My friend and I were standing under an archway, a little way back from the street, but she saw us, and gave me a glance that I shall be long in forgetting. That look was quite enough for me; I knew Miss Raymond to be Mrs. Herbert; as for Mrs. Beaumont, she had quite gone out of my head. She went into the house, and I watched it till four o'clock, when she came out, and then I followed her. It was a long chase, and I had to be very careful to keep a long way in the background, and yet not to lose sight of the woman. She took me down to the Strand, and then to Westminster, and then up St. James's Street, and along Piccadilly. I felt queerish when I saw her turn up Ashley Street; the thought that Mrs. Herbert was Mrs. Beaumont came into my mind, but it seemed too improbable to be true. I waited at the corner, keeping my eye on her all the time, and I took particular care to note the house at which she stopped. It was the house with the gay curtains, the house of flowers, the house out of which Crashaw came the night he hanged himself in his garden. I was just going away with my discovery, when I saw an empty carriage come round and draw up in front of the house, and I came to the conclusion that Mrs. Herbert was going out for a drive, and I was right. I took a hansom and followed the carriage into the Park. There, as it happened, I met a man I know, and we stood talking together a little distance from the carriage-way, to which I had my back. We had not been there for ten minutes when my friend took off his hat, and I glanced round and saw the lady I had been following all day. 'Who is that?' I said, and his answer was, 'Mrs. Beaumont; lives in Ashley Street.' Of course there could be no doubt after that. I don't know whether she saw me, but I don't think she did. I went home at once, and, on consideration, I thought that I had a sufficiently good case with which to go to Clarke."

"Why to Clarke?"

"Because I am sure that Clarke is in possession of facts about this woman, facts of which I know nothing."

"Well, what then?"

Mr. Villiers leaned back in his chair and looked reflectively at Austin for a moment before he answered:

"My idea was that Clarke and I should call on Mrs. Beaumont."

"You would never go into such a house as that? No, no, Villiers, you cannot do it. Besides, consider; what result . . ."

"I will tell you soon. But I was going to say that my information does not end here; it has been completed in an extraordinary manner.

"Look at this neat little packet of manuscript; it is paginated, you see, and I have indulged in the civil coquetry of a ribbon of red tape. It has almost a legal air, hasn't it? Run your eye over it, Austin. It is an account of the entertainment Mrs. Beaumont provided for her choicer guests. The man who wrote this escaped with his life, but I do not think he will live many years. The doctors tell him he must have sustained some severe shock to the nerves."

Austin took the manuscript, but never read it. Opening the neat pages at haphazard his eye was caught by a word and a phrase that followed it; and, sick at heart, with white lips and a cold sweat pouring like water from his temples, he flung the paper down.

"Take it away, Villiers, never speak of this again. Are you made of stone, man? Why, the dread and horror of death itself, the thoughts of the man who stands in the keen morning air on the black platform, bound, the bell tolling in his ears, and waits for the harsh rattle of the bolt, are as nothing compared to this. I will not read it; I should never sleep again."

"Very good. I can fancy what you saw. Yes, it is horrible enough; but after all, it is an old story, an old mystery played in our day, and in dim London streets instead of amidst the vineyards and the olive gardens. We know what happened to those who chanced to meet the Great God Pan, and those who are wise know that all symbols are symbols of something, not of nothing. It was, indeed, an exquisite symbol beneath which men long ago veiled their knowledge of the most awful, most secret forces which lie at the heart of all things; forces before which the souls of men must wither and die and blacken, as their bodies blacken under the electric current. Such forces cannot be named, cannot be spoken, cannot be imagined except under a veil and a symbol, a symbol to the most of us appearing a quaint, poetic fancy, to some a foolish tale. But you and I, at all events, have known something of the terror that may dwell in the secret places of life, manifested under human flesh; that which is without form taking to itself a form. Oh, Austin, how can it be? How is it that the very sunlight does not turn to blackness before this thing, the hard earth melt and boil beneath such a burden?"

Villiers was pacing up and down the room, and the beads of sweat stood out on his forehead. Austin sat silent for a while, but Villiers saw him make a sign upon his breast.

"I say again, Villiers, you will surely never enter such a house as that? You would never pass out alive."

"Yes, Austin, I shall go out alive—I, and Clarke with me."

"What do you mean? You cannot, you would not dare . . ."

"Wait a moment. The air was very pleasant and fresh this morning;

there was a breeze blowing, even through this dull street, and I thought I would take a walk. Piccadilly stretched before me a clear, bright vista, and the sun flashed on the carriages and on the quivering leaves in the park. It was a joyous morning, and men and women looked at the sky and smiled as they went about their work or their pleasure, and the wind blew as blithely as upon the meadows and the scented gorse. But somehow or other I got out of the bustle and the gaiety, and found myself walking slowly along a quiet, dull street, where there seemed to be no sunshine and no air, and where the few foot-passengers loitered as they walked, and hung indecisively about corners and archways. I walked along, hardly knowing where I was going or what I did there, but feeling impelled, as one sometimes is, to explore still further, with a vague idea of reaching some unknown goal. Thus I forged up the street, noting the small traffic of the milk-shop, and wondering at the incongruous medley of penny pipes, black tobacco, sweets, newspapers, and comic songs which here and there jostled one another in the short compass of a single window. I think it was a cold shudder that suddenly passed through me that first told me that I had found what I wanted. I looked up from the pavement and stopped before a dusty shop, above which the lettering had faded, where the red bricks of two hundred years ago had grimed to black; where the windows had gathered to themselves the fog and the dirt of winters innumerable. I saw what I required; but I think it was five minutes before I steadied myself and could walk in and ask for it in a cool voice and with a calm face. I think there must even then have been a tremor in my words, for the old man who came out from his back parlour, and fumbled slowly amongst his goods, looked oddly at me as he tied the parcel. I paid what he asked, and stood leaning by the counter, with a strange reluctance to take up my goods and go. I asked about the business, and learnt that trade was bad and the profits cut down sadly; but then the street was not what it was before traffic had been diverted, but that was done forty years ago, 'just before my father died,' he said. I got away at last, and walked along sharply; it was a dismal street indeed, and I was glad to return to the bustle and the noise. Would you like to see my purchase?"

Austin said nothing, but nodded his head slightly; he still looked white and sick. Villiers pulled out a drawer in the bamboo table, and shewed Austin a long coil of cord, hard and new; and at one end was a running noose.

"It is the best hempen cord," said Villiers, "just as it used to be made for the old trade, the man told me. Not an inch of jute from end to end."

Austin set his teeth hard, and stared at Villiers, growing whiter as he looked.

"You would not do it," he murmured at last. "You would not have blood on your hands. My God!" he exclaimed, with sudden vehemence, "you cannot mean this, Villiers, that you will make yourself a hangman?"

"No. I shall offer a choice, and leave Helen Vaughan alone with this cord in a locked room for fifteen minutes. If when we go in it is not done, I shall call the nearest policeman. That is all."

"I must go now. I cannot stay here any longer; I cannot bear this. Good-night."

"Good-night, Austin."

The door shut, but in a moment it was opened again, and Austin stood, white and ghastly, in the entrance.

"I was forgetting," he said, "that I too have something to tell. I have received a letter from Dr. Harding of Buenos Ayres. He says that he attended Meyrick for three weeks before his death."

"And does he say what carried him off in the prime of life? It was not fever?"

"No, it was not fever. According to the doctor, it was an utter collapse of the whole system, probably caused by some severe shock. But he states that the patient would tell him nothing, and that he was consequently at some disadvantage in treating the case."

"Is there anything more?"

"Yes. Dr. Harding ends his letter by saying: 'I think this is all the information I can give you about your poor friend. He had not been long in Buenos Ayres, and knew scarcely any one, with the exception of a person who did not bear the best of characters, and has since left—a Mrs. Vaughan.'"

VIII
THE FRAGMENTS

[Amongst the papers of the well-known physician, Dr. Robert Matheson, of Ashley Street, Piccadilly, who died suddenly, of apoplectic seizure, at the beginning of 1892, a leaf of manuscript paper was found, covered with pencil jottings. These notes were in Latin, much abbreviated, and had evidently been made in great haste. The MS. was only deciphered with great difficulty, and some words have up to the present time evaded all the efforts of the expert employed. The date, "xxv Jul. 1888", is written on the right-hand corner of the MS. The following is a translation of Dr. Matheson's manuscript.]

"Whether science would benefit by these brief notes if they could be published, I do not know, but rather doubt. But certainly I shall never take the responsibility of publishing or divulging one word of what is here written, not only on account of my oath freely given to those two persons who were present, but also because the details are too abominable. It is probable that, upon mature consideration, and after weighing the good and evil, I shall one day destroy this paper, or at least leave it under seal to my friend D., trusting in his discretion, to use it or to burn it, as he may think fit.

"As was befitting, I did all that my knowledge suggested to make sure that I was suffering under no delusion. At first astounded, I could hardly think, but in a minute's time I was sure that my pulse was steady and regular, and that I was in my real and true senses. I then fixed my eyes quietly on what was before me.

"Though horror and revolting nausea rose up within me, and an odour of corruption choked my breath, I remained firm. I was then privileged or accursed, I dare not say which, to see that which was on the bed, laying there black like ink, transformed before my eyes. The skin, and the flesh, and the muscles, and the bones, and the firm structure of the human body that I had thought to be unchangeable, and permanent as adamant, began to melt and dissolve.

"I knew that the body may be separated into its elements by external agencies, but I should have refused to believe what I saw. For here there was some internal force, of which I knew nothing, that caused dissolution and change.

"Here too was all the work by which man has been made repeated before my eyes. I saw the form waver from sex to sex, dividing itself from itself, and then again reunited. Then I saw the body descend to the beasts whence it ascended, and that which was on the heights go down to the depths, even to the abyss of all being. The principle of life, which makes organism, always remained, while the outward form changed.

"The light within the room had turned to blackness, not the darkness of night, in which objects are seen dimly, for I could see clearly and without difficulty. But it was the negation of light; objects were presented to my eyes, if I may say so, without any medium, in such a manner that if there had been a prism in the room I should have seen no colours represented in it.

"I watched, and at last I saw nothing but a substance as jelly. Then the ladder was ascended again . . . [*here the MS. is illegible*] . . . for one instant I saw a Form, shaped in dimness before me, which I will not farther describe. But the symbol of this form may be seen in ancient sculptures, and in paintings which survived beneath the lava, too foul to be spoken of . . . as a horrible and unspeakable shape, neither man nor beast, was changed into human form, there came finally death.

"I who saw all this, not without great horror and loathing of soul, here write my name, declaring all that I have set on this paper to be true.

"ROBERT MATHESON, Med. Dr."

*   *   *   *   *   *

. . . Such, Raymond, is the story of what I know and what I have seen. The burden of it was too heavy for me to bear alone, and yet I could tell it to none but you. Villiers, who was with me at the last, knows nothing of that awful secret of the wood, of how what we both saw die, lay upon the smooth, sweet turf amidst the summer flowers, half in sun and half in shadow, and holding the girl Rachel's hand, called and summoned those companions, and shaped in solid form, upon the earth we tread on, the horror which we can but hint at, which we can only name under a figure. I would not tell Villiers of this, nor of that resemblance, which struck me as with a blow upon my heart, when I saw the portrait, which filled the cup of terror at the end. What this can mean I dare not guess. I know that what I saw perish was not Mary, and yet in the last agony Mary's eyes looked into mine. Whether there be any one who can shew the last link in this chain of awful mystery, I do not know, but if there be any one who can do this, you, Raymond, are the man. And if you know the secret, it rests with you to tell it or not, as you please.

I am writing this letter to you immediately on my getting back to town. I have been in the country for the last few days; perhaps you may be able to guess in what part. While the horror and wonder of London was at its height—for "Mrs. Beaumont", as I have told you, was well known in society—I wrote to my friend Dr. Phillips, giving some brief outline, or rather hint, of what had happened, and asking him to tell me the name of the village where the events he had related to me occurred. He gave me the name, as he said with the less hesitation, because Rachel's father and mother were dead, and the rest of the family had gone to a relative in the State of Washington six months before. The parents, he said, had undoubtedly died of grief and horror caused by the terrible death of their daughter, and by what had gone before that death. On the evening of the day on which I received Phillips's letter I was at Caermaen, and standing beneath the moulding Roman walls, white with the winter of seventeen hundred years, I looked over the meadow where once had stood the older temple of the "God of the Deeps", and saw a house gleaming in the sunlight. It was the house where Helen had lived. I stayed at Caermaen for several days. The people of the place, I found, knew little and had guessed less. Those whom I spoke to on the matter seemed surprised that an antiquarian (as I professed myself to be) should trouble about a village tragedy, of which they gave a very commonplace version, and, as you may imagine, I told nothing of what I knew. Most of my time was spent in the great wood that rises just above the village and climbs the hillside, and goes down to the river in the valley; such another long lovely valley, Raymond, as that on which we looked one summer night, walking to and fro before your house. For many an hour I strayed through the maze of the forest, turning now to right and now to left, pacing slowly down the long alleys of undergrowth, shadowy and chill, even under the midday sun, and halting beneath great oaks; lying on the short turf of a clearing where the faint sweet scent of wild roses came to me on the wind and mixed with the heavy perfume of the elder, whose mingled odour is like the odour of the room of the dead, a vapour of incense and corruption. I stood at the edges of the wood, gazing at all the pomp and procession of the foxgloves towering amidst the bracken and shining red in the broad sunshine, and beyond them into deep thickets of close undergrowth where springs boil up from the rock and nourish the water-weeds, dank and evil. But in all my wanderings I avoided one part of the wood; it was not till yesterday that I climbed to the summit of the hill, and stood upon the ancient Roman road that threads the highest ridge of the wood. Here they had walked, Helen and Rachel, along this quiet causeway, upon the pavement of green turf, shut in on either side by high banks of red earth, and tall hedges of shining beech, and here I followed in their steps, looking out, now and again, through partings in the boughs, and seeing on one side the sweep of the wood stretching far to right and left, and sinking into the broad level, and beyond, the yellow sea, and the land over the sea. On the other side was the valley and the river, and hill following hill as wave on wave, and wood and meadow, and cornfield, and white houses gleaming, and a great wall of mountain, and far blue peaks in the north. And so at last I came to the place. The track went up a gentle slope, and widened out into an open space with a wall of thick undergrowth around it, and then, narrowing again, passed on into the distance and the faint blue mist of summer heat. And into this pleasant summer glade Rachel passed a girl, and left it, who shall say what? I did not stay long there.

In a small town near Caermaen there is a museum, containing for the most part Roman remains which have been found in the neighbourhood at various times. On the day after my arrival at Caermaen I walked over to the town in question, and took the opportunity of inspecting this museum. After I had seen most of the sculptured stones, the coffins, rings, coins, and fragments of tessellated pavement which the place contains, I was shewn a small square pillar of white stone, which had been recently discovered in the wood of which I have been speaking, and, as I found on enquiry, in that open space where the Roman road broadens out. On one side of the pillar was an inscription, of which I took a note. Some of the letters have been defaced, but I do not think there can be any doubt as to those which I supply. The inscription is as follows:

DEVOMNODENT*i*
FLA*v*IVSSENILISPOSSV*it*
PROPTERNVP*tias*
*qua*SVIDITSVBVMBRA

"To the great god Nodens (the god of the Great Deep or Abyss), Flavius Senilis has erected this pillar on account of the marriage which he saw beneath the shade."

The custodian of the museum informed me that local antiquaries were much puzzled, not by the inscription, or by any difficulty in translating it, but as to the circumstance or rite to which allusion is made.

      *   *   *   *   *   *

. . . And now, my dear Clarke, as to what you tell me about Helen Vaughan, whom you say you saw die under circumstances of the utmost and almost incredible horror. I was interested in your account, but a good deal, nay all, of what you told me I knew already. I can understand the strange likeness you remarked both in the portrait and in the actual face; you have seen Helen's mother. You remember that still summer night so many years ago, when I talked to you of the world beyond the shadows, and of the god Pan. You remember Mary. She was the mother of Helen Vaughan, who was born nine months after that night.

Mary never recovered her reason. She lay, as you saw her, all the while upon her bed, and a few days after the child was born she died. I fancy that just at the last she knew me; I was standing by the bed, and the old look came into her eyes for a second, and then she shuddered and groaned and died. It was an ill work I did that night when you were present; I broke open the door of the house of life, without knowing or caring what might pass forth or enter in. I recollect your telling me at the time, sharply enough, and rightly enough too, in one sense, that I had ruined the reason of a human being by a foolish experiment, based on an absurd theory. You did well to blame me, but my theory was not all absurdity. What I said Mary would see, she saw, but I forgot that no human eyes could look on such a vision with impunity. And I forgot, as I have just said, that when the house of life is thus thrown open, there may enter in that for which we have no name, and human flesh may become the veil of a horror one dare not express. I played with energies which I did not understand, and you have seen the ending of it. Helen Vaughan did well to bind the cord about her neck and die, though the death was horrible. The blackened face, the hideous form upon the bed, changing and melting before your eyes from woman to man, from man to beast, and from beast to worse than beast, all the strange horror that you witnessed, surprises me but little. What you say the doctor whom you sent for saw and shuddered at I noticed long ago; I knew what I had done the moment the child was born, and when it was scarcely five years old I surprised it, not once or twice but several times with a playmate, you may guess of what kind. It was for me a constant, an incarnate horror, and after a few years I felt I could bear it no longer, and I sent Helen Vaughan away. You know now what frightened the boy in the wood. The rest of the strange story, and all else that you tell me, as discovered by your friend, I have contrived to learn from time to time, almost to the last chapter. And now Helen is with her companions. . . .

A Remarkable Coincidence

I really believe, old fellow," said Mr. James Marvell to Mr. William Walters, "I really believe there are no real Bohemians left in London. Upon my word, I think we were the last of the race."

"I fancy you are right. Bohemians wear dress-clothes in these days. We didn't. I have heard of Bohemians entertaining the Prince of Wales. In our time the Prince of Wales round the corner entertained us—for a consideration. It was good beer, though. Do remember the taste? A fine solid drink I used to think it."

"I don't think I shall ever forget anything in Handel-street. I go through it sometimes on my way to the club; and, by Jove! it gives me quite a pang when I think how jolly we were at Number 20."

"How about your first romance? We didn't feel very jolly when that letter came, eh?"

"Ah, indeed! that was a blow." Mr. Walters sighed and rang the bell, and a grave and decent butler appeared. "Johnson, I want you to bring us a pint of four-ale." Marvell burst into a roar of laughter, which he tried to smother in his napkin. The butler blushed; he drank burgundy himself. "I mean, of course, Johnson, that I want you to get a bottle of that old Chateau Margaux; I wish Mr. Marvell to give me his opinion on it. Yes, as you were saying, Marvell, that was a most extraordinary thing about the romance; I never understood it, and I don't suppose I ever shall."

"It was a wonderful coincidence certainly; still it was a blow which made our fortunes. Here is the claret. Ah! a fine wine that—better than the Prince of Wales's *ordinare,* eh?"

The two friends were never tired of recalling the old days in Handel-street. Handel-street is in the gloomy wilderness of Soho, and in all that queerest of London quarters there is no street shadier, either physically or morally. It was a *cul de sac,* entered under an archway, and bounded by what had once been a nobleman's mansion and was now a warehouse; and the house in the darkest corner was Number 20. Its doorway, like other doorways, was decorated by innumerable bell-handles; within, mysterious trades were carried on in small rooms, where paint and paper had merged into a sort of neutral tint—in fact, the *couleur de Soho*. A stair as winding and narrow as the newel of a cathedral tower, led from floor to floor; and above the third and highest flight dwelt ten years ago Mr. James Marvell and Mr. William Walters, who called each other in pastoral simplicity Jim and Bill. They had two rooms; and both were of that composite order of domestic architecture known to lodging-house keepers as "sitting-room bed-room," and both commanded a view of the street, where dirty children played loud games all day, and dirtier men and women swore loud oaths most part of the night. Here, then, did the two chums, who had somehow or other joined company in the wilderness of wretched London, live together cultivating literature, not on a little oatmeal, but on a good deal of shag tobacco and a moderate allowance of beer from the "Prince of Wales." As to the manner of work they did, both history and the friends are entirely silent; it has been whispered that Marvell wrote wrappers, and Walters subedited the *Tanners' Gazette;* but this is mere rumour. At all events they both smoked all day, ate occasionally, and were generally supremely happy on next to nothing a year. It was a life of perpetual undress, of chins usually unshaven, of hours late both in the morning and at night; of occasional exultation when a chance article by one or the other was accepted; and certainly of a good deal of earnest practice in the art of literature.

This Handel-street experience had lasted for two or three years, when one morning, as Walters lounged according to custom into his friend's room, Marvell could not help noticing a strange light in his eyes and an unaccustomed restlessness in his movements.

"You seem rather queerish this morning, old chap," he said at length; "have some shag. What's happened? You look as if you hadn't slept a wink."

"I haven't. I've been thinking."

"What about?"

"I'll tell you. I believe our fortune's made. Last night after I left you and I went to bed I couldn't get to sleep; and all of a sudden I got an idea; and I really think that between us we shall be able to put together as good a novel as any one has seen lately."

"You don't say so? Fill your pipe, Bill, my boy, and tell us all about it."

Walters told his idea, waxing more and more enthusiastic as he unfolded the story: his eyes flashed, and the perspiration stood out upon his forehead, and his pipe dropped out of his hand; till at last, with something between a sob and a laugh, he asked his friend:—

"Will it do?"

"I should think it would. We'll go to work at once. You shall write out the scheme of chapters, then I'll go over it. We will take over each chapter one by one and discuss the points together. You had better do the dialogue and I will fill in the descriptions."

"All right. Go out and get some more paper, there's a good fellow; I don't feel as if I could walk a step."

The romance was begun forthwith, and carried on day by day for three months. Walters had insisted on early hours; he pointed out that if they wrote at night they would be sure to be completely knocked up; so pens were laid down every night at ten. At last the book was finished, the last corrections made, the final touches given; and one morning it was sent to the publisher's.

They waited a week, and there came a letter—and a parcel. The letter informed the collaborators that by an extraordinary coincidence—which he (the publisher) deeply regretted—he had concluded an agreement with an author (who desired strictly to preserve his anonymity) to publish a work which resembled almost to the smallest detail the MS. they had so kindly sent him. He hoped, however, that Messrs. Walters and Marvell would call upon him, as he should be glad to treat for their next novel.

It was hard—so much toil and thought so utterly wasted; but the friends agreed to make the best of it, and the result was eminently successful. They soon migrated from Handel-street and the shadow of Soho.

At present Mr. William Walters has almost forgotten how he sat up night after night recopying his story, making trifling variations here and there. He has almost forgotten also how large a cheque one Henry Smart, a young man vastly resembling William Walters, cashed at the bank. The temptation was probably too strong for him; it was a picturesque sin, certainly, to steal his own idea. But he has never done such a thing since.

The Autophone

In a small parlour—the pre-Ruskinite parlour of country lodgings—the Rev. Arthur Hammond was sitting before the rickety round table, his head upon his hands, and his eyes fixed upon an open book. For an hour or more he sat still, never turning a leaf of his volume, nor looking through the window as the sun slowly sank into a bank of clouds and the sea changed from blue to misty grey; and the far-away wash of water and the dull roar of the rising wind among the trees never reached his ears. The Rev. Arthur Hammond read on as the sun went down, but he read only one sentence over and over again, till his brain was in a whirl, and the types seemed to dance before his eyes. The sentence ran as follows:

> Personality is not a permanent but a transient thing; it lives and dies, begins and ends continually; no one can remain one and the same person two moments together.

The day had been hot and close, with one of those burning suns that sometimes shine in June and the evening seemed still hotter. Hammond had felt all day as if a weight were pressing on his head, but still he had persevered in his reading, hardly stopping to eat or drink. The next day he was going to the cathedral city to undergo his examination for priest's orders: for the last three months every moment of his spare time had been given to hard grinding study and for a week he had scarcely stirred from his books. His information on the Early Heresies was extensive and peculiar. He knew all about the Ebienites, and could explain the teachings of Basilides. He was prepared to defend St. Peter from the charge of writing "Baboo Greek", he had a good working knowledge of the Canon Law, and the Fathers were at his fingers' ends—if it be respectful to say so. The last day or two had been devoted to Butler's Analogy. Hammond had grimly struggled for the third or fourth time through the crabbed style and involved argument, and at last read "Conclusion". He leant back in his chair, supremely happy that his work was at last done and he was free to rest or do what he would. Should he go for a sail, or take a brisk walk over the hills, or call at the rector's and have a pipe? He dallied and he hesitated, carelessly turning over the leaves of the book, and at last, in mere indecision, began to read the dissertation "Of Personal Identity", a kind of philosophical appendix to the Analogy. He read carelessly, half filled his pipe and looked round for a light. The matchbox was on the mantelpiece between two shell encrusted boxes, "Presents from Baybeach", and Hammond felt too lazy to get up, and so he turned again to his book and read on. The words and phrases made but little impression on his tired brain; he felt as if everything were slowly sinking into a haze; the four walls of the little parlour seemed to hover indistinctly around him and the hot air beat palpably, as in waves, upon his temples. Suddenly his eyes fell upon the words "Personality is but a transient thing." It was like a flash of lightning—bright and yet blinding. What personality was sitting in that chair, gazing on an open book? Was it a little boy roaming among the woods and meadows in summers long ago? Or whose joys and griefs were those that now surged up in his memory? Who was that, walking with other lads across the playground, or kneeling by a deathbed? And whose were those companions, singing songs and uttering jests that made him flush for very shame? He seemed to hear a voice, hard and toneless, like the crash of a falling bough, calling "Ha ha! you have tasted the apple," and a rough man with a flushed face and a strange light in his eyes came forth from a door in a dark narrow street and shut it behind him as a girl looked out from the window. Then he heard the words "Lives and dies, begins and ends, lives and dies, begins and ends" repeated again and again, louder and louder, swelling tumultuously, and then an awful crash that burst in upon his brain.

Mr. Hammond looked up; the room was growing dark; yet he could see the twinkle of the lustres on the mantel, and he could hear, quite distinctly, the noise of tapping at his door. "Come in," he cried; and the door opened and some one stood by the sofa and began speaking to him in a low voice, yet audibly enough.

"The Rev. Arthur Hammond, I believe? Pray excuse me for intruding at such an hour; I am well aware how scanty is the leisure of the clergy; but I hope that in my case I may plead . . ."

"Pray don't apologise. I am afraid I was quite absorbed in my book and kept you waiting. What can I do for you, may I ask?"

"I have ventured to call upon you to submit to your notice an invention of mine which I think I may call the great invention of the age. I have exhibited it before many of the bishops, deans, archdeacons, and canons of the church, including your reverend diocesan; and I should like to add your name—a name, I must say, second to none among the younger generation of the clergy."

"You are very kind indeed," said Mr. Hammond dreamily. "Thank you very much; really very kind of you. By the way, you didn't happen to notice a young fellow going out of the house as you came in—a fair complexioned young man, a little like myself, but younger and, well, rather odd looking?"

"No, sir, I saw no one. Shall I now have the pleasure of exhibiting my invention?"

"Ah, to be sure—your invention. What do you call it?"

"I have named it the Autophone, the title was suggested to me by a beloved prelate and a distinguished scholar."

"Quite so; very good; the Autophone. What is the nature of the invention?"

"Allow me. You see this disk of delicate yellow metal? Kindly pass the point of your forefinger (the right hand) lightly over it from north to south. Thank you; the polarity is now established. The next thing is to set the current in action. Do you happen to have such a thing as a musical box?"

"Yes," said Hammond, growing interested and less dazed than at first, "there is an old one in that corner belonging to my landlady."

"It will answer our purpose admirably. You see I place it on the table thus. I next insert the polarised metal disk, so. Now, if you please, just give that little knob a turn; exactly!"

A babel, a tumult of voices, of voices that he knew and remembered; one striving with another, calling to him out of the deep past; and some the voices of the dead.

"Ha ha! Do you hear that, you fellows? Hammond's in luck. Didn't you see him with her? The old rascal thought it was too dark under the tree, but Davis spotted him. Didn't you, old boy?" "I should think I did. How's Mary, Hammond?" "Never you mind, Hammond. You couldn't do better. I only wish I had your luck." "Now, then, old fellow, let's have a song. Get out another bottle of whisky, Williams. Go ahead, Hammond."

The song began, and Hammond heard it across the great bridge of years; heard his own voice singing those shameful lines, and heard the laughter and the voices joining in the chorus.

"Curse you!" he cried; "whoever you are, take your infernal machine away. It's a lie; I never did this."

But the man only laughed, and the song was singing all the while, and Hammond rushed forward headlong, and fell as the thunder burst at last above the house.

They found him lying full length upon the floor, his forehead cut and bleeding and the musical box upside down on the floor beside him. It was playing "Pop goes the weasel". When the doctor came his verdict was "Brain fever."

A Double Return

The express from the west rushed through Acton with a scream, whirling clouds of dust around it; and Frank Halswell knocked out the ashes from his pipe and proceeded to gather from various quarters of the carriage his newspapers, his hat-box, his handbag, and, chief of all, a large portfolio carefully packed in brown paper. He looked at his watch, and said to himself: "6.30; we shall be at Paddington in five minutes; and only five minutes late, for a wonder." But he congratulated himself and the railway company rather too soon: a few minutes later and the train began to slacken, the speed grew slower and slower, and at last came the grinding sound of the brakes and a dead stop. Halswell looked out of the window over the dreary expanse of Wormwood Scrubbs, and heard some one in the next carriage explaining the cause of the delay with pardonable pride in his technical knowledge. "You see, them there signals is against us, and if we was to go on we should jolly well go to kingdom come, we should." Halswell looked at his watch again and drummed his heels against the floor, wondering impatiently when they would be at Paddington, when, with a sudden whirl, a down train swept by them and the western express once more moved on. Halswell rubbed his eyes; he had looked up as the down train passed, and in one of the carriages he thought he had seen his own face. It was only for a second, and he could not be sure. "It must have been a reflection," he kept on saying, "from the glass of one window to the other. Still, I fancied I saw a black coat, and mine is light. But of course it was a reflection."

The express rolled into the terminus with dignity—it was only ten minutes late, after all; and Frank Halswell bundled himself and his traps into a hansom, congratulating himself on the paucity of his bags and the absence of his trunks as he watched the excited mob rushing madly at a Redan of luggage. "153, the Mall, Kensington!" he shouted to the driver above the hubbub of the platform; and they were soon threading deftly along the dingy streets that looked so much dingier than usual after the blue mist upon the sea, the purple heather and the sunny fields. Frank (he was a very popular artist in those days—a rising man, indeed) had been on a sketching tour in Devon and Cornwall: he had wandered along the deep sheltered lanes from hill to hill, by the orchards already red and gold, by moorland and lowland, by the rocky coast and the combes sinking down to the wondrous sea.

On the Cornish roads he had seen those many ancient crosses, with their weird interlacing carving, which sometimes stand upon a mound and mark where two ways meet; and as he put his portfolio beside him he could not help feeling a glow of pride at its contents. "I fancy I shall make a pretty good show by next spring," he thought. Poor fellow! he was never to paint another picture; but he did not know it. Then, as the hansom verged westward, gliding with its ringing bells past the great mansions facing the park, Halswell's thoughts went back to the hotel at Plymouth and the acquaintance he had made there. "Yes; Kerr was an amusing fellow," he thought; "glad I gave him my card. Louie is sure to get on with him. Curious thing, too, he was wonderfully like me, if he had been only clean shaven and not 'bearded like the pard'. Dare say we shall see him before long; he said he was going to pay a short visit to London. I fancy he must be an actor; I never saw such a fellow to imitate a man's voice and gestures. I wonder what made him go off in such a hurry yesterday. Hullo! here we are; hi, cabman! there's 153."

The twin doors of the hansom banged open; the garden gate shrieked and clanged, and Halswell bounded up the steps and rapped loudly at the door. The maid opened it. Even as he said, "Thank you, Jane; your mistress quite well, I suppose?" he thought he noticed a strange look, half questioning, half surprised, in her eyes; but he ran past her, up the stairs, and burst into the pretty drawing-room. His wife was lying on the sofa; but she rose with a cry as he came in.

"Frank! Back again so soon? I am so glad! I thought you said you might have to be away a week."

"My dear Louie, what do you mean? I have been away three weeks, haven't I? I rather think I left for Devonshire in the first week of August."

"Yes, of course, my dear; but then you came back late last night."

"What! I came back last night? I slept last night at Plymouth. What are you talking about?"

"Don't be silly, Frank. You know very well you rang us all up at twelve o'clock. Just like you, to come home in the middle of the night when nobody expected you. You know you said in your last letter you were not coming until to-day."

"Louise dear, you must be dreaming. I never came here last night. Here is my bill at the hotel; you see, it is dated this morning."

Mrs. Halswell stared blankly at the bill; then she got up and rang the bell. How hot it was! The close air of the London street seemed to choke her. Halswell walked a few paces across the room, then suddenly stopped and shuddered.

"Jane, I want to ask you whether your master did not come here last night at twelve o'clock; and whether you did not get him a cab early this morning?"

"Yes, mum, at least—"

"At least what? You let him in yourself."

"Yes, mum, of course I did. But, begging your pardon, sir, I thought as how your voice didn't sound quite natural this morning when you called out to the cabman to drive to Stepney, because you had changed your mind, and didn't want to go to Waterloo."

"Good God! What are you thinking about? I never came here. I was in Plymouth."

"Frank! You are joking! Look here, you left this behind you."

She shewed him a little silver cigarette case with his initials engraved on it. It was a present from his wife, he had missed it one day when he was strolling with Kerr, and had regretted it deeply, searching in the grass in vain.

Halswell held the toy in his hand. He thought he was indeed in a dream, and through the open window came the shrieks of the newsboys, "Extry speshal! extry speshal!" The light had faded; it was getting dark. But suddenly it all flashed upon him. He remembered Kerr and the face he had caught sight of in the passing train; he remembered the strange likeness; he knew who had found the cigarette case; he knew well who it was that had come to his house.

The maid was a good girl; she had stolen away. No one knows what manner of conversation Frank and his wife had together in the darkness; but that night he went away, as it was said, to America. Mrs. Halswell was dead before the next summer.

A Wonderful Woman

On an isle of refuge, a Patmos mercifully set in the midst of an ever-roaring torrent of hansoms going from the north to the south of London and vice versa, two men, who had not seen each other for many years, met face to face one sultry afternoon in early autumn. They recognised each other simultaneously, and shook hands.

"My dear Villiers," said the elder of the two, a grizzled man of fifty, "it must be seven or eight years since we have seen anything of each other. I am glad to meet you—extremely glad to meet you again."

"You are very kind, Richardson. As you say, we managed to lose sight of each other. One does in London, I think, almost without knowing it. And how are you getting on?"

"Thank you, moderately well, I am happy to say. As you know, I am in the India trade, and of late years I have managed to increase my connection to a great extent. At present we are doing, I think I may say, respectably. Have you entered any business?"

Villiers laughed; merrily, like a boy. "No, Richardson. I have no time for business; I have definitely chosen a great subject, the study of which will occupy me for the rest of my life."

"Indeed! A scientific subject, I presume?"

"Yes; the fact is I am a student of London; I survey mankind from Cricklewood to Tooting, from Turnham Green to the Isle of Dogs. Can you speak French of Soho? Do you understand Shelta?"

"Certainly not. Mr. Jones, our corresponding clerk, is a good linguist, but I do not remember his speaking of the dialects you mention. I am afraid, Villiers, you are still an idler; I had hoped that when your poor father died you would have entered the China trade."

"No, I sold my interest in the business. In one sense my interest in it was very small indeed, but from a practical point of view it yields me a good income. Have you still got your rooms at Clement's Inn?"

Mr. Richardson blushed. He was rather a grim-looking man, with a straight mouth and a forbidding whisker. He was thoroughly good-natured, but dry and devoid of humour. But he blushed and a queer, sly smile played about his lips.

"No, Villiers, I don't live in Clement's Inn now. I am married."

"You, Richardson! You married! You really astonish me. I thought you were the typical bachelor. I must congratulate you. When did the event take place?"

"We were married three months ago. My wife and I met quite by accident; in fact, I was enabled to render her some assistance in a dispute with an insolent cab-driver; and the acquaintance ripened into affection. I am a very happy man, Villiers."

"You deserve to be, Richardson, you are a good fellow. I should like to meet your wife."

"So you shall. Are you free to-morrow? Good! Then come down and dine with us at seven. Here is my card."

The two friends parted, each darting through a momentary gap in the race of cabs. Villiers looked at the card; it referred him to "'The Limes,' Angelina Terrace, Clapham." He wondered exceedingly what manner of wife this good-hearted, dry, City man had found for himself; and his wonder sharpened the sauces at his little dinner at the Italian Restaurant in Rupert Street and gave additional zest to the Falerno. He was still wondering as he walked out of Clapham station the next day.

Villiers was some time in finding Angelina Terrace. The neighbourhood was a very new one; two or three old mansions, with their pleasant lawns and cedars, had been "developed"; the result was a maze of brand-new streets and terraces, street like to street, and terrace to terrace, and every house built after the same pattern in blinding white brick, with red facings and green Venetian blinds. The inhabitants thought it a cheerful neighbourhood, artists swore at it, and Villiers accepted it as a fresh chapter in his great study. He found the desired terrace at last, and was shewn into the drawing-room at "The Limes". He had barely time to notice that the most prominent work on the polished round table was a "Memoir of the Rev. Alex. M'Caw, of Dunblather", when Richardson came in, beaming with pleasure.

"That's right," he said; "you have broken the ice, and I hope we shall often see you. Nice cheerful place, isn't it? Better than the dingy old red-brick inn, eh? Here's my wife. This is my old friend Villiers, my dear; I was just saying that I hoped he would come down often."

Villiers had started as if he had received an electric shock, as the pretty, though demure-looking woman entered the room. He managed to join pretty well in the indifferent conversation which Richardson kept up during the dinner. Mrs. Richardson was silent; indeed, her manner to Villiers was remarkably cold. Her husband addressed himself to her now and again, calling her "my dear Agnes", but Villiers was thinking all the while of one Mary Reynolds; of certain merry dinners at this or that restaurant; of little trips to Hampton and Richmond; of jingling hansoms and St. John's Wood moons. He seemed to hear the popping of champagne corks (Mrs. Richardson drank a little water from a wine-glass) and certain strains of French song of a *fin de siècle* character; Richardson's quiet stream of talk sounded idly in his ears, like a brook murmuring far away.

Villiers looked furtively at the grave lady at the head of the table; she was wearing a diamond brooch he himself had given to Mary Reynolds. He gasped for breath.

"Yes," Richardson was saying, "my wife has some really beautiful jewellery, which she inherited from a distant cousin: Sir Lawrence Buller of Beaulieu Park, in Norfolk. That brooch, which I perceive you are admiring, is by no means the finest piece. After dinner, my dear, you must shew Villiers your jewellery; those pearl necklaces are truly magnificent."

"I don't think Mr. Villiers takes much interest in such matters."

The tone was hard and threatening. Villiers bowed and smiled in a dazed sort of way; the champagne, foaming bright in the glasses, danced before his eyes, and his ears were ringing with the daring chanson. What a strong scent of patchouli there was in the room! He felt stifled.

"You don't seem quite the thing to-night, Villiers," said Mr. Richardson, as he shewed his guest out. "Take care of the steps."

"Thanks, I'm all right now; I think the heat has been too much for me. Trying weather, isn't it? Good-night, Richardson."

Villiers went home in a kind of stupor; he felt sure he had not been misled by a chance likeness. He remembered the brooch too well.

A few days later an irresistible impulse made him find out Mr. Richardson's City address and call upon him there. The worthy man seemed constrained in his manner; he was kind, but looked anxious, like a man charged with some unpleasant duty. The climax came when Villiers proposed to accompany him home and take "pot-luck".

"My dear Villiers, you know I always liked you very much; your poor father was very kind to me; it's a great pity. But, to tell the truth, Agnes is particular; she has evidently heard some stories about you (I am afraid, Villiers, you have never lived a very strict life), and she says that as a married woman, she would not care to meet you again. It grieves me, I assure you, to have to say this; but, after all, one would not wish one's wife . . ."

Villiers had been staring in stupid astonishment, but at this point he burst into a wild peal of laughter, which echoed above the clamour of Cornhill. He roared and roared again, till the tears ran down his cheeks.

"My dear Richardson," he said at last, "I congratulate you again; you have married a wonderful woman. Good-bye."

Villiers went on his way, and as he disappeared into a hansom he was still bubbling over with unconquerable mirth.

The Lost Club

One hot afternoon in August a gorgeous young gentleman, one would say the last of his race in London, set out from the Circus end, and proceeded to stroll along the lonely expanse of Piccadilly Deserta. True to the traditions of his race, faithful even in the wilderness, he had not bated one jot or tittle of his regulation equipage; a glorious red and yellow blossom in his wholly and exquisitely-cut frock coat proclaimed him a true son of the carnation; hat and boots and chin were all polished to the highest pitch; though there had not been rain for many weeks his trouser-ends were duly turned up, and the poise of the gold-headed cane was in itself a liberal education. But ah! the heavy changes since June, when the leaves glanced green in the sunlit air, and the club windows were filled, and the hansoms flashed in long processions through the streets, and girls smiled from every carriage. The young man sighed; he thought of the quiet little evenings at the Phoenix, of encounters of the Row, of the drive to Hurlingham, and many pleasant dinners in joyous company. Then he glanced up and saw a 'bus, half empty, slowly lumbering along the middle of the street, and in front of the 'White Horse Cellars' a four-wheeler had stopped still (the driver was asleep on his seat), and in the 'Badminton' the blinds were down. He half expected to see the Briar Rose trailing gracefully over the Hotel Cosmopole; certainly the Beauty, if such a thing were left in Piccadilly, was fast asleep.

Absorbed in these mournful reflections the hapless Johnny strolled on without observing that an exact duplicate of himself was advancing on the same pavement from the opposite direction; save that the inevitable carnation was salmon colour, and the cane a silver-headed one, instruments of great magnifying power would have been required to discriminate between them. The two met; each raised his eyes simultaneously at the strange sight of a well-dressed man, and each adjured the same old-world deity.

"By Jove! old man, what the deuce are you doing here?"

The gentleman who had advanced from the direction of Hyde Park Corner was the first to answer.

"Well, to tell the truth, Austin, I am detained in town on—ah—legal business. But how is it you are not in Scotland?"

"Well, it's curious; but the fact is, I have legal business in town also."

"You don't say so? Great nuisance, ain't it? But these things must be seen to, or a fellow finds himself in no end of a mess, don't you know?"

"He does, by Jove! That's what I thought."

Mr. Austin relapsed into silence for a few moments.

"And where are you off to, Phillipps?"

The conversation had passed with the utmost gravity on both sides; at the joint mention of legal business, it was true, a slight twinkle had passed across their eyes, but the ordinary observer would have said that the weight of ages rested on those unruffled brows.

"I really couldn't say. I thought of having a quiet dinner at Azario's. The Badminton is closed, you know, for repairs or somethin', and I can't stand the Junior Wilton. Come along with me, and let's dine together."

"By Jove! I think I will. I thought of calling on my solicitor, but I dare say he can wait."

"Ah! I should think he could. We'll have some of that Italian wine—stuff in salad-oil flasks—you know what I mean."

The pair solemnly wheeled around, and solemnly paced towards the Circus, meditating, doubtless, on many things. The dinner in the little restaurant pleased them with a grave pleasure, as did the Chianti, of which they drank a good deal too much; "quite a light wine, you know," said Phillipps, and Austin agreed with him, so they emptied a quart flask between them and finished up with a couple of glasses apiece of Green Chartreuse. As they came out into the quiet street smoking vast cigars, the two slaves to duty and 'legal business' felt a dreamy delight in all things, the streets seemed full of fantasy in the dim light of the lamps, and a single star shining in the clear sky above seemed to Austin exactly of the same colour as Green Chartreuse. Phillipps agreed with him. "You know, old fellow," he said, "there are times when a fellow feels all sorts of strange things—you know, the sort of things they put in magazines, don't you know, and novels. By

Jove, Austin, old man, I feel as if I could write a novel myself."

The pair wandered aimlessly on, not quite knowing where they were going, turning from one street to another, and discoursing in a maudlin strain. A great cloud had been slowly moving up from the south, darkening the sky, and suddenly it began to rain, at first slowly with great heavy drops, and then faster and faster in a pitiless, hissing shower; the gutters flooded over, and the furious drops danced up from the stones. The two Johnnies walked on as fast as they could, whistling and calling "Hansom!" in vain; they were really getting very wet.

"Where the dickens are we?" said Phillipps. "Confound it all, I don't know. We ought to be in Oxford Street."

They walked on a little farther, when suddenly, to their great joy, they found a dry archway, leading into a dark passage or courtyard. They took shelter silently, too thankful and too wet to say anything. Austin looked at his hat; it was a wreck; and Phillipps shook himself feebly, like a tired terrier.

"What a beastly nuisance this is," he muttered: "I only wish I could see a hansom."

Austin looked into the street; the rain was still falling in torrents; he looked up the passage, and noticed for the first time that it led to a great house, which towered grimly against the sky. It seemed all dark and gloomy, except that from some chink in a shutter a light shone out. He pointed it out to Phillipps, who stared vacantly about him, then exclaimed:

"Hang it! I know where we are now. At least, I don't exactly know, you know, but I once came by here with Wylliams, and he told me there was some club or somethin' down this passage; I don't recollect exactly what he said. Hullo! why there goes Wylliams. I say, Wylliams, tell us where we are!"

A gentleman had brushed past them in the darkness and was walking fast down the passage. He heard his name and turned round, looking rather annoyed.

"Well, Phillipps, what do you want? Good evening, Austin; you seem rather wet, both of you."

"I should think we were wet; got caught in the rain. Didn't you tell me once there was some club down here? I wish you'd take us in, if you're a member."

Mr. Wylliams looked steadfastly at the two forlorn young men for a moment, hesitated, and said:

"Well, gentlemen, you may come with me if you like. But I must impose a condition; that you both give me your word of honour never to mention the club, or anything that you see while you are in it, to any individual whatsoever."

"Certainly not," replied Austin; "of course we shouldn't dream of doing so, should we, Phillipps?"

"No, no; go ahead, Wylliams, we'll keep it dark enough."

The party moved slowly down the passage till they came to the house. It was a very large house and very old; it looked as though it might have been an embassy of the last century. Wylliams whistled, knocked twice at the door, and whistled again, and it was opened by a man in black.

"Friends of yours, Mr. Wylliams?"

Wylliams nodded and they passed on.

"Now mind," he whispered, as they paused at a door, "you are not to recognise anybody, and nobody will recognise you."

The two friends nodded, and the door was opened, and they entered a vast room, brilliantly lighted with electric lamps. Men were standing in knots, walking up and down, and smoking at little tables; it was just like any club smoking room. Conversation was going on, but in a low murmur, and every now and then some one would stop talking, and look anxiously at the door at the other end of the room, and then turn round again. It was evident that they were waiting for some one or somebody. Austin and Phillipps were sitting on a sofa, lost in amazement; nearly every face was familiar to them. The flower of the Row was in that strange club room; several young noblemen, a young fellow who had just come into an enormous fortune, three or four fashionable artists and literary men, an eminent actor, and a well-known canon. What could it mean? They were all supposed to be scattered far and wide over the habitable globe, and yet here they were. Suddenly there came a loud knock at the door; and every man started, and those who were sitting got up. A servant appeared.

"The President is awaiting you, gentlemen," he said, and vanished.

One by one the members filed out, and Wylliams and the two guests brought up the rear. They found themselves in a room still larger than the first, but almost quite dark. The President sat at a long table and before him burned two candles, which barely lit up his face. It was the famous Duke of Dartington, the largest landowner in England. As soon as the members had entered he said in a cold, hard voice, "Gentlemen, you know our rules; the book is prepared. Whoever opens it at the black page is at the disposal of the committee and myself. We had better begin." Some one began to read out the names in a low distinct voice, pausing after each name, and the member called came up to the table and opened at random the pages of a big folio volume that lay between the two candles. The gloomy light made it difficult to distinguish features, but Phillipps heard a groan beside him, and recognised an old friend. His face was working fearfully, the man was evidently in an agony of terror. One by one the members opened the book; as each man did so he passed out by another door. At last there was only one left; it was Phillipps's friend. There was foam upon his lips as he passed up the table, and his hand shook as he opened up the leaves. Wylliams had passed out after whispering to the President, and had returned to his friends' side. He could hardly hold them back as the unfortunate man groaned in agony and leant against the table; he had opened the book at the black page. "Kindly come with me, Mr. D'Aubigny," said the President, and they passed out together.

"We can go now," said Wylliams, "I think the rain has gone off. Remember your promise, gentlemen. You have been at a meeting of the Lost Club. You will never see that young man again. Good-night."

"It isn't *murder*, is it?" gasped Austin.

"Oh no, not at all. Mr. D'Aubigny will, I hope, live for many years; he has disappeared, merely disappeared. Good-night; there's a hansom that will do for you."

The two friends went to their homes in dead silence. They did not meet again for three weeks, and each thought the other looked ill and shaken. They walked drearily, with grave averted faces, down Piccadilly, each afraid to begin the recollection of the terrible club. Of a sudden Phillipps stopped as if he had been shot. "Look there, Austin," he muttered, "look at that." The posters of the evening papers were spread out beside the pavement, and on one of them Austin saw in large blue letters, 'Mysterious disappearance of a Gentleman'. Austin bought a copy and turned over the leaves with shaking fingers till he found the brief paragraph:

> Mr. St. John D'Aubigny, of Stoke D'Aubigny, in Sussex, has disappeared under mysterious circumstances. Mr. D'Aubigny was staying at Strathdoon, in Scotland, and came up to London, as is stated, on business, on August 16th. It has been ascertained that he arrived safely at King's Cross, and drove to Piccadilly Circus, where he got out. It is said that he was last seen at the corner of Glass House Street, leading from Regent Street into Soho. Since the above date the unfortunate gentleman, who was much liked in London society, has not been heard of. Mr. D'Aubigny was to have been married in September. The police are extremely reticent.

"Good God! Austin, this is dreadful. You remember the date. Poor fellow, poor fellow!"

"Phillipps, I think I shall go home, I feel sick."

D'Aubigny was never heard of again. But the strangest part of the story remains to be told. The two friends called upon Wylliams, and charged him with being a member of the Lost Club, and an accomplice in the fate of D'Aubigny. The placid Mr. Wylliams at first stared at the two pale, earnest faces, and finally roared with laughter.

"My dear fellows, what on earth are you talking about? I never heard such a cock-and-bull story in my life. As you say, Phillipps, I once pointed out to you a house said to be a club, as we were walking through Soho; but that was a low gambling club, frequented by German waiters. I am afraid the fact is that Azario's Chianti was rather too strong for you. However, I will try to convince you of your mistake."

Wylliams forthwith summoned his man, who swore that he and his master were in Cairo during the whole of August, and offered to produce the hotel bills. Phillipps shook his head, and they went away. Their next step was to try and find the archway where they had taken shelter, and after a good deal of trouble they succeeded. They knocked at the door of the gloomy house, whistling as Wylliams had done. They were admitted by a respectable mechanic in a white apron, who was evidently astonished at the whistle; in fact he was inclined to suspect the influence of a 'drop too much'. The place was a billiard table factory, and had been so (as they learnt in the neighbourhood) for many years. The rooms must once have been large and magnificent, but most of them had been divided into three or four separate workshops by wooden partitions.

Phillipps sighed; he could do no more for his lost friend; but both he and Austin remained unconvinced. In justice to Mr. Wylliams, it must be stated that Lord Henry Harcourt assured Phillipps that he had seen Wylliams in Cairo about the middle of August; he thought, but could not be sure, on the 16th; and also, that the recent disappearances of some well known men about town are patient of explanations which would exclude the agency of the Lost Club.

An Underground Adventure

T he lady dressed in deep mourning would like to thank the tall gentleman, who so kindly helped her in her distress at Victoria Station on the evening of the 15th inst. Will he oblige her by meeting her outside the booking-office of the Victoria Underground Station at 6 p.m., on Friday, the 21st."

I am fond of looking through the agony columns of the leading daily organs, partly with the vague hope of seeing some day that if I call at such and such a place I shall hear of something to my advantage, and partly because I have an inherent, almost feminine, curiosity, and delight in anything in the shape of a mystery.

I saw the above about a week ago, and if you care to read further, you will see the result of my, rather to be deplored, little weakness.

A widowed lady who wished to meet a tall, kind gentleman at an underground station, suggested plots of shilling dreadfuls, and set me wondering what they had to say to each other. A brilliant idea came into my head. To-morrow evening, being the 21st, I would go to Victoria Station, and satisfy my curiosity by watching this interesting couple.

My father has instilled many excellent morals and maxims into my head. One of them is to eschew all manner of wine, tobacco, playhouses, and ball-rooms.

Consequently, I depend upon my own imagination and my childish love of adventure for my amusement, in the intervals when I am not sitting at a high desk, with my nose nearly in the ink-bottle, adding up figures for bare life.

At 5.30 the next evening I turned my face towards Victoria Station, in light-hearted anticipation of an adventure.

The time of year was November, and as a matter of course, it was damp, dark, cold, and foggy, and the station looked drear enough, both inside and out. I took up my position not far from the ticket-office, in a dark corner, where I should not be much seen. The hand of the clock pointed to three minutes to six, so I pricked up my ears and opened my eyes. A few men were loitering about, some newspaper-boys and shoe-blacks were making a commotion near the door, and a little stream of people were taking their tickets in a silent, hurried manner.

Suddenly a smartly dressed young woman strolled in, and catching sight of one of the loitering men, rushed at him. The greetings were long and loud. She was so glad to see her "dear Dick" again! What did he mean by not turning up last Sunday? and Dear Dick was pleased to see Dear Susie. Why it was ages since they'd met! It made no difference to their effusions their being in the middle of a noisy thoroughfare, quite half-a-dozen people looking on and listening.

I began to fear, with a sinking of my spirits, that this might be the beginning and the end of my adventure, when I felt a touch at my elbow, and looking round, I saw a tall, somewhat stout, well-dressed, mournful-looking, middle-aged widow lady at my side.

"I knew you would see that advertisement I put in the paper and I knew that I could depend upon you to come to me."

She spoke in clear, deliberate tones, with a slightly foreign accent. I confess my breath was completely taken away. I did not take in the situation at once. I gazed at her dumbly, and bowed, and raised my hat. Then I saw it all, and opened my mouth to try and explain the mistake, but no words came to my help.

She went on quite calmly without heeding my embarrassment—

"I recognised you at once, I have a good memory for faces. You are not so quick. You did not see me coming down the steps. But you have changed a little since I saw you"; and here she scrutinised my face with a pair of tortoise-shell-rimmed glasses. "There is a difference in you. What is it? Ah! I have it. You have shaved off your whiskers. Is that not so?"

I acquiesced.

Heaven knows, I never had any! I grew alternately hot and cold. I blushed and smiled nervously. I looked at the door, and thought desperately—Can I make a rush for it? The next moment I boldly thought, I will tell her I am not the man. But she gave me no opportunity. She talked on without a pause, sometimes sighing, sometimes smiling. I was thinking too much of my dilemma to take in what she was saying.

"Come into the waiting-room," she said, at last, in a business-like voice. "I have something of importance to say to you, which cannot be said in public." I was in for it now, and no mistake. I followed her down the long underground passage to the Great Junction waiting-room. Her quiet commanding manner made me quake in my shoes. She shewed the way into the first-class waiting-room, which was quiet and deserted. There was a table in the middle of the room. She drew a chair to it, and sat down, and signed to me to take the other. An uncomfortable silence reigned for a minute or two. At last, the widow gave a deep sigh. I did the same, and wondered what was coming next.

"I have told you enough of my history to shew you what a lonely, disconsolate life mine has been. Some women might envy me my position; but they have no conception what I have suffered. I am the Marquise de B———. You know the name well, no doubt?" (I did not, but no matter, I pretended I did.) "Since my husband's death I have been pestered with suitors—all idle, good-for-nothing fellows, the most persistent of whom is that young wretch out of whose hands you rescued me the other evening at the station. I have given him large sums of money two or three times, and entreated him to go away and torment me no longer, but he always comes back."

I was growing intensely interested, and a little less alarmed. Perhaps I really had been at the station the other evening and rescued this stout marchioness, and for a few seconds I wondered vaguely and wildly whether I was myself or some one else. The Marquise went on talking. Her voice grew, little by little, louder and more excited. Now and then she brought down her fist on the table with a thump.

I said something intended to soothe her. She looked at me with a smile, and said:

"Ah, you have a good face, and you have many noble qualities! Do not try to deny it. I am a good judge of faces, and I saw from the first that I could trust you, and that you would make me happy."

What was all this leading to? I asked myself blankly. She was looking at me with great attention, and I began to shift uneasily about on my chair.

"Are you married?" she asked, abruptly.

"No," I said, taken aback.

"Engaged?" she went on.

"No, nor engaged," I replied.

"Have you any prospect of being married?"

"None, at all, at present," I said, a little nettled by this questioning.

She gave a deep sigh of satisfaction. "I have told you that I have had an unhappy life. I have been seeking since my husband's death for some one—some kindred spirit—whom I may devote my life to making happy, and who, in his turn, will dispel the gloom of my life. I am wealthy. I am a marchioness. You are poor and lowly. I am willing to devote all to you, to lay all at your feet—to give—"

"Good heavens! Do you want to marry me?" I blurted out, jumping to my feet aghast.

"Young man," she said, sternly, "think before you speak, do not rashly refuse my offer. You do not know what you are throwing away. Say yes, and you will be the happiest man on earth. Say no, and you will repent it all your life, and will make me the most miserable of women."

I tried to make for the door, and signed wildly to her to stop, but she would not heed me. Her voice rose higher and higher.

"Do not try to stop me. I will say all I have to say, for you are the only young man I have ever set my heart upon."

I was growing desperate. "I will never marry you, not if I live to be a hundred!" I shouted. "Ask me to do anything but that."

I was in terror lest an official, hearing the commotion, might appear upon the scene. She gave a little scream, and turned crimson with fury, and I saw her totter to a chair, and sink on to it and glare at me with an expression which frightened me. It was only for a second; the next moment I had turned and bolted. I took to my heels as soon as I was fairly outside, and fled homewards; but I looked back every few seconds with a fearful nightmare-dread of seeing the widow marchioness pursuing me.

This is the first time a lady has proposed to me, and that I have had to refuse. Heaven grant that it may be the last!

The result has been an undermining and general collapse of my whole constitution.

Jocelyn's Escape

Mr. Mathews in?"

"Yes, sir; just washing his hands."

"Ask him to come into my room before he goes out for his lunch, will you?"

"Very good, sir."

Harry Jocelyn left his two clerks to their German text and round-hand, and passed through to his own office by the door marked "Private". He sat down by the fire and held out his hands to the glow, for though it was a spring day and the trees were budding in the square of the Inn and bright sunshine shone through the windows, a bitter east wind blew along the streets and whistled up the narrow passage from the Strand by which he had come. So Jocelyn made the fire blaze cheerfully, and warmed himself as he waited for Mr. Mathews.

"Come in," he said, as the two knocks pounded on the door.

"Davies told me you wanted to see me, sir."

"Yes, that's right. I only wanted to say, Mathews, that I expect a client this afternoon—a lady, and I wish her to be shewn into me directly she comes. She will be here about four o'clock, I fancy, and it's now a quarter to two; so you will be in by then, won't you?"

"Certainly, sir."

"Very good. There's nothing else, I think. You've been to Dickson's, in Bedford-row, about that will? Then that will be all for to-day."

Jocelyn wheeled round his chair to the desk, and looked out on to the square, watching the thin stream of people who passed up and down and the two or three loungers of the miscellaneous and mostly tattered kind that are to be found on sunny days in all quiet corners of London. Jocelyn was uneasy that April afternoon. He looked out a little while, and then rose from his chair and walked up and down the room for a few minutes, then stopped by his book-shelf, and, drawing out a volume of brighter yellow than that of law calf from behind Chitty and Chitty Junior on Torts, began to read it. But the French novel was soon slipped back into its hiding-place, and Jocelyn, though he expected a visit from a lady, took out a cigarette and began to smoke, now smiling and now frowning to himself over his thoughts. Jocelyn had been nervous and fidgety for some days past, and the clerks had noticed it, and entered into some speculation as to what was the matter with "the governor". Davies had seen him posting a letter with his own hands in the Strand, and when Jocelyn recognised his clerk he had looked foolish and ashamed; and Mr. Mathews was surprised on coming into the private office to see quite a pile of minute scraps of paper burning on the hearth, though the waste-basket was nearly empty. However, Mr. Mathews and the two clerks had not much time wherein to meditate whether on these or on other matters, for Jocelyn's practice was a good one—a wonderful practice, his friends said, for a man of thirty-seven to have made by his own hand, without much aid in the way of interest or connections. He had married young, before the appearance of Mr. Mathews or of the two assistants, and it was possibly the necessity for exertion which had made Jocelyn a rising man at 32, and a prosperous one at 37. Yet he looked exquisitely uncomfortable, this windy afternoon, as he sat in his chair watching the cigarette-end fuming on the tray; he looked at his watch again and again, opened the door, and peered into the outer office to see if Mathews had returned, and then renewed again his pacing up and down the room, and his watch at the window, as the day wore on and the sun sank into a cold grey haze beyond the Inn walls and the chimney-tops. The loiterers had vanished from the square, and the foot-passengers walked rapidly, inclining their heads to the wind like so many poplars, and Jocelyn took out once more his watch, and felt his heart beat fast. It was a quarter to four. He leant back in his chair, and fixed his eyes on the glass door expectantly.

"Come in!"

"Mr. James Dickson, sir."

"You can spare me a few moments, can't you, Jocelyn? That's right. I was passing this way, and I thought I should like to have some conversation with you; I shan't keep you long. Thanks, I will take a chair. You don't look very well, though, Jocelyn."

"Rather busy time of late; I've had to take papers home for several nights running. It's very good of you to come in, I'm sure; you know you have done me several good turns, Dickson, and I should be only too glad if I could be of any use to your people."

"Don't mention it, pray don't mention it. No, it's not that; it's about that man we sent over to you the other day; it struck me I might give you one or two hints which might be of service."

The elder lawyer paused, and held out his hands before the fire; he was evidently enjoying the warmth of the room after the cold blast of the streets. "More like March, isn't it?" he said at length; "my garden is terribly backward. What the country wants, you know, is rain—a good warm rain for twenty-four hours. This wind is nipping everything."

"Yes, very bitter, very bitter indeed. You were speaking of Finch's case, I suppose?"

"Quite so, of Finch's case. What I wanted to point out was this. . . ."

Mr. Dickson became scientific, but as for Jocelyn he heard not a word. He was listening for the creak and swing of the outer office-door, and for Mathews's tap on his own.

It came at last, and Jocelyn looked up.

"Come in! Well, Mathews, what is it?"

Mr. Mathews replied in a low murmur, not because he thought there was anything to conceal, but out of an inveterate habit.

"That client you spoke of, sir . . ."

"Excuse me a moment, Dickson. The lady I spoke of?" Mr. Jocelyn, possibly from habit also, spoke softly enough.

"Yes, sir, she has just come. I told her I thought you were engaged."

"Quite right. Just wait a minute, will you?"

Mr. Jocelyn walked to his desk, took a sheet of paper and wrote a few lines, and hastily put the note in an envelope.

"Take this, Mathews. I shan't be long."

"I dare say you are more accustomed to interruptions than I am," he said to Mr. Dickson when the door was shut.

"Yes, yes, we have a good many. But, as I was saying, one of the queerest features in this case of Finch's is . . ."

Mr. Dickson resumed his observations with relish, and Jocelyn sat staring at him, shivering with impatience.

The end came in due course.

"I don't think that, bearing what I have said in mind, you can go far wrong. But it's a matter that will require rather delicate handling. Good evening, Jocelyn, good evening. Don't work too hard, you know; you should take a little relaxation now and then."

"Yes, I will, Dickson. Good-night; it is very kind of you to take all this trouble."

"Not at all. Don't mind the door. I can let myself out very well."

Harry Jocelyn sat down with a vast sigh of relief. He was just going to poke up the fire and make a cheerful blaze in the dim room, when he heard the sound of voices talking in the outer office, and stopped to listen. As it happened, two or three people were racing up and down, with all the vehemence of men in a hurry on an office stair, and Jocelyn could not distinguish the voices. As the stamping ceased so also did the sound of talking and there was a knock at his door.

It was fortunate for Jocelyn that he had not made the fire blaze, and that the room was growing dim and the light uncertain. He gripped the arm of his chair and shut his teeth together, drawing a long breath.

"Well, my dear; here I am. I was telling Mr. Dickson that this was the first time I had been to your office for all the years we have been married. I thought at first of sending one of the servants; but it was so fine that I felt the drive would do me good, so I took a hansom."

"Yes; of course—yes, very pleasant. Is there anything the matter?"

"Mrs. Elstree wrote to say that her husband had been suddenly attacked with severe bronchitis, and so, of course, they can't come to dinner to-night. What do you think we had better do? It seems absurd to ask people to dinner to meet the Elstrees and then not to have them there. Don't you think we had better send telegrams? It isn't too late."

"Not at all, not at all. We'll send them at once. Come along, there's an office close by."

"But won't you send one of the clerks?"

"No, no; they're far too busy; I couldn't spare them for anything. Come on, Edith; quick! There's not a moment to lose."

Jocelyn hurried his wife out of the office and down the stairs, scarcely stopping to tell Mathews that he would not return that night; and, taking her arm, the two fairly rushed along till they got into the Strand.

"Goodness, Harry! you will walk me off my legs. There can't be such a terrible hurry."

Jocelyn slackened his pace a little and looked about him, as a man looks who has escaped a precipice but by a hair's breadth and sees from a safe place the black chasm and the sharp rocks far below. They walked on in silence, Jocelyn leaning on his wife's arm.

"Why, Harry, you are passing the telegraph office. There it is."

"So it is; I was not keeping a proper look-out. I will send the telegrams."

The telegrams were sent, and Jocelyn hailed a passing hansom, and the husband and wife drove home together. Jocelyn was very silent all the evening, and as they were sitting together by the drawing-room fire, Mrs. Jocelyn said suddenly:

"I suppose that was Mr. Mathews who shewed me in?"

"Yes, that was Mathews."

"He must be a sharp man. I have been wondering how he knew I was Mrs. Jocelyn."

"Ah! very sharp of Mr. Mathews, as you say: really very acute of him."

"Yes, and that reminds me; I have not had that cosy chat you promised me."

"Cosy chat, did you say?"

"Yes, you promised me in that funny little note you wrote me. Here it is, just as Mr. Mathews gave it me."

Jocelyn took the envelope and drew out the letter he had written in the afternoon.

> "MY DARLING DI,—Will you wait for me a little? I shall be alone in a few minutes, and then we can have a cosy little chat all to ourselves. Till then, dear, and ever—Your loving Harry J"

Jocelyn looked at his wife, who smiled.

"It's just like the little letters you used to write me before we were married," she said. "But what made you call me Di? I never heard that Di was short for Edith. But it is a very pretty little note, and I shall keep it."

"There was a lady came here last night, sir, just after you were gone. She seemed to say she had an appointment, but had been delayed."

"Did she give any name, Mathews?"

"No, sir; I asked her if she would leave her name, but she refused to do so."

"Ah, well, I dare say it isn't a matter of any consequence. If she calls again at any time you can tell her that I am out."

The Inmost Light

I

One evening in autumn, when the deformities of London were veiled in faint blue mist, and its vistas and far-reaching streets seemed splendid, Mr. Charles Salisbury was slowly pacing down Rupert Street, drawing nearer to his favourite restaurant by slow degrees. His eyes were downcast in study of the pavement, and thus it was that as he passed in at the narrow door a man who had come up from the lower end of the street jostled against him.

"I beg your pardon—wasn't looking where I was going. Why, it's Dyson!"

"Yes, quite so. How are you, Salisbury?"

"Quite well. But where have you been, Dyson? I don't think I can have seen you for the last five years?"

"No; I dare say not. You remember I was getting rather hard up when you came to my place at Charlotte Street?"

"Perfectly. I think I remember your telling me that you owed five weeks' rent, and that you had parted with your watch for a comparatively small sum."

"My dear Salisbury, your memory is admirable. Yes, I was hard up. But the curious thing is that soon after you saw me I became harder up. My financial state was described by a friend as 'stone broke'. I don't approve of slang, mind you, but such was my condition. But suppose we go in; there might be other people who would like to dine—it's a human weakness, Salisbury."

"Certainly; come along. I was wondering as I walked down whether the corner table were taken. It has a velvet back you know."

"I know the spot; it's vacant. Yes, as I was saying, I became even harder up."

"What did you do then?" asked Salisbury, disposing of his hat, and settling down in the corner of the seat, with a glance of fond anticipation at the *menu*.

"What did I do? Why, I sat down and reflected. I had a good classical education, and a positive distaste for business of any kind: that was the capital with which I faced the world. Do you know, I have heard people describe olives as nasty! What lamentable Philistinism! I have often thought, Salisbury, that I could write genuine poetry under the influence of olives and red wine. Let us have Chianti; it may not be very good, but the flasks are simply charming."

"It is pretty good here. We may as well have a big flask."

"Very good. I reflected, then, on my want of prospects, and I determined to embark in literature."

"Really; that was strange. You seem in pretty comfortable circumstances, though."

"Though! What a satire upon a noble profession. I am afraid, Salisbury, you haven't a proper idea of the dignity of an artist. You see me sitting at my desk—or at least you can see me if you care to call—with pen and ink, and simple nothingness before me, and if you come again in a few hours you will (in all probability) find a creation!"

"Yes, quite so. I had an idea that literature was not remunerative."

"You are mistaken; its rewards are great. I may mention, by the way, that shortly after you saw me I succeeded to a small income. An uncle died, and proved unexpectedly generous."

"Ah, I see. That must have been convenient."

"It was pleasant—undeniably pleasant. I have always considered it in the light of an endowment of my researches. I told you I was a man of letters; it would, perhaps, be more correct to describe myself as a man of science."

"Dear me, Dyson, you have really changed very much in the last few years. I had a notion, don't you know, that you were a sort of idler about town, the kind of man one might meet on the north side of Piccadilly every day from May to July."

"Exactly. I was even then forming myself, though all unconsciously. You know my poor father could not afford to send me to the University. I used to grumble in my ignorance at not having completed my education. That was the folly of youth, Salisbury; my University was Piccadilly.

There I began to study the great science which still occupies me."

"What science do you mean?"

"The science of the great city; the physiology of London; literally and metaphysically the greatest subject that the mind of man can conceive. What an admirable *salmi* this is; undoubtedly the final end of the pheasant. Yet I feel sometimes positively overwhelmed with the thought of the vastness and complexity of London. Paris a man may get to understand thoroughly with a reasonable amount of study; but London is always a mystery. In Paris you may say: 'Here live the actresses, here the Bohemians, and the *Ratés*'; but it is different in London. You may point out a street, correctly enough, as the abode of washerwomen; but, in that second floor, a man may be studying Chaldee roots, and in the garret over the way a forgotten artist is dying by inches."

"I see you are Dyson, unchanged and unchangeable," said Salisbury, slowly sipping his Chianti. "I think you are misled by a too fervid imagination; the mystery of London exists only in your fancy. It seems to me a dull place enough. We seldom hear of a really artistic crime in London, whereas I believe Paris abounds in that sort of thing."

"Give me some more wine. Thanks. You are mistaken, my dear fellow, you are really mistaken. London has nothing to be ashamed of in the way of crime. Where we fail is for want of Homers, not Agamemnons. *Carent quia vate sacro,* you know."

"I recall the quotation. But I don't think I quite follow you."

"Well, in plain language, we have no good writers in London who make a speciality of that kind of thing. Our common reporter is a dull dog; every story that he has to tell is spoilt in the telling. His idea of horror and of what excites horror is so lamentably deficient. Nothing will content the fellow but blood, vulgar red blood, and when he can get it he lays it on thick, and considers that he has produced a telling article. It's a poor notion. And, by some curious fatality, it is the most commonplace and brutal murders which always attract the most attention and get written up the most. For instance, I dare say that you never heard of the Harlesden case?"

"No; no, I don't remember anything about it."

"Of course not. And yet the story is a curious one. I will tell it you over our coffee. Harlesden, you know, or I expect you don't know, is quite on the out-quarters of London; something curiously different from your fine old crusted suburb like Norwood or Hampstead, different as each of these is from the other. Hampstead, I mean, is where you look for the head of your great China house with his three acres of land and pine-houses, though of late there is the artistic substratum; while Norwood is the home of the prosperous middle-class family who took the house 'because it was near the Palace', and sickened of the Palace six months afterwards; but Harlesden is a place of no character. It's too new to have any character as yet. There are the rows of red houses and the rows of white houses and the bright green Venetians, and the blistering doorways, and the little backyards they call gardens, and a few feeble shops, and then, just as you think you're going to grasp the physiognomy of the settlement, it all melts away."

"How the dickens is that? The houses don't tumble down before one's eyes, I suppose!"

"Well, no, not exactly that. But Harlesden as an entity disappears. Your street turns into a quiet lane, and your staring houses into elm-trees, and the back-gardens into green meadows. You pass instantly from town to country; there is no transition as in a small country town, no soft gradations of wider lawns and orchards, with houses gradually becoming less dense, but a dead stop. I believe the people who live there mostly go into the City. I have seen once or twice a laden 'bus bound thitherwards. But however that may be, I can't conceive a greater loneliness in a desert at midnight than there is there at mid-day. It is like a city of the dead; the streets are glaring and desolate, and as you pass it suddenly strikes you that this too is part of London. Well, a year or two ago there was a doctor living there; he had set up his brass plate and his red lamp at the very end of one of those shining streets, and from the back of the house, the fields stretched away to the north. I don't know what his reason was in settling down in such an out-of-the-way place, perhaps Dr. Black, as we call him, was a far-seeing man and looked ahead. His relations, so it appeared afterwards, had lost sight of him for many years and didn't even know he was a doctor, much less where he lived. However, there he was settled in Harlesden, with some fragments of a practice, and an uncommonly pretty wife. People used to see them walking out together in the summer evenings soon after they came to Harlesden, and, so far as could be observed, they seemed a very affectionate couple. These walks went on through the autumn, and then ceased; but, of course, as the days grew dark and the weather cold, the lanes near Harlesden might be expected to lose many of their attractions. All through the winter nobody saw anything of Mrs. Black; the doctor used to reply to his patients' enquiries that she was a 'little out of sorts, would be better, no doubt, in the spring.' But the spring came, and the summer, and no Mrs. Black appeared, and at last people began to rumour and talk amongst themselves, and all sorts of queer things were said at 'high teas', which you may possibly have heard are the only form of entertainment known in such suburbs. Dr. Black began to surprise some very odd looks cast in his direction, and the practice, such as it was, fell off before his eyes. In short, when the neighbours whispered about the matter, they whispered that Mrs. Black was dead, and that the doctor had made away with her. But this wasn't the case; Mrs. Black was seen alive in June. It was a Sunday afternoon, one of those few exquisite days that an English climate offers, and half London had strayed out into the fields, north, south, east, and west to smell the scent of the white May, and to see if the wild roses were yet in blossom in the hedges. I had gone out myself early in the morning, and had had a long ramble, and somehow or other as I was steering homeward I found myself in this very Harlesden we have been talking about. To be exact, I had a glass of beer in the 'General Gordon', the most flourishing house in the neighbourhood, and as I was wandering rather aimlessly about, I saw an uncommonly tempting gap in a hedgerow, and resolved to explore the meadow beyond. Soft grass is very grateful to the feet after the infernal grit strewn on suburban sidewalks, and after walking about for some time I thought I should like to sit down on a bank and have a smoke. While I was getting out my pouch, I looked up in the direction of the houses, and as I looked I felt my breath caught back, and my teeth began to chatter, and the stick I had in one hand snapped in two with the grip I gave it. It was as if I had had an electric current down my spine, and yet for some moment of time which seemed long, but which must have been very short, I caught myself wondering what on earth was the matter. Then I knew what had made my very heart shudder and my bones grind together in an agony. As I glanced up I had looked straight towards the last house in the row before me, and in an upper window of that house

I had seen for some short fraction of a second a face. It was the face of a woman, and yet it was not human. You and I, Salisbury, have heard in our time, as we sat in our seats in church in sober English fashion, of a lust that cannot be satiated and of a fire that is unquenchable, but few of us have any notion what these words mean. I hope you never may, for as I saw that face at the window, with the blue sky above me and the warm air playing in gusts about me, I knew I had looked into another world—looked through the window of a commonplace, brand-new house, and seen hell open before me. When the first shock was over, I thought once or twice that I should have fainted; my face streamed with a cold sweat, and my breath came and went in sobs, as if I had been half drowned. I managed to get up at last, and walk round to the street, and there I saw the name 'Dr. Black' on the post by the front gate. As fate or my luck would have it, the door opened and a man came down the steps as I passed by. I had no doubt it was the doctor himself. He was of a type rather common in London; long and thin, with a pasty face and a dull black moustache. He gave me a look as we passed each other on the pavement, and though it was merely the casual glance which one foot-passenger bestows on another, I felt convinced in my mind that here was an ugly customer to deal with. As you may imagine, I went my way a good deal puzzled and horrified too by what I had seen; for I had paid another visit to the 'General Gordon', and had got together a good deal of the common gossip of the place about the Blacks. I didn't mention the fact that I had seen a woman's face in the window; but I heard that Mrs. Black had been much admired for her beautiful golden hair, and round what had struck me with such a nameless terror, there was a mist of flowing yellow hair, as it was an aureole of glory round the visage of a satyr. The whole thing bothered me in an indescribable manner; and when I got home I tried my best to think of the impression I had received as an illusion, but it was no use. I knew very well I had seen what I have tried to describe to you, and I was morally certain that I had seen Mrs. Black. And then there was the gossip of the place, the suspicion of foul play, which I knew to be false, and my own conviction that there was some deadly mischief or other going on in that bright red house at the corner of Devon Road: how to construct a theory of a reasonable kind out of these two elements. In short, I found myself in a world of mystery; I puzzled my head over it and filled up my leisure moments by gathering together odd threads of speculation, but I never moved a step towards any real solution, and as the summer days went on the matter seemed to grow misty and indistinct, shadowing some vague terror, like a nightmare of last month. I suppose it would before long have faded into the background of my brain—I should not have forgotten it, for such a thing could never be forgotten—but one morning as I was looking over the paper my eye was caught by a heading over some two dozen lines of small type. The words I had seen were simply: 'The Harlesden Case', and I knew what I was going to read. Mrs. Black was dead. Black had called in another medical man to certify as to cause of death, and something or other had aroused the strange doctor's suspicions and there had been an inquest and *post-mortem*. And the result? That, I will confess, did astonish me considerably; it was the triumph of the unexpected. The two doctors who made the autopsy were obliged to confess that they could not discover the faintest trace of any kind of foul play; their most exquisite tests and reagents failed to detect the presence of poison in the most infinitesimal quantity. Death, they found, had been caused by a somewhat obscure and scientifically interesting form of brain disease. The tissue of the brain and the molecules of the grey matter had undergone a most extraordinary series of changes; and the younger of the two doctors, who has some reputation, I believe, as a specialist in brain trouble, made some remarks in giving his evidence which struck me deeply at the time, though I did not then grasp their full significance. He said: 'At the commencement of the examination I was astonished to find appearances of a character entirely new to me, notwithstanding my somewhat large experience. I need not specify these appearances at present, it will be sufficient for me to state that as I proceeded in my task I could scarcely believe that the brain before me was that of a human being at all.' There was some surprise at this statement, as you may imagine, and the coroner asked the doctor if he meant that the brain resembled that of an animal. 'No,' he replied, 'I should not put it in that way. Some of the appearances I noticed seemed to point in that direction, but others, and these were the more surprising, indicated a nervous organisation of a wholly different character from that either of man or the lower animals.' It was a curious thing to say, but of course the jury brought in a verdict of death from natural causes, and, so far as the public was concerned, the case came to an end. But after I had read what the doctor said I made up my mind that I should like to know a good deal more, and I set to work on what seemed likely to prove an interesting investigation. I had really a good deal of trouble, but I was successful in a measure. Though why—my dear fellow, I had no notion at the time. Are you aware that we have been here nearly four hours? The waiters are staring at us. Let's have the bill and be gone."

The two men went out in silence, and stood a moment in the cool air, watching the hurrying traffic of Coventry Street pass before them to the accompaniment of the ringing bells of hansoms and the cries of the newsboys; the deep far murmur of London surging up ever and again from beneath these louder noises.

"It is a strange case, isn't it?" said Dyson at length. "What do you think of it?"

"My dear fellow, I haven't heard the end, so I will reserve my opinion. When will you give me the sequel?"

"Come to my rooms some evening; say next Thursday. Here's the address. Good-night; I want to get down to the Strand." Dyson hailed a passing hansom, and Salisbury turned northward to walk home to his lodgings.

II

Mr. Salisbury, as may have been gathered from the few remarks which he had found it possible to introduce in the course of the evening, was a young gentleman of a peculiarly solid form of intellect, coy and retiring before the mysterious and the uncommon, with a constitutional dislike of paradox. During the restaurant dinner he had been forced to listen in almost absolute silence to a strange tissue of improbabilities strung together with the ingenuity of a born meddler in plots and mysteries, and it was with a feeling of weariness that he crossed Shaftesbury Avenue, and dived into the recesses of Soho, for his lodgings were in a modest neighbourhood to the north of Oxford Street. As he walked he speculated on the probable fate of Dyson, relying on literature, unbefriended by a thoughtful relative, and could not help concluding that so much subtlety united to a too vivid imagination would in all likelihood have been rewarded with a pair of sandwich-boards or a super's banner. Absorbed in this train of thought, and admiring the perverse dexterity which could transmute the face of a sickly woman and a case of brain disease into the crude elements of romance, Salisbury strayed on through the dimly-lighted streets, not noticing the gusty wind which drove sharply round corners and whirled the stray rubbish of the pavement into the air in eddies, while black clouds gathered over the sickly yellow moon. Even a stray drop or two of rain blown into his face did not rouse him from his meditations, and it was only when with a sudden rush the storm tore down upon the street that he began to consider the expediency of finding some shelter. The rain, driven by the wind, pelted down with the violence of a thunder-storm, dashing up from the stones and hissing through the air, and soon a perfect torrent of water coursed along the kennels and accumulated in pools over the choked-up drains. The few stray passengers who had been loafing rather than walking about the street had scuttered away, like frightened rabbits, to some invisible places of refuge, and though Salisbury whistled loud and long for a hansom, no hansom appeared. He looked about him, as if to discover how far he might be from the haven of Oxford Street, but strolling carelessly along, he had turned out of his way, and found himself in an unknown region, and one to all appearance devoid even of a public-house where shelter could be bought for the modest sum of twopence. The street lamps were few and at long intervals, and burned behind grimy glasses with the sickly light of oil, and by this wavering glimmer Salisbury could make out the shadowy and vast old houses of which the street was composed. As he passed along, hurrying, and shrinking from the full sweep of the rain, he noticed the innumerable bell-handles, with names that seemed about to vanish of old age graven on brass plates beneath them, and here and there a richly carved penthouse overhung the door, blackening with the grime of fifty years. The storm seemed to grow more and more furious; he was wet through, and a new hat had become a ruin, and still Oxford Street seemed as far off as ever; it was with deep relief that the dripping man caught sight of a dark archway which seemed to promise shelter from the rain if not from the wind. Salisbury took up his position in the driest corner and looked about him; he was standing in a kind of passage contrived under part of a

house, and behind him stretched a narrow footway leading between
blank walls to regions unknown. He had stood there for some time,
vainly endeavouring to rid himself of some of his superfluous moisture, and listening for the passing wheel of a hansom, when his attention was aroused by a loud noise coming from the direction of the
passage behind, and growing louder as it drew nearer. In a couple of
minutes he could make out the shrill, raucous voice of a woman,
threatening and renouncing and making the very stones echo with her
accents, while now and then a man grumbled and expostulated.
Though to all appearance devoid of romance, Salisbury had some relish for street rows, and was, indeed, somewhat of an amateur in the
more amusing phases of drunkenness; he therefore composed himself
to listen and observe with something of the air of a subscriber to grand
opera. To his annoyance, however, the tempest seemed suddenly to be
composed, and he could hear nothing but the impatient steps of the
woman and the slow lurch of the man as they came towards him.
Keeping back in the shadow of the wall, he could see the two drawing
nearer; the man was evidently drunk, and had much ado to avoid frequent collision with the wall as he tacked across from one side to the
other, like some bark beating up against a wind. The woman was looking straight in front of her, with tears streaming from her blazing eyes,
but suddenly as they went by the flame blazed up again, and she burst
forth into a torrent of abuse, facing round upon her companion.

"You low rascal, you mean, contemptible cur," she went on, after
an incoherent storm of curses, "you think I'm to work and slave for
you always, I suppose, while you're after that Green Street girl and
drinking every penny you've got? But you're mistaken, Sam—indeed,
I'll bear it no longer. Damn you, you dirty thief, I've done with you
and your master too, so you can go your own errands, and I only hope
they'll get you into trouble."

The woman tore at the bosom of her dress, and taking something
out that looked like paper, crumpled it up and flung it away. It fell at
Salisbury's feet. She ran out and disappeared in the darkness, while the
man lurched slowly into the street, grumbling indistinctly to himself in
a perplexed tone of voice. Salisbury looked out after him, and saw him
maundering along the pavement, halting now and then and swaying
indecisively, and then starting off at some fresh tangent. The sky had

cleared, and white fleecy clouds were fleeting across the moon, high in the heaven. The light came and went by turns, as the clouds passed by, and, turning round as the clear, white rays shone into the passage, Salisbury saw the little ball of crumpled paper which the woman had cast down. Oddly curious to know what it might contain, he picked it up and put it in his pocket, and set out afresh on his journey.

III

Salisbury was a man of habit. When he got home, drenched to the skin, his clothes hanging lank about him, and a ghastly dew besmearing his hat, his only thought was of his health, of which he took studious care. So, after changing his clothes and encasing himself in a warm dressing-gown, he proceeded to prepare a sudorific in the shape of hot gin and water, warming the latter over one of those spirit-lamps which mitigate the austerities of the modern hermit's life. By the time this preparation had been exhibited, and Salisbury's disturbed feelings had been soothed by a pipe of tobacco, he was able to get into bed in a happy state of vacancy, without a thought of his adventure in the dark archway, or of the weird fancies with which Dyson had seasoned his dinner. It was the same at breakfast the next morning, for Salisbury made a point of not thinking of any thing until that meal was over; but when the cup and saucer were cleared away, and the morning pipe was lit, he remembered the little ball of paper, and began fumbling in the pockets of his wet coat. He did not remember into which pocket he had put it, and as he dived now into one and now into another, he experienced a strange feeling of apprehension lest it should not be there at all, though he could not for the life of him have explained the importance he attached to what was in all probability mere rubbish. But he sighed with relief when his fingers touched the crumpled surface in an inside pocket, and he drew it out gently and laid it on the little desk by his easy-chair with as much care as if it had been some rare jewel. Salisbury sat smoking and staring at his find for a few minutes, an odd temptation to throw the thing in the fire and have done with it struggling with as odd a speculation as to its possible contents, and as to the reason why the infuriated woman should have flung a bit of paper from her with such vehemence. As might be expected, it was the latter feeling that conquered in the end, and yet it was with something like repugnance that he at last took the paper and unrolled it, and laid it out before him. It was a piece of common dirty paper, to all appearance torn out of a cheap exercise-book, and in the middle were a few lines written in a queer cramped hand. Salisbury bent his head and stared eagerly at it for a moment, drawing a long breath, and then fell back in his chair gazing blankly before him, till at last with a sudden revulsion he burst into a peal of laughter, so long and loud and uproarious that the landlady's baby in the floor below awoke from sleep and echoed his mirth with hideous yells. But he laughed again and again, and took the paper up to read a second time what seemed such meaningless nonsense.

> "Q. has had to go and see his friends in Paris," it began. "Traverse Handel S. 'Once around the grass, and twice around the lass, and thrice around the maple-tree.'"

Salisbury took up the paper and crumpled it as the angry woman had done, and aimed it at the fire. He did not throw it there, however, but tossed it carelessly into the well of the desk, and laughed again. The sheer folly of the thing offended him, and he was ashamed of his own eager speculation, as one who pores over the high-sounding announcements in the agony column of the daily paper, and finds nothing but advertisement and triviality. He walked to the window, and stared out at the languid morning life of his quarter; the maids in slatternly print dresses washing door-steps, the fishmonger and the butcher on their rounds, and the tradesmen standing at the doors of their small shops, drooping for lack of trade and excitement. In the distance a blue haze gave some grandeur to the prospect, but the view as a whole was depressing, and would only have interested a student of the life of London, who finds something rare and choice in its every aspect. Salisbury turned away in disgust, and settled himself in the easy-chair, upholstered in a bright shade of green, and decked with yellow gimp, which was the pride and attraction of the apartments. Here he composed himself to his morning's occupation—the perusal of a novel that dealt with sport and love in a manner that suggested the collaboration of a stud-groom and a ladies' college. In an ordinary way, however, Salisbury would have been carried on by the interest of the story up to lunch-time, but this morning he fidgeted in and out of his chair, took the book up and laid it down again, and swore at last to himself and at himself in mere irritation. In point of fact the jingle of the paper found in the archway had "got into his head", and do what he would he could not help muttering over and over, "Once around the grass, and twice around the lass, and thrice around the maple-tree." It became a positive pain, like the foolish burden of a music-hall song, everlastingly quoted, and sung at all hours of the day and night, and treasured by the street boys as an unfailing resource for six months together. He went out into the streets, and tried to forget his enemy in the jostling of the crowds and the roar and clatter of the traffic, but presently he would find himself stealing quietly aside, and pacing some deserted byway, vainly puzzling his brains, and trying to fix some meaning to phrases that were meaningless. It was a positive relief when Thursday came, and he remembered that he had made an appointment to go and see Dyson; the flimsy reveries of the self-styled man of letters appeared entertaining when compared with this ceaseless iteration, this maze of thought from which there seemed no possibility of escape. Dyson's abode was in one of the quietest of the quiet streets that lead down from the Strand to the river, and when Salisbury passed from the narrow stairway into his friend's room, he saw that the uncle had been beneficent indeed. The floor glowed and flamed with all the colours of the East; it was, as Dyson pompously remarked, "a sunset in a dream", and the lamplight, the twilight of London streets, was shut out with strangely worked curtains, glittering here and there with threads of gold. In the shelves of an oak *armoire* stood jars and plates of old French china, and the black and white of etchings not to be found in the Haymarket or in Bond Street, stood out against the splendour of a Japanese paper. Salisbury sat down on the settle by the hearth, and sniffed the mingled fumes of incense and tobacco, wondering and dumb before all this splendour after the green rep and the oleographs, the gilt-framed mirror, and the lustres of his own apartment.

"I am glad you have come,' said Dyson. "Comfortable little room, isn't it? But you don't look very well, Salisbury. Nothing disagreed with you, has it?"

"No; but I have been a good deal bothered for the last few days. The fact is I had an odd kind of—of—adventure, I suppose I may call it, that night I saw you, and it has worried me a good deal. And the provoking part of it is that it's the merest nonsense—but, however, I will tell you all about it, by and by. You were going to let me have the rest of that odd story you began at the restaurant."

"Yes. But I am afraid, Salisbury, you are incorrigible. You are a slave to what you call matter of fact. You know perfectly well that in your heart you think the oddness in that case is of my making, and that it is all really as plain as the police reports. However, as I have begun, I will go on. But first we will have something to drink, and you may as well light your pipe."

Dyson went up to the oak cupboard, and drew from its depths a rotund bottle and two little glasses, quaintly gilded.

"It's Benedictine," he said. "You'll have some, won't you?"

Salisbury assented, and the two men sat sipping and smoking reflectively for some minutes before Dyson began.

"Let me see," he said at last, "we were at the inquest, weren't we? No, we had done with that. Ah, I remember. I was telling you that on the whole I had been successful in my enquiries, investigation, or whatever you like to call it, into the matter. Wasn't that where I left off?"

"Yes, that was it. To be precise, I think 'though' was the last word you said on the matter."

"Exactly. I have been thinking it all over since the other night, and I have come to the conclusion that that 'though' is a very big 'though' indeed. Not to put too fine a point on it, I have had to confess that what I found out, or thought I found out, amounts in reality to nothing. I am as far away from the heart of the case as ever. However, I may as well tell you what I do know. You may remember my saying that I was impressed a good deal by some remarks of one of the doctors who gave evidence at the inquest. Well, I determined that my first step must be to try if I could get something more definite and intelligible out of that doctor. Somehow or other I managed to get an introduction to the man, and he gave me an appointment to come and see him. He turned out to be a pleasant, genial fellow; rather young and not in the least like the typical medical man, and he began the conference by offering me whisky and cigars. I didn't think it worth while to beat about the bush, so I began by saying that part of his evidence at the Harlesden inquest struck me as very peculiar, and I gave him the printed report, with the sentences in question underlined. He just glanced at the slip, and gave me a queer look. 'It struck you as peculiar, did it?' said he. 'Well, you must remember that the Harlesden case was very peculiar. In fact, I think I may safely say that in some features it was unique—quite unique.' 'Quite so,' I replied, 'and that's exactly why it interests me, and why I want to know more about it. And I thought that if anybody could give me any information it would be you. What is your opinion of the matter?'

"It was a pretty downright sort of question, and my doctor looked rather taken aback.

"'Well,' he said, 'as I fancy your motive in enquiring into the question must be mere curiosity, I think I may tell you my opinion with tolerable freedom. So, Mr., Mr. Dyson? if you want to know my theory, it is this: I believe that Dr. Black killed his wife.'

"'But the verdict,' I answered, 'the verdict was given from your own evidence.'

"'Quite so; the verdict was given in accordance with the evidence of my colleague and myself, and, under the circumstances, I think the jury acted very sensibly. In fact, I don't see what else they could have done. But I stick to my opinion, mind you, and I say this also. I don't wonder at Black's doing what I firmly believe he did. I think he was justified.'

"'Justified! How could that be?' I asked. I was astonished, as you may imagine, at the answer I had got. The doctor wheeled round his chair and looked steadily at me for a moment before he answered.

"'I suppose you are not a man of science yourself? No; then it would be of no use my going into detail. I have always been firmly opposed myself to any partnership between physiology and psychology. I believe that both are bound to suffer. No one recognises more decidedly than I do the impassable gulf, the fathomless abyss that separates the world of consciousness from the sphere of matter. We know that every change of consciousness is accompanied by a rearrangement of the molecules in the grey matter; and that is all. What the link between them is, or why they occur together, we do not know, and most authorities believe that we never can know. Yet, I will tell you that as I did my work, the knife in my hand, I felt convinced, in spite of all theories, that what lay before me was not the brain of a dead woman—

not the brain of a human being at all. Of course I saw the face; but it was quite placid, devoid of all expression. It must have been a beautiful face, no doubt, but I can honestly say that I would not have looked in that face when there was life behind it for a thousand guineas, no, nor for twice that sum.'

"'My dear sir,' I said, 'you surprise me extremely. You say that it was not the brain of a human being. What was it, then?'

"'The brain of a devil.' He spoke quite coolly, and never moved a muscle. 'The brain of a devil,' he repeated, 'and I have no doubt that Black found some way of putting an end to it. I don't blame him if he did. Whatever Mrs. Black was, she was not fit to stay in this world. Will you have anything more? No? Good-night, good-night.'

"It was a queer sort of opinion to get from a man of science, wasn't it? When he was saying that he would not have looked on that face when alive for a thousand guineas, or two thousand guineas, I was thinking of the face I had seen, but I said nothing. I went again to Harlesden, and passed from one shop to another, making small purchases, and trying to find out whether there was anything about the Blacks which was not already common property, but there was very little to hear. One of the tradesmen to whom I spoke said he had known the dead woman well; she used to buy of him such quantities of grocery as were required for their small household, for they never kept a servant, but had a charwoman in occasionally, and she had not seen Mrs. Black for months before she died. According to this man Mrs. Black was 'a nice lady', always kind and considerate, and so fond of her husband and he of her, as every one thought. And yet, to put the doctor's opinion on one side, I knew what I had seen. And then after thinking it over, and putting one thing with another, it seemed to me that the only person likely to give me much assistance would be Black himself, and I made up my mind to find him. Of course he wasn't to be found in Harlesden; he had left, I was told, directly after the funeral. Everything in the house had been sold, and one fine day Black got into the train with a small portmanteau, and went, nobody knew where. It was a chance if he were ever heard of again, and it was by a mere chance that I came across him at last. I was walking one day along Gray's Inn Road, not bound for anywhere in particular, but looking about me, as usual, and holding on to my hat, for it was a gusty day in early March, and the wind was making the treetops in the Inn rock and quiver. I had come up from the Holborn end, and I had almost got to Theobald's Road when I noticed a man walking in front of me, leaning on a stick, and to all appearance very feeble. There was something about his look that made me curious, I don't know why, and I began to walk briskly with the idea of overtaking him, when of a sudden his hat blew off and came bounding along the pavement to my feet. Of course I rescued the hat, and gave it a glance as I went towards its owner. It was a biography in itself; a Piccadilly maker's name in the inside, but I don't think a beggar would have picked it out of the gutter. Then I looked up and saw Dr. Black of Harlesden waiting for me. A queer thing, wasn't it? But, Salisbury, what a change! When I saw Dr. Black come down the steps of his house at Harlesden he was an upright man, walking firmly with well-built limbs; a man, should say, in the prime of his life. And now before me there crouched this wretched creature, bent and feeble, with shrunken cheeks, and hair that was whitening fast, and limbs that trembled and shook together, and misery in his eyes. He thanked me for bringing him his hat, saying, 'I don't think I should ever have got it, I can't run much now. A gusty day, sir, isn't it?' and with this he was turning away, but by little and little I contrived to draw him into the current of conversation, and we walked together eastward. I think the man would have been glad to get rid of me; but I didn't intend to let him go, and he stopped at last in front of a miserable house in a miserable street. It was, I verily believe, one of the most wretched quarters I have ever seen: houses that must have been sordid and hideous enough when new, that had gathered foulness with every year, and now seemed to lean and totter to their fall. 'I live up there,' said Black, pointing to the tiles, 'not in the front—in the back. I am very quiet there. I won't ask you to come in now, but perhaps some other day—' I caught him up at that, and told him I should be only too glad to come and see him. He gave me an odd sort of glance, as if he were wondering what on earth I or anybody else could care about him, and I left him fumbling with his latch-key. I think you will say I did pretty well when I tell you that within a few weeks I had made myself an intimate friend of Black's. I shall never forget the first time I went to his room; I hope I shall never see such abject, squalid misery again. The foul paper, from which all pattern or trace of a pattern had long vanished, subdued and penetrated with the grime of the evil street, was hanging in mouldering pennons from the wall. Only at the end of the room was it possible to stand upright, and the sight of the wretched bed and the odour of corruption that pervaded the place made me turn faint and sick. Here I found him munching a piece of bread; he seemed surprised to find that I had kept my promise, but he gave me his chair and sat on the bed while we talked. I used to go to see him often, and we had long conversations together, but he never mentioned Harlesden or his wife. I fancy that he supposed me ignorant of the matter, or thought that if I had heard of it, I should never connect the respectable Dr. Black of Harlesden with a poor garreteer in the backwoods of London. He was a strange man, and as we sat together smoking, I often wondered whether he were mad or sane, for I think the wildest dreams of Paracelsus and the Rosicrucians would appear plain and sober fact compared with the theories I have heard him earnestly advance in that grimy den of his. I once ventured to hint something of the sort to him. I suggested that something he had said was in flat contradiction to all science and all experience. 'No,' he answered, 'not all experience, for mine counts for something. I am no dealer in unproved theories; what I say I have proved for myself, and at a terrible cost. There is a region of knowledge which you will never know, which wise men seeing from afar off shun like the plague, as well they may, but into that region I have gone. If you knew, if you could even dream of what may be done, of what one or two men have done in this quiet world of ours, your very soul would shudder and faint within you. What you have heard from me has been but the merest husk and outer covering of true science—that science which means death, and that which is more awful than death, to those who gain it. No, when men say that there are strange things in the world, they little know the awe and the terror that dwell always with them and about them.' There was a sort of fascination about the man that drew me to him, and I was quite sorry to have to leave London for a month or two; I missed his odd talk. A few days after I came back to town I thought I would look him up, but when I gave the two rings at the bell that used to summon him, there was no answer. I rang and rang again, and was just turning to go away, when the door opened and a dirty woman asked me what I wanted. From her look I fancy she took me for a plain-clothes officer after one of her lodgers, but when I enquired if Mr. Black were in, she gave me a stare of another kind. 'There's no Mr. Black lives here,' she said. 'He's gone. He's dead this six weeks. I always thought he was a bit queer in his head, or else had been and got into some trouble or other. He used to go out every morning from ten till one, and one Monday morning we heard him come in, and go into his room and shut the door, and a few minutes after, just as we was a-sitting down to our dinner, there was such a scream that I thought I should have gone right off. And then we heard a stamping, and down he came, raging and cursing most dreadful, swearing he had been robbed of something that was worth millions. And then he just dropped down in the passage, and we thought he was dead. We got him up to his room, and put him on his bed, and I just sat there and waited, while my 'usband he went for the doctor. And there was the winder wide open, and a little tin box he had lying on the floor open and empty, but of course nobody could possible have got in at the winder, and as for him having anything that was worth anything, it's nonsense, for he was often weeks and weeks behind with his rent, and my 'usband he threatened often and often to turn him into the street, for, as he said, we've got a living to myke like other people—and, of course, that's true; but, somehow, I didn't like to do it, though he was an odd kind of a man, and I fancy had been better off. And then the doctor came and looked at him, and said as he couldn't do nothing, and that night he died as I was a-sitting by his bed; and I can tell you that, with one thing and another, we lost money by him, for the few bits of clothes as he had were worth next to nothing when they came to be sold.' I gave the woman half a sovereign for her trouble, and went home thinking of Dr. Black and the epitaph she had made him, and wondering at his strange fancy that he had been robbed. I take it that he had very little to fear on that score, poor fellow; but I suppose that he was really mad, and died in a sudden access of his mania. His landlady said that once or twice when she had had occasion to go into his room (to dun the poor wretch for his rent, most likely), he would keep her at the door for about a minute, and that when she came in she would find him putting away his tin box in the corner by the window; I suppose he had become possessed with the idea of some great treasure, and fancied himself a wealthy man in the midst of all his misery. *Explicit,* my tale is ended, and you see that though I knew Black, I knew nothing of his wife or of the history of her death.—That's the Harlesden case, Salisbury, and I think it interests me all the more deeply because there does not seem the shadow of a possibility that I or any one else will ever know more about it. What do you think of it?"

"Well, Dyson, I must say that I think you have contrived to surround the whole thing with a mystery of your own making. I go for the doctor's solution: Black murdered his wife, being himself in all probability an undeveloped lunatic."

"What? Do you believe, then, that this woman was something too awful, too terrible to be allowed to remain on the earth? You will remember that the doctor said it was the brain of a devil?"

"Yes, yes, but he was speaking, of course, metaphorically. It's really quite a simple matter if you only look at it like that."

"Ah, well, you may be right; but yet I am sure you are not. Well, well, it's not good discussing it any more. A little more Benedictine? That's right; try some of this tobacco. Didn't you say that you had been bothered by something—something which happened that night we dined together?"

"Yes, I have been worried, Dyson, worried a great deal. I— But it's such a trivial matter—indeed, such an absurdity—that I feel ashamed to trouble you with it."

"Never mind, let's have it, absurd or not."

With many hesitations, and with much inward resentment of the folly of the thing, Salisbury told his tale, and repeated reluctantly the absurd intelligence and the absurder doggerel of the scrap of paper, expecting to hear Dyson burst out into a roar of laughter.

"Isn't it too bad that I should let myself be bothered by such stuff as that?" he asked, when he had stuttered out the jingle of once, and twice, and thrice.

Dyson had listened to it all gravely, even to the end, and meditated for a few minutes in silence.

"Yes," he said at length, "it was a curious chance, your taking shelter in that archway just as those two went by. But I don't know that I should call what was written on the paper nonsense; it is bizarre certainly, but I expect it has a meaning for somebody. Just repeat it again, will you, and I will write it down. Perhaps we might find a cipher of some sort, though I hardly think we shall."

Again had the reluctant lips of Salisbury slowly to stammer out the rubbish that he abhorred, while Dyson jotted it down on a slip of paper.

"Look over it, will you?" he said, when it was done; "it may be important that I should have every word in its place. Is that all right?"

"Yes; that is an accurate copy. But I don't think you will get much out of it. Depend upon it, it is mere nonsense, a wanton scribble. I must be going now, Dyson. No, no more; that stuff of yours is pretty strong. Good-night."

"I suppose you would like to hear from me, if I did find out anything?"

"No, not I; I don't want to hear about the thing again. You may regard the discovery, if it is one, as your own."

"Very well. Good-night."

IV

A good many hours after Salisbury had returned to the company of the green rep chairs, Dyson still sat at his desk, itself a Japanese romance, smoking many pipes, and meditating over his friend's story. The bizarre quality of the inscription which had annoyed Salisbury was to him an attraction, and now and again he took it up and scanned thoughtfully what he had written, especially the quaint jingle at the end. It was a token, a symbol, he decided, and not a cipher, and the woman who had flung it away was in all probability entirely ignorant of its meaning; she was but the agent of the "Sam" she had abused and discarded, and he too was again the agent of some one unknown; possibly of the individual styled Q, who had been forced to visit his French friends. But what to make of "Traverse Handel S." Here was the root and source of the enigma, and not all the tobacco of Virginia seemed likely to suggest any clue here. It seemed almost hopeless, but Dyson regarded himself as the Wellington of mysteries, and went to bed feeling assured that sooner or later he would hit upon the right track. For the next few days he was deeply engaged in his literary labours, labours which were a profound mystery even to the most intimate of his friends, who searched the railway bookstalls in vain for the result of so many hours spent at the Japanese bureau in company with strong tobacco and black tea. On this occasion Dyson confined himself to his room for four days, and it was with genuine relief that he laid down his pen and went out into the streets in quest of relaxation and fresh air. The gas-lamps were being lighted, and the fifth edition of the evening papers was being howled through the streets, and Dyson, feeling that he wanted quiet, turned away from the clamorous Strand, and began to trend away to the north-west. Soon he found himself in streets that echoed to his footsteps, and crossing a broad new thoroughfare, and verging still to the west, Dyson discovered that he had penetrated to the depths of Soho. Here again was life; rare vintages of France and Italy, at prices which seemed contemptibly small, allured the passer-by; here were cheeses, vast and rich, here olive oil, and here a grove of Rabelaisian sausages; while in a neighbouring shop the whole Press of Paris appeared to be on sale. In the middle of the roadway a strange miscellany of nations sauntered to and fro, for there cab and hansom rarely ventured; and from window over window the inhabitants looked forth in pleased contemplation of the scene. Dyson made his way slowly along, mingling with the crowd on the cobblestones, listening to the queer babel of French and German, and Italian and English, glancing now and again at the shop-windows with their levelled batteries of bottles, and had almost gained the end of the street, when his attention was arrested by a small shop at the corner, a vivid contrast to its neighbours. It was the typical shop of the poor quarter; a shop entirely English. Here were vended tobacco and sweets, cheap pipes of clay and cherrywood; penny exercise-books and pen-holders jostled for precedence with comic songs, and story papers with appalling cuts shewed that romance claimed its place beside the actualities of the evening paper, the bills of which fluttered at the doorway. Dyson glanced up at the name above the door, and stood by the kennel trembling, for a sharp pang, the pang of one who has made a discovery, had for a moment left him incapable of motion. The name over the shop was Travers. Dyson looked up again, this time at the corner of the wall above the lamp-post, and read in white letters on a blue ground the words "Handel Street, W.C.", and the legend was repeated in fainter letters just below. He gave a little sigh of satisfaction, and without more ado walked boldly into the shop, and stared full in the face of the fat man who was sitting behind the counter. The fellow rose to his feet, and returned the stare a little curiously, and then began in stereotyped phrase—

"What can I do for you, sir?"

Dyson enjoyed the situation and a dawning perplexity on the man's face. He propped his stick carefully against the counter and leaning over it, said slowly and impressively—

"Once around the grass, and twice around the lass, and thrice around the maple-tree."

Dyson had calculated on his words producing an effect, and he was not disappointed. The vendor of the miscellanies gasped, openmouthed like a fish, and steadied himself against the counter. When he spoke, after a short interval, it was in a hoarse mutter, tremulous and unsteady.

"Would you mind saying that again, sir? I didn't quite catch it."

"My good man, I shall most certainly do nothing of the kind. You heard what I said perfectly well. You have got a clock in your shop, I see; an admirable timekeeper, I have no doubt. Well, I give you a minute by your own clock."

The man looked about him in a perplexed indecision, and Dyson felt that it was time to be bold.

"Look here, Travers, the time is nearly up. You have heard of Q, I think. Remember, I hold your life in my hands. Now!"

Dyson was shocked at the result of his own audacity. The man shrank and shrivelled in terror, the sweat poured down a face of ashy white, and he held up his hands before him.

"Mr. Davies, Mr. Davies, don't say that—don't for Heaven's sake. I didn't know you at first, I didn't indeed. Good God! Mr. Davies, you wouldn't ruin me? I'll get it in a moment."

"You had better not lose any more time."

The man slunk piteously out of his own shop, and went into a back parlour. Dyson heard his trembling fingers fumbling with a bunch of keys, and the creak of an opening box. He came back presently with a small package neatly tied up in brown paper in his hands, and still, full of terror, handed it to Dyson.

"I'm glad to be rid of it," he said. "I'll take no more jobs of this sort."

Dyson took the parcel and his stick, and walked out of the shop with a nod, turning round as he passed the door. Travers had sunk into his seat, his face still white with terror, with one hand over his eyes, and Dyson speculated a good deal as he walked rapidly away as to what queer chords those could be on which he had played so roughly. He hailed the first hansom he could see and drove home, and when he had lit his hanging lamp, and laid his parcel on the table, he paused for a moment, wondering on what strange thing the lamplight would soon shine. He locked his door, and cut the strings, and unfolded the paper layer after layer, and came at last to a small wooden box, simply but solidly made. There was no lock, and Dyson had simply to raise the lid, and as he did so he drew a long breath and started back. The lamp seemed to glimmer feebly like a single candle, but the whole room blazed with light—and not with light alone, but with a thousand colours, with all the glories of some painted window; and upon the walls of his room and on the familiar furniture, the glow flamed back and seemed to flow again to its source, the little wooden box. For there upon a bed of soft wool lay the most splendid jewel, a jewel such as Dyson had never dreamed of, and within it shone the blue of far skies, and the green of the sea by the shore, and the red of the ruby, and deep violet rays, and in the middle of all it seemed aflame as if a fountain of fire rose up, and fell, and rose again with sparks like stars for drops. Dyson gave a long deep sigh, and dropped into his chair, and put his hands over his eyes to think. The jewel was like an opal, but from a long experience of the shop-windows he knew there was no such thing as an opal one-quarter or one-eighth of its size. He looked at the stone again, with a feeling that was almost awe, and placed it gently on the table under the lamp, and watched the wonderful flame that shone and sparkled in its centre, and then turned to the box, curious to know whether it might contain other marvels. He lifted the bed of wool on which the opal had reclined, and saw beneath, no more jewels, but a little old pocket-book, worn and shabby with use. Dyson opened it at the first leaf, and dropped the book again appalled. He had read the name of the owner, neatly written in blue ink:

> STEVEN BLACK, M.D.,
> Oranmore,
> Devon Road,
> Harlesden.

It was several minutes before Dyson could bring himself to open the book a second time; he remembered the wretched exile in his garret; and his strange talk, and the memory too of the face he had seen at the window, and of what the specialist had said, surged up in his mind, and as he held his finger on the cover, he shivered, dreading what might be written within. When at last he held it in his hand, and turned the pages, he found that the first two leaves were blank, but the third was covered with clear, minute writing, and Dyson began to read with the light of the opal flaming in his eyes.

V

"Ever since I was a young man"—the record began—"I devoted all my leisure and a good deal of time that ought to have been given to other studies to the investigation of curious and obscure branches of knowledge. What are commonly called the pleasures of life had never any attractions for me, and I lived alone in London, avoiding my fellow-students, and in my turn avoided by them as a man self-absorbed and unsympathetic. So long as I could gratify my desire of knowledge of a peculiar kind, knowledge of which the very existence is a profound secret to most men, I was intensely happy, and I have often spent whole nights sitting in the darkness of my room, and thinking of the strange world on the brink of which I trod. My professional studies, however, and the necessity of obtaining a degree, for some time forced my more obscure employment into the background, and soon after I had qualified I met Agnes, who became my wife. We took a new house in this remote suburb, and I began the regular routine of a sober practice, and for some months lived happily enough, sharing in the life about me, and only thinking at odd intervals of that occult science which had once fascinated my whole being. I had learnt enough of the paths I had begun to tread to know that they were beyond all expression difficult and dangerous, that to persevere meant in all probability the wreck of a life, and that they led to regions so terrible, that the mind of man shrinks appalled at the very thought. Moreover, the quiet and the peace I had enjoyed since my marriage had wiled me away to a great extent from places where I knew no peace could dwell. But suddenly—I think indeed it was the work of a single night, as I lay awake on my

bed gazing into the darkness—suddenly, I say, the old desire, the former longing, returned, and returned with a force that had been intensi-
fied ten times by its absence; and when the day dawned and I looked
out of the window, and saw with haggard eyes the sunrise in the east, I
knew that my doom had been pronounced; that as I had gone far, so
now I must go farther with unfaltering steps. I turned to the bed where
my wife was sleeping peacefully, and lay down again, weeping bitter
tears, for the sun had set on our happy life and had risen with a dawn
of terror to us both. I will not set down here in minute detail what followed; outwardly I went about the day's labour as before, saying nothing to my wife. But she soon saw that I had changed; I spent my spare
time in a room which I had fitted up as a laboratory, and often I crept
upstairs in the grey dawn of the morning, when the light of many
lamps still glowed over London; and each night I had stolen a step
nearer to that great abyss which I was to bridge over, the gulf between
the world of consciousness and the world of matter. My experiments
were many and complicated in their nature, and it was some months
before I realised whither they all pointed, and when this was borne in
upon me in a moment's time, I felt my face whiten and my heart still
within me. But the power to draw back, the power to stand before the
doors that now opened wide before me and not to enter in, had long
ago been absent; the way was closed, and I could only pass onward.
My position was as utterly hopeless as that of the prisoner in an utter
dungeon, whose only light is that of the dungeon above him; the doors
were shut and escape was impossible. Experiment after experiment
gave the same result, and I knew, and shrank even as the thought
passed through my mind, that in the work I had to do there must be
elements which no laboratory could furnish, which no scales could ever measure. In that work, from which even I doubted to escape with
life, life itself must enter; from some human being there must be
drawn that essence which men call the soul, and in its place (for in the
scheme of the world there is no vacant chamber)—in its place would
enter in what the lips can hardly utter, what the mind cannot conceive
without a horror more awful than the horror of death itself. And when
I knew this, I knew also on whom this fate would fall; I looked into my
wife's eyes. Even at that hour, if I had gone out and taken a rope and
hanged myself, I might have escaped, and she also, but in no other

way. At last I told her all. She shuddered, and wept, and called on her dead mother for help, and asked me if I had no mercy, and I could only sigh. I concealed nothing from her; I told her what she would become, and what would enter in where her life had been; I told her of all the shame and of all the horror. You who will read this when I am dead—if indeed I allow this record to survive—you who have opened the box and have seen what lies there, if you could understand what lies hidden in that opal! For one night my wife consented to what I asked of her, consented with the tears running down her beautiful face, and hot shame flushing red over her neck and breast, consented to undergo this for me. I threw open the window, and we looked together at the sky and the dark earth for the last time; it was a fine star-light night, and there was a pleasant breeze blowing, and I kissed her on her lips, and her tears ran down upon my face. That night she came down to my laboratory, and there, with shutters bolted and barred down, with curtains drawn thick and close, so that the very stars might be shut out from the sight of that room, while the crucible hissed and boiled over the lamp, I did what had to be done, and led out what was no longer a woman. But on the table the opal flamed and sparkled with such light as no eyes of man have ever gazed on, and the rays of the flame that was within it flashed and glittered, and shone even to my heart. My wife had only asked one thing of me; that when there came at last what I had told her, I would kill her. I have kept that promise."

There was nothing more. Dyson let the little pocket-book fall, and turned and looked again at the opal with its flaming inmost light, and then with unutterable irresistible horror surging up in his heart, grasped the jewel, and flung it on the ground, and trampled it beneath his heel. His face was white with terror as he turned away, and for a moment stood sick and trembling, and then with a start he leapt across the room and steadied himself against the door. There was an angry hiss, as of steam escaping under great pressure, and as he gazed, motionless, a volume of heavy yellow smoke was slowly issuing from the very centre of the jewel, and wreathing itself in snakelike coils above it. And then a thin white flame burst forth from the smoke, and shot up into the air and vanished; and on the ground there lay a thing like a cinder, black and crumbling to the touch.

The Three Impostors;
or, The Transmutations

PROLOGUE

And Mr. Joseph Walters is going to stay the night?" said the smooth, clean-shaven man to his companion, an individual not of the most charming appearance, who had chosen to make his ginger-coloured moustache merge into a pair of short chin-whiskers.

The two stood at the hall door, grinning evilly at each other; and presently a girl ran quickly down the stairs, and joined them. She was quite young, with a quaint and piquant rather than a beautiful face, and her eyes were of a shining hazel. She held a neat paper parcel in one hand, and laughed with her friends.

"Leave the door open," said the smooth man to the other, as they were going out. "Yes, by ——," he went on with an ugly oath, "we'll leave the front door on the jar. He may like to see company, you know."

The other man looked doubtfully about him.

"Is it quite prudent, do you think, Davies," he said, pausing with his hand on the mouldering knocker. "I don't think Lipsius would like it. What do you say, Helen?"

"I agree with Davies. Davies is an artist, and you are common-place, Richmond, and a bit of a coward. Let the door stand open, of course. But what a pity Lipsius had to go away! He would have enjoyed himself."

"Yes," replied the smooth Mr. Davies, "that summons to the west was very hard on the doctor."

The three passed out, leaving the hall door, cracked and riven with frost and wet, half-open, and they stood silent for a moment under the ruinous shelter of the porch.

"Well," said the girl, "it is done at last. We shall hurry no more on the track of the young man with spectacles."

"We owe a great deal to you," said Mr. Davies politely; "the doctor said so before he left. But have we not all three some farewells to make? I, for my part, propose to say good-bye here, before this picturesque but mouldy residence, to my friend, Mr. Burton, dealer in the antique and curious," and the man lifted his hat with an exaggerated bow.

"And I," said Richmond, "bid adieu to Mr. Wilkins, the private secretary, whose company has, I confess, become a little tedious."

"Farewell to Miss Lally, and to Miss Leicester also," said the girl, making as she spoke a delicious curtsy. "Farewell to all occult adventure; the farce is played."

Mr. Davies and the lady seemed full of grim enjoyment, but Richmond tugged at his whiskers nervously.

"I feel a bit shaken up," he said. "I've seen rougher things in the States, but that crying noise he made gave me a sickish feeling. And then the smell—; but my stomach was never very strong."

The three friends moved away from the door, and began to walk slowly up and down what had been a gravel path, but now lay green and pulpy with damp mosses. It was a fine autumn evening, and a faint sunlight shone on the yellow walls of the old deserted house, and shewed the patches of gangrenous decay, and all the stains, the black drift of rain from the broken pipes, the scabrous blots where the bare bricks were exposed, the green weeping of a gaunt laburnum that stood beside the porch, and ragged marks near the ground where the reeking clay was gaining on the worn foundations. It was a queer, rambling old place, the centre perhaps two hundred years old, with dormer windows sloping from the tiled roof, and on each side there were Georgian wings; bow windows had been carried up to the first floor, and two dome-like cupolas that had once been painted a bright green were now grey and neutral. Broken urns lay upon the path, and a heavy mist seemed to rise from the unctuous clay; the neglected shrubberies, grown all tangled and unshapen, smelt dank and evil, and there was an atmosphere all about the deserted mansion that proposed thoughts of an open grave. The three friends looked dismally at the rough grasses and the nettles that grew thick over lawn and flower-beds; and at the sad water-pool in the midst of the weeds. There, above green and oily scum instead of lilies, stood a rusting Triton on the rocks, sounding a dirge through a shattered horn; and beyond, beyond the sunk fence and the far meadows, the sun slid down and shone red through the bars of the elm-trees.

Richmond shivered and stamped his foot.

"We had better be going soon," he said; "there is nothing else to be done here."

"No," said Davies; "it is finished at last. I thought for some time we should never get hold of the gentleman with the spectacles. He was a clever fellow, but, Lord! he broke up badly at last. I can tell you, he looked white at me when I touched him on the arm in the bar. But where could he have hidden the thing? We can all swear it was not on him."

The girl laughed, and they turned away, when Richmond gave a violent start.

"Ah!" he cried, turning to the girl, "what have you got there? Look, Davies, look; it's all oozing and dripping."

The young woman glanced down at the little parcel she was carrying, and partially unfolded the paper.

"Yes, look, both of you," she said; "it's my own idea. Don't you think it will do nicely for the doctor's museum? It comes from the right hand, the hand that took the Gold Tiberius."

Mr. Davies nodded with a good deal of approbation, and Richmond lifted his ugly high-crowned bowler, and wiped his forehead with a dingy handkerchief.

"I'm going," he said; "you two can stay if you like."

The three went round by the stable-path, past the withered wilderness of the old kitchen-garden, and struck off by a hedge at the back, making for a particular point in the road. About five minutes later two gentlemen, whom idleness had led to explore these forgotten outskirts of London, came sauntering up the shadowy carriage-drive. They had spied the deserted house from the road, and as they observed all the heavy desolation of the place, they began to moralise in the great style, with considerable debts to Jeremy Taylor.

"Look, Dyson," said the one, as they drew nearer; "look at those upper windows; the sun is setting, and, though the panes are dusty, yet—

'The grimy sash an oriel burns.'"

"Phillipps," replied the elder and (it must be said) the more pompous of the two, "I yield to fantasy; I cannot withstand the influence of the grotesque. Here, where all is falling into dimness and dissolution, and we walk in cedarn gloom, and the very air of heaven goes mouldering to the lungs, I cannot remain commonplace. I look at that deep glow on the panes, and the house lies all enchanted; that very room, I tell you, is within all blood and fire."

ADVENTURE OF THE GOLD TIBERIUS

The acquaintance between Mr. Dyson and Mr. Charles Phillipps arose from one of those myriad chances which are every day doing their work in the streets of London. Mr. Dyson was a man of letters, and an unhappy instance of talents misapplied. With gifts that might have placed him in the flower of his youth among the most favoured of Bentley's favourite novelists, he had chosen to be perverse; he was, it is true, familiar with scholastic logic, but he knew nothing of the logic of life, and he flattered himself with the title of artist, when he was in fact but an idle and curious spectator of other men's endeavours. Amongst many delusions, he cherished one most fondly, that he was a strenuous worker; and it was with a gesture of supreme weariness that he would enter his favourite resort, a small tobacco-shop in Great Queen Street, and proclaim to any one who cared to listen that he had seen the rising and setting of two successive suns. The proprietor of the shop, a middle-aged man of singular civility, tolerated Dyson partly out of good nature, and partly because he was a regular customer. He was allowed to sit on an empty cask, and to express his sentiments on literary and artistic matters till he was tired, or the time for closing came; and if no fresh customers were attracted, it is believed that none was turned away by his eloquence. Dyson was addicted to wild experiments in tobacco; he never wearied of trying new combinations; and one evening he had just entered the shop, and given utterance to his last preposterous formula, when a young fellow, of about his own age, who had come in a moment later, asked the shopman to duplicate the order on his account, smiling politely, as he spoke, to Mr. Dyson's address. Dyson felt profoundly flattered, and after a few phrases the two entered into conversation, and in an hour's time the tobacconist saw the new friends sitting side by side on a couple of casks, deep in talk.

"My dear sir," said Dyson, "I will give you the task of the literary man in a phrase. He has got to do simply this—to invent a wonderful story, and to tell it in a wonderful manner."

"I will grant you that," said Mr. Phillipps, "but you will allow me to insist that in the hands of the true artist in words all stories are marvellous, and every circumstance has its peculiar wonder. The matter is of little consequence, the manner is everything. Indeed, the highest skill is shewn in taking matter apparently commonplace and transmuting it by the high alchemy of style into the pure gold of art."

"That is indeed a proof of great skill, but it is great skill exerted foolishly, or at least unadvisedly. It is as if a great violinist were to shew us what marvellous harmonies he could draw from a child's banjo."

"No, no, you are really wrong. I see you take a radically mistaken view of life. But we must thresh this out. Come to my rooms; I live not far from here."

It was thus that Mr. Dyson became the associate of Mr. Charles Phillipps, who lived in a quiet square not far from Holborn. Thenceforth they haunted each other's rooms at intervals, sometimes regular, and occasionally the reverse, and made appointments to meet at the shop in Queen Street, where their talk robbed the tobacconist's profit of half its charm. There was a constant jarring of literary formulas, Dyson exalting the claims of the pure imagination; while Phillipps, who was a student of physical science, and something of an ethnologist, insisted that all literature ought to have a scientific basis. By the mistaken benevolence of deceased relatives both young men were placed out of reach of hunger, and so, meditating high achievements, idled their time pleasantly away, and revelled in the careless joys of a Bohemianism devoid of the sharp seasoning of adversity.

One night in June Mr. Phillipps was sitting in his room in the calm retirement of Red Lion Square. He had opened the window, and was smoking placidly, while he watched the movement of life below. The sky was clear, and the afterglow of sunset had lingered long about it. The flushing twilight of a summer evening vied with the gas-lamps in the square, and fashioned a chiaroscuro that had in it something unearthly; and the children, racing to and fro upon the pavement, the lounging idlers by the public, and the casual passers-by rather flickered and hovered in the play of lights than stood out substantial things. By degrees in the houses opposite one window after another leapt out a square of light; now and again a figure would shape itself against a blind and vanish, and to all this semi-theatrical magic the runs and flourishes of brave Italian opera played a little distance off on a piano-organ seemed an appropriate accompaniment, while the deep-muttered bass of the traffic of Holborn never ceased. Phillipps enjoyed the scene and its effects; the light in the sky faded and turned to darkness, and the square gradually grew silent, and still he sat dreaming at the window, till the sharp peal of the house-bell roused him, and looking at his watch, he found that it was past ten o'clock. There was a knock at the door, and his friend Mr. Dyson entered, and, according to his custom, sat down in an arm-chair and began to smoke in silence.

"You know, Phillipps," he said at length, "that I have always battled for the marvellous. I remember your maintaining in that chair that one has no business to make use of the wonderful, the improbable, the odd coincidence in literature, and you took the ground that it was wrong to do so, because as a matter of fact the wonderful and the improbable don't happen, and men's lives are not really shaped by odd coincidence. Now, mind you, if that were so, I would not grant your conclusion, because I think the 'criticism-of-life' theory is all nonsense; but I deny your premiss. A most singular thing has happened to me to-night."

"Really, Dyson, I am very glad to hear it. Of course, I oppose your argument, whatever it may be; but if you would be good enough to tell me of your adventure, I should be delighted."

"Well, it came about like this. I have had a very hard day's work; indeed I have scarcely moved from my old bureau since seven o'clock last night. I wanted to work out that idea we discussed last Tuesday, you know, the notion of the fetish-worshipper?"

"Yes, I remember. Have you been able to do anything with it?"

"Yes; it came out better than I expected; but there were great difficulties, the usual agony between the conception and the execution. Anyhow, I got it done about seven o'clock to-night, and I thought I should like a little of the fresh air. I went out and wandered rather aimlessly about the streets; my head was full of my tale, and I didn't much notice where I was going. I got into those quiet places to the north of

Oxford Street as you go west, the genteel residential neighbourhood of stucco and prosperity. I turned east again without knowing it, and it was quite dark when I passed along a sombre little by-street, ill-lighted and empty. I did not know at the time in the least where I was, but I found out afterwards that it was not very far from Tottenham Court Road. I strolled idly along, enjoying the stillness; on one side there seemed to be the back premises of some great shop; tier after tier of dusty windows lifted up into the night, with gibbet-like contrivances for raising heavy goods, and below large doors, fast closed and bolted, all dark and desolate. Then there came a huge pantechnicon ware-house; and over the way a grim blank wall, as forbidding as the wall of a gaol, and then the headquarters of some volunteer regiment, and af-terwards a passage leading to a court where waggons were standing to be hired; it was, one might almost say, a street devoid of inhabitants, and scarce a window shewed the glimmer of a light. I was wondering at the strange peace and dimness there, where it must be close to some roaring main artery of London life, when suddenly I heard the noise of dashing feet tearing along the pavement at full speed, and from a nar-row passage, a mews or something of that kind, a man was discharged as from a catapult under my very nose, and rushed past me, flinging something from him as he ran. He was gone, and down another street in an instant, almost before I knew what had happened; but I didn't much bother about him, I was watching something else. I told you he had thrown something away; well, I watched what seemed a line of flame flash through the air and fly quivering over the pavement, and in spite of myself I could not help tearing after it. The impetus lessened, and I saw something like a bright halfpenny roll slower and slower, and then deflect towards the gutter, hover for a moment on the edge, and dance down into a drain. I believe I cried out in positive despair, though I hadn't the least notion what I was hunting; and then, to my joy, I saw that, instead of dropping into a sewer, it had fallen flat across two bars. I stooped down and picked it up and whipped it into my pocket, and I was just about to walk on when I heard again that sound of dashing footsteps. I don't know why I did it, but as a matter of fact I dived down into the mews, or whatever it was, and stood as much in the shadow as possible. A man went by with a rush a few paces from where I was standing, and I felt uncommonly pleased that I was hiding. I couldn't make out much feature, but I saw his eyes gleaming and his teeth shewing, and he had an ugly-looking knife in one hand, and I thought things would be very unpleasant for gentleman number one if the second robber, or robbed, or what you like, caught him up. I can tell you, Phillipps, a fox-hunt is exciting enough, when the horn blows clear on a winter morning, and the hounds give tongue, and the red-coats charge away, but it's nothing to a man-hunt, and that's what I had a slight glimpse of to-night. There was murder in the fellow's eyes as he went by, and I don't think there was much more than fifty seconds between the two. I only hope it was enough."

Dyson leant back in his arm-chair, relit his pipe, and puffed thoughtfully. Phillipps began to walk up and down the room, musing over the story of violent death fleeting in chase along the pavement, the knife shining in the lamplight, the fury of the pursuer, and the terror of the pursued.

"Well," he said at last, "and what was it, after all, that you rescued from the gutter?"

Dyson jumped up, evidently quite startled. "I really haven't a notion. I didn't think of looking. But we shall see."

He fumbled in his waistcoat pocket, drew out a small and shining object, and laid it on the table. It glowed there beneath the lamp with the radiant glory of rare old gold; and the image and the letters stood out in high relief, clear and sharp, as if it had but left the mint a month before. The two men bent over it, and Phillipps took it up and examined it closely.

"Imp. Tiberius Cæsar Augustus," he read the legend, and then looking at the reverse of the coin, he stared in amazement, and at last turned to Dyson with a look of exultation.

"Do you know what you have found?" he said.

"Apparently a gold coin of some antiquity," said Dyson coolly.

"Quite so, a gold Tiberius. No, that is wrong. You have found *the* gold Tiberius. Look at the reverse."

Dyson looked and saw the coin was stamped with the figure of a faun standing amidst reeds and flowing water. The features, minute as they were, stood out in delicate outline; it was a face lovely and yet terrible, and Dyson thought of the well-known passage of the lad's play-mate, gradually growing with his growth and increasing with his stature till the air was filled with the rank fume of the goat.

"Yes," he said; "it is a curious coin. Do you know it?"

"I know about it. It is one of the comparatively few historical objects in existence; it is all storied like those jewels we have read of. A whole cycle of legend has gathered round the thing; the tale goes that it formed part of an issue struck by Tiberius to commemorate an infamous excess. You see the legend on the reverse: 'Victoria.' It is said that by an extraordinary accident the whole issue was thrown into the melting-pot, and that only this one coin escaped. It glints through history and legend, appearing and disappearing, with intervals of a hundred years in time, and continents in place. It was 'discovered' by an Italian humanist, and lost and rediscovered. It has not been heard of since 1727, when Sir Joshua Byrde, a Turkey merchant, brought it home from Aleppo, and vanished with it a month after he had shewn it to the virtuosi, no man knew or knows where. And here it is!"

"Put it in your pocket, Dyson," he said, after a pause. "I would not let any one have a glimpse of the thing if I were you. I would not talk about it. Did either of the men you saw see you?"

"Well, I think not. I don't think the first man, the man who was vomited out of the dark passage, saw anything at all; and I am sure that he could not have seen me."

"And you didn't really see them. You couldn't recognise either the one or the other if you met him in the street to-morrow?"

"No, I don't think I could. The street, as I said, was dimly lighted, and they ran like madmen."

The two men sat silent for some time, each weaving his own fancies of the story; but the lust of the marvellous was slowly overpowering Dyson's more sober thoughts.

"It is all more strange than I fancied," he said at last. "It is queer enough what I saw; a man is sauntering along a quiet, sober, everyday London street, a street of grey houses and blank walls, and there, for a moment, a veil seems drawn aside, and the very fume of the pit steams up through the flagstones, the ground glows, red-hot, beneath his feet, and he seems to hear the hiss of the infernal caldron. A man flying in mad terror for his life, and furious hate pressing hot on his steps with knife drawn ready; here, indeed, is horror; but what is all that to what you have told me? I tell you, Phillipps, I see the plot thicken; our steps will henceforth be dogged with mystery, and the most ordinary incidents will teem with significance. You may stand out against it, and shut your eyes, but they will be forced open; mark my words, you will have to yield to the inevitable. A clue, tangled if you like, has been placed by chance in our hands; it will be our business to follow it up. As for the guilty person or persons in this strange case, they will be unable to escape us, our nets will be spread far and wide over this great city, and suddenly, in the streets and places of public resort, we shall in some way or other be made aware that we are in touch with the unknown criminal. Indeed I almost fancy I see him slowly approaching this quiet square of yours; he is loitering at street corners, wandering, apparently without aim, down far-reaching thoroughfares, but all the while coming nearer and nearer, drawn by an irresistible magnetism, as ships were drawn to the Loadstone Rock in the Eastern tale."

"I certainly think," replied Phillipps, "that if you pull out that coin and flourish it under people's noses as you are doing at the present moment, you will very probably find yourself in touch with the criminal, or a criminal. You will undoubtedly be robbed with violence. Otherwise, I see no reason why either of us should be troubled. No one saw you secure the coin, and no one knows you have it. I, for my part, shall sleep peacefully, and go about my business with a sense of security and a firm dependence on the natural order of things. The events of the evening, the adventure in the street, have been odd, I grant you, but I resolutely decline to have any more to do with the matter, and, if necessary, I shall consult the police. I will not be enslaved by a gold Tiberius, even though it swims into my ken in a manner which is somewhat melodramatic."

"And I, for my part," said Dyson, "go forth like a knight-errant in search of adventure. Not that I shall need to seek; rather adventure will seek me; I shall be like a spider in the midst of his web, responsive to every movement, and ever on the alert."

Shortly afterwards Dyson took his leave, and Mr. Phillipps spent the rest of the night in examining some flint arrow-heads which he had purchased. He had every reason to believe that they were the work of a modern and not a palæolithic man; still he was far from gratified when a close scrutiny shewed him that his suspicions were well founded. In his anger at the turpitude which would impose on an ethnologist, he completely forgot Dyson and the gold Tiberius; and when he went to bed at first sunlight, the whole tale had faded utterly from his thoughts.

The Encounter of the Pavement

Mr. Dyson, walking leisurely along Oxford Street, and staring with bland enquiry at whatever caught his attention, enjoyed in all its rare flavours the sensation that he was really very hard at work. His observation of mankind, the traffic, and the shop windows tickled his faculties with an exquisite bouquet; he looked serious, as one looks on whom charges of weight and moment are laid; and he was attentive in his glances to right and left, for fear lest he should miss some circumstance of more acute significance. He had narrowly escaped being run over at a crossing by a charging van, for he hated to hurry his steps, and indeed the afternoon was warm; and he had just halted by a place of popular refreshment, when the astounding gestures of a well-dressed individual on the opposite pavement held him enchanted and gasping like a fish. A treble line of hansoms, carriages, vans, cabs, and omnibuses was tearing east and west, and not the most daring adventurer of the crossings would have cared to try his fortune; but the person who had attracted Dyson's attention seemed to rage on the very edge of the pavement, now and then darting forward at the hazard of instant death, and at each repulse absolutely dancing with excitement, to the rich amusement of the passers-by. At last a gap that would have tried the courage of a street-boy appeared between the serried lines of vehicles, and the man rushed across in a frenzy, and escaping by a hair's-breadth, pounced upon Dyson as a tiger pounces on her prey. "I saw you looking about you," he said, sputtering out his words in his intense eagerness; "would you mind telling me this? Was the man who came out of the Aerated Bread Shop and jumped into the hansom three minutes ago a youngish-looking man with dark whiskers and spectacles? Can't you speak, man? For heaven's sake, can't you speak? Answer me; it's a matter of life and death."

The words bubbled and boiled out of the man's mouth in the fury of his emotion, his face went from red to white, and the beads of sweat stood out on his forehead; he stamped his feet as he spoke, and tore with his hand at his coat, as if something swelled and choked him, stopping the passage of his breath.

"My dear sir," said Dyson, "I always like to be accurate. Your observation was perfectly correct. As you say, a youngish man—a man, I should say, of somewhat timid bearing—ran rapidly out of the shop here, and bounced into a hansom that must have been waiting for him, as it went eastwards at once. Your friend also wore spectacles, as you say. Perhaps you would like me to call a hansom for you to follow the gentleman?"

"No, thank you; it would be a waste of time." The man gulped down something which appeared to rise in his throat, and Dyson was alarmed to see him shaking with hysterical laughter; he clung hard to a lamp-post, and swayed and staggered like a ship in a heavy gale.

"How shall I face the doctor?" he murmured to himself. "It is too hard to fail at the last moment." Then he seemed to recollect himself; he stood straight again, and looked quietly at Dyson.

"I owe you an apology for my violence," he said at last. "Many men would not be so patient as you have been. Would you mind adding to your kindness by walking with me a little way? I feel a little sick; I think it's the sun."

Dyson nodded assent, and devoted himself to a quiet scrutiny of this strange personage as they moved on together. The man was dressed in quiet taste, and the most scrupulous observer could find nothing amiss with the fashion or make of his clothes; yet, from his hat to his boots, everything seemed inappropriate. His silk hat, Dyson thought, should have been a high bowler of odious pattern, worn with a baggy morning-coat, and an instinct told him that the fellow did not commonly carry a clean pocket-handkerchief. The face was not of the most agreeable pattern, and was in no way improved by a pair of bulbous chin-whiskers of a ginger hue, into which moustaches of like colour merged imperceptibly. Yet, in spite of these signals hung out by nature, Dyson felt that the individual beside him was something more than compact of vulgarity. He was struggling with himself, holding his feelings in check; but now and again passion would mount black to his face, and it was evidently by a supreme effort that he kept himself from raging like a madman. Dyson found something curious, and a little terrible, in the spectacle of an occult emotion thus striving for the mastery, and threatening to break out at every instant with violence; and they had gone some distance before the person whom he had met by so odd a hazard was able to speak quietly.

"You are really very good," he said. "I apologise again; my rudeness was really most unjustifiable. I feel my conduct demands an explanation, and I shall be happy to give it to you. Do you happen to know of any place near here where one could sit down? I should really be very glad."

"My dear sir," said Dyson solemnly, "the only café in London is close by. Pray do not consider yourself as bound to offer me any explanation, but at the same time I should be most happy to listen to you. Let us turn down here."

They walked down a sober street and turned into what seemed a narrow passage past an iron-barred gate thrown back. The passage was paved with flagstones, and decorated with handsome shrubs in pots on either side, and the shadow of the high walls made a coolness which was very agreeable after the hot breath of the sunny street. Presently the passage opened out into a tiny square, a charming place, a morsel of France transplanted into the heart of London. High walls rose on either side, covered with glossy creepers, flower-beds beneath were gay with nasturtiums, and marigolds, and odorous with mignonette, and in the centre of the square a fountain, hidden by greenery, sent a cool shower continually plashing into the basin beneath. Chairs and tables were disposed at convenient intervals, and at the other end of the court broad doors had been thrown back; beyond was a long, dark room, and the turmoil of traffic had become a distant murmur. Within the room one or two men were sitting at the tables, writing and sipping, but the courtyard was empty.

"You see, we shall be quiet," said Dyson. "Pray sit down here, Mr.—?"

"Wilkins. My name is Henry Wilkins."

"Sit here, Mr. Wilkins. I think you will find that a comfortable seat. I suppose you have not been here before? This is the quiet time; the place will be like a hive at six o'clock, and the chairs and tables will overflow into that little alley there."

A waiter came in response to the bell; and after Dyson had politely enquired after the health of M. Annibault, the proprietor, he ordered a bottle of the wine of Champigny.

"The wine of Champigny," he observed to Mr. Wilkins, who was evidently a good deal composed by the influence of the place, "is a Tourainian wine of great merit. Ah, here it is; let me fill your glass. How do you find it?"

"Indeed," said Mr. Wilkins, "I should have pronounced it a fine Burgundy. The bouquet is very exquisite. I am fortunate in lighting upon such a good Samaritan as yourself: I wonder you did not think me mad. But if you knew the terrors that assailed me, I am sure you would no longer be surprised at conduct which was certainly most un-justifiable."

He sipped his wine, and leant back in his chair, relishing the drip and trickle of the fountain, and the cool greenness that hedged in this little port of refuge.

"Yes," he said at last, "that is indeed an admirable wine. Thank you; you will allow me to offer you another bottle?"

The waiter was summoned, and descended through a trap-door in the floor of the dark apartment and brought up the wine. Mr. Wilkins lit a cigarette, and Dyson pulled out his pipe.

"Now," said Mr. Wilkins, "I promised to give you an explanation of my strange behaviour. It is rather a long story, but I see, sir, that you are no mere cold observer of the ebb and flow of life. You take, I think, a warm and an intelligent interest in the chances of your fellow-creatures, and I believe you will find what I have to tell not devoid of interest."

Mr. Dyson signified his assent to these propositions; and though he thought Mr. Wilkins's diction a little pompous, prepared to interest himself in his tale. The other, who had so raged with passion half an hour before, was now perfectly cool, and when he had smoked out his cigarette, he began in an even voice to relate the

NOVEL OF THE DARK VALLEY.

I am the son of a poor but learned clergyman in the west of Eng-land— But I am forgetting, these details are not of special interest. I will briefly state, then, that my father, who was, as I have said, a learned man, had never learnt the specious arts by which the great are flattered, and would never condescend to the despicable pursuit of self-advertisement. Though his fondness for ancient ceremonies and quaint customs, combined with a kindness of heart that was un-equalled and a primitive and fervent piety, endeared him to his moor-land parishioners, such were not the steps by which clergy then rose in the Church, and at sixty my father was still incumbent of the little ben-efice he had accepted in his thirtieth year. The income of the living was barely sufficient to support life in the decencies which are expected of the Anglican parson; and when my father died a few years ago, I, his only child, found myself thrown upon the world with a slender capital of less than a hundred pounds, and all the problem of existence before me. I felt that there was nothing for me to do in the country, and as usually happens in such cases, London drew me like a magnet. One day in August, in the early morning, while the dew still glittered on the turf, and on the high green banks of the lane, a neighbour drove me to the railway station, and I bade good-bye to the land of the broad moors and unearthly battlements of the wild tors. It was six o'clock as we neared London; the faint, sickly fume of the brickfields about Ac-ton came in puffs through the open window, and a mist was rising from the ground. Presently the brief view of successive streets, prim and uniform, struck me with a sense of monotony; the hot air seemed to grow hotter; and when we had rolled beneath the dismal and squalid houses, whose dirty and neglected backyards border the line near Pad-dington, I felt as if I should be stifled in this fainting breath of Lon-don. I got a hansom and drove off, and every street increased my gloom; grey houses with blinds drawn down, whole thoroughfares al-most desolate, and the foot-passengers who seemed to stagger wearily along rather than walk, all made me feel a sinking at heart. I put up for the night at a small hotel in a street leading from the Strand, where my father had stayed on his few brief visits to the town; and when I went out after dinner, the real gaiety and bustle of the Strand and Fleet Street could cheer me but little, for in all this great city there was no single human being whom I could claim even as an acquaintance. I will not weary you with the history of the next year, for the adventures of a man who sinks are too trite to be worth recalling. My money did not last me long; I found that I must be neatly dressed, or no one to whom I applied would so much as listen to me; and I must live in a street of decent reputation if I wished to be treated with common civility. I applied for various posts, for which, as I now see, I was completely devoid of qualification; I tried to become a clerk without having the smallest notion of business habits; and I found, to my cost, that a general knowledge of literature and an execrable style of penmanship are far from being looked upon with favour in commercial circles. I had read one of the most charming of the works of a famous novelist of the present day, and I frequented the Fleet Street taverns in the hope of making literary friends, and so getting the introductions which I understood were indispensable in the career of letters. I was disappointed; I once or twice ventured to address gentlemen who were sitting in adjoining boxes, and I was answered, politely indeed, but in a manner that told me my advances were unusual. Pound by pound, my small resources melted; I could no longer think of appearances; I migrated to a shy quarter, and my meals became mere observances. I went out at one and returned to my room at two, but nothing but a milk-cake had occurred in the interval. In short, I became acquainted with misfortune; and as I sat amidst slush and ice on a seat in Hyde Park, munching a piece of bread, I realised the bitterness of poverty, and the feelings of a gentleman reduced to something far below the condition of a vagrant. In spite of all discouragement I did not desist in my efforts to earn a living. I consulted advertisement columns, I kept my eyes open for a chance, I looked in at the windows of stationers' shops, but all in vain. One evening I was sitting in a Free Library, and I saw an advertisement in one of the papers. It was something like this: "Wanted by a gentleman a person of literary tastes and abilities as secretary and amanuensis. Must not object to travel." Of course I knew that such an advertisement would have answers by the hundred, and I thought my own chances of securing the post extremely small; however, I applied at the address given, and wrote to Mr. Smith, who was staying at the West End. I must confess that my heart gave a jump when I received a note a couple of days later, asking me to call at the Cosmopole at my earliest convenience. I do not know, sir, what your experiences of life may have been, and so I cannot tell you whether you have known such moments. A slight sickness, my heart beating rather more rapidly than usual, a choking in the throat, and a difficulty of utterance; such were my sensations as I walked to the Cosmopole; I had to mention the name twice before the hall porter could understand me, and as I went upstairs my hands were wet. I was a good deal struck by Mr. Smith's appearance; he looked younger than I did, and there was something mild and hesitating about his expression. He was reading when I came in, and he looked up when I gave my name. "My dear sir," he said, "I am really delighted to see you. I have read very carefully the letter you were good enough to send me. Am I to understand that this document is in your own handwriting?" He shewed me the letter I had written, and I told him I was not so fortunate as to be able to keep a secretary myself. "Then, sir," he went on, "the post I advertised is at your service. You have no objection to travel, I presume?" As you may imagine, I closed pretty eagerly with the offer he made, and thus I entered the service of Mr. Smith. For the first few weeks I had no special duties; I had received a quarter's salary, and a handsome allowance was made me in lieu of board and lodging. One morning, however, when I called at the hotel according to instructions, my master informed me that I must hold myself in readiness for a sea-voyage, and, to spare unnecessary detail, in the course of a fortnight we had landed at New York. Mr. Smith told me that he was engaged on a work of a special nature, in the compilation of which some peculiar researches had to be made; in short, I was given to understand that we were to travel to the far West.

After about a week had been spent in New York we took our seats in the cars, and began a journey tedious beyond all conception. Day after day, and night after night, the great train rolled on, threading its way through cities the very names of which were strange to me, passing at slow speed over perilous viaducts, skirting mountain ranges and pine forests, and plunging into dense tracts of wood, where mile after mile and hour after hour the same monotonous growth of brushwood met the eye, and all along the continual clatter and rattle of the wheels upon the ill-laid lines made it difficult to hear the voices of our fellow-passengers. We were a heterogeneous and ever-changing company; often I woke up in the dead of night with a sudden grinding jar of the breaks, and looking out found that we had stopped in the shabby street of some frame-built town, lighted chiefly by the flaring windows of the saloon. A few rough-looking fellows would often come out to stare at the cars, and sometimes passengers got down, and sometimes there was a party of two or three waiting on the wooden sidewalk to get on board. Many of the passengers were English; humble households torn up from the moorings of a thousand years, and bound for some problematical paradise in the alkali desert or the Rockies. I heard the men talking to one another of the great profits to be made on the virgin soil of America, and two or three, who were mechanics, expatiated on the wonderful wages given to skilled labour on the railways and in the factories of the States. This talk usually fell dead after a few minutes, and I could see a sickness and dismay in the faces of these men as they looked at the ugly brush or at the desolate expanse of the prairie, dotted here and there with frame-houses, devoid of garden or flowers or trees, standing all alone in what might have been a great grey sea frozen into stillness. Day after day the waving sky-line, and the desolation of a land without form or colour or variety, appalled the hearts of such of us as were Englishmen, and once in the night as I lay awake I heard a woman sobbing and asking what she had done to come to such a place. Her husband tried to comfort her in the broad speech of Gloucestershire, telling her the ground was so rich that one had only to plough it up and it would grow sunflowers of itself, but she cried for her mother and their old cottage and the beehives like a little child. The sadness of it all overwhelmed me, and I had no heart to think of other matters; the question of what Mr. Smith could have to do in such a country, and of what manner of literary research could be carried on in the wilderness, hardly troubled me. Now and again my situation struck me as peculiar; I had been engaged as a literary assistant at a handsome salary, and yet my master was still almost a stranger to me; sometimes he would come to where I was sitting in the cars and make a few banal remarks about the country, but for the most part of the journey he sat by himself, not speaking to any one, and so far as I could judge, deep in his thoughts. It was, I think, on the fifth day from New York when I received the intimation that we should shortly leave the cars; I had been watching some distant mountains which rose wild and savage before us, and I was wondering if there were human beings so unhappy as to speak of home in connection with those piles of lumbered rock, when Mr. Smith touched me lightly on the shoulder. "You will be glad to be done with the cars, I have no doubt, Mr. Wilkins," he said. "You were looking at the mountains, I think? Well, I hope we shall be there to-night. The train stops at Reading, and I dare say we shall manage to find our way."

A few hours later the breaksman brought the train to a standstill at the Reading depôt, and we got out. I noticed that the town, though of course built almost entirely of frame-houses, was larger and busier than any we had passed for the last two days. The depôt was crowded; and as the bell and whistle sounded, I saw that a number of persons were preparing to leave the cars, while an even greater number were waiting to get on board. Besides the passengers, there was a pretty dense crowd of people, some of whom had come to meet or to see off their friends and relatives, while others were merely loafers. Several of our English fellow-passengers got down at Reading, but the confusion was so great that they were lost to my sight almost immediately. Mr. Smith beckoned me to follow him, and we were soon in the thick of the mass; and the continual ringing of bells, the hubbub of voices, the shrieking of whistles, and the hiss of escaping steam, confused my senses, and I wondered dimly, as I struggled after my employer, where we were going, and how we should be able to find our way through an unknown country. Mr. Smith had put on a wide-brimmed hat, which he had sloped over his eyes, and as all the men wore hats of the same pattern, it was with some difficulty that I distinguished him in the crowd. We got free at last, and he struck down a side street, and made one or two sharp turns to right and left. It was getting dusk, and we seemed to be passing through a shy portion of the town; there were few people about in the ill-lighted streets, and these few were men of the unprepossessing pattern. Suddenly we stopped before a corner house. A man was standing at the door, apparently on the look-out for some one, and I noticed that he and Smith gave sharp glances one to the other.

"From New York City, I expect, mister?"

"From New York."

"All right; they're ready, and you can have 'em when you choose. I know my orders, you see, and I mean to run this business through."

"Very well, Mr. Evans, that is what we want. Our money is good, you know. Bring them round."

I had stood silent, listening to this dialogue and wondering what it meant. Smith began to walk impatiently up and down the street, and the man Evans was still standing at his door. He had given a sharp whistle, and I saw him looking me over in a quiet, leisurely way, as if to make sure of my face for another time. I was thinking what all this could mean, when an ugly, slouching lad came up a side passage, leading two raw-boned horses.

"Get up, Mr. Wilkins, and be quick about it," said Smith; "we ought to be on our way."

We rode off together into the gathering darkness, and before long I looked back and saw the far plain behind us, with the lights of the town glimmering faintly; and in front rose the mountains. Smith guided his horse on the rough track as surely as if he had been riding along Piccadilly, and I followed as well as I could. I was weary and exhausted, and scarcely took note of anything; I felt that the track was a gradual ascent, and here and there I saw great boulders by the road. The ride made but little impression on me. I have a faint recollection of passing through a dense black pine forest, where our horses had to pick their way among the rocks, and I remember the peculiar effect of the rarefied air as we kept still mounting higher and higher. I think I must have been half asleep for the latter half of the ride, and it was with a shock that I heard Smith saying—

"Here we are, Wilkins. This is Blue Rock Park. You will enjoy the view to-morrow. To-night we will have something to eat, and then go to bed."

A man came out of a rough-looking house and took the horses, and we found some fried steak and coarse whiskey awaiting us inside. I had come to a strange place. There were three rooms—the room in which we had supper, Smith's room, and my own. The deaf old man who did the work slept in a sort of shed, and when I woke up the next morning and walked out I found that the house stood in a sort of hollow amongst the mountains; the clumps of pines and some enormous bluish-grey rocks that stood here and there between the trees had given the place the name of Blue Rock Park. On every side the snow-covered mountains surrounded us, the breath of the air was as wine, and when I climbed the slope and looked down, I could see that, so far as any human fellowship was concerned, I might as well have been wrecked on some small island in mid-Pacific. The only trace of man I could see was the rough log-house where I had slept, and in my ignorance I did not know that there were similar houses within comparatively easy distance, as distance is reckoned in the Rockies. But at the moment, the utter, dreadful loneliness rushed upon me, and the thought of the great plain and the great sea that parted me from the world I knew caught me by the throat, and I wondered if I should die there in that mountain hollow. It was a terrible instant, and I have not yet forgotten it. Of course, I managed to conquer my horror; I said I should be all the stronger for the experience, and I made up my mind to make the best of everything. It was a rough life enough, and rough enough board and lodging. I was left entirely to myself. Smith I scarcely ever saw, nor did I know when he was in the house. I have often thought he was far away, and have been surprised to see him walking out of his room, locking the door behind him, and putting the key in his pocket; and on several occasions, when I fancied he was busy in his room, I have seen him come in with his boots covered with dust and dirt. So far as work went I enjoyed a complete sinecure; I had nothing to do but to walk about the valley, to eat, and to sleep. With one thing and another I grew accustomed to the life, and managed to make myself pretty comfortable, and by degrees I began to venture farther away from the house, and to explore the country. One day I had contrived to get into the neighbouring valley, and suddenly I came upon a group of men sawing timber. I went up to them, hoping that perhaps some of them might be Englishmen; at all events, they were human beings, and I should hear articulate speech; for the old man I have mentioned, besides being half blind and stone deaf, was wholly dumb so far as I was concerned. I was prepared to be welcomed in rough and ready fashion, without much of the forms of politeness, but the grim glances and the short, gruff answers I received astonished me. I saw the men glance oddly at each other; and one of them, who had stopped work, began fingering a gun, and I was obliged to return on my path uttering curses on the fate which had brought me into a land where men were more brutish than the very brutes. The solitude of the life began to oppress me as with a nightmare, and a few days later I determined to walk to a kind of station some miles distant, where a rough inn was kept for the accommodation of hunters and tourists. English gentlemen occasionally stopped there for the night, and I thought I might perhaps fall in with some one of better manners than the inhabitants of the country. I found, as I had expected, a group of men lounging about the door of the log-house that served as a hotel, and as I came nearer I could see that heads were put together and looks interchanged, and when I walked up the six or seven trappers stared at me in stony ferocity, and with something of the disgust that one eyes a loathsome and venomous snake. I felt that I could bear it no longer, and I called out—

"Is there such a thing as an Englishman here, or any one with a little civilisation?"

One of the men put his hand to his belt, but his neighbour checked him, and answered me—

"You'll find we've got some of the resources of civilisation before very long, mister, and I expect you'll not fancy them extremely. But, anyway, there's an Englishman tarrying here, and I've no doubt he'll be glad to see you. There you are; that's Mr. D'Aubernoun."

A young man, dressed like an English country squire, came and stood at the door, and looked at me. One of the men pointed to me and said—

"That's the individual we were talking about last night. Thought you might like to have a look at him, squire, and here he is."

The young fellow's good-natured English face clouded over, and he glanced sternly at me, and turned away with a gesture of contempt and aversion.

"Sir," I cried, "I do not know what I have done to be treated in this manner. You are my fellow-countryman, and I expected some courtesy."

He gave me a black look and made as if he would go in, but he changed his mind and faced me.

"You are rather imprudent, I think, to behave in this manner. You must be counting on a forbearance which cannot last very long, which may last a very short time indeed. And let me tell you this, sir, you may call yourself an Englishman, and drag the name of England through the dirt, but you need not count on any English influence to help you. If I were you, I would not stay here much longer."

He went into the inn, and the men quietly watched my face as I stood there, wondering whether I was going mad. The woman of the house came out and stared at me as if I were a wild beast or a savage, and I turned to her, and spoke quietly—

"I am very hungry and thirsty. I have walked a long way. I have plenty of money. Will you give me something to eat and drink?"

"No, I won't," she said. "You had better quit this."

I crawled home like a wounded beast, and lay down on my bed. It was all a hopeless puzzle to me; I knew nothing but rage, and shame, and terror, and I suffered little more when I passed by a house in an adjacent valley, and some children who were playing outside ran from me shrieking. I was forced to walk to find some occupation; I should have died if I had sat down quietly in Blue Rock Park and looked all day at the mountains; but wherever I saw a human being I saw the same glance of hatred and aversion, and once as I was crossing a thick brake I heard a shot and the venomous hiss of a bullet close to my ear.

One day I heard a conversation which astounded me; I was sitting behind a rock resting, and two men came along the track and halted. One of them had got his feet entangled in some wild vines, and swore fiercely, but the other laughed, and said they were useful things sometimes.

"What the hell do you mean?"

"Oh, nothing much. But they're uncommon tough, these here vines, and sometimes rope is skerse and dear."

The man who had sworn chuckled at this, and I heard them sit down and light their pipes.

"Have you seen him lately?" asked the humorist.

"I sighted him the other day, but the darned bullet went high. He's got his master's luck, I expect, sir, but it can't last much longer. You heard about him going to Jinks's and trying his brass, but the young Britisher downed him pretty considerable, I can tell you."

"What the devil is the meaning of it?"

"I don't know, but I believe it'll have to be finished, and done in the old style too. You know how they fix the niggers?"

"Yes, sir, I've seen a little of that. A couple of gallons of kerosene'll cost a dollar at Brown's store, but I should say it's cheap anyway."

They moved off after this, and I lay still behind the rock, the sweat pouring down my face. I was so sick that I could barely stand, and I walked home as slowly as an old man, leaning on my stick. I knew that the two men had been talking about me, and I knew that some terrible death was in store for me. That night I could not sleep; I tossed on the rough bed and tortured myself to find out the meaning of it all. At last, in the very dead of night, I rose from the bed and put on my clothes, and went out. I did not care where I went, but I felt that I must walk till I had tired myself out. It was a clear moonlight night, and in a couple of hours I found I was approaching a place of dismal reputation in the mountains, a deep cleft in the rocks, known as Black Gulf Cañon. Many years before an unfortunate party of Englishmen and English-women had camped here and had been surrounded by Indians. They were captured, outraged, and put to death with almost inconceivable tortures, and the roughest of the trappers or woodsmen gave the cañon a wide berth even in the daytime. As I crushed through the dense brushwood which grew above the cañon I heard voices; and wondering who could be in such a place at such a time, I went on, walking more carefully, and making as little noise as possible. There was a great tree growing on the very edge of the rocks, and I lay down and looked out from behind the trunk. Black Gulf Cañon was below me, the moonlight shining bright into its very depths from mid-heaven, and casting shadows as black as death from the pointed rock, and all the sheer rock on the other side, overhanging the cañon, was in darkness. At intervals a light veil obscured the moonlight, as a filmy cloud fleeted across the moon, and a bitter wind blew shrill across the gulf. I looked down, as I have said, and saw twenty men standing in a semicircle round a rock; I counted them one by one, and knew most of them. They were the vilest of the vile, more vile than any den in London could shew, and there was murder, worse than murder, on the heads of not a few. Facing them and me stood Mr. Smith, with the rock before him, and on the rock was a great pair of scales, such as are used in the stores. I heard his voice ringing down the cañon as I lay beside the tree, and my heart turned cold as I heard it.

"Life for gold," he cried, "a life for gold. The blood and the life of an enemy for every pound of gold."

A man stepped and raised one hand, and with the other flung a bright lump of something into the pan of the scales, which clanged down, and Smith muttered something in his ear. Then he cried again—

"Blood for gold, for a pound of gold, the life of an enemy. For every pound of gold upon the scales, a life."

One by one the men came forward, each lifting up his right hand; and the gold was weighed in the scales, and each time Smith leant forward and spoke to each man in his ear. Then he cried again—

"Desire and lust for gold on the scales. For every pound of gold enjoyment of desire."

I saw the same thing happen as before; the uplifted hand and the metal weighed, and the mouth whispering, and black passion on every face.

Then, one by one, I saw the men again step up to Smith. A muttered conversation seemed to take place. I could see that Smith was explaining and directing, and I noticed that he gesticulated a little as one who points out the way, and once or twice he moved his hands quickly as if he would shew that the path was clear and could not be missed. I kept my eyes so intently on his figure that I noted little else, and at last it was with a start that I realised the cañon was empty. A moment before I thought I had seen the group of villainous faces, and the two standing, a little apart, by the rock; I had looked down a moment, and when I glanced again into the cañon there was no one there. In dumb terror I made my way home, and I fell asleep in an instant from exhaustion. No doubt I should have slept on for many hours, but when I woke up the sun was only rising, and the light shone in on my bed. I had started up from sleep with the sensation of having received a violent shock; and as I looked in confusion about me, I saw, to my amazement, that there were three men in the room. One of them had his hand on my shoulder and spoke to me—

"Come, mister, wake up. Your time's up now, I reckon, and the boys are waiting for you outside, and they're in a big hurry. Come on; you can put on your clothes; it's kind of chilly this morning."

I saw the other two men smiling sourly at each other, but I understood nothing. I simply pulled on my clothes and said I was ready.

"All right; come on, then. You go first, Nichols, and Jim and I will give the gentleman an arm."

They took me out into the sunlight, and then I understood the meaning of the dull murmur that had vaguely perplexed me while I was dressing. There were about two hundred men waiting outside, and some women too, and when they saw me there was a low muttering growl. I did not know what I had done, but that noise made my heart beat and the sweat come out on my face. I saw confusedly, as through a veil, the tumult and tossing of the crowd, discordant voices were speaking, and amongst all those faces there was not one glance of mercy, but a fury of lust that I did not understand. I found myself presently walking in a sort

of procession up the slope of the valley, and on every side of me there
were men with revolvers in their hands. Now and then a voice struck
me, and I heard words as sentences of which I could form no connected
story. But I understood that there was one sentence of execration; I
heard scraps of stories that seemed strange and improbable. Some one
was talking of men, lured by cunning devices from their homes and
murdered with hideous tortures, found writhing like wounded snakes in
dark and lonely places, only crying for some one to stab them to the
heart, and so end their torments; and I heard another voice speaking of
innocent girls who had vanished for a day or two, and then come back
and died, blushing red with shame even in the agonies of death. I wondered what it all meant, and what was to happen; but I was so weary
that I walked on in a dream, scarcely longing for anything but sleep. At
last we stopped. We had reached the summit of the hill overlooking
Blue Rock Valley, and I saw that I was standing beneath a clump of
trees where I had often sat. I was in the midst of a ring of armed men,
and I saw that two or three men were very busy with piles of wood,
while others were fingering a rope. Then there was a stir in the crowd,
and a man was pushed forward. His hands and feet were tightly bound
with cord; and though his face was unutterably villainous, I pitied him
for the agony that worked his features and twisted his lips. I knew him;
he was amongst those that had gathered round Smith in Black Gulf
Cañon. In an instant he was unbound and stripped naked, borne beneath one of the trees, and his neck encircled by a noose that went
around the trunk. A hoarse voice gave some kind of order; there was a
rush of feet, and the rope tightened; and there before me I saw the
blackened face and the writhing limbs and the shameful agony of
death. One after another half a dozen men, all of whom I had seen in
the cañon the night before, were strangled before me, and their bodies
were flung forth on the ground. Then there was a pause, and the man
who had roused me a short while before came up to me, and said—

"Now, mister, it's your turn. We give you five minutes to cast up
your accounts, and when that's clocked, by the living God, we will
burn you alive at that tree."

It was then I awoke and understood. I cried out—

"Why, what have I done? Why should you hurt me? I am a harmless man; I never did you any wrong." I covered my face with my

hands; it seemed so pitiful, and it was such a terrible death.

"What have I done?" I cried again. "You must take me for some other man. You cannot know me."

"You black-hearted devil," said the man at my side, "we know you well enough. There's not a man within thirty miles of this that won't curse Jack Smith when you are burning in hell."

"My name is not Smith," I said, with some hope left in me. "My name is Wilkins. I was Mr. Smith's secretary, but I knew nothing of him."

"Hark at the black liar," said the man. "Secretary be damned! You were clever enough, I dare say, to slink out at night and keep your face in the dark, but we've tracked you out at last. But your time's up. Come along."

I was dragged to the tree and bound to it with chains; I saw the piles of wood heaped all about me, and shut my eyes. Then I felt myself drenched all over with some liquid, and looked again, and a woman grinned at me. She had just emptied a great can of petroleum over me and over the wood. A voice shouted, "Fire away!" and I fainted, and knew nothing more.

When I opened my eyes I was lying on a bed in a bare, comfortless room. A doctor was holding some strong salts to my nostrils, and a gentleman standing by the bed, whom I afterwards found to be the sheriff, addressed me.

"Say, mister," he began, "you've had an uncommon narrow squeak for it. The boys were just about lighting up when I came along with the posse, and I had as much as I could do to bring you off, I can tell you. And, mind you, I don't blame them; they had made up their minds, you see, that you were the head of the Black Gulf gang, and at first nothing I could say would persuade them you weren't Jack Smith. Luckily, a man from here named Evans, that came along with us, allowed he had seen you with Jack Smith, and that you were yourself. So we brought you along and gaoled you, but you can go if you like when you're through with this faint turn."

I got on the cars next day, and in three weeks I was in London; again almost penniless. But from that time my fortune seemed to change; I made influential friends in all directions; bank directors courted my company, and editors positively flung themselves into my arms. I had only to choose my career, and after a while I determined that I was meant by nature for a life of comparative leisure. With an ease that seemed almost ridiculous, I obtained a well-paid position in connection with a prosperous political club. I have charming chambers in a central neighbourhood, close to the parks, the club chef exerts himself when I lunch or dine, and the rarest vintages in the cellar are always at my disposal. Yet, since my return to London, I have never known a day's security or peace; I tremble when I awake lest Smith should be standing at my bed, and every step I take seems to bring me nearer to the edge of the precipice. Smith, I knew, had escaped free from the raid of the Vigilantes, and I grew faint at the thought that he would in all probability return to London, and that suddenly and un-prepared I should meet him face to face. Every morning as I left my house I would peer up and down the street, expecting to see that dreaded figure awaiting me; I have delayed at street-corners, my heart in my mouth, sickening at the thought that a few quick steps might bring us together; I could not bear to frequent the theatres or music-halls, lest by some bizarre chance he should prove to be my neighbour. Sometimes I have been forced, against my will, to walk out at night, and then in silent squares the shadows have made me shudder, and in the medley of meetings in the crowded thoroughfares I have said to myself, "It must come sooner or later; he will surely return to London, and I shall see him when I feel most secure." I scanned the newspapers for hint or intimation of approaching danger, and no small type nor report of trivial interest was allowed to pass unread. Especially I read and re-read the advertisement columns, but without result; months passed by, and I was undisturbed till, though I felt far from safe, I no longer suffered from the intolerable oppression of instant and ever-present terror. This afternoon, as I was walking quietly along Oxford Street, I raised my eyes and looked across the road, and then at last I saw the man who had so long haunted my thoughts.

Mr. Wilkins finished his wine, and leant back in his chair, looking sadly at Dyson; and then, as if a thought struck him, fished out of an inner pocket a leather letter-case, and handed a newspaper cutting across the table.

Dyson glanced closely at the slip, and saw that it had been extract-ed from the columns of an evening paper. It ran as follows:—

WHOLESALE LYNCHING.

SHOCKING STORY.

"A Dalziel telegram from Reading (Colorado) states that advices received there from Blue Rock Park report a frightful instance of popular vengeance. For some time the neighbourhood has been terrorised by the crimes of a gang of desperadoes, who, under the cover of a carefully planned organisation, have perpetrated the most infamous cruelties on men and women. A Vigilance Committee was formed, and it was found that the leader of the gang was a person named Smith, living in Blue Rock Park. Action was taken, and six of the worst in the band were summarily strangled in the presence of two or three hundred men and women. Smith is said to have escaped."

"This is a terrible story," said Dyson; "I can well believe that your days and nights are haunted by such fearful scenes as you have described. But surely you have no need to fear Smith? He has much more cause to fear you. Consider: you have only to lay your information before the police, and a warrant would be immediately issued for his arrest. Besides, you will, I am sure, excuse me for what I am going to say."

"My dear sir," said Mr. Wilkins, "I hope you will speak to me with perfect freedom."

"Well, then, I must confess that my impression was that you were rather disappointed at not being able to stop the man before he drove off. I thought you seemed annoyed that you could not get across the street."

"Sir, I did not know what I was about. I caught sight of the man, but it was only for a moment, and the agony you witnessed was the agony of suspense. I was not perfectly certain of the face, and the horrible thought that Smith was again in London overwhelmed me. I shuddered at the idea of this incarnate fiend, whose soul is black with shocking crimes, mingling free and unobserved amongst the harmless crowds, meditating perhaps a new and more fearful cycle of infamies. I tell you, sir, that an awful being stalks through the streets, a being before whom the sunlight itself should blacken, and the summer air grow chill and dank. Such thoughts as these rushed upon me with the force of a whirlwind; I lost my senses."

"I see. I partly understand your feelings, but I would impress on you that you have nothing really to fear. Depend upon it, Smith will not molest you in any way. You must remember he himself has had a warning; and indeed, from the brief glance I had of him, he seemed to me to be a frightened-looking man. However, I see it is getting late, and if you will excuse me, Mr. Wilkins, I think I will be going. I dare say we shall often meet here."

Dyson walked off smartly, pondering the strange story chance had brought him, and finding on cool reflection that there was something a little strange in Mr. Wilkins's manner, for which not even so weird a catalogue of experiences could altogether account.

ADVENTURE OF THE MISSING BROTHER

Mr. Charles Phillipps was, as has been hinted, a gentleman of pronounced scientific tastes. In his early days he had devoted himself with fond enthusiasm to the agreeable study of biology, and a brief monograph on the Embryology of the Microscopic Holothuria had formed his first contribution to the *belles lettres*. Later he had somewhat relaxed the severity of his pursuits, and had dabbled in the more frivolous subjects of palæontology and ethnology; he had a cabinet in his sitting-room whose drawers were stuffed with rude flint implements, and a charming fetish from the South Seas was the dominant note in the decorative scheme of the apartment. Flattering himself with the title of materialist, he was in truth one of the most credulous of men, but he required a marvel to be neatly draped in the robes of Science before he would give it any credit, and the wildest dreams took solid shape to him if only the nomenclature were severe and irreproachable. He laughed at the witch, but quailed before the powers of the hypnotist, lifting his eyebrows when Christianity was mentioned, but adoring protyle and the ether. For the rest, he prided himself on a boundless scepticism; the average tale of wonder he heard with nothing but contempt, and he would certainly not have credited a word or syllable of Dyson's story of the pursuer and pursued, unless the gold coin had been produced as visible and tangible evidence. As it was, he half suspected that Dyson had imposed upon him; he knew his friend's disordered fancies, and his habit of conjuring up the marvellous to account for the entirely commonplace; and, on the whole, he was inclined to think that the so-called facts in the odd adventure had been gravely distorted in the telling. Since the evening on which he had listened to the tale he paid Dyson a visit, and had delivered himself of some serious talk on the necessity of accurate observation, and the folly, as he put it, of using a kaleidoscope instead of a telescope in the view of things, to which remarks his friend had listened with a smile that was extremely sardonic. "My dear fellow," Dyson had remarked at last, "you will allow me to tell you that I see your drift perfectly. However, you will be astonished to hear that I consider you to be the visionary, while I am a sober and serious spectator of human life. You have gone round the circle; and while you fancy yourself far in the golden land of new philosophies, you are in reality a dweller in a metaphorical Clapham; your scepticism has defeated itself and become a monstrous credulity; you are, in fact, in the position of the bat or owl, I forget which it was, who denied the existence of the sun at noonday, and I shall be astonished if you do not one day come to me full of contrition for your manifold intellectual errors, with a humble resolution to see things in their true light for the future." This tirade had left Mr. Phillipps unimpressed; he considered Dyson as hopeless, and he went home to gloat over some primitive stone implements that a friend had sent him from India. He found that his landlady, seeing them displayed in all their rude formlessness upon the table, had removed the collection to the dustbin, and had replaced it by lunch; and the afternoon was spent in malodorous research. Mrs. Brown, hearing these stones spoken of as very valuable knives, had called him in his hearing "poor Mr. Phillipps", and between rage and evil odours he spent a sorry afternoon. It was four o'clock before he had completed his work of rescue; and overpowered with the flavours of decaying cabbage leaves, Phillipps felt that he must have a walk to gain an appetite for the evening meal. Unlike Dyson, he walked fast, with his eyes on the pavement, absorbed in his thoughts, and oblivious of the life around him; and he could not have told by what streets he had passed, when he suddenly lifted up his eyes and found himself in Leicester Square. The grass and flowers pleased him, and he welcomed the opportunity of resting for a few minutes, and glancing round, he saw a bench which had only one occupant, a lady, and as she was seated at one end, Phillipps took up a position at the other extremity, and began to pass in angry review the events of the afternoon. He had noticed as he came up to the bench that the person already there was neatly dressed, and to all appearance young; her face he could not see, as it was turned away in apparent contemplation of the shrubs, and, moreover, shielded with her hand; but it would be doing wrong to Mr. Phillipps to imagine that his choice of seat was dictated by any hopes of an affair of the heart, he had simply preferred the company of one lady to that of five dirty children, and having seated himself, was immersed directly in thoughts of his misfortunes. He had meditated changing his lodgings; but now, on a judicial review of the case in all its bearings, his calmer judgment told him that the race of landladies is like to the race of the leaves, and that there was but little to choose between them. He resolved, however, to talk to Mrs. Brown, the offender, very coolly and yet severely, to point out the extreme indiscretion of her conduct, and to express a hope for better things in the future. With this decision registered in his mind, Phillipps was about to get up from the seat and move off, when he was intensely annoyed to hear a stifled sob, evidently from the lady, who still continued her contemplation of the shrubs and flower-beds. He clutched his stick desperately, and in a moment would have been in full retreat, when the lady turned her face towards him, and with mute entreaty bespoke his attention. She was a young girl with a quaint and piquant rather than a beautiful face, and she was evidently in the bitterest distress. Mr. Phillipps sat down again, and cursed his chances heartily. The young lady looked at him with a pair of charming eyes of a shining hazel, which shewed no trace of tears, though a handkerchief was in her hand; she bit her lip, and seemed to struggle with some overpowering grief, and her whole attitude was all-beseeching and imploring. Phillipps sat on the edge of the bench gazing awkwardly at her, and wondering what was to come next, and she looked at him still without speaking.

"Well, madam," he said at last, "I understood from your gesture that you wished to speak to me. Is there anything I can do for you? Though, if you will pardon me, I cannot help saying that that seems highly improbable."

"Ah, sir," she said in a low, murmuring voice, "do not speak harshly to me. I am in sore straits, and I thought from your face that I could safely ask your sympathy, if not your help."

"Would you kindly tell me what is the matter?" said Phillipps. "Perhaps you would like some tea?"

"I knew I could not be mistaken," the lady replied. "That offer of refreshment bespeaks a generous mind. But tea, alas! is powerless to console me. If you will let me, I shall endeavour to explain my trouble."

"I should be glad if you would."

"I shall do so, and I shall try to be brief, in spite of the numerous complications which have made me, young as I am, tremble before what seems the profound and terrible mystery of existence. Yet the grief which now racks my very soul is but too simple; I have lost my brother."

"Lost your brother! How on earth can that be?"

"I see I must trouble you with a few particulars. My brother, then, who is by some years my elder, is a tutor in a private school in the extreme north of London. The want of means deprived him of the advantages of a University education; and lacking the stamp of a degree, he could not hope for that position which his scholarship and his talents entitled him to claim. He was thus forced to accept the post of classical master at Dr. Saunderson's Highgate Academy for the sons of gentlemen, and he has performed his duties with perfect satisfaction to his principal for some years. My personal history need not trouble you; it will be enough if I tell you that for the last month I have been governess in a family residing at Tooting. My brother and I have always cherished the warmest mutual affection; and though circumstances into which I need not enter have kept us apart for some time, yet we have never lost sight of one another. We made up our minds that unless one of us was absolutely unable to rise from a bed of sickness, we should never let a week pass by without meeting, and some time ago we chose this square as our rendezvous on account of its central position and its convenience of access. And indeed, after a week of distasteful toil, my brother felt little inclination for much walking, and we have often spent two or three hours on this bench, speaking of our prospects and of happier days, when we were children. In the early spring it was cold and chilly; still we enjoyed the short respite, and I think that we were often taken for a pair of lovers, as we sat close together, eagerly talking. Saturday after Saturday we have met each other here; and though the doctor told him it was madness, my brother would not allow the influenza to break the appointment. That was some time ago; last Saturday we had a long and happy afternoon, and separated more cheerfully than usual, feeling that the coming week would be bearable, and resolving that our next meeting should be if possible still more pleasant. I arrived here at the time agreed upon, four o'clock, and sat down and watched for my brother, expecting every moment to see him advancing towards me from the gate at the north side of the square. Five minutes passed by, and he had not arrived; I thought he must have missed his train, and the idea that our interview would be cut short by twenty minutes, or perhaps half an hour, saddened me; I had hoped we should be so happy together today. Suddenly, moved by I know not what impulse, I turned abruptly round, and how can I describe to you my astonishment when I saw my brother advancing slowly towards me from the southern side of the square, accompanied by another person? My first thought, I remember, had in it something of resentment that this man, whoever he was, should intrude himself into our meeting; I wondered who it could possibly be, for my brother had, I may say, no intimate friends. Then as I looked still at the advancing figures, another feeling took possession of me; it was a sensation of bristling fear, the fear of the child in the dark, unreasonable and unreasoning, but terrible, clutching at my heart as with the cold grip of a dead man's hands. Yet I overcame the feeling, and looked steadily at my brother, waiting for him to speak, and more closely at his companion. Then I noticed that this man was leading my brother rather than walking arm-in-arm with him; he was a tall man, dressed in quite ordinary fashion. He wore a high bowler hat, and, in spite of the warmth of the day, a plain black overcoat, tightly buttoned, and I noticed his trousers, of a quiet black and grey stripe. The face was commonplace too, and indeed I cannot recall any special features, or any trick of expression; for though I looked at him as he came near, curiously enough his face made no impression on me—it was as though I had seen a well-made mask. They passed in front of me, and to my unutterable astonishment, I heard my brother's voice speaking to me, though his lips did not move, nor his eyes look into mine. It was a voice I cannot describe, though I knew it, but the words came to my ears as if mingled with splashing water and the sound of a shallow brook flowing amidst stones. I heard, then, the words, 'I cannot stay,' and for a moment the heavens and the earth seemed to rush together with the sound of thunder, and I was thrust forth from the world into a black void without beginning and without end. For, as my brother passed me, I saw the hand that held him by the arm, and seemed to guide him, and in one moment of horror I realised that it was a formless thing that has mouldered for many years in the grave. The flesh was peeled in strips from the bones, and hung apart dry and granulated, and the fingers that encircled my brother's arm were all unshapen, claw-like things, and one was but a stump from which the end had rotted off. When I recovered my senses I saw the two passing out by the gate. I paused for a moment, and then with a rush of fire to my heart I knew that no horror could stay me, but that I must follow my brother and save him, even though all hell rose up against me. I ran out, and looked up the pavement, and saw the two figures walking amidst the crowd. I ran across the road, and saw them turn up that side street, and I reached the corner a moment later. In vain I looked to right and left, for neither my brother nor his strange guardian was in sight; two elderly men were coming down arm-in-arm, and a telegraph boy was walking lustily along whistling. I remained there a moment horror-struck, and then I bowed my head and returned to this seat, where you found me. Now, sir, do you wonder at my grief? Oh, tell me what has happened to my brother, or I feel I shall go mad!"

Mr. Phillipps, who had listened with exemplary patience to this tale, hesitated a moment before he spoke.

"My dear madam," he said at length, "you have known how to engage me in your service, not only as a man, but as a student of science. As a fellow-creature I pity you most profoundly; you must have suffered extremely from what you saw, or rather from what you fancied you saw. For, as a scientific observer, it is my duty to tell you the plain truth, which, indeed, besides being true, must also console you. Allow me to ask you then to describe your brother."

"Certainly," said the lady eagerly; "I can describe him accurately. My brother is a somewhat young-looking man; he is pale, has small black whiskers, and wears spectacles. He has rather a timid, almost a frightened expression, and looks about him nervously from side to side. Think, think! Surely you must have seen him. Perhaps you are an *habitué* of this engaging quarter; you may have met him on some previous Saturday. I may have been mistaken in supposing that he turned up that side street; he may have gone on, and you may have passed each other. Oh, tell me, sir, whether you have not seen him!"

"I am afraid I do not keep a very sharp look-out when I am walking," said Phillipps, who would have passed his mother unnoticed; "but I am sure your description is admirable. And now will you describe the person who, you say, held your brother by the arm?"

"I cannot do so. I told you his face seemed devoid of expression or salient feature. It was like a mask."

"Exactly; you cannot describe what you have never seen. I need hardly point out to you the conclusion to be drawn; you have been the victim of an hallucination. You expected to see your brother, you were alarmed because you did not see him, and unconsciously, no doubt, your brain went to work, and finally you saw a mere projection of your own morbid thoughts—a vision of your absent brother, and a mere confusion of terrors incorporated in a figure which you can't describe. Of course your brother has been in some way prevented from coming to meet you as usual. I expect you will hear from him in a day or two."

The lady looked seriously at Mr. Phillipps, and then for a second there seemed almost a twinkling as of mirth about her eyes, but her face clouded sadly at the dogmatic conclusions to which the scientist was led so irresistibly.

"Ah!" she said, "you do not know. I cannot doubt the evidence of my waking senses. Besides, perhaps I have had experiences even more terrible. I acknowledge the force of your arguments, but a woman has intuitions which never deceive her. Believe me, I am not hysterical; feel my pulse, it is quite regular."

She stretched out her hand with a dainty gesture, and a glance that enraptured Phillipps in spite of himself. The hand held out to him was soft and white and warm, and as, in some confusion, he placed his fingers on the purple vein, he felt profoundly touched by the spectacle of love and grief before him.

"No," he said, as he released her wrist, "as you say, you are evidently quite yourself. Still, you must be aware that living men do not possess dead hands. That sort of thing doesn't happen. It is, of course, barely possible that you did see your brother with another gentleman, and that important business prevented him from stopping. As for the wonderful hand, there may have been some deformity, a finger shot off by accident, or something of that sort."

The lady shook her head mournfully.

"I see you are a determined rationalist," she said. "Did you not hear me say that I have had experiences even more terrible? I too was once a sceptic, but after what I have known I can no longer doubt."

"Madam," replied Mr. Phillipps, "no one shall make me deny my faith. I will never believe, nor will I pretend to believe that two and two make five, nor will I on any pretences admit the existence of two-sided triangles."

"You are a little hasty," rejoined the lady. "But may I ask you if you ever heard the name of Professor Gregg, the authority on ethnology and kindred subjects?"

"I have done much more than merely hear of Professor Gregg," said Phillipps. "I always regarded him as one of our most acute and clear-headed observers; and his last publication, the *Textbook of Ethnology*, struck me as being admirable in its kind. Indeed, the book had but come into my hands when I heard of the terrible accident which cut short Gregg's career. He had, I think, taken a country house in the West of England for the summer, and is supposed to have fallen into a river. So far as I remember, his body was never recovered."

"Sir, I am sure that you are discreet. Your conversation seems to declare as much, and the very title of that little work of yours which you mentioned assures me that you are no empty trifler. In a word, I feel that I may depend on you. You appear to be under the impression that Professor Gregg is dead; I have no reason to believe that that is the case."

"What?" cried Phillipps, astonished and perturbed. "You do not hint that there was anything disgraceful? I cannot believe it. Gregg was a man of the clearest character; his private life was one of great benevolence; and though I myself am free from delusions, I believe him to have been a sincere and devout Christian. Surely you cannot mean to insinuate that some disreputable history forced him to flee the country?"

"Again you are in a hurry," replied the lady. "I said nothing of all this. Briefly, then, I must tell you that Professor Gregg left his house one morning in full health both of mind and body. He never returned, but his watch and chain, a purse containing three sovereigns in gold, and some loose silver, with a ring that he wore habitually, were found three days later on a wild and savage hillside, many miles from the river. These articles were placed beside a limestone rock of fantastic form; they had been wrapped into a parcel with a kind of rough parchment which was secured with gut. The parcel was opened, and the inner side of the parchment bore an inscription done with some red substance; the characters were undecipherable, but seemed to be a corrupt cuneiform."

"You interest me intensely," said Phillipps. "Would you mind continuing your story? The circumstance you have mentioned seems to me of the most inexplicable character, and I thirst for elucidation."

The young lady seemed to meditate for a moment, and she then proceeded to relate the

NOVEL OF THE BLACK SEAL.

I must now give you some fuller particulars of my history. I am the daughter of a civil engineer, Steven Lally by name, who was so unfortunate as to die suddenly at the outset of his career, and before he had accumulated sufficient means to support his wife and her two children. My mother contrived to keep the small household going on resources which must have been incredibly small; we lived in a remote country village, because most of the necessaries of life were cheaper than in a town, but even so we were brought up with the severest economy. My father was a clever and well-read man, and left behind him a small but select collection of books, containing the best Greek, Latin, and English classics, and these books were the only amusement we possessed. My brother, I remember, learnt Latin out of Descartes' *Meditationes*, and I, in place of the little tales which children are usually told to read, had nothing more charming than a translation of the *Gesta Romanorum*. We grew up thus, quiet and studious children, and in course of time my brother provided for himself in the manner I have mentioned. I continued to live at home; my poor mother had become an invalid, and demanded my continual care, and about two years ago she died after many months of painful illness. My situation was a terrible one; the shabby furniture barely sufficed to pay the debts I had been forced to contract, and the books I dispatched to my brother, knowing how he would value them. I was absolutely alone; I was aware how poorly my brother was paid; and though I came up to London in the hope of finding employment, with the understanding that he would defray my expenses, I swore it should only be for a month, and that if I could not in that time find some work, I would starve rather than deprive him of the few miserable pounds he had laid by for his day of trouble. I took a little room in a distant suburb, the cheapest that I could find; I lived on bread and tea, and I spent my time in vain answering of advertisements, and vainer walks to addresses I had noted. Day followed on day, and week on week, and still I was unsuccessful, till at last the term I had appointed drew to a close, and I saw before me the grim prospect of slowly dying of starvation. My landlady was good-natured in her way; she knew the slenderness of my means, and I am sure that she would not have turned me out of doors; it remained for me then to go away, and to try to die in some quiet place. It was winter then and a thick white fog gathered in the early part of the afternoon, becoming more dense as the day wore on; it was a Sunday, I remember, and the people of the house were at chapel. At about three o'clock I crept out and walked away as quickly as I could, for I was weak from abstinence. The white mist wrapped all the streets in silence, a hard frost had gathered thick upon the bare branches of the trees, and frost crystals glittered on the wooden fences, and on the cold, cruel ground beneath my feet. I walked on, turning to right and left in utter haphazard, without caring to look up at the names of the streets, and all that I remember of my walk on that Sunday afternoon seems but the broken fragments of an evil dream. In a confused vision I stumbled on, through roads half-town and half-country, grey fields melting into the cloudy world of mist on one side of me, and on the other comfortable villas with a glow of firelight flickering on the walls, but all unreal; red brick walls and lighted windows, vague trees, and glimmering country, gas-lamps beginning to star the white shadows, the vanishing perspectives of the railway line beneath high embankments, the green and red of the signal lamps,—all these were but momentary pictures flashed on my tired brain and senses numbed by hunger. Now and then I would hear a quick step ringing on the iron road, and men would pass me well wrapped up, walking fast for the sake of warmth, and no doubt eagerly foretasting the pleasures of a glowing hearth, with curtains tightly drawn about the frosted panes, and the welcomes of their friends; but as the early evening darkened and night approached, foot-passengers got fewer and fewer, and I passed through street after street alone. In the white silence I stumbled on, as desolate as if I trod the streets of a buried city; and as I grew more weak and exhausted, something of the horror of death was folding thickly round my heart. Suddenly, as I turned a corner, some one accosted me courteously beneath the lamp-post, and I heard a voice asking if I could kindly point the way to Avon Road. At the sudden shock of human accents I was prostrated, and my strength gave way; I fell all huddled on the sidewalk, and wept and sobbed and laughed in violent hysteria. I had gone out prepared to die, and as I stepped across the threshold that had sheltered me, I consciously bade adieu to all hopes and all remembrances; the door clanged behind me with the noise of thunder, and I felt that an iron curtain had fallen on the brief passages of my life, that henceforth I was to walk a little way in a world of gloom and shadow; I entered on the stage of the first act of death. Then came my wandering in the mist, the whiteness wrapping all things, the void streets, and muffled silence, till when that voice spoke to me it was as if I had died and life returned to me. In a few minutes I was able to compose my feelings, and as I rose I saw that I was confronted by a middle-aged gentleman of pleasing appearance, neatly and correctly dressed. He looked at me with an expression of great pity, but before I could stammer out my ignorance of the neighbourhood, for indeed I had not the slightest notion of where I had wandered, he spoke.

"My dear madam," he said, "you seem in some terrible distress. You cannot think how you alarmed me. But may I enquire the nature of your trouble? I assure you that you can safely confide in me."

"You are very kind," I replied, "but I fear there is nothing to be done. My condition seems a hopeless one."

"Oh, nonsense, nonsense! You are too young to talk like that. Come, let us walk down here, and you must tell me your difficulty. Perhaps I may be able to help you."

There was something very soothing and persuasive in his manner, and as we walked together I gave him an outline of my story, and told of the despair that had oppressed me almost to death.

"You were wrong to give in so completely," he said, when I was silent. "A month is too short a time in which to feel one's way in London. London, let me tell you, Miss Lally, does not lie open and undefended; it is a fortified place, fossed and double-moated with curious intricacies. As must always happen in large towns, the conditions of life have become hugely artificial; no mere simple palisade is run up to oppose the man or woman who would take the place by storm, but serried lines of subtle contrivances, mines, and pitfalls which it needs a strange skill to overcome. You, in your simplicity, fancied you had only to shout for these walls to sink into nothingness, but the time is gone for such startling victories as these. Take courage; you will learn the secret of success before long."

"Alas! sir," I replied, "I have no doubt your conclusions are correct, but at the present moment I seem to be in a fair way to die of starvation. You spoke of a secret; for heaven's sake tell it me, if you have any pity for my distress."

He laughed genially. "There lies the strangeness of it all. Those who know the secret cannot tell it if they would; it is positively as ineffable as the central doctrine of Freemasonry. But I may say this, that you yourself have penetrated at least the outer husk of the mystery," and he laughed again.

"Pray do not jest with me," I said. "What have I done, *que sçais-je?* I am so far ignorant that I have not the slightest idea of how my next meal is to be provided."

"Excuse me. You ask what you have done. You have met me. Come, we will fence no longer. I see you have self-education, the only education which is not infinitely pernicious, and I am in want of a governess for my two children. I have been a widower for some years; my name is Gregg. I offer you the post I have named, and shall we say a salary of a hundred a year?"

I could only stutter out my thanks, and slipping a card with his address, and a banknote by way of earnest, into my hand, Mr. Gregg bade me good-bye, asking me to call in a day or two.

Such was my introduction to Professor Gregg, and can you wonder that the remembrance of despair and the cold blast that had blown from the gates of death upon me made me regard him as a second father? Before the close of the week I was installed in my new duties. The professor had leased an old brick manor-house in a western suburb of London, and here, surrounded by pleasant lawns and orchards, and soothed with the murmur of ancient elms that rocked their boughs above the roof, the new chapter of my life began. Knowing as you do the nature of the professor's occupations, you will not be surprised to hear that the house teemed with books, and cabinets full of strange, and even hideous, objects filled every available nook in the vast low rooms. Gregg was a man whose one thought was for knowledge, and I too before long caught something of his enthusiasm, and strove to enter into his passion for research. In a few months I was perhaps more his secretary than the governess of the two children, and many a night I have sat at the desk in the glow of the shaded lamp while he, pacing up and down in the rich gloom of the firelight, dictated to me the substance of his *Textbook of Ethnology.* But amidst these more sober and accurate studies I always detected a something hidden, a longing and desire for some object to which he did not allude; and now and then he would break short in what he was saying and lapse into reverie, intranced, as it seemed to me, by some distant prospect of adventurous discovery. The textbook was at last finished, and we began to receive proofs from the printers, which were intrusted to me for a first reading, and then underwent the final revision of the professor. All the while his weariness of the actual business he was engaged on increased, and it was with the joyous laugh of a schoolboy when term is over that he one day handed me a copy of the book. "There," he said, "I have kept my word; I promised to write it, and it is done with. Now I shall be free to live for stranger things; I confess it, Miss Lally, I covet the renown of Columbus; you will, I hope, see me play the part of an explorer."

"Surely," I said, "there is little left to explore. You have been born a few hundred years too late for that."

"I think you are wrong," he replied; "there are still, depend upon it, quaint, undiscovered countries and continents of strange extent. Ah, Miss Lally! believe me, we stand amidst sacraments and mysteries full of awe, and it doth not yet appear what we shall be. Life, believe me, is no simple thing, no mass of grey matter and congeries of veins and muscles to be laid naked by the surgeon's knife; man is the secret which I am about to explore, and before I can discover him I must cross over weltering seas indeed, and oceans and the mists of many thousand years. You know the myth of the lost Atlantis; what if it be true, and I am destined to be called the discoverer of that wonderful land?"

I could see the excitement boiling beneath his words, and in his face was the heat of the hunter; before me stood a man who believed himself summoned to tourney with the unknown. A pang of joy possessed me when I reflected that I was to be in a way associated with him in the adventure, and I too burned with the lust of the chase, not pausing to consider that I knew not what we were to unshadow.

The next morning Professor Gregg took me into his inner study, where, ranged against the wall, stood a nest of pigeon-holes, every drawer neatly labelled, and the results of years of toil classified in a few feet of space.

"Here," he said, "is my life; here are all the facts which I have gathered together with so much pains, and yet it is all nothing. No, nothing to what I am about to attempt. Look at this"; and he took me to an old bureau, a piece fantastic and faded, which stood in a corner of the room. He unlocked the front and opened one of the drawers.

"A few scraps of paper," he went on, pointing to the drawer, "and a lump of black stone, rudely annotated with queer marks and scratches—that is all that drawer holds. Here you see is an old envelope with the dark red stamp of twenty years ago, but I have pencilled a few lines at the back; here is a sheet of manuscript, and here some cuttings from obscure local journals. And if you ask me the subject-matter of the collection, it will not seem extraordinary—a servant-girl at a farmhouse, who disappeared from her place and has never been heard of, a child supposed to have slipped down some old working on the mountains, some queer scribbling on a limestone rock, a man murdered with a blow from a strange weapon; such is the scent I have to go upon. Yes, as you say, there is a ready explanation for all this; the girl may have run away to London, or Liverpool, or New York; the child may be at the bottom of the disused shaft; and the letters on the rock may be the idle whims of some vagrant. Yes, yes, I admit all that; but I know I hold the true key. Look!" and he held out a slip of yellow paper.

Characters found inscribed on a limestone rock on the Grey Hills, I read, and then there was a word erased, presumably the name of a county, and a date some fifteen years back. Beneath was traced a number of uncouth characters, shaped somewhat like wedges or daggers, as strange and outlandish as the Hebrew alphabet.

"Now the seal," said Professor Gregg, and he handed me the black stone, a thing about two inches long, and something like an old-fashioned tobacco-stopper, much enlarged.

I held it up to the light, and saw to my surprise the characters on the paper repeated on the seal.

"Yes," said the professor, "they are the same. And the marks on the limestone rock were made fifteen years ago, with some red substance. And the characters on the seal are four thousand years old at least. Perhaps much more."

"Is it a hoax?" I said.

"No, I anticipated that. I was not to be led to give my life to a practical joke. I have tested the matter very carefully. Only one person besides myself knows of the mere existence of that black seal. Besides, there are other reasons which I cannot enter into now."

"But what does it all mean?" I said. "I cannot understand to what conclusion all this leads."

"My dear Miss Lally, that is a question I would rather leave unanswered for some little time. Perhaps I shall never be able to say what secrets are held here in solution; a few vague hints, the outlines of village tragedies, a few marks done with red earth upon a rock, and an ancient seal. A queer set of data to go upon? Half a dozen pieces of evidence, and twenty years before even so much could be got together; and who knows what mirage or *terra incognita* may be beyond all this? I look across deep waters, Miss Lally, and the land beyond may be but a haze after all. But still I believe it is not so, and a few months will shew whether I am right or wrong."

He left me, and alone I endeavoured to fathom the mystery, wondering to what goal such eccentric odds and ends of evidence could lead. I myself am not wholly devoid of imagination, and I had reason to respect the professor's solidity of intellect; yet I saw in the contents of the drawer·but the materials of fantasy, and vainly tried to conceive what theory could be founded on the fragments that had been placed before me. Indeed, I could discover in what I had heard and seen but the first chapter of an extravagant romance; and yet deep in my heart I burned with curiosity, and day after day I looked eagerly in Professor

Gregg's face for some hint of what was to happen.

It was one evening after dinner that the word came.

"I hope you can make your preparations without much trouble," he said suddenly to me. "We shall be leaving here in a week's time."

"Really!" I said in astonishment. "Where are we going?"

"I have taken a country house in the west of England, not far from Caermaen, a quiet little town, once a city, and the headquarters of a Roman legion. It is very dull there, but the country is pretty, and the air is wholesome."

I detected a glint in his eyes, and guessed that this sudden move had some relation to our conversation of a few days before.

"I shall just take a few books with me," said Professor Gregg, "that is all. Everything else will remain here for our return. I have got a holiday," he went on, smiling at me, "and I shan't be sorry to be quit for a time of my old bones and stones and rubbish. Do you know," he went on, "I have been grinding away at facts for thirty years; it is time for fancies."

The days passed quickly; I could see that the professor was all quivering with suppressed excitement, and I could scarce credit the eager appetence of his glance as we left the old manor house behind us and began our journey. We set out at midday, and it was in the dusk of the evening that we arrived at a little county station. I was tired and excited, and the drive through the lanes seems all a dream. First the deserted streets of a forgotten village, while I heard Professor Gregg's voice talking of the Augustan Legion and the clash of arms, and all the tremendous pomp that followed the eagles; then the broad river swimming to full tide with the last afterglow glimmering duskily in the yellow water, the wide meadows, the cornfields whitening, and the deep lane winding on the slope between the hills and the water. At last we began to ascend, and the air grew rarer. I looked down and saw the pure white mist tracking the outline of the river like a shroud, and a vague and shadowy country; imaginations and fantasy of swelling hills and hanging woods, and half-shaped outlines of hills beyond, and in the distance the glare of the furnace fire on the mountain, growing by turns a pillar of shining flame and fading to a dull point of red. We were slowly mounting a carriage drive, and then there came to me the cool breath and the secret of the great wood that was above us; I seemed to wander in its deepest depths, and there was the sound of trickling water, the scent of the green leaves, and the breath of the summer night. The carriage stopped at last, and I could scarcely distinguish the form of the house as I waited a moment at the pillared porch. The rest of the evening seemed a dream of strange things bounded by the great silence of the wood and the valley and the river.

The next morning, when I awoke and looked out of the bow window of the big, old-fashioned bedroom, I saw under a grey sky a country that was still all mystery. The long, lovely valley, with the river winding in and out below, crossed in mid-vision by a mediæval bridge of vaulted and buttressed stone, the clear presence of the rising ground beyond, and the woods that I had only seen in shadow the night before, seemed tinged with enchantment, and the soft breath of air that sighed in at the opened pane was like no other wind. I looked across the valley, and beyond, hill followed on hill as wave on wave, and here a faint blue pillar of smoke rose still in the morning air from the chimney of an ancient grey farmhouse, there was a rugged height crowned with dark firs, and in the distance I saw the white streak of a road that climbed and vanished into some unimagined country. But the boundary of all was a great wall of mountain, vast in the west, and ending like a fortress with a steep ascent and a domed tumulus clear against the sky.

I saw Professor Gregg walking up and down the terrace path below the windows, and it was evident that he was revelling in the sense of liberty, and the thought that he had for a while bidden good-bye to task-work. When I joined him there was exultation in his voice as he pointed out the sweep of valley and the river that wound beneath the lovely hills.

"Yes," he said, "it is a strangely beautiful country; and to me, at least, it seems full of mystery. You have not forgotten the drawer I shewed you, Miss Lally? No; and you guessed that I have come here not merely for the sake of the children and the fresh air?"

"I think I have guessed as much as that," I replied; "but you must remember I do not know the mere nature of your investigations; and as for the connection between the search and this wonderful valley, it is past my guessing."

He smiled queerly at me. "You must not think I am making a mystery for the sake of a mystery," he said. "I do not speak out because, so far, there is nothing to be spoken, nothing definite, I mean, nothing that can be set down in hard black and white, as dull and sure and irreproachable as any blue-book. And then I have another reason: Many years ago a chance paragraph in a newspaper caught my attention, and focused in an instant the vagrant thoughts and half-formed fancies of many idle and speculative hours into a certain hypothesis. I saw at once that I was treading on a thin crust; my theory was wild and fantastic in the extreme, and I would not for any consideration have written a hint of it for publication. But I thought that in the company of scientific men like myself, men who knew the course of discovery, and were aware that the gas that blazes and flares in the gin-palace was once a wild hypothesis—I thought that with such men as these I might hazard my dream—let us say Atlantis, or the philosopher's stone, or what you like—without danger of ridicule. I found I was grossly mistaken; my friends looked blankly at me and at one another, and I could see something of pity, and something also of insolent contempt, in the glances they exchanged. One of them called on me next day, and hinted that I must be suffering from overwork and brain exhaustion. 'In plain terms,' I said, 'you think I am going mad. I think not'; and I shewed him out with some little appearance of heat. Since that day I vowed that I would never whisper the nature of my theory to any living soul; to no one but yourself have I ever shewn the contents of that drawer. After all, I may be following a rainbow; I may have been misled by the play of coincidence; but as I stand here in this mystic hush and silence amidst the woods and the wild hills, I am more than ever sure that I am hot on the scent. Come, it is time we went in."

To me in all this there was something both of wonder and excitement; I knew how in his ordinary work Professor Gregg moved step by step, testing every inch of the way, and never venturing on assertion without proof that was impregnable. Yet I divined more from his glance and the vehemence of his tone than from the spoken word, that he had in his every thought the vision of the almost incredible continually with him; and I, who was with some share of imagination no little of a sceptic, offended at a hint of the marvellous, could not help asking myself whether he were cherishing a monomania, and barring out from this one subject all the scientific method of his other life.

Yet, with this image of mystery haunting my thoughts, I surrendered wholly to the charm of the country. Above the faded house on the hillside began the great forest—a long, dark line seen from the opposing hills, stretching above the river for many a mile from north to south, and yielding in the north to even wilder country, barren and savage hills, and ragged common-land, a territory all strange and unvisited, and more unknown to Englishmen than the very heart of Africa. The space of a couple of steep fields alone separated the house from the wood, and the children were delighted to follow me up the long alleys of undergrowth, between smooth pleached walls of shining beech, to the highest point in the wood, whence one looked on one side across the river and the rise and fall of the country to the great western mountain wall, and on the other over the surge and dip of the myriad trees of the forest, over level meadows and the shining yellow sea to the faint coast beyond. I used to sit at this point on the warm sunlit turf which marked the track of the Roman Road, while the two children raced about hunting for the whinberries that grew here and there on the banks. Here beneath the deep blue sky and the great clouds rolling, like olden galleons with sails full-bellied, from the sea to the hills, as I listened to the whispered charm of the great and ancient wood, I lived solely for delight, and only remembered strange things when we would return to the house and find Professor Gregg either shut up in the little room he had made his study, or else pacing the terrace with the look, patient and enthusiastic, of the determined seeker.

One morning, some eight or nine days after our arrival, I looked out of my window and saw the whole landscape transmuted before me. The clouds had dipped low and hidden the mountain in the west; a southern wind was driving the rain in shifting pillars up the valley, and the little brooklet that burst the hill below the house now raged, a red torrent, down the river. We were perforce obliged to keep snug within-doors; and when I had attended to my pupils, I sat down in the morning-room where the ruins of a library still encumbered an old-fashioned bookcase. I had inspected the shelves once or twice, but their contents had failed to attract me; volumes of eighteenth-century sermons, an old book on farriery, a collection of *Poems* by "persons of quality", Prideaux's *Connection,* and an odd volume of Pope, were the boundaries of the library, and there seemed little doubt that everything of interest or value had been removed. Now however, in desperation, I began to re-examine the musty sheepskin and calf bindings, and found, much to my delight, a fine old quarto printed by the Stephani, containing the three books of Pomponius Mela, *De Situ Orbis,* and other of the ancient geographers. I knew enough of Latin to steer my way through an ordinary sentence, and I soon became absorbed in the odd mixture of fact and fancy—light shining on a little space of the world, and beyond, mist and shadow and awful forms. Glancing over the clear-printed pages, my attention was caught by the heading of a chapter in Solinus, and I read the words:—

"MIRA DE INTIMIS GENTIBUS LIBYAE, DE LAPIDE HEXECONTALITHO,"

—"The wonders of the people that inhabit the inner parts of Libya, and of the stone called Sixtystone."

The odd title attracted me, and I read on:—

"Gens ista avia et secreta habitat, in montibus horrendis fœda mysteria celebrat. De hominibus nihil aliud illi praeferunt quam figuram, ab humano ritu prorsus exulant, oderunt deum lucis. Stridunt potius quam loquuntur; vox absona nee sine horrore auditur. Lapide quodam gloriantur, quem Hexecontalithon vocant; dicunt enim hunc lapidem sexaginta notas ostendere. Cujus lapidis nomen secretum ineffabile colunt: quod Ixaxar."

"This folk," I translated to myself, "dwells in remote and secret places, and celebrates foul mysteries on savage hills. Nothing have they in common with men save the face, and the customs of humanity are wholly strange to them; and they hate the sun. They hiss rather than speak; their voices are harsh, and not to be heard without fear. They boast of a certain stone, which they call Sixtystone; for they say that it displays sixty characters. And this stone has a secret unspeakable name; which is Ixaxar."

I laughed at the queer inconsequence of all this, and thought it fit for Sinbad the Sailor, or other of the supplementary Nights. When I saw Professor Gregg in the course of the day, I told him of my find in the bookcase, and the fantastic rubbish I had been reading. To my surprise he looked up at me with an expression of great interest.

"That is really very curious," he said. "I have never thought it worth while to look into the old geographers, and I dare say I have missed a good deal. Ah, that is the passage, is it? It seems a shame to rob you of your entertainment, but I really think I must carry off the book."

The next day the professor called me to come to the study. I found him sitting at a table in the full light of the window, scrutinising something very attentively with a magnifying glass.

"Ah, Miss Lally," he began, "I want to use your eyes. This glass is pretty good, but not like my old one that I left in town. Would you mind examining the thing yourself, and telling me how many characters are cut on it?"

He handed me the object in his hand. I saw that it was the black seal he had shewn me in London, and my heart began to beat with the thought that I was presently to know something. I took the seal, and, holding it up to the light, checked off the grotesque dagger-shaped characters one by one.

"I make sixty-two," I said at last.

"Sixty-two? Nonsense; it's impossible. Ah, I see what you have done, you have counted that and that," and he pointed to two marks which I had certainly taken as letters with the rest.

"Yes, yes," Professor Gregg went on, "but those are obvious scratches, done accidentally; I saw that at once. Yes, then that's quite right. Thank you very much, Miss Lally."

I was going away, rather disappointed at my having been called in merely to count the number of marks on the black seal, when suddenly there flashed into my mind what I had read in the morning.

"But, Professor Gregg," I cried, breathless, "the seal, the seal. Why, it is the stone Hexecontalithos that Solinus writes of; it is Ixaxar."

"Yes," he said, "I suppose it is. Or it may be a mere coincidence. It never does to be too sure, you know, in these matters. Coincidence killed the professor."

I went away puzzled at what I had heard, and as much as ever at a loss to find the ruling clue in this maze of strange evidence. For three days the bad weather lasted, changing from driving rain to a dense mist, fine and dripping, and we seemed to be shut up in a white cloud that veiled all the world away from us. All the while Professor Gregg was darkling in his room, unwilling, it appeared, to dispense confidences or talk of any kind, and I heard him walking to and fro with a quick, impatient step, as if he were in some way wearied of inaction. The fourth morning was fine, and at breakfast the professor said briskly—

"We want some extra help around the house; a boy of fifteen or sixteen, you know. There are a lot of little odd jobs that take up the maids' time which a boy could do much better."

"The girls have not complained to me in any way," I replied. "Indeed, Anne said there was much less work than in London, owing to there being so little dust."

"Ah, yes, they are very good girls. But I think we shall do much better with a boy. In fact, that is what has been bothering me for the last two days."

"Bothering you?" I said in astonishment, for as a matter of fact the professor never took the slightest interest in the affairs of the house.

"Yes," he said, "the weather, you know. I really couldn't go out in that Scotch mist; I don't know the country very well, and I should have lost my way. But I am going to get the boy this morning."

"But how do you know there is such a boy as you want anywhere about?"

"Oh, I have no doubt as to that. I may have to walk a mile or two at the most, but I am sure to find just the boy I require."

I thought the professor was joking, but though his tone was airy enough there was something grim and set about his features that puzzled me. He got his stick, and stood at the door looking meditatively before him, and as I passed through the hall he called to me.

"By the way, Miss Lally, there was one thing I wanted to say to you. I dare say you may have heard that some of these country lads are not over bright; idiotic would be a harsh word to use, and they are usually called 'naturals,' or something of the kind. I hope you won't mind if the boy I am after should turn out not too keen-witted; he will be perfectly harmless, of course, and blacking boots doesn't need much mental effort."

With that he was gone, striding up the road that led to the wood, and I remained stupefied; and then for the first time my astonishment was mingled with a sudden note of terror, arising I knew not whence, and all unexplained even to myself, and yet I felt about my heart for an instant something of the chill of death, and that shapeless, formless dread of the unknown that is worse than death itself. I tried to find courage in the sweet air that blew up from the sea, and in the sunlight after rain, but the mystic woods seemed to darken around me; and the vision of the river coiling between the reeds, and the silver grey of the ancient bridge, fashioned in my mind symbols of vague dread, as the mind of a child fashions terror from things harmless and familiar.

Two hours later Professor Gregg returned. I met him as he came down the road, and asked quietly if he had been able to find a boy.

"Oh yes," he answered; "I found one easily enough. His name is Jervase Cradock, and I expect he will make himself very useful. His father has been dead for many years, and the mother, whom I saw, seemed very glad at the prospect of a few shillings extra coming in on Saturday nights. As I expected, he is not too sharp, has fits at times, the mother said; but as he will not be trusted with the china, that doesn't much matter, does it? And he is not in any way dangerous, you know, merely a little weak."

"When is he coming?"

"To-morrow morning at eight o'clock. Anne will shew him what he has to do, and how to do it. At first he will go home every night, but perhaps it may ultimately turn out more convenient for him to sleep here, and only go home for Sundays."

I found nothing to say to all this; Professor Gregg spoke in a quiet tone of matter-of-fact, as indeed was warranted by the circumstance; and yet I could not quell my sensation of astonishment at the whole affair. I knew that in reality no assistance was wanted in the house-work, and the professor's prediction that the boy he was to engage might prove a little "simple", followed by so exact a fulfilment, struck me as bizarre in the extreme. The next morning I heard from the housemaid that the boy Cradock had come at eight, and that she had been trying to make him useful. "He doesn't seem quite all there, I don't think, miss," was her comment, and later in the day I saw him helping the old man who worked in the garden. He was a youth of about fourteen, with black hair and black eyes and an olive skin, and I saw at once from the curious vacancy of his expression that he was mentally weak. He touched his forehead awkwardly as I went by, and I heard him answering the gardener in a queer, harsh voice that caught my attention; it gave me the impression of some one speaking deep below under the earth, and there was a strange sibilance, like the hiss-

ing of the phonograph as the pointer travels over the cylinder. I heard
that he seemed anxious to do what he could, and was quite docile and
obedient, and Morgan the gardener, who knew his mother, assured me
he was perfectly harmless. "He's always been a bit queer," he said,
"and no wonder, after what his mother went through before he was
born. I did know his father, Thomas Cradock, well, and a very fine
workman he was too, indeed. He got something wrong with his lungs
owing to working in the wet woods, and never got over it, and went
off quite sudden like. And they do say as how Mrs. Cradock was quite
off her head; anyhow, she was found by Mr. Hillyer, Ty Coch, all
crouched up on the Grey Hills, over there, crying and weeping like a
lost soul. And Jervase, he was born about eight months afterwards,
and as I was saying, he was a bit queer always; and they do say when he
could scarcely walk he would frighten the other children into fits with
the noises he would make."

A word in the story had stirred up some remembrance within me,
and, vaguely curious, I asked the old man where the Grey Hills were.

"Up there," he said, with the same gesture he had used before;
"you go past the Fox and Hounds, and through the forest, by the old
ruins. It's a good five mile from here, and a strange sort of a place. The
poorest soil between this and Monmouth, they do say, though it's
good feed for sheep. Yes, it was a sad thing for poor Mrs. Cradock."

The old man turned to his work, and I strolled on down the path
between the espaliers, gnarled and gouty with age, thinking of the story
I had heard, and groping for the point in it that had some key to my
memory. In an instant it came before me; I had seen the phrase "Grey
Hills" on the slip of yellowed paper that Professor Gregg had taken
from the drawer in his cabinet. Again I was seized with pangs of mingled curiosity and fear; I remembered the strange characters copied
from the limestone rock, and then again their identity with the inscription on the age-old seal, and the fantastic fables of the Latin geogra-
pher. I saw beyond doubt that, unless coincidence had set all the scene
and disposed all these bizarre events with curious art, I was to be a
spectator of things far removed from the usual and customary traffic
and jostle of life. Professor Gregg I noted day by day; he was hot on
his trail, growing lean with eagerness; and in the evenings, when the
sun was swimming on the verge of the mountain, he would pace the

terrace to and fro with his eyes on the ground, while the mist grew white in the valley, and the stillness of the evening brought far voices near, and the blue smoke rose a straight column from the diamond-shaped chimney of the grey farmhouse, just as I had seen it on the first morning. I have told you I was of sceptical habit; but though I understood little or nothing, I began to dread, vainly proposing to myself the iterated dogmas of science that all life is material, and that in the system of things there is no undiscovered land, even beyond the remotest stars, where the supernatural can find a footing. Yet there struck in on this the thought that matter is as really awful and unknown as spirit, that science itself but dallies on the threshold, scarcely gaining more than a glimpse of the wonders of the inner place.

There is one day that stands up from amidst the others as a grim red beacon, betokening evil to come. I was sitting on a bench in the garden, watching the boy Cradock weeding, when I was suddenly alarmed by a harsh and choking sound, like the cry of a wild beast in anguish, and I was unspeakably shocked to see the unfortunate lad standing in full view before me, his whole body quivering and shaking at short intervals as though shocks of electricity were passing through him, his teeth grinding, foam gathering on his lips, and his face all swollen and blackened to a hideous mask of humanity. I shrieked with terror, and Professor Gregg came running; and as I pointed to Cradock, the boy with one convulsive shudder fell face forward, and lay on the wet earth, his body writhing like a wounded blind-worm, and an inconceivable babble of sounds bursting and rattling and hissing from his lips. He seemed to pour forth an infamous jargon, with words, or what seemed words, that might have belonged to a tongue dead since untold ages, and buried deep beneath Nilotic mud, or in the inmost recesses of the Mexican forest. For a moment the thought passed through my mind, as my ears were still revolted with that infernal clamour, "Surely this is the very speech of hell," and then I cried out again and again, and ran away shuddering to my inmost soul. I had seen Professor Gregg's face as he stooped over the wretched boy and raised him, and I was appalled by the glow of exultation that shone on every lineament and feature. As I sat in my room with drawn blinds, and my eyes hidden in my hands, I heard heavy steps beneath, and I was told afterwards that Professor Gregg had carried Cradock to his study, and had locked the door. I heard voices murmur indistinctly, and I trembled to think of what might be passing within a few feet of where I sat; I longed to escape to the woods and sunshine, and yet I dreaded the sights that might confront me on the way; and at last, as I held the handle of the door nervously, I heard Professor Gregg's voice calling to me with a cheerful ring. "It's all right now, Miss Lally," he said. "The poor fellow has got over it, and I have been arranging for him to sleep here after to-morrow. Perhaps I may be able to do something for him."

"Yes," he said later, "it was a very painful sight, and I don't wonder you were alarmed. We may hope that good food will build him up a little, but I am afraid he will never be really cured," and he affected the dismal and conventional air with which one speaks of hopeless illness; and yet beneath it I detected the delight that leapt up rampant within him, and fought and struggled to find utterance. It was as if one glanced down on the even surface of the sea, clear and immobile, and saw beneath raging depths, and a storm of contending billows. It was indeed to me a torturing and offensive problem that this man, who had so bounteously rescued me from the sharpness of death, and shewed himself in all the relations of life full of benevolence, and pity, and kindly forethought, should so manifestly be for once on the side of the demons, and take a ghastly pleasure in the torments of an afflicted fellow-creature. Apart, I struggled with the horned difficulty, and strove to find the solution; but without the hint of a clue, beset by mystery and contradiction. I saw nothing that might help me, and began to wonder whether, after all, I had not escaped from the white mist of the suburb at too dear a rate. I hinted something of my thought to the professor; I said enough to let him know that I was in the most acute perplexity, but the moment after regretted what I had done when I saw his face contort with a spasm of pain.

"My dear Miss Lally," he said, "you surely do not wish to leave us? No, no, you would not do it. You do not know how I rely on you; how confidently I go forward, assured that you are here to watch over my children. You, Miss Lally, are my rearguard; for let me tell you the business in which I am engaged is not wholly devoid of peril. You have not forgotten what I said the first morning here; my lips are shut by an old and firm resolve till they can open to utter no ingenious hypothesis or vague surmise but irrefragable fact, as certain as a demonstration in mathematics. Think over it, Miss Lally: not for a moment would I endeavour to keep you here against your own instincts, and yet I tell you frankly that I am persuaded it is here, here amidst the woods, that your duty lies."

I was touched by the eloquence of his tone, and by the remembrance that the man, after all, had been my salvation, and I gave him my hand on a promise to serve him loyally and without question. A few days later the rector of our church—a little church, grey and severe and quaint, that hovered on the very banks of the river and watched the tides swim and return—came to see us, and Professor Gregg easily persuaded him to stay and share our dinner. Mr. Meyrick was a member of an antique family of squires, whose old manor-house stood amongst the hills some seven miles away, and thus, rooted in the soil, the rector was a living store of all the old, fading customs and lore of the country. His manner, genial, with a deal of retired oddity, won on Professor Gregg; and towards the cheese, when a curious Burgundy had begun its incantations, the two men glowed like the wine, and talked of philology with the enthusiasm of a burgess over the peerage. The parson was expounding the pronunciation of the Welsh *ll,* and producing sounds like the gurgle of his native brooks, when Professor Gregg struck in.

"By the way," he said, "that was a very odd word I met the other day. You know my boy, poor Jervase Cradock? Well, he has got the bad habit of talking to himself, and the day before yesterday I was walking in the garden here and heard him; he was evidently quite unconscious of my presence. A lot of what he said I couldn't make out, but one word struck me distinctly. It was such an odd sound, half-sibilant, half-guttural, and as quaint as those double *ls* you have been demonstrating. I do not know whether I can give you an idea of the sound; 'Ishakshar' is perhaps as near as I can get. But the *k* ought to be a Greek *chi* or a Spanish *j.* Now what does it mean in Welsh?"

"In Welsh?" said the parson. "There is no such word in Welsh, nor any word remotely resembling it. I know the book-Welsh, as they call it, and the colloquial dialects as well as any man, but there's no word like that from Anglesea to Usk. Besides, none of the Cradocks speaks a word of Welsh; it's dying out about here."

"Really. You interest me extremely, Mr. Meyrick. I confess the word didn't strike me as having the Welsh ring. But I thought it might be some local corruption."

"No, I never heard such a word, or anything like it. Indeed," he added, smiling whimsically, "if it belongs to any language, I should say it must be that of the fairies—the Tylwydd Têg, as we call them."

The talk went on to the discovery of a Roman villa in the neighbourhood; and soon after I left the room, and sat down apart to wonder at the drawing together of such strange clues of evidence. As the professor had spoken of the curious word, I had caught the glint of his eye upon me; and though the pronunciation he gave was grotesque in the extreme, I recognised the name of the stone of sixty characters mentioned by Solinus, the black seal shut up in some secret drawer of the study, stamped for ever by a vanished race with signs that no man could read, signs that might, for all I knew, be the veils of awful things done long ago, and forgotten before the hills were moulded into form.

When the next morning I came down, I found Professor Gregg pacing the terrace in his eternal walk.

"Look at that bridge," he said when he saw me; "observe the quaint and Gothic design, the angles between the arches, and the silvery grey of the stone in the awe of the morning light. I confess it seems to me symbolic; it should illustrate a mystical allegory of the passage from one world to another."

"Professor Gregg," I said quietly, "it is time that I knew something of what has happened, and of what is to happen."

For the moment he put me off, but I returned again with the same question in the evening, and then Professor Gregg flamed with excitement. "Don't you understand yet?" he cried. "But I have told you a good deal; yes, and shewn you a good deal; you have heard pretty nearly all that I have heard, and seen what I have seen; or at least," and his voice chilled as he spoke, "enough to make a good deal clear as noonday. The servants told you, I have no doubt, that the wretched boy Cradock had another seizure the night before last; he awoke me with cries in that voice you heard in the garden, and I went to him, and God forbid you should see what I saw that night. But all this is useless; my time here is drawing to a close; I must be back in town in three weeks, as I have a course of lectures to prepare, and need all my books about me. In a very few days it will all be over, and I shall no longer hint, and no longer be liable to ridicule as a madman and a quack. No, I shall speak plainly, and I shall be heard with such emotions as perhaps no other man has ever drawn from the breasts of his fellows."

He paused, and seemed to grow radiant with the joy of great and wonderful discovery.

"But all that is for the future, the near future certainly, but still the future," he went on at length. "There is something to be done yet; you will remember my telling you that my researches were not altogether devoid of peril? Yes, there is a certain amount of danger to be faced; I did not know how much when I spoke on the subject before, and to a certain extent I am still in the dark. But it will be a strange adventure, the last of all, the last demonstration in the chain."

He was walking up and down the room as he spoke, and I could hear in his voice the contending tones of exultation and despondence, or perhaps I should say awe, the awe of a man who goes forth on unknown waters, and I thought of his allusion to Columbus on the night he had laid his book before me. The evening was a little chilly, and a fire of logs had been lighted in the study where we were; the remittent flame and the glow on the walls reminded me of the old days. I was sitting silent in an arm-chair by the fire, wondering over all I had heard, and still vainly speculating as to the secret springs concealed from me under all the phantasmagoria I had witnessed, when I became suddenly aware of a sensation that change of some sort had been at work in the room, and that there was something unfamiliar in its aspect. For some time I looked about me, trying in vain to localise the alteration that I knew had been made; the table by the window, the chairs, the faded settee were all as I had known them. Suddenly, as a sought-for recollection flashes into mind, I knew what was amiss. I was facing the professor's desk, which stood on the other side of the fire, and above the desk was a grimy-looking bust of Pitt, that I had never seen there before. And then I remembered the true position of this work of art; in the furthest corner by the door was an old cupboard, projecting into the room, and on the top of the cupboard, fifteen feet from the floor, the bust had been, and there, no doubt, it had delayed, accumulating dirt, since the early years of the century.

I was utterly amazed, and sat silent still, in a confusion of thought.

There was, so far as I knew, no such thing as a step-ladder in the house, for I had asked for one to make some alterations in the curtains of my room, and a tall man standing on a chair would have found it impossible to take down the bust. It had been placed, not on the edge of the cupboard, but far back against the wall; and Professor Gregg was, if anything, under the average height.

"How on earth did you manage to get down Pitt?" I said at last.

The professor looked curiously at me, and seemed to hesitate a little.

"They must have found you a step-ladder, or perhaps the gardener brought in a short ladder from outside?"

"No, I have had no ladder of any kind. Now, Miss Lally," he went on with an awkward simulation of jest, "there is a little puzzle for you; a problem in the manner of the inimitable Holmes; there are the facts, plain and patent; summon your acuteness to the solution of the puzzle. For Heaven's sake," he cried with a breaking voice, "say no more about it! I tell you, I never touched the thing," and he went out of the room with horror manifest on his face, and his hand shook and jarred the door behind him.

I looked round the room in vague surprise, not at all realising what had happened, making vain and idle surmises by way of explanation, and wondering at the stirring of black waters by an idle word and the trivial change of an ornament. "This is some petty business, some whim on which I have jarred," I reflected; "the professor is perhaps scrupulous and superstitious over trifles, and my question may have outraged unacknowledged fears, as though one killed a spider or spilled the salt before the very eyes of a practical Scotchwoman." I was immersed in these fond suspicions, and began to plume myself a little on my immunity from such empty fears, when the truth fell heavily as lead upon my heart, and I recognised with cold terror that some awful influence had been at work. The bust was simply inaccessible; without a ladder no one could have touched it.

I went out to the kitchen and spoke as quietly as I could to the housemaid.

"Who moved that bust from the top of the cupboard, Anne?" I said to her. "Professor Gregg says he has not touched it. Did you find an old step-ladder in one of the outhouses?"

The girl looked at me blankly.

"I never touched it," she said. "I found it where it is now the other morning when I dusted the room. I remember now, it was Wednesday morning, because it was the morning after Cradock was taken bad in the night. My room is next to his, you know, miss," the girl went on piteously, "and it was awful to hear how he cried and called out names that I couldn't understand. It made me feel all afraid; and then master came, and I heard him speak, and he took down Cradock to the study and gave him something."

"And you found that bust moved the next morning?"

"Yes, miss. There was a queer sort of smell in the study when I came down and opened the windows; a bad smell it was, and I wondered what it could be. Do you know, miss, I went a long time ago to the Zoo in London with my cousin Thomas Barker, one afternoon that I had off, when I was at Mrs. Prince's in Stanhope Gate, and we went into the snake-house to see the snakes, and it was just the same sort of smell; very sick it made me feel, I remember, and I got Barker to take me out. And it was just the same kind of a smell in the study, as I was saying, and I was wondering what it could be from, when I see that bust with Pitt cut in it, standing on the master's desk, and I thought to myself, Now who has done that, and how have they done it? And when I came to dust the things, I looked at the bust, and I saw a great mark on it where the dust was gone, for I don't think it can have been touched with a duster for years and years, and it wasn't like finger-marks, but a large patch like, broad and spread out. So I passed my hand over it, without thinking what I was doing, and where that patch was it was all sticky and slimy, as if a snail had crawled over it. Very strange, isn't it, miss? and I wonder who can have done it, and how that mess was made."

The well-meant gabble of the servant touched me to the quick; I lay down upon my bed, and bit my lip that I should not cry out loud in the sharp anguish of my terror and bewilderment. Indeed, I was almost mad with dread; I believe that if it had been daylight I should have fled hot foot, forgetting all courage and all the debt of gratitude that was due to Professor Gregg, not caring whether my fate were that I must starve slowly, so long as I might escape from the net of blind and panic fear that every day seemed to draw a little closer round me. If I knew, I thought, if I knew what there were to dread, I could guard against it; but here, in this lonely house, shut in on all sides by the olden woods and the vaulted hills, terror seems to spring inconsequent from every covert, and the flesh is aghast at the half-heard murmurs of horrible things. All in vain I strove to summon scepticism to my aid, and endeavoured by cool common-sense to buttress my belief in a world of natural order, for the air that blew in at the open window was a mystic breath, and in the darkness I felt the silence go heavy and sorrowful as a mass of requiem, and I conjured images of strange shapes gathering fast amidst the reeds, beside the wash of the river.

In the morning, from the moment that I set foot in the breakfast-room, I felt that the unknown plot was drawing to a crisis; the professor's face was firm and set, and he seemed hardly to hear our voices when we spoke.

"I am going out for a rather long walk," he said when the meal was over. "You mustn't be expecting me, now, or thinking anything has happened if I don't turn up to dinner. I have been getting stupid, lately, and I dare say a miniature walking tour will do me good. Perhaps I may even spend the night in some little inn, if I find any place that looks clean and comfortable."

I heard this, and knew by my experience of Professor Gregg's manner that it was no ordinary business or pleasure that impelled him. I knew not, nor even remotely guessed, where he was bound, nor had I the vaguest notion of his errand, but all the fear of the night before returned; and as he stood, smiling, on the terrace, ready to set out, I implored him to stay, and to forget all his dreams of the undiscovered continent.

"No, no, Miss Lally," he replied still smiling, "it's too late now. *Vestigia nulla retrorsum,* you know, is the device of all true explorers, though I hope it won't be literally true in my case. But, indeed, you are wrong to alarm yourself so; I look upon my little expedition as quite commonplace; no more exciting than a day with the geological hammers. There is a risk, of course, but so there is on the commonest excursion. I can afford to be jaunty; I am doing nothing so hazardous as 'Arry does a hundred times over in the course of every Bank Holiday. Well, then, you must look more cheerfully; and so good-bye till to-morrow at latest."

He walked briskly up the road, and I saw him open the gate that marks the entrance of the wood, and then he vanished in the gloom of the trees.

All the day passed heavily with a strange darkness in the air, and again I felt as if imprisoned amidst the ancient woods, shut in an olden land of mystery and dread, and as if all was long ago and forgotten by the living outside. I hoped and dreaded; and when the dinner-hour came I waited, expecting to hear the professor's step in the hall, and his voice exulting at I knew not what triumph. I composed my face to welcome him gladly, but the night descended dark, and he did not come.

In the morning, when the maid knocked at my door, I called out to her, and asked if her master had returned; and when she replied that his bedroom stood open and empty, I felt the cold clasp of despair. Still, I fancied he might have discovered genial company, and would return for luncheon, or perhaps in the afternoon, and I took the children for a walk in the forest, and tried my best to play and laugh with them, and to shut out the thoughts of mystery and veiled terror. Hour after hour I waited, and my thoughts grew darker; again the night came and found me watching, and at last, as I was making much ado to finish my dinner, I heard steps outside and the sound of a man's voice.

The maid came in and looked oddly at me. "Please, miss," she began, "Mr. Morgan the gardener wants to speak to you for a minute, if you didn't mind."

"Shew him in, please," I answered, and I set my lips tight.

The old man came slowly into the room, and the servant shut the door behind him.

"Sit down, Mr. Morgan," I said; "what is it that you want to say to me?"

"Well, miss, Mr. Gregg he gave me something for you yesterday morning, just before he went off; and he told me particular not to hand it up before eight o'clock this evening exactly, if so be as he wasn't back home again before, and if he should come home before I was just to return it to him in his own hands. So, you see, as Mr. Gregg isn't here yet, I suppose I'd better give you the parcel directly."

He pulled out something from his pocket, and gave it to me, half rising. I took it silently, and seeing that Morgan seemed doubtful as to what he was to do next, I thanked him and bade him good-night, and he went out. I was left alone in the room with the parcel in my hand—

a paper parcel neatly sealed and directed to me, with the instructions Morgan had quoted, all written in the professor's large loose hand. I broke the seals with a choking at my heart, and found an envelope inside, addressed also, but open, and I took the letter out.

"MY DEAR MISS LALLY," it began,—"To quote the old logic manual, the case of your reading this note is a case of my having made a blunder of some sort, and, I am afraid, a blunder that turns these lines into a farewell. It is practically certain that neither you nor any one else will ever see me again. I have made my will with provision for this eventuality, and I hope you will consent to accept the small remembrance addressed to you, and my sincere thanks for the way in which you joined your fortunes to mine. The fate which has come upon me is desperate and terrible beyond the remotest dreams of man; but this fate you have a right to know—if you please. If you look in the left-hand drawer of my dressing-table, you will find the key of the escritoire, properly labelled. In the well of the escritoire is a large envelope sealed and addressed to your name. I advise you to throw it forthwith into the fire; you will sleep better of nights if you do so. But if you must know the history of what has happened, it is all written down for you to read."

The signature was firmly written below, and again I turned the page and read out the words one by one, aghast and white to the lips, my hands cold as ice, and sickness choking me. The dead silence of the room, and the thought of the dark woods and hills closing me in on every side, oppressed me, helpless and without capacity, and not knowing where to turn for counsel. At last I resolved that though knowledge should haunt my whole life and all the days to come, I must know the meaning of the strange terrors that had so long tormented me, rising grey, dim, and awful, like the shadows in the wood at dusk. I carefully carried out Professor Gregg's directions, and not without reluctance broke the seal of the envelope, and spread out his manuscript before me. That manuscript I always carry with me, and I see that I cannot deny your unspoken request to read it. This, then, was what I read that night, sitting at the desk, with a shaded lamp beside me.

The young lady who called herself Miss Lally then proceeded to recite

The Statement of William Gregg, F.R.S., etc.

It is many years since the first glimmer of the theory which is now almost, if not quite, reduced to fact dawned on my mind. A somewhat extensive course of miscellaneous and obsolete reading had done a good deal to prepare the way, and, later, when I became somewhat of a specialist, and immersed myself in the studies known as ethnological, I was now and then startled by facts that would not square with orthodox scientific opinion, and by discoveries that seemed to hint at something still hidden for all our research. More particularly I became convinced that much of the folk-lore of the world is but an exaggerated account of events that really happened, and I was especially drawn to consider the stories of the fairies, the good folk of the Celtic races. Here I thought I could detect the fringe of embroidery and exaggeration, the fantastic guise, the little people dressed in green and gold sporting in the flowers, and I thought I saw a distinct analogy between the name given to this race (supposed to be imaginary) and the description of their appearance and manners. Just as our remote ancestors called the dreadful beings "fair" and "good" precisely because they dreaded them, so they had dressed them up in charming forms, knowing the truth to be the very reverse. Literature, too, had gone early to work, and had lent a powerful hand in the transformation, so that the playful elves of Shakespeare are already far removed from the true original, and the real horror is disguised in a form of prankish mischief. But in the older tales, the stories that used to make men cross themselves as they sat round the burning logs, we tread a different stage; I saw a widely opposed spirit in certain histories of children and of men and women who vanished strangely from the earth. They would be seen by a peasant in the fields walking towards some green and rounded hillock, and seen no more on earth; and there are stories of mothers who have left a child quietly sleeping, with the cottage door rudely barred with a piece of wood, and have returned, not to find the plump and rosy little Saxon, but a thin and wizened creature, with sallow skin and black, piercing eyes, the child of another race. Then, again, there were myths darker still; the dread of witch and wizard, the lurid evil of the Sabbath, and the hint of demons who mingled with the daughters of men. And just as we have turned the terrible "fair folk" into a company of benignant, if freakish, elves, so we have hidden from us the black foulness of the witch and her companions under a popular *diablerie* of old women and broomsticks and a comic cat with tail on end. So the Greeks called the hideous furies benevolent ladies, and thus the northern nations have followed their example. I pursued my investigations, stealing odd hours from other and more imperative labours, and I asked myself the question: Supposing these traditions to be true, who were the demons who are reported to have attended the Sabbaths? I need not say that I laid aside what I may call the supernatural hypothesis of the Middle Ages, and came to the conclusion that fairies and devils were of one and the same race and origin; invention, no doubt, and the Gothic fancy of old days, had done much in the way of exaggeration and distortion; yet I firmly believe that beneath all this imagery there was a black background of truth. As for some of the alleged wonders, I hesitated. While I should be very loath to receive any one specific instance of modern spiritualism as containing even a grain of the genuine, yet I was not wholly prepared to deny that human flesh may now and then, once perhaps in ten million cases, be the veil of powers which seem magical to us—powers which, so far from proceeding from the heights and leading men thither, are in reality survivals from the depth of being. The amœba and the snail have powers which we do not possess; and I thought it possible that the theory of reversion might explain many things which seem wholly inexplicable. Thus stood my position; I saw good reason to believe that much of the tradition, a vast deal of the earliest and uncorrupted tradition of the so-called fairies, represented solid fact, and I thought that the purely supernatural element in these traditions was to be accounted for on the hypothesis that a race which had fallen out of the grand march of evolution might have retained, as a survival, certain powers which would be to us wholly miraculous. Such was my theory as it stood conceived in my mind; and working with this in view, I seemed to gather confirmation from every side, from the spoils of a tumulus or a barrow, from a local paper reporting an antiquarian meeting in the country, and from general literature of all kinds. Amongst other instances, I remember being struck by the phrase "articulate-speaking men" in Homer, as if the writer knew or had heard of men whose speech was so rude that it could hardly be termed articulate; and on my hypothesis of a race who had lagged far behind the rest, I could easily conceive that such a folk would speak a jargon but little removed from the inarticulate noises of brute beasts.

Thus I stood, satisfied that my conjecture was at all events not far removed from fact, when a chance paragraph in a small country print one day arrested my attention. It was a short account of what was to all appearance the usual sordid tragedy of the village—a young girl unaccountably missing, and evil rumour blatant and busy with her reputation. Yet, I could read between the lines that all this scandal was purely hypocritical, and in all probability invented to account for what was in any other manner unaccountable. A flight to London or Liverpool, or an undiscovered body lying with a weight about its neck in the foul depths of a woodland pool, or perhaps murder—such were the theories of the wretched girl's neighbours. But as I idly scanned the paragraph, a flash of thought passed through me with the violence of an electric shock: what if the obscure and horrible race of the hills still survived, still remained haunting the wild places and barren hills, and now and then repeating the evil of Gothic legend, unchanged and unchangeable as the Turanian Shelta, or the Basques of Spain? I have said that the thought came with violence; and indeed I drew in my breath sharply, and clung with both hands to my elbow-chair, in a strange confusion of horror and elation. It was as if one of my *confrères* of physical science, roaming in a quiet English wood, had been suddenly stricken aghast by the presence of the slimy and loathsome terror of the ichthyosaurus, the original of the stories of the awful worms killed by valorous knights, or had seen the sun darkened by the pterodactyl, the dragon of tradition. Yet as a resolute explorer of knowledge, the thought of such a discovery threw me into a passion of joy, and I cut out the slip from the paper and put it in a drawer in my old bureau, resolved that it should be but the first piece in a collection of the strangest significance. I sat long that evening dreaming of the conclusions I should establish, nor did cooler reflection at first dash my confidence. Yet as I began to put the case fairly, I saw that I might be building on an unstable foundation; the facts might possibly be in accordance with local opinion, and I regarded the affair with a mood of some reserve. Yet I resolved to remain perched on the look-out, and I hugged to myself the thought that I alone was watching and wakeful, while the great crowd of thinkers and searchers stood heedless and indifferent, perhaps letting the most prerogative facts pass by unnoticed.

Several years elapsed before I was enabled to add to the contents of the drawer; and the second find was in reality not a valuable one, for it was a mere repetition of the first, with only the variation of another and distant locality. Yet I gained something; for in the second case, as in the first, the tragedy took place in a desolate and lonely country, and so far my theory seemed justified. But the third piece was to me far more decisive. Again, amongst outland hills, far even from a main road of traffic, an old man was found done to death, and the instrument of execution was left beside him. Here, indeed, there were rumour and conjecture, for the deadly tool was a primitive stone axe, bound by gut to the wooden handle, and surmises the most extravagant and improbable were indulged in. Yet, as I thought with a kind of glee, the wildest conjectures went far astray; and I took the pains to enter into correspondence with the local doctor, who was called at the inquest. He, a man of some acuteness, was dumbfoundered. "It will not do to speak of these things in country places," he wrote to me; "but frankly, Professor Gregg, there is some hideous mystery here. I have obtained possession of the stone axe, and have been so curious as to test its powers. I took it into the back-garden of my house one Sunday afternoon when my family and the servants were all out, and there, sheltered by the poplar hedges, I made my experiments. I found the thing utterly unmanageable; whether there is some peculiar balance, some nice adjustment of weights, which require incessant practice, or whether an effectual blow can be struck only by a certain trick of the muscles, I do not know; but I can assure you that I went into the house with but a sorry opinion of my athletic capacities. It was like an inexperienced man trying 'putting the hammer'; the force exerted seemed to return on oneself, and I found myself hurled backwards with violence, while the axe fell harmless to the ground. On another occasion I tried the experiment with a clever woodman of the place; but this man, who had handled his axe for forty years, could do nothing with the stone implement, and missed every stroke most ludicrously. In short, if it were not so supremely absurd, I should say that for four thousand years no one on earth could have struck an effective blow with the tool that undoubtedly was used to murder the old man." This, as may be imagined, was to me rare news; and afterwards, when I heard the whole story, and learned that the unfortunate old man had babbled tales of what might be seen at night on a certain wild hillside, hinting at un-heard-of wonders, and that he had been found cold one morning on the very hill in question, my exultation was extreme, for I felt I was leaving conjecture far behind me. But the next step was of still greater importance. I had possessed for many years an extraordinary stone seal—a piece of dull, black stone, two inches long from the handle to the stamp, and the stamping end a rough hexagon an inch and a quar-ter in diameter. Altogether, it presented the appearance of an enlarged tobacco-stopper of an old-fashioned make. It had been sent to me by an agent in the East, who informed me that it had been found near the site of the ancient Babylon. But the characters engraved on the seal were to me an intolerable puzzle. Somewhat of the cuneiform pattern, there were yet striking differences, which I detected at the first glance, and all efforts to read the inscription on the hypothesis that the rules for deciphering the arrow-headed writing would apply proved futile. A riddle such as this stung my pride, and at odd moments I would take the Black Seal out of the cabinet, and scrutinise it with so much idle perseverance that every letter was familiar to my mind, and I could have drawn the inscription from memory without the slightest error. Judge, then, of my surprise when I one day received from a corre-spondent in the west of England a letter and an enclosure that posi-tively left me thunderstruck. I saw carefully traced on a large piece of paper the very characters of the Black Seal, without alteration of any kind, and above the inscription my friend had written: *Inscription found on a limestone rock on the Grey Hills, Monmouthshire. Done in some red earth, and quite recent.* I turned to the letter. My friend wrote: "I sent you the enclosed inscription with all due reserve. A shepherd who passed by the stone a week ago swears that there was then no mark of any kind. The characters, as I have noted, are formed by drawing some red earth over the stone, and are of an average height of one inch. They look to me like a kind of cuneiform character, a good deal altered, but this, of course, is impossible. It may be either a hoax, or more probably some scribble of the gypsies, who are plentiful enough in this wild country. They have, as you are aware, many hieroglyphics which they use in communicating with one another. I happened to visit the stone in question two days ago in connection with a rather painful incident which has occurred here."

As may be supposed, I wrote immediately to my friend, thanking him for the copy of the inscription, and asking him in a casual manner the history of the incident he mentioned. To be brief, I heard that a woman named Cradock, who had lost her husband a day before, had set out to communicate the sad news to a cousin who lived some five miles away. She took a short cut which led by the Grey Hills. Mrs. Cradock, who was then quite a young woman, never arrived at her relative's house. Late that night a farmer who had lost a couple of sheep, supposed to have wandered from the flock, was walking over the Grey Hills, with a lantern and his dog. His attention was attracted by a noise, which he described as a kind of wailing, mournful and pitiable to hear; and, guided by the sound, he found the unfortunate Mrs. Cradock crouched on the ground by the limestone rock, swaying her body to and fro, and lamenting and crying in so heartrending a manner that the farmer was, as he says, at first obliged to stop his ears, or he would have run away. The woman allowed herself to be taken home, and a neighbour came to see to her necessities. All the night she never ceased her crying, mixing her lament with words of some unintelligible jargon, and when the doctor arrived he pronounced her insane. She lay on her bed for a week, now wailing, as people said, like one lost and damned for eternity, and now sunk in a heavy coma; it was thought that grief at the loss of her husband had unsettled her mind, and the medical man did not at one time expect her to live. I need not say that I was deeply interested in this story, and I made my friend write to me at intervals with all the particulars of the case. I heard then that in the course of six weeks the woman gradually recovered the use of her faculties, and some months later she gave birth to a son, christened Jervase, who unhappily proved to be of weak intellect. Such were the facts known to the village; but to me, while I whitened at the suggested thought of the hideous enormities that had doubtless been committed, all this was nothing short of conviction, and I incautiously hazarded a hint of something like the truth to some scientific friends. The moment the words had left my lips I bitterly regretted having spoken, and thus given way the great secret of my life, but with a good deal of relief mixed with indignation I found my fears altogether misplaced, for my friends ridiculed me to my face, and I was regarded as a madman; and beneath a natural anger I chuckled to myself, feeling as secure amidst these blockheads as if I had confided what I knew to the desert sands.

But now, knowing so much, I resolved I would know all, and I concentrated my efforts on the task of deciphering the inscription on the Black Seal. For many years I made this puzzle the sole object of my leisure moments; for the greater portion of my time was, of course, devoted to other duties, and it was only now and then that I could snatch a week of clear research. If I were to tell the full history of this curious investigation, this statement would be wearisome in the extreme, for it would contain simply the account of long and tedious failure. By what I knew already of ancient scripts I was well equipped for the chase, as I always termed it to myself. I had correspondents amongst all the scientific men in Europe, and, indeed, in the world, and I could not believe that in these days any character, however ancient and however perplexed, could long resist the search-light I should bring to bear upon it. Yet, in point of fact, it was fully fourteen years before I succeeded. With every year my professional duties increased, and my leisure became smaller. This no doubt retarded me a good deal; and yet, when I look back on those years, I am astonished at the vast scope of my investigation of the Black Seal. I made my bureau a centre, and from all the world and from all the ages I gathered transcripts of ancient writing. Nothing, I resolved, should pass me unawares, and the faintest hint should be welcomed and followed up. But as one covert after another was tried and proved empty of result, I began in the course of years to despair, and to wonder whether the Black Seal were the sole relic of some race that had vanished from the world and left no other trace of its existence—had perished, in fine, as Atlantis is said to have done, in some great cataclysm, its secrets perhaps drowned beneath the ocean or moulded into the heart of the hills. The thought chilled my warmth a little, and though I still persevered, it was no longer with the same certainty of faith. A chance came to the rescue. I was staying in a considerable town in the north of England, and took the opportunity of going over the very creditable museum that had for some time been established in the place. The curator was one of my correspondents; and, as we were looking through one of the mineral cases, my attention was struck by a specimen, a piece of black stone some four inches square, the appearance of which reminded me in a measure of the Black Seal. I took it up carelessly, and was turning it over in my hand, when I saw, to my astonishment, that the under side was inscribed. I said, quietly enough, to my friend the curator that the specimen interested me, and that I should be much obliged if he would allow me to take it with me to my hotel for a couple of days. He, of course, made no objection, and I hurried to my rooms and found that my first glance had not deceived me. There were two inscriptions; one in the regular cuneiform character, another in the character of the Black Seal, and I realised that my task was accomplished. I made an exact copy of the two inscriptions; and when I got to my London study, and had the Seal before me, I was able seriously to grapple with the great problem. The interpreting inscription on the museum specimen, though in itself curious enough, did not bear on my quest, but the transliteration made me master of the secret of the Black Seal. Conjecture, of course, had to enter into my calculations; there was here and there uncertainty about a particular ideograph, and one sign recurring again and again on the seal baffled me for many successive nights. But at last the secret stood open before me in plain English, and I read the key of the awful transmutation of the hills. The last word was hardly written, when with fingers all trembling and unsteady I tore the scrap of paper into the minutest fragments, and saw them flame and blacken in the red hollow of the fire, and then I crushed the grey films that remained into finest powder. Never since then have I written those words; never will I write the phrases which tell how man can be reduced to the slime from which he came, and be forced to put on the flesh of the reptile and the snake. There was now but one thing remaining. I knew, but I desired to see, and I was after some time able to take a house in the neighbourhood of the Grey Hills, and not far from the cottage where Mrs. Cradock and her son Jervase resided. I need not go into a full and detailed account of the apparently inexplicable events which have occurred here, where I am writing this. I knew that I should find in Jervase Cradock something of the blood of the "Little People", and I found later that he had more than once encountered his kinsmen in lonely places in that lonely land. When I was summoned one day to the garden, and found him in a seizure speaking or hissing the ghastly jargon of the Black Seal, I am afraid that exultation prevailed over pity. I heard bursting from his lips the secrets of the underworld, and the word of dread, "Ishakshar", the signification of which I must be excused from giving.

But there is one incident I cannot pass over unnoticed. In the waste hollow of the night I awoke at the sound of those hissing syllables I knew so well; and on going to the wretched boy's room, I found him convulsed and foaming at the mouth, struggling on the bed as if he strove to escape the grasp of writhing demons. I took him down to my room and lit the lamp, while he lay twisting on the floor, calling on the power within his flesh to leave him. I saw his body swell and become distended as a bladder, while the face blackened before my eyes; and then at the crisis I did what was necessary according to the directions on the Seal, and putting all scruple on one side, I became a man of science, observant of what was passing. Yet the sight I had to witness was horrible, almost beyond the power of human conception and the most fearful fantasy. Something pushed out from the body there on the floor, and stretched forth, a slimy, wavering tentacle, across the room, grasped the bust upon the cupboard, and laid it down on my desk.

When it was over, and I was left to walk up and down all the rest of the night, white and shuddering, with sweat pouring from my flesh, I vainly tried to reason with myself: I said, truly enough, that I had seen nothing really supernatural, that a snail pushing out his horns and drawing them in was but an instance on a smaller scale of what I had witnessed; and yet horror broke through all such reasonings and left me shattered and loathing myself for the share I had taken in the night's work.

There is little more to be said. I am going now to the final trial and encounter; for I have determined that there shall be nothing wanting, and I shall meet the "Little People" face to face. I shall have the Black Seal and the knowledge of its secrets to help me, and if I unhappily do not return from my journey, there is no need to conjure up here a picture of the awfulness of my fate.

Pausing a little at the end of Professor Gregg's statement, Miss Lally continued her tale in the following words:—

Such was the almost incredible story that the professor had left behind him. When I had finished reading it, it was late at night, but the next morning I took Morgan with me, and we proceeded to search the Grey Hills for some trace of the lost professor. I will not weary you with a description of the savage desolation of that tract of country, a tract of utterest loneliness, of bare green hills, dotted over with grey limestone boulders, worn by the ravages of time into fantastic semblances of men and beasts. Finally, after many hours of weary searching, we found what I told you—the watch and chain, the purse, and the ring—wrapped in a piece of coarse parchment. When Morgan cut the gut that bound the parcel together, and I saw the professor's property, I burst into tears, but the sight of the dreaded characters of the Black Seal repeated on the parchment froze me to silent horror, and I think I understood for the first time the awful fate that had come upon my late employer.

I have only to add that Professor Gregg's lawyer treated my account of what had happened as a fairy tale, and refused even to glance at the documents I laid before him. It was he who was responsible for the statement that appeared in the public press, to the effect that Professor Gregg had been drowned, and that his body must have been swept into the open sea.

Miss Lally stopped speaking, and looked at Mr. Phillipps, with a glance of some enquiry. He, for his part, was sunken in a deep reverie of thought; and when he looked up and saw the bustle of the evening gathering in the square, men and women hurrying to partake of dinner, and crowds already besetting the music-halls, all the hum and press of actual life seemed unreal and visionary, a dream in the morning after an awakening.

"I thank you," he said at last, "for your most interesting story; interesting to me, because I feel fully convinced of its exact truth."

"Sir," said the lady, with some energy of indignation, "you grieve and offend me. Do you think I should waste my time and yours by concocting fictions on a bench in Leicester Square?"

"Pardon me, Miss Lally, you have a little misunderstood me. Before you began I knew that whatever you told would be told in good faith, but your experiences have a far higher value than that of *bona fides*. The most extraordinary circumstances in your account are in perfect harmony with the very latest scientific theories. Professor Lodge would, I am sure, value a communication from you extremely; I was charmed from the first by his daring hypothesis in explanation of the wonders of Spiritualism (so called), but your narrative puts the whole matter out of the range of mere hypothesis."

"Alas! sir, all this will not help me. You forget, I have lost my brother under the most startling and dreadful circumstances. Again, I ask you, did you not see him as you came here? His black whiskers, his spectacles, his timid glance to right and left; think, do not these particulars recall his face to your memory?"

"I am sorry to say I have never seen any one of the kind," said Phillipps, who had forgotten all about the missing brother. "But let me ask you a few questions. Did you notice whether Professor Gregg . . ."

"Pardon me, sir, I have stayed too long. My employers will be expecting me. I thank you for your sympathy. Good-bye."

Before Mr. Phillipps had recovered from his amazement at this abrupt departure Miss Lally had disappeared from his gaze, passing into the crowd that now thronged the approaches to the Empire. He walked home in a pensive frame of mind, and drank too much tea. At ten o'clock he had made his third brew, and had sketched out the outlines of a little work to be called *Protoplasmic Reversion.*

INCIDENT OF THE PRIVATE BAR

Mr. Dyson often meditated at odd moments over the singular tale he had listened to at the Café de la Touraine. In the first place, he cherished a profound conviction that the words of truth were scattered with a too niggardly and sparing hand over the agreeable history of Mr. Smith and the Black Gulf Cañon; and secondly, there was the undeniable fact of the profound agitation of the narrator, and his gestures on the pavement, too violent to be simulated. The idea of a man going about London haunted by the fear of meeting a young man with spectacles struck Dyson as supremely ridiculous; he searched his memory for some precedent in romance, but without success; he paid visits at odd times to the little café, hoping to find Mr. Wilkins there; and he kept a sharp watch on the great generation of the spectacled men, without much doubt that he would remember the face of the individual whom he had seen dart out of the aerated bread shop. All his peregrinations and researches, however, seemed to lead to nothing of value, and Dyson needed all his warm conviction of his innate detective powers and his strong scent for mystery to sustain him in his endeavours. In fact, he had two affairs on hand; and every day, as he passed through streets crowded or deserted, lurked in the obscure districts and watched at corners, he was more than surprised to find that the affair of the gold coin persistently avoided him, while the ingenious Wilkins, and the young man with spectacles, whom he dreaded, seemed to have vanished from the pavements.

He was pondering these problems one evening in a house of call in the Strand, and the obstinacy with which the persons he so ardently desired to meet hung back gave the modest tankard before him an additional touch of bitter. As it happened, he was alone in his compartment, and, without thinking, he uttered aloud the burden of his meditations. "How bizarre it all is!" he said, "a man walking the pavement with the dread of a timid-looking young man with spectacles continually hovering before his eyes. And there was some tremendous feeling at work, I could swear to that." Quick as thought, before he had finished the sentence, a head popped round the barrier, and was withdrawn again; and while Dyson was wondering what this could mean, the door of the compartment was swung open, and a smooth, clean-shaven, and smiling gentleman entered.

"You will excuse me, sir," he said politely, "for intruding on your thoughts, but you made a remark a minute ago."

"I did," said Dyson; "I have been puzzling over a foolish matter, and I thought aloud. As you heard what I said, and seem interested, perhaps you may be able to relieve my perplexity?"

"Indeed, I scarcely know; it is an odd coincidence. One has to be cautious. I suppose, sir, that you would have no repulsion in assisting the ends of justice."

"Justice," replied Dyson, "is a term of such wide meaning, that I too feel doubtful about giving an answer. But this place is not altogether fit for such a discussion; perhaps you would come to my rooms?"

"You are very kind; my name is Burton, but I am sorry to say I have not a card with me. Do you live near here?"

"Within ten minutes' walk."

Mr. Burton took out his watch, and seemed to be making a rapid calculation.

"I have a train to catch," he said; "but after all, it is a late one. So if you don't mind, I think I will come with you. I am sure we should have a little talk together. We turn up here?"

The theatres were filling as they crossed the Strand; the street seemed alive, and Dyson looked fondly about him. The glittering lines of gas-lamps, with here and there the blinding radiance of an electric light, the hansoms that flashed to and fro with ringing bells, the laden 'buses, and the eager hurrying east and west of the foot-passengers, made his most enchanting picture; and the graceful spire of St. Mary le Strand on the one hand, and the last flush of sunset on the other, were to him a cause of thanksgiving, as the gorse blossom to Linnæus. Mr. Burton caught his look of fondness as they crossed the street.

"I see you can find the picturesque in London," he said. "To me this great town is as I see it is to you—the study and the love of life. Yet how few there are that can pierce the veils of apparent monotony and meanness! I have read in a paper, which is said to have the largest circulation in the world, a comparison between the aspects of London and Paris, a comparison which should be positively laureate as the great masterpiece of fatuous stupidity. Conceive if you can a human being of ordinary intelligence preferring the Boulevards to our London streets; imagine a man calling for the wholesale destruction of our most charming city, in order that the dull uniformity of that whited sepulchre called Paris should be reproduced here in London. Is it not positively incredible?"

"My dear sir," said Dyson, regarding Burton with a good deal of interest, "I agree most heartily with your opinions, but I really can't share your wonder. Have you heard how much George Eliot received for *Romola?* Do you know what the circulation of *Robert Elsmere* was? Do you read *Tit-Bits* regularly? To me, on the contrary, it is constant matter for wonder and thanksgiving that London was not boule-vardized twenty years ago. I praise that exquisite jagged skyline that stands up against the pale greens and fading blues and flushing clouds of sunset, but I wonder even more than I praise. As for St. Mary le Strand, its preservation is a miracle, nothing more or less. A thing of exquisite beauty *versus* four 'buses abreast! Really, the conclusion is too obvious. Didn't you read the letter of the man who proposed that the whole mysterious system, the immemorial plan of computing Easter, should be abolished off-hand, because he doesn't like his son having his holidays as early as March 25th? But shall we be going on?"

They had lingered at the corner of a street on the north side of the Strand, enjoying the contrasts and the glamour of the scene. Dyson pointed the way with a gesture, and they strolled up the comparatively deserted streets, slanting a little to the right, and thus arriving at Dyson's lodging on the verge of Bloomsbury. Mr. Burton took a comfortable arm-chair by the open window, while Dyson lit the candles and produced the whisky and soda and cigarettes.

"They tell me these cigarettes are very good," he said; "but I know nothing about it myself. I hold at last that there is only one tobacco, and that is shag. I suppose I could not tempt you to try a pipeful?"

Mr. Burton smilingly refused the offer, and picked out a cigarette from the box. When he had smoked it half through, he said with some hesitation—

"It is really kind of you to have me here, Mr. Dyson; the fact is that the interests at issue are far too serious to be discussed in a bar, where, as you found for yourself, there may be listeners, voluntary or involuntary, on each side. I think the remark I heard you make was something about the oddity of an individual going about London in deadly fear of a young man with spectacles?"

"Yes; that was it."

"Well, would you mind confiding to me the circumstances that gave rise to the reflection?"

"Not in the least. It was like this." And he ran over in brief outline the adventure in Oxford Street, dwelling on the violence of Mr. Wilkins's gestures, but wholly suppressing the tale told in the café. "He told me he lived in constant terror of meeting this man; and I left him when I thought he was cool enough to look after himself," said Dyson, ending his narrative.

"Really," said Mr. Burton. "And you actually saw this mysterious person?"

"Yes."

"And could you describe him?"

"Well, he looked to me a youngish man, pale and nervous. He had small black side-whiskers, and wore rather large spectacles."

"But this is simply marvellous! You astonish me. For I must tell you that my interest in the matter is this. I'm not in the least in terror of meeting a dark young man with spectacles, but I shrewdly suspect a person of that description would much rather not meet me. And yet the account you give of the man tallies exactly. A nervous glance to right and left—is it not so? And, as you observed, he wears prominent spectacles, and has small black whiskers. There cannot be, surely, two people exactly identical—one a cause of terror, and the other, I should imagine, extremely anxious to get out of the way. But have you seen this man since?"

"No, I have not; and I have been looking out for him pretty keenly. But of course he may have left London, and England too, for the matter of that."

"Hardly, I think. Well, Mr. Dyson, it is only fair that I should explain my story, now that I have listened to yours. I must tell you, then, that I am an agent for curiosities and precious things of all kinds. An odd employment, isn't it? Of course, I wasn't brought up to the business; I gradually fell into it. I have always been fond of things queer and rare, and by the time I was twenty I had made half a dozen collections. It is not generally known how often farm-labourers come upon rarities; you would be astonished if I told you what I have seen turned up by the plough. I lived in the country in those days, and I used to buy anything the men on the farms brought me; and I had the queerest set of rubbish, as my friends called my collection. But that's how I got the scent of the business, which means everything; and, later on, it struck me that I might very well turn my knowledge to account and add to my income. Since those early days I have been in most quarters of the world, and some very valuable things have passed through my hands, and I have had to engage in difficult and delicate negotiations. You have possibly heard of the Khan opal—called in the East 'The Stone of a Thousand and One Colours'? Well, perhaps the conquest of that stone was my greatest achievement. I call it myself the stone of the thousand and one lies, for I assure you that I had to invent a cycle of folk-lore before the Rajah who owned it would consent to sell the thing. I subsidised wandering story-tellers, who told tales in which the opal played a frightful part; I hired a holy man—a great ascetic—to prophesy against the thing in the language of Eastern symbolism; in short, I frightened the Rajah out of his wits. So, you see, there is room for diplomacy in the traffic I am engaged in. I have to be ever on my guard, and I have often been sensible that unless I watched every step and weighed every word, my life would not last me much longer. Last April I became aware of the existence of a highly valuable antique gem; it was in southern Italy, and in the possession of persons who were ignorant of its real value. It has always been my experience that it is precisely the ignorant who are most difficult to deal with. I have met farmers who were under the impression that a shilling of George I. was a find of almost incalculable value; and all the defeats I have sustained have been at the hands of people of this description. Reflecting on these facts, I saw that the acquisition of the gem would be an affair demanding the nicest diplomacy; I might possibly have got it by offering a sum approaching its real value, but I need not point out to you that such a proceeding would be most unbusinesslike. Indeed, I doubt whether it would have been successful; for the cupidity of such persons is aroused by a sum which seems enormous, and the low cunning which serves them in place of intelligence immediately suggests that the object for which such an amount is offered must be worth at least double. Of course, when it is a matter of an ordinary curiosity—an old jug, a carved chest, or a queer brass lantern—one does not much care; the cupidity of the owner defeats its object; the collector laughs and goes away, for he is aware that such things are by no means unique. But this gem I fervently desired to possess; and as I did not see my way to giving more than a hundredth part of its value, I was conscious that all my, let us say, imaginative and diplomatic powers would have to be exerted. I am sorry to say that I came to the conclusion that I could not undertake to carry the matter through single-handed, and I determined to confide in my assistant, a young man named William Robbins, whom I judged to be by no means devoid of capacity. My idea was that Robbins should get himself up as a low-class dealer in precious stones; he could patter a little Italian, and would go to the town in question and manage to see the gem we were after, possibly by offering some trifling articles of jewellery for sale, but that I left to be decided. Then my work was to begin, but I will not trouble you with a tale told twice over. In due course, then, Robbins went off to Italy with an assortment of uncut stones and a few rings, and some jewellery I bought in Birmingham on purpose for his expedition. A week later I followed him, travelling leisurely, so that I was a fortnight later in arriving at our common destination. There was a decent hotel in the town, and on my enquiring of the landlord whether there were many strangers in the place, he told me very few; he had heard there was an Englishman staying in a small tavern, a pedlar, he said, who sold beautiful trinkets very cheaply, and wanted to buy old rubbish. For five or six days I took life leisurely, and I must say I enjoyed myself. It was part of my plan to make the people think I was an enormously rich man; and I knew that such items as the extravagance of my meals, and the price of every bottle of wine I drank, would not be suffered, as Sancho Panza puts it, to rot in the landlord's breast. At the end of the week I was fortunate enough to make the acquaintance of Signor Melini, the owner of the gem I coveted, at the café, and with his ready hospitality, and my geniality, I was soon established as a friend of the house. On my third or fourth visit I managed to make the Italians talk about the English pedlar, who, they said, spoke a most detestable Italian. 'But that does not matter,' said the Signora Melini, 'for he has beautiful things, which he sells very very cheap.' 'I hope you may not find he has cheated you,' I said, 'for I must tell you that English people give these fellows a very wide berth. They usually make a great parade of the cheapness of their goods, which often turn out to be double the price of better articles in the shops.' They would not hear of this, and Signora Melini insisted on shewing me the three rings and the bracelet she had bought of the pedlar. She told me the price she had paid; and after scrutinising the articles carefully, I had to confess that she had made a bargain, and indeed Robbins had sold her the things at about fifty per cent below market value. I admired the trinkets as I gave them back to the lady, and I hinted that the pedlar must be a somewhat foolish specimen of his class. Two days later, as I was taking my vermouth at the café with Signor Melini, he led the conversation back to the pedlar, and mentioned casually that he had shewn the man a little curiosity, for which he had made rather a handsome offer. 'My dear sir,' I said, 'I hope you will be careful. I told you that the travelling tradesman does not bear a very high reputation in England; and notwithstanding his apparent simplicity, this fellow may turn out to be an arrant cheat. May I ask you what is the nature of the curiosity you have shewn him?' He told me it was a little thing, a pretty little stone with some figures cut on it: people said it was old. 'I should like to examine it;' I replied, 'as it happens I have seen a good deal of these gems. We have a fine collection of them in our Museum at London.' In due course I was shewn the article, and I held the gem I so coveted between my fingers. I looked at it coolly, and put it down carelessly on the table. 'Would you mind telling me, Signor,' I said, 'how much my fellow-countryman offered you for this?' 'Well,' he said, 'my wife says the man must be mad; he said he would give me twenty lire for it.'

"I looked at him quietly, and took up the gem and pretended to examine it in the light more carefully; I turned it over and over, and finally pulled out a magnifying glass from my pocket, and seemed to search every line in the cutting with minutest scrutiny. 'My dear sir,' I said at last, 'I am inclined to agree with Signora Melini. If this gem were genuine, it would be worth some money; but as it happens to be a rather bad forgery, it is not worth twenty centesimi. It was sophisticated, I should imagine, some time in the last century, and by a very unskilful hand.' 'Then we had better get rid of it,' said Melini. 'I never thought it was worth anything myself. Of course, I am sorry for the pedlar, but one must let a man know his own trade. I shall tell him we will take the twenty lire.' 'Excuse me,' I said, 'the man wants a lesson. It would be a charity to give him one. Tell him that you will not take anything under eighty lire, and I shall be much surprised if he does not close with you at once.'

"A day or two later I heard that the English pedlar had gone away, after debasing the minds of the country people with Birmingham art jewellery; for I admit that the gold sleeve-links like kidney beans, the silver chains made apparently after the pattern of a dog-chain, and the initial brooches have always been heavy on my conscience. I cannot acquit myself of having indirectly contributed to debauch the taste of a simple folk; but I hope that the end I had in view may finally outbalance this heavy charge. Soon afterwards I paid a farewell visit at the Melinis', and the signor informed me with an oily chuckle that the plan I had suggested had been completely successful. I congratulated him on his bargain, and went away after expressing a wish that Heaven might send many such pedlars in his path.

"Nothing of interest occurred on my return journey. I had arranged that Robbins was to meet me at a certain place on a certain day, and I went to the appointment full of the coolest confidence; the gem had been conquered, and I had only to reap the fruits of victory. I am sorry to shake that trust in our common human nature which I am sure you possess, but I am compelled to tell you that up to the present date I have never set eyes on my man Robbins, or on the antique gem in his custody. I have found out that he actually arrived in London, for he was seen three days before my arrival in England by a pawnbroker of my acquaintance, consuming his favourite beverage—four ale—in the tavern where we met to-night. Since then he has not been heard of. I hope you will now pardon my curiosity as to the history and adventures of dark young men with spectacles. You will, I am sure, feel for me in my position; the savour of life has disappeared for me; it is a bitter thought that I have rescued one of the most perfect and exquisite specimens of antique art from the hands of ignorant, and indeed unscrupulous persons, only to deliver it into the keeping of a man who is evidently utterly devoid of the very elements of commercial morality."

"My dear sir," said Dyson, "you will allow me to compliment you on your style; your adventures have interested me exceedingly. But, forgive me, you just now used the word morality; would not some persons take exception to your own methods of business? I can conceive, myself, flaws of a moral kind being found in the very original conception you have just described to me; I can imagine the Puritan shrinking in dismay from your scheme, pronouncing it unscrupulous—nay, dishonest."

Mr. Burton helped himself very frankly to some more whisky.

"Your scruples entertain me," he said. "Perhaps you have not gone very deeply into these questions of ethics. I have been compelled to do so myself, just as I was forced to master a system of book-keeping. Without book-keeping, and still more without a system of ethics, it is impossible to conduct a business such as mine. But I assure you that I am often profoundly saddened, as I pass through the crowded streets and watch the world at work, by the thought of how few amongst all these hurrying individuals, black-hatted, well dressed, educated we may presume sufficiently,—how few amongst them have any reasoned system of morality. Even you have not weighed the question; although you study life and affairs, and to a certain extent penetrate the veils and masks of the comedy of man, even you judge by empty conventions, and the false money which is allowed to pass current as sterling coin. Allow me to play the part of Socrates; I shall teach you nothing that you do not know. I shall merely lay aside the wrappings of prejudice and bad logic, and shew you the real image which you possess in your soul. Come, then. Do you allow that happiness is anything?"

"Certainly," said Dyson.

"And happiness is desirable or undesirable?"

"Desirable, of course."

"And what shall we call the man who gives happiness? Is he not a philanthropist?"

"I think so."

"And such a person is praiseworthy, and the more praiseworthy in the proportion of the persons whom he makes happy?"

"By all means."

"So that he who makes a whole nation happy is praiseworthy in the extreme, and the action by which he gives happiness is the highest virtue?"

"It appears so, O Burton," said Dyson, who found something very exquisite in the character of his visitor.

"Quite so; you find the several conclusions inevitable. Well, apply them to the story I have told you. I conferred happiness on myself by obtaining (as I thought) possession of the gem; I conferred happiness on the Melinis by getting them eighty lire instead of an object for which they had not the slightest value, and I intended to confer happiness on the whole British nation by selling the thing to the British Museum, to say nothing of the happiness a profit of about nine thousand per cent. would have conferred on me. I assure you, I regard Robbins as an interferer with the cosmos and fair order of things. But that is nothing; you perceive that I am an apostle of the very highest morality; you have been forced to yield to argument."

"There certainly seems a great deal in what you advance," said Dyson. "I admit that I am a mere amateur of ethics, while you, as you say, have brought the most acute scrutiny to bear on these perplexed and doubtful questions. I can well understand your anxiety to meet the fallacious Robbins, and I congratulate myself on the chance which has made us acquainted. But you will pardon my seeming inhospitality; I see it is half-past eleven, and I think you mentioned a train."

"A thousand thanks, Mr. Dyson. I have just time, I see. I will look you up some evening if I may. Good-night."

The Decorative Imagination

In the course of a few weeks Dyson became accustomed to the constant incursions of the ingenious Mr. Burton, who shewed himself ready to drop in at all hours, not averse to refreshment, and a profound guide in the complicated questions of life. His visits at once terrified and delighted Dyson, who could no longer seat himself at his bureau secure from interruption while he embarked on literary undertakings, each one of which was to be a masterpiece. On the other hand, it was a vivid pleasure to be confronted with views so highly original; and if here and there Mr. Burton's reasonings seemed tinged with fallacy, yet Dyson freely yielded to the joy of strangeness, and never failed to give his visitor a frank and hearty welcome. Mr. Burton's first enquiry was always after the unprincipled Robbins, and he seemed to feel the stings of disappointment when Dyson told him that he had failed to meet this outrage on all morality, as Burton styled him, vowing that sooner or later he would take vengeance on such a shameless betrayal of trust.

One evening they had sat together for some time discussing the possibility of laying down for this present generation and our modern and intensely complicated order of society some rules of social diplomacy, such as Lord Bacon gave to the courtiers of King James I. "It is a book to make," said Mr. Burton, "but who is there capable of making it? I tell you, people are longing for such a book; it would bring fortune to its publisher. Bacon's Essays are exquisite, but they have now no practical application; the modern strategist can find but little use in a treatise *De Re Militari,* written by a Florentine in the fifteenth century. Scarcely more dissimilar are the social conditions of Bacon's time and our own; the rules that he lays down so exquisitely for the courtier and diplomatist of James the First's age will avail us little in the rough-and-tumble struggle of to-day. Life, I am afraid, has deteriorated; it gives little play for fine strokes such as formerly advanced men in the state. Except in such businesses as mine, where a chance does occur now and then, it has all become, as I said, an affair of rough and tumble; men still desire to attain, it is true, but what is their *moyen de parvenir?* A mere imitation—and not a gracious one—of the arts of the soap vendor and the proprietor of baking-powder. When I think of these things, my dear Dyson, I confess that I am tempted to despair of my century."

"You are too pessimistic, my dear fellow; you set up too high a standard. Certainly, I agree with you, that the times are decadent in many ways. I admit a general appearance of squalor; it needs much philosophy to extract the wonderful and the beautiful from the Cromwell Road or the Nonconformist conscience. Australian wines of fine Burgundy character, the novels alike of the old women and the new women, popular journalism,—these things, indeed, make for depression. Yet we have our advantages: before us is unfolded the greatest spectacle the world has ever seen—the mystery of the innumerable, unending streets, the strange adventures that must infallibly arise from so complicated a press of interests. Nay, I will say that he who has stood in the ways of a suburb, and has seen them stretch before him all shining, void, and desolate at noonday, has not lived in vain. Such a sight is in reality more wonderful than any perspective of Bagdad or Grand Cairo. And, to set on one side the entertaining history of the gem which you told me, surely you must have had many singular adventures in your own career?"

"Perhaps not so many as you would think; a good deal—the larger part of my business—has been as commonplace as linen-drapery. But, of course, things happen now and then. It is ten years since I established my agency, and I suppose that a house- and estate-agent who had been in trade for an equal time could tell you some queer stories. But I must give you a sample of my experiences some night."

"Why not to-night?" said Dyson. "This evening seems to me admirably adapted for an odd chapter. Look out into the street; you can catch a view of it if you crane your neck from that chair of yours. Is it not charming? The double row of lamps growing closer in the distance, the hazy outline of the plane-tree in the square, and the lights of the hansoms swimming to and fro, gliding and vanishing; and above, the sky all clear and blue and shining. Come, let us have one of your *cent nouvelles nouvelles.*"

"My dear Dyson, I am delighted to amuse you." With these words Mr. Burton prefaced the

NOVEL OF THE IRON MAID.

I think the most extraordinary event which I can recall took place about five years ago. I was then still feeling my way; I had declared for business, and attended regularly at my office; but I had not succeeded in establishing a really profitable connection, and consequently I had a good deal of leisure time on my hands. I have never thought fit to trouble you with the details of my private life; they would be entirely devoid of interest. I must briefly say, however, that I had a numerous circle of acquaintance, and was never at a loss as to how to spend my evenings. I was so fortunate as to have friends in most of the ranks of the social order; there is nothing so unfortunate, to my mind, as a specialised circle, wherein a certain round of ideas is continually traversed and retraversed. I have always tried to find out new types and persons whose brains contained something fresh to me; one may chance to gain information even from the conversation of city men on an omnibus. Amongst my acquaintance I knew a young doctor, who lived in a far outlying suburb, and I used often to brave the intolerably slow railway journey to have the pleasure of listening to his talk. One night we conversed so eagerly together over our pipes and whisky that the clock passed unnoticed; and when I glanced up, I realised with a shock that I had just five minutes in which to catch the last train. I made a dash for my hat and stick, jumped out of the house and down the steps, and tore at full speed up the street. It was no good, however; there was a shriek of the engine-whistle, and I stood there at the station door and saw far on the long, dark line of the embankment a red light shine and vanish, and a porter came down and shut the door with a bang.

"How far to London?" I asked him.

"A good nine miles to Waterloo Bridge." And with that he went off.

Before me was the long suburban street, its dreary distance marked by rows of twinkling lamps, and the air was poisoned by the faint, sickly smell of burning bricks; it was not a cheerful prospect by any means, and I had to walk through nine miles of such streets, deserted as those of Pompeii. I knew pretty well what direction to take, so I set out wearily, looking at the stretch of lamps vanishing in perspective; and as I walked, street after street branched off to right and left, some far-reaching, to distances that seemed endless, communicating with other systems of thoroughfare, and some mere protoplasmic streets, beginning in orderly fashion with serried two-storied houses, and ending suddenly in waste, and pits, and rubbish-heaps, and fields whence the magic had departed. I have spoken of systems of thoroughfare, and I assure you that walking alone through these silent places I felt fantasy growing on me, and some glamour of the infinite. There was here, I felt, an immensity as in the outer void of the universe; I passed from unknown to unknown, my way marked by lamps like stars, and on either hand was an unknown world where myriads of men dwelt and slept, street leading into street, as it seemed to world's end. At first the road by which I was travelling was lined with houses of unutterable monotony, a wall of grey brick pierced by two stories of windows, drawn close to the very pavement; but by degrees I noticed an improvement, there were gardens, and these grew larger; the suburban builder began to allow himself a wider scope; and for a certain distance each flight of steps was guarded by twin lions of plaster, and scents of flowers prevailed over the fume of heated bricks. The road began to climb a hill, and looking up a side street I saw the half moon rise over plane-trees, and there on the other side was as if a white cloud had fallen, and the air around it was sweetened as with incense; it was a may-tree in full bloom. I pressed on stubbornly, listening for the wheels and the clatter of some belated hansom; but into that land of men who go to the city in the morning and return in the evening the hansom rarely enters, and I had resigned myself once more to the walk, when I suddenly became aware that some one was advancing to meet me along the sidewalk. The man was strolling rather aimlessly; and though the time and the place would have allowed an unconventional style of dress, he was vested in the ordinary frockcoat, black tie, and silk hat of civilisation. We met each other under the lamp, and, as often happens in this great town, two casual passengers brought face to face found each in the other an acquaintance.

"Mr. Mathias, I think?" I said.

"Quite so. And you are Frank Burton. You know you are a man with a Christian name, so I won't apologise for my familiarity. But may I ask where you are going?"

I explained the situation to him, saying I had traversed a region as unknown to me as the darkest recesses of Africa. "I think I have only about five miles further," I concluded.

"Nonsense! you must come home with me. My house is close by; in fact, I was just taking my evening walk when we met. Come along; I dare say you will find a makeshift bed easier than a five-mile walk."

I let him take my arm and lead me along, though I was a good deal surprised at so much geniality from a man who was, after all, a mere casual club acquaintance. I suppose I had not spoken to Mr. Mathias half a dozen times; he was a man who would sit silent in an arm-chair for hours, neither reading nor smoking, but now and again moistening his lips with his tongue and smiling queerly to himself. I confess he had never attracted me, and on the whole I should have preferred to continue my walk. But he took my arm and led me up a side street, and stopped at a door in a high wall. We passed through the still, moonlit garden, beneath the black shadow of an old cedar, and into an old red-brick house with many gables. I was tired enough, and I sighed with relief as I let myself fall into a great leather arm-chair. You know the infernal grit with which they strew the sidewalk in those suburban districts; it makes walking a penance, and I felt my four-mile tramp had made me more weary than ten miles on an honest country road. I looked about the room with some curiosity; there was a shaded lamp, which threw a circle of brilliant light on a heap of papers lying on an old brass-bound secretaire of the last century, but the room was all vague and shadowy, and I could only see that it was long and low, and that it was filled with indistinct objects which might be furniture. Mr. Mathias sat down in a second arm-chair, and looked about him with that odd smile of his. He was a queer-looking man, clean shaven, and white to the lips. I should think his age was something between fifty and sixty.

"Now I have got you here," he began, "I must inflict my hobby on you. You knew I was a collector? Oh yes, I have devoted many years to collecting curiosities, which I think are really curious. But we must have a better light."

He advanced into the middle of the room, and lit a lamp which hung from the ceiling; and as the bright light flashed round the wick, from every corner and space there seemed to start a horror. Great wooden frames, with complicated apparatus of ropes and pulleys, stood against the wall; a wheel of strange shape had a place beside a thing that looked like a gigantic gridiron; little tables glittered with bright steel instruments carelessly put down as if ready for use; a screw and vice loomed out, casting ugly shadows, and in another nook was a saw with cruel jagged teeth.

"Yes," said Mr. Mathias, "they are, as you suggest, instruments of torture—of torture and death. Some—many, I may say—have been used; a few are reproductions after ancient examples. Those knives were used for flaying; that frame is a rack, and a very fine specimen. Look at this; it comes from Venice. You see that sort of collar, something like a big horse-shoe? Well, the patient, let us call him, sat down quite comfortably, and the horse-shoe was neatly fitted round his neck. Then the two ends were joined with a silken band, and the executioner began to turn a handle connected with the band. The horse-shoe contracted very gradually as the band tightened, and the turning continued till the man was strangled. It all took place quietly, in one of those queer garrets under the leads. But these things are all European; the Orientals are, of course, much more ingenious. These are the Chinese contrivances; you have heard of the 'Heavy Death'? It is my hobby, this sort of thing. Do you know, I often sit here, hour after hour, and meditate over the collection. I fancy I see the faces of the men who have suffered, faces lean with agony, and wet with sweats of death growing distinct out of the gloom, and I hear the echoes of their cries for mercy. But I must shew you my latest acquisition. Come into the next room."

I followed Mr. Mathias out. The weariness of the walk, the late hour, and the strangeness of it all made me feel like a man in a dream; nothing would have surprised me very much. The second room was as the first, crowded with ghastly instruments; but beneath the lamp was a wooden platform, and a figure stood on it. It was a large statue of a naked woman, fashioned in green bronze, the arms were stretched out, and there was a smile on the lips; it might well have been intended for a Venus, and yet there was about the thing an evil and a deadly look.

Mr. Mathias looked at it complacently. "Quite a work of art, isn't it?" he said. "It's made of bronze, as you see, but it has long had the name of the Iron Maid. I got it from Germany, and it was only unpacked this afternoon; indeed, I have not yet had time to open the letter of advice. You see that very small knob between the breasts? Well, the victim was bound to the Maid, the knob was pressed, and the arms slowly tightened round the neck. You can imagine the result."

As Mr. Mathias talked, he patted the figure affectionately. I had turned away, for I sickened at the sight of the man and his loathsome treasure. There was a slight click, of which I took no notice; it was not much louder than the tick of a clock; and then I heard a sudden whirr, the noise of machinery in motion, and I faced round. I have never forgotten the hideous agony on Mathias's face as those relentless arms tightened about his neck; there was a wild struggle as of a beast in the toils, and then a shriek that ended in a choking groan. The whirring noise had suddenly changed into a heavy droning. I tore with all my might at the bronze arms, and strove to wrench them apart, but I could do nothing. The head had slowly bent down, and the green lips were on the lips of Mathias.

Of course, I had to attend at the inquest. The letter which had accompanied the figure was found unopened on the study table. The German firm of dealers cautioned their client to be most careful in touching the Iron Maid, as the machinery had been put in thorough working order.

For many revolving weeks Mr. Burton delighted Dyson by his agreeable conversation, diversified by anecdote, and interspersed with the narration of singular adventures. Finally, however, he vanished as suddenly as he had appeared, and on the occasion of his last visit he contrived to loot a copy of his namesake's *Anatomy*. Dyson, considering this violent attack on the rights of property, and certain glaring inconsistencies in the talk of his late friend, arrived at the conclusion that his stories were fabulous, and that the Iron Maid only existed in the sphere of a decorative imagination.

The Recluse of Bayswater

Amongst the many friends who were favoured with the occasional pleasure of Mr. Dyson's society was Mr. Edgar Russell, realist and obscure struggler, who occupied a small back room on the second floor of a house in Abingdon Grove, Notting Hill. Turning off from the main street, and walking a few paces onward, one was conscious of a certain calm, a drowsy peace, which made the feet inclined to loiter, and this was ever the atmosphere of Abingdon Grove. The houses stood a little back, with gardens where the lilac, and laburnum, and blood-red may blossomed gaily in their seasons, and there was a corner where an older house in another street had managed to keep a back garden of real extent, a walled-in garden, whence there came a pleasant scent of greenness after the rains of early summer, where old elms held memories of the open fields, where there was yet sweet grass to walk on. The houses in Abingdon Grove belonged chiefly to the nondescript stucco period of thirty-five years ago, tolerably built, with passable accommodation for moderate incomes; they had largely passed into the state of lodgings, and cards bearing the inscription "Furnished apartments" were not infrequent over the doors. Here, then, in a house of sufficiently good appearance, Mr. Russell had established himself; for he looked upon the traditional dirt and squalor of Grub Street as a false and obsolete convention, and preferred, as he said, to live within sight of green leaves. Indeed, from his room one had a magnificent view of a long line of gardens, and a screen of poplars shut out the melancholy back premises of Wilton Street during the summer months. Mr. Russell lived chiefly on bread and tea, for his means were of the smallest; but when Dyson came to see him, he would send out the slavey for six ale, and Dyson was always at liberty to smoke as much of his tobacco as he pleased. The landlady had been so unfortunate as to have her drawing-room floor vacant for many months; a card had long proclaimed the void within; and Dyson, when he walked up the steps one evening in early autumn, had a sense that something was missing, and, looking at the fanlight, saw the appealing card had disappeared.

"You have let your first floor, have you?" he said, as he greeted Mr. Russell.

"Yes; it was taken about a fortnight ago by a lady."

"Indeed," said Dyson, always curious; "a young lady?"

"Yes; I believe so. She is a widow, and wears a thick crape veil. I have met her once or twice on the stairs and in the street; but I should not know her face."

"Well," said Dyson, when the beer had arrived, and the pipes were in full blast, "and what have you been doing? Do you find the work getting any easier?"

"Alas!" said the young man, with an expression of great gloom, "the life is a purgatory, and all but a hell. I write, picking out my words, weighing and balancing the force of every syllable, calculating the minutest effects that language can produce, erasing and rewriting, and spending a whole evening over a page of manuscript. And then, in the morning, when I read what I have written— Well, there is nothing to be done but to throw it in the wastepaper basket, if the verso has been already written on, or to put it in the drawer if the other side happens to be clean. When I have written a phrase which undoubtedly embodies a happy turn of thought, I find it dressed up in feeble commonplace; and when the style is good, it serves only to conceal the baldness of superannuated fancies. I sweat over my work, Dyson—every finished line means so much agony. I envy the lot of the carpenter in the side street who has a craft which he understands. When he gets an order for a table he does not writhe with anguish; but if I were so unlucky as to get an order for a book, I think I should go mad."

"My dear fellow, you take it all too seriously. You should let the ink flow more readily. Above all, firmly believe, when you sit down to write, that you are an artist, and that whatever you are about is a masterpiece. Suppose ideas fail you, say, as I heard one of our most exquisite artists say, 'It's of no consequence; the ideas are all there, at the bottom of that box of cigarettes!' You, indeed, smoke a pipe, but the application is the same. Besides, you must have some happy moments; and these should be ample consolation."

"Perhaps you are right. But such moments are so few; and then there is the torture of a glorious conception matched with execution beneath the standard of the Family Story Paper. For instance, I was happy for two hours a night or two ago; I lay awake and saw visions. But then the morning!"

"What was your idea?"

"It seemed to me a splendid one: I thought of Balzac and the *Co-médie Humaine,* of Zola and the Rougon-Macquart family. It dawned on me that I would write the history of a street. Every house should form a volume. I fixed upon the street, I saw each house, and read as clearly as in letters the physiology and psychology of each; the little byway stretched before me in its actual shape—a street that I know and have passed down a hundred times, with some twenty houses, prosperous and mean, and lilac bushes in purple blossom. And yet it was, at the same time, a symbol, a *via dolorosa* of hopes cherished and disappoint-ed, of years of monotonous existence without content or discontent, of tragedies and obscure sorrows; and on the door of one of those houses I saw the red stain of blood, and behind a window two shad-ows, blackened and faded, on the blind, as they swayed on tightened cords—the shadows of a man and a woman hanging in a vulgar gaslit parlour. These were my fancies; but when pen touched paper they shrivelled and vanished away."

"Yes," said Dyson, "there is a lot in that. I envy you the pains of transmuting vision into reality, and, still more, I envy you the day when you will look at your bookshelf and see twenty goodly books upon the shelves—the series complete and done for ever. Let me entreat you to have them bound in solid parchment, with gold lettering. It is the only real cover for a valiant book. When I look in at the windows of some choice shop, and see the bindings of levant morocco, with pretty tools and panellings, and your sweet contrasts of red and green, I say to my-self, 'These are not books, but *bibelots.*' A book bound so—a true book, mind you—is like a Gothic statue draped in brocade of Lyons."

"Alas!" said Russell, "we need not discuss the binding—the books are not begun."

The talk went on as usual till eleven o'clock, when Dyson bade his friend good-night. He knew the way downstairs, and walked down by himself; but, greatly to his surprise, as he crossed the first-floor landing the door opened slightly, and a hand was stretched out, beckoning.

Dyson was not the man to hesitate under such circumstances. In a moment he saw himself involved in adventure; and, as he told himself, the Dysons had never disobeyed a lady's summons. Softly, then, with due regard for the lady's honour, he would have entered the room, when a low but clear voice spoke to him—

"Go downstairs and open the door and shut it again rather loudly. Then come up to me; and for Heaven's sake, walk softly."

Dyson obeyed her commands, not without some hesitation, for he was afraid of meeting the landlady or the maid on his return journey. But, walking like a cat, and making each step he trod on crack loudly, he flattered himself that he had escaped observation; and as he gained the top of the stairs the door opened wide before him, and he found himself in the lady's drawing-room, bowing awkwardly.

"Pray be seated, sir. Perhaps this chair will be the best; it was the favoured chair of my landlady's deceased husband. I would ask you to smoke, but the odour would betray me. I know my proceedings must seem to you unconventional; but I saw you arrive this evening, and I do not think you would refuse to help a woman who is so unfortunate as I am."

Mr. Dyson looked shyly at the young lady before him. She was dressed in deep mourning, but the piquant smiling face and charming hazel eyes ill accorded with the heavy garments and the mouldering surface of the crape.

"Madam," he said gallantly, "your instinct has served you well. We will not trouble, if you please, about the question of social conventions; the chivalrous gentleman knows nothing of such matters. I hope I may be privileged to serve you."

"You are very kind to me, but I knew it would be so. Alas! sir, I have had experience of life, and I am rarely mistaken. Yet man is too often so vile and so misjudging that I trembled even as I resolved to take this step, which, for all I knew, might prove to be both desperate and ruinous."

"With me you have nothing to fear," said Dyson. "I was nurtured in the faith of chivalry, and I have always endeavoured to remember the proud traditions of my race. Confide in me, then, and count upon my secrecy, and if it prove possible, you may rely on my help."

"Sir, I will not waste your time, which I am sure is valuable, by idle parleyings. Learn, then, that I am a fugitive, and in hiding here; I place myself in your power; you have but to describe my features, and I fall into the hands of my relentless enemy."

Mr. Dyson wondered for a passing instant how this could be, but he only renewed his promise of silence, repeating that he would be the embodied spirit of dark concealment.

"Good," said the lady, "the Oriental fervour of your style is delightful. In the first place, I must disabuse your mind of the conviction that I am a widow. These gloomy vestments have been forced on me by strange circumstance; in plain language, I have deemed it expedient to go disguised. You have a friend, I think, in the house, Mr. Russell? He seems of a coy and retiring nature."

"Excuse me, madam," said Dyson, "he is not coy, but he is a realist; and perhaps you are aware that no Carthusian monk can emulate the cloistral seclusion in which a realistic novelist loves to shroud himself. It is his way of observing human nature."

"Well, well," said the lady; "all this, though deeply interesting, is not germane to our affair. I must tell you my history."

With these words the young lady proceeded to relate the

NOVEL OF THE WHITE POWDER.

My name is Leicester; my father, Major-General Wyn Leicester, a distinguished officer of artillery, succumbed five years ago to a complicated liver complaint acquired in the deadly climate of India. A year later my only brother, Francis, came home after an exceptionally brilliant career at the University, and settled down with the resolution of a hermit to master what has been well called the great legend of the law. He was a man who seemed to live in utter indifference to everything that is called pleasure; and though he was handsomer than most men, and could talk as merrily and wittily as if he were a mere vagabond, he avoided society, and shut himself up in a large room at the top of the house to make himself a lawyer. Ten hours a day of hard reading was at first his allotted portion; from the first light in the east to the late afternoon he remained shut up with his books, taking a hasty half-hour's lunch with me as if he grudged the wasting of the moments, and going out for a short walk when it began to grow dusk. I thought that such relentless application must be injurious, and tried to cajole him from the crabbed text-books, but his ardour seemed to grow rather than diminish, and his daily tale of hours increased. I spoke to him seriously, suggesting some occasional relaxation, if it were but an idle afternoon with a harmless novel; but he laughed, and said that he read about feudal tenures when he felt in need of amusement, and scoffed at the notions of theatres, or a month's fresh air. I confessed that he looked well, and seemed not to suffer from his labours, but I knew that such unnatural toil would take revenge at last, and I was not mistaken. A look of anxiety began to lurk about his eyes, and he seemed languid, and at last he avowed that he was no longer in perfect health; he was troubled, he said, with a sensation of dizziness, and awoke now and then of nights from fearful dreams, terrified and cold with icy sweats. "I am taking care of myself," he said, "so you must not trouble; I passed the whole of yesterday afternoon in idleness, leaning back in that comfortable chair you gave me, and scribbling nonsense on a sheet of paper. No, no; I will not overdo my work; I shall be well enough in a week or two depend upon it."

Yet in spite of his assurances I could see that he grew no better, but rather worse; he would enter the drawing-room with a face all miserably wrinkled and despondent, and endeavour to look gaily when my eyes fell on him, and I thought such symptoms of evil omen, and was frightened sometimes at the nervous irritation of his movements, and at glances which I could not decipher. Much against his will, I prevailed on him to have medical advice, and with an ill grace he called in our old doctor.

Dr. Haberden cheered me after examination of his patient.

"There is nothing really much amiss," he said to me. "No doubt he reads too hard and eats hastily, and then goes back again to his books in too great a hurry, and the natural sequence is some digestive trouble and a little mischief in the nervous system. But I think—I do indeed, Miss Leicester—that we shall be able to set this all right. I have written him a prescription which ought to do great things. So you have no cause for anxiety."

My brother insisted on having the prescription made up by a chemist in the neighbourhood. It was an odd, old-fashioned shop, devoid of the studied coquetry and calculated glitter that make so gay a shew on the counters and shelves of the modern apothecary; but Francis liked the old chemist, and believed in the scrupulous purity of his drugs. The medicine was sent in due course, and I saw that my brother took it regularly after lunch and dinner. It was an innocent-looking white powder, of which a little was dissolved in a glass of cold water; I stirred it in, and it seemed to disappear, leaving the water clear and colourless. At first Francis seemed to benefit greatly; the weariness vanished from his face, and he became more cheerful than he had ever been since the time when he left school; he talked gaily of reforming himself, and avowed to me that he had wasted his time.

"I have given too many hours to law," he said, laughing; "I think you have saved me in the nick of time. Come, I shall be Lord Chancellor yet, but I must not forget life. You and I will have a holiday together before long; we will go to Paris and enjoy ourselves, and keep away from the Bibliothèque Nationale."

I confessed myself delighted with the prospect.

"When shall we go?" I said. "I can start the day after to-morrow if you like."

"Ah! that is perhaps a little too soon; after all, I do not know London yet, and I suppose a man ought to give the pleasures of his own country the first choice. But we will go off together in a week or two, so try and furbish up your French. I only know law French myself, and I am afraid that wouldn't do."

We were just finishing dinner, and he quaffed off his medicine with a parade of carousal as if it had been wine from some choicest bin.

"Has it any particular taste?" I said.

"No; I should not know I was not drinking water," and he got up from his chair and began to pace up and down the room as if he were undecided as to what he should do next.

"Shall we have coffee in the drawing-room?" I said; "or would you like to smoke?"

"No, I think I will take a turn; it seems a pleasant evening. Look at the afterglow; why, it is as if a great city were burning in flames, and down there between the dark houses it is raining blood fast, fast. Yes, I will go out; I may be in soon, but I shall take my key; so good-night, dear, if I don't see you again."

The door slammed behind him, and I saw him walk lightly down the street, swinging his malacca cane, and I felt grateful to Dr. Haberden for such an improvement.

I believe my brother came home very late that night, but he was in a merry mood the next morning.

"I walked on without thinking where I was going," he said, "enjoying the freshness of the air, and livened by the crowds as I reached more frequented quarters. And then I met an old college friend, Orford, in the press of the pavement, and then—well, we enjoyed ourselves. I have felt what it is to be young and a man; I find I have blood in my veins, as other men have. I made an appointment with Orford for to-night; there will be a little party of us at the restaurant. Yes; I shall enjoy myself for a week or two, and hear the chimes at midnight, and then we will go for our little trip together."

Such was the transmutation of my brother's character that in a few days he became a lover of pleasure, a careless and merry idler of western pavements, a hunter out of snug restaurants, and a fine critic of fantastic dancing; he grew fat before my eyes, and said no more of Paris, for he had clearly found his paradise in London. I rejoiced, and yet wondered a little; for there was, I thought, something in his gaiety that indefinitely displeased me, though I could not have defined my feeling. But by degrees there came a change; he returned still in the cold hours of the morning, but I heard no more about his pleasures, and one morning as we sat at breakfast together I looked suddenly into his eyes and saw a stranger before me.

"Oh, Francis!" I cried. "Oh, Francis, Francis, what have you done?" and rending sobs cut the words short. I went weeping out of the room; for though I knew nothing, yet I knew all, and by some odd play of thought I remembered the evening when he first went abroad to prove his manhood, and the picture of the sunset sky glowed before me; the clouds like a city in burning flames, and the rain of blood. Yet I did battle with such thoughts, resolving that perhaps, after all, no great harm had been done, and in the evening at dinner I resolved to press him to fix a day for our holiday in Paris. We had talked easily enough, and my brother had just taken his medicine, which he continued all the while. I was about to begin my topic, when the words forming in my mind vanished, and I wondered for a second what icy and intolerable weight oppressed my heart and suffocated me as with the unutterable horror of the coffin-lid nailed down on the living.

We had dined without candles; the room had slowly grown from twilight to gloom, and the walls and corners were indistinct in the shadow. But from where I sat I looked out into the street; and as I thought of what I would say to Francis, the sky began to flush and shine, as it had done on a well-remembered evening, and in the gap between two dark masses that were houses an awful pageantry of flame appeared—lurid whorls of writhed cloud, and utter depths burning, grey masses like the fume blown from a smoking city, and an evil glory blazing far above shot with tongues of more ardent fire, and below as if there were a deep pool of blood. I looked down to where my brother sat facing me, and the words were shaped on my lips, when I saw his hand resting on the table. Between the thumb and forefinger of the closed hand there was a mark, a small patch about the size of a sixpence, and somewhat of the colour of a bad bruise. Yet, by some sense I cannot define, I knew that what I saw was no bruise at all; oh! if human flesh could burn with flame, and if flame could be black as pitch, such was that before me. Without thought or fashioning of words grey horror shaped within me at the sight, and in an inner cell it was known to be a brand. For the moment the stained sky became dark as midnight, and when the light returned to me I was alone in the silent room, and soon after I heard my brother go out.

Late as it was, I put on my hat and went to Dr. Haberden, and in his great consulting room, ill lighted by a candle which the doctor brought in with him, with stammering lips, and a voice that would break in spite of my resolve, I told him all, from the day on which my brother began to take the medicine down to the dreadful thing I had seen scarcely half an hour before.

When I had done, the doctor looked at me for a minute with an expression of great pity on his face.

"My dear Miss Leicester," he said, "you have evidently been anxious about your brother; you have been worrying over him, I am sure. Come, now, is it not so?"

"I have certainly been anxious," I said. "For the last week or two I have not felt at ease."

"Quite so; you know, of course, what a queer thing the brain is?"

"I understand what you mean; but I was not deceived. I saw what I have told you with my own eyes."

"Yes, yes, of course. But your eyes had been staring at that very curious sunset we had to-night. That is the only explanation. You will see it in the proper light to-morrow, I am sure. But, remember, I am always ready to give any help that is in my power; do not scruple to come to me, or to send for me if you are in any distress."

I went away but little comforted, all confusion and terror and sorrow, not knowing where to turn. When my brother and I met the next day, I looked quickly at him, and noticed, with a sickening at heart, that the right hand, the hand on which I had clearly seen the patch as of a black fire, was wrapped up with a handkerchief.

"What is the matter with your hand, Francis?" I said in a steady voice.

"Nothing of consequence. I cut a finger last night, and it bled rather awkwardly. So I did it up roughly to the best of my ability."

"I will do it neatly for you, if you like."

"No, thank you, dear; this will answer very well. Suppose we have breakfast; I am quite hungry."

We sat down, and I watched him. He scarcely ate or drank at all, but tossed his meat to the dog when he thought my eyes were turned away; there was a look in his eyes that I had never yet seen, and the thought flashed across my mind that it was a look that was scarcely human. I was firmly convinced that awful and incredible as was the thing I had seen the night before, yet it was no illusion, no glamour of bewildered sense, and in the course of the morning I went again to the doctor's house.

He shook his head with an air puzzled and incredulous, and seemed to reflect for a few minutes.

"And you say he still keeps up the medicine? But why? As I understand, all the symptoms he complained of have disappeared long ago; why should he go on taking the stuff when he is quite well? And by the by, where did he get it made up? At Sayce's? I never send any one there; the old man is getting careless. Suppose you come with me to the chemist's; I should like to have some talk with him."

We walked together to the shop; old Sayce knew Dr. Haberden, and was quite ready to give any information.

"You have been sending that in to Mr. Leicester for some weeks, I think, on my prescription," said the doctor, giving the old man a pencilled scrap of paper.

The chemist put on his great spectacles with trembling uncertainty, and held up the paper with a shaking hand.

"Oh yes," he said, "I have very little of it left; it is rather an uncommon drug, and I have had it in stock some time. I must get in some more, if Mr. Leicester goes on with it."

"Kindly let me have a look at the stuff," said Haberden, and the chemist gave him a glass bottle. He took out the stopper and smelt the contents, and looked strangely at the old man.

"Where did you get this?" he said, "and what is it? For one thing, Mr. Sayce, it is not what I prescribed. Yes, yes, I see the label is right enough, but I tell you this is not the drug."

"I have had it a long time," said the old man in feeble terror; "I got it from Burbage's in the usual way. It is not prescribed often, and I have had it on the shelf for some years. You see there is very little left."

"You had better give it to me," said Haberden. "I am afraid something wrong has happened."

We went out of the shop in silence, the doctor carrying the bottle neatly wrapped in paper under his arm.

"Dr. Haberden," I said, when we had walked a little way—"Dr. Haberden."

"Yes," he said, looking at me gloomily enough.

"I should like you to tell me what my brother has been taking twice a day for the last month or so."

"Frankly, Miss Leicester, I don't know. We will speak of this when we get to my house."

We walked on quickly without another word till we reached Dr. Haberden's. He asked me to sit down, and began pacing up and down the room, his face clouded over, as I could see, with no common fears.

"Well," he said at length, "this is all very strange; it is only natural that you should feel alarmed, and I must confess that my mind is far from easy. We will put aside, if you please, what you told me last night and this morning, but the fact remains that for the last few weeks Mr. Leicester has been impregnating his system with a drug which is completely unknown to me. I tell you, it is not what I ordered; and what the stuff in the bottle really is remains to be seen."

He undid the wrapper, and cautiously tilted a few grains of the white powder on to a piece of paper, and peered curiously at it.

"Yes," he said, "it is like the sulphate of quinine, as you say; it is flaky. But smell it."

He held the bottle to me, and I bent over it. It was a strange, sickly smell, vaporous and overpowering, like some strong anæsthetic.

"I shall have it analysed," said Haberden; "I have a friend who has devoted his whole life to chemistry as a science. Then I we shall have something to go upon. No, no; say no more about that other matter; I cannot listen to that; and take my advice and think no more about it yourself."

That evening my brother did not go out as usual after dinner.

"I have had my fling," he said with a queer laugh, "and I must go back to my old ways. A little law will be quite a relaxation after so sharp a dose of pleasure," and he grinned to himself, and soon after went up to his room. His hand was still all bandaged.

Dr. Haberden called a few days later.

"I have no special news to give you," he said. "Chambers is out of town, so I know no more about that stuff than you do. But I should like to see Mr. Leicester, if he is in."

"He is in his room," I said; "I will tell him you are here."

"No, no, I will go up to him; we will have a little quiet talk together. I dare say that we have made a good deal of fuss about a very little; for, after all, whatever the powder may be, it seems to have done him good."

The doctor went upstairs, and standing in the hall I heard his knock, and the opening and shutting of the door; and then I waited in the silent house for an hour, and the stillness grew more and more intense as the hands of the clock crept round. Then there sounded from above the noise of a door shut sharply, and the doctor was coming down the stairs. His footsteps crossed the hall, and there was a pause at the door; I drew a long, sick breath with difficulty, and saw my face white in a little mirror, and he came in and stood at the door. There was an unutterable horror shining in his eyes; he steadied himself by holding the back of a chair with one hand, his lower lip trembled like a horse's, and he gulped and stammered unintelligible sounds before he spoke.

"I have seen that man," he began in a dry whisper. "I have been sitting in his presence for the last hour. My God! And I am alive and in my senses! I, who have dealt with death all my life, and have dabbled with the melting ruins of the earthly tabernacle. But not this, oh! not this," and he covered his face with his hands as if to shut out the sight of something before him.

"Do not send for me again, Miss Leicester," he said with more composure. "I can do nothing in this house. Good-bye."

As I watched him totter down the steps, and along the pavement towards his house, it seemed to me that he had aged by ten years since the morning.

My brother remained in his room. He called out to me in a voice I hardly recognised that he was very busy, and would like his meals brought to his door and left there, and I gave the order to the servants. From that day it seemed as if the arbitrary conception we call time had been annihilated for me; I lived in an ever-present sense of horror, going through the routine of the house mechanically, and only speaking a few necessary words to the servants. Now and then I went out and paced the streets for an hour or two and came home again; but whether I were without or within, my spirit delayed before the closed door of the upper room, and, shuddering, waited for it to open. I have said that I scarcely reckoned time; but I suppose it must have been a fortnight after Dr. Haberden's visit that I came home from my stroll a little refreshed and lightened. The air was sweet and pleasant, and the hazy form of green leaves, floating cloudlike in the square, and the smell of blossoms, had charmed my senses, and I felt happier and walked more briskly. As I delayed a moment at the verge of the pavement, waiting for a van to pass by before crossing over to the house, I happened to look up at the windows, and instantly there was the rush and swirl of deep cold waters in my ears, my heart leapt up and fell down, down as into a deep hollow, and I was amazed with a dread and terror without form or shape. I stretched out a hand blindly through the folds of thick darkness, from the black and shadowy valley, and held myself from falling, while the stones beneath my feet rocked and swayed and tilted, and the sense of solid things seemed to sink away from under me. I had glanced up at the window of my brother's study, and at that moment the blind was drawn aside, and something that had life stared out into the world. Nay, I cannot say I saw a face or any human likeness; a living thing, two eyes of burning flame glared at me, and they were in the midst of something as formless as my fear, the symbol and presence of all evil and all hideous corruption. I stood shuddering and quaking as with the grip of ague, sick with unspeakable agonies of fear and loathing, and for five minutes I could not summon force or motion to my limbs. When I was within the door, I ran up the stairs to my brother's room, and knocked.

"Francis, Francis," I cried, "for Heaven's sake, answer me. What is the horrible thing in your room? Cast it out, Francis; cast it from you."

I heard a noise as of feet shuffling slowly and awkwardly, and a choking, gurgling sound, as if some one was struggling to find utterance, and then the noise of a voice, broken and stifled, and words that I could scarcely understand.

"There is nothing here," the voice said. "Pray do not disturb me. I am not very well to-day."

I turned away, horrified, and yet helpless. I could do nothing, and I wondered why Francis had lied to me, for I had I seen the appearance beyond the glass too plainly to be deceived, though it was but the sight of a moment. And I sat still, conscious that there had been something else, something I had seen in the first flash of terror, before those burning eyes had looked at me. Suddenly I remembered; as I lifted my face the blind was being drawn back, and I had had an instant's glance of the thing that was moving it, and in my recollection I knew that a hideous image was engraved for ever on my brain. It was not a hand; there were no fingers that held the blind, but a black stump pushed it aside, the mouldering outline and the clumsy movement as of a beast's paw had glowed into my senses before the darkling waves of terror had overwhelmed me as I went down quick into the pit. My mind was aghast at the thought of this, and of the awful presence that dwelt with my brother in his room; I went to his door and cried to him again, but no answer came. That night one of the servants came up to me and told me in a whisper that for three days food had been regularly placed at the door and left untouched; the maid had knocked, but had received no answer; she had heard the noise of shuffling feet that I had noticed. Day after day went by, and still my brother's meals were brought to his door and left untouched; and though I knocked and called again and again, I could get no answer. The servants began to talk to me; it appeared they were as alarmed as I; the cook said that when my brother first shut himself up in his room she used to hear him come out at night and go about the house; and once, she said, the hall door had opened and closed again, but for several nights she had heard no sound. The climax came at last; it was in the dusk of the evening, and I was sitting in the darkening dreary room when a terrible shriek jarred and rang harshly out of the silence, and I heard a frightened scurry of feet dashing down the stairs. I waited, and the servant-maid staggered into the room and faced me, white and trembling.

"Oh, Miss Helen!" she whispered; "oh! for the Lord's sake, Miss Helen, what has happened? Look at my hand, miss; look at that hand!"

I drew her to the window, and saw there was a black wet stain upon her hand.

"I do not understand you," I said. "Will you explain to me?"

"I was doing your room just now," she began. "I was turning down the bed-clothes, and all of a sudden there was something fell upon my hand, wet, and I looked up, and the ceiling was black and dripping on me."

I looked hard at her and bit my lip.

"Come with me," I said. "Bring your candle with you."

The room I slept in was beneath my brother's, and as I went in I felt I was trembling. I looked up at the ceiling, and saw a patch, all black and wet, and a dew of black drops upon it, and a pool of horrible liquor soaking into the white bed-clothes.

I ran upstairs and knocked loudly.

"Oh, Francis, Francis, my dear brother," I cried, "what has happened to you?"

And I listened. There was a sound of choking, and a noise like water bubbling and regurgitating, but nothing else, and I called louder, but no answer came.

In spite of what Dr. Haberden had said, I went to him; with tears streaming down my cheeks I told him all that had happened, and he listened to me with a face set hard and grim.

"For your father's sake," he said at last, "I will go with you, though I can do nothing."

We went out together; the streets were dark and silent, and heavy with heat and a drought of many weeks. I saw the doctor's face white under the gas-lamps, and when we reached the house his hand was shaking.

We did not hesitate, but went upstairs directly. I held the lamp, and he called out in a loud, determined voice—

"Mr. Leicester, do you hear me? I insist on seeing you. Answer me at once."

There was no answer, but we both heard that choking noise I have mentioned.

"Mr. Leicester, I am waiting for you. Open the door this instant, or I shall break it down." And he called a third time in a voice that rang and echoed from the walls—

"Mr. Leicester! For the last time I order you to open the door."

"Ah!" he said, after a pause of heavy silence, "we are wasting time here. Will you be so kind as to get me a poker, or something of the kind?"

I ran into a little room at the back where odd articles were kept, and found a heavy adze-like tool that I thought might serve the doctor's purpose.

"Very good," he said, "that will do, I dare say. I give you notice, Mr. Leicester," he cried loudly at the keyhole, "that I am now about to break into your room."

Then I heard the wrench of the adze, and the woodwork split and cracked under it; with a loud crash the door suddenly burst open, and for a moment we started back aghast at a fearful screaming cry, no human voice, but as the roar of a monster, that burst forth inarticulate and struck at us out of the darkness.

"Hold the lamp," said the doctor, and we went in and glanced quickly round the room.

"There it is," said Dr. Haberden, drawing a quick breath; "look, in that corner."

I looked, and a pang of horror seized my heart as with a white-hot iron. There upon the floor was a dark and putrid mass, seething with corruption and hideous rottenness, neither liquid nor solid, but melting and changing before our eyes, and bubbling with unctuous oily bubbles like boiling pitch. And out of the midst of it shone two burning points like eyes, and I saw a writhing and stirring as of limbs, and something moved and lifted up what might have been an arm. The doctor took a step forward, raised the iron bar, and struck at the burning points; he drove in the weapon, and struck again and again in the fury of loathing. At last the thing was quiet.

A week or two later, when I had to some extent recovered from the terrible shock, Dr. Haberden came to see me.

"I have sold my practice," he began, "and to-morrow I am sailing on a long voyage. I do not know whether I shall ever return to England; in all probability I shall buy a little land in California, and settle there for the remainder of my life. I have brought you this packet, which you may open and read when you feel able to do so. It contains the report of Dr. Chambers on what I submitted to him. Good-bye, Miss Leicester, good-bye."

When he was gone I opened the envelope; I could not wait, and proceeded to read the papers within. Here is the manuscript, and if you will allow me, I will read you the astounding story it contains.

"My dear Haberden," the letter began, "I have delayed inexcusably in answering your questions as to the white substance you sent me. To tell you the truth, I have hesitated for some time as to what course I should adopt, for there is a bigotry and an orthodox standard in physical science as in theology, and I knew that if I told you the truth I should offend rooted prejudices which I once held dear myself. However, I have determined to be plain with you, and first I must enter into a short personal explanation.

"You have known me, Haberden, for many years as a scientific man; you and I have often talked of our profession together, and discussed the hopeless gulf that opens before the feet of those who think to attain to truth by any means whatsoever except the beaten way of experiment and observation in the sphere of material things. I remember the scorn with which you have spoken to me of men of science who have dabbled a little in the unseen, and have timidly hinted that perhaps the senses are not, after all, the eternal, impenetrable bounds of all knowledge, the everlasting walls beyond which no human being has ever passed. We have laughed together heartily, and I think justly, at the 'occult' follies of the day, disguised under various names—the mesmerisms, spiritualisms, materialisations, theosophies, all the rabble rant of imposture, with their machinery of poor tricks and feeble conjuring, the true back-parlour magic of shabby London streets. Yet, in

spite of what I have said, I must confess to you that I am no materialist, taking the word of course in its usual signification. It is now many
years since I have convinced myself—convinced myself, a sceptic, remember—that the old iron-bound theory is utterly and entirely false.
Perhaps this confession will not wound you so sharply as it would
have done twenty years ago; for I think you cannot have failed to notice that for some time hypotheses have been advanced by men of
pure science which are nothing less than transcendental, and I suspect
that most modern chemists and biologists of repute would not hesitate
to subscribe the *dictum* of the old Schoolman, *Omnia exeunt in mysterium,*
which means, I take it, that every branch of human knowledge if traced
up to its source and final principles vanishes into mystery. I need not
trouble you now with a detailed account of the painful steps which led
me to my conclusions; a few simple experiments suggested a doubt as
to my then standpoint, and a train of thought that rose from circumstances comparatively trifling brought me far; my old conception of
the universe has been swept away, and I stand in a world that seems as
strange and awful to me as the endless waves of the ocean seen for the
first time, shining, from a peak in Darien. Now I know that the walls
of sense that seemed so impenetrable, that seemed to loom up above
the heavens and to be founded below the depths, and to shut us in for
evermore, are no such everlasting impassable barriers as we fancied,
but thinnest and most airy veils that melt away before the seeker, and
dissolve as the early mist of the morning about the brooks. I know that
you never adopted the extreme materialistic position; you did not go
about trying to prove a universal negative, for your logical sense with-
held you from that crowning absurdity; but I am sure that you will find
all that I am saying strange and repellent to your habits of thought.
Yet, Haberden, what I tell you is the truth, nay, to adopt our common
language, the sole and scientific truth, verified by experience; and the
universe is verily more splendid and more awful than we used to
dream. The whole universe, my friend, is a tremendous sacrament; a
mystic, ineffable force and energy, veiled by an outward form of matter; and man, and the sun and the other stars, and the flower of the
grass, and the crystal in the test-tube, are each and every one as spiritual, as material, and subject to an inner working.

"You will perhaps wonder, Haberden, whence all this tends; but I think a little thought will make it clear. You will understand that from such a standpoint the whole view of things is changed, and what we thought incredible and absurd may be possible enough. In short, we must look at legend and belief with other eyes, and be prepared to accept tales that had become mere fables. Indeed this is no such great demand. After all, modern science will concede as much, in a hypocritical manner; you must not, it is true, believe in witchcraft, but you may credit hypnotism; ghosts are out of date, but there is a good deal to be said for the theory of telepathy. Give superstition a Greek name, and believe in it, should almost be a proverb.

"So much for my personal explanation. You sent me, Haberden, a phial, stoppered and sealed, containing a small quantity of flaky white powder, obtained from a chemist who has been dispensing it to one of your patients. I am not surprised to hear that this powder refused to yield any results to your analysis. It is a substance which was known to a few many hundred years ago, but which I never expected to have submitted to me from the shop of a modern apothecary. There seems no reason to doubt the truth of the man's tale; he no doubt got, as he says, the rather uncommon salt you prescribed from the wholesale chemist's; and it has probably remained on his shelf for twenty years, or perhaps longer. Here what we call chance and coincidence begin to work; during all these years the salt in the bottle was exposed to certain recurring variations of temperature, variations probably ranging from 40° to 80°. And, as it happens, such changes, recurring year after year at irregular intervals, and with varying degrees of intensity and duration, have constituted a process, and a process so complicated and so delicate, that I question whether modern scientific apparatus directed with the utmost precision could produce the same result. The white powder you sent me is something very different from the drug you prescribed; it is the powder from which the wine of the Sabbath, the *Vinum Sabbati,* was prepared. No doubt you have read of the Witches' Sabbath, and have laughed at the tales which terrified our ancestors; the black cats, and the broomsticks, and dooms pronounced against some old woman's cow. Since I have known the truth I have often reflected that it is on the whole a happy thing that such burlesque as this is believed, for it serves to conceal much that it is better should not be known generally. However, if you care to read the appendix to Payne Knight's monograph, you will find that the true Sabbath was something very different, though the writer has very nicely refrained from printing all he knew. The secrets of the true Sabbath were the secrets of remote times surviving into the Middle Ages, secrets of an evil science which existed long before Aryan man entered Europe. Men and women, seduced from their homes on specious pretences, were met by beings well qualified to assume, as they did assume, the part of devils, and taken by their guides to some desolate and lonely place, known to the initiate by long tradition, and unknown to all else. Perhaps it was a cave in some bare and wind-swept hill, perhaps some inmost recess of a great forest, and there the Sabbath was held. There, in the blackest hour of night, the *Vinum Sabbati* was prepared, and this evil graal was poured forth and offered to the neophytes, and they partook of an infernal sacrament; *sumentes calicem principis inferorum,* as an old author well expresses it. And suddenly, each one that had drunk found himself attended by a companion, a shape of glamour and unearthly allurement, beckoning him apart, to share in joys more exquisite, more piercing than the thrill of any dream, to the consummation of the marriage of the Sabbath. It is hard to write of such things as these, and chiefly because that shape that allured with loveliness was no hallucination, but, awful as it is to express, the man himself. By the power of that Sabbath wine, a few grains of white powder thrown into a glass of water, the house of life was riven asunder and the human trinity dissolved, and the worm which never dies, that which lies sleeping within us all, was made tangible and an external thing, and clothed with a garment of flesh. And then, in the hour of midnight, the primal fall was repeated and re-presented, and the awful thing veiled in the mythos of the Tree in the Garden was done anew. Such was the *nuptiæ Sabbati.*

"I prefer to say no more; you, Haberden, know as well as I do that the most trivial laws of life are not to be broken with impunity; and for so terrible an act as this, in which the very inmost place of the temple was broken open and defiled, a terrible vengeance followed. What began with corruption ended also with corruption."

Underneath is the following in Dr. Haberden's writing:—

"The whole of the above is unfortunately strictly and entirely true. Your brother confessed all to me on that morning when I saw him in his room. My attention was first attracted to the bandaged hand, and I forced him to shew it me. What I saw made me, a medical man of many years standing, grow sick with loathing, and the story I was forced to listen to was infinitely more frightful than I could have believed possible. It has tempted me to doubt the Eternal Goodness which can permit nature to offer such hideous possibilities; and if you had not with your own eyes seen the end, I should have said to you—disbelieve it all. I have not, I think, many more weeks to live, but you are young, and may forget all this.

"JOSEPH HABERDEN, M.D."

In the course of two or three months I heard that Dr. Haberden had died at sea shortly after the ship left England.

Miss Leicester ceased speaking, and looked pathetically at Dyson, who could not refrain from exhibiting some symptoms of uneasiness.

He stuttered out some broken phrases expressive of his deep interest in her extraordinary history, and then said with a better grace—

"But pardon me, Miss Leicester, I understood you were in some difficulty. You were kind enough to ask me to assist you in some way."

"Ah," she said, "I had forgotten that; my own present trouble seems of such little consequence in comparison with what I have told you. But as you are so good to me, I will go on. You will scarcely believe it, but I found that certain persons suspected, or rather pretended to suspect, that I had murdered my brother. These persons were relatives of mine, and their motives were extremely sordid ones; but I actually found myself subject to the shameful indignity of being watched. Yes, sir, my steps were dogged when I went abroad, and at home I found myself exposed to constant if artful observation. With my high spirit this was more than I could brook, and I resolved to set my wits to work and elude the persons who were shadowing me. I was so fortunate as to succeed; I assumed this disguise, and for some time have lain snug and unsuspected. But of late I have reason to believe that the pursuer is on my track; unless I am greatly deceived, I saw yesterday the detective who is charged with the odious duty of observing my movements. You, sir, are watchful and keen-sighted; tell me, did you see any one lurking about this evening?"

"I hardly think so," said Dyson, "but perhaps you would give me some description of the detective in question."

"Certainly; he is a youngish man, dark, with dark whiskers. He has adopted spectacles of large size in the hope of disguising himself effectually, but he cannot disguise his uneasy manner, and the quick, nervous glances he casts to right and left."

This piece of description was the last straw for the unhappy Dyson, who was foaming with impatience to get out of the house, and would gladly have sworn eighteenth-century oaths, if propriety had not frowned on such a course.

"Excuse me, Miss Leicester," he said with cool politeness, "I cannot assist you."

"Ah," she said sadly, "I have offended you in some way. Tell me what I have done, and I will ask you to forgive me."

"You are mistaken," said Dyson, grabbing his hat, but speaking with some difficulty; "you have done nothing. But, as I say, I cannot help you. Perhaps," he added, with some tinge of sarcasm, "my friend Russell might be of service."

"Thank you," she replied; "I will try him," and the lady went off into a shriek of laughter, which filled up Mr. Dyson's cup of scandal and confusion.

He left the house shortly afterwards, and had the peculiar delight of a five-mile walk, through streets which slowly changed from black to grey, and from grey to shining passages of glory for the sun to brighten. Here and there he met or overtook strayed revellers, but he reflected that no one could have spent the night in a more futile fashion than himself; and when he reached his home he had made resolves for reformation. He decided that he would abjure all Milesian and Arabian methods of entertainment, and subscribe to Mudie's for a regular supply of mild and innocuous romance.

STRANGE OCCURRENCE IN CLERKENWELL

Mr. Dyson had inhabited for some years a couple of rooms in a moderately quiet street in Bloomsbury, where, as he somewhat pompously expressed it, he held his finger on the pulse of life without being deaf-ened with the thousand rumours of the main arteries of London. It was to him a source of peculiar, if esoteric, gratification that from the adjacent corner of Tottenham Court Road a hundred lines of omni-buses went to the four quarters of the town; he would dilate on the fa-cilities for visiting Dalston, and dwell on the admirable line that knew extremest Ealing and the streets beyond Whitechapel. His rooms, which had been originally "furnished apartments", he had gradually purged of their more peccant parts; and though one would not find here the glowing splendours of his old chambers in the street off the Strand, there was something of severe grace about the appointments which did credit to his taste. The rugs were old, and of the true faded beauty; the etchings, nearly all of them proofs printed by the artist, made a good show with broad white margins and black frames, and there was no spurious black oak. Indeed, there was but little furniture of any kind: a plain and honest table, square and sturdy, stood in one corner; a seventeenth-century settle fronted the hearth; and two wood-en elbow-chairs and a bookshelf of the Empire made up the equip-ment, with an exception worthy of note. For Dyson cared for none of these things, his place was at his own bureau, a quaint old piece of lacquered-work, at which he would sit for hour after hour, with his back to the room, engaged in the desperate pursuit of literature, or, as he termed his profession, the chase of the phrase. The neat array of pigeon-holes and drawers teemed and overflowed with manuscripts and note-books, the experiments and efforts of many years; and the inner well, a vast and cavernous receptacle, was stuffed with accumulated ideas. Dyson was a craftman who loved all the detail and the technique of his work intensely; and if, as has been hinted, he deluded himself a little with the name of artist, yet his amusements were eminently harmless, and, so far as can be ascertained, he (or the publishers) had chosen the good part of not tiring the world with printed matter.

Here, then, Dyson would shut himself up with his fancies, experi-menting with words, and striving, as his friend the recluse of Bayswa-ter strove, with the almost invincible problem of style, but always with a fine confidence, extremely different from the chronic depression of the realist. He had been almost continuously at work on some scheme that struck him as wellnigh magical in its possibilities since the night of his adventure with the ingenious tenant of the first floor in Abingdon Grove; and as he laid down the pen with a glow of triumph, he reflected that he had not viewed the streets for five days in succession. With all the enthusiasm of his accomplished labour still working in his brain, he put away his papers and went out, pacing the pavement at first in that rare mood of exultation which finds in every stone upon the way the possibilities of a masterpiece. It was growing late, and the autumn evening was drawing to a close amidst veils of haze and mist, and in the stilled air the voices, and the roaring traffic, and incessant feet seemed to Dyson like the noise upon the stage when all the house is silent. In the square the leaves rippled down as quick as summer rain, and the street beyond was beginning to flare with the lights in the butcher's shops and the vivid illumination of the greengrocer. It was a Saturday night, and the swarming populations of the slums were turning out in force; the battered women in rusty black had begun to paw the lumps of cagmag, and others gloated over unwholesome cabbages, and there was a brisk demand for four ale. Dyson passed through these night-fires with some relief; he loved to meditate, but his thoughts were not as De Quincey's after his dose; he cared not two straws whether onions were dear or cheap, and would not have exulted if meat had fallen to twopence a pound. Absorbed in the wilderness of the tale he had been writing, weighing nicely the points of plot and construction, relishing the recollection of this and that happy phrase, and dreading failure here and there, he left the rush and whistle of the gas-flares behind him, and began to touch upon pavements more deserted.

He had turned, without taking note, to the northward, and was passing through an ancient fallen street, where now notices of floors and offices to let hung out, but still about it lingered the grace and the stiffness of the Age of Wigs—a broad roadway, a broad pavement, and on each side a grave line of houses with long and narrow windows flush with the walls, all of mellowed brickwork. Dyson walked with quick steps, as he resolved that short work must be made of a certain episode; but he was in that happy humour of invention, and another chapter rose in the inner chamber of his brain, and he dwelt on the circumstances he was to write down with curious pleasure. It was charming to have the quiet streets to walk in, and in his thought he made a whole district the cabinet of his studies, and vowed he would come again. Heedless of his course, he struck off to the east again, and soon found himself involved in a squalid network of grey two-storied houses, and then in the waste void and elements of brickwork, the passages and unmade roads behind great factory walls, encumbered with the refuse of the neighbourhood, forlorn, ill-lighted, and desperate. A brief turn, and there rose before him the unexpected, a hill suddenly lifted from the level ground, its steep ascent marked by the lighted lamps, and eager as an explorer, Dyson found his way to the place, wondering where his crooked paths had brought him. Here all was again decorous, but hideous in the extreme. The builder, some one lost in the deep gloom of the early 'twenties, had, conceived the idea of twin villas in grey brick, shaped in a manner to recall the outlines of the Parthenon, each with its classic form broadly marked with raised bands of stucco. The name of the street was all strange, and for a further surprise the top of the hill was crowned with an irregular plot of grass and fading trees, called a square, and here again the Parthenon-motive had persisted. Beyond, the streets were curious, wild in their irregularities, here a row of sordid, dingy dwellings, dirty and disreputable in appearance, and there, without warning, stood a house, genteel and prim, with wire blinds and brazen knocker, as clean and trim as if it had been the doctor's house in some benighted little country town. These surprises and discoveries began to exhaust Dyson, and he hailed with delight the blazing windows of a public-house, and went in with the intention of testing the beverage provided for the dwellers in this region, as remote as Libya and Pamphylia and the parts about Mesopotamia. The babble of voices from within warned him that he was about to assist at the true parliament of the London workman, and he looked about him for that more retired entrance called private. When he had settled himself on an exiguous bench, and had ordered some beer, he began to listen to the jangling talk in the public bar beyond; it was a senseless argument, alternately furious and maudlin, with appeals to Bill and Tom, and mediæval survivals of speech, words that Chaucer wrote belched out with zeal and relish, and the din of pots jerked down and coppers rapped smartly on the zinc counter made a thorough bass for it all. Dyson was calmly smoking his pipe between the sips of beer, when an indefinite-looking figure slid rather than walked into the compartment. The man started violently when he saw Dyson placidly sitting in the corner, and glanced keenly about him. He seemed to be on wires, controlled by some electric machine, for he almost bolted out of the door when the barman asked with what he could serve him, and his hand shivered as he took the glass. Dyson inspected him with a little curiosity. He was muffled up almost to the lips, and a soft felt hat was drawn down over his eyes; he looked as if he shrank from every glance, and a more raucous voice suddenly uplifted in the public bar seemed to find in him a sympathy that made him shake and quiver like a jelly. It was pitiable to see any one so thrilled with nervousness, and Dyson was about to address some trivial remark of casual enquiry to the man, when another person came into the compartment, and, laying his hand on his arm, muttered something in an undertone, and vanished as he came. But Dyson had recognised him as the smooth-tongued and smooth-shaven Burton, who had displayed so sumptuous a gift for lying; and yet he thought little of it, for his whole faculty of observation was absorbed in the lamentable and yet grotesque spectacle before him. At the first touch of the hand on his arm the unfortunate man had wheeled round as if spun on a pivot, and shrank back with a low, piteous cry, as if some dumb beast were caught in the toils. The blood fled away from the wretch's face, and the skin became grey as if a shadow of death had passed in the air and fallen on it, and Dyson caught a choking whisper—

"Mr. Davies! For God's sake, have pity on me, Mr. Davies! On my oath, I say—" and his voice sank to silence as he heard the message, and strove in vain to bite his lip, and summon up to his aid some tinge of manhood. He stood there a moment, wavering as the leaves of an aspen, and then he was gone out into the street, as Dyson thought silently, with his doom upon his head. He had not been gone a minute when it suddenly flashed into Dyson's mind that he knew the man; it was undoubtedly the young man with spectacles for whom so many ingenious persons were searching; the spectacles indeed were missing, but the pale face, the dark whiskers, and the timid glances were enough to identify him. Dyson saw at once that by a succession of hazards he had unawares hit upon the scent of some desperate conspiracy, wavering as the track of a loathsome snake in and out of the highways and byways of the London cosmos; the truth was instantly pictured before him, and he divined that all unconscious and unheeding he had been privileged to see the shadows of hidden forms, chasing and hurrying, and grasping and vanishing across the bright curtain of common life, soundless and silent, or only babbling fables and pretences. For him in an instant the jargoning of voices, the garish splendour, and all the vulgar tumult of the public-house became part of magic; for here before his eyes a scene in this grim mystery play had been enacted, and he had seen human flesh grow grey with a palsy of fear; the very hell of cowardice and terror had gaped wide within an arm's-breadth. In the midst of these reflections the barman came up and stared at him as if to hint that he had exhausted his right to take his ease, and Dyson bought another lease of the seat by an order for more beer. As he pondered the brief glimpse of tragedy, he recollected that with his first start of haunted fear the young man with whiskers had drawn his hand swiftly from his greatcoat pocket, and that he had heard something fall to the ground; and pretending to have dropped his pipe, Dyson began to grope in the corner, searching with his fingers. He touched something and drew it gently to him, and with one brief glance, as he put it quietly in his pocket, he saw it was a little old-fashioned note-book, bound in faded green morocco.

He drank down his beer at a gulp, and left the place, overjoyed at his fortunate discovery, and busy with conjecture as to the possible importance of the find. By turns he dreaded to find perhaps mere blank leaves, or the laboured follies of a betting-book, but the faded morocco cover seemed to promise better things, and to hint at mysteries. He piloted himself with no little difficulty out of the sour and squalid quarter he had entered with a light heart, and emerging at Gray's Inn Road, struck off down Guilford Street and hastened home, only anxious for a lighted candle and solitude.

Dyson sat down at his bureau, and placed the little book before him; it was an effort to open the leaves and dare disappointment. But in desperation at last he laid his finger between the pages at haphazard, and rejoiced to see a compact range of writing with a margin, and as it chanced, three words caught his glance and stood out apart from the mass. Dyson read—

"the Gold Tiberius,"

and his face flushed with fortune and the lust of the hunter.

He turned at once to the first leaf of the pocket-book, and proceeded to read with rapt interest the

HISTORY OF THE YOUNG MAN WITH SPECTACLES.

From the filthy and obscure lodging, situated, I verily believe, in one of the foulest slums of Clerkenwell, I indite this history of a life which, daily threatened, cannot last very much longer. Every day—nay, every hour, I know too well my enemies are drawing their nets closer about me; even now I am condemned to be a close prisoner in my squalid room, and I know that when I go out I shall go to my destruction. This history, if it chance to fall into good hands, may, perhaps, be of service in warning young men of the dangers and pitfalls that most surely must accompany any deviation from the ways of rectitude.

My name is Joseph Walters. When I came of age I found myself in possession of a small but sufficient income, and I determined that I would devote my life to scholarship. I do not mean the scholarship of these days; I had no intention of associating myself with men whose lives are spent in the unspeakably degrading occupation of "editing" classics, befouling the fair margins of the fairest books with idle and superfluous annotation, and doing their utmost to give a lasting disgust of all that is beautiful. An abbey church turned to the base use of a stable or a bakehouse is a sorry sight; but more pitiable still is a masterpiece spluttered over with the commentator's pen, and his hideous mark "cf."

For my part, I chose the glorious career of scholar in its ancient sense; I longed to possess encyclopædic learning, to grow old amongst books, to distil day by day, and year after year, the inmost sweetness of all worthy writings. I was not rich enough to collect a library, and I was therefore forced to betake myself to the reading-room of the British Museum.

O dim, far-lifted, and mighty dome, Mecca of many minds, mausoleum of many hopes, sad house where all desires fail! For there men enter in with hearts uplifted, and dreaming minds, seeing in those exalted stairs a ladder to fame, in that pompous portico the gate of knowledge, and going in, find but vain vanity, and all but in vain. There, when the long streets are ringing, is silence, there eternal twilight, and the odour of heaviness. But there the blood flows thin and cold, and the brain burns adust; there is the hunt of shadows, and the chase of embattled phantoms; a striving against ghosts, and a war that has no victory. O dome, tomb of the quick! surely in thy galleries, where no reverberant voice can call, sighs whisper ever, and mutterings of dead hopes; and there men's souls mount like moths towards the flame, and fall scorched and blackened beneath thee, O dim, far-lifted, and mighty dome!

Bitterly do I now regret the day when I took my place at a desk for the first time, and began my studies. I had not been an *habitué* of the place for many months, when I became acquainted with a serene and benevolent gentleman, a man somewhat past middle age, who nearly always occupied a desk next to mine. In the reading-room it takes little to make an acquaintance—a casual offer of assistance, a hint as to the search in the catalogue, and the ordinary politeness of men who constantly sit near each other; it was thus I came to know the man calling himself Dr. Lipsius. By degrees I grew to look for his presence, and to miss him when he was away, as was sometimes the case, and so a friendship sprang up between us. His immense range of learning was placed freely at my service; he would often astonish me by the way in which he would sketch out in a few minutes the bibliography of a given subject, and before long I had confided to him my ambitions.

"Ah," he said, "you should have been a German. I was like that myself when I was a boy. It is a wonderful resolve, an infinite career. I will know all things; yes, it is a device indeed. But it means this—a life of labour without end, and a desire unsatisfied at last. The scholar has to die, and die saying, 'I know very little!'"

Gradually, by speeches such as these, Lipsius seduced me: he would praise the career, and at the same time hint that it was as hopeless as the search for the philosopher's stone, and so by artful suggestions, insinuated with infinite address, he by degrees succeeded in undermining all my principles. "After all," he used to say, "the greatest of all sciences, the key to all knowledge, is the science and art of pleasure. Rabelais was perhaps the greatest of all the encyclopædic scholars; and he, as you know, wrote the most remarkable book that has ever been written. And what does he teach men in this book? Surely the joy of living. I need not remind you of the words, suppressed in most of the editions, the key of all the Rabelaisian mythology, of all the enigmas of his grand philosophy, *Vivez joyeux*. There you have all his learning; his work is the institutes of pleasure as the fine art; the finest art there is; the art of all arts. Rabelais had all science, but he had all life too. And we have gone a long way since his time. You are enlightened, I think; you do not consider all the petty rules and by-laws that a corrupt society has made for its own selfish convenience as the immutable decrees of the eternal."

Such were the doctrines that he preached; and it was by such insidious arguments, line upon line, here a little and there a little, that he at last succeeded in making me a man at war with the whole social system. I used to long for some opportunity to break the chains and to live a free life, to be my own rule and measure. I viewed existence with the eyes of a pagan, and Lipsius understood to perfection the art of stimulating the natural inclinations of a young man hitherto a hermit. As I gazed up at the great dome I saw it flushed with the flames and colours of a world of enticement unknown to me, my imagination played me a thousand wanton tricks, and the forbidden drew me as surely as a lodestone draws on iron. At last my resolution was taken, and I boldly asked Lipsius to be my guide.

He told me to leave the Museum at my usual hour, half-past four, to walk slowly along the northern pavement of Great Russell Street, and to wait at the corner of the street till I was addressed, and then to obey in all things the instructions of the person who came up to me. I carried out these directions, and stood at the corner looking about me anxiously, my heart beating fast, and my breath coming in gasps. I waited there for some time, and had begun to fear I had been made the object of a joke, when I suddenly became conscious of a gentleman who was looking at me with evident amusement from the opposite pavement of Tottenham Court Road. He came over, and raising his hat, politely begged me to follow him, and I did so without a word, wondering where we were going, and what was to happen. I was taken to a house of quiet and respectable aspect in a street lying to the north of Oxford Street, and my guide rang the bell. A servant shewed us into a large room, quietly furnished, on the ground floor. We sat there in silence for some time, and I noticed that the furniture, though unpretending, was extremely valuable. There were large oak presses, two book-cases of extreme elegance, and in one corner a carved chest which must have been mediæval. Presently Dr. Lipsius came in and welcomed me with his usual manner, and after some desultory conversation my guide left the room. Then an elderly man dropped in and began talking to Lipsius, and from their conversation I understood that my friend was a dealer in antiques; they spoke of the Hittite seal, and of the prospects of further discoveries, and later, when two or three more persons had joined us, there was an argument as to the possibility of a systematic exploration of the pre-Celtic monuments in England. I was, in fact, present at an archæological reception of an informal kind; and at nine o'clock, when the antiquaries were gone, I stared at Lipsius in a manner that shewed I was puzzled, and sought an explanation.

"Now," he said, "we will go upstairs."

As we passed up the stairs, Lipsius lighting the way with a hand-lamp, I heard the sound of a jarring lock and bolts and bars shot on at the front door. My guide drew back a baize door and we went down a passage, and I began to hear odd sounds, a noise of curious mirth; then he pushed me through a second door, and my initiation began. I cannot write down what I witnessed that night; I cannot bear to recall what went on in those secret rooms fast shuttered and curtained so that no light should escape into the quiet street; they gave me red wine to drink, and a woman told me as I sipped it that it was wine of the Red Jar that Avallaunius had made. Another asked me how I liked the wine of the Fauns, and I heard a dozen fantastic names, while the stuff boiled in my veins, and stirred, I think, something that had slept within me from the moment I was born. It seemed as if my self-consciousness deserted me; I was no longer a thinking agent, but at once subject and object; I mingled in the horrible sport, and watched the mystery of the Greek groves and fountains enacted before me, saw the reeling dance and heard the music calling as I sat beside my mate, and yet I was outside it all, and viewed my own part an idle spectator. Thus with strange rites they made me drink the cup, and when I woke up in the morning I was one of them, and had sworn to be faithful. At first I was shewn the enticing side of things; I was bidden to enjoy myself and care for nothing but pleasure, and Lipsius himself indicated to me as the acutest enjoyment the spectacle of the terrors of the unfortunate persons who were from time to time decoyed into the evil house. But after a time it was pointed out to me that I must take my share in the work, and so I found myself compelled to be in my turn a seducer; and thus it is on my conscience that I have held many to the deaths of the pit.

One day Lipsius summoned me to his private room, and told me that he had a difficult task to give me. He unlocked a drawer and gave me a sheet of type-written paper, and bade me read it.

It was without place, or date, or signature, and ran as follows:—

> Mr. James Headley, F.S.A., will receive from his agent in Armenia, on the 12th inst., a unique coin, the gold Tiberius. It bears on the reverse a faun with the legend VICTORIA. It is believed that this coin is of immense value. Mr. Headley will come up to town to shew the coin to his friend, Professor Memys, of Chenies Street, Oxford Street, on some date between the 13th and the 18th.

Dr. Lipsius chuckled at my face of blank surprise when I laid down this singular communication.

"You will have a good chance of shewing your discretion," he said. "This is not a common case; it requires great management and infinite tact. I am sure I wish I had a Panurge in my service, but we will see what you can do."

"But is it not a joke?" I asked him. "How can you know—or rather, how can this correspondent of yours know—that a coin has been despatched from Armenia to Mr. Headley? And how is it possible to fix the period in which Mr. Headley will take it into his head to come up to town? It seems to me a lot of guesswork."

"My dear Mr. Walters," he replied, "we do not deal in guesswork here. It would bore you if I went into all these little details, the cogs and wheels, if I may say so, which move the machine. Don't you think it is much more amusing to sit in front of the house and be astonished than to be behind the scenes and see the mechanism? Better tremble at the thunder, believe me, than see the man rolling the cannon-ball. But, after all, you needn't bother about the how and why; you have your share to do. Of course, I shall give you full instructions, but a great deal depends on the way the thing is carried out. I have often heard very young men maintain that style is everything in literature, and I can assure you that the same maxim holds good in our far more delicate profession. With us style is absolutely everything, and that is why we have friends like yourself."

I went away in some perturbation; he had no doubt designedly left everything in mystery, and I did not know what part I should have to play. Though I had assisted at scenes of hideous revelry, I was not yet dead to all echo of human feeling, and I trembled lest I should receive the order to be Mr. Headley's executioner.

A week later, it was on the sixteenth of the month, Dr. Lipsius made me a sign to come into his room.

"It is for to-night," he began. "Please to attend carefully to what I am going to say, Mr. Walters, and on peril of your life, for it is a dangerous matter,—on peril of your life, I say, follow these instructions to the letter. You understand? Well, to-night at about half-past seven, you will stroll quietly up the Hampstead Road till you come to Vincent Street. Turn down here and walk along, taking the third turning to your right, which is Lambert Terrace. Then follow the terrace, cross the road, and go along Hertford Street, and so into Lillington Square. The second turning you will come to in the square is called Sheen Street; but in reality it is more a passage between blank walls than a street. Whatever you do, take care to be at the corner of this street at eight o'clock precisely. You will walk along it, and just at the bend where you lose sight of the square, you will find an old gentleman with white beard and whiskers. He will in all probability be abusing a cabman for having brought him to Sheen Street instead of Chenies Street. You will go up to him quietly and offer your services; he will tell you where he wants to go, and you will be so courteous as to offer to shew him the way. I may say that Professor Memys moved into Chenies Street a month ago; thus Mr. Headley has never been to see him there, and, moreover, he is very short-sighted, and knows little of the topography of London. Indeed, he has quite lived the life of a learned hermit at Audley Hall.

"Well, need I say more to a man of your intelligence? You will bring him to this house, he will ring the bell, and a servant in quiet livery will let him in. Then your work will be done, and I am sure done well. You will leave Mr. Headley at the door, and simply continue your walk, and I shall hope to see you the next day. I really don't think there is anything more I can tell you."

These minute instructions I took care to carry out to the letter. I confess that I walked up the Tottenham Court Road by no means blindly, but with an uneasy sense that I was coming to a decisive point in my life. The noise and rumour of the crowded pavements were to me but dumb-show; I revolved again and again in ceaseless iteration the task that had been laid on me, and I questioned myself as to the possible results. As I got near the point of turning, I asked myself whether danger were not about my steps; the cold thought struck me that I was suspected and observed, and every chance foot-passenger who gave me a second glance seemed to me an officer of police. My time was running out, the sky had darkened, and I hesitated, half resolved to go no farther, but to abandon Lipsius and his friends for ever. I had almost determined to take this course, when the conviction suddenly came to me that the whole thing was a gigantic joke, a fabrication of rank improbability. Who could have procured the information about the Armenian agent? I asked myself. By what means could Lipsius have known the particular day and the very train that Mr. Headley was to take? how engage him to enter one special cab amongst the dozens waiting at Paddington? I vowed it a mere Milesian tale, and went forward merrily, turned down Vincent Street, and threaded out the route that Lipsius had so carefully impressed upon me. The various streets he had named were all places of silence and an oppressive cheap gentility; it was dark, and I felt alone in the musty squares and crescents, where people pattered by at intervals, and the shadows were growing blacker. I entered Sheen Street, and found it as Lipsius had said, more a passage than a street; it was a byway, on one side a low wall and neglected gardens, and grim backs of a line of houses, and on the other a timberyard. I turned the corner, and lost sight of the square, and then, to my astonishment, I saw the scene of which I had been told. A hansom cab had come to a stop beside the pavement, and an old man, carrying a handbag, was fiercely abusing the cabman, who sat on his perch the image of bewilderment.

"Yes, but I'm sure you said Sheen Street, and that's where I brought you," I heard him saying as I came up, and the old gentleman boiled in a fury, and threatened police and suits at law.

The sight gave me a shock, and in an instant I resolved to go through with it. I strolled on, and without noticing the cabman, lifted my hat politely to old Mr. Headley.

"Pardon me, sir," I said, "but is there any difficulty? I see you are a traveller; perhaps the cabman has made a mistake. Can I direct you?"

The old fellow turned to me, and I noticed that he snarled and shewed his teeth like an ill-tempered cur as he spoke.

"This drunken fool has brought me here," he said. "I told him to drive to Chenies Street, and he brings me to this infernal place. I won't pay him a farthing, and I meant to have given him a handsome sum. I am going to call for the police and give him in charge."

At this threat the cabman seemed to take alarm; he glanced round, as if to make sure that no policeman was in sight, and drove off grumbling loudly, and Mr. Headley grinned savagely with satisfaction at having saved his fare, and put back one and sixpence into his pocket, the "handsome sum" the cabman had lost.

"My dear sir," I said, "I am afraid this piece of stupidity has annoyed you a great deal. It is a long way to Chenies Street, and you will have some difficulty in finding the place unless you know London pretty well."

"I know it very little," he replied. "I never come up except on important business, and I've never been to Chenies Street in my life."

"Really? I should be happy to shew you the way. I have been for a stroll, and it will not at all inconvenience me to take you to your destination."

"I want to go to Professor Memys, at number 15. It's most annoying to me; I'm short-sighted, and I can never make out the numbers on the doors."

"This way, if you please," I said, and we set out.

I did not find Mr. Headley an agreeable man; indeed, he grumbled the whole way. He informed me of his name, and I took care to say, "The well-known antiquary?" and thenceforth I was compelled to listen to the history of his complicated squabbles with publishers, who treated him, as he said, disgracefully; the man was a chapter in the Irritability of Authors. He told me that he had been on the point of making the fortune of several firms, but had been compelled to abandon the design owing to their rank ingratitude. Besides these ancient histories of wrong, and the more recent misadventure of the cabman, he had another grievous complaint to make. As he came along in the train, he had been sharpening a pencil, and the sudden jolt of the engine as it drew up at a station had driven the penknife against his face, inflicting a small triangular wound just on the cheek-bone, which he shewed me. He denounced the railway company, heaped imprecations on the head of the driver, and talked of claiming damages. Thus he grumbled all the way, not noticing in the least where he was going; and so unamiable did his conduct appear to me, that I began to enjoy the trick I was playing on him.

Nevertheless, my heart beat a little faster as we turned into the street where Lipsius was waiting. A thousand accidents, I thought, might happen; some chance might bring one of Headley's friends to meet us; perhaps, though he knew not Chenies Street, he might know the street where I was taking him; in spite of his short-sight, he might possibly make out the number; or, in a sudden fit of suspicion, he might make an enquiry of the policeman at the corner. Thus every step upon the pavement, as we drew nearer to the goal, was to me a pang and a terror, and every approaching passenger carried a certain threat of danger. I gulped down my excitement with an effort, and made shift to say pretty quietly—

"Number 15, I think you said? That is the third house from this. If you will allow me, I will leave you now; I have been delayed a little, and my way lies on the other side of Tottenham Court Road."

He snarled out some kind of thanks, and I turned my back and walked swiftly in the opposite direction. A minute or two later I looked round, and saw Mr. Headley standing on the doorstep, and then the door opened and he went in. For my part, I gave a sigh of relief; I hastened to get away from the neighbourhood, and endeavoured to enjoy myself in merry company.

The whole of the next day I kept away from Lipsius. I felt anxious, but I did not know what had happened, or what was happening, and a reasonable regard for my own safety told me that I should do well to remain quietly at home. My curiosity, however, to learn the end of the odd drama in which I had played a part stung me to the quick, and late in the evening I made up my mind to see how events had turned out. Lipsius nodded when I came in, and asked if I could give him five minutes' talk. We went to his room, and he began to walk up and down, while I sat waiting for him to speak.

"My dear Mr. Walters," he said at length, "I congratulate you warmly; your work was done in the most thorough and artistic manner. You will go far. Look."

He went to his escritoire and pressed a secret spring; a drawer flew out, and he laid something on the table. It was a gold coin; I took it up and examined it eagerly, and read the legend about the figure of the faun.

"Victoria," I said, smiling.

"Yes; it was a great capture, which we owe to you. I had great difficulty in persuading Mr. Headley that a little mistake had been made; that was how I put it. He was very disagreeable, and indeed ungentlemanly, about it; didn't he strike you as a very cross old man?"

I held the coin, admiring the choice and rare design, clear cut as if from the mint; and I thought the fine gold glowed and burnt like a lamp.

"And what finally became of Mr. Headley?" I said at last.

Lipsius smiled, and shrugged his shoulders.

"What on earth does it matter?" he said. "He might be here, or there, or anywhere; but what possible consequence could it be? Besides, your question rather surprises me; you are an intelligent man, Mr. Walters. Just think it over, and I'm sure you won't repeat the question."

"My dear sir," I said, "I hardly think you are treating me fairly. You have paid me some handsome compliments on my share in the capture, and I naturally wish to know how the matter ended. From what I saw of Mr. Headley, I should think you must have had some difficulty with him."

He gave me no answer for the moment, but began again to walk up and down the room, apparently absorbed in thought.

"Well," he said at last, "I suppose there is something in what you say. We are certainly indebted to you. I have said that I have a high opinion of your intelligence, Mr. Walters. Just look here, will you?"

He opened a door communicating with another room, and pointed.

There was a great box lying on the floor, a queer, coffin-shaped thing. I looked at it, and saw it was a mummy case, like those in the British Museum, vividly painted in the brilliant Egyptian colours, with I knew not what proclamation of dignity or hopes of life immortal. The mummy swathed about in the robes of death was lying within, and the face had been uncovered.

"You are going to send this away?" I said, forgetting the question I had put.

"Yes; I have an order from a local museum. Look a little more closely, Mr. Walters."

Puzzled by his manner, I peered into the face, while he held the lamp. The flesh was black with the passing of the centuries; but as I looked I saw upon the right cheek-bone a small triangular scar, and the secret of the mummy flashed upon me: I was looking at the dead body of the man whom I had decoyed into that house.

There was no thought or design of action in my mind. I held the accursed coin in my hand, burning me with a foretaste of hell, and I fled as I would have fled from pestilence and death, and dashed into the street in blind horror, not knowing where I went. I felt the gold coin grasped in my clenched fist, and throwing it away, I knew not where, I ran on and on through by-streets and dark ways, till at last I issued out into a crowded thoroughfare and checked myself. Then as consciousness returned I realised my instant peril, and understood what would happen if I fell into the hands of Lipsius. I knew that I had put forth my finger to thwart a relentless mechanism rather than a man. My recent adventure with the unfortunate Mr. Headley had taught me that Lipsius had agents in all quarters; and I foresaw that if I fell into his hands, he would remain true to his doctrine of style, and cause me to die a death of some horrible and ingenious torture. I bent my whole mind to the task of outwitting him and his emissaries, three of whom I knew to have proved their ability for tracking down persons who for various reasons preferred to remain obscure. These servants of Lipsius were two men and a woman, and the woman was incomparably the most subtle and the most deadly. Yet I considered that I too had some portion of craft, and I took my resolve. Since then I have matched myself day by day and hour by hour against the ingenuity of Lipsius and his myrmidons. For a time I was successful; though they beat furiously after me in the covert of London, I remained *perdu*, and watched with some amusement their frantic efforts to recover the scent lost in two or three minutes. Every lure and wile was put forth to entice me from my hiding-place; I was informed by the medium of the public prints that what I had taken had been recovered, and meetings were proposed in which I might hope to gain a great deal without the slightest risk. I laughed at their endeavours, and began a little to despise the organisation I had so dreaded, and ventured more abroad. Not once or twice, but several times, I recognised the two men who were charged with my capture, and I succeeded in eluding them at close quarters; and a little too hastily I decided that I had nothing to dread, and that my craft was greater than theirs. But in the meanwhile, while I congratulated myself on my cunning, the third of Lipsius's emissaries was weaving her nets; and in an evil hour I paid a visit to an old friend, a literary man named Russell, who lived in a quiet street in Bayswater. The woman, as I found out too late, a day or two ago occupied rooms in the same house, and I was followed and tracked down. Too late, as I have said, I recognised that I had made a fatal mistake, and that I was besieged. Sooner or later I shall find myself in the power of an enemy without pity; and so surely as I leave this house I shall go to receive doom. I hardly dare to guess how it will at last fall upon me; my imagination, always a vivid one, paints to me appalling pictures of the unspeakable torture which I shall probably endure; and I know that I shall die with Lipsius standing near and gloating over the refinements of my suffering and my shame.

Hours, nay minutes, have become precious to me. I sometimes pause in the midst of anticipating my tortures, to wonder whether even now I cannot hit upon some supreme stroke, some design of infinite subtlety, to free myself from the toils. But I find that the faculty of combination has left me; I am as the scholar in the old myth, deserted by the power which has helped me hitherto. I do not know when the supreme moment will come, but sooner or later it is inevitable; before long I shall receive sentence, and from the sentence to execution will not be long.

I cannot remain here a prisoner any longer. I shall go out to-night when the streets are full of crowds and clamours, and make a last effort to escape.

It was with profound astonishment that Dyson closed the little book, and thought of the strange series of incidents which had brought him into touch with the plots and counterplots connected with the Gold Tiberius. He had bestowed the coin carefully away, and he shuddered at the bare possibility of its place of deposit becoming known to the evil band who seemed to possess such extraordinary sources of information.

It had grown late while he read, and he put the pocket-book away, hoping with all his heart that the unhappy Walters might even at the eleventh hour escape the doom he dreaded.

ADVENTURE OF THE DESERTED RESIDENCE

"A wonderful story, as you say, an extraordinary sequence and play of coincidence. I confess that your expressions when you first shewed me the Gold Tiberius were not exaggerated. But do you think that Walters has really some fearful fate to dread?"

"I cannot say. Who can presume to predict events when life itself puts on the robe of coincidence and plays at drama? Perhaps we have not yet reached the last chapter in the queer story. But, look, we are drawing near to the verge of London; there are gaps, you see, in the serried ranks of brick, and a vision of green fields beyond."

Dyson had persuaded the ingenious Mr. Phillipps to accompany him on one of those aimless walks to which he was himself so addicted. Starting from the very heart of London, they had made their way westward through the stony avenues, and were now just emerging from the red lines of an extreme suburb, and presently the half-finished road ended, a quiet lane began, and they were beneath the shade of elm-trees. The yellow autumn sunlight that had lit up the bare distance of the suburban street now filtered down through the boughs of the trees and shone on the glowing carpet of fallen leaves, and the pools of rain glittered and shot back the gleam of light. Over all the broad pastures there was peace and the happy rest of autumn before the great winds begin, and afar off London lay all vague and immense amidst the veiling mist; here and there a distant window catching the sun and kindling with fire, and a spire gleaming high, and below the streets in shadow, and the turmoil of life. Dyson and Phillipps walked on in silence beneath the high hedges, till at a turn of the lane they saw a mouldering and ancient gate standing open, and the prospect of a house at the end of a moss-grown carriage drive.

"There is a survival for you," said Dyson; "it has come to its last days, I imagine. Look how the laurels have grown gaunt and weedy, and black and bare beneath; look at the house, covered with yellow wash, and patched with green damp. Why, the very notice-board, which informs all and singular that the place is to be let, has cracked and half fallen."

"Suppose we go in and see it," said Phillipps; "I don't think there is anybody about."

They turned up the drive, and walked slowly towards this remnant of old days. It was a large, straggling house, with curved wings at either end, and behind a series of irregular roofs and projections, shewing that the place had been added to at divers dates; the two wings were roofed in cupola fashion, and at one side, as they came nearer, they could see a stableyard, and a clock turret with a bell, and the dark masses of gloomy cedars. Amidst all the lineaments of dissolution there was but one note of contrast: the sun was setting beyond the elm-trees, and all the west and south were in flames; on the upper windows of the house the glow shone reflected, and it seemed as if blood and fire were mingled. Before the yellow front of the mansion, stained, as Dyson had remarked, with gangrenous patches, green and blackening, stretched what had once been, no doubt, a well-kept lawn, but it was now rough and ragged, and nettles and great docks, and all manner of coarse weeds, struggled in the places of the flower-beds. The urns had fallen from their pillars beside the walk, and lay broken in shards upon the ground, and everywhere from grass-plot and path a fungoid growth had sprung up and multiplied, and lay dank and slimy like a festering sore upon the earth. In the middle of the rank grass of the lawn was a desolate fountain; the rim of the basin was crumbling and pulverised with decay, and within the water stood stagnant, with green scum for the lilies that had once bloomed there; rust had eaten into the bronze flesh of the Triton that stood in the middle, and the conch-shell he held was broken.

"Here," said Dyson, "one might moralise over decay and death. Here all the stage is decked out with the symbols of dissolution; the cedarn gloom and twilight hang heavy around us, and everywhere within the pale dankness has found a harbour, and the very air is changed and brought to accord with the scene. To me, I confess, this deserted house is as moral as a graveyard, and I find something sub-lime in that lonely Triton, deserted in the midst of his water-pool. He is the last of the gods; they have left him, and he remembers the sound of water falling on water, and the days that were sweet."

"I like your reflections extremely," said Phillipps; "but I may mention that the door of the house is open."

"Let us go in, then."

The door was just ajar, and they passed into the mouldy hall and looked in at a room on one side. It was a large room, going far back, and the rich, old, red flock paper was peeling from the walls in long strips, and blackened with vague patches of rising damp; the ancient clay, the dank reeking earth rising up again, and subduing all the work of men's hands after the conquest of many years. The floor was thick with the dust of decay, and the painted ceiling fading from all gay colours and light fancies of cupids in a career, and disfigured with sores of dampness, seemed transmuted into other work. No longer the amorini chased one another pleasantly, with limbs that sought not to advance, and hands that merely simulated the act of grasping at the wreathed flowers; but it appeared some savage burlesque of the old careless world and of its cherished conventions, and the dance of the Loves had become a Dance of Death; black pustules and festering sores swelled and clustered on fair limbs and smiling faces shewed corruption, and the fairy blood had boiled with the germs of foul disease; it was a parable of the leaven working, and worms devouring for a banquet the heart of the rose.

Strangely, under the painted ceiling, against the decaying walls, two old chairs still stood alone, the sole furniture of the empty place. High-backed, with curving arms and twisted legs, covered with faded gold leaf, and upholstered in tattered damask, they too were a part of the symbolism, and struck Dyson with surprise. "What have we here?" he said. "Who has sat in these chairs? Who, clad in peach-bloom satin, with lace ruffles and diamond buckles, all golden, *a conté fleurettes* to his companion? Phillipps, we are in another age. I wish I had some snuff to offer you, but failing that, I beg to offer you a seat, and we will sit and smoke tobacco. A horrid practice, but I am no pedant."

They sat down on the queer old chairs, and looked out of the dim and grimy panes to the ruined lawn, and the fallen urns, and the deserted Triton.

Presently Dyson ceased his imitation of eighteenth-century airs; he no longer pulled forward imaginary ruffles, or tapped a ghostly snuff-box.

"It's a foolish fancy," he said at last; "but I keep thinking I hear a noise like some one groaning. Listen; no, I can't hear it now. There it is again! Did you notice it, Phillipps?"

"No, I can't say I heard anything. But I believe that old places like this are like shells from the shore, ever echoing with noises. The old beams, mouldering piecemeal, yield a little and groan; and such a house as this I can fancy all resonant at night with voices, the voices of matter so slowly and so surely transformed into other shapes, the voice of the worm that gnaws at last the very heart of the oak, the voice of stone grinding on stone, and the voice of the conquest of Time."

They sat still in the old arm-chairs, and grew graver in the musty ancient air, the air of a hundred years ago.

"I don't like the place," said Phillipps, after a long pause. "To me it seems as if there were a sickly, unwholesome smell about it, a smell of something burning."

"You are right; there is an evil odour here. I wonder what it is. Hark! Did you hear that?"

A hollow sound, a noise of infinite sadness and infinite pain, broke in upon the silence, and the two men looked fearfully at one another, horror, and the sense of unknown things, glimmering in their eyes.

"Come," said Dyson, "we must see into this," and they went into the hall and listened in the silence.

"Do you know," said Phillipps, "it seems absurd, but I could almost fancy that the smell is that of burning flesh."

They went up the hollow-sounding stairs, and the odour became thick and noisome, stifling the breath, and a vapour, sickening as the smell of the chamber of death, choked them. A door was open, and they entered the large upper room, and clung hard to one another, shuddering at the sight they saw.

A naked man was lying on the floor, his arms and legs stretched wide apart, and bound to pegs that had been hammered into the boards. The body was torn and mutilated in the most hideous fashion, scarred with the marks of red-hot irons, a shameful ruin of the human shape. But upon the middle of the body a fire of coals was smouldering; the flesh had been burnt through. The man was dead, but the smoke of his torment mounted still, a black vapour.

"The young man with spectacles," said Mr. Dyson.

The Red Hand

THE PROBLEM OF THE FISH-HOOKS

There can be no doubt whatever," said Mr. Phillipps, "that my theory is the true one; these flints are prehistoric fish-hooks."

"I dare say; but you know that in all probability the things were forged the other day with a door-key."

"Stuff!" said Phillipps; "I have some respect, Dyson, for your literary abilities, but your knowledge of ethnology is insignificant, or rather non-existent. These fish-hooks satisfy every test; they are perfectly genuine."

"Possibly, but as I said just now, you go to work at the wrong end. You neglect the opportunities that confront you and await you, obvious, at every corner; you positively shrink from the chance of encountering primitive man in this whirling and mysterious city, and you pass the weary hours in your agreeable retirement of Red Lion Square fumbling with bits of flint, which are, as I said, in all probability, rank forgeries."

Phillipps took one of the little objects, and held it up in exasperation.

"Look at that ridge," he said. "Did you ever see such a ridge as that on a forgery?"

Dyson merely grunted and lit his pipe, and the two sat smoking in rich silence, watching through the open window the children in the square as they flitted to and fro in the twilight of the lamps, as elusive as bats flying on the verge of a dark wood.

"Well," said Phillipps at last, "it is really a long time since you have been round. I suppose you have been working at your old task."

"Yes," said Dyson, "always the chase of the phrase. I shall grow old in the hunt. But it is a great consolation to meditate on the fact that there are not a dozen people in England who know what style means."

"I suppose not; for the matter of that, the study of ethnology is far from popular. And the difficulties! Primitive man stands dim and very far off across the great bridge of years."

"By the way," he went on after a pause, "what was that stuff you were talking just now about shrinking from the chance of encountering primitive man at the corner, or something of the kind? There are certainly people about here whose ideas are very primitive."

"I wish, Phillipps, you would not rationalise my remarks. If I recollect the phrase correctly, I hinted that you shrank from the chance of encountering primitive man in this whirling and mysterious city, and I meant exactly what I said. Who can limit the age of survival? The troglodyte and the lake-dweller, perhaps representatives of yet darker races, may very probably be lurking in our midst, rubbing shoulders with frock-coated and finely-draped humanity, ravening like wolves at heart and boiling with the foul passions of the swamp and the black cave. Now and then as I walk in Holborn or Fleet Street I see a face which I pronounce abhorred, and yet I could not give a reason for the thrill of loathing that stirs within me."

"My dear Dyson, I refuse to enter myself in your literary 'trying-on' department. I know that survivals do exist, but all things have a limit, and your speculations are absurd. You must catch me your troglodyte before I will believe in him."

"I agree to that with all my heart," said Dyson, chuckling at the case with which he had succeeded in "drawing" Phillips. "Nothing could be better. It's a fine night for a walk," he added, taking up his hat.

"What nonsense you are talking, Dyson!" said Phillipps. "However, I have no objection to taking a walk with you: as you say, it is a pleasant night."

"Come along then," said Dyson, grinning, "but remember our bargain."

The two men went out into the square, and threading one of the narrow passages that serve as exits, struck towards the north-east. As they passed along a flaring causeway they could hear at intervals between the clamour of the children and the triumphant *Gloria* played on a piano-organ the long deep hum and roll of the traffic in Holborn, a sound so persistent that it echoed like the turning of everlasting wheels. Dyson looked to right and left and conned the way, and presently they were passing through a more peaceful quarter, touching on deserted squares and silent streets black as midnight. Phillipps had lost all count of direction, and as by degrees the region of faded respectability gave place to the squalid, and dirty stucco offended the eye of the artistic observer, he merely ventured the remark that he had never seen a neighbourhood more unpleasant or more commonplace.

"More mysterious, you mean," said Dyson. "I warn you, Phillipps, we are now not upon the scent."

They dived yet deeper into the maze of brickwork; some time before they had crossed a noisy thoroughfare running east and west, and now the quarter seemed all amorphous, without character; here a decent house with sufficient garden, here a faded square, and here factories surrounded by high, blank walls, with blind passages and dark corners; but all ill-lighted and unfrequented and heavy with silence.

Presently, as they paced down a forlorn street of two-story houses, Dyson caught sight of a dark and obscure turning.

"I like the look of that," he said; "it seems to me promising." There was a street lamp at the entrance, and another, a mere glimmer, at the further end. Beneath the lamp, on the pavement, an artist had evidently established his academy in the daytime, for the stones were all a blur of crude colours rubbed into each other, and a few broken fragments of chalk lay in a little heap beneath the wall.

"You see people do occasionally pass this way," said Dyson, pointing to the ruins of the screever's work. "I confess I should not have thought it possible. Come, let us explore."

On one side of this byway of communication was a great timber-yard, with vague piles of wood looming shapeless above the enclosing wall; and on the other side of the road a wall still higher seemed to enclose a garden, for there were shadows like trees, and a faint murmur of rustling leaves broke the silence. It was a moonless night, and clouds that had gathered after sunset had blackened, and midway between the feeble lamps the passage lay all dark and formless, and when one stopped and listened, and the sharp echo of reverberant footsteps ceased, there came from far away, as from beyond the hills, a faint roll of the noise of London. Phillipps was bolstering up his courage to declare that he had had enough of the excursion, when a loud cry from Dyson broke in upon his thoughts.

"Stop, stop for Heaven's sake, or you will tread on it! There! almost under your feet!" Phillipps looked down, and saw a vague shape, dark, and framed in surrounding darkness, dropped strangely on the pavement, and then a white cuff glimmered for a moment as Dyson lit a match, which went out directly.

"It's a drunken man," said Phillipps very coolly.

"It's a murdered man," said Dyson, and he began to call for police with all his might, and soon from the distance running footsteps echoed and grew louder, and cries sounded.

A policeman was the first to come up.

"What's the matter?" he said, as he drew to a stand, panting. "Anything amiss here?" for he had not seen what was on the pavement.

"Look!" said Dyson, speaking out of the gloom. "Look there! My friend and I came down this place three minutes ago, and that is what we found."

The man flashed his light on the dark shape and cried out.

"Why, it's murder," he said; "there's blood all about him, and a puddle of it in the gutter there. He's not dead long, either. Ah! there's the wound! It's in the neck."

Dyson bent over what was lying there. He saw a prosperous gentleman, dressed in smooth, well-cut clothes. The neat whiskers were beginning to grizzle a little; he might have been forty-five an hour before; and a handsome gold watch had half slipped out of his waistcoat pocket. And there in the flesh of the neck, between chin and ear, gaped a great wound, clean cut, but all clotted with dry blood, and the white of the cheeks shone like a lighted lamp above the red.

Dyson turned, and looked curiously about him; the dead man lay across the path with his head inclined towards the wall, and the blood from the wound streamed away across the pavement, and lay a dark puddle, as the policeman had said, in the gutter. Two more policemen had come up, the crowd gathered, humming from all quarters, and the officers had as much as they could do to keep the curious at a distance. The three lanterns were flashing here and there, searching for more evidence, and in the gleam of one of them Dyson caught sight of an object in the road, to which he called the attention of the policeman nearest to him.

"Look, Phillipps," he said, when the man had secured it and held it up. "Look, that should be something in your way!"

It was a dark flinty stone, gleaming like obsidian, and shaped to a broad edge something after the manner of an adze. One end was rough, and easily grasped in the hand, and the whole thing was hardly five inches long. The edge was thick with blood.

"What is that, Phillipps?" said Dyson; and Phillipps looked hard at it.

"It's a primitive flint knife," he said. "It was made about ten thousand years ago. One exactly like this was found near Aubury, in Wiltshire, and all the authorities gave it that age."

The policeman stared astonished at such a development of the case; and Phillipps himself was all aghast at his own words. But Mr. Dyson did not notice him. An inspector who had just come up and was listening to the outlines of the case, was holding a lantern to the dead man's head. Dyson, for his part, was staring with a white heat of curiosity at something he saw on the wall, just above where the man was lying; there were a few rude marks done in red chalk.

"This is a black business," said the inspector at length; "does anybody know who it is?"

A man stepped forward from the crowd. "I do, governor," he said, "he's a big doctor, his name's Sir Thomas Vivian; I was in the 'orspital abart six months ago, and he used to come round; he was a very kind man."

"Lord," cried the inspector, "this is a bad job indeed. Why, Sir Thomas Vivian goes to the Royal Family. And there's a watch worth a hundred guineas in his pocket, so it isn't robbery."

Dyson and Phillipps gave their cards to the authorities, and moved off, pushing with difficulty through the crowd that was still gathering, gathering fast; and the alley that had been lonely and desolate now swarmed with white staring faces and hummed with the buzz of rumour and horror, and rang with the commands of the officers of police. The two men, once free from this swarming curiosity, stepped out briskly, but for twenty minutes neither spoke a word.

"Phillipps," said Dyson, as they came into a small but cheerful street, clean and brightly lit, "Phillipps, I owe you an apology. I was wrong to have spoken as I did to-night. Such infernal jesting," he went on, with heat, "as if there were no wholesome subjects for a joke. I feel as if I had raised an evil spirit."

"For Heaven's sake say nothing more," said Phillipps, choking down horror with visible effort. "You told the truth to me in my room; the troglodyte, as you said, is still lurking about the earth, and in these very streets around us, slaying for mere lust of blood."

"I will come up for a moment," said Dyson when they reached Red Lion Square, "I have something to ask you. I think there should be nothing hidden between us at all events."

Phillipps nodded gloomily, and they went up to the room, where everything hovered indistinct in the uncertain glimmer of the light from without. When the candle was lighted and the two men sat facing each other, Dyson spoke.

"Perhaps," he began, "you did not notice me peering at the wall just above the place where the head lay. The light from the inspector's lantern was shining full on it, and I saw something that looked queer to me, and I examined it closely. I found that some one had drawn in red chalk a rough outline of a hand—a human hand—upon the wall. But it was the curious position of the fingers that struck me; it was like this"; and he took a pencil and a piece of paper and drew rapidly, and then handed what he had done to Phillipps. It was a rough sketch of a hand seen from the back, with the fingers clenched, and the top of the thumb protruded between the first and second fingers, and pointed downwards, as if to something below.

"It was just like that," said Dyson, as he saw Phillipps's face grow still whiter. "The thumb pointed down as if to the body; it seemed almost a live hand in ghastly gesture. And just beneath there was a small mark with the powder of the chalk lying on it—as if some one had commenced a stroke and had broken the chalk in his hand. I saw the bit of chalk lying on the ground. But what do you make of it?"

"It's a horrible old sign," said Phillipps—"one of the most horrible signs connected with the theory of the evil eye. It is used still in Italy, but there can be no doubt that it has been known for ages. It is one of the survivals; you must look for the origin of it in the black swamp whence man first came."

Dyson took up his hat to go.

"I think, jesting apart," said he, "that I kept my promise, and that we were and are hot on the scent, as I said. It seems as if I had really shewn you primitive man, or his handiwork at all events."

INCIDENT OF THE LETTER

About a month after the extraordinary and mysterious murder of Sir Thomas Vivian, the well-known and universally respected specialist in heart disease, Mr. Dyson called again on his friend Mr. Phillipps, whom he found, not, as usual, sunk deep in painful study, but reclining in his easy-chair in an attitude of relaxation. He welcomed Dyson with cordiality.

"I am very glad you have come," he began; "I was thinking of looking you up. There is no longer the shadow of doubt about the matter."

"You mean the case of Sir Thomas Vivian?"

"Oh, no, not at all. I was referring to the problem of the fish-hooks. Between ourselves, I was a little too confident when you were here last, but since then other facts have turned up; and only yesterday I had a letter from a distinguished F.R.S. which quite settles the affair. I have been thinking what I should tackle next; and I am inclined to believe that there is a good deal to be done in the way of so-called un-decipherable inscriptions."

"Your line of study pleases me," said Dyson. "I think it may prove useful. But in the meantime, there was surely something extremely mysterious about the case of Sir Thomas Vivian."

"Hardly, I think. I allowed myself to be frightened that night; but there can be no doubt that the facts are patient of a comparatively commonplace explanation."

"Really! What is your theory then?"

"Well, I imagine that Vivian must have been mixed up at some period of his life in an adventure of a not very creditable description, and that he was murdered out of revenge by some Italian whom he had wronged."

"Why Italian?"

"Because of the hand, the sign of the *mano in fica*. That gesture is now only used by Italians. So you see that what appeared the most ob-scure feature in the case turns out to be illuminant."

"Yes, quite so. And the flint knife?"

"That is very simple. The man found the thing in Italy, or possibly stole it from some museum. Follow the line of least resistance, my dear fellow, and you will see there is no need to bring up primitive man from his secular grave beneath the hills."

"There is some justice in what you say," said Dyson. "As I understand you, then, you think that your Italian, having murdered Vivian, kindly chalked up that hand as a guide to Scotland Yard?"

"Why not? Remember a murderer is always a madman. He may plot and contrive nine-tenths of his scheme with the acuteness and the grasp of a chess-player or a pure mathematician; but somewhere or other his wits leave him and he behaves like a fool. Then you must take into account the insane pride or vanity of the criminal; he likes to leave his mark, as it were, upon his handiwork."

"Yes, it is all very ingenious; but have you read the reports of the inquest?"

"No, not a word. I simply gave my evidence, left the court, and dismissed the subject from my mind."

"Quite so. Then if you don't object I should like to give you an account of the case. I have studied it rather deeply, and I confess it interests me extremely."

"Very good. But I warn you I have done with mystery. We are to deal with facts now."

"Yes, it is fact that I wish to put before you. And this is fact the first. When the police moved Sir Thomas Vivian's body they found an open knife beneath him. It was an ugly-looking thing such as sailors carry, with a blade that the mere opening rendered rigid, and there the blade was all ready, bare and gleaming, but without a trace of blood on it, and the knife was found to be quite new; it had never been used. Now, at the first glance it looks as if your imaginary Italian were just the man to have such a tool. But consider a moment. Would he be likely to buy a new knife expressly to commit murder? And, secondly, if he had such a knife, why didn't he use it, instead of that very odd flint instrument?

"And I want to put this to you. You think the murderer chalked up the hand after the murder as a sort of 'melodramatic Italian assassin his mark' touch. Passing over the question as to whether the real criminal ever does such a thing, I would point out that, on the medical evidence, Sir Thomas Vivian hadn't been dead for more than an hour. That would place the stroke at about a quarter to ten, and you know it was perfectly dark when we went out at 9.30. And that passage was singularly gloomy and ill-lighted, and the hand was drawn roughly, it is true, but correctly and without the bungling of strokes and the bad shots that are inevitable when one tries to draw in the dark or with shut eyes. Just try to draw such a simple figure as a square without looking at the paper, and then ask me to conceive that your Italian, with the rope waiting for his neck, could draw the hand on the wall so firmly and truly, in the black shadow of that alley. It is absurd. By consequence, then, the hand was drawn early in the evening, long before any murder was committed; or else—mark this, Phillipps—it was drawn by some one to whom darkness and gloom were familiar and habitual; by some one to whom the common dread of the rope was unknown!

"Again: a curious note was found in Sir Thomas Vivian's pocket. Envelope and paper were of a common make, and the stamp bore the West Central postmark. I will come to the nature of the contents later on, but it is the question of the handwriting that is so remarkable. The address on the outside was neatly written in a small clear hand, but the letter itself might have been written by a Persian who had learnt the English script. It was upright, and the letters were curiously contorted, with an affectation of dashes and backward curves which really reminded me of an Oriental manuscript, though it was all perfectly legible. But—and here comes the poser—on searching the dead man's waistcoat pockets a small memorandum book was found; it was almost filled with pencil jottings. These memoranda related chiefly to matters of a private as distinct from a professional nature; there were appointments to meet friends, notes of theatrical first-nights, the address of a good hotel in Tours, and the title of a new novel—nothing in any way intimate. And the whole of these jottings were written in a hand nearly identical with the writing of the note found in the dead man's coat pocket! There was just enough difference between them to enable the expert to swear that the two were not written by the same person. I will just read you so much of Lady Vivian's evidence as bears on this point of the writing; I have the printed slip with me. Here you see she says: 'I was married to my late husband seven years ago; I never saw any letter addressed him in a hand at all resembling that on the envelope produced, nor have I ever seen writing like that in the letter before me. I never saw my late husband using the memorandum book, but I am sure he did write everything in it; I am certain of that because we stayed last May at the Hotel du Faisan, Rue Royale, Tours, the address of which is given in the book; I remember his getting the novel "A Sentinel" about six weeks ago. Sir Thomas Vivian never liked to miss the first-nights at the theatres. His usual hand was perfectly different from that used in the notebook.'

"And now, last of all, we come back to the note itself. Here it is in facsimile. My possession of it is due to the kindness of Inspector Cleeve, who is pleased to be amused at my amateur inquisitiveness. Read it, Phillipps; you tell me you are interested in obscure inscriptions; here is something for you to decipher."

Mr. Phillipps, absorbed in spite of himself in the strange circumstances Dyson had related, took the piece, of paper, and scrutinised it closely. The handwriting was indeed bizarre in the extreme, and, as Dyson had noted, not unlike the Persian character in its general effect, but it was perfectly legible.

"Read it aloud," said Dyson, and Phillipps obeyed.

"'Hand did not point in vain. The meaning of the stars is no longer obscure. Strangely enough, the black heaven vanished, or was stolen yesterday, but that does not matter in the least, as I have a celestial globe. Our old orbit remains unchanged; you have not forgotten the number of my sign, or will you appoint some other house? I have been on the other side of the moon, and can bring something to shew you.'"

"And what do you make of that?" said Dyson.

"It seems to me mere gibberish," said Phillipps; "you suppose it has a meaning?"

"Oh, surely; it was posted three days before the murder; it was found in the murdered man's pocket; it is written in a fantastic hand which the murdered man himself used for his private memoranda. There must be purpose under all this, and to my mind there is something ugly enough hidden under the circumstances of this case of Sir Thomas Vivian."

"But what theory have you formed?"

"Oh, as to theories, I am still in a very early stage; it is too soon to state conclusions. But I think I have demolished your Italian. I tell you, Phillipps, again, the whole thing has an ugly look to my eyes. I cannot do as you do, and fortify myself with cast-iron propositions to the effect that this or that doesn't happen, and never has happened. You note that the first word in the letter is 'hand'. That seems to me, taken with what we know about the hand on the wall, significant enough, and what you yourself told me of the history and meaning of the symbol, its connection with a world-old belief and faiths of dim far-off years, all this speaks of mischief, for me at all events. No; I stand pretty well to what I said to you half in joke that night before we went out. There are sacraments of evil as well as of good about us, and we live and move to my belief in an unknown world, a place where there are caves and shadows and dwellers in twilight. It is possible that man may sometimes return on the track of evolution, and it is my belief that an awful lore is not yet dead."

"I cannot follow you in all this," said Phillipps; "it seems to interest you strangely. What do you propose to do?"

"My dear Phillipps," replied Dyson, speaking in a lighter tone, "I am afraid I shall have to go down a little in the world. I have a prospect of visits to the pawnbrokers before me, and the publicans must not be neglected. I must cultivate a taste for four ale; shag tobacco I already love and esteem with all my heart."

SEARCH FOR THE VANISHED HEAVEN

For many days after the discussion with Phillipps, Mr. Dyson was resolute in the line of research he had marked out for himself. A fervent curiosity and an innate liking for the obscure were great incentives, but especially in this case of Sir Thomas Vivian's death (for Dyson began to boggle a little at the word "murder") there seemed to him an element that was more than curious. The sign of the red hand upon the wall, the tool of flint that had given death, the almost identity between the handwriting of the note and the fantastic script reserved religiously, as it appeared, by the doctor for trifling jottings, all these diverse and variegated threads joined to weave in his mind a strange and shadowy picture, with ghastly shapes dominant and deadly, and yet ill-defined, like the giant figures wavering in an ancient tapestry. He thought he had a clue to the meaning of the note, and in his resolute search for the "black heaven", which had vanished, he beat furiously about the alleys and obscure streets of central London, making himself a familiar figure to the pawnbroker, and a frequent guest at the more squalid pot-houses.

For a long time he was unsuccessful, and he trembled at the thought that the "black heaven" might be hid in the coy retirements of Peckham, or lurk perchance in distant Willesden, but finally, improbability, in which he put his trust, came to the rescue. It was a dark and rainy night, with something in the unquiet and stirring gusts that savoured of approaching winter, and Dyson, beating up a narrow street not far from the Gray's Inn Road, took shelter in an extremely dirty "public", and called for beer, forgetting for the moment his preoccupations, and only thinking of the sweep of the wind about the tiles and the hissing of the rain through the black and troubled air. At the bar there gathered the usual company: the frowsy women and the men in shiny black, those who appeared to mumble secretly together, others who wrangled in interminable argument, and a few shy drinkers who stood apart, each relishing his dose, and the rank and biting flavour of cheap spirit. Dyson was wondering at the enjoyment of it all, when suddenly there came a sharper accent. The folding-doors swayed open, and a middle-aged woman staggered towards the bar, and clutched the pewter rim as if she stepped a deck in a roaring gale. Dyson glanced at her attentively as a pleasing specimen of her class; she was decently dressed in black, and carried a black bag of somewhat rusty leather, and her intoxication was apparent and far advanced. As she swayed at the bar, it was evidently all she could do to stand upright, and the barman, who had looked at her with disfavour, shook his head in reply to her thick-voiced demand for a drink. The woman glared at him, transformed in a moment to a fury, with bloodshot eyes, and poured forth a torrent of execration, a stream of blasphemies and early English phraseology.

"Get out of this," said the man; "shut up and be off, or I'll send for the police."

"Police, you —— ," bawled the woman, "I'll —— well give you something to fetch the police for!" and with a rapid dive into her bag she pulled out some object which she hurled furiously at the barman's head.

The man ducked down, and the missile flew over his head and smashed a bottle to fragments, while the woman with a peal of horrible laughter rushed to the door, and they could hear her steps pattering fast over the wet stones.

The barman looked ruefully about him.

"Not much good going after her," he said, "and I'm afraid what she's left won't pay for that bottle of whisky." He fumbled amongst the fragments of broken glass, and drew out something dark, a kind of square stone it seemed, which he held up.

"Valuable cur'osity," he said, "any gent like to bid?"

The *habitués* had scarcely turned from their pots and glasses during these exciting incidents; they gazed a moment, fishily, when the bottle smashed, and that was all, and the mumble of the confidential was resumed and the jangle of the quarrelsome, and the shy and solitary sucked in their lips and relished again the rank flavour of the spirit.

Dyson looked quickly at what the barman held before him.

"Would you mind letting me see it?" he said; "it's a queer-looking thing, isn't it?"

It was a small black tablet, apparently of stone, about four inches long by two and a half broad, and as Dyson took it he felt rather than saw that he touched the secular with his flesh. There was some kind of carving on the surface, and, most conspicuous, a sign that made Dyson's heart leap.

"I don't mind taking it," he said quietly. "Would two shillings be enough?"

"Say half a dollar," said the man, and the bargain was concluded. Dyson drained his pot of beer, finding it delicious, and lit his pipe, and went out deliberately soon after. When he reached his apartment he locked the door, and placed the tablet on his desk, and then fixed himself in his chair, as resolute as an army in its trenches before a beleaguered city. The tablet was full under the light of the shaded candle, and scrutinising it closely, Dyson saw first the sign of the hand with the thumb protruding between the fingers; it was cut finely and firmly on the dull black surface of the stone, and the thumb pointed downward to what was beneath.

"It is a mere ornament," said Dyson to himself, "perhaps symbolical ornament, but surely not an inscription, or the signs of any words ever spoken."

The hand pointed to a series of fantastic figures, spirals and whorls of the finest, most delicate lines, spaced at intervals over the remaining surface of the tablet. The marks were as intricate and seemed almost as much as without design as the pattern of a thumb impressed on a pane of glass.

"Is it some natural marking?" thought Dyson; "there have been queer designs, likenesses of beasts and flowers, in stones with which man's hand had nothing to do"; and he bent over the stone with a magnifier, only to be convinced that no hazard of nature could have delineated those varied labyrinths of line. The whorls were different sizes; some were less than the twelfth of an inch in diameter, and the largest was a little smaller than a sixpence, and under the glass the regularity and accuracy of the cutting were evident, and in the smaller spirals the lines were graduated at intervals of a hundredth of an inch. The whole thing had a marvellous and fantastic look, and gazing at the mystic whorls beneath the hand, Dyson became subdued with an impression of vast and far-off ages, and of a living being that had touched the stone with enigmas before the hills were formed, when the hard rocks still boiled with fervent heat.

"The 'black heaven' is found again," he said, "but the meaning of the stars is likely to be obscure for everlasting so far as I am concerned."

London stilled without, and a chill breath came into the room as Dyson sat gazing at the tablet shining duskily under the candle-light; and at last, as he closed the desk over the ancient stone, all his wonder at the case of Sir Thomas Vivian increased tenfold, and he thought of the well-dressed prosperous gentleman lying dead mystically beneath the sign of the hand, and the insupportable conviction seized him that between the death of this fashionable West-end doctor and the weird spirals of the tablet there were most secret and unimaginable links.

For days he sat before his desk gazing at the tablet, unable to resist its lodestone fascination, and yet quite helpless, without ever the hope of solving the symbols so secretly inscribed. At last, desperate, he called in Mr. Phillipps in consultation, and told in brief the story of the finding the stone.

"Dear me!" said Phillipps, "this is extremely curious; you have had a find indeed. Why it looks to me even more ancient than the Hittite seal. I confess the character, if it is a character, is entirely strange to me. These whorls are really very quaint."

"Yes, but I want to know what they mean. You must remember this tablet is the 'black heaven' of the letter found in Sir Thomas Vivian's pocket; it bears directly on his death."

"Oh, no, that is nonsense! This is, no doubt, an extremely ancient tablet, which has been stolen from some collection. Yes, the hand makes an odd coincidence, but only a coincidence after all."

"My dear Phillipps, you are a living example of the truth of the axiom that extreme scepticism is mere credulity. But can you decipher the inscription?"

"I undertake to decipher anything," said Phillipps. "I do not believe in the insoluble. These characters are curious, but I cannot fancy them to be inscrutable."

"Then take the thing away with you and make what you can of it. It has begun to haunt me; I feel as if I had gazed too long into the eyes of the Sphinx."

Phillipps departed with the tablet in an inner pocket. He had not much doubt of success, for he had evolved thirty-seven rules for the solution of inscriptions. Yet when a week had passed and he called to see Dyson there was no vestige of triumph on his features. He found his friend in a state of extreme irritation, pacing up and down in the room like a man in a passion. He turned with a start as the door opened.

"Well," said Dyson, "you have got it? What is it all about?"

"My dear fellow, I am sorry to say I have completely failed. I have tried every known device in vain. I have even been so officious as to submit it to a friend at the Museum, but he, though a man of prime authority on the subject, tells me that he is quite at fault. It must be some wreckage of a vanished race, almost, I think—a fragment of another world than ours. I am not a superstitious man, Dyson, and you know that I have no truck with even the noble delusions, but I confess I yearn to be rid of this small square of blackish stone. Frankly, it has given me an ill week; it seems to me troglodytic and abhorred."

Phillipps drew out the tablet and laid it on the desk before Dyson.

"By the way," he went on, "I was right at all events in one particular; it has formed part of some collection. There is a piece of grimy paper on the back that must have been a label."

"Yes, I noticed that," said Dyson, who had fallen into deepest disappointment; "no doubt the paper is a label. But as I don't much care where the tablet originally came from, and only wish to know what the inscription means, I paid no attention to the paper. The thing is a hopeless riddle, I suppose, and yet it must surely be of the greatest importance."

Phillipps left soon after, and Dyson, still despondent, took the tablet in his hand and carelessly turned it over. The label had so grimed that it seemed merely a dull stain, but as Dyson looked at it idly, and yet attentively, he could see pencil-marks, and he bent over it eagerly, with his glass to his eye. To his annoyance, he found that part of the paper had been torn away, and he could only with difficulty make out odd words and pieces of words. First he read something that looked like "inroad", and then beneath, "stony-hearted step—" and a tear cut off the rest. But in an instant a solution suggested itself, and he chuckled with huge delight.

"Certainly," he said aloud, "this is not only the most charming but the most convenient quarter in all London; here I am, allowing for the accidents of side streets, perched on a tower of observation."

He glanced triumphantly out of the window across the street to the gate of the British Museum. Sheltered by the boundary wall of that agreeable institution, a "screever", or artist in chalks, displayed his brilliant impressions on the pavement, soliciting the approval and the coppers of the gay and serious.

"This," said Dyson, "is more than delightful! An artist is provided to my hand."

THE ARTIST OF THE PAVEMENT

Mr. Phillipps, in spite of all disavowals—in spite of the wall of sense of whose enclosure and limit he was wont to make his boast—yet felt in his heart profoundly curious as to the case of Sir Thomas Vivian. Though he kept a brave face for his friend, his reason could not decently resist the conclusion that Dyson had enunciated, namely, that the whole affair had a look both ugly and mysterious. There was the weapon of a vanished race that had pierced the great arteries; the red hand, the symbol of a hideous faith, that pointed to the slain man; and then the tablet which Dyson declared he had expected to find, and had certainly found, bearing the ancient impress of the hand of malediction, and a legend written beneath in a character compared with which the most antique cuneiform was a thing of yesterday. Besides all this, there were other points that tortured and perplexed. How to account for the bare knife found unstained beneath the body? And the hint that the red hand upon the wall must have been drawn by some one whose life was passed in darkness thrilled him with a suggestion of dim and infinite horror. Hence he was in truth not a little curious as to what was to come, and some ten days after he had returned the tablet he again visited the "mystery-man", as he privately named his friend.

Arrived in the grave and airy chambers in Great Russell Street, he found the moral atmosphere of the place had been transformed. All Dyson's irritation had disappeared, his brow was smoothed with complacency, and he sat at a table by the window gazing out into the street with an expression of grim enjoyment, a pile of books and papers lying unheeded before him.

"My dear Phillipps, I am delighted to see you! Pray excuse my moving. Draw your chair up here to the table, and try this admirable shag tobacco."

"Thank you," said Phillipps, "judging by the flavour of the smoke, I should think it is a little strong. But what on earth is all this? What are you looking at?"

"I am on my watch-tower. I assure you that the time seems short while I contemplate this agreeable street and the classic grace of the Museum portico."

"Your capacity for nonsense is amazing," replied Phillipps, "but have you succeeded in deciphering the tablet? It interests me."

"I have not paid much attention to the tablet recently," said Dyson. "I believe the spiral character may wait."

"Really! And how about the Vivian murder?"

"Ah, you do take an interest in that case? Well, after all, we cannot deny that it was a queer business. But is not 'murder' rather a coarse word? It smacks a little, surely, of the police poster. Perhaps I am a trifle decadent, but I cannot help believing in the splendid word; 'sacrifice', for example, is surely far finer than 'murder'."

"I am all in the dark," said Phillipps. "I cannot even imagine by what track you are moving in this labyrinth."

"I think that before very long the whole matter will be a good deal clearer for us both, but I doubt whether you will like hearing the story."

Dyson lit his pipe afresh and leant back, not relaxing, however, in his scrutiny of the street. After a somewhat lengthy pause, he startled Phillipps by a loud breath of relief as he rose from the chair by the window and began to pace the floor.

"It's over for the day," he said, "and, after all, one gets a little tired."

Phillipps looked with enquiry into the street. The evening was darkening, and the pile of the Museum was beginning to loom indistinct before the lighting of the lamps, but the pavements were thronged and busy. The artist in chalks across the way was gathering together his materials, and blurring all the brilliance of his designs, and a little lower down there was the clang of shutters being placed in position. Phillipps could see nothing to justify Mr. Dyson's sudden abandonment of his attitude of surveillance, and grew a little irritated by all these thorny enigmas.

"Do you know, Phillipps," said Dyson, as he strolled at ease up and down the room, "I will tell you how I work. I go upon the theory of improbability. The theory is unknown to you? I will explain. Suppose I stand on the steps of St. Paul's and look out for a blind man lame of the left leg to pass me, it is evidently highly improbable that I shall see such a person by waiting for an hour. If I wait two hours the improbability is diminished, but is still enormous, and a watch of a whole day would give little expectation of success. But suppose I take up the same position day after day, and week after week, don't you perceive that the improbability is lessening constantly—growing smaller day after day? Don't you see that two lines which are not parallel are gradually approaching one another, drawing nearer and nearer to a point of meeting, till at last they do meet, and improbability has vanished altogether? That is how I found the black tablet: I acted on the theory of improbability. It is the only scientific principle I know of which can enable one to pick out an unknown man from amongst five million."

"And you expect to find the interpreter of the black tablet by this method?"

"Certainly."

"'And the murderer of Sir Thomas Vivian also?"

"Yes, I expect to lay my hands on the person concerned in the death of Sir Thomas Vivian in exactly the same way."

The rest of the evening, after Phillipps had left, was devoted by Dyson to sauntering in the streets, and afterwards, when the night grew late, to his literary labours, or the chase of the phrase, as he called it. The next morning the station by the window was again resumed. His meals were brought to him at the table, and he ate with his eyes on the street. With briefest intervals, snatched reluctantly from time to time, he persisted in his survey throughout the day, and only at dusk, when the shutters were put up and the "screever" ruthlessly deleted all his labour of the day, just before the gas-lamps began to star the shadows, did he feel at liberty to quit his post. Day after day this ceaseless glance upon the street continued, till the landlady grew puzzled and aghast at such a profitless pertinacity.

But at last, one evening, when the play of lights and shadows was scarce beginning, and the clear cloudless air left all distinct and shining, there came the moment. A man of middle age, bearded and bowed, with a touch of grey about the ears, was strolling slowly along the northern pavement of Great Russell Street from the eastern end. He looked up at the Museum as he went by, and then glanced involuntarily at the art of the "screever", and at the artist himself, who sat beside his pictures, hat in hand. The man with the beard stood still an instant, swaying slightly to and fro as if in thought, and Dyson saw his fists shut tight, and his back quivering, and the one side of his face in view twitched and grew contorted with the indescribable torment of approaching epilepsy. Dyson drew a soft hat from his pocket, and dashed the door open, taking the stair with a run.

When he reached the street the person he had seen so agitated had turned about, and, regardless of observation, was racing wildly towards Bloomsbury Square, with his back to his former course.

Mr. Dyson went up to the artist of the pavement, and gave him some money, observing quietly, "You needn't trouble to draw that thing again." Then he too turned about, and strolled idly down the street in the opposite direction to that taken by the fugitive. So the distance between Dyson and the man with the bowed head grew steadily greater.

STORY OF THE TREASURE HOUSE

"There are many reasons why I chose your rooms for the meeting in preference to my own. Chiefly, perhaps, because I thought the man would be more at his ease on neutral ground."

"I confess, Dyson," said Phillipps, "that I feel both impatient and uneasy. You know my standpoint: hard matter of fact, materialism if you like, in its crudest form. But there is something about all this affair of Vivian that makes me a little restless. And how did you induce the man to come?"

"He has an exaggerated opinion of my powers. You remember what I said about the doctrine of improbability? When it does work out, it gives results which seem very amazing to a person who is not in the secret. That is eight striking, isn't it? And there goes the bell."

They heard footsteps on the stair, and presently the door opened, and a middle-aged man, with a bowed head, bearded, and with a good deal of grizzling hair about his ears, came into the room. Phillipps glanced at his features, and recognised the lineaments of terror.

"Come in, Mr. Selby," said Dyson. "This is Mr. Phillipps, my intimate friend and our host for this evening. Will you take anything? Then perhaps we had better hear your story—a very singular one, I am sure."

The man spoke in a voice hollow and a little quavering, and a fixed stare that never left his eyes seemed directed to something awful that was to remain before him by day and night for the rest of his life.

"You will, I am sure, excuse preliminaries," he began; "what I have to tell is best told quickly. I will say, then, that I was born in a remote part of the west of England, where the very outlines of the woods and hills, and the winding of the streams in the valleys, are apt to suggest the mystical to any one strongly gifted with imagination. When I was quite a boy there were certain huge and rounded hills, certain depths of hanging wood, and secret valleys bastioned round on every side that filled me with fancies beyond the bourne of rational expression, and as I grew older and began to dip into my father's books, I went by instinct, like the bee, to all that would nourish fantasy. Thus, from a course of obsolete and occult reading, and from listening to certain wild legends in which the older people still secretly believe, I grew firmly convinced of the existence of treasure, the hoard of a race extinct for ages, still hidden beneath the hills, and my every thought was directed to the discovery of the golden heaps that lay, as I fancied, within a few feet of the green turf. To one spot, in especial, I was drawn as if by enchantment; it was a tumulus, the doomed memorial of some forgotten people, crowning the crest of a vast mountain range; and I have often lingered there on summer evenings, sitting on the great block of limestone at the summit, and looking out far over the yellow sea towards the Devonshire coast. One day as I dug heedlessly with the ferrule of my stick at the mosses and lichens which grew rank over the stone, my eye was caught by what seemed a pattern beneath the growth of green; there was a curving line, and marks that did not look altogether the work of nature. At first I thought I had bared some rare fossil, and I took out my knife and scraped away at the moss till a square foot was uncovered. Then I saw two signs which startled me; first, a closed hand, pointing downwards, the thumb protruding between the fingers, and beneath the hand a whorl or spiral, traced with exquisite accuracy in the hard surface of the rock. Here, I persuaded myself, was an index to the great secret, but I chilled at the recollection of the fact that some antiquarians had tunnelled the tumulus through and through, and had been a good deal surprised at not finding so much as an arrowhead within. Clearly, then, the signs on the limestone had no local significance; and I made up my mind that I must search abroad. By sheer accident I was in a measure successful in my quest. Strolling by a cottage, I saw some children playing by the roadside; one was holding up some object in his hand, and the rest were going through one of the many forms of elaborate pretence which make up a great part of the mystery of a child's life. Something in the object held by the little boy attracted me, and I asked him to let me see it. The plaything of these children consisted of an oblong tablet of black stone; and on it was inscribed the hand pointing downwards, just as I had seen it on the rock, while beneath, spaced over the tablet, were a number of whorls and spirals, cut, as it seemed to me, with the utmost care and nicety. I bought the toy for a couple of shillings; the woman of the house told me it had been lying about for years; she thought her husband had found it one day in the brook which ran in front of the cottage; it was a very hot summer, and the stream was almost dry, and he saw it amongst the stones. That day I tracked the brook to a well of water gushing up cold and clear at the head of a lonely glen in the mountains. That was twenty years ago, and I only succeeded in deciphering the mysterious inscription last August. I must not trouble you with irrelevant details of my life; it is enough for me to say that I was forced, like many another man, to leave my old home and come to London. Of money I had very little, and I was glad to find a cheap room in a squalid street off the Gray's Inn Road. The late Sir Thomas Vivian, then far poorer and more wretched than myself, had a garret in the same house, and before many months we became intimate friends, and I had confided to him the object of my life. I had at first great difficulty in persuading him that I was not giving my days and my nights to an enquiry altogether hopeless and chimerical; but when he was convinced he grew keener than myself, and glowed at the thought of the riches which were to be the prize of some ingenuity and patience. I liked the man intensely, and pitied his case; he had a strong desire to enter the medical profession, but he lacked the means to pay the smallest fees, and indeed he was, not once or twice, but often reduced to the very verge of starvation. I freely and solemnly promised that, under whatever chances, he should share in my heaped fortune when it came, and this promise to one who had always been poor, and yet thirsted for wealth and pleasure in a manner unknown to me, was the strongest incentive. He threw himself into the task with eager interest, and applied a very acute intellect and unwearied patience to the solution of the characters on the tablet. I, like other ingenious young men, was curious in the matter of handwriting, and I had invented or adapted a fantastic script which I used occasionally, and which took Vivian so strongly that he was at the pains to imitate it. It was arranged between us that if we were ever parted, and had occasion to write on the affair that was so close to our hearts, this queer hand of my invention was to be used, and we also contrived a semi-cypher for the same purpose. Meanwhile we exhausted ourselves in efforts to get at the heart of the mystery, and after a couple of years had gone by I could see that Vivian began to sicken a little of the adventure, and one night he told me with some emotion that he feared both our lives were being passed away in idle and hopeless endeavour. Not many months afterwards he was so happy as to receive a considerable legacy from an aged and distant relative whose very existence had been almost forgotten by him; and with money at the bank, he became at once a stranger to me. He had passed his preliminary examination many years before, and he forthwith decided to enter at St. Thomas's Hospital, and he told me that he must look out for a more convenient lodging. As we said good-bye, I reminded him of the promise I had given, and solemnly renewed it; but Vivian laughed with something between pity and contempt in his voice and expression as he thanked me. I need not dwell on the long struggle and misery of my existence, now doubly lonely; I never wearied or despaired of final success, and every day saw me at work, the tablet before me, and only at dusk would I go out and take my daily walk along Oxford Street, which attracted me I think by the noise and motion and glitter of lamps.

"This walk grew with me to a habit; every night, and in all weathers, I crossed the Gray's Inn Road and struck westward, sometimes choosing a northern track, by the Euston Road and Tottenham Court Road, sometimes I went by Holborn, and sometimes by the way of Great Russell Street. Every night I walked for an hour to and fro on the northern pavement of Oxford Street, and the tale of De Quincey and his name for the Street, 'Stony-hearted step-mother', often recurred to my memory. Then I would return to my grimy den and spend hours more in endless analysis of the riddle before me.

"The answer came to me one night a few weeks ago; it flashed into my brain in a moment, and I read the inscription, and saw that after all I had not wasted my days. 'The place of the treasure house of them that dwell below,' were the first words, I read, and then followed minute indications of the spot in my own country where the great works of gold were to be kept for ever. Such a track was to be followed, such a pitfall avoided; here the way narrowed almost to a fox's hole, and there it broadened, and so at last the chamber would be reached. I determined to lose no time in verifying my discovery—not that I doubted at that great moment, but I would not risk even the smallest chance of disappointing my old friend Vivian, now a rich and prosperous man. I took the train for the West, and one night, with chart in hand, traced out the passage of the hills, and went so far that I saw the gleam of gold before me. I would not go on; I resolved that Vivian must be with me; and I only brought away a strange knife of flint which lay on the path, as confirmation of what I had to tell. I returned to London, and was a good deal vexed to find the stone tablet had disappeared from my rooms. My landlady, an inveterate drunkard, denied all knowledge of the fact, but I have little doubt she had stolen the thing for the sake of the glass of whisky it might fetch. However, I knew what was written on the tablet by heart, and I had also made an exact facsimile of the characters, so the loss was not severe. Only one thing annoyed me: when I first came into possession of the stone, I had pasted a piece of paper on the back and had written down the date and place of finding, and later on I had scribbled a word or two, a trivial sentiment, the name of my street, and such-like idle pencillings on the paper; and these memories of days that had seemed so hopeless were dear to me: I had thought they would help to remind me in the future of the hours when I had hoped against despair. However, I wrote at once to Sir Thomas Vivian, using the handwriting I have mentioned and also the quasi-cypher. I told him of my success, and after mentioning the loss of the tablet and the fact that I had a copy of the inscription, I reminded him once more of my promise, and asked him either to write or call. He replied that he would see me in a certain obscure passage in Clerkenwell well known to us both in the old days, and at seven o'clock one evening I went to meet him. At the corner of this byway, as I was walking to and fro, I noticed the blurred pictures of some street artist, and I picked up a piece of chalk he had left behind him, not much thinking what I was doing. I paced up and down the passage, wondering a good deal, as you may imagine, as to what manner of man I was to meet after so many years of parting, and the thoughts of the buried time coming thick upon me, I walked mechanically without raising my eyes from the ground. I was startled out of my reverie by an angry voice and a rough enquiry why I didn't keep to the right side of the pavement, and looking up I found I had confronted a prosperous and important gentleman, who eyed my poor appearance with a look of great dislike and contempt. I knew directly it was my old comrade, and when I recalled myself to him, he apologised with some show of regret, and began to thank me for my kindness, doubtfully, as if he hesitated to commit himself, and, as I could see, with the hint of a suspicion as to my sanity. I would have engaged him at first in reminiscences of our friendship, but I found Sir Thomas viewed those days with a good deal of distaste, and replying politely to my remarks, continually edged in 'business matters', as he called them. I changed my topics, and told him in greater detail what I have told you. Then I saw his manner suddenly change; as I pulled out the flint knife to prove my journey 'to the other side of the moon', as we called it in our jargon, there came over him a kind of choking eagerness, his features were somewhat discomposed, and I thought I detected a shuddering horror, a clenched resolution, and the efforts to keep quiet succeed one another in a manner that puzzled me. I had occasion to be a little precise in my particulars, and it being still light enough, I remembered the red chalk in my pocket, and drew the hand on the wall. 'Here, you see, is the hand,' I said, as I explained its true meaning, 'note where the thumb issues from between the first and second fingers,' and I would have gone on, and had applied the chalk to the wall to continue my diagram, when he struck my hand down, much to my surprise. 'No, no,' he said, 'I do not want all that. And this place is not retired enough; let us walk on, and do you explain everything to me minutely.' I complied readily enough, and he led me away, choosing the most unfrequented byways, while I drove in the plan of the hidden house word by word. Once or twice as I raised my eyes I caught Vivian looking strangely about him; he seemed to give a quick glint up and down, and glance at the houses; and there was a furtive and anxious air about him that displeased me. 'Let us walk on to the north,' he said at length, 'we shall come to some pleasant lanes where we can discuss these matters, quietly; my night's rest is at your service.' I declined, on the pretext that I could not dispense with my visit to Oxford Street, and went on till he understood every turning and winding and the minutest detail as well as myself. We had returned on our footsteps, and stood again in the dark passage, just where I had drawn the red hand on the wall, for I recognised the vague shape of the trees whose branches hung above us. 'We have come back to our starting-point,' I said; 'I almost think I could put my finger on the wall where I drew the hand. And I am sure you could put your finger on the mystic hand in the hills as well as I. Remember between stream and stone.'

"I was bending down, peering at what I thought must be my drawing, when I heard a sharp hiss of breath, and started up, and saw Vivian with his arm uplifted and a bare blade in his hand, and death threatening in his eyes. In sheer self-defence I caught at the flint weapon in my pocket, and dashed at him in blind fear of my life, and the next instant he lay dead upon the stones.

"I think that is all," Mr. Selby continued after a pause, "and it only remains for me to say to you, Mr. Dyson, that I cannot conceive what means enabled you to run me down."

"I followed many indications," said Dyson, "and I am bound to disclaim all credit for acuteness, as I have made several gross blunders. Your celestial cypher did not, I confess, give me much trouble; I saw at once that terms of astronomy were substituted for common words and phrases. You had lost something black, or something black had been stolen from you; a celestial globe is a copy of the heavens, so I knew you meant you had a copy of what you had lost. Obviously, then, I came to the conclusion that you had lost a black object with characters or symbols written or inscribed on it, since the object in question certainly contained valuable information, and all information must be written or pictured. 'Our old orbit remains unchanged'; evidently our old course or arrangement. 'The number of my sign' must mean the number of my house, the allusion being to the signs of the zodiac. I need not say that 'the other side of the moon' can stand for nothing but some place where no one else has been; and 'some other house' is some other place of meeting, the 'house' being the old term 'house of the heavens'. Then my next step was to find the 'black heaven' that had been stolen, and by a process of exhaustion I did so."

"You have got the tablet?"

"Certainly. And on the back of it, on the slip of paper you have mentioned, I read 'inroad', which puzzled me a good deal, till I thought of Gray's Inn Road; you forgot the second *n*. 'Stony-hearted step—' immediately suggested the phrase of De Quincey you have alluded to; and I made the wild but correct shot, that you were a man who lived in or near the Gray's Inn Road, and had the habit of walking in Oxford Street, for you remember how the opium eater dwells on his wearying promenades along that thoroughfare? On the theory of improbability, which I have explained to my friend here, I concluded that occasionally, at all events, you would choose the way Guilford Street, Russel Square, and Great Russell Street, and I knew that if I watched long enough I should see you. But how was I to recognise my man? I

noticed the screever opposite my rooms, and got him to draw every
day a large hand, in the gesture so familiar to us all, upon the wall behind him. I thought that when the unknown person did pass he would
certainly betray some emotion at the sudden vision of the sign, to him
the most terrible of symbols. You know the rest. Ah, as to catching
you an hour later, that was, I confess, a refinement. From the fact of
your having occupied the same rooms for so many years, in a neighbourhood moreover where lodgers are migratory to excess, I drew the
conclusion that you were a man of fixed habit, and I was sure that after
you had got over your fright you would return for the walk down Oxford Street. You did, by way of New Oxford Street, and I was waiting
at the corner."

"Your conclusions are admirable," said Mr. Selby. "I may tell you
that I had my stroll down Oxford Street the night Sir Thomas Vivian
died. And I think that is all I have to say."

"Scarcely," said Dyson. "How about the treasure?"

"I had rather we did not speak of that," said Mr. Selby, with a
whitening of the skin about the temples.

"Oh, nonsense, sir, we are not blackmailers. Besides, you know
you are in our power."

"Then, as you put it like that, Mr. Dyson, I must tell you I returned
to the place. I went on a little farther than before."

The man stopped short; his mouth began to twitch, his lips moved
apart, and he drew in quick breaths, sobbing.

"Well, well," said Dyson, "I dare say you have done comfortably."

"Comfortably," Selby went on, constraining himself with an effort,
"yes, so comfortably that hell burns hot within me for ever. I only
brought one thing away from that awful house within the hills; it was
lying just beyond the spot where I found the flint knife."

"Why did you not bring more?"

The whole bodily frame of the wretched man visibly shrank and
wasted; his face grew yellow as tallow, and the sweat dropped from his
brows. The spectacle was both revolting and terrible, and when the
voice came, it sounded like the hissing of a snake.

"Because the keepers are still there, and I saw them, and because
of this," and he pulled out a small piece of curious gold-work and held
it up.

"There," he said, "that is the Pain of the Goat."

Phillipps and Dyson cried out together in horror at the revolting obscenity of the thing.

"Put it away, man; hide it, for Heaven's sake, hide it!"

"I brought that with me; that is all," he said. "You do not wonder that I did not stay long in a place where those who live are a little higher than the beasts, and where what you have seen is surpassed a thousandfold?"

"Take this," said Dyson, "I brought it with me in case it might be useful"; and he drew out the black tablet, and handed it to the shaking, horrible man.

"And now," said Dyson, "will you go out?"

The two friends sat silent a little while, facing one another with restless eyes and lips that quivered.

"I wish to say that I believe him,'" said Phillipps.

"My dear Phillipps," said Dyson as he threw the windows wide open, "I do not know that, after all, my blunders in this queer case were so very absurd."

The Shining Pyramid

I

THE ARROW-HEAD CHARACTER

Haunted, you said?"

"Yes, haunted. Don't you remember, when I saw you three years ago, you told about your place in the west with the ancient woods hanging all about it, and the wild, domed hills, and the ragged land? It has always remained a sort of enchanted picture in my mind as I sit at my desk and hear the traffic rattling in the street in the midst of whirling London. But when did you come up?"

"The fact is, Dyson, I have only just got out of the train. I drove to the station early this morning and caught the 10.45."

"Well, I am very glad you looked in on me. How have you been getting on since we last met? There is no Mrs. Vaughan, I suppose?"

"No," said Vaughan, "I am still a hermit, like yourself. I have done nothing but loaf about."

Vaughan had lit his pipe and sat in the elbow chair, fidgeting and glancing about him in a somewhat dazed and restless manner. Dyson had wheeled round his chair when his visitor entered and sat with one arm fondly reclining on the desk of his bureau, and touching the litter of manuscript.

"And you are still engaged in the old task?" said Vaughan, pointing to the pile of papers and the teeming pigeon-holes.

"Yes, the vain pursuit of literature, as idle as alchemy, and as entrancing. But you have come to town for some time I suppose; what shall we do to-night?"

"Well, I rather wanted you to try a few days with me down in the west. It would do you a lot of good, I'm sure."

"You are very kind, Vaughan, but London in September is hard to leave. Doré could not have designed anything more wonderful and mystic than Oxford Street as I saw it the other evening; the sunset flaming, the blue haze transmuting the plain street into a road 'far in the spiritual city'."

"I should like you to come down though. You would enjoy roaming over our hills. Does this racket go on all day and all night? It quite bewilders me; I wonder how you can work through it. I am sure you would revel in the great peace of my old home among the woods."

Vaughan lit his pipe again, and looked anxiously at Dyson to see if his inducements had had any effect, but the man of letters shook his head, smiling, and vowed in his heart a firm allegiance to the streets.

"You cannot tempt me," he said.

"Well, you may be right. Perhaps, after all, I was wrong to speak of the peace of the country. There, when a tragedy does occur, it is like a stone thrown into a pond; the circles of disturbance keep on widening, and it seems as if the water would never be still again."

"Have you ever any tragedies where you are?"

"I can hardly say that. But I was a good deal disturbed about a month ago by something that happened; it may or may not have been a tragedy in the usual sense of the word."

"What was the occurrence?"

"Well, the fact is a girl disappeared in a way which seems highly mysterious. Her parents, people of the name of Trevor, are well-to-do farmers, and their eldest daughter Annie was a sort of village beauty; she was really remarkably handsome. One afternoon she thought she would go and see her aunt, a widow who farms her own land, and as the two houses are only about five or six miles apart, she started off, telling her parents she would take the short cut over the hills. She never got to her aunt's, and she never was seen again. That's putting it in a few words."

"What an extraordinary thing! I suppose there are no disused mines, are there, on the hills? I don't think you quite run to anything so formidable as a precipice?"

"No; the path the girl must have taken had no pitfall of any description; it is just a track over wild, bare hillside, far, even, from a by-road. One may walk for miles without meeting a soul, but it is all perfectly safe."

"And what do people say about it?"

"Oh, they talk nonsense—among themselves. You have no notion as to how superstitious English cottagers are in out-of-the-way parts like mine. They are as bad as the Irish, every whit, and even more secretive."

"But what do they say?"

"Oh, the poor girl is supposed to have 'gone with the fairies', or to have been 'taken by the fairies'. Such stuff!" he went on, "one would laugh if it were not for the real tragedy of the case."

Dyson looked somewhat interested.

"Yes," he said, "'fairies' certainly strike a little curiously on the ear in these days. But what do the police say? I presume they do not accept the fairy-tale hypothesis?"

"No; but they seem quite at fault. What I am afraid of is that Annie Trevor must have fallen in with some scoundrels on her way. Castletown is a large seaport, you know, and some of the worst of the foreign sailors occasionally desert their ships and go on the tramp up and down the country. Not many years ago a Spanish sailor named Garcia murdered a whole family for the sake of plunder that was not worth sixpence. They are hardly human, some of these fellows, and I am dreadfully afraid the poor girl must have come to an awful end."

"But no foreign sailor was seen by any one about the country?"

"No; there is certainly that; and of course country people are quick to notice any one whose appearance and dress are a little out of the common. Still it seems as if my theory were the only possible explanation."

"There are no data to go upon," said Dyson, thoughtfully. "There was no question of a love affair, or anything of the kind, I suppose?"

"Oh, no, not a hint of such a thing. I am sure if Annie were alive she would have contrived to let her mother know of her safety."

"No doubt, no doubt. Still it is barely possible that she is alive and yet unable to communicate with her friends. But all this must have disturbed you a good deal."

"Yes, it did; I hate a mystery, and especially a mystery which is probably the veil of horror. But frankly, Dyson, I want to make a clean breast of it; I did not come here to tell you all this."

"Of course not," said Dyson, a little surprised at Vaughan's uneasy manner. "You came to have a chat on more cheerful topics."

"No, I did not. What I have been telling you about happened a month ago, but something which seems likely to affect me more personally has taken place within the last few days, and to be quite plain, I came up to town with the idea that you might be able to help me. You recollect that curious case you spoke to me about at our last meeting; something about a spectacle-maker."

"Oh, yes, I remember that. I know I was quite proud of my acumen at the time; even to this day the police have no idea why those peculiar yellow spectacles were wanted. But, Vaughan, you really look quite put out; I hope there is nothing serious?"

"No. I think I have been exaggerating, and I want you to reassure me. But what has happened is very odd."

"And what has happened?"

"I am sure that you will laugh at me, but this is the story. You must know there is a path, a right of way, that goes through my land, and to be precise, close to the wall of the kitchen garden. It is not used by many people; a woodman now and again finds it useful, and five or six children who go to school in the village pass twice a day. Well, a few days ago I was taking a walk about the place before breakfast, and I happened to stop to fill my pipe just by the large doors in the garden wall. The wood, I must tell you, comes to within a few feet of the wall, and the track I spoke of runs right in the shadow of the trees. I thought the shelter from a brisk wind that was blowing rather pleasant, and I stood there smoking with my eyes on the ground. Then something caught my attention. Just under the wall, on the short grass, a number of small flints were arranged in a pattern; something like this": and Mr. Vaughan caught at a pencil and piece of paper, and dotted down a few strokes.

"You see," he went on, "there were, I should think, twelve little stones neatly arranged in lines, and spaced at equal distances, as I have shewn it on the paper. They were pointed stones, and the points were very carefully directed one way."

"Yes," said Dyson, without much interest, "no doubt the children you have mentioned had been playing there on their way from school. Children, as you know, are very fond of making such devices with oyster shells or flints or flowers, or with whatever comes in their way."

"So I thought; I just noticed these flints were arranged in a sort of pattern and then went on. But the next morning I was taking the same round, which, as a matter of fact, is habitual with me, and again I saw at the same spot a device in flints. This time it was really a curious pattern; something like the spokes of a wheel, all meeting at a common centre, and this centre formed by a device which looked like a bowl; all, you understand, done in flints."

"You are right," said Dyson, "that seems odd enough. Still it is reasonable that your half-a-dozen children are responsible for these fantasies in stone."

"Well, I thought I would set the matter at rest. The children pass the gate every evening at half-past five, and I walked by at six, and found the device just as I had left it in the morning. The next day I was up and about at a quarter to seven, and I found the whole thing had been changed. There was a pyramid outlined in flints upon the grass. The children I saw going by an hour and a half later, and they ran past the spot without glancing to right or left. In the evening I watched them going home, and this morning when I got to the gate at six o'clock there was a thing like a half moon waiting for me."

"So then the series runs thus: firstly ordered lines, then the device of the spokes and the bowl, then the pyramid, and finally, this morning, the half moon. That is the order, isn't it?"

"Yes; that is right. But do you know it has made me feel very uneasy? I suppose it seems absurd, but I can't help thinking that some kind of signalling is going on under my nose, and that sort of thing is disquieting."

"But what have you to dread? You have no enemies?"

"No; but I have some very valuable old plate."

"You are thinking of burglars then?" said Dyson, with an accent of considerable interest, "but you must know your neighbours. Are there any suspicious characters about?"

"Not that I am aware of. But you remember what I told you of the sailors."

"Can you trust your servants?"

"Oh, perfectly. The plate is preserved in a strong room; the butler, an old family servant, alone knows where the key is kept. There is nothing wrong there. Still, everybody is aware that I have a lot of old

silver, and all country folks are given to gossip. In that way information may have got abroad in very undesirable quarters."

"Yes, but I confess there seems something a little unsatisfactory in
the burglar theory. Who is signalling to whom? I cannot see my way to
accepting such an explanation. What put the plate into your head in
connection with these flint signs, or whatever one may call them?"

"It was the figure of the Bowl," said Vaughan. "I happen to possess a very large and very valuable Charles II punch-bowl. The chasing
is really exquisite, and the thing is worth a lot of money. The sign I described to you was exactly the same shape as my punch-bowl."

"A queer coincidence certainly. But the other figures or devices:
you have nothing shaped like a pyramid?"

"Ah, you will think that queerer. As it happens, this punch bowl of
mine, together with a set of rare old ladles, is kept in a mahogany chest
of a pyramidal shape. The four sides slope upwards, the narrow towards the top."

"I confess all this interests me a good deal," said Dyson. "Let us
go on then. What about the other figures; how about the Army, as we
may call the first sign, and the Crescent or Half-moon?"

"Ah, there is no reference that I can make out of these two. Still,
you see I have some excuse for curiosity at all events. I should be very
vexed to lose any of the old plate; nearly all the pieces have been in the
family for generations. And I cannot get it out of my head that some
scoundrels mean to rob me, and are communicating with one another
every night."

"Frankly," said Dyson, "I can make nothing of it; I am as much in
the dark as yourself. Your theory seems certainly the only possible explanation, and yet the difficulties are immense."

He leaned back in his chair, and the two men faced each other,
frowning, and perplexed by so bizarre a problem.

"By the way," said Dyson, after a long pause, "what is your geological formation down there?"

Mr. Vaughan looked up, a good deal surprised by the question.

"Old red sandstone and limestone, I believe," he said. "We are just
beyond the coal measures, you know."

"But surely there are no flints either in the sandstone or the limestone?"

"No, I never see any flints in the fields. I confess that did strike me as a little curious."

"I should think so! It is very important. By the way, what size were the flints used in making these devices?"

"I happen to have brought one with me; I took it this morning."

"From the Half-moon?"

"Exactly. Here it is."

He handed over a small flint, tapering to a point, and about three inches in length.

Dyson's face blazed up with excitement as he took the thing from Vaughan.

"Certainly," he said, after a moment's pause, "you have some curious neighbours in your country. I hardly think they can harbour any designs on your punch-bowl. Do you know this is a flint arrow-head of vast antiquity, and not only that, but an arrow-head of a unique kind? I have seen specimens from all parts of the world, but there are features about this thing that are quite peculiar."

He laid down his pipe, and took out a book from a drawer.

"We shall just have time to catch the 5.45 to Castletown," he said.

II
THE EYES ON THE WALL

Mr. Dyson drew in a long breath of the air of the hills and felt all the enchantment of the scene about him. It was very early morning, and he stood on the terrace in the front of the house. Vaughan's ancestor had built on the lower slope of a great hill, in the shelter of a deep and ancient wood that gathered on three sides about the house, and on the fourth side, the south-west, the land fell gently away and sank to the valley, where a brook wound in and out in mystic esses, and the dark and gleaming alders tracked the stream's course to the eye. On the terrace in that sheltered place no wind blew, and far beyond, the trees were still. Only one sound broke in upon the silence, and Dyson heard the noise of the brook singing far below, the song of clear and shining water rippling over the stones, whispering and murmuring as it sank to dark deep pools. Across the stream, just below the house, rose a grey stone bridge, vaulted and buttressed, a fragment of the Middle Ages, and then beyond the bridge the hills rose again, vast and rounded like bastions, covered here and there with dark woods and thickets of undergrowth, but the heights were all bare of trees, shewing only grey turf and patches of bracken, touched here and there with the gold of fading fronds. Dyson looked to the north and south, and still he saw the wall of the hills, and the ancient woods, and the stream drawn in and out between them; all grey and dim with morning mist beneath a grey sky in a hushed and haunted air.

Mr. Vaughan's voice broke in upon the silence.

"I thought you would be too tired to be about so early," he said. "I see you are admiring the view. It is very pretty, isn't it, though I suppose old Meyrick Vaughan didn't think much about the scenery when he built the house. A queer grey, old place, isn't it?"

"Yes, and how it fits into the surroundings; if seems of a piece with the grey hills and the grey bridge below."

"I am afraid I have brought you down on false pretences, Dyson," said Vaughan, as they began to walk up and down the terrace. "I have been to the place, and there is not a sign of anything this morning."

"Ah, indeed. Well, suppose we go round together."

They walked across the lawn and went by a path through the ilex shrubbery to the back of the house. There Vaughan pointed out the track leading down to the valley and up to the heights above the wood, and presently they stood beneath the garden wall, by the door.

"Here, you see, it was," said Vaughan, pointing to a spot on the turf. "I was standing just where you are now that morning I first saw the flints."

"Yes, quite so. That morning it was the Army, as I call it; then the Bowl, then the Pyramid, and, yesterday, the Half-moon. What a queer old stone that is," he went on, pointing to a block of limestone rising out of the turf just beneath the wall. "It looks like a sort of dwarf pillar, but I suppose it is natural."

"Oh, yes, I think so. I imagine it was brought here, though, as we stand on the red sandstone. No doubt it was used as a foundation stone for some older building."

"Very likely." Dyson was peering about him attentively, looking from the ground to the wall, and from the wall to the deep wood that hung almost over the garden and made the place dark even in the morning.

"Look here," said Dyson at length, "it is certainly a case of children this time. Look at that."

He was bending down and staring at the dull red surface of the mellowed bricks of the wall. Vaughan came up and looked hard where Dyson's finger was pointing, and could scarcely distinguish a faint mark in deeper red.

"What is it?" he said. "I can make nothing of it."

"Look a little more closely. Don't you see it is an attempt to draw the human eye?"

"Ah, now I see what you mean. My sight is not very sharp. Yes, so it is, it is meant for an eye, no doubt, as you say. I thought the children learnt drawing at school."

"Well, it is an odd eye enough. Do you notice the peculiar almond shape; almost like the eye of a Chinaman?"

Dyson looked meditatively at the work of the undeveloped artist, and scanned the wall again, going down on his knees in the minuteness of his inquisition.

"I should like very much," he said at length, "to know how a child in this out of the way place could have any idea of the shape of the Mongolian eye. You see the average child has a very distinct impression of the subject; he draws a circle, or something like a circle, and puts a dot in the centre. I don't think any child imagines that the eye is really made like that; it's just a convention of infantile art. But this almond-shaped thing puzzles me extremely. Perhaps it may be derived from a gilt Chinaman on a tea-canister in the grocer's shop. Still that's hardly likely."

"But why are you so sure it was done by a child?"

"Why! Look at the height. These old-fashioned bricks are little more than two inches thick; there are twenty courses from the ground to the sketch if we call it so; that gives a height of three and a half feet. Now, just imagine you are going to draw something on this wall. Exactly; your pencil, if you had one, would touch the wall somewhere on the level with your eyes, that is, more than five feet from the ground. It seems, therefore, a very simple deduction to conclude that this eye on the wall was drawn by a child about ten years old."

"Yes, I had not thought of that. Of course one of the children must have done it."

"I suppose so; and yet as I said, there is something singularly un-childlike about those two lines, and the eyeball itself, you see, is almost an oval. To my mind, the thing has an odd, ancient air; and a touch that is not altogether pleasant. I cannot help fancying that if we could see a whole face from the same hand it would not be altogether agreeable. However, that is nonsense, after all, and we are not getting farther in our investigations. It is odd that the flint series has come to such an abrupt end."

The two men walked away towards the house, and as they went in at the porch there was a break in the grey sky, and a gleam of sunshine on the grey hill before them.

All the day Dyson prowled meditatively about the fields surrounding the house. He was thoroughly and completely puzzled by the trivial circumstances he proposed to elucidate, and now he again took the flint arrow-head from his pocket, turning it over and examining it with deep attention. There was something about the thing that was altogether different from the specimens he had seen at the museums and private collections; the shape was of a distinct type, and around the edge there was a line of little punctured dots, apparently a suggestion of ornament. Who, thought Dyson, could possess such things in so remote a place; who, possessing the flints, could have put them to the fantastic use of designing meaningless figures under Vaughan's garden wall? The rank absurdity of the whole affair offended him unutterably; and as one theory after another rose in his mind only to be rejected, he felt strongly tempted to take the next train back to town. He had seen the silver plate which Vaughan treasured, and had inspected the punch-bowl, the gem of the collection, with close attention; and what he saw and his interview with the butler convinced him that a plot to rob the strong box was out of the limits of enquiry. The chest in which the bowl was kept, a heavy piece of mahogany, evidently dating from the beginning of the century, was certainly strongly suggestive of a pyramid, and Dyson was at first inclined to the inept manœuvres of the detective, but a little sober thought convinced him of the impossibility of the burglary hypothesis, and he cast wildly about for something more satisfying. He asked Vaughan if there were any gypsies in the neighbourhood, and heard that the Romany had not been seen for years. This dashed him a good deal, as he knew the gypsy habit of leaving queer hieroglyphics on the line of march, and had been much elated when the thought occurred to him. He was facing Vaughan by the old-fashioned hearth when he put the question, and leaned back in his chair in disgust at the destruction of his theory.

"It is odd," said Vaughan, "but the gypsies never trouble us here. Now and then the farmers find traces of fires in the wildest part of the hills, but nobody seems to know who the fire-lighters are."

"Surely that looks like gypsies?"

"No, not in such places as those. Tinkers and gypsies and wanderers of all sorts stick to the roads and don't go very far from the farm-houses."

"Well, I can make nothing of it. I saw the children going by this afternoon, and, as you say, they ran straight on. So we shall have no more eyes on the wall at all events."

"No, I must waylay them one of these days and find out who is the artist."

The next morning when Vaughan strolled in his usual course from the lawn to the back of the house he found Dyson already awaiting him by the garden door, and evidently in a state of high excitement, for he beckoned furiously with his hand, and gesticulated violently.

"What is it?" asked Vaughan. "The flints again?"

"No; but look here, look at the wall. There; don't you see it?"

"There's another of those eyes!"

"Exactly. Drawn, you see, at a little distance from the first, almost on the same level, but slightly lower."

"What on earth is one to make of it? It couldn't have been done by the children; it wasn't there last night, and they won't pass for another hour. What can it mean?"

"I think the very devil is at the bottom of all this," said Dyson. "Of course, one cannot resist the conclusion that these infernal almond eyes are to be set down to the same agency as the devices in the arrow-heads; and where that conclusion is to lead us is more than I can tell. For my part, I have to put a strong check on my imagination, or it will run wild."

"Vaughan," he said as they turned away from the wall, "has it struck you that there is one point—a very curious point—in common between the figures done in flints and the eyes drawn on the wall?"

"What is that?" asked Vaughan, on whose face there had fallen a certain shadow of indefinite dread.

"It is this. We know that the signs of the Army, the Bowl, the Pyramid, and the Half-moon must have been done at night. Presumably they were meant to be seen at night. Well, precisely the same reasoning applies to those eyes on the wall."

"I do not quite see your point."

"Oh, surely. The nights are dark just now, and have been very cloudy, I know, since I came down. Moreover, those overhanging trees would throw that wall into deep shadow even on a clear night."

"Well?"

"What struck me was this. What very peculiarly sharp eyesight, they, whoever 'they' are, must have to be able to arrange arrow-heads in intricate order in the blackest shadow of the wood, and then draw the eyes on the wall without a trace of bungling, or a false line."

"I have read of persons confined in dungeons for many years who have been able to see quite well in the dark," said Vaughan.

"Yes," said Dyson, "there was the abbé in *Monte Cristo*. But it is a singular point."

III

THE SEARCH FOR THE BOWL

"Who was that old man that touched his hat to you just now?" said Dyson, as they came to the bend of the lane near the house.

"Oh, that was old Trevor. He looks very broken, poor old fellow."

"Who is Trevor?"

"Don't you remember? I told you the story that afternoon I came to your rooms—about a girl named Annie Trevor, who disappeared in the most inexplicable manner about five weeks ago. That was her father."

"Yes, yes, I recollect now. To tell the truth I had forgotten all about it. And nothing has been heard of the girl?"

"Nothing whatever. The police are quite at fault."

"I am afraid I did not pay very much attention to the details you gave me. Which way did the girl go?"

"Her path would take her right across those wild hills above the house; the nearest point in the track must be about two miles from here."

"Is it near that little hamlet I saw yesterday?"

"You mean Croesyceiliog, where the children came from? No; it goes more to the north."

"Ah, I have never been that way."

They went into the house, and Dyson shut himself up in his room, sunk deep in doubtful thought, but yet with the shadow of a suspicion growing within him that for a while haunted his brain, all vague and fantastic, refusing to take definite form. He was sitting by the open window and looking out on the valley and saw, as if in a picture, the intricate winding of the brook, the grey bridge, and the vast hills rising beyond; all still and without a breath of wind to stir the mystic hanging woods, and the evening sunshine glowed warm on the bracken, and down below a faint mist, pure white, began to rise from the stream. Dyson sat by the window as the day darkened and the huge bastioned hills loomed vast and vague, and the woods became dim and more shadowy; and the fancy that had seized him no longer appeared altogether impossible. He passed the rest of the evening in a reverie, hardly hearing what Vaughan said; and when he took his candle in the hall, he paused a moment before bidding his friend good-night.

"I want a good rest," he said. "I have got some work to do to-morrow."

"Some writing, you mean?"

"No. I am going to look for the Bowl."

"The Bowl! If you mean my punch-bowl, that is safe in the chest."

"I don't mean the punch-bowl. You may take my word for it that your plate has never been threatened. No; I will not bother you with any suppositions. We shall in all probability have something much stronger than suppositions before long. Good-night, Vaughan."

The next morning Dyson set off after breakfast. He took the path by the garden-wall, and noted that there were now eight of the weird almond eyes dimly outlined on the brick.

"Six days more," he said to himself, but as he thought over the theory he had formed, he shrank, in spite of strong conviction, from such a wildly incredible fancy. He struck up through the dense shadows of the wood, and at length came out on the bare hillside, and climbed higher and higher over the slippery turf, keeping well to the north, and following the indications given him by Vaughan. As he went on, he seemed to mount ever higher above the world of human life and customary things; to his right he looked at a fringe of orchard and saw a faint blue smoke rising like a pillar; there was the hamlet from which the children came to school, and there the only sign of life, for the woods embowered and concealed Vaughan's old grey house. As he reached what seemed the summit of the hill, he realised for the first time the desolate loneliness and strangeness of the land; there was nothing but grey sky and grey hill, a high, vast plain that seemed to stretch on for ever and ever, and a faint glimpse of a blue-peaked mountain far away and to the north. At length he came to the path, a slight track scarcely noticeable, and from its position and by what Vaughan had told him he knew that it was the way the lost girl, Annie Trevor, must have taken. He followed the path on the bare hill-top, noticing the great limestone rocks that cropped out of the turf, grim and hideous, and of an aspect as forbidding as an idol of the South Seas; and suddenly he halted, astonished, although he had found what he searched for. Almost without warning the ground shelved suddenly away on all sides, and Dyson looked down into a circular depression, which might well have been a Roman amphitheatre, and the ugly crags of limestone rimmed it round as if with a broken wall. Dyson walked round the hollow, and noted the position of the stones, and then turned on his way home.

"This," he thought to himself, "is more than curious. The Bowl is discovered, but where is the Pyramid?"

"My dear Vaughan," he said, when he got back, "I may tell you that I have found the Bowl, and that is all I shall tell you for the present. We have six days of absolute inaction before us; there is really nothing to be done."

IV

THE SECRET OF THE PYRAMID

"I have just been round the garden," said Vaughan one morning. "I have been counting those infernal eyes, and I find there are fourteen of them. For heaven's sake, Dyson, tell me what the meaning of it all is."

"I should be very sorry to attempt to do so. I may have guessed this or that, but I always make it a principle to keep my guesses to myself. Besides, it is really not worth while anticipating events; you will remember my telling you that we had six days of inaction before us? Well, this is the sixth day, and the last of idleness. To-night I propose we take a stroll."

"A stroll! Is that all the action you mean to take?"

"Well, it may shew you some very curious things. To be plain, I want you to start with me at nine o'clock this evening for the hills. We may have to be out all night, so you had better wrap up well, and bring some of that brandy."

"Is it a joke?" asked Vaughan, who was bewildered with strange events and strange surmises.

"No, I don't think there is much joke in it. Unless I am much mistaken we shall find a very serious explanation of the puzzle. You will come with me, I am sure?"

"Very good. Which way do you want to go?"

"By the path you told me of; the path Annie Trevor is supposed to have taken."

Vaughan looked white at the mention of the girl's name.

"I did not think you were on that track," he said. "I thought it was the affair of those devices in flint and of the eyes on the wall that you were engaged on. It's no good saying any more, but I will go with you."

At a quarter to nine that evening the two men set out, taking the path through the wood, and up the hill-side. It was a dark and heavy night, and the sky was thick with clouds, and the valley full of mist, and all the way they seemed to walk in a world of shadow and gloom, hardly speaking, and afraid to break the haunted silence. They came out at last on the steep hill-side, and instead of the oppression of the wood there was the long, dim sweep of the turf, and higher, the fantastic limestone rocks hinted horror through the darkness, and the wind sighed as it passed across the mountain to the sea, and in its passage beat chill about their hearts. They seemed to walk on and on for hours, and the dim outline of the hill still stretched before them, and the haggard rocks still loomed through the darkness, when suddenly Dyson whispered, drawing his breath quickly, and coming close to his companion.

"Here," he said, "we will lie down. I do not think there is anything yet."

"I know the place," said Vaughan, after a moment. "I have often been by in the daytime. The country people are afraid to come here, I believe; it is supposed to be a fairies' castle, or something of the kind. But why on earth have we come here?"

"Speak a little lower," said Dyson. "It might not do us any good if we are overheard."

"Overheard here! There is not a soul within three miles of us."

"Possibly not; indeed, I should say certainly not. But there might be a body somewhat nearer."

"I don't understand you in the least," said Vaughan, whispering to humour Dyson, "but why have we come here?"

"Well, you see this hollow before us is the Bowl. I think we had better not talk even in whispers."

They lay full length upon the turf; the rock between their faces and the Bowl, and now and again, Dyson, slouching his dark, soft hat over his forehead, put out the glint of an eye, and in a moment drew back, not daring to take a prolonged view. Again he laid an ear to the ground and listened, and the hours went by, and the darkness seemed to blacken, and the faint sign of the wind was the only sound.

Vaughan grew impatient with this heaviness of silence, this watching for indefinite terror; for to him there was no shape or form of apprehension, and he began to think the whole vigil a dreary farce.

"How much longer is this to last?" he whispered to Dyson, and Dyson who had been holding his breath in the agony of attention put his mouth to Vaughan's ear and said:

"Will you listen?" with pauses between each syllable, and in the voice with which the priest pronounces the awful words.

Vaughan caught the ground with his hands, and stretched forward, wondering what he was to hear. At first there was nothing, and then a low and gentle noise came very softly from the Bowl, a faint sound, almost indescribable, but as if one held the tongue against the roof of the mouth and expelled the breath. He listened eagerly and presently the noise grew louder, and became a strident and horrible hissing as if the pit beneath boiled with fervent heat, and Vaughan, unable to remain in suspense any longer, drew his cap half over his face in imitation of Dyson, and looked down to the hollow below.

It did, in truth, stir and seethe like an infernal caldron. The whole of the sides and bottom tossed and writhed with vague and restless forms that passed to and fro without the sound of feet, and gathered thick here and there and seemed to speak to one another in those tones of horrible sibilance, like the hissing of snakes, that he had heard. It was as if the sweet turf and the cleanly earth had suddenly become quickened with some foul writhing growth. Vaughan could not draw back his face, though he felt Dyson's finger touch him, but he peered into the quaking mass and saw faintly that there were things like faces and human limbs, and yet he felt his inmost soul chill with the sure belief that no fellow soul or human thing stirred in all that tossing and hissing host. He looked aghast, choking back sobs of horror, and at length the loathsome forms gathered thickest about some vague object in the middle of the hollow, and the hissing of their speech grew more venomous, and he saw in the uncertain light the abominable limbs, vague and yet too plainly seen, writhe and intertwine, and he thought he heard, very faint, a low human moan striking through the noise of speech that was not of man. At his heart something seemed to whisper ever "the worm of corruption, the worm that dieth not", and grotesquely the image was pictured to his imagination of a piece of putrid offal stirring through and through with bloated and horrible creeping things. The writhing of the dusky limbs continued, they seemed clustered round the dark form in the middle of the hollow, and the sweat dripped and poured off Vaughan's forehead, and fell cold on his hand beneath his face.

Then, it seemed done in an instant, the loathsome mass melted and fell away to the sides of the Bowl, and for a moment Vaughan saw in the middle of the hollow the tossing of human arms. But a spark gleamed beneath, a fire kindled, and as the voice of a woman cried out loud in a shrill scream of utter anguish and terror, a great pyramid of flame spired up like a bursting of a pent fountain, and threw a blaze of light upon the whole mountain. In that instant Vaughan saw the myriads beneath; the things made in the form of men but stunted like children hideously deformed, the faces with the almond eyes burning with evil and unspeakable lusts; the ghastly yellow of the mass of naked flesh; and then as if by magic the place was empty, while the fire roared and crackled, and the flames shone abroad.

"You have seen the Pyramid," said Dyson in his ear, "the Pyramid of fire."

V

THE LITTLE PEOPLE

"Then you recognise the thing?"

"Certainly. It is a brooch that Annie Trevor used to wear on Sundays; I remember the pattern. But where did you find it? You don't mean to say that you have discovered the girl?"

"My dear Vaughan, I wonder you have not guessed where I found the brooch. You have not forgotten last night already?"

"Dyson," said the other, speaking very seriously, "I have been turning it over in my mind this morning while you have been out. I have thought about what I saw, or perhaps I should say about what I thought I saw, and the only conclusion I can come to is this, that the thing won't bear recollection. As men live, I have lived soberly and honestly, in the fear of God, all my days, and all I can do is believe that I suffered from some monstrous delusion, from some phantasmagoria of the bewildered senses. You know we went home together in silence, not a word passed between us as to what I fancied I saw; had we not better agree to keep silence on the subject? When I took my walk in the peaceful morning sunshine, I thought all the earth seemed full of praise, and passing by that wall I noticed there were no more signs recorded, and I blotted out those that remained. The mystery is over, and we can live quietly again. I think some poison has been working for the last few weeks; I have trod on the verge of madness, but I am sane now."

Mr. Vaughan had spoken earnestly, and bent forward in his chair and glanced at Dyson with something of entreaty.

"My dear Vaughan," said the other, after a pause, "what's the use of this? It is much too late to take that tone; we have gone too deep. Besides you know as well as I that there is no delusion in the case; I wish there were with all my heart. No, in justice to myself I must tell you the whole story, so far as I know it."

"Very good," said Vaughan with a sigh, "if you must, you must."

"Then," said Dyson, "we will begin with the end if you please. I found this brooch you have just identified in the place we have called the Bowl. There was a heap of grey ashes, as if a fire had been burning, indeed, the embers were still hot, and this brooch was lying on the ground, just outside the range of the flame. It must have dropped accidentally from the dress of the person who was wearing it. No, don't interrupt me; we can pass now to the beginning, as we have had the end. Let us go back to that day you came to see me in my rooms in London. So far as I can remember, soon after you came in you mentioned, in a somewhat casual manner, that an unfortunate and mysterious incident had occurred in your part of the country; a girl named Annie Trevor had gone to see a relative, and had disappeared. I confess freely that what you said did not greatly interest me; there are so many reasons which may make it extremely convenient for a man and more especially a woman to vanish from the circle of their relations and friends. I suppose, if we were to consult the police, one would find that in London somebody disappears mysteriously every other week, and the officers would, no doubt, shrug their shoulders, and tell you that by the law of averages it could not be otherwise. So I was very culpably careless to your story, and besides, there is another reason for my lack of interest; your tale was inexplicable. You could only suggest a blackguard sailor on the tramp, but I discarded the explanation immediately. For many reasons, but chiefly because the occasional criminal, the amateur in brutal crime, is always found out, especially if he selects the country as the scene of his operations. You will remember the case of that Garcia you mentioned; he strolled into a railway station the day after the murder, his trousers covered with blood, and the works of the Dutch clock, his loot, tied in a neat parcel. So rejecting this, your only suggestion, the whole tale became, as I say, inexplicable, and, therefore, profoundly uninteresting. Yes, *therefore,* it is a perfectly valid conclusion. Do you ever trouble your head about problems which you know to be insoluble? Did you ever bestow much thought on the old puzzle of Achilles and the Tortoise? Of course not, because you knew it was a hopeless quest, and so when you told me the story of a country girl who had disappeared I simply placed the whole thing down in the category of the insoluble, and thought no more about the matter. I was mistaken, so it has turned out; but if you remember, you immediately passed on to an affair which interested you more intensely, because personally. I need not go over the very singular narrative of the flint signs; at first I thought it all trivial, probably some children's game, and if not that a hoax of some sort; but your shewing me the arrow-head awoke my acute interest. Here, I saw, there was something widely removed from the commonplace, and matter of real curiosity; and as soon as I came here I set to work to find the solution, repeating to myself again and again the signs you had described. First came the sign we have agreed to call the Army; a number of serried lines of flints, all pointing in the same way. Then the lines, like the spokes of a wheel, all converging towards the figure of a Bowl, then the triangle or Pyramid, and last of all the Half-moon. I confess that I exhausted conjecture in my efforts to unveil this mystery, and as you will understand it was a duplex or rather triplex problem. For I had not merely to ask myself: what do these figures mean? but also, who can possibly be responsible for the designing of them? And again, who can possibly possess such valuable things, and knowing their value thus throw them down by the wayside? This line of thought led me to suppose that the person or persons in question did not know the value of unique flint arrow-heads, and yet this did not lead me far, for a well-educated man might easily be ignorant on such a subject. Then came the complication of the eye on the wall, and you remember that we could not avoid the conclusion that in the two cases the same agency was at work. The peculiar position of these eyes on the wall made me enquire if there was such a thing as a dwarf anywhere in the neighbourhood, but I found that there was not, and I knew that the children who pass by every day had nothing to do with the matter. Yet I felt convinced that whoever drew the eyes must be from three-and-a-half to four feet high, since, as I pointed out at the time, any one who draws on a perpendicular surface chooses by instinct a spot about level with his face. Then again, there was the question of the peculiar shape of the eyes; that marked Mongolian character of which the English countryman could have no conception, and for a final cause of confusion the obvious fact that the designer or designers must be able practically to see in the dark. As you remarked, a man who has been confined for many years in an extremely dark cell or dungeon might acquire that power; but since the days of Edmond Dantès, where would such it person be found in Europe? A sailor, who had been immured for a considerable period in some horrible Chinese *oubliette,* seemed the individual I was in search of, and though it looked improbable, it was not absolutely impossible that a sailor or, let us say, a man employed on shipboard, should be a dwarf. But how to account for my imaginary sailor being in possession of prehistoric arrow-heads? And the possession granted, what was the meaning and object of these mysterious signs of flint, and the almond-shaped eyes? Your theory of a contemplated burglary I saw, nearly from the first, to be quite untenable, and I confess I was utterly at a loss for a working hypothesis. It was a mere accident which put me on the track; we passed poor old Trevor, and your mention of his name and of the disappearance of his daughter, recalled the story which I had forgotten, or which remained unheeded. Here, then, I said to myself, is another problem, uninteresting, it is true, by itself; but what if it prove to be in relation with all these enigmas which torture me? I shut myself in my room, and endeavoured to dismiss all prejudice from my mind, and I went over everything *de novo,* assuming for theory's sake that the disappearance of Annie Trevor had some connection with the flint signs and the eyes on the wall. This assumption did not lead me very far, and I was on the point of giving the whole problem up in despair, when a possible significance of the Bowl struck me. As you know there is a 'Devil's Punch-bowl' in Surrey, and I saw that the symbol might refer to some feature in the country. Putting the two extremes together, I determined to look for the Bowl near the path which the lost girl had taken, and you know how I found it. I interpreted the sign by what I knew, and read the first, the Army, thus: 'there is to be a gathering or assembly at the Bowl in a fortnight (that is the Half-moon) to see the Pyramid, or to build the Pyramid.' The eyes, drawn one by one, day by day, evidently checked off the days, and I knew that there would be fourteen and no more. Thus far the way seemed pretty plain; I would not trouble myself to enquire as to the nature of the assembly, or as to who was to assemble in the loneliest and most dreaded place among these lonely hills. In Ireland or China or the west of America the question would have been easily answered; a muster of the disaffected, the meeting of a secret society, Vigilantes summoned to report: the thing would be simplicity itself; but in this quiet corner of England, inhabited by quiet folk, no such suppositions were possible for a moment. But I knew that I should have an opportunity of seeing and watching the assembly, and I did not care to perplex myself with hopeless research; and in place of reasoning a wild fancy entered into judgment: I remembered what people had said about Annie Trevor's disappearance, that she had been 'taken by the fairies'. I tell you, Vaughan, I am a sane man as you are, my brain is not, I trust, mere vacant space to let to any wild improbability, and I tried my best to thrust the fantasy away. And the hint came of the old name of fairies, 'the little people', and the very probable belief that they represent a tradition of the prehistoric Turanian inhabitants of the country, who were cave dwellers: and then I realised with a shock that I was looking for a being under four feet in height, accustomed to live in darkness, possessing stone instruments, and familiar with the Mongolian cast of features! I say this, Vaughan, that I should be ashamed to hint at such visionary stuff to you, if it were not for that which you saw with your very eyes last night, and I say that I might doubt the evidence of my senses, if they were not confirmed by yours. But you and I cannot look each other in the face and pretend delusion; as you lay on the turf beside me I felt your flesh shrink and quiver, and I saw your eyes in the light of the flame. And so I tell you without any shame what was in my mind last night as we went through the wood and climbed the hill, and lay hidden beneath the rock.

"There was one thing that should have been most evident that puzzled me to the very last. I told you how I read the sign of the Pyramid; the assembly was to see a pyramid, and the true meaning of the symbol escaped me to the last moment. The old derivation from πυρ, fire, though false, should have set me on the track, but it never occurred to me.

"I think I need say very little more. You know we were quite help-less, even if we had foreseen what was to come. Ah, the particular place where these signs were displayed? Yes, that is a curious question. But this house is, so far as I can judge, in a pretty central situation amongst the hills; and possibly, who can say yes or no, that queer, old limestone pillar by your garden wall was a place of meeting before the Celt set foot in Britain. But there is one thing I must add: I don't regret our inability to rescue the wretched girl. You saw the appearance of those things that gathered thick and writhed in the Bowl; you may be sure that what lay bound in the midst of them was no longer fit for earth."

"So?" said Vaughan.

"So she passed in the Pyramid of Fire," said Dyson, "and they passed again to the under-world, to the places beneath the hills."

Appendix

Folklore and Legends of the North

The ideas of Aristotle became the fixed ideas of the Middle Ages. This was well enough in logic, but in physics it was a bar to all progress, and the poverty, or rather the nullity, of the mediæval chemistry and biology is the only excuse for the ignorant epithet "dark" applied to ages which contained some of the acutest thinkers that the world has ever seen. In sciences which are tentative and depend upon research and enquiry there must be no axioms, and no infallible pronouncements; if men of science had certainly believed that a deal board was impervious to light, we should never have seen the shadow-pictures of the unknown rays. This horror of the axiom is well established in the minds of those who deal with the sensible properties of matter, but when we cross the boundary and try to trace the secrets of the soul, we find ourselves at once in the intellectual atmosphere of the Aristotelian tyranny of the Middle Ages. The curious may study early consciousness, beliefs, and legends as deeply as they please—on the condition that they bear in mind the axiom that the unusual never happens, that the supernatural (or supernormal) does not exist, and never has existed.

Unfortunately, Mr. Léon Pineau, the author of the learned and entertaining *Les Vieux Chants Populaires Scandinaves* (Émile Bouillon, Paris, 10f.), has given in his fullest adhesion to this scientific dogma. The first *fasciculus* of the work, which is before us, has for its subject the Magical Songs of the "Époque Sauvage"; and the book, besides being a study in comparative literature, is also a history of Northern folk-lore, and more particularly of the stories of transformation. M. Pineau lays down the laws of the primordial consciousness in an elaborate preface. Here is his demonstration. In the beginning primitive man had one and only one object—the struggle for life. Those who fought against him in this struggle were other men—and animals. *Therefore*, he came to the conclusion that there was no distinction between animal and human con-

sciousness, and he naturally called himself by the name of some animal. Hence arose the "tribe of the Wolfs", and hence, in process of
time, totemism, the belief that this tribe was descended from a wolf.
Indeed, the author has heard a farmer's wife in Touraine talking to her
goat as if it could understand her; *therefore,* this belief of animal descent
still exists. Later, man discovered that he had a "double", a soul, and
so, of course, had animals, since animals and men are the same, and
since for primitive man all things are animated, not only animals, but
stars and rocks and winds have "doubles" also. Next, primitive man
dreamed a dream; his double had gone abroad. No doubt animals and
trees and the sun had similar experiences; *therefore,* there were wandering doubles everywhere, and by consequence a man might find himself
turned into an animal. This, briefly, is the theory on which the author
explains every song, every legend, and every belief that he encounters
in his Scandinavian researches. Later, in the book, it is true, we find
traces of "sun myth", and "corruption of language"; but these are, in
the phrase of the geologists, mere "traces", and the whole work is vir-
tually founded on the above analysis of the primitive consciousness. It
will be seen that M. Pineau inclines rather to the doctrine of Mr. Andrew Lang than to that of Mr. Herbert Spencer, since he apparently
holds animism to be part of the original human thought, but we find
no indication of Mr. Lang's fruitful suggestion that myths are the result
of misunderstood ritual.

Now, although there are links in M. Pineau's chain of argument
that seem weak, yet there is no doubt a good deal to be said for his position. It is possible that sometimes our early ancestor, having formed
designs against a hare, found himself thwarted by a bear; it is possible
that he argued from this that the bear was a creature of like passions
with himself, capable of similar designs and of superior strategy.

But M. Pineau has only one explanation for the strange beliefs of
early man—a series of hazardous deductions from uncertain premiss-
es. Mr. Herbert Spencer tells us that primitive man came on earth sane,
and without delusions of an animistic kind, but that afterwards he
dreamed and entangled himself in a mesh of vain superstitions. Mr.
Andrew Lang says that from the first man was an animist, and he
thinks that a wild belief was strengthened by the occurrence of "hallu-
cinations" of the dead and the living. One need hardly trouble to men-

tion the good old teaching of the eighteenth century and the rationalists—that everything was invented by the art of crafty priests trading on the simplicity of a clear-headed and virtuous people; and, perhaps, the "sun myth" and the "corruption of language" theories are more extinct than the superstitions which they professed to elucidate.

But are any or all of these explanations adequate? Does any one of them cover the whole field of legend and belief?

Let us take an example from the work of M. Pineau. He lays stress on the peculiar importance of the "runes" in Northern folk-lore; by runes and runic art all the marvels are achieved, by them the lover wins his mistress, by runic charms the ship is brought safe into the haven or overwhelmed by the storm, by runes the good sword kills, by runes the maiden becomes a deer amidst the woods. And the runes, it seems agreed, were the mystery of the dwarfs; again and again we meet the daughter of the dwarf-king by a Christian mother, who teaches her lover the magic art of those potent letters and words. M. Pineau, very properly, interprets these dwarfs to mean the aboriginal Turanian race which inhabited Europe before the coming of the Aryans, and passes on, without dwelling on the subject. But can we not get more out of the dwarfs? Every one is aware of the great part played by the fairies in old legend, and in spite of the "literary" fairy, the tricksy elf of Shakespeare, and the minor divinity, sometimes benevolent and sometimes maleficent, of Perrault, there yet survives in Ireland the older conception of the "good people", the "fair folk", who must be given a pleasant name precisely because they are evil. Of recent years abundant proof has been given that a short, non-Aryan race once dwelt beneath ground, in hillocks, throughout Europe, their raths have been explored, and the weird old tales of green hills all lighted up at night have received confirmation. Much in the old legends may be explained by a reference to this primitive race. The stories of changelings, and captive women, become clear on the supposition that the "fairies" occasionally raided the houses of the invaders. And M. Pineau, after saying that everything in Scandinavian folk-lore is effected by runes, admits that the runes came from the dwarfs. We might deduce the whole mythology from a confused recollection of the relations existing between the tall Aryans and the short Turanians, but how fallacious such an explanation would be! No doubt the fairies count for something. The ballad of Sir Tœnne of Alsoe, for example, may very well be a poetical and decorated account of an event which really happened when the "good folk" inhabited the lonely rounded hillocks, and haunted the remotest recesses of the forest. One day, the song tells, Sir Tœnne went hunting in the woods, and there encountered the "daughter of the dwarf", surrounded by her maidens. She took her harp, and began to "play the runes".

> And the harp sang afar
> And the wild world of the wood was still,
> And the bird upon the bough left his lay,
> And the little hawk high in the hedge
>   Fluttered his feathers.
> The field grew fair with flowers,
> And bright the boughs with leaves,
>   So strong sang the runes.
> Sir Tœnne spurred his steed,
> Yet he could not fare free.

The knight was obliged to follow the "dwarf" girl to the mountain (the fairy rath), where the "wife of the dwarf" tells him that she was born a Christian, and carried away by the dwarfs. To adopt the manner of the bard, the whole song may very well be sooth; such incidents may have often occurred in the early history of the Aryan invasion, and there are many of the old ballads and traditions which may be explained on similar grounds. But though all "magic" is worked by runes, and though the runes came from the fairies or "dwarfs", yet we must beware of making the "little people" responsible for all the marvels of story. M. Pineau forces the whole wonderland to rest on his somewhat doubtful argument as to the primitive consciousness; we must not let ourselves be entangled into following his example, and, above all, we must beware of M. Pineau's almost suppressed but all-pervading minor premiss—the supernormal never happens.

A large portion of the book deals with metamorphoses, with songs telling of how the princess was changed into a doe, how the wicked stepmother made her stepdaughter assume the form of a pair of scissors. That all such stories arose from the fact that primitive men, fighting with beasts, concluded that a beast and a man were the same thing, that after a few dreams they found out that not only all men but all beasts have doubles, and that not only beasts but all existence, from the sun to a sword, has its double, and therefore, since these "doubles" wandered away from their bodies, any one thing could be easily changed into any other thing appears to be an unthinkable proposition. We have said that the whole chain of argument seems so weak that, even if we allow M. Pineau's very doubtful deductions to stand good, there are many other factors which may have gone to the making of this curious superstition.

In the first place, "lycanthropy" is a fact of human nature. Men and women have actually been possessed by the belief that they are wolves or other animals, and they have, no doubt, acted on their delusion. In the old legends we are told that such a person was a woman by day and a wolf by night, and no doubt the "fit" which transformed the human being into a creature of blind ferocity, running on all fours, gnashing its teeth and tearing to pieces all whom it encountered, occurred when the darkness came on, at the hour in which all that is morbid in mind and body is strongest. The were-wolf, then, is not a superstition but a fact, and a fact which goes very far in clearing up the early belief in metamorphosis.

Secondly, the whole group of stories which deal with mermen, mermaids, Melusines and "ladies from the sea" may be explained in a manner which renders our author's theory quite superfluous. Mr. J. Russell-Jeaffreson, the author of *The Faröe Islands* (Sampson Low, 7s. 6d.), relates the legend of a man who went sealing, and hid himself by the shore.

> In the morning the seals came up on to the rocks. But what was his surprise on their landing to see them slip out of their skins and assume the form of very beautiful damsels.

We know how the story must proceed. The fisherman, of course, catches one of the seal-maidens before she can put on her skin, and takes her home and marries her, and they become the parents of a large family. The skin is kept carefully locked up by the husband, but one day he leaves the key at home, and the seal-wife returns to her old shape and her beloved element. The legend has been told again and again, but Mr. Jeaffreson's tale has a touch of actuality that is new, inasmuch as he was assured that the descendants of the mermaid were alive and had webbing between their fingers. Now this legend, and all legends that resemble it, may be clearly traced to the sea-going Lapps, who, covered with seal-skins, drove their canoes through the stormiest waters and sometimes visited, not only the Faröe Islands, but the coasts of Scotland. The seal-skin, which covered the man or woman, was attached to the boat and kept out of the water, and without this protection the Lapp was helpless.

Thirdly, there can be no doubt that the collective memory of the human race is a very long one. At the present day, in quiet Somerset and Derbyshire villages, there are women who follow the same arts, and, on some matters, think the same thoughts as the sorceresses of antique Babylon. The readers of Mr. Elworthy's admirable book on the "Evil Eye" will remember the instances of modern witchcraft, and the account of the horrible objects which have been found within the last ten years, hidden in the chimney-corners of witches' cottages. The methods of sorcery have not changed, the clay images are made as they have always been made, and here is a memory that goes back at least 6,000 years. If, then, the people of our modern England, surrounded by every hostile influence, have remembered the black art of Babylon, what shall we say of the memory of early man? For no doubt the singers of these Northern songs worked on old materials—one song may be the product of a hundred revisions. The earliest men of whom we know anything were artists, and scratched pictures of the creatures they hunted on horn, and where there is the art of line, there will be the art of literature; consequently, the earliest form of any given song may probably have been chanted by Palæolithic poets. And who shall put a limit to the dim and remote antiquity of which these old makers knew by a still older tradition? Is it not possible, and, indeed, probable, that these earliest inventors had an inherited memory of a time when men had scarcely emerged from the company and state of the beasts, when individuals, here and there, fell out of the great march of evolution and lapsed into the low condition from which they had scarcely risen? Here, then, is another cause which in all likelihood influenced the belief in the possibility of a man becoming an animal. So far as we are aware, no legend tells that a beast became human; though if M. Pineau's theory were satisfactory we should expect to find many instances of reversed metamorphosis. A princess may turn into a swan, but a swan never becomes a princess.

Fourthly, there may be the influence of the human consciousness. We know what strange, almost incredible, tricks the mind of man can play on itself; how children (those eternal "primitives") can "make believe"; how an actor can for the moment change his personality, how a dreamer may lose all idea of self-consciousness, and become another person, and, more rarely, an inanimate object; how a lunatic accomplishes for himself the wildest transmutations in idea. The imagination of primitive man, luxuriant to extravagance, and almost wholly unrestrained, must have been capable of feats of which we can form but a poor and inadequate conception.

And, lastly, there is hypnotic suggestion, called witchcraft by our ancestors, and the primitive hypnotist is, no doubt, responsible for many of the metamorphoses which startled the early community. And after we have allowed for all the sources, there still remains the great question of Montaigne—What do we know? Every day thinkers are becoming more and more convinced of the absurdity of saying that anything is impossible, every day it becomes clearer that the universe and man are mysteries. The Marquis of Lorne in *Adventures in Legend* (Constable, 6s.) tells of a recent case of undoubted "second-sight", the scene of which was at Loch Awe, close to a hotel, crowded every summer by tourists. A young man was drowned a year or two ago in the loch, and his body could not be recovered. At last an old woman in Perthshire, who had never seen the loch, was consulted, and by her vision and description of the loch and the islands the mother of the drowned lad succeeded in an extraordinary manner in obtaining the body. In a recent number of the *National Review*, Dr. Herbert Coryn gives the case of the lady who saw a heavy window-sash fall on three of her child's fingers, cutting them off. After dressing the wounds the surgeon turned to the mother, whom he found moaning and complaining of pain in the hand. "Three fingers corresponding to those injured in the child were discovered to be swollen and inflamed. Purulent sloughing set in." So a mental impression can affect the tissues of the flesh; and what is this but magic? And if this be possible in our late civilisation, what might not have been possible in the far-off ages which moulded the human consciousness? Let M. Pineau consider again all this matter of legend and magic. He will find, we believe, many marvels which his philosophy cannot explain, which cannot for a moment be understood in the light of his crude hypothesis. And as the "worms" and "dragons" of the ancient songs, and the "roc" of the Arabian tales are doubtless memories of the iguanadons and plesiosauri and pterodactyls, so the wildest myth may prove to be founded on a, perhaps, wilder reality.

Preface to "The Great God Pan" (1916)

The Great God Pan" was first published in December, 1894. So
the book is of full age, and I am glad to take the opportunity of
a new edition to recall those early 'nineties when the tale was
written and published—those 'nineties of which I was not even a small
part, but no part at all. For those were the days of "The Yellow Book",
of "Keynotes", and the "Keynotes Series", of Aubrey Beardsley and
"The Woman Who Did", of many portentous things in writing and
drawing and publishing. "The Great God Pan" had the good fortune
to issue from The Bodley Head, which was the centre of the whole
movement, and no doubt the book profited by the noise that the
movement was making. But this was in a sense an illegitimate profit;
since the story was conceived and written in solitude, and came from
far off lonely days spent in a land remote from London, and from literary societies and sodalities. So far as it stands for anything, it stands,
not for the ferment of the 'nineties, but for the visions that a little boy
saw in the late 'sixties and early 'seventies.

We all know the saying, *Si jeunesse savait*. I have respected it for
some years, and it is only lately that I have begun to have very grave
doubts as to the truth of the implied statement. "If only youth understood" . . . but I have a very strong suspicion that if youth did understand it would be as unprofitable and unfruitful as the most barren
years of old age. I believe that youth attains, so far as it does attain, just
because it does not understand. The logical understanding is the prison-
house of Wordsworth's supreme and magistral ode; it is the house of
prudent artifice, of the calculations of means to the end; it is the region
where things can be done by recipe, where effects are all foreseen and
intended. It is the house of matter and the house of mechanism. And
when youth does anything well or pretty well, it is because youth has
not wholly been overcast by the shadows of the prison-walls; it is be-

cause it does not understand. Nay; it is so even with age. Cervantes understood quite clearly that he was going to write a clever burlesque of the romances of chivalry, that he was going to make people laugh with a great deal of low comedy and broad farce and funny "business"; he understood, too, that he was to redeem his book from the charge of sheer vulgarity by inserting here and there some real literature, in the shape of certain elegant tales of sentiment and passion. He understood all this; but he did not in the least understand that he was to do something infinitely greater than all this; and so he did it and made "Don Quixote" a high, immortal masterpiece. This was the achievement of a youth recovered, of the happy state of ignorance restored; it is the clearest example that I know of the law that youth succeeds because it does not understand.

Here a horrible descent has to be made; so let it be made quickly. It is necessary to come down from the high and shining and remote peaks to the homely hillocks, in other words to explain how I came to write "The Great God Pan". I found out, long years afterwards, how it was done, how my effects were produced; but I am very certain that I understood nothing about the real origins and essences of the story while I was writing it. It all came from a lonely house standing on the slope of a hill, under a great wood, above a river in the country where I was born.

Llanddewi Rectory where I was bred looks out over a wonderful and enchanting country. The hill on which the house stands slopes down through apple orchards to a wild brake or thicket of undergrowth and bracken; in the heart of this little wood the well bubbles over and sends a brooklet to swell the Soar brook. Beyond the brake rising ground again, where Llanddewi Church stands amidst dark yews, age-old; hills rise higher to right and left of it, those to the right deeply wooded. I have often spent an afternoon gazing at the woods in summer weather, watching the sheen of the sun and the stirring of the wind on those nearest, and thinking of what Ulysses said of his dear Zacynthus "wooded, quivering with leaves". Then, beyond again, another height, Llanhenoc, and the distance was closed by the vast green wall of Wentwood, a remnant, still great, of the Wood of Gwent that once covered all the land of the lower Usk and the Wye. And just visible beneath this forest was the white of a house, which they told me was called Bertholly.

And for some reason, or for no reason, this house which stood on the boundaries and green walls of my young world became an object of mysterious attraction to me. It became one of the many symbols of the world of wonder that were offered to me, it became, as it were, a great word in the secret language by which the mysteries were communicated. I thought of it always with something of awe, even of dread; its appearance was significant of . . . I knew not what. Thus for many years; but I suppose I may have been twelve or thirteen when I saw Bertholly near at hand. My father had taken me to see a neighbouring clergyman who lived at a place called Tredonoc, and Tredonoc goes down to the banks of the Usk. On our way there we passed through a maze of hills and valleys, through woods, by deep lanes, by paths over sunken lands; we could see no distances. But after the call on the rector had been made, we went on a little and, cresting a slight hill, saw suddenly before us a dream of mystic beauty—the valley of the Usk. Still, after many years have passed, after many things have been broken for ever, I remember how it overwhelmed me and possessed me, as the soul is overwhelmed and subdued by the first kiss of the Beloved.

And there, under the great green of the forest, high above the mystic, silvery esses of the river was Bertholly, more inexplicable, more wonderful, more significant, the nearer it was seen.

Stevenson, I think, knew of the emotions which I am trying to express. To his mind the matter presented itself thus: there are certain scenes, certain hills and valleys and groves of pines which demand that a story shall be written about them. I would refine; I would say that the emotions aroused by these external things reverberating in the heart, are indeed the story; or all that signifies in the story. But, our craft being that of letters, we must express what we feel through the medium of words. And once words are granted, we fall into the region of the logical understanding, we are forced to devise incidents and circumstances and plots, to "make up a story"; we translate a hill into a tale, conceive lovers to explain a brook, turn the perfect into the imperfect. The musician must be happier in his art, if he be not the sorry slave of those sorry follies which mimic the lowing of cattle by some big brazen horn. The true musician exercises a perfect art; there is no descent into the logic of plots for him.

For me; these thoughts of Bertholly in the awe of the forest and the breath of the winding river remained through many years, as something to be expressed. And to these were joined the dream I had made to myself of Caerleon-on-Usk, the town where I was born, a very ancient place, once the home of the legions, the centre of an exiled Roman culture in the heart of Celtdom. I had seen a man looking at a bright gold coin that his gardener brought him from the making of a new fruit border. It shone in the sunlight: but there were eighteen hundred years upon it. I had seen the vase of glass, iridescent, wonderful as an opal, after those long centuries of sojourn in the earth, which, as they say, uttered sweet rich odours as it came up out of its deep aeonian grave. I had stood, dreaming under the mouldering remnants of the Roman city wall as the sun set red over Twyn Barlwm, I had noted the leering lineaments of Faunus built as an ornament into the wall of a modern house in Caerleon. In fine, there was a dream ever with me of the ancient city and the former rites that it had witnessed; with the old hills and the old woods a deep green circle about it. Such, I believe, were the fountains of my story. Of course, I leave out the centre of it all, that is the heart of the author; but that is a secret hidden from him and revealed to the reviewers, certain of whom I propose presently to quote.

Well; I found myself in the year 1890 twenty-seven years old, and in some sort of way a man of letters. Let me hasten to explain that nobody of the slightest consequence knew anything about me or my doings; I had no literary connections of any kind or sort. But I had translated Margaret of Navarre's "Heptameron", and Béroalde de Verville's "Moyen de Parvenir", and I had written a volume of tales in the manner of the Renaissance, a volume called "The Chronicle of Clemendy". Altogether, I had acquired that ill habit of writing, that queer itch which so works that the patient if he be neither writing nor thinking of something to be written is bored and dull and unhappy. So I wrote.

I began like many a better man, on "turnovers" for *The Globe*. *The Globe* paid a guinea, but I found out that the *St. James's Gazette* paid two pounds for the same number of words, so I wrote as much as I could for the *St. James's Gazette*. These things were at first "essays" or articles upon things in general, on books, on country sights, on summer days or snowy lanes in winter, on old songs, old proverbs—or anything that got into my head. Then I chanced to meet Oscar Wilde, and dined with him, and at dinner he told me the plot of a story written by a friend of his, which he said was "wonderful". It did not seem to me so sheerly wonderful; I did not see why I should not think of a plot as good or almost as good—always reserving, of course, my first principle, which has been so choice a comfort all my literary life: that nothing that I have written, am writing, or am to write can possibly be of the faintest use or profit to myself or to anybody else. But, anyhow, I tried my hand at a slight whimsical story (it was about a famous dinner-giving baronet who turned out to be his own cook) sent it to the *St. James's,* and to my joy and surprise they printed it, and so I commenced story writer. My tales were strangely enough "society" tales; strangely enough, because I know about as much of "society" as of the habits of the Great Horned Owl.

How it was that I did not send the tale of "The Great God Pan" to the *St. James's Gazette* I do not know. But in this summer of 1890 there was founded a new weekly paper called *The Whirlwind.* It advocated Jacobite principles, and it printed tales, and so when I thought of what is now the first chapter of "The Great God Pan" I sent it to *The Whirlwind,* and there it appeared. I had no notion that there would be anything to follow this first chapter; and it was many months later, sometime in January, 1891, that I set out to write one of my short "society" tales, "The City of Resurrections", which is now the third chapter in the book. I finished the story and found it would never do, the occult horror suggested in it did not consort with the "social" framework: and suddenly it dawned on me that this short tale was a continuation of the *Whirlwind* story; that there were many other chapters to write: in brief, that I had somehow got hold of an idea. I was happy for a whole evening; while I thought of the curious and beautiful thing I was to invent. I thought of this curious and beautiful thing when I read through the proof sheets of the completed book for the first time, and then I groaned, realising what a great gulf was fixed (for me) between the idea and the fact.

But this is all too fast. I wrote, with horrid difficulty, with sick despairs, with a sinking heart, with hope ever failing, all but the last chapter of the book. Of course, I had got the whole thing plotted out

carefully on paper, and as I went on story after story of my card-castle
fell into ruins; this device, I found, would by no means serve; that incident would never convey the meaning intended. But somehow the
thing was done; all but the last chapter; and that I could not do at all.
There was no help for it, and I put the manuscript away, and had pretty well resigned myself to its remaining unfinished for ever. It was not
until the following June that a possible way of ending the book occurred to me, and so in June, 1891, it was all finished. I sent the manuscript to Messrs. Blackwood of Edinburgh; and they very civilly
declined it, praising its cleverness—it is not at all clever—but "shrinking", if I remember, "from the central idea". I forget whether I tried
other publishers vainly; but "The Great God Pan" was accepted by
Mr. John Lane of the Bodley Head, and published by him in 1894.

And then the reviews began to come in, and then the fun began;
and I must confess that I enjoyed it all very much. For I would find
this sort of thing waiting for me on the breakfast table:

> . . . It is not Mr. Machen's fault but his misfortune, that one shakes with
> laughter rather than with dread over the contemplation of his psychologi-
> cal bogey.—*Observer.*
>
> His horror, we regret to say, leaves us quite cold. Gallant gentlemen
> commit suicide at the mere sight of the accursed thing; here be murders,
> inquests, alarums, and excursions—and our flesh obstinately refuses to
> creep. Why? Possibly because we have had a surfeit of this morbid thau-
> maturgy of late, and "ken the biggin' o't."—*Chronicle.*
>
> In the hands of a student of occultism might be made very powerful.
> As it is, they just fail.—*Sunday Times.*
>
> If Mr. Arthur Machen's object were to make our flesh creep, we can
> only speak for ourselves and say that we have read the book without an
> emotion . . . the story is, in fact, most elaborately absurd . . . as meaning-
> less as an allegory as it is absurd from any other point of view.—
> *Westminster.*
>
> Not the ghost of a creepy feeling will this story produce in the mind of
> anybody who reads it.—*Echo.*
>
> His bogles don't scare. In his next attempt, however, he may come out
> on the right side.—*Sketch.*
>
> "Really," laughed the Hostess, "is the Yellow Book a disease?" . . .
> "Yes," continued the Philosopher, meditatively, . . . "and as for 'The
> House of Shame', and 'The Great God Pan'—well there are some kinds

of maladies which are not mentioned outside medical treatises!"—W. L. Courtney, in *The Daily Telegraph*.

We are afraid he only succeeds in being ridiculous. The book is, on the whole, the most acutely and intentionally disagreeable we have yet seen in English. We could say more, but refrain from doing so for fear of giving such a work advertisement.—*Manchester Guardian*.

In all the glory of the binder's and printer's arts, we have two tales of no great distinction.—*National Observer*.

This book is gruesome, ghastly, and dull . . . the majority of readers will turn from it in utter disgust.—*Lady's Pictorial*.

These tricks have also their ludicrous side.—*Guardian*.

It is an incoherent nightmare of sex and the supposed horrible mysteries behind it, such as might conceivably possess a man who was given to a morbid brooding over these matters, but which would soon lead to insanity if unrestrained. . . . innocuous from its absurdity.—*Westminster* (Second Notice).

So well they kept the bridge in the brave days of old! I have turned the leaves of the scrap-book in which I have religiously preserved these cuttings with a tender melancholy, which, nevertheless, is not altogether sad. Indeed, I have felt more in the mood of the man who finds a crushed flower or a leaf in an old book that he seldom opens, that he has not looked into for years. He remembers the affair, whatever it was; he recognises that it was all over and done with very long ago, that it was a silly business at the best: and yet, the little faded flower brings back that night in spring, and makes him feel a boy again. He is wiser now; but then the white boughs of the May hung just over the walls of Paradise. So I have read once more these little faded flowers of speech, and feel a boy again. Or rather, a sort of a boy, a boy of thirty who has been very nearly starved to death in a London lodging-house, who has toiled and despaired over the impossible alchemy of letters, finding nothing but ashes in his crucible, who has given many lonely years to the work. Such a boy I find once more in the leaves of my old scrap-book. I salute him across the great bridge of years and bid him farewell.

Introduction to
The Three Impostors (1923)

In the course of a quarter of a century—and a little more—I have received a good many letters of serious enquiry about *The Three Impostors*. My correspondents ask me in various terms and turns of phrase whether there is any foundation for the strange circumstances and tales narrated in the book. Only the other day an American clergyman wrote to me as follows: "There are few priests," he says, "that have not stumbled upon the unknown as dramatically as you depict it, not as realistically. Of course a thousand reasons prevent their publication. I know that most of these stories are very much coloured; but there are truths, stranger than even the most vivid fiction. Is it possible that these stories have, as we say, a *fundamentum in re*? I would be pleased indeed to know from you if I am not making too bold?"

The letter is typical of many others. I began to get them pretty soon after *The Three Impostors* was published in 1895. Then, on the whole, I was rather displeased than pleased at the question. We have our funny little ways, our amusing little points of pride and dignity, all of us, authors as well as the rest, and I was strongly inclined to resent the implication that I had embroidered rather than invented. I remember when "The Great God Pan" was issued, a friend of mine said, "I suppose it is just an old legend that was going down in your part of the country when you were a boy?" I was quite cross. I said to myself, and I daresay to others, "These barbarians can't bear to acknowledge that anybody can 'make up' anything. They know they couldn't do anything of the kind themselves and the suggestion that, for all that, the thing is done now and again annoys them." I was proud of having invented "The Great God Pan": I was not going to have the credit of that fact taken away on the strength of a legend which never existed. And so with *The Three Impostors*. I wanted to impress on all enquirers that the

530

whole thing came out of my head—I forgot to add "and Stevenson's"—
and that I had taken a great deal of trouble over the tales, and that
there was no foundation in fact for anything between the two covers
of the book. So far, from the point of view of the touchy author; but if
this had been put out of the case and I had been asked whether I
thought that anything like the experience of Professor Gregg—see the
"Novel of the Black Seal"—had occurred in actuality, I should have
said, "Of course not!" And if a similar question had been put as to the
"Novel of the White Powder", I am afraid I should have replied,
"Don't talk such damned nonsense!"

And farther, if I had been asked about the general atmosphere of
the book, the Arabian Nightish aspect of London, the strange encounters, the stranger disappearances, I should certainly have stated with
some firmness that I had never come across anything of the sort, that
no queer characters had ever crossed my track, that my walks about
Soho and Islington, Barnsbury and Clerkenwell were void of all adventures. I would have said, I think, that London streets, like most things,
were dull and grey and uninteresting. "And so," I might likely enough
have added, "we pretend they are wonderful and enchanting, just because it's delightful to do so, just as children are always pretending and
making believe."

That, then, was my general attitude on these points in 1895 and for
some years afterwards. I was quite sure that there was not and could
not be the faintest foundation in fact for any of my tales, and I was
quite sure too that London was not a bit like an Arabian Night. I hardly think that I should be quite so positive today, if I were asked these
old questions all over again. So many things have happened since the
mid-nineties of the last century.

As to the "Arabian" atmosphere of London, for example, I must
admit modifications in my point of view. I think it was in the June of
1900 that I was sitting in the New Lyric Club in Coventry Street, taking
tea with a young friend of mine. He was telling me of some singular
adventures in which he was then involved. It seemed that he had made
a deadly enemy and that, furthermore, this enemy was a notorious
Black Magician. This personage—who is, I may, say, an actual personage—was guilty of the most hideous misdeeds. In the pursuit, doubt-

less, of his favourite art of Black Magic he had entrapped women into his house and had suspended them naked in cupboards, hanging in the air by hooks run through the flesh of their arms. There were other tales of strange horror which I forget. But not this. My friend had offended the magician; I do not think I heard what the offence had been. But he went in dread of his life.

"He has hired a gang down Lambeth way to smash me up and kill me if possible, and he is paying each of them eight-and-six-a day."

I listened stupefied; more stupefied still when I heard of the threatening letters sealed with a "Rosicrucian Seal" that had been received. I can't say whether I believed or disbelieved, or how much I believed and how much I disbelieved. I don't know to this day what relation this queer tale bore to the hard solid facts; though I must say that some years later I myself received a minatory epistle, sealed with a "Rosicrucian Seal" which I have always put down to the credit of the Adept of the Black Art. But I was not bothering about the possible truth or possible falsity of the tale that I had been told; I was thinking of its queerness, of its incongruity with the comfortable chairs of the New Lyric Club, and the view of Coventry Street as seen from the window. I do not think that I realised with whom I had been talking till I got home to my chambers in Verulam Buildings, Gray's Inn. Then I recalled my friend's face and aspect as he told his story; certain phrases came into my mind: "youngish looking man with dark whiskers and spectacles . . . of somewhat timid bearing he is pale, has small black whiskers and wears spectacles. He has rather a timid, almost a frightened expression and looks about him nervously from side to side." And so on, and so on; and it was with a shock that I realised that I had been talking with The Young Man in Spectacles, and that he came out of *The Three Impostors*. I must add that I had first met him in a secret Assembly, more harmless than the gatherings of the terrible Lipsius, but quite as queer. The Young Man in Spectacles! It was astounding, but it was undeniable; and the discovery opened my eyes to the fact that Miss Lally had also come up out of the book into my life and was involving me daily in strange adventures, in meetings and encounters that would have charmed the ear of the Caliph Haroun-al-Raschid, relating as she went on her incalculable way the most wonderful and unexpected tales. Miss Lally and The Young Man in Spectacles met

more than once in my rooms. Naturally, they did not recognise each
other since neither had read my book. But I shall never forget the gravity with which Miss Lally related to the Young Man in Spectacles the
"Novel of My Aunt, the Enchantress". The aunt, I remember, burned
curious gums obtained from the East before rising into the air; and
when this operation was to be performed, the room had to be hung
round with curtains distant one foot from the walls, and nine inches
from the ground. It was, indeed, a sumptuous fable. And, to resume the
old manner for a moment: "The Young Man in Spectacles listened with
the gravest attention to the history of the Enchanting Aunt, asking
many questions of a highly pertinent character, and expressing himself
as more particularly satisfied with the singular circumstance of the dra-
peries before the walls of the magic chamber. He took notes on many
points, and went away with a countenance which fully expressed the
serious nature of the communication which he had received."

Indeed, the tale had been told with such grave earnestness, with
such an attention to the smallest minutiæ of detail, that I myself could
not help thinking that it was a tale about something, that it was an illumination of some sort of a text. I therefore questioned Miss Lally
pretty closely after the departure of the Young Man, whereupon she
informed me with happy laughter that all was quite devoid of truth. I
think she had an aunt; but that was all the fact; the rest was fiction.

And the insurgence of Miss Lally and the spectacled one from the
pages of the printed book was only one, amongst many, extraordinary
circumstances that now gathered thick about me. One day, for example, I got a letter from my publisher asking me to call upon him. I went
at once, thinking that he wished to commission a new masterpiece. He
did not quite want to do that. He explained to me that he had an acquaintance; a distant cousin, if I remember, whose existence annoyed
him. I forget what poor Rundle had done, so far as I know nothing in
particular, beyond being there, but, anyhow, he offended the publisher
and could I help? I was not asked to murder Rundle; I was simply to
found a secret society. Into this the poor fellow was to be entrapped,
and from the moment of his capture his life was to be a burden to
him. The agents of the Society were to beset all his ways; he was to be
accosted suddenly in the street and sent on impossible errands; he was
to keep appointments with mysterious persons, and these appoint-

ments were to end in nothing but annoyance and deep confusion; he was to be terrified by dark threats; doom was to hover like a fiery cloud above his devoted head. Cheerfully, I undertook the business; when in an Arabian Night behave like the Arabian Nighters. But, somehow, the Secret Society was never founded; there must have been some strange intrusion of cool reason into the wild world which I inhabited, that London which I had once thought so commonplace.

It is just possible, it strikes me, that many people have found the odd encounters related in *The Three Impostors,* to be of a highly improbable nature. Indeed as I have confessed, I thought so myself as I was writing of them. But experience, the experiences of 1899–1900, thoroughly convinced me that I was wrong. I became subject at this time to the oddest encounters at every turning, in every quarter of London. Total strangers would accost me on one excuse or another. I have counted ten such unexpected meetings in a day. They would babble confused things, narrate odd adventures, things, I would say, without head or tail or reason, and then sink back into the great deep of the London multitude from which they had emerged. These were utter strangers and remained such; but there were others whom I knew, who were equally entertaining and extravagant; but were so only for a certain appointed season. Thus, a gentleman, who is now one of the most serious of men, used to meet me at the Café de l'Europe in Leicester Square and come home with me to my rooms in Verulam Buildings, and there discourse amazing fables, with such eloquence, weightiness, humour, vivacity, that I was convinced of the truth of every word that was uttered. What added to the charm was the fact that after ten o'clock at night my friend seldom spoke English. He addressed me in French, and I may say that, having lived a good deal in Touraine, I have heard few Frenchmen who could speak their native tongue with so pure and winning and perfect an intonation. And I heard from men familiar with German and Italian that he excelled in these tongues also; and a Spaniard could have taught him nothing of Spanish. Well, infinitely to my delight, this personage would come home with me as I say, and tell tales till far into the night. I remember a few scraps of one of these fables. It related to a well known London restaurant which we may call Pergolesi's. My friend, as he puts it, had been one of the fondatori, the earliest customers of the establishment. There were others with him, many of them well known, even famous men, in later years.

"We noticed," the story went on, "night after night, a very beautiful woman who sat in a corner, apart by herself. There was something entrancing, something almost mystic about her beauty. No one knew who she was. Somehow I succeeded—I need not trouble you with an account of the little stratagems that I may have employed—I succeeded in making her acquaintance. We became, shall I say, friends? After a few months I had reason to suppose that she was a secret agent of the Russian Government. I found myself beset with hints, with half-expressed questions. I parried them as well as I could. At last I discovered that the continuance of the lady's favour depended on my willingness to betray the secrets of my country. I refused; in spite of tears, prayers, endearments; I refused.

"That night I was sitting in our drawing-room. I was in an arm-chair, facing a mirror, and in this mirror I could see reflected the curtains hanging across the entrance to an inner room. Suddenly, the lady appeared, parting the curtains. Her feet were bare. I could not hear her, but I saw her slowly advancing into the room. One hand was raised; in it there was a revolver, levelled at my head. I hardly knew what I did, but I cried out, 'Au moins, madame, tirez juste!'

"She burst into tears and the revolver fell from her hand. I never saw her from that night. She fled!"

I think it was some years before I began to hesitate to myself about this adventure. Indeed, for all I know, every word of it may be true. But: I have no reason for supposing that my friend was ever acquainted with the secrets of the British Government; so . . . what could he have betrayed, if he had been willing to betray?

Still; that doesn't matter. The point is that for many months my life was more Three-Impostory than *The Three Impostors*. I relished all the queer atmosphere of "Arabian" in consequence which I had enjoyed describing, though I didn't believe there ever was or would be anything like it in actuality. I was and am convinced of my error. London will turn into Bagdad in an instant: if you have the true wand of transmutation.

So much for the atmosphere of the framework of *The Three Impostors*; now as to the "foundation in fact" question, where the stories are con-

cerned. This is a much more doubtful and difficult matter. I have attempted to deal with it in a book called *Things Near and Far*. Does the
impossible ever happen? Well, the utmost I would say is this; that I
have had experiences which debar me from returning the absolute
negative of earlier years; the years in which I was writing the book and
the years afterwards. These experiences of mine were trifling enough
but they suggest the possibility of far greater things and far more extraordinary things for those with the necessary qualifications. For, if
you think of it, from the scratched pictures of primitive man, the images he drew on the reindeer horn, you may infer all the majesty of
pictorial art, all the mighty names and the magistral achievements of
the ages. There are, I believe, savage tribes who cannot count beyond
ten; yet all the science of numbers is latent in that decad of theirs. The
savage scratches, the savage numberings at least prove the possibility
of great art and high mathematics; and so I am inclined to urge that the
things which I have known may suggest the probable existence of a
world very far and remote from the world of common experience.

It may turn out after all that the weavers of fantasy are the veritable
realists.

On Re-Reading *The Three Impostors* and the Wonder Story

The "Novel of the Black Seal" and the "Novel of the White Powder" are, I suppose, the only things of much account in this volume. Each of these tales is an experiment in the art of the wonder story, the story of events which are beyond the ordinary range of human observation, of events which we roughly call impossible.

Of course, there are many theories of the impossible. It was only the other day that a casual acquaintance, a man I have seen half a dozen times perhaps in the last four years, assured me with every appearance of conviction that he had seen a small table rise two or three or four—I forget how many—feet into the air. No; it was not done in the dark; the electric lights were full on. No; the medium was not near the table, nor could she exercise any kind of mechanical influence on the table. But the table most certainly rose into the air.

Well; what is one to say? There are all sorts of answers: "you lie", "you were deceived by a Maskelyne apparatus", "you were 'hypnotised' by the medium so that you thought you saw the table rise", and I daresay that there are other retorts. I have used the hypnotism explanation because it is one that is frequently given to explain wonders of all sorts including the famous Rope Trick of India. But so far as I know, hypnotism demands the full and deliberate consent of the subject. A man cannot be hypnotised unawares. He must know what is to be done and give up his will to the experiment and the experimenter; and so I cannot see how my acquaintance can have been hypnotised into seeing the table rise and yet be unaware that he was so hypnotised.

But, be pleased to note, I am not saying, nor even implying that it is impossible for tables to rise in the air without the use of mechanism. I do not know whether such an event be possible or impossible. I merely know that I have never seen a table rise, nor anything at all like such a circumstance. It seems to me highly improbable that such a thing should happen, and I shall require very sure and clear evidence before I believe that it can and does happen.

And so with the tales in *The Three Impostors*, with the "Novel of the Black Seal". Here there are certain slender foundations of fact. It is undoubtedly true, for example, that the pre-Celtic race who inhabited this country before history begins were cave-dwellers, living in hollows in the earth. I do not know whether they had always lived thus or whether these caverns were places of refuge against the invading and conquering Celt. Moreover, I have such faith in tradition that I think it highly probable that the tales of children and others "taken by the fairies", the Little People of the Hills, are fanciful representations of actual events. And the changeling? The little fair Celtic baby vanishing from the snug place of the hearth one dusky evening while father and mother Celt were hard by on the mountain bringing down the turf; and they to come back home—I must really suit my idiom to the matter—and find a little wizened, olive-coloured black-eyed infant by the fire? I have no doubt such a thing happened again and again.

There and so far the hypothesis of Professor Gregg is entirely justified; but the next step is a huge one. The Professor had, he said, evidence to shew that the Little People still existed. Well, and after all, that is true in a sense. I have known many Welshmen, as dark as any Southern Italian with dead black crinkly hair, and with oddly shaped heads underneath it. These are, no doubt, Turanians, descendants of the pre-Celtic inhabitants of Britain; but the caves in which they dwell are called "Capel Adullam", "Capel Ebezener", "Capel Bryn Sion". Professor Gregg went much farther. He said that the people still lived in hidden caverns in wild and lonely lands, and, specifically, amongst the Grey Hill, Monmouthshire, which, you can see for yourself soon after your train has come up from the Severn Tunnel. Well, the Professor may have had evidence for this, but his is the only case that we know of; and I am afraid we must say that here the tale becomes wildly improbable. Then it takes not so much a step as a leap into the darkness. The Little People are not merely pre-Celtic, they are almost, if not quite, pre-human. Their bodies are not as the bodies of men; their limbs can be extruded and withdrawn in the fashion of the horns of the snail. This strange circumstance was suggested to me by a hypothesis of Sir Oliver Lodge's as to some of the feats of Eusapia Palladino; the hypothesis has now become firmly established as a belief in spiritualistic circles, and they call the extruded matter ectoplasm. With all this I have nothing to do; but I must say that I this point the tale of the Black Seal approaches very near to the line of the impossible, taking that word in its common and colloquial significance.

There are many degrees, then, of the unlikely, and it is with these degrees, from the lowest to the highest, that the inventor of strange fictions has to deal. The "Novel of the White Powder" is, perhaps, more wildly unlikely that the "Novel of the Black Seal". The latter, as I have shewn, has a certain substratum of truth, there were once little people who lived under the hills. But the mythos on which the "White Powder" fantasy is based is a sheer invention of my own. There never was such a thing as the *Vinum Sabbati;* but more, there never were any legends about such a thing, no supposition that there might once on a time have been such a thing.

And as there are varying degrees, from the somewhat improbable to the, practically, impossible from the point of view of the writer; so there are varying degrees of assent given by the reader. I suppose that Daniel Defoe's story of the apparition of Mrs. Veal is not strictly within the limits of art, though it is certainly an amazing piece of artifice. For here the writer's object was to make the reader believe that the whole tale was no tale at all, but a piece of actuality, that it had all happened. Newspapers were in their infancy, it was often more convenient and more profitable for a man who knew of some extraordinary event to cast his account into the form of a pamphlet rather than that of a newspaper article. And many hundreds of people in the eighteenth century gave to the story of Mrs. Veal exactly the credit that we give to a newspaper article headed "Earthquake in Chile". Boswell, if I remember, quoted Mrs. Veal as evidence for the existence of ghosts, and Johnson gave the oddest reply; something like: "No, Sir, the woman confessed that the whole story was an imposture." The fact is that there was no woman; there was only Daniel Defoe.

But this is not art. The landscape painter does not want you to try to ascend his mountain or to take a header into his sea. He demands from you an assent, but not an assent of this order. And so the writer of the wonder story demands a kind of momentary assent, and it is his business to lure the reader on gently, to direct his attention in the first place to things which are credible and even probable, and so from step to step, by imperceptible degrees, to draw him down into a fantastic cave of marvels, so that he is amazed as he reads the last line, and awakes and behold! it was a dream!

Bibliography

I. *Book Publications of Machen's Fiction*

A Chapter from the Book Called The Ingenious Gentleman Don Quijote de la Mancha Which by Some Mischance Has Not Till Now Been Printed. London: George Redway, [1887]. [Reprinted in *Tales of the Strange and the Supernatural* (1925?) as "The Priest and the Barber."]

The Chronicle of Clemendy. London: Privately Printed for the Society of Pantegruelists, [March 1888]. New York: Privately Printed for the Society of Pantegruelists [Boni & Liveright], 1923. London: Martin Secker, 1925. New York: Alfred A. Knopf, 1926. London: Martin Secker/ Adelphi Library, 1927. London: Martin Secker/Adelphi Library, [1927].

The Great God Pan and The Inmost Light. London: John Lane; Boston: Roberts Brothers, 1894. Boston: Roberts Brothers, 1894. London: John Lane, 1895. London: Grant Richards, [1913]. London: Martin Secker/New Adelphi Library, 1926. [*Contents:* "The Great God Pan"; "The Inmost Light." The Secker edition adds "The Red Hand."]

The Three Impostors. London: John Lane; Boston: Roberts Brothers, 1895. New York: Alfred A. Knopf, 1923. London: Martin Secker/New Adelphi Library, 1926.

The House of Souls. London: E. Grant Richards, 1906. Boston: Dana Estes & Co., 1906. New York: Albert & Charles Boni, 1915. New York: Frank Shay, 1917. [*Contents:* "A Fragment of Life"; "The White People"; "The Great God Pan"; "The Inmost Light"; *The Three Impostors;* "The Red Hand."]

The Hill of Dreams. London: E. Grant Richards, 1907. Boston: Dana

Estes, 1907. New York: Albert & Charles Boni, 1915. New York: Frank Shay, 1917. London: Martin Secker, 1922. New York: Alfred A. Knopf, 1923. London: Martin Secker, 1924. London: Secker & Warburg, 1927. [Serialised in *Horlick's Magazine* 2 (July 1904): 1–12; (August 1904): 129–39; (September 1904): 225–33; (October 1904): 353–62; (November 1904): 417–27; (December 1904): 545–56 (as "The Garden of Avallaunius").]

The Angels of Mons: The Bowmen and Other Legends of the War. London: Simpkin, Marshall, Hamilton, Kent & Co., 1915 (2nd ed. 1915). New York: G. P. Putnam's Sons, 1915. [*Contents:* "The Bowmen"; "The Soldiers' Rest"; "The Monstrance"; "The Dazzling Light"; "The Bowmen and Other Noble Ghosts," by "The Londoner" (pseudonym of Oswald Barron, F. S. A.). Second edition adds the stories "The Little Nations" and "The Men from Troy."]

The Great Return. London: Faith Press, 1915.

The Great God Pan. London: Simpkin, Marshall, Hamilton, Kent & Co., 1916.

The Terror: A Fantasy. London: Duckworth, 1917. New York: Robert M. McBride & Co., 1917 (as *The Terror: A Mystery*). London: Duckworth, 1927.

The House of Souls. New York: Alfred A. Knopf, 1922. London: Grant Richards, 1923. [*Contents:* "A Fragment of Life"; "The White People"; "The Great God Pan"; "The Inmost Light."]

The Secret Glory. London: Martin Secker, 1922. New York: Alfred A. Knopf, 1922. London: Martin Secker, 1928. [Incorporates "The Marriage of Panurge," *Academy* 72 (22 June 1907): 607–9; *Wave* 1, no. 1 (January 1922): 2–7; in *Holy Terrors* (1946). "The Martyr," *Academy* 73 (20 July 1907): 702–4; in *The Shining Pyramid* (1923); in *The Shining Pyramid* (1925). "Levavi Oculos," *Academy* 73 (21 September 1907): 923–25. "The Parting," *Academy* 73 (23 November 1907): 166–69. "The Schoolmaster's Dream," *Academy* 74 (25 January 1908): 387–90. "Symbols," *Academy* 74 (23 May 1908): 808–10. "The Hidden Mystery,"

Academy 74 (6 June 1908): 856–58; in *The Shining Pyramid* (1923); In *Out of the Earth and Other Sketches* (1925?); in *The Cosy Room and Other Stories* (1936). "Enchanted Café," *Academy* 75 (27 June 1908): 927–28 (as part of the column "From a Notebook"). "In Convertendo," *Academy* 75 (15 August 1908): 157–58; in *The Shining Pyramid* (1923); in *The Shining Pyramid* (1925). "The Secret Glory," *Gypsy* 1 (May 1915): 79–89; (May 1916): 139–45.]

Works (Caerleon Edition). London: Martin Secker; Edinburgh: Dunedin Press, 1923. 9 vols. [*Contents:* Vol. 1: "The Great God Pan," "The Inmost Light," "The Red Hand"; Vol. 2: *The Three Impostors;* Vol. 6: "A Fragment of Life," "The White People"; Vol. 7: *The Terror; The Bowmen and Other Legends of the War;* "The Great Return." Vols. 3–5, 8, and 9 contain no fiction.]

The Shining Pyramid. Edited by Vincent Starrett. Chicago: Covici-McGee, 1923. [*Contents* (fiction only): "The Shining Pyramid"; "Out of the Earth"; "The Lost Club"; "A Wonderful Woman."]

The Glorious Mystery. Edited by Vincent Starrett. Chicago: Covici-McGee, 1924. [*Contents* (fiction only): "The Rose Garden"; "Fragments of Paper" (i.e., "Psychology"); "The Holy Things"; "Scrooge: 1920."]

Ornaments in Jade. New York: Alfred A. Knopf, 1924. [*Contents:* "The Rose Garden"; "The Turanians"; "The Idealist"; "Witchcraft"; "The Ceremony"; "Psychology"; "Torture"; "Midsummer"; "Nature"; "The Holy Things."]

Tales of the Strange and the Supernatural. Girard, KS: Haldeman-Julius, [1925?]. [*Contents:* "The Priest and the Barber"; "The Lost Club"; "A Wonderful Woman"; "The Shining Pyramid."]

Out of the Earth and Other Sketches. Girard, KS: Haldeman-Julius, [1925?]. [*Contents* (fiction only): "Out of the Earth."]

The Shining Pyramid. London: Martin Secker, 1925. New York: Alfred A. Knopf, 1925. [*Contents* (fiction only): "The Shining Pyramid"; "Out of the Earth"; "The Happy Children."]

A Fragment of Life. London: Martin Secker, 1928. [*Contents:* "A Fragment of Life"; "The White People."]

The Children of the Pool and Other Stories. London: Hutchinson, 1936. [*Contents:* "The Exalted Omega"; "The Children of the Pool"; "The Bright Boy"; "The Tree of Life"; "Out of the Picture"; "Change."]

The Cosy Room and Other Stories. London: Rich & Cowan, 1936. [*Contents:* "A Double Return"; "A Wonderful Woman"; "The Lost Club"; "The Holy Things"; "Psychology"; "Torture"; "Witchcraft"; "The Turanians"; "The Rose Garden"; "The Ceremony"; "Midsummer"; "Nature"; "The Hidden Mystery"; "Munitions of War"; "Drake's Drum"; "A New Christmas Carol"; "The Islington Mystery"; "The Gift of Tongues"; "The Cosy Room"; "Awaking"; "Opening the Door"; "The Compliments of the Season"; "N."]

The Great God Pan and Other Weird Tales. New York: Editions for the Armed Services, [c. 1943]. [*Contents:* "The Great God Pan"; "The White People"; "The Inmost Light"; "The Recluse of Bayswater" (segment of *The Three Impostors*).]

Holy Terrors. Harmondsworth: Penguin, 1946. [*Contents:* "The Bright Boy"; "The Tree of Life"; "Opening the Door"; "The Marriage of Panurge" (segment of *The Secret Glory*); "The Holy Things"; "Psychology"; "The Turanians"; "The Rose Garden"; "The Ceremony"; "The Soldiers' Rest"; "The Happy Children"; "The Cosy Room"; "Munitions of War"; "The Great Return."]

Tales of Horror and the Supernatural. New York: Alfred A. Knopf, 1948. London: Richards Press, 1949. [*Contents:* "Novel of the Black Seal"; "Novel of the White Powder"; "The Great God Pan"; "The White People"; "The Inmost Light"; "The Shining Pyramid"; "The Bowmen"; "The Great Return"; "The Happy Children"; "The Bright Boy"; "Out of the Earth"; "N"; "The Children of the Pool"; *The Terror.*]

II. Individual Publications of Short Stories

"The Autophone." *St. James's Gazette* (21 August 1890): 6.

"A Double Return." *St. James's Gazette* (11 September 1890): 6–7 (unsigned). In *The Cosy Room and Other Stories* (1936).

"The Great God Pan." *Whirlwind* 2 (13 December 1890): 170–71 (ch. 1 only). In *The Great God Pan and The Inmost Light* (1894). In *The House of Souls* (1906). In *The Great God Pan* (1916). In *The House of Souls* (1922). In *Works,* Vol. 1 (1923). In *The Great God Pan and Other Weird Tales* (1943). In *Tales of Horror and the Supernatural* (1948).

"The Inmost Light." In *The Great God Pan and The Inmost Light* (1894). In The House of Souls (1906). In *The House of Souls* (1922). In *Works,* Vol. 1 (1923). In The *Great God Pan and Other Weird Tales* (1943). In *Tales of Horror and the Supernatural* (1948).

"Jocelyn's Escape." *World* (17 June 1891): 31–32, 36.

"The Lost Club." *Whirlwind* 2 (20 December 1890): 182–84. In *The Shining Pyramid* (1923). In *Tales of the Strange and the Supernatural* (1925?). In *The Cosy Room and Other Stories* (1936).

"The Red Hand." *Chapman's Magazine* 2 (December 1895): 390–418. In *The House of Souls* (1906). In *Works,* Vol. 1 (1923). In *The Great God Pan and The Inmost Light* (Secker ed. [1926]).]

"A Remarkable Coincidence." *St. James's Gazette* (26 August 1890): 6.

"The Shining Pyramid." *Unknown World* 2 (15 May 1895): 148–55; (15 June 1895): 197–203. In *The Shining Pyramid* (1923). In *Tales of the Strange and the Supernatural* (1925?). In *The Shining Pyramid* (1925). In *Tales of Horror and the Supernatural* (1948).

"The Spagyric Quest of Beroaldus Cosmopolita." In *Thesaurus Incantatus.* London: Thomas Marvell [i.e., Machen and Harry Spurr], [1888].

The Three Impostors. In *The Three Impostors* (1895). In *The House of Souls* (1906). In *Works,* Vol. 2 (1923). In *The Great God Pan and Other Weird*

Tales (1943) ("The Recluse of Bayswater" only). ["The Novel of the Iron Maid" first published in *St. James's Gazette* (13 September 1890): 6 (unsigned; as "The Iron Maid").]

"An Underground Adventure." *Whirlwind* 2 (27 December 1890): 196–97 (unsigned).

"A Wonderful Woman." *Whirlwind* 2 (6 December 1890): 182–84 (unsigned). In *The Shining Pyramid* (1923). In *Tales of the Strange and the Supernatural* (1925?).

Appendix:

"Folklore and Legends of the North." *Literature* (24 September 1898): 238–39.

Preface to "The Great God Pan." London: Simpkin, Marshall, Hamilton, Kent & Co., 1916.

Introduction to *The Three Impostors.* New York: Alfred A. Knopf, 1923. vii–xix.

"On Re-Reading *The Three Impostors* and the Wonder Story." Ms., Wisconsin Historical Society (Madison, WI).